Mother's Day Collection 2024

MEREDITH WEBBER

CHRISTINE RIMMER

CHRISTY JEFFRIES

TANYA MICHAELS

MILLS & BOON

CONTENTS

ONE NIGHT TO FOREVER FAMILY   5
Meredith Webber

THE RIGHT REASON TO MARRY   165
Christine Rimmer

MAKING ROOM FOR THE RANCHER   353
Christy Jeffries

HILL COUNTRY CUPID   551
Tanya Michaels

One Night To Forever Family

Merideth Webber

Meredith Webber lives on the sunny Gold Coast in Queensland, Australia, but takes regular trips west into the Outback, fossicking for gold or opal. These breaks in the beautiful and sometimes cruel red earth country provide her with an escape from the writing desk and a chance for her mind to roam free—not to mention getting some much needed exercise. They also supply the kernels of so many stories that it's hard for her to stop writing!

Books by Meredith Webber

Harlequin Medical

Bondi Bay Heroes

Healed by Her Army Doc

The Halliday Family

A Forever Family for the Army Doc
Engaged to the Doctor Sheikh
A Miracle for the Baby Doctor
From Bachelor to Daddy

New Year Wedding for the Crown Prince
A Wife for the Surgeon Sheikh
The Doctors' Christmas Reunion
Conveniently Wed in Paradise

Visit the Author Profile page
at millsandboon.com.au for more titles.

Dear Reader,

For many years, I have enjoyed visits to the regional city of Port Macquarie, on the midcoast of New South Wales. It has appeared, under different names, in a number of my books, and I always see it in my mind's eye as I write.

Twelve months ago, I was fortunate enough to be taken on a tour of the new hospital there, and the first seed of an idea for a book was planted.

A chance meeting with an intensive care specialist made me realize just how much training goes into producing these vital members of the hospital community—six years on top of their six years of medical training, then a further year for pediatric intensive care here in Australia.

And that's how, for me anyway, a story is born— two random things coming together. All I had to do was add a hero and heroine and it was done.

For some reason, the idea of a friends-to-lovers story was niggling in my mind, and it seemed a while since I'd used that scenario. So I let it take shape, added characters, and the story was born.

Meredith Webber

CHAPTER ONE

SAM REILLY KNEW she shouldn't be walking into a large hospital with a well-travelled and probably germ-laden backpack towering over her, the soft roll of the sleeping bag on the top pushing her head forward so she probably resembled a bedraggled turtle as she made her way towards the reception desk.

She leant against the counter, easing the weight on her back slightly.

'I know I don't look much,' she said to the polite woman on the other side of the desk, 'but the road out from where I was working was washed away in a typhoon and it's taken me a month to get here. I need a shower, some scrubs, and if possible a white coat so that I can present myself as a reasonably competent doctor up in the PICU. My name's Sam Reilly—well, Samantha, really, but people call me Sam.'

'*You're* the new PICU doctor? I was told to expect you but, oh, my dear, you can't possibly go up there looking like that! Think of the germs you're probably carrying.'

'Exactly!' Sam said, 'Which is why I need that shower and something clean to wear. Can you help me out?'

The woman eyed her doubtfully.

'I guess you'd be okay in the ED staffroom. There are always plenty of clean sets of scrubs in there—showers, too, of course. Just continue down this passage and you'll find it on the left.' The woman hesitated. 'It's often a bit messy,' she added, as if a scrawny, redheaded backpacker might not have understood messy...

'And I'm not?' Sam queried with a smile.

Apart from a youngish man, sleeping like the dead on a most uncomfortable-looking couch, the staffroom was empty—but it *was* only six in the morning and he'd probably been on duty all night.

The showers were easy to find, but the cubicles were small, so Sam set her backpack down in the adjoining changing room, removed the sleeping bag—why on earth had she not thrown it away?—and dug into her pack for the meagre selection of new clothes she'd bought at Bangkok airport.

Four bras, four pairs of knickers, three pairs of socks and a new pair of sneakers, which had cost more than double all her other purchases put together. She found her toiletries, too, deodorant, toothpaste and brush, a wide-toothed comb that could handle her unruly locks, and a couple of strong hair clips she hoped could hold those locks in place.

Next, she removed a plastic-wrapped bundle and took out her stethoscope, watch and tiny torch.

A cupboard on one side of the changing room yielded sets of scrubs stacked under small, medium and large labels. Sam selected a large, which would swim on her small frame but experience told her she needed them for her height, though she'd also need something to use as a belt to hold up the trousers.

And finally, leaving everything she wanted to wear on the small bench in the cubicle, she stripped off and stepped under the water, cold at first but then so deliciously warm she could have stayed there for hours.

Unfortunately, the time she'd spent with her mother in the

small hospital near the Thai-Cambodian border—three weeks that had become seven when the typhoon had taken out the access road—had taught her the importance of clean water. She used soap from the dispenser on the wall to wash her hair and then the rest of her body, sluicing away the stiffness of thirty hours', mostly uncomfortable, travel, and whatever foreign microbes she might have been carrying.

Once clean she roughly towelled her hair as dry as she could get it, used another towel on her body, then dressed in new underwear and the scrub suit—way too big but still better than a medium that would have her ankles and wrists sticking out.

She dragged the comb through her hair, taming it sufficiently to pull it up onto the top of her head and secure it with a couple of clips. Somewhere there'd be a supply of bandanas—one to cover her hair and another she could possibly use as a belt—but in the meantime, with a white coat purloined from the cupboard—she felt presentable enough to find a café or canteen and have breakfast before fronting up for work.

In the outer passage, she found a row of lockers and spotted an empty one with a key in the door. She dumped her gear into it, locked it and pocketed the key. Now to find the canteen and some much-needed food.

Excitement at being back at work and back at home—back where she belonged, even if *was* a new hospital in a new city—made her want to skip along the corridor, but hunger was gnawing at her stomach. She'd been travelling for hours and she knew she had to eat before starting work as a senior PICU physician.

Andy looked up from the meal he was eating, unsure whether it was dinner or breakfast—just that he'd needed it after a more than hectic night on call for the PICU. The little boy with the burns to the soles of his feet had reacted badly to the pain relief they'd given him in the Emergency Department and had had to be stabilised before they could turn their attention to his injuries.

Redheaded little boy…

Andy smiled to himself. He'd once heard a statistic about children with self-inflicted burns that suggested nearly all of them were redheaded boys, and since he'd heard it he'd been surprised by how often it had turned out to be true.

Just then, he noticed another redhead who entered the canteen. She was anything but a boy, and he felt an all-too-familiar jolt in his chest.

He'd known she was coming, of course—how could he not? As head of the PICU he'd read her résumé and been present at her interview. But the interview itself had been by a very static-filled radio link-up to some obscure place on the Thai border with Cambodia, and he hadn't seen her.

Not physically at least.

But in his mind's eye, she'd been as clear as day—a tall, redheaded woman who strode through life towards whatever it could throw at her, prepared to meet and beat any challenge.

Except that the last time he'd seen her she'd been in a hospital bed, the scattering of freckles across her nose and cheeks standing out against sheet-white skin, fury flashing in her pale green eyes as she'd told him to get out and never come back…

'Now!' she'd added in a strangled voice, and he'd left—walked away, his heart heavy with the loss of his best friend and aching for the woman on the bed who had looked so lost and vulnerable. Sorrow, anger and grief had churned inside him—fear for her, too—and words he should never have said had come out of his mouth. But now his head had told him just how stupid he had been, virtually accusing her of Nick's death, adding to her pain, while his heart?

Who knew where his heart had been back then…?

Life had thrown plenty at her since then, yet here she was—shoulders back, head held high, walking into the place as if she owned it.

Hiding the butterflies in her stomach—surely she'd worked in enough places to no longer have that uneasy feeling when she entered somewhere new—Sam crossed the canteen towards the self-serve shelves. She slotted onto the end of a small queue of people either coming off duty and needing food because they'd been too busy to eat all night or going on duty but needing sustenance before they tackled a new day.

She grabbed a packet of sandwiches and a bottle of some greeny-yellow juice and headed for the checkout, suddenly aware of a prickly feeling on her skin, as though someone was watching her.

She glanced around at what appeared to be a typical crowd in any hospital canteen at change of shifts, with subdued conversation and exhaustion leaking into the air. Sam paid her bill and headed for an empty table she'd spotted on the far side of the room. She had an hour before she was due to report to the head of department, but she'd eat then go on up to the ward, explain who she was and familiarise herself with the place—once she'd found a belt.

'You've gone all out to impress your new colleagues in that outfit,' a voice said above her head, and as her heart registered just who the voice belonged to, Andy Wilkie lowered his tall, solid frame into the chair opposite her.

'Andy?'

Damn her voice! The word came out as a pathetic squeak!

'What are you doing here?'

Much better—practically a demand...

'Did you not do *any* research on the place before you applied for a job?'

Andy's expressive eyebrows lifted above blue, blue eyes. Sardonically?

Damn the man!

'I saw the ad online in an internet café in Bangkok. I'd just got off a flight from London and knew my stay with Mum would only be a few weeks, so I shot off an application and résumé while I was there. But I didn't have time to look into either the hospital or the staffing side of things.'

She hoped she sounded more composed than she felt, because

the realisation that she'd be working with Andy had caused panic and despair to swell inside her.

The same Andy who'd blamed her for his best friend's death...

Which she probably had been...

But that was her guilt to cope with, her memories to haunt her, and right now she had to make some rational explanation about why this had come as a total shock. This was the start of a whole new life for her—she had to put the past behind her and start afresh.

She slammed the door closed on those painful memories, and remembered instead the good times when she, Nick and Andy had been friends—good friends who had laughed together. Although she'd seen less of Andy after she'd married Nick...

But right now she had to explain. Preferably without sounding as if she was making excuses.

'I was spending a few weeks working in a small hospital—more a clinic, really—near the Thai border with Cambodia when the phone interview was set up. Actually, the interview on my side was mostly static. Were you one of the voices on the phone?'

'Of course!' he replied, no glimmer of expression on his face. 'I am, after all, the department head.'

Her boss!

Andy had employed her in spite of what had happened between them in the past?

'But *you* must have known it was me. After all, you had my application and résumé,' she said, trying to ease the tension in her body, praying it wasn't revealed in her voice. 'You gave me the job.'

He half smiled, and while her heart skipped a beat at the sign of this softening on his part, his voice was still cool and unemotional as he said, 'You were by far the best applicant. Anyone who's done eighteen months in the PICU in the biggest children's hospital in London has had more experience than all the other applicants put together.'

Sam closed her eyes, just briefly, stilling the confusion inside her.

She could do this.

She could work with Andy.

Actually, she doubted there were many better than Andy to work with. He'd headed east to America after Nick's death, while she'd fled west, first to Perth on the other side of the country and then London—the other side of the world—before spending three weeks that had grown to nearly seven with her mother in the tiny medical outpost on the Thai-Cambodian border.

Of course she could do it!

Play it cool!

'I'm sorry about the scrubs, but we had a typhoon a month ago just when I was due to leave, and the road to the nearest town was washed away. I finally got out, and onto a flight from Bangkok last night, changed flights in Sydney, and came straight from the local airport.'

'With no clothes?'

He sounded so disbelieving she had to smile.

'I could hardly take my winter clothes to Thailand, but I did buy some new undies at the airport in Bangkok,' she assured him, 'and as today was to be an orientation day, I'm hoping I'll have some time later to get out and buy something new. I'll need to book into a hotel, too, until I find somewhere to stay.'

He shook his head—disbelief at her story clear in his eyes.

'I'd have been here a month ago if it hadn't been for the typhoon. Plenty of time to have found things to wear and a place to live!' she said, cross with herself for the defensive justification.

'Well, eat up and we'll do the business side of things, and then I'll show you around the hospital. Just get some clothes, but don't bother with a hotel. I can give you a bed at my apartment for a night or two.'

He flung the words at her so casually—coolly—she didn't have a clue how to take them.

Simple politeness?

Or exasperation that she was so disorganised?

'You don't have to do that. I'll be fine in a hotel,' she told him, not adding that she'd also be far more comfortable away from him.

Staying with Andy? The very thought had tension tightening her nerves...

He studied her, eyes revealing nothing, although the words, when they came, were cold—their meaning clear.

'You *are* the widow of my best friend, of course you should stay with me, Sam.'

The best friend you think I killed, Sam thought as she drained the rest of her juice to help swallow the dry piece of sandwich.

But given that, could she really stay with him, even for a few days while she found somewhere else to live?

Although the offer might just be a peace offering. And it wasn't going to be for ever, she might have found somewhere else to stay by tomorrow...

And they *had* been friends.

And just what were you thinking? Andy asked himself. Inviting her to stay like that?

Especially as just seeing her again had stirred up so much consternation in his gut.

Even in baggy scrubs and her wet hair bunched somehow on the top of her head, she was still one of the most attractive women he'd ever met.

But she'd ended up with Nick—and, as far as Nick was concerned, she'd belonged to him. But could a woman as strong-willed and determined as Sam ever *belong* to anyone? Nick had certainly thought so, and somehow she'd made their marriage work. Though, knowing Nick, that wouldn't have been easy...

Why was he thinking of the past when it was the immediate future he needed to solve?

It could be weeks before she found a place, months even, because the summer holiday season was approaching fast and accommodation owners made more money with short-term holiday rentals at this time of the year.

So why the hell had he suggested she stay with him, even for a couple of nights?

Exhaustion was the answer. He'd been operating the department without a first-class number two for nearly six months, the previous incumbent having left in a huff for not getting the top job. Others had filled in, of course, but none of them had wanted to take on too much responsibility for a job they'd never get.

But he'd asked her now and he had to live with her answer. Maybe she'd feel just as uncomfortable about the arrangement as he did and would find somewhere else really quickly.

But there was no time for conjecture, Sam was already on her feet, pushing back her chair, the far too big scrubs sliding down her legs to reveal a startling pair of lacy purple panties.

Scarlet with embarrassment, she grabbed the trousers and pulled them up, glaring at him as she muttered, 'There was very little choice of underwear at Bangkok airport!'

'Great colour!' he said, mainly to see her blush deepen. 'Pity you can't wear them on the outside like a superhero.'

She looked seriously at him and he guessed she was wondering how things would be between them, working together in the PICU.

'I'm no super-hero,' she said quietly. 'But I've learned a lot and can do my job.'

And having put him right back in his place, she offered a small smile before adding, 'But right now I need a bit of string or something to hold up these trousers.'

She marched ahead of him out of the canteen, one hand holding the errant scrub trousers tightly to her waist.

He followed close behind her, his head still asking why the

hell he'd done this—chosen her for the job when he'd known it would mean the pair of them working closely together.

Yes, she'd been the best candidate and he had no doubt she'd be superb, but that strong niggle of attraction—he'd always hesitated to call it more—he'd felt from the first moment he and Nick had laid eyes on her, in the staff's favourite bar across the road from their old hospital, had never really gone away.

He flinched with embarrassment as he remembered that night. He and Nick had done Rock, Paper, Scissors to see who'd ask her out and the rest, as the saying went, was history. Sam and Nick had been married within three months, and he'd managed to distance himself from the happy couple as much as possible. Nick had been his friend from childhood—no way could he be lusting after Nick's wife...

'Something to keep my trousers up,' that same woman reminded him, bringing him out of the past and back to the present—and to the decision that as Nick's widow Sam was even more unattainable.

'There'll be a bungy cord in the janitors' room—everyone needs bungy cords.'

He ducked in front of her to lead the way, but as he passed, he couldn't help wondering how *she* was feeling about this. She'd certainly been startled to see him, so obviously hadn't had time to learn much about the new hospital or its PICU staffing.

He opened a door on the right and rummaged around through miscellaneous junk, finally finding not a bungy cord but a ball of twine.

'Put your hands out from your sides while I measure how much we'll need,' he said, stepping behind her and unrolling the twine, wrapping it around her waist—not easy when one hand still held tightly to the trousers—until his fingers met at the front.

'Leave enough to tie a bow,' she said, grabbing at the other side of the trousers before they slid down again. 'I don't want to be cutting myself out of it later.'

He didn't answer—couldn't. This was Sam, right here in front of him, more or less in his arms...

He'd denied this attraction, even to himself, for the three long years she and Nick had been married. He'd avoided her—avoided seeing her with Nick—and now she was here, and her closeness filled his senses. The smell of her seemed to invade his whole body.

It was hard to deny his attraction now, when she was so close.

So why the hell had he asked her to stay with him?

And why had she agreed? Especially given how much he must have hurt her with his accusation as she had lain in hospital...

Or had she agreed?

Not in as many words.

She just hadn't outright refused.

There'd surely be a hotel available—could he find her one? Or would that look churlish?

Yep!

And it wasn't as if he'd asked her to live with him, He'd just offered her a bed until she found something else.

Soon, he hoped...

He pulled back, away from her, the twine ball clutched in his hands. He had to get a life, find a diversion, take out a woman, any woman—anything to keep Sam out of his system.

He found a knife and cut the length, then handed it to her to tie it around her own waist, easing further away from her, his mind churning with the knowledge that she still had such an effect on him.

Sam tied the twine around her waist then turned the top of the trousers over it so the tunic hung neatly over them—more or less. Fiddling, fiddling, giving herself time to get over the startling discovery that Andy's arms around her—innocent as the movement had been—had brought heat to her cheeks and sent shivers down her spine.

Prolonged abstinence—that's all it was! In the three years since Nick's death she'd had only one relationship and although occasional sex had been involved in it, it had been more comfort than physical fulfilment that she'd wanted.

But Andy?

She'd met him and Nick together, and although it had been Nick who'd asked her out then courted her into a whirlwind marriage, she'd always liked Andy, had felt a kind of kinship with him. There'd always been something steady and reliable about Andy, though she'd seen less of him after her marriage.

Now he marched away after handing her the twine, and she had to hurry to catch up with him, falling in almost beside him, just a half-step back.

Deference to the boss, or fear that being closer might disturb her in some way?

Nonsense. It was simply because of the past that she was feeling uneasy…

He used a card to access what was obviously a staff elevator and punched the number for the fourth floor.

'You'll get one of these with your information pack,' he told her, 'and sometime today you'll need to have a photo taken to put on your ID—it only takes a few minutes.'

End of conversation, the elevator doors opened and they stepped into a corridor, Andy turning left and pushing through pneumatic doors.

They'd barely entered when a nurse appeared.

'Andy, they need someone down in the ED, eighteen-month-old with a temp of thirty-nine C, listless, flushed, unresponsive.'

'Come with me,' Andy said to Sam as he turned on his heel and headed back to the elevator.

'These two elevators are staff only. Well, they're used for moving patients as well, but the hospital is fairly new and the design is really brilliant, which makes working here a dream.'

He paused, then added, 'How often have you stood in an elevator and known there are at least three people in it who'd like to ask you a question about a patient?'

'And often did,' she added as she nodded her agreement.

This was good, this was work. She could not only handle working with Andy but she would enjoy it, aware that he was extremely good at what he did.

If she locked the past away where it belonged, treated Andy like any other colleague, and just concentrated on work…

He led the way into the ED, which was strangely quiet early in the morning, and a nurse hailed him as he walked in.

'We've put her in an isolation room—she's pink but that could just be the fever,' she explained.

'Or measles,' Andy ground out savagely.

He walked into the room and leant over the child, Sam slipping around to the other side of the bed, the small girl on it staring blankly at the ceiling. Her eyes were red, her nose oozing mucus, and flat red spots covered her forehead and were appearing as they watched, down her face and neck and onto her torso.

Speaking quietly to the child, Andy eased her mouth open and peered inside, finding tell-tale signs of measles in there as well.

'We need to check with her parents if she's been vaccinated, although somehow I doubt it as the measles vaccine provides almost one hundred percent protection.

'What checks have you done so far?' he asked the nurse.

'We've removed her clothes and sponged her down, given her twenty milligrams of paracetamol, tried to get some water into her but she's so unresponsive I was afraid she'd choke.'

Andy nodded.

'We'll admit her, take her up to PICU and isolate her up there. We can use IV fluids and add ibuprofen six hourly via her drip.' He paused, drew a deep breath, then said, 'I'd better talk to the parents. Who brought her in?'

'The father, but he had to leave. Both parents are lawyers apparently, but I have a phone number for him.'

Sam followed, trying to thrust images of the sick child from her mind, wondering just how this had happened in this day and age of preventative measures. But as Andy used the card for the elevator, another thought struck her.

'You've just come off duty, haven't you? Why are you following up on this infant?'

'You've never worked a few hours after your shift ended?' he asked, and she shrugged because, of course, she, and probably thousands of other doctors, had.

'Thought not,' he said. 'But I've not just come off night shift—it's one of the few perks of the job that I don't do night shifts. I came in earlier and then again at about four to see a child on the ward who was having breathing problems.'

He smiled, and although it was a tired smile, it affected her, deep inside, in a way she certainly didn't want to think about.

Andy had been Nick's friend, and for all the irritations she might have felt in her marriage, the difficulties and disappointments, she still felt loyalty to Nick's memory, and somehow being attracted to his best friend was surely the ultimate disloyalty...

And, anyway, it was just a smile!

Andy had always had a nice smile.

They left the elevator, and Andy led her to the main monitoring desk, pointing out the way all the rooms could be monitored at once and introducing her to Karen, who was the head nurse on duty that morning.

She watched as his eyes scanned the monitors, and knew he'd been taking a mental note of every patient, even leaning over the desk and picking up a paper file to check on something he'd seen.

He explained the new admission to Karen, adding, 'Keep trying the number they have for the father in case the ED didn't get hold of him. Let him know where we are at and how to find us.'

A short discussion on their other patients, then Andy turned away, leading Sam along a corridor and returning to the conversation they'd been having.

'Actually, it was my last shift on call, and I'd worked my schedule so I could be here for your orientation before heading off this afternoon for a rest and to try to get my biorhythms back into sync.'

'I thought biorhythms had been totally debunked,' she said as the elevator doors slid open.

'Not totally and anyway it always seems to me that it's a better word to use because it's more than the physical side of yourself—well, myself anyway—that has to sort itself out after being on call, but the emotional and intellectual sides as well. I don't know about you, but I don't think well after a change of shifts—not until the sleep thing is sorted.'

'And the emotional side?' Sam asked as she followed him along the corridor.

'Oh, that's been totally stuffed for years,' he said. 'Unless you're involved with someone else who works ridiculous hours and often has to dash off at two in the morning for an emergency, a normal relationship is impossible.'

'Is there such a thing as a normal relationship?' she couldn't resist asking, thinking of the trials and anxiety she'd often felt in her marriage to Nick. But they'd reached the room where the little girl was already up from the ED and was being intubated by a nurse in full sterile covering, while Andy was looking intently at the chart he'd collected from the door.

With ninety-nine percent of his attention on the child in front of him, that tiny one percent had been caught by something in Sam's voice as she'd asked that question. The one about relationships…

Had her and Nick's marriage not been the one of connubial bliss he and everyone else had always thought it?

Nick had certainly painted it that way.

'We'll need to find out about her family,' he said, dragging that errant one percent back into place. 'Siblings, parents and grandparents, children she might mix with in day care or kindy.'

'I know most kindergartens won't accept unimmunised children. I'm not certain whether family day care is covered by it,' Sam told him, although he'd been speaking to the nurse.

'Her family—or at least one of them—should be with her,' the nurse muttered, but Andy ignored them both.

'There's a phone number for the father. When you speak to him just check out all you can about anyone she's been in contact with. If she has siblings who haven't been vaccinated, we need to get them in—or get them to their local doctor—for vaccination now. If she's been with other children at risk, we need to find them and get them vaccinated too.'

'Within seventy-two hours,' Sam finished for him. 'I could do that.'

He frowned at her.

'You're here for orientation,' he reminded her, a little too sharply because what he could only put down to lack of sleep was making him overly aware of Sam by his side. Reminding him he'd been foolish enough to ask her to stay with him at his apartment.

He stepped aside and wrote up the protocols for the day, handed the chart to the nurse, saying, 'I'd have liked to speak to a family member before admitting her, but I couldn't leave her in the ED. We'll have to explain that to someone later.'

He left the room, Sam on his heels.

'Why Intensive Care not the children's ward?' she asked, and he seized on the question to shake off the weirdness going on with this woman's reappearance in his life. Dear God, he'd known she was coming—had been looking forward to working with her again, given the experience she'd gained—and stupidest of all, he'd thought that long-ago attraction would surely have burnt out...

He banished the distracting thoughts, put them down to tiredness. This was work, a child's life was at stake.

'We can isolate her better here, watch for any signs of complication.'

'Pneumonia, encephalitis?'

'Ear infections,' he added, shaking his own head as if that might dislodge the softness of her voice.

Forcing his mind back to work, he led her towards the nurses' station, situated in the centre of the ward where a team of five nurses monitored the live feeds from all the PICU beds while two clerical staff handled phones and paperwork.

'This is Dr Sam Reilly,' he said as several of them looked up. 'She starts here tomorrow and I'm showing her around.'

He waved Sam forward before adding, 'No point in introducing you all now, she'll meet you in time.'

He turned to one of the clerical workers.

'I've just admitted a three-year-old girl with measles and put her in Isolation Room Two. Could you chase up the electronic file from the ED and make sure the room's online for monitoring?'

'We use paper files that stay with the patient, as well as electronic,' he said to Sam as he whisked away, aware she was just a step behind him—aware, too, that he should slow, they should walk together, as colleagues did.

But although he'd been prepared for her arrival, even looked forward to seeing her again, having her on his team, the fact that her physical presence still perturbed him had thrown his mind into chaos.

It was only temporary, this reaction. They hadn't parted on the best of terms—no, they'd parted on the worst of terms, he'd hurt her badly—so this would pass.

Soon, he hoped...

He thought back to that day in shame, but he'd seen her there in the hospital bed, so pale she'd have disappeared against the white pillow case if the scattering of freckles across her nose and the tangled red hair hadn't stood out so clearly.

She'd been injured, but just the sight of her—the pain he'd

read on her face—had knotted something in his gut, something that he'd tried to burn away with anger.

And now?

Now she was a colleague, and he had to think of her that way, because that was surely the only way she thought of him, She'd certainly never given the slightest indication that she was interested in him—in anyone but Nick, in fact...

'Abby has encephalitis,' he said, forcing his mind back to work as he led Sam into another room.

The young girl in the bed opened her eyes and smiled wanly at them.

'We've no idea what brought it on, have we, Abs?' he added, coming closer to take Abby's hand, 'but we do know she's on the mend.'

He motioned Sam forward.

'This is Sam, Abby, a new doctor and a very good one. We'll let her have a go at your records and see what she can sniff out, eh?'

Abby smiled again, then her eyes closed and she drifted back to sleep.

Andy handed the file he'd picked up from the back of the door to Sam, but kept his eyes on the sleeping girl.

Abby was thirteen, the same age Sarah had been when she'd died—Sarah, his beautiful, loving, always happy sister...

Sam flipped through the pages, noting the myriad tests that had been carried out on the sick child, realising that nothing had shown up as a possible trigger.

'Had she had a sore throat—could it have been as simple as a cold virus that triggered the swelling in her brain?' she asked as she slotted the file back in its place on the door, knowing she could read up on it on the computer later.

'Or some autoimmune thing, we've been thinking,' Andy replied, obviously still puzzled over the case. 'In fact, we did the regular tests, then stopped worrying what might have caused it and simply treated her. She's a little more alert every day, so I'm hopeful, given time and rest, she'll make a full recovery.'

'So much of what we do in PICU is rest and monitoring, isn't it?' Sam said, hoping she sounded rational and professional, although this being with Andy, trying to pretend he was nothing more than a colleague, was tying her stomach in knots.

And then he grinned at her.

'Ah, but the monitoring needs to be constant,' he said, while her head whirled. But Andy had always had that teasing grin so why...?

She dragged her mind back into gear and caught up with the conversation.

'Which is why the children are here and not down in the normal kids' wards. Come and meet Ryan—he's one of our frequent flyers.'

Sam laughed at the familiar phrase, reminding herself that this was work.

'Premmie?' she asked, and Andy nodded.

'He's two years old now, but still susceptible to any damn virus floating past in the air.'

'Usually RSV?' Sam asked, aware that respiratory syncytial virus, with its respiratory and breathing difficulties, was common in premature children.

Andy nodded.

'It's bronchiolitis this time. All the small passages in his lungs are inflamed, but six months ago it was pneumonia.'

'Poor kid,' Sam said, entering the room and peering down at the small form in the small cot. The little boy was probably only two thirds the size of a normal two-year-old, though what was really 'normal' with any child?

But she was intrigued by the small mask taped to the little boy's face and the tube from it leading back to a tiny CPAP machine.

'Non-invasive positive air pressure?' she said, intrigued

why the usual nasal prongs weren't delivering oxygen to the little body.

'We're finding, particularly with smaller children, that it's easier to get them off the oxygen when we use the continuous pressure air pump. There've been various small trials on it, and no definitive data as yet, but it works for young Ryan here, so we stick to it.'

Aware there was no treatment apart from oxygen to help their battling lungs, fluid to keep them hydrated, and paracetamol to keep the child's temperature down, Sam followed Andy out the door. Studying him, thinking...

He would have had the final decision on her employment, yet he'd employed her anyway—even though he obviously blamed her for Nick's death.

She shut the box in her mind that held memories of that day. This was now a new life, and Andy would be, inevitably, a big part of it so sometime soon that box had to be opened and some of the contents discussed. Their last encounter especially needed some explanations and she knew they couldn't go forward with it in both their minds, blocking out any proper conversation or even, possibly, friendship.

But in the meantime, Andy was right here—her boss—and she had to prove herself to him.

He was tall—taller than Nick had been—and he carried himself well, except for stooping slightly to hide his height as he was wont to do. He was good looking, too, with his dark hair and blue eyes.

But not married—well, apparently not—there was no ring on his finger.

And why would you be checking that out? she asked herself. He doesn't even like you.

'We talked about monitoring earlier.'

The words brought her mind back to the job. It was probably a bit of jet lag that had it wandering so far and so fast.

'And though it seems such a simple thing, it's paramount. It means we can see when they're about to crash and need resuscitation, or stop breathing and need urgent intubation, or have a seizure and need protective care and medication to ease it.'

He frowned slightly, turning to look directly at her, before adding, 'Though why I'm justifying our work to someone who is as experienced as you I don't know!'

Blue eyes looked steadily into her wishy-washy green ones, and about a million synapses in her brain fired to chaotic life.

Breathe!

'You forget I've just come from a hospital that's barely more than a shed with some beds, and the most sophisticated medical machinery was an X-ray machine that we couldn't work because of a lack of electricity.'

Andy stared at her. 'Seriously?' he said, and she smiled, relaxing as she talked about the place she'd grown to love. A place where her mother, a nurse, had worked for so many years it had become her home.

'Well, we did have a generator and when we had fuel for it, and it actually decided to work for a while, we could get the occasional X-ray. Whoever had donated the X-ray machine to the clinic had included plenty of film, so from time to time it was very handy. Mind you, I wasn't there for long enough to get totally frustrated by the lack of technology, but it was very educational in its own way!'

Andy shook his head, and she followed him into the next room, where a very pale girl of about twelve, was lying listlessly on a bed. Her eyes were open but whether she was seeing them, Sam didn't know.

'Kayla has recently been diagnosed with Type One diabetes, but it took a while for her GP to get to the root of her problem.'

'Or for her to agree to even see a doctor,' Sam suggested, and saw the girl give a wan smile. 'A lot of girls going into the teenage years complain of being tired, of having headaches, or they're irritable. So it isn't always picked up on at home and they don't always get to a doctor until something drastic happens.'

'You're right, of course,' Andy agreed, and Sam was just deciding that this would be okay—this working with Andy—but then he smiled, and it was such an open, warm, typical Andy smile that something inside her began to crack.

Could it be the film of the ice she'd sheathed around her heart when Nick had died?

CHAPTER TWO

IT TOOK ANOTHER hour to visit the other patients in the ICU, including the little girl with measles who'd now been installed in an isolation room.

'Has someone been in touch with the family?' Andy asked the nurse who was checking the drip stand.

'The ED phoned the number the father left, but couldn't get him, but we'll keep trying. He could already have realised the implications and be taking his other children for vaccination.'

Sam nodded, hoping this was true, but Andy wasn't appeased.

'Come on,' he said brusquely. 'We're done here. I'll make sure one of the nurses gets on to someone in that family and tells them they need vaccinations urgently. It's probably best I don't talk to them when I'm tired and—'

'Angry?' Sam offered, and he shrugged.

'More frustrated,' he said slowly. 'You see a child so sick from a preventable disease and wonder what people are thinking of. Anyway, it's time I left. I'll take you back to my place, and you can do some shopping.'

Very frustrated, Sam realised, so she kept her mouth shut until he'd led her out of the hospital and into the car park, opening the door of a dark saloon.

The flashback hit her without warning—Nick's voice, loud and insistent, the car swerving. Then nothing...

She knew she couldn't get into the car; couldn't get in with an angry—or frustrated—driver.

Not again.

Not after the last time.

'I have to go back and get my things,' she said. 'My backpack. But you go. I think I'll stick to my initial plan and get a hotel for a couple of weeks until I find somewhere more permanent.'

The tightness she'd read on his face vanished like mist burnt off by the sun, and now anxiety drew its lines in his skin.

'Hey, it's okay,' he said. 'I just get a bit upset when I butt up against parents like that.'

'Like what?' she retorted. 'A couple where both parents choose to work? Where neither wants to set aside the expensive training they've had, largely through public funds, to be with their children twenty-four seven? You don't know those people, Andy. For all you know, he could be representing a young girl in a rape case and can't afford *not* to be in court this morning, and the mother could be helping refugees in an off-shore detention centre.'

He stared at her.

'You're saying they could both have legitimate reasons *not* to be with their child?'

'I am,' she said. 'I know there are parents who aren't totally involved in their children's lives, but we can't judge *all* working parents. Half the doctors at this hospital are working parents. Is a surgeon going to cancel a possibly life-saving op to sit with his sick child?'

Andy said nothing but she could see the idea taking root in his mind.

'So he'd focus on what had to be done—put his personal

anxiety aside for as long as it took to get the best result for his patient—and then go back to the child.'

'Of course he would. Ninety percent of parents would.'

Andy studied her for what seemed like for ever.

'You've given this a lot of thought,' he finally said, and saw a deep sadness cloud her pale eyes.

But all she said was, 'Indeed I have,' before she turned and walked back towards the hospital.

He went after her, catching up in a few strides.

'Hey!'

He turned her so she faced towards him and used one finger to tilt her head so he could look into those tantalising eyes.

'Why don't you forget about a hotel for a while? Come and stay with me while you find somewhere permanent,' he said, hoping it didn't sound like a plea. 'It'll be fun—like the old days, although we probably won't see that much of each other because our shifts won't coincide, but...'

He paused and tried a smile.

'But when we *are* together, you can teach me not to judge, and remind me that every picture could be telling many different stories.'

She stood there, lips pursed—kissable, but he definitely wasn't going there—and he remembered she'd always done that when she was thinking.

When they'd all been friends.

'Okay!' she said, 'but I still need to get my backpack.'

He followed her back to the building, surprised when she led him into the ED staff lounge.

'I needed a shower before I ventured anywhere further into the hospital,' she explained, digging a key out of the pocket of her scrubs and leading him to a locker.

He watched as she unlocked the locker and reached in to haul out what seemed like an enormous backpack.

Sliding it out of her hands, he slung it over his shoulder, bending at the knees in faked collapse.

'It's not *that* heavy!' she told him, although he did win a smile.

Silly really, but the smile made the weight lighter, and he led the way back towards his car, feeling alive and alert, despite the early start. And if a tiny whisper suggested they should have parted when she'd suggested it earlier, he could easily ignore it.

It would be good to have Sam back in his life.

It *would*!

'It's not far from the hospital—my place,' Andy said, as Sam settled herself into the comfortable passenger seat in his car, 'but at night I like to use the car, the streets are dark and you never know who's hanging around.'

It was such an ordinary conversation Sam should have felt relaxed, but instead she was wondering why she hadn't insisted on going to a hotel. It wasn't that she didn't enjoy Andy's company—she always had, although she'd seen a lot less of him after she'd married Nick. He and Andy would meet up for a drink when she was on a late shift, or Andy would be busy when she and Nick were having friends over.

Then, so upset by what had been just his unthinking reaction to the accident, she'd refused to see him again while she'd been in hospital. But she'd been hurt by his angry words—hurt, if she was honest, because they had been too close to the truth.

But working with him meant they'd be colleagues, and colleagues were often friends, and she and Andy—

For heaven's sake, stop analysing everything. Whatever happened to your philosophy of taking each day as it came. That's what got you through the accident, and that's what you have to do here.

She glanced towards him, pleased he was concentrating on the road so she could study him for a moment. And wonder if perhaps she'd always felt a slight attraction towards him?

She shook her head.

'Bad thoughts?' he asked. He'd obviously seen her frown and head shake.

'No, just wondering where we are and how long it will take me to find my way around a new place.'

'You'd never been here before? Never had a holiday on the coast?'

She shook her head again.

'Mum worked full time—and I mean full time—two jobs usually, just to keep us fed and watered. Any extra money was put aside for the university education she insisted I had to have. Holidays never entered the picture.'

'Well, I'll just have to educate you. Port Fortesque was first settled way back, much of the original building done by convicts,' he explained. 'It was a stopping-off place for boats going north from Sydney to the new penal colony in Moreton Bay, which is now in Queensland but back then was part of New South Wales. There are still some lovely old buildings here, especially the lighthouse. We should go there for dinner tonight to welcome you back to Oz. They've turned the lighthouse-keeper's cottage into a fine restaurant.'

She'd let him talk, let his voice wash over her, although—

'I don't need fine dining,' she told him, 'and I definitely don't want you running around after me. You'll want a relaxing, early night after your four a.m. start, and I've got shopping to do and clothes to sort and wash.'

She paused, aware that what she was about to say was for her own protection. Andy was too darned attractive for his own good, and the less she saw of him outside working hours the better.

'I also need to get onto a real-estate website. There might even be a self-contained B&B I can use as a base until I get to know the area. In London, there were dozens of them set up close to hospitals.'

He glanced her way.

'Whatever suits you best,' he said, his voice noticeably cooler.

Surely he hadn't been *looking forward* to her staying with him. Wouldn't that put a crimp in his social life, for a start?

Although what did *she* know about his social life? Except that he'd be sure to have one. The Andy who'd been half of Nick and Andy had always had a beautiful woman in his life.

An image of Andy walking into his flat with a beautiful woman, chatting politely for a while before disappearing into his bedroom, had Sam feeling distinctly uncomfortable. Which was a totally ridiculous reaction as Andy's social life was none of her business, whether she was sharing his apartment or not.

Nothing to do with her.

At all!

He'd been—probably still would have been—her husband's best friend. She'd known him as long as she'd known Nick—which, much as she'd loved him, had, at times, seemed a very long three years—but Andy had always been there whenever he'd been needed, with a smile on his face and a ready laugh on his lips.

Except after the accident...

He'd been pointing out landmarks as they passed, the river with its old wharf now only used to tie up visiting pleasure yachts, the surf beaches between rocky headlands to the south of the river mouth.

The sun sparkled on the ocean, making magic in the air, so when Andy turned into the drive that led to the basement of newish block of apartments, pressed a fob for the metal doors to rise, she began to regret accepting his offer.

It might be hard to leave the views this place must have, the rocky headlands curling protectively around the surf beach, a stretch of golden sand, the broken waves rushing up the beach as the tide came in.

'I thought you said it wasn't far from the hospital,' she said, as Andy expertly parked his car and came round to open her door.

She beat him to it, but only just, so she stood to find him so close they could have kissed.

If they hadn't been separated by the car door.

If this had been that kind of relationship.

And just where had *those* thoughts come from?

She might have felt a sudden awareness of Andy as a man, but she was probably the last woman in the world *he'd* consider getting involved with!

'I brought you the long way around to see some of the sights, but the hospital is only ten minutes directly west, twenty minutes on foot. Though I must warn you...' he added with a smile that raised goose-bumps on her skin.

What was wrong with her?

She tuned back into Andy's conversation.

'There are some steep hills to tackle if you're walking to work. This was once a rocky peninsula that reached out into the sea. There's actually good diving on it further out, colourful soft corals and tiny, brilliant fish darting in and out of it. Do you dive?'

'Dive?'

She invested the word with such disbelief Andy had to smile.

'You might not remember, but I come from a land-locked village in the top western corner of the state. We're lucky when we have a good enough wet season to have a swim in the local dam,' she told him. 'Plus, as you may have noticed, I have the kind of skin that turns beetroot red after about five minutes in the sun. The English climate really suited me!'

He did remember now—remembered more and more about her. She had two laughs, an infectious giggle and a full-blown laugh that was a sound of sheer delight.

And he'd asked her to stay with him?

He must have been out of his mind, especially when he loved to come home to the peace and quiet of his apartment after a busy day.

And now he was leaning on the top of the car door, talking about diving, of all things, and thinking about laughter from a time that seemed so far in the past it was practically ancient history.

Except that she was, and always would be, to him, quite lovely, with her vivid hair and pale skin, her easy smile and laughter.

Did he not want this light-hearted moment to end?

Or was he afraid that once she'd imprinted herself on his living space, he'd find it hard to reclaim it as his own?

His attraction to her had led him to distance himself from her and Nick after the wedding—not far, just far enough. Protection really, but she'd stayed in his head, usually laughing at some silly—

'Do you not want me to see your apartment, or have you sent an urgent message to some woman to vacate the place for a while?'

Her teasing smile plucked at his nerves, so it took him a moment to recover.

'Tribes of women having to vacate it,' he managed to say lightly, fully opening the car door for her and heading to the trunk to retrieve her backpack.

But the tension he felt as the elevator rose to the eleventh floor strengthened the feeling that maybe this hadn't been one of his better ideas.

Perhaps even his worst since the rock, paper, scissors fiasco all those years ago.

His mind did a quick mental scan of the state of his place. He liked it neat and tidy, but he'd left in a rush this morning. Although, while his bedroom might be a bit chaotic, she'd hardly be inspecting that. And this thought caused nearly as many strange reactions in his body as her pursed and kissable lips had earlier.

Enough!

This was Sam, his best friend's widow, remember, invited to stay while she sorted herself out.

A few days—a week—she was already talking about real-estate sites...

The problem was he'd known she was coming, but he'd been unprepared for actually seeing her again. *And* he'd been unprepared for the memories her presence had evoked.

He'd been attracted to her as far back as the day he and Nick had first met her, and he'd hoped she'd say no when Nick asked her out...

He'd telephone Susie later today, get his social life organised.

'Oh, but it's beautiful!'

Sam's words made him turn to see her gazing, wide-eyed, at his view.

'It takes in so much—the rocky headland, the sea, and then the sky. How lucky are you?'

He could hear the genuine delight in her voice, and for a moment wanted to tell her she could always stay on here, pay a little rent if it made her feel better. There was plenty of room...

Are you mad?

He hid more than a few qualms as he led her deeper into the apartment. This was not a good idea, given that he still felt a lingering attraction to her. Especially when, in his heart, he still blamed her for Nick's death, only too aware that never driving over the speed limit was a part of Nick's mild OCD.

In fact, the whole situation was a bloody mess.

'I like this room that looks back towards the mountains,' Sam was saying while he stood in the passage, clutching her backpack, random thoughts jostling in his head.

'Here, give me that.'

Her words broke the spell.

'I'll find something clean and relatively suitable to go shopping in and leave you to catch up on your sleep.'

He set her backpack down on the bedroom floor, aware of some new tension in the air. Had she guessed what he'd been thinking? Not that she needed to guess his thoughts about the accident—he'd more or less accused her of causing it.

'The bed's made up—friends and family are always turning up, so I leave it with clean sheets on,' he said awkwardly as he backed out of the room. 'I'll find some spare keys you can use.'

This was *not* a good idea, Sam decided when Andy had disappeared. They'd barely met again, and yet she felt unsettled when she was with him. It was an awareness, really—even an attraction—yet this was the man who'd blamed her for Nick's death, probably still did...

Not that she had time to be worrying about a little awkwardness, let alone attraction. She'd lost a month of preparation back in Cambodia and she had a lot of organising to do. Clothes first—sensible clothes for work, that's all she'd need for a while. A new swimming costume, there'd be days when she'd be able to fit in a swim before work, before the sun got too hot...

She opened her bag and rummaged through it, finding some long loose trousers and a tunic top—the kind of thing she'd been wearing all the time at the little clinic. The clothes might look a little odd in the shopping mall at Port Fortesque but they were clean and decent.

Once showered and dressed, she found Andy in the kitchen. 'We passed a shopping mall on the way here. If I just go out the front door and turn left, I'll find it, won't I?'

He smiled at her outfit—making her think again of awkwardness and attraction, and definitely finding a real-estate office online...

'They're clean and respectable,' she told him, defending her choice of clothing. 'The shopping mall?'

'Left and left again at the second street, you can't miss it,' he said, the smile still teasing at his lips. 'Phone me if you buy so much you need a lift home.'

He crossed to the bar on one side of the kitchen, undoubtedly used for most meals, and picked up a card and a set of keys.

'The fob opens the garage doors, the flat one you swipe for the elevator, the big key is for the front entrance and this lovely purple one is for my front door. Eleventh floor, Apartment Two. My number's on the card. Okay?'

She took them from him, their fingers tangling around the flat elevator key, sending such a weird sensation through Sam she involuntarily looked up to see if Andy had also felt it.

But although that teasing smile still hovered on his lips, he showed no sign of any sudden reaction.

Which was hardly surprising...

Sam departed, tucking the keys into her small backpack, reminding herself that was something else she should buy—a handbag.

She shook her head. Her small backpack had served her well for the past three years. It had originally been Nick's, but he'd replaced it with a much smarter leather briefcase once he'd been promoted. She'd found it when she'd been cleaning out their flat and realised how handy it would be for her travels.

Besides, it was so long since she'd used a handbag she'd feel foolish with one, and she certainly wasn't going down the brief-case road. But she *did* have a small, pretty, handwoven bag with a long strap that would hold her wallet and a few tissues. She could always take that if she ever *did* go out at night.

The mall loomed in front of her, and she wondered just what it would offer in the way of clothes-buying options.

She needn't have worried, because all the old familiar stores were there, and within half an hour she had a selection of slacks, long shorts, skirts, T-shirts and shirts, and two swimming costumes. She'd stuck with basics—black and white with a few floral and striped tops to brighten things up—but as she walked out—newly bought shopping weighing down her arms—she passed a small boutique offering a fifty percent off sale.

The clothes were beautiful, mainly linen and silk, and simple in style but shrieking elegance. She tried to persuade herself that she'd never wear such clothes, but a pale green linen shift drew her like a magnet, while a black silk dress with a low scooped neckline and flaring skirt refused to be left behind. Sandals, shoes and a pair of comfy slides for the beach soon followed and she spent the walk home telling herself there'd surely be a Christmas party at the hospital so, depending on how formal it might be, either the shift or the black dress would do.

Back when she'd been growing up, buying her own clothes for the first time, her mother had always assured her that a little black dress could go anywhere. And her mother's LBD had gone many places—the single mother of a growing daughter not having had the money to spend on a range of 'going out' dresses!

'You didn't strike me a shopper,' Andy greeted her when she walked back in.

'I'm not,' she said. 'But having discarded all my London clothes before I left, and with the few Cambodian outfits not really suitable here, I had to start again. Basic shopping from the skin out, plus toiletries and odds and ends. I decided that being second in charge meant I had to at least look respectable.'

He smiled, eyes gleaming so she knew a tease was coming.

'Going to give me a fashion parade? You could start with the purple undies!'

She shook her head, but she was smiling too. This was the old Andy—often teasing her to see her blush, Nick laughing with him at the result.

Enough memories.

Be practical.

'You must be ready for an early night after your four a.m. start. As you've been good enough to take me in, would you like me to send out for a takeaway? Although I did grab a few groceries on the way home. I'd be happy to do a Cambodian stir-fry.'

'You cook?'

He sounded astounded.

In fact, so astounded Sam felt a little stab of pain. She'd always cooked and enjoyed it, but Nick had liked to give their friends the impression that she was a pampered princess, and he had always cooked the meals when they'd had guests.

She'd grown to hate it, but had kept quiet about it, at first putting it down to Nick showing off and only later realising it was part of his problem; his need to be the best in other people's eyes, both as a husband and a cook—even a doctor...

And she'd put up with it because she'd loved Nick, and she'd been determined to make their marriage work. Right up until the end—that last fateful day...

Focus!

'Well?' she demanded of Andy, possibly a little too abruptly.

He'd been frowning off into the distance, and turned, startled, back towards her.

'Well, what?'

'Would you like me to cook dinner?'

'Well, yes, of course,' he managed to say. 'If you really want to.'

'I do.' she said firmly, although she'd had to close her eyes for an instant to control a rising heat of anger.

So not only had Nick done his best to make *her* feel useless, but Andy's reaction had made her realise he'd convinced his friends of that as well.

The kitchen was neat and functional. No wok, but she could cook in a frying pan.

'Do you eat chicken?' she called to Andy, last seen standing on the balcony looking out to sea.

'Love it,' he said, sounding so close she started and spun around to find him on the other side of the breakfast bar.

'And you,' he asked, 'would you like a beer as you slave away over a hot stove?'

'Love one,' she said. 'You might not know it, but Cambodia has some very good beers, and one always goes down well while I'm cooking.'

He put the small stubby of beer in a foam holder beside the chopping board she was using to finely slice spring onions, bok choy, capsicum, carrots, snow peas and cabbage.

'Thanks,' she said, setting down her knife and lifting the beer. 'Cheers!' she said, and clinked it with Andy's.

'Welcome home!' he replied, smiling at her as if he meant it, and she had to turn away to hide the silly tears that had, for no good reason, filled her eyes.

Andy watched as Sam sliced and diced, taking a sip from her beer occasionally.

He'd thought he'd known this woman who'd been married to his best friend for three years, yet small things were causing him to question all he'd known.

Not that it mattered. They'd be working and living—temporarily at least—together, plenty of time to get to know her. And if he was right about glimpsing a sheen of tears in her eyes when he'd said welcome home, then there was a lot about her to get to know.

He'd always admired her for the way she'd handled Nick, who hadn't always been the easiest of friends to have.

Nick had always wanted to win, to be the best.

Andy closed his eyes on memories and concentrated on the woman in his kitchen. Tall and lean in the loose-fitting, distinctly Asian outfit, she'd bunched her hair up on top of her head to keep it out of the way, and was humming to herself as she worked.

'You seem to enjoy cooking,' he said, watching as she opened a bottle of sesame oil she'd obviously bought earlier and poured a fine stream into the pan.

'Love it,' she said, echoing the words he'd said earlier, but turning to smile at him at the same time.

Tears—if they had been tears—now gone.

The pan sizzled as she slid the sliced chicken in and tossed it around so it would cook quickly. The vegetables followed, more sizzling, more tossing and turning.

She pulled her shopping bag towards her with her free hand, and half turned to him.

'I've cheated with the rice. Can you cut the top off the packet and microwave it for two minutes for me, please?'

He put down his beer and lifted the packet.

'Chilli and coconut, my favourite,' he said, as he did his part in the dinner preparation. 'I've come to regard microwave rice as one to the world's great inventions.'

She grinned at him, then added a variety of sauces to the stir-fry—small amounts but the aroma made the dish come alive.

'Right, rice into bowls, some eating utensils, and we're done,' she said, turning off the gas beneath the pan and raising her beer to her lips again.

Her eyes were shining, with pleasure now, he was sure, and as he watched the pale skin on her throat move as she swallowed the beer, a feeling in his gut told him this cohabitation might not be such a good idea.

But as they ate, sitting at the small table on the balcony, the moon silvering the sea, and the soft shushing of the waves the only noise, Andy found himself enjoying the company, the laughter Sam brought with the stories of her travels, and the allure of his beautiful companion, fine skin pale in the moonlight, stray strands of red-gold hair tumbling in long curls to her shoulders.

They talked of many things beyond her travels—the hospital, Andy's time in the US—but never Nick, for all he'd been an important part of both their lives. She thought Andy's conversation had swerved that way from time to time, but she'd turned the question or remark away, not yet ready to discuss this part of their past.

And aware she might never be able to…

Except she should—had to really—or it would fester and ruin any chance of a friendship between them.

She took a deep breath and launched right into it.

'That night at the hospital, Andy. I was upset when you said Nick would never have spee—'

'I should never have said it,' he interrupted. 'Never said anything so hurtful to you. Since we offered you the job, I've had this last month to think about how to apologise, trying to work out what—'

She reached out and touched his lips with one finger to stop his words.

'Me first,' she said, looking directly into his eyes, desperate to see understanding there, though at the moment there was only concern.

'I loved Nick to distraction,' she said quietly, 'but later I grew to hate our marriage. Not Nick—the love was still there always—but I hated what I'd let myself become, hated that I'd given so much of myself away to be what he wanted me to be, to fit into *his* life the way he wanted me to—the way *he* felt a wife should.'

She paused and looked down into her lap where her hands were tightly clasped, fingers twined into each other as she struggled with the emotion of those days.

'But that day—in the car—it suddenly got too much and the temper I was sure I'd conquered just erupted again, and I threw all the unkind and hurtful things I could find at him, at the man I loved...'

Another silence and she looked into Andy's face again.

It told her nothing, and a cold certainty that she'd ruined any friendship they'd had and the one they might have had in the future spread through her.

But she had to finish.

'You were right,' she said, almost gabbling the words to get them said. 'I probably did cause the accident. I was as angry as I've ever been, yelling at him—him yelling back at me, both unwilling to give an inch. Then, suddenly it was over, a loud bang, and I was in hospital, Nick dead...'

She bowed her head, so he didn't see the tears—tears of pain for what else she'd lost that day.

'So you were spot on,' she finished, battling to keep her voice steady. 'Nick wouldn't have broken the speed limit, but he was as angry as I was, hurt and hurtful.'

She waited, praying silently that Andy would understand, wondering why life had to be so complicated.

But all he did was reach one hand across the table and squeeze her fingers.

Then he smiled, a weary, tired smile but one that still lit up his eyes.

'Oh, Sam, you shouldn't still be blaming yourself. I know I made things so much worse for you with my cruel, thoughtless words. And I've been wondering for a month how I could apologise to you. I had no right to say that to you—to hurt you further. Of course it wasn't your fault—you weren't driving, Nick was, and no matter the provocation *he* was the one speeding.'

He took both her hands in his now, and added, 'Can you forgive me? Can we be friends?'

She squeezed his fingers.

'Friends,' she said.

They sat a little longer, their hands still clasped, until Sam began to feel uncomfortable.

'You should be in bed,' she told him, needing to get away, to think about what had just happened between them, but first and foremost to remove her fingers, which seemed to be quite happy sitting there in his light clasp.

Andy had been trying to ignore their tangled fingers—ignore the tension rising in his body.

He stood up, probably a little too abruptly.

'I should, and so should you,' he said, clamping his lips together as beer and a single glass of wine had weakened his resistance, and the suggestion they could share a bed threatened to escape his lips.

As if, given how she'd just said she still loved Nick...

Or *had* still loved him?

He brought reality back with talk of work—safe talk.

'I did tell you, didn't I, that we'll be working together? Same shifts for the first few days, just until you settle in and get to know our routines and procedure protocols. Basic stuff, but I always found it difficult moving hospitals, so it seemed like a good idea.'

'That's great!' Sam said, a bright smile underlining the words. 'So, what time do we need to leave?'

Her enthusiasm *and* the smile made him wonder if it had been all *that* great an idea, but he battled on.

'We'll leave about seven-thirty,' he said, forcing the distraction of this beautiful woman away with practical words. 'See you then?'

CHAPTER THREE

'SEE YOU THEN?'

The words echoed in Sam's head as she made her way to her bedroom.

Did he not eat breakfast before he left for work?

And what was she supposed to do?

She remembered how she'd hated staying with a friend for the first time, never sure when to get out of bed—would everyone be up, or would she wake them?

And she'd certainly need breakfast but could she just open and shut cupboards in Andy's kitchen until she found breakfast-type food?

Not that she regretted him leaving so suddenly. Something had shifted between them after they'd talked about Nick. It was as if the breeze had strengthened in some way and caused vibrations in her body, a sense so fine she knew it had to be imagined.

Or hoped it had to be imagined…

Yet Andy's abrupt departure had eased that tension at least, although he'd left her wondering just what it was she felt.

Andy was just Andy—a friend from years back—and his having her to stay was nothing more than a sign of that.

But, practically, could they get back to the easy friendship they'd had when she'd first met him? From the way he'd spoken, he'd obviously regretted the harsh words he'd said to her after the accident, so she could put that behind her and go forward.

In friendship… Something, she realised now, she wouldn't like to lose.

She closed her bedroom door and was pulling off her T-shirt when there was a light tap from outside.

'I should have said there's plenty of food in the pantry and refrigerator, or there's a café on ground level that opens early to do breakfasts.'

She moved closer to the door, awareness of him just outside prickling her skin.

'Thanks,' she said. 'The café sounds good!'

She was close enough now to press her hand against the wood, aware he was just as close on the other side.

Was his hand also against the door?

Did she want it to be?

Did *he* want it to be?

She waited, wondering if he'd suggest they eat breakfast in the café together.

Should *she* suggest it?

But all she heard was a shuffle of feet on carpet and a quiet, 'Goodnight!'

She stayed where she was, hand on the door, trying to disentangle the various emotions this nothing of a conversation had just stirred up in her.

Had she *wanted* him to come in?

She shook her head to that one, although she wasn't totally convinced.

Had *he* wanted her to ask him in?

Well, on that point she had no idea at all, but would guess not. Andy was far too…proper, really for something so crass…

They were going to work together—be colleagues—and relationships with colleagues grew muddled. She and Nick had discovered that.

Nick.

She'd thought three years would have made it easier to think about him—even talk about him—but the resentment and anger she'd begun to feel towards the end of their marriage had surfaced again when she'd started talking earlier. Perhaps it was best to leave things as they were...

She moved away from the door, stripped off her clothes and stepped under the shower in the little en suite bathroom.

But once in bed, a book propped on her knees, she wondered again about her agreement to stay with Andy—if only for a short time...

She did have breakfast in the café but ate alone—fruit toast and strong tea. No sign of Nick, no sound of him in the apartment before she'd left it.

But that was explained when she returned, and he was in the kitchen, mixing up some type of green sludge—presumably a healthy smoothie—a beach towel wrapped around his waist and his bare chest still damp in patches from an early morning swim.

She'd walk to work in future, she decided then and there. That way she wouldn't have to work out why that bare chest, tanned and sculpted by the swimming and whatever other exercise he did, had caused a hitch in her breathing, and a warmth to fill her body.

'I can walk to the hospital today,' she said, the words shooting out of her mouth. 'It'll do me good.'

He swallowed a mouthful of his green sludge and shook his head.

'I'll be five minutes,' he told her, 'I've had my shower, and—'

Dear Heaven, he was naked under that towel!

The warmth became heat, which she knew would be showing in her cheeks.

'No, I need the exercise, and it will be good to get a feel for the place.'

She grabbed the little backpack, checked the keys were in it, and with a casual wave of her hand escaped out the door.

What she really needed was a real-estate office or to start searching online for somewhere else to live.

No way could she continue to live with Andy now he'd started to affect her the way he did. Neither could she really find another man—just a friend with benefits—to ease her frustration, not while she was living with Andy. *That* would be far too awkward!

She needed to move out, find somewhere of her own. Somewhere she could think about the future, put Nick behind her for ever, and, in the classic phrase, move on!

How had she got herself into this?

But as she walked up onto the top of the next hill and looked north this time, to the river's mouth and beyond it to the sweeping, golden beach and brilliant, dark blue ocean, a sense of peace stole over her.

Coming here *had been* a good decision.

And having a friend—for that was all Andy was—to show her around was also a good thing.

She walked on, breathing in the sea air, her feet beating out a rhythm that echoed in her head—Andy is a friend, Andy is a friend…

Rosa, the three-year-old with measles, was their first stop, after being alerted by a nurse that her condition hadn't improved.

'In fact, it's worsened,' Sam said as she read through the chart, while Andy bent over the cot.

'Yes,' he said. 'The night duty doctor phoned, and we discussed using the cooling pads.'

Sam had been looking at the small pads on Rosa's wrists, neck and temples, white against the raw redness of the rash that now covered her body.

'We're just getting new ones for the inside of her elbows,' the nurse explained, 'and her father's been here all night.'

She pointed to the big adjustable chair that could be tipped back to allow someone in it to at least doze.

'He's gone home to see his other children and take them to their local GP for vaccinations, then he'll be back.' She paused. 'He's devastated,' she said. 'Blames himself.'

Sam took one glance at Andy's face and stepped into the conversation.

'Some people genuinely believe the vaccination could harm their child. They fear it, no matter how much education we do.'

Andy shook his head. 'Were you always Little Miss Sunshine, refusing to see any bad in people?' he said, but it was more a tease than a sarcastic remark.

She grinned at him. 'I try,' she said.

They moved on to the boy with the burnt feet, Jonah. He was sleeping, and as Andy studied his chart, Sam looked at the bandages and shook her head.

'How on earth can you burn the bottom of your feet?' she asked, and it was Andy's turn to smile.

'He lives near the beach and, apparently, he was clever enough to know he'd probably end up in serious trouble if he started a fire in the scrub on the headland. So he decided to experiment with a small one on a sandy patch hidden in amongst the rocks at the point. Had a great time, then his mother called him for dinner, and he covered it over with sand.'

'And walked on it?' Sam guessed.

'Worse,' Andy said. 'He stamped the sand down to make sure the fire was out.'

Sam shook her head. 'His poor parents,' she said. 'They must wonder what on earth he'll get up to next.'

They discussed his treatment—the worst of the wounds had been debrided, and both feet were now bound in bandages to prevent infection. Given his improvement, he could go into a general children's ward later that day.

Together they checked the most seriously ill children, three of them in isolation rooms following chemotherapy. Then Andy excused himself to attend a department heads' meeting, and Sam was left to visit the other children—twenty-three in all, quite a number for a provincial city's ICU.

'They come in from all the outlying areas,' the nurse with her explained. 'The district hospitals don't have the specialists or Intensive Care.'

'Certainly not as up to date as this place,' Sam said, constantly surprised by the facilities in the unit.

A loud beep took both of them to the small alcove where the child with RSV lay limply in his cot. One glance at the bedside monitor told Sam what was happening. His struggle to breathe, even with the ventilation, had caused his overworked heart to stop beating.

As the nurse pressed the button for a crash cart, Sam started chest compressions, the heel of her hand on the little breast bone, pressing hard and counting.

'Remove his mask for a minute and suction his trachea, in case the oxygen isn't getting through' she said to the nurse, as Andy, no doubt alerted to the crisis, appeared.

'His chest is rising and falling so the ventilator is keeping him oxygenated.'

Andy felt for a pulse, shook his head.

'Epinephrine?' Sam asked, and he shook his head again.

'There are so many questions about the use of it in the long term these days,' he said. 'It will probably restart his heart but could also cause brain damage. We'll shock him. You've got his weight?'

The nurse read it out from the chart and Sam watched as Andy translated it to voltage, using four joules per kilogram. The nurse was already attaching miniature pads to the small chest while Andy set the machine.

They stood clear and the little body jerked, Sam bending

over him ready to begin chest compressions again, although the steady heart-rate lines were already running across the monitor.

It had been a heart-stopping moment—literally for the child—and the tension had somehow thickened the air in the room, while all eyes remained on the monitor, dreading they'd see that line waver.

Sam turned to practical matters, beginning compressions again, aware that continuing compressions for a couple of minutes helped the failing heart regain its normal momentum.

The nurses were cleaning up and wheeling the crash cart away, but Andy continued to study the boy.

'We need to go back in his history to see if there was any suggestion of an abnormality in his heart from birth.' He shook his head before answering his own question. 'Surely not. Premmies are always tested every which way, scanned and checked on an almost daily basis.'

Sam smiled to herself. Back when she'd first met Nick and Andy, and had worked with Andy when she'd been on a month's student placement and he a junior registrar, she'd often heard him debating his thoughts aloud.

'What about an atrial septum defect?' she suggested. 'They can sometimes be so small they're not picked up until adulthood, although they do affect the lungs as well as the heart.'

Andy smiled at her, which, given the situation, shouldn't have had the slightest effect on her, but when he added, 'I knew I'd got you here for a reason,' she felt a flush of pride.

'We'll let the little fellow rest for an hour,' he continued, while she told herself it really *was* pride, not something else that had caused the heat, 'then see what an ultrasound can find.'

'They're often picked up in adults with a murmur,' Sam said, concentrating on their small patient and sticking the buds of her stethoscope in her ears. 'If it was audible it would have been picked up before now, but I'll just have a listen in case the stoppage made it clearer.'

She blew on the pad to warm it, then pressed it gently to the little chest, hearing the beat of his heart, steady and regular now, and perhaps just a whisper of something else.

Andy listened too, but shook his head. 'We'll leave it for the ultrasound.'

He paused, thoughtful again. 'Although if it does show something up, we then have a decision to make—or the heart specialists will.'

'Operate to close it, or just leave it and watch?'

He nodded, frowning now at the child who'd had such a bad start to his life.

They checked the rest of their patients, including a large lad of twelve who looked out of place in the PICU.

'He took a knock on the football field, lost consciousness, then had a grand mal seizure,' Andy explained. 'The neurologist who admitted him wanted him monitored for forty-eight hours before he does an EEG to see if there's a likelihood of recurrent seizures.'

He watched Sam flicking through the lad's chart, pleased he had such good support from his number two, even though working with Sam felt disorientating in some way. For so long she'd just been Nick's girl and that's the way he'd forced himself to think of her from the time they'd started going out together—Nick's girlfriend, Nick's partner, Nick's wife.

But Nick had been lost to both of them and now she was just Sam—a woman he'd been attracted to, and, he rather thought, still was...

And he'd been stupid enough to ask her to stay!

'His CT scan showed no visible damage,' she said, glancing up at him with a flash of pale green eyes. 'No bleeds or clots, no abnormalities that could have caused it, so it was likely the result of the concussion.'

He nodded, aware some response was needed, but—

You've got a patient! an inner voice said sternly, and he

turned his full attention on the boy, asking him simple questions, noticing his patient's growing exasperation.

'And before you ask, I don't know who the prime minister is, and I didn't know it before either. It's a stupid question,' the lad said.

'So, tell me about your mates instead,' Andy suggested, and listened while the boy rattled off the names of his friends and gave them brief descriptions of each of them.

Andy smiled at him. 'I don't think there's much wrong with your brain, and the EEG—that's just short for electroencephalogram, which you must admit is a bit of a mouthful—will show if there's likely to be a recurrence, and you'll need to be on medication to stop it happening again.'

'But that would mean no more football,' the lad complained.

'No football for four weeks anyway,' he told the lad.

'Try tennis—it's much better for your head,' Sam suggested, but a little frown between her eyebrows made Andy wonder what was bothering her.

'Let's get a coffee,' he suggested as they left the boy to his video game. 'We'll talk about the children we've seen and you can tell me what you think.'

He led her into the small, comfortable staffroom and turned on the coffee machine.

'You okay?' he asked, carefully not looking at her but aware of her presence.

Aware of *her*...

Wondering if he'd made a mistake in appointing her when there was a close connection between them and he'd always been attracted to her.

Then reminding himself he couldn't have not employed her. She had been far and away the best candidate.

Wondering, also, why she hadn't answered.

It had been the kind of question that usually got a reply immediately.

So he had to turn, *had* to look at her, had to put up with the disturbances her presence was causing him, because she *was* the best and his patients deserved that.

'*Are* you okay?' he asked this time.

She smiled at him, but it was such a pathetic effort he forgot about the coffee, and his personal concerns, and sat down beside her on the couch.

'What is it?' he said, trying to sound gently persuasive but missing it by a mile.

Even to him the question sounded abrupt to the point of rudeness, but it had been the best he could do when every fibre in his being was telling him to put his arm around her—tell her that whatever it was they'd work it out.

Hold her...

Comfort her...

That might be what she needed right now, but was it what *he* wanted?

Forget that, think about her. It's what a friend would do—any friend.

But *were* they friends?

They'd certainly made peace between them...

She smiled again, a better effort, and added a half-laugh.

'Stupid, really,' she said. 'But I was looking at young Nathan and wondering if I could let my child play football.'

She studied him for a moment before adding, 'When you've got children—a family of your own—how do you make those decisions? Do they worry constantly, every parent, or is it worse for us because we see what *can* happen?'

He thought of the children he'd probably never have—the women who hadn't wanted to risk having a child with him—the scars that had made him stop thinking about a family, about any permanent relationship...

'I'm not sure,' he said, 'about other parents but I think it's probably easier not to have them, then you don't have to worry at all. That's where I've got to in my thinking.'

He knew it was a flippant answer but he didn't want to go into all of that with Sam when she was obviously upset.

Thrusting the confusion of thoughts out of his head, Andy returned to his coffee-making. But he *had* to think about Sam's questions because there'd been genuine concern in her voice, as if having a family was important to her and she'd need to know how to handle things.

Had she and Nick been arguing about that?

Nick certainly wouldn't have wanted a family—it would have diverted the attention from him. He chose instead to just answer her original question.

'About sport, that lad could just as easily have fallen out of a tree and hit his head or tripped at home. I guess most parents just do what they think is best at the time and hope their children survive childhood.'

She made a sound that could have been agreement but continued to look pensive—even worried.

He carried over a coffee, realising as he placed it down in front of her that he hadn't even asked how she took it, and wondering why he'd remembered her coffee preferences from the past.

'You remembered?' she said, looking up at him, her eyes wide with surprise.

'It wasn't a hard choice to remember,' he said. 'Black no sugar.'

He carried his own coffee over, along with a tin of assorted biscuits.

'Like white, skimmed milk and half a teaspoon of sugar?'

She spoke lightly, but he heard a hint of tension beneath the words and wondered, not for the first time, how she'd ever managed to live with Nick's little peculiarities.

She'd loved him to distraction, she'd said, but had come to hate who she'd become in fitting into his mould of her.

He understood that. He'd known Nick nearly all his life and

had accepted his pedantic ways—for the most part—as simply Nick being Nick.

But he'd been able to walk away; to find someone else to play with, someone else to discuss their studies with, when Nick had become too controlling.

Sam had not only loved the man, she'd been married to him. Hard to walk away from that.

Impossible, Andy guessed, to find someone else...

He watched as she dunked a biscuit in her coffee and sucked on the soggy end, drank some coffee, *then* looked across the table at him.

'You've probably read the latest studies on OCD, linking it to serotonin issues,' she said quietly. 'I tried to persuade Nick to try some anti-anxiety medication, which works for some people, but, as you know, he really couldn't see he had a problem.'

Which made Andy remember the accident, and his own personal conviction, at the time, that Nick would never have driven above the legal limit, could never speed—it was part of his make-up.

Perfectionism was how Nick had termed it.

So, now the fact they'd had an argument had been revealed, rather than solving things, it had made Andy more curious. It must have been about something really important, drastic even, for Nick to have reacted the way he had.

Had it been about them having a family?

Sam had finished her coffee. 'Back to work?' she asked.

'There's no rush. The staff know where we are. And we *did* come here to discuss the patients.'

He hesitated, wanting to ask how she was finding things but knowing it was far too early for such a question.

And, anyway, what he really wanted to know was more about her—about her life over the last three years—and how she felt about Nick now. Was she still mourning him?

Well, he wanted to know everything really.

Which was so unsettling a thought he stood up, collected her cup and the biscuits and made a business of washing the dishes, aware of her standing, moving towards the door—every nerve ending in his skin alive to her movement...

Weirdest coffee break she could remember, Sam thought, leaving her cup on the table because carrying it over to the taps would have meant getting close to Andy again.

She escaped from the comfortable room to the routine movement on the ward but couldn't escape her thoughts. Thoughts that must have been written clearly on her face earlier because Andy had been so concerned—so caring—when he'd sat her down and asked if she was okay.

Which she really wasn't, considering it was so close to the anniversary...

But she'd welcomed the coffee break, sure they'd be discussing patients or talking about the hospital in general—even gossiping, which was the most common pursuit in staffroom coffee breaks. All of which would have got her mind off her own bleak thoughts.

But, no, somehow, without really speaking, they'd ended up discussing Nick.

And children—that had been the other topic, and a revealing one. Andy had spoken lightly but it sounded as if he'd, for some reason, already decided not to have children.

For a moment she wondered why, then realised all this was just another way to keep her mind off the upcoming date.

Work! That was a far better answer.

Her first stop was at the nurses' station to check that families of children who might have been in contact with young Rosa had been alerted by the hospital staff.

'Yes, we've got on to the private day care place she went to twice a week. Only five kids in all, and the woman who runs the place said she's spoken to all the parents, but we got names and telephone numbers and spoke to them again ourselves.'

The nurse—Damian, his name tag read—frowned. 'It's not the children I've been worried about but the old people,' he said.

'Old people?' Sam echoed, as she felt Andy materialise by her side.

'Yes. Rosa also went to a playgroup. The nanny took her one day each week. It was run in a nursing home. Apparently, the residents loved having the little ones running around.'

Sam closed her eyes, considering how quickly something like measles might spread through such a place.

'It might not be too bad,' Andy said, coming to stand beside her. 'A lot of older people have the measles vaccine when they're expecting their first grandchild. It's actually recommended by most GPs.'

'But would they all remember whether they've had it or not? And can we really vaccinate everyone in the place, given that many of them would have complex health problems?'

Sam had turned towards Andy as she spoke so read her own concern in his face.

'I'll get on to the people at Infections Diseases Control—talk to them,' he said. 'But I think it's going to be safer to vaccinate them all.'

'Is this really our problem?' another nurse asked, and Andy and Sam both turned back towards her.

'Who else's would it be?' Sam demanded. 'It's not as if we have to do the actual work, but we need to get authorities alerted to what's going on. And they, in turn, can make the decisions, even publicise the risk if they feel it's necessary.'

The nurse nodded, though she still seemed unconvinced.

'It's a very real risk,' Sam told her. 'A measles outbreak—even with a limited number of patients—almost inevitably results in some deaths.'

She turned away, disturbed by her own words, wanting to go back and check on Rosa.

And, if she was honest, wanting to put some space between herself and Andy, who'd been standing beside her for far too long. This awareness thing she was feeling would disrupt her work if she didn't get it under control. It wasn't as if Andy would ever be interested in her, given how he'd seen her role in the accident.

And hadn't he said that the reason he'd asked her to stay had been because she was the widow of his best friend?

Hardly a romantic invitation.

Rosa was still febrile. The drugs and cooling packs would be keeping her temperature below a really dangerous level, but she was still a very sick little girl.

Sam watched the monitors. Her heart rate was a little elevated but it would be, blood oxygen level fine, but it was being helped by the nasal cannula providing supplemental oxygen. A tube dripped fluid and drugs into her little body, but what else could they do?

She knew this was the problem with choosing to work with seriously ill children—some of them could not be saved. But deep inside she felt that wasn't good enough. They *all* deserved a chance at life—something her child had never had…

A nurse distracted her with a message about one of the chemo patients, and she was pleased to turn her attention from such dismal thoughts. She met the oncology consultant in the child's room, and from then on it seemed as if the world had conspired to keep her mind fully focussed on work.

Sometime in the early afternoon she grabbed a cup of tea and an apple in the staffroom and was looking forward to the end of the day when she could finally relax.

But Rosa's condition had worsened and neither she nor Andy felt happy about leaving the child. Andy made the excuse of paperwork while she stayed with the father in the room, bathing the little girl's body with a cool, damp cloth.

'She's not going to make it, is she?' the father asked at one stage, and Sam couldn't answer. He sat back in his chair and bent forward, elbows on knees, face bowed into his upturned hands, his despair seeping into the room.

* * *

Rosa died at four minutes past midnight in her father's arms, Sam standing with a protective arm around the man's shoulders, tears glistening in her eyes.

After a few minutes the duty doctor and nurses moved in quietly, taking care of both the father and the formalities.

Andy slipped his arm around Sam's shoulders and led her firmly out to his car, aware of a terrible tension in her body.

But as he walked around to the driver's door, he looked up at the star-bright sky and wondered what the hell was going on. He'd understood Sam's desire to stay and care for Rosa, but when he'd forced her to leave the child for long enough to eat earlier in the evening he'd seen the tension in her body, and he'd had the sense of someone holding themselves together with only the greatest difficulty.

Now she sat, rigid in the seat beside him, her hands knotted in her lap, and instinct told him to get her home—unfamiliar though that home might be. She needed to be somewhere away from the hospital, somewhere he could put his arm around her shoulders when he asked her what was wrong.

But they only made it to the elevator of his apartment block before he saw the tears on her cheeks, so he held her as they rose, steered her gently into the apartment, and enfolded her against his body as soon as they were inside.

'Tell me,' he said quietly, sliding his fingers into her hair to tug her head back gently so he could see her face, flushed and tear-stained.

She looked at him, so much pain in her eyes—pain he couldn't understand—but still he felt it. He tried to ask, to get her to talk explain, but found he couldn't speak, words weren't enough.

He brushed his lips across hers, murmuring her name, aware this might be a very wrong response yet feeling her take something from it—feeling passion, heat, and some unable-to-be-spoken agony as she kissed him back.

Somewhere in his head a voice was yelling warnings, but his body felt her urgency and responded to it.

The kiss deepened, her hands now on his back, tugging at his shirt so she was touching his skin—cold hands, cold fingers digging into his skin, dragging him closer and closer. His hands exploring now, feeling the dip of her waist, the curve of her hips, moving lower to press her into him.

Then clothes were shed in an undignified scramble, Sam pushing his hands away and quickly peeling garments off herself.

They kissed again, and that magic moment of skin touching skin swept over Andy as he guided them both towards his bedroom, to the rumpled, unmade bed he'd had no time to straighten that morning.

In some dim recess of her brain Sam was aware this was madness—they had to go on living together—but right now, on the anniversary of her own baby's death, she needed the release— the oblivion—of sex.

So, as Andy's lips moved down her neck, as his hand grasped her breast, fingers teasing at the nipple, she groaned with the sheer, mindless pleasure of it, bit into his shoulder, and pressed her body hard against his.

They fell together onto the bed, mindlessly engrossed in pleasure—in pleasing each other and being pleased, teasing and being teased—until Sam could take no more and guided him into her body, revelling at how natural it was, moving in an age-old rhythm that eventually brought with it total release.

A long time later, it seemed, Sam woke to find Andy propped on his elbow, looking down at her, and as she watched, he reached out and wiped a tear from her cheek, holding it up for her inspection.

She rubbed her hands across her face, hoping to obliterate any more tell-tale signs there might be, then slid carefully out of his bed, wanting to take a rumpled sheet to wrap around her naked body but feeling that would make her look as if she was ashamed.

Which she probably was, but right now leaving was the best thing she could do, before he started asking questions.

Andy was far too astute for his own good!

But at the door she did turn to say thank you, adding honestly, as heat flooded her cheeks, 'I really needed that.'

He gave her a mocking smile that didn't quite hide the hurt she saw in his eyes.

'Any time. Only too happy to oblige.'

She fled, not wanting to make things more complicated than they already were. What they'd shared had been surprisingly intense and fulfilling for first time lovers, but that was all it could be. For all she knew, he had a woman in his life already.

And having a relationship with a colleague wasn't a good idea.

She showered, dressed for work, and came out to find him already gone. No doubt to the beach for his morning swim.

Images of his naked body danced before her eyes and she knew she didn't want to be around when he returned, even though he'd not be entirely naked. She grabbed her things and headed for the café. Avocado and smoked salmon on toast sounded good, and if she kept her mind on food, and then on work, she wouldn't be thinking about how good it had felt to be held in Andy's arms—*or* what today's date meant to her and how hard she was going to find it…

CHAPTER FOUR

THEY WORKED THROUGH the day, carefully polite with each other but equally careful not to get too close. Fortunately, it was busy, some children transferred back to children's wards while new patients came in.

Two were high priority, one an oncology patient who'd received a stem-cell transplant from a non-family member and needed a total isolation room, which meant anyone entering the room, staff included, needed mask, gloves, booties and a long gown.

It was the mask Sam was having trouble with, in the small airlock area outside the isolation room. The strings had somehow become entangled with her hair and as someone else came in, she closed her lips tightly to capture the swear words that wanted to escape.

'Here, let me!'

His voice, right there behind her, stopped her breath, and the touch of his strong hands releasing her fingers and the tape from her hair stole her ability to breathe.

'It didn't mean anything, you know that, don't you?' The

words tumbled out with a desperation she couldn't control. 'Can we forget it happened? I was upset, overwrought. The clock ticked past midnight and it just brought it all back. It's the anniversary, you see.'

He must have finished untangling her mask for now both hands rested on her shoulders, drew her back against his body.

'What happened?' he said gravely, and all the pent-up anxiety left her body in a long sigh.

'I can't talk about it today. But thank you, Andy,' she said quietly, then she stepped away because, contrary to what she had said, being held against him was extremely comforting.

Even enticing?

Definitely exciting to many parts of her body.

But she had to focus on work.

The small boy was Jake Andrews, and as Sam entered the room, he was sleeping. To one side sat the dedicated nurse, while on the other side his mother slept, not in a comfortable chair but on a narrow hospital bed, as sterile as the room itself.

While Andy examined their patient, Sam read through the notes, sighing again to herself when she realised what this child and his family had already been through. Superstitiously, she crossed her gloved fingers, hoping this time the treatment would succeed.

'I don't know that crossing gloved fingers works as well as un-gloved ones,' Andy murmured to her a little later as they stripped off their protective gear and threw it into the various bins.

She smiled and although her own body was asking what harm there'd be in a purely sexual relationship with him for a while, her brain was yelling to forget such folly. Andy hadn't the slightest interest in her. In fact, given how he'd felt about Nick's accident she was surprised that he seemed to tolerate her at all, let alone offer her a bed.

Although, as he'd said to her that first afternoon, she *was* the widow of his best friend...

And if that reminder filled her with a deep sadness, well, that was her problem.

She left the changing room, but Andy was close behind her.

'Our next arrival, Grant Williams, was riding his bicycle home from a mate's last night and was knocked over by a hit-and-run driver. It took a while to stabilise him, both at the scene and in the ED.'

'After which,' Sam guessed, 'he spent a good deal of time in Theatre getting put back together again.'

He'd also been put into an induced coma, Sam discovered when they reached his room, where his two anxious parents sat.

'Did someone speak to you about his condition?' she asked quietly, although both parents looked too shell-shocked to have taken much in.

'Broken pelvis, broken leg, fractured shoulder, cracked head,' the father recited, and was about to continue when Sam intervened.

'Did they tell you he's been put into an induced coma so he's deeply asleep, unconscious really, which will give his body, and particularly his brain, a little time to recover.'

'Someone said something,' the mother said quietly, and Sam smiled at her.

'What it means is that he won't regain consciousness until the specialists think he's well enough to cope with it all. That won't be for a few days, so although I know you want to be near him, you're better off going home and getting some rest. One of you might like to come back a little later just to sit and talk quietly to him, smooth his skin. But when the specialists decide to bring him out of the coma, we'll contact you so you can both be here, and you'll be the first people he sees.'

'What if we don't want to go home? If we both want to stay with our boy?'

The aggression in the man's voice suggested he was already exhausted so Sam knew she'd have to tread very carefully.

She was assembling her most persuasive arguments when

she heard someone come into the room behind her and knew it was Andy.

'Of course you may stay if you wish,' he said, speaking directly to the father. 'But it's likely to be three or four days—perhaps longer—before the specialists decide to reverse the drug that's helping his body and mind deal with what happened. When that decision is made, we'll let you know so you can be here to reassure him he's safe.'

The father nodded and put his arm around his wife.

'Maybe the doctor's right, love,' he said. 'We'll be no good to him if we're exhausted, now, will we?'

She gave a wan smile but stood up at his urging, and after the lightest of kisses on her son's pale cheek left the room.

Sam was wondering why it still was—in a world where women often outnumbered men as doctors—that a man's explanation of a situation still held more weight. With other men, at least.

Musing on this, she missed the first bit of Andy's conversation.

'So I've a three-day conference in Sydney from tomorrow, but the welcome stuff starts this evening.'

She caught up as they followed the couple out the door. 'I wouldn't go if I felt you still needed me here, but you'll be fine.'

He walked away, paused, then turned to look at her, hesitating, before adding, 'I'll leave the car keys on the kitchen table—use it if you like.'

Another glance her way. 'And definitely use it if you're called out at night. I'll get a cab to the airport.'

Although, when she considered them again, those two looks towards her had told her everything, as well as his abrupt departure to a conference in Sydney.

He was ruling a line under what had happened between them the previous night, just as she had done earlier.

But would three days be enough for her body to get with the programme?

To stop fizzing with excitement at the sound of his voice and flaring with heat if he accidentally brushed up against her?

It had been bad enough discovering she was physically attracted to Andy when they'd met again, but it was far worse now, when every square inch of her skin knew the feel of his skin against it and seemed determined *not* to forget that night.

And yet...

Andy walked out through the front entrance to his apartment building, confident he'd find a cab cruising past. Confident, also, that he was doing the right thing—getting right away from the beguiling woman who was his best friend's widow,

He'd never been good with calendar dates so he hadn't had a clue that it had been the torturous pain of loss that had driven Sam into his arms the previous night. She'd been so willing, so hot really, responding with a ferocity he'd been foolish enough to believe was because she felt as much attraction to him as he did to her.

The intensity of the experience had stunned him, to the extent that his body felt as if she'd imprinted herself on his skin.

Cursing quietly under his breath, he threw his overnight bag into the taxi, pleased he had the diversion of a trip to Sydney, although Antarctica might have been a better option. But a couple of days away from the distraction that was Sam would help him get his life back on track—get things into perspective again...

Possibly!

He shook his head, so lost in his memories of the passion they'd shared he barely heard the cabbie's conversation.

Something about football, perhaps?

Left to her own devices, Sam visited the rest of her patients, discussing each of them with the dedicated nurse on duty with the child.

Whoever had trained these nurses in the fairly new hospital had done an excellent job because all the ones she saw today—

and had seen earlier—were really invested in their patients, showing empathy as well as caring.

It was a special job, nursing in a PICU, and although the majority of nurses who chose to work there were empathetic, she'd known a few who just did their job—and did it well—but stayed detached from the child and his or her family.

And she was thinking about this, why? she wondered when she sat down at her desk to write up some notes and check the medication orders.

She knew the answer.

Thinking about anything was better than thinking about the previous night—and the way she'd behaved.

Like a wanton hussy, her old secondary school teacher would have said. Throwing yourself into that man's arms…

But that man was Andy, and although she'd seen less of him after her marriage she'd always been impressed by his dedication to his work—impressed by him as a genuinely nice person.

In fact, it had been his decision to leave the hurly-burly of the Emergency Department that Nick had loved so much to work in Intensive Care and then Paediatric ICU that had influenced her own decision.

Though just why she was thinking of Andy on the anniversary of Nick's death, she wasn't sure. She pressed her hand against her flat stomach and forced her mind back to work.

A call from the nurse with the oncology patient killed any wayward thoughts and she went back to his room, gloved and gowned, and managed the mask herself this time before quietly opening the door.

Jake lay pale and wan on the bed, but a nasty rash was appearing on his torso.

'Have you called his oncologist? Sam asked, and the nurse nodded.

'It's most likely a reaction to one of the drugs he's on to suppress his immune system so his body doesn't reject the new stem cells, but I'll take some blood to test for infection.'

Sam was watching the monitor as she spoke, seeking any variation in the patterns of his heart rate or his blood oxygen level, listening to his chest, feeling the slightly raised nature of the rash.

She used a port in his left arm to extract some blood and labelled the three phials she'd taken while the nurse organised for someone to collect them from the changing room to get them to the laboratory as quickly as possible.

'Fluid overload,' Sam muttered to herself, and checked the drip to see how much fluid had gone into him since the last check, then his catheter bag to ensure he was getting rid of fluid.

Graft versus host disease was the most common complication and the rash could be a symptom of that. It was mostly seen within the first three months after a transplant but could occur up to three years afterwards.

She'd written up the information of all she'd done, including the tests she'd ordered, when the oncologist appeared and took the chart from her.

He was a silver-haired man with a tanned skin and a charming smile, and he spoke to young Jake like a family friend, reassuring the boy that they'd sort things out.

'What did you request with the bloods?' he asked Sam, turning away from the chart.

'Infection, low platelets, and any sign of organ failure,' she said, and he nodded.

'The results will be copied to me, and I'll be right back if they show anything. In the meantime, we might use a little more supplemental oxygen, and I'd suggest a simple mix of bicarbonate of soda and water on the rash to help ease the irritation.'

Sam smiled at him. 'It was my mother's panacea for all ills and certainly helped me survive chicken pox.'

The oncologist gave a theatrical shiver. 'Don't even think of things like that. The poor lad has enough possible complications without introducing childhood diseases. I'm thinking he might need another blood transfusion, but we'll wait for the test results. Then, of course, there's a possibility the stem cells didn't take, and he'll need more of them.'

Sam looked at the frail figure lying on the bed and prayed that the rash was nothing more than a reaction to one of the drugs coursing through his body in the drip fluid.

The nurse was already speaking to someone to arrange the soothing liquid and Sam would have left to see other patients, but she caught sight of Jake's mother gowning up in the ante-room, and waited to speak to her, to update her on what was going on.

For parents of children who were up to the stage of trialling bone-marrow transplants to save their child's life, the hospital processes were well known. They'd had to cope with the highs and lows of the previous treatments and procedures and the hope and despair that came with each one.

For Jake's mother, this was just one more bridge to cross, her faith in finding a cure for him never wavering.

Could she have handled that as well as most of the parents she saw did? Sam wondered.

If her child had lived…

She shut the memory down, but not before tears had pricked her eyes.

Three years today. It was stupid to even think about it!

But at least Andy hadn't been around to see her momentary weakness…

Andy boarded the plane for the short flight to Sydney with a strange sense of relief. Sam had drawn a line under what had happened the previous evening, which was, he was almost certainly sure, a good thing.

So why was he feeling a nagging sense of…

What?

Regret?

Not exactly...

No, he wouldn't think about it—particularly not how she'd felt in his arms, or the heat of her body as he'd slid into her—her cries of passion as she'd clung to him in that final release.

Get your head straight, Andy.

This was Sam! She'd needed comfort, and he'd been there to give it to her.

A tightening of his stomach muscles suggested that he was damned glad he *had* been there. Heaven forbid, she might have gone off with anyone!

Not, he told himself sternly, that it would have been any of his business if she had. He'd known she was grieving for Rosa, the child who'd died. That was only natural, all of them felt an unnecessary loss like that very deeply, but on top of the date of her own loss...

No, he couldn't begin to imagine what her feelings had been, and furthermore it was time to stop this pointless speculation and concentrate on the reason he was on the plane.

Not to escape Sam but to hear one of the US's top PICU physicians speak about making the experience for families more comfortable.

He prided himself on how well they did it at his hospital. He'd been consulted about it as it was being built, and, having spent so much time in hospital with his patient, smiling sister, he knew just how uncomfortable places they could be, and he'd had a raft of ideas to offer the designers. And you could always learn something from other hospitals, even if it was what not to do.

But his focus was obviously shot to pieces for surely one of the first among any '*not* to do' lists of his own was take your best friend's widow to bed!

Even if she'd been so willing, so excited, in turn both tender and torturous and loving, so totally irresistible he'd lost himself in her, lost all inhibitions, and had responded with a passion he knew he'd never experienced before.

He was jolted out of his heated memories as the plane landed in Sydney, and he shut the memories away.

He was here to learn, to pick up ideas to take back to his hospital that hopefully would produce better outcomes for his patients and their families.

His and Sam's patients—and *that* was definitely the last time he would think about her.

Today…

It was weird returning to Andy's apartment without him being there.

Weird and definitely unsettling!

There'd been a small, discreet 'Manager' sign on the door on the ground-floor apartment, opposite the café, and she'd thought it wouldn't hurt to ask about an apartment—maybe there'd be a one-bedroomed, which was all she'd need.

She knocked on the door, which was opened almost immediately by a youngish man with a slightly unkempt look about him who was clutching a puffy black garbage bag in one hand.

'Sorry, just on my way to the bins. I can't put this down without spilling the lot, so would you like to wait, or maybe walk with me?'

'I'm happy to do either, but all I really wanted to ask was whether you had an apartment for rent. Just for me.'

She found she'd fallen in beside him as she spoke, so kept walking.

'One bedroom?' he asked.

'Well, that's all I'd really need.'

She'd sleep on the couch if her mother came, but, given her mother's life, it wasn't all that probable.

'Yeah, there's one available,' he said, leading her down a concrete stairwell into the basement garage. 'But we're coming up to the Christmas holidays when all the empty apartments double in price. I'm only the manager for about forty different owners—most of them absentee owners—and some of them only rent out over Christmas, because that pays the bills on the place and they can use it themselves any time over the rest of the year.'

'So I'd be paying double normal price?'

'From next weekend when the season starts, yes,' he said, rather gloomily.

Intrigued, Sam asked, 'You don't like the holiday season?'

He shook his head. 'I don't dislike it,' he said, 'but it's just so much extra work, and the young people I employ for the season as cleaners also want to have fun so they're not exactly reliable.'

They'd reached the bins, corralled behind a high wooden fence, and he lifted the lid of one to dump the bag, before turning to a nearby tap to wash his hands.

'I do have a couple of rooms in my place I let out as B and Bs, only the second B is a chit for the café across the hall. They each have an en suite bathroom and a small open kitchen-cum-sitting area with a hotplate and a microwave and TV and such. If that'd suit you?'

'I think that would be more than enough for me,' Sam told him, and was about to shake his hand on the deal when she thought of Andy. Would he think her ungrateful?

Even rude?

'Can I let you know later?' she asked the manager as they emerged into the foyer once again.

'Sure, I'm Rod, by the way.'

Sam took his hand and shook it.

'Sam,' she said, and smiled at him.

'But you'd be living with a stranger—a man you don't even know,' Andy protested when she put the idea to him on his return on Saturday afternoon.

'I'm renting a room,' Sam corrected him. 'That's not exactly living with someone!'

'You could do that here,' he argued. 'Heaven knows, I don't need it, but you could pay rent if it would make you feel better.'

He paused. 'It's because of what happened, isn't it?' he said, as grumpy as she'd ever heard the usually upbeat Andy.

'Not entirely,' she said. 'You know very well I've always intended to get my own place, and I like what I've seen of this area.' She hesitated. 'And, given you're the only person I know in this city, I thought it would be nice to be near you.'

'Just not in my apartment—in some other man's!'

Sam looked at him in disbelief. 'Andy, you're being ridiculous! The fact is, as Rod pointed out, summer holidays are a week away and rents on regular accommodation double for two months. He can't charge double for his rooms, so it works out well for me because it gives me a chance to settle in, get to know my way around, meet other people, make friends, then maybe, when the holidays end, find something permanent.'

She watched as he bit back the words she was sure he wanted to say, before muttering something about taking a shower and disappearing in the direction of his bedroom.

But did he *really* want her to stay?

Or was it simply a kindness to an old friend, something he was doing for Nick as much as her?

The question made her stomach hurt, as if, deep down, she'd wanted him to want her to stay for herself...

She shook her head, aware such thoughts were madness...

He *was* being ridiculous, and he knew it, but as Andy stalked off to his bedroom, it was all he could do to keep from grinding his teeth.

And his reason for this sudden, and quite irrational, anger?

He shook his head, not wanting to think about it, but still it gnawed away inside him, to the extent that he turned back towards the living room, where Sam stood at the window, silhouetted by the moon rising over the waters in front of her.

And, suddenly, he didn't want to argue with her—didn't want discord between them.

He walked closer, his footsteps on the timber floor causing her to half turn towards him.

'I thought it would be for the best,' she said, in such a small voice he knew he'd upset her with his tirade. 'I mean, it can't be helping your love life any, having me living with you. And maybe if I ever decide to chance such a thing again, it would be awkward for me as well.'

'What love life?' he snorted. 'That's not high on my list of priorities! Anyway, how many intensivists do you know who can manage a relationship successfully?'

'Plenty!' she snapped, any hurt she may have felt burned off by sudden anger. 'And this entire conversation is stupid. You took me in when I had nowhere to stay and for that I'm grateful, but it was never meant to be for ever and, providing I don't see any evidence of rats when I look at Rod's rooms tomorrow, I'm moving on. I've only delayed because I thought it would be polite to discuss it with you first. Not that this conversation has had any resemblance to a discussion.'

And this time it was Sam who stalked off, leaving him standing by the tall windows, gazing out to sea.

He'd heard—even understood—her final, angry words, but it was something she'd said earlier that had snagged in his mind.

Something about 'should she ever decide to *chance* such a thing again'...

'Chance' was a strange word for her to have used.

It implied risk. Had her marriage to Nick not been the nuptial bliss Nick had always made it out to be?

Had she found it harder than he had realised to live with Nick's mild OCD?

Though had it really been mild?

He shook his head.

Questions to which, he was reasonably sure, he'd never find answers, yet for some unfathomable reason he'd have liked to know...

CHAPTER FIVE

THE ROOM ROD offered Sam had a view out over the ocean and she was immediately entranced.

The bedroom was small, divided, she realised, in some clever way to make room for the small sitting room, a few cupboards, refrigerator, sink and microwave tucked into a corner, and to Sam's delight, a small barbecue out on the balcony, along with a couple of easy outdoor chairs and a table.

'It's perfect,' she told Rod, beaming with delight. 'I'll take it.'

'You're supposed to ask how much the rent is,' Rod reminded her, and Sam shook her head.

'I'm sure it's not over my budget. Not that I have a budget.'

But they did discuss the rent, and a good deal besides, out on the balcony, with the fresh north-easterly sea breeze cooling the air around them.

'So, you work with Andy,' Ron said, and Sam nodded.

'He's an old friend of my dead husband,' she explained. 'And he took me in when I arrived to save me going to a hotel while I got my bearings.'

'Nice,' Rod said. 'He's a good man.'

Something about the conversation was making Sam feel uncomfortable—talking about Andy with a stranger?—so she made the excuse that she'd need to pack her few things, took the keys Rod gave her and, after learning which key did what, she departed.

Andy, who'd been in a meeting when she'd left the hospital, was back when she walked in, new keys in her hand.

'Does your room have a lock?' he asked, looking at them dangling from her fingers.

She frowned at him, disturbed by the inference that she'd need a lock. To keep Rod out?

Surely not!

'You should change it,' Andy said, and Sam shook her head in disbelief.

'You think he'll come creeping into my room in the dead of night and ravish me?' she snapped, the anger she'd thought she'd learned to control sparking suddenly. 'I should be so lucky!'

Really shouldn't have said that, she muttered in her head as she strode towards her bedroom. It was just that Andy was being so darned unreasonable about this. He should be glad to be getting rid of her, not acting like her moral guardian!

She shut the bedroom door and leaned back against it, taking deep breaths to sweep away the anger he'd aroused, especially as the real reason she was moving out was because of him.

Well, not him as such, but the way she was beginning to feel about him—and seeing him at home as well as at work—well, it was just too much...

She had to pack.

She opened the door, intending to go out, find Andy, apologise for losing her temper then ask politely if she could borrow a suitcase for a few hours to stop her new clothes getting crumpled and wrinkly in her old backpack. But Andy was right there, outside the door, and her immediate reaction was not suspicion about his presence but a flood of attraction.

'I'm sorry!'

Their voices formed a chorus, but Andy recovered first.

'I don't know why I was upset,' he said. 'I guess I was kind of enjoying you being around. It's been a while since I've had company at home.'

Sam grinned at him.

'It's only been five days and you were away for two of them,' she pointed out, 'and, anyway, I'll still be around at work.'

He nodded but remained where he was—rooted in the passage.

Her turn to talk, obviously.

'I was wondering if I could borrow a suitcase just for this evening, to take my clothes down to Rod's.' She paused, before adding, 'And to say I'm sorry I lost my temper earlier.'

She tried a smile, but knew it was probably fairly pathetic. 'Every time I think I've conquered my wretched temper, something happens and I'm blowing up again.'

Another pause.

'Although you did provoke it, you must admit, talking about changing the locks!'

He laughed now, a joyous sound that made her toes curl inside her sneakers. She *so* had to get away from him, if only after work hours.

'So you're apologising but blaming me at the same time,' he teased, his eyes twinkling in such a way she had to forcibly clamp her hand to her side to stop herself reaching out and touching his face.

She *had* to move! Had to get away from this man who could have her hormones rioting with the twinkle in his eyes.

'I'll get you a case,' he was saying as he moved away from her, and she ran her hands through her unruly hair and clutched her head, trying to restore some balance to her mind in the hope it would do the same for her body.

He'd asked her to stay because she was Nick's widow and though he'd proved an exciting and satisfying lover when she'd thrown herself into his arms, that was no indication that he was in any way attracted to her.

In fact, the way he'd been so quick to agree with her about drawing a line under the incident proved that she was no more than an acquaintance—or friend at best...

And if that thought caused a tiny ache in her chest, then that was her problem, not his.

Andy dug into the back of his small storeroom, dislodging a broom and mop he rarely used because he was blessed with a cleaning man who came once a week, and left his often untidy apartment spotless.

Was it because they'd had sex that he'd been behaving irrationally about Sam moving out?

Great sex, admittedly, but that's all it had been...

He'd answered a need in her, for which she was grateful, but she'd made it very clear that that was that. Which was just as well as he was having a lot of trouble working out just how he felt about Sam.

He was definitely attracted to her, now more than ever, it appeared. But attraction usually—well, often—led to love, and in his mind there was a huge blockage that would stop such a process.

Actually, there were two problems—the discomfort about her being his friend's widow, and the big one—what if she was still in love with Nick?

Would the latter explain her desperate need on the anniversary of his death?

She'd said she'd hated what she'd become as his wife, but she'd also said she'd loved him to distraction.

And the way she'd said it suggested the love part had been paramount, so probably she still loved him.

Enough to stop her loving someone else?

Hell's teeth, get the suitcase and take it to her. Stop trying to fathom what's going on in someone else's head when you can't work out what's going on in your own. And given the mess you've made of the love business in the past, it certainly shouldn't be entering the equation.

You've given up on it, remember? Twice burnt by it. Surely that was enough for any man to realise he was better off single—free to enjoy brief encounters with willing women who might come his way.

He grabbed the suitcase and backed out of the small room, then pushed the case down the corridor, but his mind was right back on Sam, only this time he was telling himself he was done thinking about her—done guessing about her marriage and Nick and whether she still loved him.

Telling himself the easiest way to find out was to ask.

Right!

March up to Sam and say, 'Are you still in love with Nick?'

Honestly, man, for a supposedly intelligent human being you haven't got a clue!

He knocked on her door.

'I'll just leave the case here,' he said, but before he had time to turn away she'd flung open the door.

'Don't rush off,' she said, clearing a space on the bed between small piles of clothing. 'I won't be long, and I thought I could take you to dinner at the café as a thank you for having me.'

'You don't have to do that,' he said, but he did go into the room, sitting down where she'd made a space for him on the bed, watching her as she efficiently cleared the bed of clothing and packed it into the suitcase.

Watching her and wondering...

'I was only too happy to give you a bed.'

She looked up at him from where she knelt, a question in her eyes.

'Because I was your best friend's widow,' she said. A statement not a question after all.

'More than that, Sam,' he said. 'We'd been friends, you and I, back when we all met.' Even to him that sounded weak—

mawkish—so he quickly added, 'Besides which you were a new member of the team, and had nowhere booked to stay. I'd have offered the bed to whoever it was.'

'Okay,' she said, as if his explanation had sorted out something in her mind, which was good because it had only made him feel even more confused...

She turned her attention back to the packing, filling the edges around the neatly folded skirts and shirts with toiletries and, yes, the purple underwear!

He smiled to himself then realised she'd caught him for the rosy colour was rising in her cheeks.

'It's best I move,' she said quietly, then zipped the case shut and pulled it upright onto its rollers. 'But I'd still like to take you to dinner.'

He stood up and took the case, rolling it towards the door, turning to say, 'Ah, but I felt it was my turn to cook. I bought steaks and some stuff for a salad.'

'In a packet, no doubt?' she teased, and he felt a sense of relief—a sense that everything was all right between them again.

On the surface, at least.

Well, he'd just have to live with that.

Though in his heart he hoped that before too long they'd be able to talk—talk properly—about the past.

About their feelings?

And the future?

He shook his head. He and Sam may have enjoyed one glorious night of sex, but as far as she was concerned that was that. There'd been no suggestion—at any time really—that she might be feeling the same attraction towards him as he did towards her.

He'd grill the steak.

With her clothing installed in her new home, Sam returned to join Andy on his balcony, and now sat, sipping at a glass of white wine he'd produced, and watching him at the barbecue.

Out to her right, a low rising moon had silvered the ocean,

whose soft murmur, this calm evening, filled her with a sense of peace.

A rare sense of peace, given she was with Andy.

But the muddle of emotions she usually felt with him—the attraction, the sense that it was wrong, the awareness that it probably wasn't reciprocated, especially now he *knew* she had been instrumental in his best friend's death—all those worries seemed to have slipped from her shoulders. Tonight she was just going to enjoy the sheer pleasure of being in a beautiful place with a friend.

'I feel good,' she said, and he turned to look at her, eyebrows raised.

Surprised?

'Well, you have to admit it's been a frenetic week,' she said. 'Getting here was bad enough, I kept worrying I wouldn't make it in time to start on Monday, then finding out you're my boss—which is good, don't get me wrong—then all the stuff with Rosa and the anniversary—my mind and body have been in turmoil.'

'And now?' he prompted, turning back to prod the meat—or just not wanting to look at her when she answered?

'Now I feel at peace,' she said. 'As if I can go forward into a whole new life stretching out in front of me. New hospital to work in, new staff to meet and get to know, and this beautiful town to explore. The beach, the sea, the sand—rock pools out on the headland, I'm sure—a whole new world.'

She paused, and as he carefully lifted the steaks onto two waiting plates, she added, 'I ran away, you see, after the accident. Couldn't face any of it, especially the thought of a life without Nick. But a couple of months ago, when I was offered a better post in London, I thought about it for, oh, all of two seconds, because I suddenly knew it was time to go home.'

'And now you're here?' he asked as he set the plates down on the table.

'I know it was the right decision, so really, why wouldn't I be feeling good?'

He nodded, as if satisfied with her answer and disappeared inside, reappearing with the salad bowl and cutlery and sitting down opposite her. 'Eat!' he said, smiling.

Which she did—they both did—so for a while there was no more talk and when it did resume it was work talk mixed with travel talk—his work in Boston, hers in London, comparisons of hospital systems, staffing arrangements. It was all nice, safe, work-related talk that skated fairly easily over the muddle of emotions she'd landed in when she'd met Andy again, and the mess she'd made of things the night Rosa had died.

They'd have to talk about that, too, sometime, she knew, but now to just sit in the soft moonlight with Andy, relaxed by the sound of the sea, was enough.

Might have to be enough always.

She pushed *that* thought away.

Jake's father was with him when they did their rounds on Monday morning, and looked as anxious as Andy felt. They didn't yet have the results of all the blood tests, but those they did have offered no clue as to what might have caused the rash.

Sam was explaining this to the father when Andy was paged to an emergency in the ED.

He excused himself and left Sam to get on with the round. She'd contact him if she needed any help. With the shift change on Thursday, they'd be working together less often, which, he decided as he made his way downstairs, would be a good thing. The urge to touch Sam, just lightly on the shoulder, as he'd left Jake's room had been almost overwhelming.

That, he reminded himself as he went down to the ED, was why relationships between colleagues could be difficult.

Even now, when he *wasn't* in a relationship with her, she was far too often in his thoughts and far, far too often those thoughts could be distracting.

And distraction was one thing a PICU physician just could not afford.

He was relieved when the elevator disgorged him outside the ED, and his focus returned immediately to work.

He heard, first, that it was a child saved from drowning, then, as he walked into the resus room, he realised the pale, anxious father was an old acquaintance—a fellow medical student he'd last seen in the Sydney hospital where Sam had been admitted after the accident.

Ned Radcliffe—the name came back to him as he held out his hand in greeting—but he could have been Santa Claus for all the notice Ned took of him. One hundred percent of his attention was focussed on the boy of about three who lay, unmoving, on the examination couch.

'Edward Radcliffe, two years four months, non-responsive when the ambos reached him,' a nurse said quietly to Andy. 'Father had been giving CPR, ambos took over and heart restarted. He's on oxygen, but he's remained deeply unconscious.'

'Any sign of a head injury?' Andy asked, almost automatically, his mind on the child and how they might achieve the best possible outcomes for the small boy and his family.

'No, the ambos checked and the duty doctor here checked. Apparently, he went straight in.'

'How long would he have been in there, Ned?' Andy asked, and the father frowned as he heard the question, his eyes still on his son.

'I would say less than five minutes. I opened the pool fence gate to get a toy the dog had left in the garden, and turned to throw it back to the dog. But Chippy ignored it and raced back into the pool enclosure, barking like crazy, and that's when I realised Eddie must have followed me in.'

He looked at Andy now and frowned, then said, 'Andy?' in a bewildered voice.

'That's right, Ned. I'm head of the PICU here. We'll be admitting Eddie. He'll get the best of care.'

He turned back to the child, considerably pleased by the knowledge of such a short immersion.

'Hello, Eddie,' he said, in a loud voice, but there was no response, not even when he clapped his hands beside the little head. Neither did Eddie retract his foot when Andy stuck a pin into the sole of it, testing for physical response.

'We'll take him to Radiography on the way up to the PICU. I'll order an EEG and MRI,' he said to the nurse as he wrote up the requests. 'Do you want to stay with him, Ned?'

Ned nodded. 'I'll phone my wife on the way, let her know what's going on.'

He looked at Andy, a plea for reassurance in his eyes. 'Do you think...?'

Andy patted him on the shoulder.

'You were right there on the spot and did the best possible thing in giving CPR immediately. His heartbeat returned quickly, and he wasn't in the pool for long. They're all good indicators, Ned.'

An orderly arrived to transfer the boy, via Radiography, to the PICU, so Andy returned to the ward, aware the radiography he'd ordered probably wouldn't show much at this stage but still wanting a baseline from which to work.

He found Sam at the desk, and told her what was happening, asking if she'd known Ned.

She shook her head, but obviously hadn't taken much notice of the question because she asked, 'Would you consider continuous EEG monitoring?'

He shrugged. 'I'd been thinking of it, why?'

She grinned at him. 'I often wonder if it does much good and I think it must freak most parents out, seeing all those electrodes attached to their child's head. It's almost yelling "brain injury" at them.'

He shook his head. 'I must admit I've never thought of that aspect to it, but I'm really hoping he'll be responsive by the time he gets up to us.'

* * *

'And his father—this Ned—was he at university with you?'
Sam asked, aware she'd usually have put an 'and Nick' at the
end of that question.

But the peaceful, pleasant evening she'd enjoyed with Andy
the previous night had left her more aware of Andy than when
she'd been living with him.

And *that* had been bad enough!

Then she'd been able to put it down to proximity, especially
after the night together, but now she was beginning to wonder
if the awareness was more than physical attraction—not that
she was even going to think about the L word.

Love had been too hard, like a prison she couldn't escape.

The arrival of young Eddie blocked all extraneous thoughts
from her mind, especially as his father was beaming with joy.

'He reacted to the noise of the MRI in spite of the earmuffs,'
he told them, although the little boy lay still, eyes closed again.

'He opened his eyes and moved his legs.'

'That's great, Ned, but we'll still keep him here and do further tests. The bloods should be back soon, and they'll tell us
more, but everything is looking positive for the moment.'

'I'll phone my wife,' Ned said, and disappeared out of the
room.

'He didn't want us to see him crying,' Sam said softly.

'And you,' Andy asked, looking intently into her eyes. 'Are
you worrying again about the myriad things that can endanger
a child and how a parent can protect them from everything?'

She shot him a quick smile. 'No, I was thinking how lucky
they were to have such an intelligent dog!'

And with that she walked away, because of course she'd been
worrying about how parents managed to survive their children's childhoods, Though the likelihood of her ever having to
go through such agony was diminishing fast.

She'd known when she'd chosen to go into intensive care
that it would be six hard years before she became qualified,

then another six months before she qualified for paediatric intensive care. She'd done those final six months in London and had stayed another six months because the hospital had offered so many learning opportunities.

So now, at thirty-five, it wasn't that she was running out of time to have a child, but running out of time to have children—a family, something she'd dreamed about since she'd been a child herself, brought up by a single mother who'd been banished from her own family as a disgrace.

CHAPTER SIX

SAM WAS STANDING at the monitor desk, checking through some lab results, when she saw Ned again, returning to the hospital, this time with a woman she guessed must be his wife.

He stopped to introduce her to Sam, who was slightly startled when the woman said, 'Oh, I know who you are.'

'Oh, yes?' Sam said politely.

'Yes, of course. You were the new doctor at the hospital where Nick and Andy worked and they both fancied you. You must remember, Ned—they tossed a coin to see which one would ask her out and Nick won. How is Nick, by the way?'

'Nick was killed in an accident three years ago,' Sam said, but her mind was whirling.

He and Andy had actually *tossed up* to see who asked her out?

For some reason, the idea disturbed her. Made her feel like a cheap prize at a funfair.

The woman, whose name she'd forgotten almost as soon as she'd heard it—was it Ann?—and Ned were now arguing about whether or not he'd been in the pub that night, making Sam feel even worse.

Although, she decided, maybe it was keeping their minds off their concerns for Eddie.

'Eddie's doing well,' she said, glad to have found a way to interrupt things she didn't want to hear. 'You must both be pleased.'

But it didn't help much as Ann was now berating her husband for his carelessness in letting little Eddie fall in the pool.

'We *are* pleased,' Ned said, ignoring his wife's accusations with an ease that suggested they argued often. 'How long do you want to keep him in?'

'Overnight at least,' Sam told him, then watched as he steered his wife, still talking, to Eddie's room.

She moved on to see Jake, who was brighter today, his test results showing positive signs that the stem-cell transplant had taken. His father was with him today, explaining to Sam that he'd taken some personal time off work so his wife could have a proper rest at home.

'With two other children, it's hectic, but both our sets of parents help out all they can. My mum's staying with us at the moment, and the other kids love it as she spoils them rotten, doesn't she, Jake?'

Jake smiled, and touched his father's gloved hand.

'Me too,' Jake said, and pointed to a stuffed alligator that looked ready to eat the child.

Andy came into the changing cubicle as she was pulling off her gown, and although her body felt the usual rush of attraction that was becoming part of her normal life, it was Ann's earlier words that came back to her.

'Did you and Nick actually toss a coin to decide which of you would ask me out?' she demanded as pique at such behaviour overcame the silly attraction thing.

'Not at all,' Andy said, in an offended tone. 'We did rock, paper, scissors!'

Sam frowned at him, aware he thought the whole thing a joke, but feeling…slighted by it?

'And after you lost, that was it?' she muttered at him, as she hauled off the rest of her protective gear. 'You must have been really keen!'

And without waiting for a reply, she stalked out of the tiny room.

But once away from Andy, she tried to understand why hearing the silly nonsense had upset her so much.

It had been years ago, she'd married Nick, so how or why he'd asked her out shouldn't matter a jot.

A call from the ED made her push the past away, although she was aware it would niggle away deep inside her no matter how much she ignored it.

'We've isolated another girl, and the red spots in her mouth with their tiny pinpricks of white in the centre confirm it's measles,' Phil, the young intern on duty, told her as she came into the emergency department.

He led the way to one of the two isolation rooms in the ED and introduced the patient, Ruby, and her parents, Alice and Bob.

Not knowing the local area, Sam asked the intern to stay so they could try to work out if the two cases were connected in any way.

While she examined the little girl, a year older than Rosa had been, she listened to Phil's questions, and from the way he shook his head she realised there wasn't an obvious overlap in the two children's activities or friends.

'I'll admit her to our Paediatric Intensive Care unit,' Sam told the parents, 'but that's just because we can isolate her better than on the normal children's ward, where the contagion could spread.'

She left instructions on the chart and returned to the PICU, her mind puzzling over this second admission. She knew immunisation rates in the country as a whole were above ninety percent—she'd looked it up when Rosa had been admitted—yet two children in a regional city, two children out of the—at the most—ten percent not immunised had contracted the disease.

'Who does what?' she asked Andy, when she caught him in the staffroom and explained her concern. 'Do the Infectious Diseases people have staff who follow the trail of the two children, or do the police do it, or do we do it?'

Andy frowned at the question, and as she looked at him the question of whether she'd have gone out with him if he'd won their stupid game popped into her head.

Forget it!

But she knew she probably wouldn't have. Knew it was the kind of question that could bob into her head as she fell asleep at night or walked on the beach, thinking of nothing in particular.

'I think the infectious diseases staff use the police if they need them,' Andy was saying, while her mind wandered. 'We'll inform them of this second case, and they can publicise it, warning parents of the dangers, suggesting unimmunised children should be done before it becomes more widespread.'

'Has there been anything special here recently?' Sam asked. 'A local agricultural show, surfing contest people might have watched, a circus, or funfair of some kind?'

'Somewhere people from all walks of life could have met,' Andy said, more or less to himself. 'You're right, that's something they'll look into, I'm sure. And there *was* the annual show about a week before you came, and it had a big sideshow alley and all the fun of the fair.'

'I think I'd rather you said there'd been nothing like that, because if it came from a travelling fair anyone could be the carrier, and who knows where they went next.'

He grinned at her, which made her think she *would* have gone out with him—way back when...

'Which makes me doubly glad it's someone else's job to locate him or her,' he was saying. 'Have you admitted the new case?'

'She should be on her way up. Her name's Ruby, and she's not as feverish as Rosa was, but I thought it best to keep her away from other children so she'll go into another of our isolation rooms.'

'I'll see her before I go,' Andy said, and Sam realised with a slight shock that this was the first day of a new shift. She'd known about it, had it noted in her diary, knew exactly when she would and wouldn't be at work, but suddenly Andy was departing and, for all she'd have a registrar or a young resident on duty with her at all times, she'd be in charge.

Andy must have read what she was thinking in her face, for he reached out and touched her shoulder.

'You handled it all extremely well when I was in Sydney, remember, and I'll only be a phone call away,' he told her. 'It's the paperwork more than the patients that'll get you down!'

'I'll be fine,' she said, as forcefully as she could, but again guessed he'd read her doubts.

'Of course, you will,' he assured her. 'And you're off on Sunday—well, on call—so bring your phone and I'll take you for a drive around the place if you like, show you some of the sights of the great Port Fortesque!'

'That sounds good,' Sam said, although she had more doubts about that plan than she did about running the department in his absence.

Andy walked away, not at all concerned over Sam's ability to keep the place running, more concerned that she'd been upset over his and Nick's silly bet.

But she *had* agreed to go out with him on Sunday, although as he was the only person she knew in the area, that didn't mean much.

He went back to his office and tidied his desk, then decided to call in on young Eddie before he left.

His mother was sitting with him, reading a story to the bright, alert child.

'He could really come home now, couldn't he?' she said, smiling sweetly at Andy.

'Tomorrow,' he said firmly. 'We want some follow-up bloods and another EEG, but Dr Reilly will discharge him tomorrow, probably by eleven-thirty.'

'Oh, pooh!' the woman said. 'I was hoping Sam would be off duty tomorrow. I was going to ask the two of you to dinner at the weekend. Ned was so pleased to meet up with you again, especially as we're new in town. He's just joined a practice on the north side. I didn't want to leave Sydney, but he thought it would be better to bring Eddie up in the country.'

She gave a theatrical shudder and added, 'This was a compromise, and look what just happened.'

Andy closed his eyes and thanked the merciful fates that Sam was not around because he was pretty sure she wouldn't want this gossipy woman—it had to be she who'd told Sam about the rock, paper, scissors fiasco—linking their names like that.

He checked Eddie's file, spoke briefly to the bright little boy, and escaped before Ann could think of another plan.

'Would you have asked me out if you'd won the bet?'

It was the first question Sam asked when she climbed into his car on Sunday morning, dressed in pristine white slacks and a black and white striped shirt, her usually unruly hair somehow knotted rather severely on the top of her head.

Her question had come just in time to stop him saying she looked terrific and Andy had to concentrate on getting out of the underground garage far more intently than he needed to. But once on the road, taking the one that led to the lighthouse first, he knew he'd have to answer.

'Of course,' he said.

He didn't need to glance her way to know she was frowning—he could actually feel her tension in the air.

'But couldn't you have asked at another time?'

The question made him frown.

'Once you were going out with Nick? Of course not!'

'Because I was somehow marked as his?' she demanded, as he pulled into the parking area near the track that led to the top of the headland.

He turned to face her, puzzled by the question—trying to think back to that fateful time.

'Not marked as his—I don't think I thought that way. It's just, well, you were going out with him—why would I assume you'd say yes to me? And how would he have felt if I'd done such a thing? And what would he have thought of you—well, of us both—if you'd said yes? Life just doesn't work that way.'

She'd been staring out the window at the sea, but as she turned back towards him he wanted to ask her if she would have said yes, but it was all so pointless.

'What happened, happened,' he said, reaching out to touch her cheek with one finger. 'There aren't any set rules or guidelines for life, you know. We just have to stumble along as best we can, doing what we feel is right at the time, and hopefully not having too many regrets when we look back at the past.'

She smiled and touched her hand to his.

'We tend to remember the regrets—the bad things, more than the good, don't we?' she said, giving his hand a squeeze before opening the car door, signalling, without a doubt, that that particular conversation was over.

They climbed the hill to the top of the rocky outcrop, coming out on the grassy knoll with the wide Pacific Ocean stretching out on both sides of them.

Sam threw her arms wide and turned to him in sheer delight.

'This is what I dreamt about—all the time I was in London, and while I was with Mum in the wilds of South-East Asia. I dreamt of living near the ocean. Working in Perth gave me a taste for it, for being close to the sea and beaches—although with my skin I really should have stayed in London or gone even further north to Scotland. But I think Aussies need the ocean— well, I do,' she said, her face aglow with the wonder of it.

So it seemed natural to take advantage of those out-flung arms and wrap his around her body, holding her close—a friendly hug—for all his body screamed for more.

They drew apart but somehow were holding hands, and walked across the grass to the brilliant white lighthouse and the squat building that had been the keeper's cottage nestled beside it.

They climbed to the top and from there looked back over the countryside that surrounded the sprawling coastal city.

'It's mainly dairy farms, some cattle properties and plenty of hobby farms, where people keep everything from goats to llamas,' he told her. 'There are local markets on the second and fourth Sunday of the month. You'd be surprised what you can buy there. Everything from local wines and beers, to hats, and mats, and guinea pigs.'

'Well, that's next Sunday accounted for,' she said. 'And next Saturday or maybe on one of my early finish days next week, I want to have a look for a car, just something small to get me to the hospital at night when I'm on call.'

She turned to him and put her finger against his lips.

'Don't bother telling me I can always take yours,' she said, 'because I wouldn't dream of it. And, anyway, you might be using it.'

She frowned, as if about to say more, but other people arrived at the top and the moment passed.

Could this count as courting? he wondered as they made their way back to the car, her hand still captive in his.

Such an old-fashioned word, but he couldn't remember ever being so uncertain with a woman—uncertain how to proceed, wondering whether, if he rushed things, he might spoil what they already had—which *had* to be friendship.

But if he were to court her, start with occasional dates maybe…

Dear God, it all seemed so infantile when they were both mature people and had already slept together!

But he couldn't help but be aware of the distance she usually kept between them; her avoidance of an accidental touch, let alone a real one. And instinct told him it was to do with her marriage, her previous experience that had either been so great she'd never stopped loving Nick, or so tricky she didn't want to repeat it.

Could he ask?

Get her to talk about it?

Not really, when either love or loyalty to Nick would colour her reply. And given the failure of love in *his* life, he doubted he'd be able to judge which it was.

And, to be honest, he'd been wary of proximity himself—of getting too close, of touching her by accident.

Yet, still hand in hand, they reached the car, and the mood was broken.

'Nick would have asked me out if you'd won,' Sam said quietly, and Andy felt his gut clench as the words told him with a stark certainty that Nick was never far from her thoughts.

Sam used the excuse of needing to shop for food and sort out her new living quarters to turn down Andy's invitation to spend the afternoon at the local gallery before an early dinner—even just fish and chips by the shore.

The morning had been confusing enough.

Spending non-work time with Andy had been wonderful and having seen more of this beautiful place where she'd ended up had made her delighted with her decision.

But Andy's hug, the hand-holding had stirred up memories of their night together, and her body ached for more intimacy— for kisses and touches, for being held, and whispered words...

But to get more involved with Andy was really impossible. In Andy's mind this might appear to be a prelude to marriage and even after three years the M word brought up an image of a black hole into which she'd disappear.

Andy was as different from Nick as it was possible for a man to be, and he'd be a loving, supportive husband and wonderful father to the children she really wanted to have.

But would *she* change, as she had with Nick?

She didn't blame Nick for the person she'd become within the marriage because it had been something she hadn't liked in herself. She'd felt as if she was always trying to prove something, and somehow always failing...

Growing up with only a mother and with no extended family around by which to judge people's marriages, she'd had no idea she'd find it as overwhelming as she had.

But Andy was different, and having found her way back to being herself again, surely she wouldn't lose that with Andy.

Would it be a risk?

She'd been lying on her bed while these thoughts had worked their way through her head, coming back now to the fact that it would be wrong to have an affair with Andy because he'd be hurt when she ended it. And, what's more, she'd have to find another job, as working with him afterwards would be just too hard.

Actually, working with him during an affair would also be hard—the discretion part of it almost impossible, and that, too, would damage Andy more than her.

And wasn't all this futile? Hand-holding hardly counted as a declaration of love!

She climbed resolutely off the bed, changed into one of her new swimming costumes, slathered fifty-plus sun block all over her skin, pulled on a light shift as a cover-up, and headed for the beach.

An hour battling the waves would chase all these gloomy thoughts away. And, besides, Andy might just have been holding her hand because they were friends.

She slipped on her sandals, slapped on her hat and, with a towel slung over her shoulder, she set off.

Perhaps if she talked to Andy about these things it would help.

Or would she be making a complete fool of herself, if he wasn't the slightest bit interested in her—even attracted to her?

Just because he had been once, it didn't mean much six years later...

Hoping an hour out on the waves would clear his head and tangled thoughts, Andy changed into board shorts and a light wetsuit, went back to the garage to get his board from the lock-up section in front of his car, and headed for the beach.

He was sitting on his board out beyond the breakers, hoping for one last good wave to carry him all the way back to the beach. If it didn't come, he'd paddle into shore, but it was so peaceful and serene out here, he didn't mind a wait.

The wave, when it did come, was a beauty, and he caught the top of it before it curved into a barrel, crouching on the board to get his body into this green curl of the ocean, exultant as he rode out the other end.

A loud cheer from the beach told him he wasn't alone, and as he rode the wash of the now-broken wave through to the sand, he realised it was Sam.

'I didn't know you could surf,' she said, then frowned. 'In fact,' she added in a puzzled voice, 'I really know nothing about you—the now you, not the six-years-ago you. I've been rude, babbling on about me and my travels, but what of you?'

She'd stretched her towel on the beach and was sitting on it, spreading sunscreen on her arms and legs—long, long, and quite lovely, legs.

'Who are you, Andy Wilkie?' she said, smiling up at him as he stripped off the top half of his wetsuit, letting it dangle from his waist, and picked up his towel. 'And what have *you* been doing? I know we talked briefly about Boston and our travels. In fact, I read a paper you wrote from there—the dangers of hyperthermia in children, I seem to remember. But the real Andy Wilkie. You're not married, unless you have a wife tucked away in a cupboard somewhere, so what's been happening in your life?'

She patted the sand beside her, and when he'd dried off his face and torso he sat down next to her. She'd obviously been swimming, for her hair hung in wet tendrils down her back, and clustered ringlets curled around her face.

'Did you ever marry?' she asked, bringing his attention back to what was obviously going to be an inquisition.

'Got close to it twice,' he said, and immediately felt guilty that he'd said it so casually—with such a lack of feeling.

But wasn't it the truth?

'Wrong women?' Sam persisted, and this time, looking at her as he answered, he could say truthfully, 'Maybe I was the wrong man.'

'I doubt that,' she said. 'You're one of the good guys, but I assume that took up quite a bit of the six years, wooing and winning not one but two wrong women. But there has to be more—a grand passion?'

That he definitely wasn't going to answer!

'Several not so grand passions,' he did say, because he didn't want her persisting. 'But fun relationships with no expectations at the end of them. Really, Sam, you must know yourself how hard it is to keep a relationship alive when one, or in my case often both, the parties are involved in either emergency medicine or PICU.'

'We should have been skin specialists—they hardly ever get called out at night,' she said, but she was smiling, and he knew her passion for the job they did was as strong as his.

It was time to change the conversation, but he'd missed his chance. Sam was already asking, 'Were there reasons?'

He looked blankly at her. 'Reasons for what?'

She gave an exasperated sigh. 'For neither of the relationships going on to marriage? And don't talk to me about work pressures. The majority of specialists in all fields manage to make marriage work and the ones who don't probably wouldn't have stayed married if they were bank managers or garbage collectors.'

'Garbage collectors?' he echoed, and she had to smile.

'You know perfectly well what I mean! What happened?'

Tell her, or not tell her?

He thought how peaceful this was—or had been—just being with Sam, enjoying her company and the beautiful setting. Medical matters had been the last things on their minds.

So he told another truth...

'I just wasn't right for them,' he said, 'or perhaps they weren't right for me. It was a long time ago, Sam, and I've settled into a life I'm comfortable with—comfortable in. I like my life just as it is. Work does have pressures, as you know, and to be able to come home and just relax and renew myself is exactly what I need.'

Liar, a voice was yelling in his head, although it was only a partial lie. He really *did* like his nice, uncomplicated lifestyle.

'Nonsense,' Sam told him. 'You've got to get out and about. You're far too good a man to be frittering your life away on brief romances. You'd make a wonderful father—anyone who sees you with a patient would realise that in an instant!'

He could tell she was winding up towards more marital advice, so it really *was* time to change the conversation.

'So now you've obviously done all you needed to do in your enormous new living space,' he said to her, 'you've got no excuse—so how about fish and chips on the beach? I know the best fish and chip shop in Port F.'

And to his surprise she smiled, and said, 'You're on! But I like calamari and chips if that's okay, and I do need to shower and do something to control my hair before we can leave. Will we walk?'

'It's not too far,' he said, his mind racing ahead to the possibility of holding hands—if not on the way there, at least on the way back.

You are nuts, he told himself, but his mind had already moved on to a dark spot at the end of the esplanade that would be perfect for a very chaste kiss...

But right now she was standing up so he picked up her towel, took it a little further downwind on the beach and shook the sand from it before handing it back to her.

She seemed surprised by the gesture but simply thanked him, then wrapped the towel around her body, covering her swimsuit but leaving the lovely length of leg for him to enjoy.

Which he probably shouldn't be enjoying as much as he was.

'Are you checking out my legs?'

Sam's sudden question brought him out of this consideration.

'Yes, I was,' he told her, 'and very lovely legs they are too. And you must remember it's allowable on Aussie beaches for men to admire women's legs. It's one of the reasons we have beaches!'

She laughed and told him he was talking nonsense, but the colour in her cheeks suggested she hadn't minded it, nonsense or not!

They *did* hold hands, and although Sam suspected Andy had used the excuse of helping her up the first steep hill to take hers, she found it was comfortable, her fingers wrapped securely in his, and did nothing to stop the small pleasure.

They ate their paper-wrapped meals sitting on a bench that overlooked the river, dog walkers strolling by, seagulls clamouring around their feet for the occasional dropped scrap.

And they talked of work—Sam bringing Andy up to date on the progress of their current patients, explaining that Ryan had picked up quite a lot and could possibly go home the following day.

'Although you know him better than I do. So I decided to leave that decision to you.'

She fed her last chip to the clamouring seagulls and crumpled up the paper.

'Have you enjoyed it?' Andy asked, and she smiled at him.

'The fish and chips by the river? Enormously!' she said.

He grinned at her, sending tendrils of delight threading through her body.

'You know very well we were talking about work!' he scolded. 'Have you enjoyed your first two weeks?'

She turned to him.

'Loved it,' she said. 'And that's mainly thanks to you for making it so easy for me to fit in.'

He looked at her for a moment, then said, 'I think you'd fit in anywhere.'

They walked back, Andy leading her to a track that would take them up through the scrub to the top of the hill near the apartment block. But when he stopped beneath a dramatic pandanus palm, and drew her into his arms, she looked into his dimly lit eyes and had to ask, 'Are you courting me?'

His answer was a light kiss on her lips.

'Would you like me to?'

She shook her head, unable to really answer that, but she nestled closer to his body, finally pulling away enough to say, 'I'm not sure I'm good courting material, Andy.'

'Because?' he asked, kissing her cheek, then the hollow beneath her ear.

'I wasn't good at marriage,' she blurted out, because Andy's kisses were tantalising, and her body, as well as her brain, was going haywire. 'I loved Nick, but it wasn't enough somehow. And I lost myself somewhere in it. Mum was away, in South America most of the time, but I doubt she'd have been much help, because she'd never been in a long-term relationship. And how could I ask a friend how their marriage worked?'

He kissed her lips again, and before she dissolved into the bliss of being kissed by Andy—which she had done all too recently—she eased away again.

'Nick wouldn't have been easy to live with,' Andy pointed out, still holding her loosely in his arms.

'That's no excuse for my failure,' Sam told him, her voice thick with remembered unhappiness. 'I just don't know, Andy.'

He turned, but kept one arm around her waist as he steered them both back onto the path.

'I doubt you lost of all of yourself,' he said gently, 'because to me you're every bit the Sam I used to know, only wiser, but just as fierce in protection of something you believe is right, and passionate about your patients.'

'Doesn't mean I'm good marriage material, though,' she said gloomily.

'Well,' he said, 'as I've already told you, I didn't even make it to a wedding, so I can't judge anyone else. But do we have to look that far ahead? What about now?'

Sam was tempted, so tempted, yet still something held her back.

'We're colleagues,' she reminded him.

'And surely professional enough to keep our work lives separate?' he countered. 'So forget about the future and let's try just for now?'

She wished she could see his face, but the track was narrow and dark so he led her by the hand, about half a step ahead.

Just for now. The words echoed in her head, sounding far too tempting, while somewhere deep inside her body some traitorous little impulse was dancing up and down with joy at the thought of an affair with Andy.

But whether either of them could do 'just for now' without someone getting hurt was a totally different question.

They came out on the top of the hill, meeting up with the reality of streetlights, apartment blocks and occasional traffic.

'You don't have to decide this right now,' Andy told her, wrapping his arm around her waist again now they could walk side by side. 'Just think about it for—oh, a few minutes, maybe an hour?'

He was smiling, sure they'd reached the place he wanted to be, but still caution held her back.

'Tomorrow,' she said, 'and, because I'm not nearly as sure as you are about the "professional at work" side of things, I'll tell you when you knock off tomorrow.'

'What about when your shift ends, then?' he said with a smile, and she shook her head.

'I'm on early, as you well know, and I'm going out to look at cars when I finish work, so we'll leave it till your shift ends, thank you very much. I'll even cook us dinner if I can use your kitchen, and perhaps your balcony to eat on.'

She could see his face now, and guessed he was holding back an urge to say he'd look at cars with her, or maybe they wouldn't need two cars, but he did hold back, and she squeezed his hand.

Maybe it *would* work out—if only just for now...

CHAPTER SEVEN

SAM LOVED EARLY-MORNING SHIFTS. The wards were quiet, lacking the buzz and bustle that seemed to build up during the day, and many of the children were still asleep.

Those who were awake were usually chatty. Kayla, her diabetes now stabilised with the knowledge and drugs she'd need to keep it that way, was due to go to the wards, where she'd spend a day with one of her parents and a specialised nurse to run through the pin-prick blood test she'd need to do several times a day with her special device, and practise using the syringe with which she'd be injecting her insulin.

Sam sat with her for a few minutes, talking to her about what lay ahead, reassuring her that she'd soon be able to manage it all without stress, telling stories of six-year-olds she'd seen who had been doing their own injections for a year.

Then on to Grant, who was due to be brought out of his coma today. So much rested on this, although evidence of mild brain damage might not be noticeable for some time.

But the shock for the child, waking to find so much plaster on his body, one leg suspended above the bed by a sling around his ankle, his other leg held together with an external frame, would be the most immediate problem.

'How do I explain it all to him?' his mother, who was sitting by the bed, asked.

Sam smiled at her. 'With any luck he'll find it exciting—something to tell all the kids at school. But he'll be woozy for a day or two, so don't get alarmed. As far as all our tests show, there was no substantial damage to his brain, just some slight swelling, which has gone down now.'

She waved her hand towards the sling.

'Boredom's going to be the main thing—he's not going to be able to move around much for a while. Does he have some kind of device with games on that he can use while lying in bed?'

His mother gave a huff of rueful laughter.

'He has some hand-held thing he plays with all the time. In fact, I feel so guilty because that's why he was out on his bike. I told him if he didn't put the silly device away and get out in the fresh air, I'd confiscate it for good.'

'You can't blame yourself,' Sam told her, knowing it would do no good at all. How often had she told herself she wasn't to blame for Nick's death when she knew full well it was the argument that had caused it.

It wasn't rational, she knew that, but it lingered anyway, as this would with Grant's mother...

Abby was sufficiently recovered to be transferred to a ward, and Sam was writing up the protocols for it when a shiver down her spine told Andy had just walked into the room.

'You're early,' she said, not turning to look at him in case her too-ready blush gave her away.

'Wanted to see Abby before she left us,' he said, going to stand by the bed and taking Abby's hand.

'Happy to be getting out of here, Abs?' he said, and the girl smiled radiantly at him.

'But I'll miss you all,' she said, the words belying the smile. 'You've all been so kind, especially you, Dr Wilkie!'

Now *she* was blushing, and Sam bumped Andy's arm as they left the room.

'Do all the teenage girls fall for you, Dr Wilkie?'

'Behave yourself,' Andy said sternly, but the twinkle in his eyes told her how hard this 'just colleagues thing' could prove to be.

'Why *are* you here early?' Sam asked, as they stood outside the door, the file in Sam's hands between them so it *could* look like a normal colleague conversation.

'Paperwork,' he said briefly, but she knew it was more than that.

He'd wanted to see her just as much as she'd wanted to see him, and how they were both going to get through their shifts when the air between them was so charged it was a wonder the lights weren't flickering.

'Go do your paperwork!' Sam said, needing to get away from him so she could sort out what was going on in her head *and* her body.

He left, but it didn't help much.

How hadn't she felt this charge last night, when they'd been so serious and adult about not committing too much? How stupid had that been? Surely if they'd gone to bed last night, she'd have been satisfied enough not to want to rip his clothes off in the hospital corridor this morning.

Focus!

She forced Andy from her mind and concentrated on the patients, possibly a little too hard because one mother asked her if everything was all right in the panicky voice parents got when a doctor was looking worried.

'She's fine,' Sam said. 'I was just wondering if she was ready to go to a children's ward today or to leave it until tomorrow.'

'It would suit me better tomorrow,' the mother told her, 'so I can bring in some everyday clothes for her. I noticed when someone showed me the ward she'll be going to that the children were in day clothes, not pyjamas.'

'Then tomorrow it is,' Sam said. 'And you're right, she'll feel more at ease if she's wearing day clothes like the others.'

It was a nothing conversation, but it brought Sam's mind back into balance. This was work, and her mind was now firmly fixed on it, and would remain there for the rest of the shift.

Which, as it turned out, was a nightmare.

A call from the ED with a third measles case, this time a boy of eleven. Sam went straight down and although the boy wasn't particularly sick, she knew he could deteriorate. Plus the fact that they could isolate him best in the PICU meant she had a new patient.

Peter Collins—a nice-looking kid—was obviously unhappy about being in hospital.

'But I'm not that sick!' he complained to Sam, when she visited him on his arrival in the PICU.

'We don't want you spreading the disease any further,' Sam told him, as she read through the information the ED had collected on him.

'It says here he has had all his immunisations,' she said, turning to Mrs Collins who was telling Peter to behave himself. 'Did they include measles?'

Mrs Collins nodded. 'I'm sure they did—we had to show the papers to his kindy—but I don't know what happened to them after that. It was years ago.'

'Well, it might explain why he's not as badly affected as the other two,' Sam said. 'But we're trying to track the source. Did Peter go to the show that was on here not long ago?'

Mrs Collins nodded. 'We all went. It was just after Peter's birthday and some of the family had given him money to go on all the rides.'

'Can you remember what rides you went on?' Sam asked her patient, then had to listen to how rad the dodgem cars were and why he hadn't gone on the Ferris Wheel—far too high and he'd have been sick—but had loved the ghost train, and the hall of mirrors, but mostly he'd been on the dodgems.

Sam shook her head.

The other two children were surely too young to have been on dodgem cars but at least the authorities now had someone they could track through the fair.

She left Peter and his mother and sat down at the main desk to get on to the details of the contact they now had at infectious diseases control.

'We'll send someone to talk to Peter and his mother,' the voice promised. 'It will give us two visits to compare—we haven't liked to disturb Rosa's family at this time. And we'll have to publicise this now. Be ready for a few journalists, TV cameras, et cetera.'

'My boss can do that,' Sam said firmly, and the woman laughed.

'If you can get Andy Wilkie to front the cameras, you're a better woman than I am,' she said.

'No way—no, never!' Andy told Sam very firmly when she came to his office at the end of her shift to tell him journalists would be on their way.

'But why not?' Sam asked, frowning at him, the spark that had flared between them earlier tamped down now under the pressure of work.

'I just don't do it!' he said bluntly. 'This is a small regional hospital, and once the press latch onto someone they can use as an "expert" or "hospital spokesperson—"' he put the words in inverted commas with his fingers '—they never let him or her go.'

He paused then spread out his hands.

'Have you ever done it? They put powder all over your face and shine bright lights into your eyes so you look like a startled rabbit. Only in my case I look like a very tall, gangly, startled rabbit. Never! The Administrator can do it. He can get all the info he needs off the computer, and he'll handle the press far better than I would.'

But still Sam frowned, apparently not at all placated by his flood of words.

'What?' he asked, and now she smiled.

'You must have done it at some time,' she pointed out, 'to know you look like a very tall, startled rabbit.'

'I did it when Nick died,' he said, voice flat and cold, obviously still distressed by the memory. 'I was there at the hospital that day. Some people knew I was his friend and sicced a reporter onto me.'

Holy cow! What had he done, blurting that out?

He didn't need to see Sam's stricken face to realise that, just like that, he'd spread all the horror of the past on his desk in front of her—in front of them both—because she'd know immediately why he'd been at the hospital that day. He'd been there to yell at her!

'Shit!' he said, and buried his face in his hands. 'I'm sorry, Sam, so sorry.'

But sorry was too late. She'd been transported as rapidly as he had back to that dreadful day, and now the tentative attraction that had flared between them, piping hot only a few hours earlier, had vanished beneath the weight of old, and very cold, memories.

'I understand,' she finally said, in a voice devoid of feeling. 'I'm sure they'll find someone else to do it.' And with that she was gone.

This relationship was never going to work.

No matter how he felt about Sam, the past would always be there, hovering in the background, ready to leap out and bite them at the most unexpected moments.

Sam left work feeling unsettled and anxious. She'd thrust Andy back into those memories with her teasing him about being on TV, but did that mean…

You are over Nick, she told herself firmly. You won't ever

forget him, the great times with Nick and the love she'd had for him, but it was time to move on.

And given the effect Andy was having on her, surely he was the man to move on with?

For now, at least.

Although those last two words made her stomach ache. If she wanted even just for now, she somehow had to show Andy that everything was all right between them.

Somehow...

Tom Carey was the first man she'd seen in a suit since her arrival—very smooth and efficient, rattling off numbers she really didn't understand, or want to learn about.

But she'd already spotted the car she wanted, a vivid yellow, compact four-wheel drive tucked into a back corner of the showroom.

'But will you need a four-wheel drive? Wouldn't a nice sedan—a small one—suit you better?'

'Not if I'm going to explore the places around Port on my days off,' she told him, pleased the name the locals used had come easily to her lips. 'I saw from up on the lighthouse hill that the country begins quickly on the outskirts of town, and while I don't intend to do any dangerous off-road driving, I'll be more comfortable in something that doesn't hate country roads.'

Tom took her across to look at the interior of the car, though she assured him she didn't need to see the engine as she had no idea what it was supposed to look like.

'Want to take it for a spin?' Tom asked, and she smiled and nodded.

It was a glorious car to drive, not too high off the ground but high enough to see over many of the cars around her.

'I love it,' she told Tom, then realised that probably wasn't a good bargaining point, but it already had its price written on the back window, and with new cars she wouldn't have a lot of bargaining power, but she tried anyway.

'Can I get the window tinting included in the price?' she asked, and Tom agreed without any argument so she guessed the company allowed for that in its profit margin.

Fifteen minutes of paperwork later, the car insured and registered, she drove out of the dealership filled with the joy and pride of ownership.

Remembering the uneasiness between her and Andy before she'd left the hospital, she drove to the shopping centre and picked up all she'd need to cook a decent meal for the two of them, deciding on roast lamb because she knew people living alone rarely bothered with a roast dinner.

The residual chill she'd felt in Andy's office remained with her, but it hadn't completely doused the heat that had flared between them earlier, and if she wanted to retrieve that—wanted to be with Andy, even just for now—she had to make things right between them again.

Rod had given her a remote to access the garage and she drove in proudly, finding the double space for Unit One and parking her car beside what was presumably Rod's.

Would Andy guess it was hers when he drove in past it?

She smiled at the thought then bundled her groceries out of the car and up in the elevator to Andy's floor, pleased she still had his keys.

But even as she marinated the roast in rosemary and lemon, and prepared the vegetables so everything was ready to go into the oven when he returned home, misgivings swirled in her stomach and she was tempted to open the bottle of quality shiraz she'd bought and have a drink to settle her nerves.

Better to go downstairs for a shower and change of clothes, she decided, but as she reached the elevator, it stopped and Andy stepped out.

He took her in his arms and held her close.

'I was so sure I'd ruined everything, bringing up the past like that. I just didn't realise what I was saying. I was so adamant about not appearing on television again I wasn't thinking.'

He nuzzled his lips against her neck, then kissed her lips, the kiss deepening as the charge she'd felt this morning returned.

'I was just going down for a shower,' she murmured weakly.

'I need one too,' he told her, so somehow it was inevitable they both ended up in his shower, exploring each other with touch and kisses, less frantic this time, prolonging their pleasure until satisfaction could wait no longer, and they joined beneath the running water, gloriously slick, and cool, intensifying the experience.

'Well, that's going to make dinner a little late,' she said, smiling at him as she towelled her hair dry, marvelling at the sight of him naked, his body lithe yet muscular from his swimming and surfing. 'And I need to get clean clothes from my room but don't want to go down there wrapped in a towel.'

He slipped out of the bathroom, returning with a T-shirt with a large dog on the front of it and a pair of his boxers.

'They've an elastic waist so should stay up on you, although maybe not for long,' he teased, his blue eyes glinting with mischief.

But Sam had a dinner to prepare, so she put on the offered clothes and headed for the kitchen, turned on the oven, and when it had heated put the meat and vegetables into it.

'And wine, too?' Andy said, when he returned, similarly attired in a baggy shirt and boxers, explaining when she raised her eyebrows, 'I thought it'd be nice to match.'

He opened the wine and poured two glasses, kissing her lightly on the lips as he handed one to her.

'Let's sit outside,' she said, and headed for the balcony, quite sure where kisses would lead if they stayed in the kitchen.

'I didn't think you'd come,' he said, as they raised their glasses in a toast. 'But you'll be pleased to know I did the interview. I decided I'd let Nick's death colour my life for far too long. I knew I'd hurt you when I brought the whole darned thing up again this morning, so I did my powdered, startled rabbit thing not long after you left. If you want to see it, we'll probably catch it on the late local news.'

She smiled at him.

'If we happen to be around to catch the late local news!'

Sam felt herself blush as she said it. That was surely flirting, and she'd never flirted much—certainly not with Nick, who could so easily take something the wrong way. But Andy winked at her, and she knew everything was going to be all right.

Andy looked out over the ocean, dark now as the moon hadn't yet shown itself. He felt at peace, and knew it was to do with the woman sitting beside him.

Fate had brought this woman back into his life, and now she was here, with him—and even if it *was* just for now, he could be content with it—just for now, anyway...

He understood some of her reservations about relationships, he'd known Nick well enough to know he wouldn't have wanted to work with him. With Nick, everything had to be a contest, with him as the winner, and throughout their friendship, from childhood on, Andy had been content with that.

Winning had never seemed important to him.

Being the best he could—that was something else—but coming second, or even thirty-first, had never bothered him.

And then there were the disasters of his own relationships, failures that had led him to wonder if they were worth the investment he'd put into them; that had led him to step back from too much commitment to anyone.

'Want to share?' Sam asked, and he was startled out of his thoughts.

'Share what?' he said, aware he certainly didn't want to share those particular thoughts, especially not with Sam.

'The myriad thoughts that were chasing across your face—and not all of them good, I suspect.'

He shrugged the words away. 'Just random things floating

past, nothing deep and meaningful,' he said. 'I suppose just sitting here with you is enough for me at the moment.'

He smiled at her, sitting with her feet up on the railing of his balcony, her long legs sending a frisson of excitement through him.

'Do you want me to do anything about the dinner—turn something over in the oven, get the cutlery?'

'Just sit and relax,' she said, sipping at her drink. 'And after dinner, if you like, I'll take you for a drive in my new car.'

'You bought a car? Why didn't you say? We could have gone straight down and looked at it.'

'Yes?' she teased, and he had to laugh, but her lack of excitement over such a purchase bemused him. Buying a new car, for him, was right up there with surfing big waves as far as excitement went.

But Sam?

He studied her for a moment, saw her in profile as she watched the moon put in its appearance over the ocean. She was different, this woman. He sensed she had an inner calmness of spirit that meant she could cope with whatever life threw at her. Someone at ease with herself.

Yes, she'd been upset about Rosa, but in no way had it affected her work, or her capacity to empathise with all the other patients and their families, all of whom he knew, even after a week or two, liked and trusted her implicitly.

If he'd been the peevish type, he might have resented her easy popularity—the way nurses would turn to her, parents seek her out—but instead he was proud, not only because he'd appointed her but because she was Sam, and he was happy for her.

Sam sipped her drink, delighting in the peace and quiet of the early evening, happy she could sit like this with Andy, not having to talk, or plan, or, in fact, do anything much.

Shortly she'd have to get up and check on their dinner, but right now all she had to do was sit, comfortable in his presence, relishing his closeness—the feeling of a bond between them that worked without words.

'Sure I can't do anything for you in the kitchen?' he asked and she turned to smile at him, shaking her head.

'Starving, are you?' she teased. 'You can't hurry a roast dinner. I'll take care of it, but we can sit a while longer.'

She paused, remembering the bad moments they'd had earlier in the day, *and* the outcome when he'd arrived home.

This could work, but being with Andy, enjoying the physical side of things, could she let it go when the 'just for now' ended?

She rather doubted it, so with a less content feeling she lowered her legs and headed for the kitchen to pull the lamb out of the oven and wrap it in foil to let it rest, then called Andy, asking him to set the table while she served up.

Which involved coming into the kitchen to get the cutlery and, it appeared, seizing her by the waist and waltzing her around the kitchen island, before releasing her to get on with her job.

But that carefree impulse had left her smiling and wondering again if 'just for now' *would* be enough.

The drive was forgotten as the meal became an erotic feast, feeding titbits to each other, feet tangling beneath the table, hands touching, stroking, the meal in the end only three-quarters eaten as the need grew too great and they moved to the bedroom to pursue the by now red-hot attraction.

Sam woke at three and slid out of the bed, careful not to wake Andy. She pulled on yesterday's clothes to make her way down to her own small living space, showered and slipped into bed. She'd get a couple of hours' good sleep before her alarm told her the new day was waiting for her.

Andy wasn't surprised to find Sam gone when he awoke the next morning. Her work shift began at seven and he'd slept until close to eight. But as he touched the cold sheets beside him, he wished she was still there.

Not for sex, although that would have been nice—but just for company. And with nearly two hours before *he* had to be at work, he could afford to lie here for a while and think about her.

He felt comfortable with Sam—talking to her, being with her, even knowing she was close by when they were on the ward.

And somehow, to him, he decided, that was nearly as good as the sex—though it was great sex—something you couldn't really say about most new relationships—well, in his case anyway.

To get his mind off that particular subject, he ran through the patients on the ward, mentally checking where they all were in their treatment. Grant was a worry. X-rays and scans of his head had revealed little damage to his brain—no swelling, no obvious injuries at all, and although the anaesthetist had reversed the anaesthetic he'd been given to keep him calm for a few days, he'd remained unresponsive.

A neurosurgeon was due to visit him today, and Andy closed his eyes briefly, praying there was nothing the other specialists had missed.

And Jake's rash—still no answer to that.

He drifted back to sleep...

Colin Forbes had appeared as Sam was finishing her first round, checking on any changes to patients' statuses during the night, noting down any problems or anomalies that would require more attention later.

But right now there was a visiting neurologist standing at the monitor desk, going through Grant's file.

'He was alert immediately after the accident?' he asked, when Sam had introduced herself.

'Alert and responding to questions the ambos put to him,' Sam confirmed. 'It was because of the extent of his physical injuries that the surgeons who patched him up decided to put him into an induced coma for a few days, to allow the healing process to begin.'

'And they reversed it, when?'

'Yesterday, late afternoon.'

'And no change?'

'None!' Sam told him, drawing a vacant monitor towards her and pulling up Grant's scans and X-rays.

'Did they do an MRI?' Colin asked, and Sam shook her head.

'Get one done now and ask Radiography to copy to me. Now let's see the boy.'

Sam spoke to the nurse about organising someone to take Grant down to Radiography, then led the specialist to Grant's room, where his mother was reading to the unresponsive boy.

'Good stuff!' Colin told her, then introduced himself. 'The more stimulation a coma patient has the better,' he said, before adding, 'although plenty dispute that. But you keep it up, touch him, talk to him, let him smell things and feel things. It can't do any harm, and who knows what will help.'

Grant's mother happily agreed, saying to Sam as Colin left the room, 'What a lovely man!'

And indeed he was. Sam totally agreed with his notions about providing stimulation for coma patients.

But little Jake was her main problem, his rash far worse. She'd wondered if it could be measles, however unlikely that would be given the child's isolation, but she did return to his bedside to open his mouth, trying to find tell-tale spots among the ulcers the chemo had caused, which was impossible.

Aware he'd been home before the bone-marrow transplant, she wondered if he might have been taken to the fair for a treat.

'Oh, no—no way!' Mrs Wilson responded. 'We kept him well away from any other children and definitely away from crowds. We wanted him as well as possible for the transplant.'

Sam examined him gently, aware he was in a world of misery right now.

The rash was confined to his torso, which really ruled out the wild supposition of measles, the rash usually starting from the face down.

'Could the donor have had some infection?' Mrs Collins asked, but Sam shook her head.

'The donor cells are tested, and then treated to ensure they're totally clear of any infection. But for some reason he's just reacted badly to the transfusion.'

'But on the upside,' a voice behind her said, and this time Andy had come into the room without shivers running up or down her spine, 'it might just be a rash and it will clear up in a couple of days.'

Mrs Collins smiled at him, and Sam wondered at the ease with which Andy could reassure both patients and their families.

They left Jake's room together, Sam explaining the neurologist's visit and his wanting an MRI for Grant.

Andy frowned, and shook his head.

'Surely they'd have picked up anything when they did that in the ED before he was operated on,' he said.

'Unless there was a small bleed, and it's just continued to bleed. He's not on anti-coagulants—I checked what the surgeons had ordered, but—'

'You're right—a small bleed could have been missed,' Andy finished for her.

And, as if summoned by their thoughts, two uniformed police officers appeared.

'Grant Williams. We were told he'd be conscious again today,' one of them said.

'Might have been but even if he was, he wouldn't be in any fit state to answer questions,' Sam told the two men. 'He's badly injured, and he's still in a coma, but you must realise that even when he comes out of it, he'll be sleepy and confused.'

'That right?' one of them asked, turning to Andy as if he needed a male viewpoint on the situation.

'Dr Reilly is in charge of the patient, so she should know,' he said, and Sam felt her pique at the policeman's question subside.

The two men left, and she turned to thank Andy for his support, but he just grinned at her.

'Actually, I did it to save that poor fellow from one of your pithy set-downs. I could see the colour rising in your face.'

'Wretch!' she muttered at him, then added, 'But I *am* worried about Grant—worried we've missed something important.'

'Let's wait for the MRI and the neurologist's report before we start worrying. The kid's had a rough few days—he needs time as much as anything else.'

A nurse appeared at that moment with a request from the ED, for someone to see a child with status epilepticus.

'I'll go down,' Andy said, but Sam was already on her way.

'You're not on duty for another two hours,' she reminded him, although inside she was rather hoping he'd come in early because he wanted to see her, maybe even brush against her— as she'd wanted to do with him.

Mind on job, she scolded herself as she arrived on the ground floor, though the thoughts she'd just dismissed did make her wonder again whether relationships between close colleagues were a good idea.

The child, Ahmed, was four years old, Sam read from his paper file as the ED doctor explained.

'Suffers from epilepsy but usually controlled by drugs. Mother gave oral dose of a benzodiazepine, and the ambos established an IV line and gave a second dose. We have a breathing tube in place, blood sugar is low, so we gave a bolus of glucose IV but he's still—well, you can see...'

The little boy was stiff, but his limbs were twitching and his little body twisting.

'We'll admit him,' Sam said, aware they might have to begin second-level drugs, and do further blood and neurological tests. She was pleased to see the neurologist who'd been visiting Grant was listed as the child's regular specialist. Perhaps he was still in the hospital or had rooms nearby.

Colin Forbes was not only in the hospital, but was in the PICU, at the monitor desk, reading a report on Grant from Radiography.

'Look at this,' he said to Sam, turning a monitor so she could see the screen. 'Here!' he said, using a pen to point to a darker mass of matter towards the back of the skull. 'Poor lad was hit so hard by that damn vehicle he had a contra coup injury to the left side at the back of his brain—just a small contusion but it has bled. From his injuries, we know the car hit him on the right side, and his brain must have jolted forward then back against his skull. It wouldn't have been picked up earlier because it wasn't bleeding directly after the accident, then he went up to surgery and it was missed.'

'Would it be causing his lack of response to the reversal of the coma?' Sam asked, but Dr Forbes shrugged.

'Possibly. A case of delayed concussion maybe—that's always possible. But let's just wait and see. It could resolve itself in a day or two.'

Not something Sam wanted to say to the parents, but she knew the specialist was right.

She told him about Ahmed, who should have arrived in the unit by now, and led the way to the room that had been allotted to him. Sam explained the treatment he'd received from the onset of the seizure, and to her surprise he asked, 'And what would you use next?'

'I suggested downstairs they use a second-line anti-epileptic drug like phenytoin, and if that doesn't work by the time they get him transferred, paraldehyde diluted with point nine percent saline.'

He smiled at her. 'You really don't need me, but as Ahmed is one of my patients, I'll definitely see him. I'd like to speak to his mother about the circumstances around the seizure—whether it was brought on by anything, or if the severity of his seizures has been increasing.'

Ahmed was settled in a bed, an ECG connected to his frail chest, the nurse checking the IV line hadn't kinked during the transfer.

Sam checked the file and saw that phenytoin had been administered in the ED more than five minutes ago, and although Ahmed's body seemed less rigid, the twitching continued.

'Go ahead with paraldehyde,' Colin told her, and keep me posted on his progress.'

CHAPTER EIGHT

AND SO THE days progressed, some patients leaving, new ones arriving, but the small core of seriously ill children remaining with them. Grant had regained consciousness but remained in the PICU because of the severity of his injuries and Colin Forbes's desire to keep an eye on his head injury.

But Jake was causing the most concern, the source of his rash still unidentified, although as yet he was showing no sign of rejecting the transfusion of stem cells he'd received. However, far from improving, he remained limp and listless.

Sam had gone from a week of early shifts to six days of night shifts so she'd seen far less of Andy, grabbing a meal together occasionally if he was home from work before she left for her shift.

She'd finished her final night shift and was looking forward to a full day's sleep, possibly two or three, and sat in her office, writing up some notes. She'd visit Jake before she left, his condition still the main source of concern in the unit.

But as she came out into the airlock room to disrobe, there

was Andy, looking so great even robed in white paper that her heart flipped.

'How's our boy?' he asked, although his eyes said other things. Things that made her blush.

She pulled off her mask to smile properly at him, and was untying her gown when she started to feel sick. She ripped off her gown and raced out of the room, still wearing her booties and gloves, heading post haste for the staff lounge and its bathrooms.

Flushed with heat, she knelt by the lavatory, throwing up everything she'd snacked on during the night.

Then, clammy, and still feeling distinctly wonky, she sat back on the floor. She was aware she had to get up, wash out her mouth, wash her face and hands, and generally sort herself out, but she was unable, for the moment, to move.

Snacking on night shift was normal, mainly because the time seemed all wrong for eating a large meal, but what had she eaten that could do this to her? A couple of cups of tea with biscuits, coffee at some stage, and a sandwich from the machine in the corridor. She couldn't even remember what had been in it, but that seemed the most likely culprit.

Hauling herself to her feet, she made her way out to the washroom to clean herself up and remove her gloves and booties, dumping them in the disposal bin.

Andy was waiting outside when she opened the door.

'Are you all right?' he asked, concern clouding his features.

'Fine now,' she said, 'but I must have eaten something that disagreed with me.'

'Or you've a virus of some kind. Maybe even something you brought back from South-East Asia. You'll have to go home, Sam,' he said. 'I can't risk you being here, maybe passing on something contagious to the children.'

'I *am* going home,' she reminded him. 'End of night shift, four days off, remember, but I doubt it's some bug I picked up before I came—just too long ago. It's something I ate. I'll be fine once I've had a sleep.'

He stepped towards her and she knew he wanted to hold her as much as she wanted to be held—not a done thing in a staff common room.

'I'll call in and see you when I get off,' he said, reaching out and touching her lightly on the shoulder. 'For now, go home and rest—we'll talk later,' he said quietly, then turned away, leaving Sam feeling weak and sick and badly in need of a hug that just hadn't come.

Sorry she hadn't driven her new car to work, Sam trudged home, feeling quite well now but upset that she hadn't finished the handover and had let the team down—let Andy down!

She'd get her car and go to a pathology lab in town, ask for all the tests they could think of for possible overseas viral or bacterial complaints. But not today—today she'd sleep...

By the following morning, she felt so well she knew it couldn't possibly be anything other than something she'd eaten that had disagreed with her. She phoned Andy to explain how well she was, but only midway through the conversation the sick feeling returned, bile rising in her throat, so she said a hasty goodbye and headed for her own small bathroom.

Where, fifteen minutes later, sitting on a different cool, tiled floor, her brain began to work again, and she had to close her mind against the answer it had reached.

Surely not?

It couldn't be!

But it had been over two weeks since Rosa's death, and she knew from the last time that a pregnancy was dated from the date of the last period, and that morning sickness could begin within three to four weeks of that date.

Which, to her, last time, had seemed totally unreasonable!

But this time?

It was impossible!

How could she possibly be pregnant after one night of grief-driven lust?

True, there'd been more nights together since, but she'd gone onto the Pill, and Andy had been scrupulous in using protection until it was well into her system.

So, what the hell was Andy going to think?

She went cold all over, dreading a repeat of the storm her previous pregnancy had caused—remembering the tragedy that it had led to. Not that she had long to find out what Andy thought...

Deciding the best thing to do would be to cook him dinner that evening, and as they relaxed over fine food she'd—well, probably blurt it out!

She'd leave a note on her door that she was up in his apartment, and—

Stop!

First and foremost was the decision *she* had to make.

How did *she* feel?

What did *she* want?

The first was easy—she was delighted at the thought—and the answer lay in the second question—a baby.

She'd already lost one baby and although it had been barely the size of a fist, her arms had ached for it.

This baby she would keep.

And, yes, it would be difficult as she still wanted to work—would *have* to work in order to provide a decent life for herself and her child.

And, really, apart from wanting to keep working, she owed it to Andy, who'd employed her, to stay on. But working women had options these days, and a hospital as new as Port's would almost certainly have a crèche and day-care centre tucked away somewhere in its building.

So, that was *her* decisions made.

In, what, in all of three minutes?

You really gave this a lot of thought, Sam!

But chiding herself didn't stop the secret glee she clutched inside her, ignoring all she knew about the uncertainties tied to the first months of any pregnancy.

It would be the start of her family, her mum's longed-for grandchild. She hugged herself in sheer delight...

Her happy secret kept her going all day as she shopped and prepared a meal for herself and Andy, but about the time he was due to arrive home it occurred to her that Andy would be entitled to some say in this matter. After all, it would be his baby too...

Although if he didn't want a baby, wasn't ready, or thought they should be married but didn't fancy that idea, she'd be quite happy to raise the baby on her own.

All Andy had to decide was whether he'd like to take an interest in it—or even accept a fatherhood role—be part of its life for ever.

The glow was fading slightly, especially now she'd *really* considered Andy and his reaction. He might be horrified.

Probably would be horrified...

She had to stop thinking about it, and definitely stop projecting all the possible reactions Andy might have to hear the news before she became too worried about it that telling him would be impossible.

She *did* blurt it out in the end, but at least not until they'd eaten, and she'd stacked their dirty plates and cutlery in the dishwasher and left the kitchen sparkling clean. Eventually she'd joined him on the balcony, a glass of sparkling mineral water in her hand.

He'd taken her hand to draw her closer but she'd resisted, thinking it best not to be too close, actually edging her chair a little further away.

All the things she'd been going to say, all the ways of telling him she'd practised, vanished in a split second as she clutched her water more tightly in her hand and came out with an abrupt, 'I'm pregnant!'

And apart from seeing his face freeze in reaction, she took

no further notice of him as everything else she wanted to say came rushing after those two words.

'I didn't have a virus and this happened last time, the early morning sickness thing, and I'm happy to bring the baby up on my own, or if you want involvement then that's okay too, and I know it will interfere with my work but I'll make sure it interferes as little as possible because I want to keep working and—'

He held up his hand like a policeman, signalling her to stop, and as her flow of words did stop he said, 'What last time? And how come you get to say if my involvement is okay or not? And, anyway, we need to talk about this, Sam!' He paused, then added, 'Seriously talk, Sam.'

Feeling completely deflated, Sam waited, and when he said nothing else, anxiety began to grow where the joy had once been. And well aware of how quickly anxiety could lead to anger, she had to prod.

'So talk,' she said, pleased her voice didn't shake too much as she spoke.

He squeezed the fingers of the hand she was surprised to find he still held.

'This is hard,' he began, 'but, seriously, Sam, you shouldn't have this baby.'

Sam stared at him in total shock. She'd been prepared for him not wanting involvement, even for him to be angry at the place they'd landed in, but for his first reaction to be a termination, without any discussion or reasoning, that blew her mind.

And took her right back to three years ago when Nick had made a similar pronouncement, only his had been a blunt, 'Get rid of it!'

And ten minutes later he'd been dead.

Red mist gathered in her head and she knew she had to leave, snatching back her hand and rushing off the balcony, through the living room and out the front door, only vaguely aware of Andy saying something to her, getting up to follow her and knocking over his chair on the way.

But she was gone, racing down the fire stairs rather than waiting for the lift, needing to get back into the small space that was her own, where she could hold herself and breathe and remember the excitement she'd been feeling all day long.

Andy let her go.

She had another three days off then a late shift. Hopefully she'd feel well enough to keep working.

Oh, for heaven's sake, why the hell are you thinking about Sam's work hours and shifts? You have to see her, tell her, explain, sort things out.

This wasn't the end of the world.

Then something she'd said—something else—echoed in his bemused brain.

'This happened last time!'

When had she been pregnant before?

Not by Nick, surely, given Nick's steely determination that they both finish their specialty courses before they even thought about a family.

And, slowly, a glimmer of light appeared. She'd said she probably *had* caused the accident—that they'd been arguing—and knowing Nick, nothing would have made him angrier than an announcement by Sam that she was pregnant...

He sighed, remembering the harsh words he'd flung at her at a time when her whole world must have been crashing down around her—when the pain of loss would have been crushing her usually indomitable spirit.

But that was the past, and right now he had problems of his own to solve.

Sam had been happy, her face aglow as she'd announced her pregnancy, and he'd said exactly the worst possible thing.

But how to explain?

How to tell her that genetic testing only identified eighty-five to ninety percent of carriers, which was great, of course, but oh hell and damnation, he'd already been through all this before, the first time after his engagement, but the second time he'd explained first.

And neither of those women, who had professed to loving him deeply and wholly, had wanted to go ahead with a marriage to him.

Could he watch Sam walk away if he told her—*when* he told her?

Especially now, when he'd known this 'just for now' talk was nonsense and he wanted her—loved her—more than anything else in his life. Probably had done for years.

He closed his eyes to the beauty around him and tried to think, but his mind refused to work, blocked by fear of losing Sam.

He had to see her, talk to her, explain…

Sam lay on her bed and stared at the ceiling, her hands cradling her stomach, although it had yet to produce the slightest of bumps.

Stupid, that's what she'd been, reacting like that—like a spoilt child told she couldn't have what she wanted.

She should go back.

Andy must have had a reason for saying what he had.

Surely he did!

But memories of that other time cut too deep—the bitterness, the implacability of Nick's attitude, the anger then the crash—made her dread the conversation that she knew, only too well, she'd have to have with Andy sometime.

But not tonight. Tonight she was far too irrational; the two rejections somehow melding into one.

She had another three days off. She'd sleep and read, and maybe go to the beach or drive around the town, and tomorrow night—surely by tomorrow night—she'd be able to talk sensibly and calmly to Andy, explain how she felt, assure him she could do it on her own, that he needn't be involved.

She shook her head.

Andy *not* be involved?

She'd seen enough of him around the ward to know he'd make a fantastic father. So maybe it was her? Maybe she was okay 'just for now' but not for long term, as a mother of his children.

Dear heaven, she had to stop thinking like this, stop her mind going round and round in circles. She should pick up a book and lose herself in it until she fell asleep. She'd been on night duty, she was tired...

She had a shower, thinking it would soothe her—help her sleep—but Andy's words were a constant echo in her head— *Really, Sam, you shouldn't have this baby...*

Rod woke her with a soft tapping at the door, calling her name. Face crumpled from sleep, hair like a haystack from her tossing and turning all night, she went to it, opening it a crack.

'Andy is here. He wants to see you, just for a minute, before he goes to work.'

Rod was looking anxiously at her and a sideways glance at her mirrored wardrobe doors told her just how bad she *did* look.

Then the nausea came—she'd slept late and not eaten—and she had to flee, managing a garbled, 'Sorry,' to Rod as she shut the door in his face and rushed to the bathroom.

And as she sat on a cool, tiled floor yet again, her stomach empty and the muscles around it complaining, she wondered if Andy was right.

Maybe she *shouldn't* have this baby?

But the mere word 'baby' made her smile, and she hugged her body and told herself she'd manage, get through this, and make a life for herself and her child.

The text was there when she awoke the second time.

I've booked a table for dinner at the Lighthouse Restaurant for tonight at eight. Bring a warm wrap so we can sit out-

side and talk. I'll knock on Rod's door about seven forty-five.
Please let me know.

They *did* need to talk, but there was something very remote
about the text—something detached—one colleague to another,
rather than a text between lovers.

Not that love had ever been mentioned, although now Sam
thought about *that* she felt distinctly unhappy. As if somewhere
in the just-for-now scenario, love had entered the picture.

On her side, anyway.

So a cool, unemotional, colleague-type text made her heart
ache.

But love wasn't the issue right now, she reminded herself.
This was about the baby—someone she could love unreservedly!

She'd bought fresh bread the previous day and was trialling
dry toast and a cup of tea for breakfast, hoping it would quell
the nausea so her work days wouldn't be disrupted.

And if it worked, she'd head for the beach this morning,
slathering on sunscreen and not staying long—just time for a
swim and a short sunbake to dry off.

Andy stared at his phone. Sam had replied to his text, but somehow the single word—Okay—made him feel worse than no
reply.

No, he couldn't feel worse, but what the hell did Okay tell
him? Abso-bloody-lutely nothing, that was what!

Somehow he made it through the day, pleased to see improvement in most of his patients, although some of the new admissions were causing problems, including a fourth measles case.

Given the high percentage of children who *did* receive all
their immunisations, he hated to think how many there would
have been if more parents had opted out.

But at least the people at Infectious Diseases had isolated the
carrier now, an older man who'd fallen ill in Port, but unfor-

tunately he hadn't been ill enough to take to his bed and keep away from the general population.

'It was just a cold and a sore throat,' he'd told his interviewer. 'Yes, maybe a bit of a rash, but I didn't connect the two. You can brush against something, get a rash anywhere!'

It was the only real diversion in a long work day, which finally ended with a Heads of Department meeting that dragged on and on.

He'd finally stood up, apologising but saying he had to leave for another appointment, surprising not a few of the other department heads, who all assumed he had no life outside the hospital.

Not that they'd been wrong about that—not until recently, anyway...

Now, as he drove home—having driven to work to avoid being late—his gut was clenching and his nausea was probably rivalling Sam's morning sickness. Just thinking those two words filled him with so much confusion he had to shut down his wretched imagination and concentrate on practical matters, like what shirt to wear.

Did it matter?

Not one jot, he suspected, but he had to think about something.

Sam had been waiting by the door and opened it when Andy knocked.

Her mind had played out so many scenarios of this moment, most of them as formal as his text, so she was totally undone when he opened his arms and drew her close, murmuring, 'Oh, my love, I'm so sorry!'

Hugging her to him, rocking her in his arms, just holding her.

'This *is* the main entry foyer and a public space,' a voice behind Andy said, and they broke apart, Sam glaring at Rod's huge smile and furious with herself for blushing.

Grabbing hold of Andy's hand, she said, 'Come on, let's go!' and all but dragged him out the front door.

Andy's car was sitting in one of the drop-off, pick-up bays.

'I thought we'd walk,' she said, embarrassed now by her reaction to Rod's tease.

'Driving, we can talk,' Andy said, turning so he could take both her hands in his. 'And we *do* need to talk.'

She looked up into his anxious blue eyes.

'It's not the baby, Sam. There's nothing I'd like more,' he said quietly, then he opened the car door for her, and she slid into the seat.

'But there's something I need to tell you,' he added, as he joined her in the car.

Sam waited, her anxiety, which had vanished in Andy's warm hug, slowly squirming its way inside her once again.

They drove up to the lighthouse, the moon sparkling on the ocean below, the night picture perfect. As was the restaurant, with elegant starched white tablecloths and gleaming silver and glassware, while the outside deck looked north along the coastline and the ocean, occasional clusters of lights suggesting small beachside hamlets.

But it wasn't until they each had glasses of sparkling mineral water in their hands, and the waiter had departed with their orders, that Andy broke the tension that had been gathering between them.

'It's a genetic thing,' he said, and she knew she'd frowned because he held up his hand to stop her questions. 'I'm a carrier for cystic fibrosis. I had a younger sister who had it, so I was tested as well. It means you will need to be tested because most carriers have no idea they are carrying it, unless they've been impacted by a relative with the disease.'

'And you were?' she asked, thinking of very sick children with CF that she'd cared for in the past. 'You *had* a sister? She died?'

She saw the sadness in his eyes, but he waved her questions away, needing, she guessed, to get said what he wanted to tell her.

'Unfortunately testing only reveals eighty-five to ninety percent of carriers. There are rare mutations that aren't revealed.'

He sounded so stressed she reached out and took his hand, aware that this was very difficult for him, while her own mind whirled through possible consequences. Survival rates for cystic fibrosis were much better these days, and if a sufferer could get a heart-lung transplant they had a good chance of leading a good life.

But it was a condition that limited a child's life enormously, and not something she would ever want to see a child of hers go through.

'So, I get tested to see if I'm a carrier,' she said, 'and hope I'm not one, for a start. I guess there's nothing we can do about the chances of my being one of the five to ten percent who might have it but don't get picked up?'

She could hear the hesitation in her voice and knew how hard it was for him to tell her this.

Andy nodded. 'Yes, but in case you are in that group, we should test the foetus too,' he said. 'CVS testing at ten to twelve weeks or amniocentesis at sixteen to twenty weeks, although even if we are both carriers there's only a one in four chance the baby would have it.'

Sam could only stare at him, aware he'd lived with this for most of his life so the facts and figures rolled off his tongue.

CVS—chorionic villus sampling—was where a small number of cells were taken from the placenta close to where it attached to the uterus. Her hand went automatically to her belly, as if she could hold the baby safe from this intrusion.

'Did your parents know?' she asked, wondering if she'd be willing to take the chance of having children if something like this could occur.

Andy shook his head. 'As far back as either of their parents or grandparents were concerned, no one remembered a child who was seriously ill from birth.'

He paused, then added, 'Not that that mattered. They had Sarah and she was a blessing to our family. She was so funny and smart, Sam, and so unconcerned about the difficulties she faced every day.'

He paused.

'We loved her,' he said simply, but his voice was tight, and Sam reached out to hold his hand. Some other time they'd talk more about Sarah, but for now she had to concentrate on her child—their child...

She'd get tested for CF, and if she wasn't found to be a carrier, there was only a minimal chance of her being one of the rare ones, and even if she was... She shuddered at the thought then pushed it away—all the odds were in her favour, although she knew nothing of her father's family, nothing of her father, for that matter.

'If I'm not a carrier then there's no problem,' she said.

'We'd still have to test the baby,' Andy told her. 'Remember the small percentage of people with the rare mutation that testing doesn't reveal.'

Sam sighed and shook her head, unable to take it all in, staring down at the table and fiddling with her cutlery, twirling her knife on the stiffly starched tablecloth.

'Let's wait and see,' she said. 'At the moment it's just all ifs and buts and maybes—all hypothetical. Whatever my test reveals, I'll get the foetus tested and go from there. Okay?'

Andy had to smile at Sam, refusing to get carried away with possibilities, or be concerned over things that might never eventuate. He might mull over it all, and run through dozens of scenarios in his head, but she just got on with things—meeting problems head on. Practical, loving Sam.

Their meals arrived, and as they ate they talked about the food, how good it was, how special to be eating with the ocean right there below them, yet he knew Sam's brain would be working through consequences, and that this was only a temporary lull in the main conversation.

And as the waiter took their plates and left them with a dessert menu, the topic did resume again.

'There's a huge amount of research being done about CF at the moment,' she said, 'and treatments are improving all the time. Imagine if a heart-lung transplant had been available for your sister, Sarah.'

She was smiling at the thought, and Andy could only shake his head. He'd hit Sam with what must have been quite frightening news and here she was thinking of the positives.

Although... Andy knew she was speaking calmly and rationally, but his mind had snagged back at the testing part of her conversation. Sam's use of the little words 'I' and 'I'll' had rattled him. Surely it should have been 'we' and 'us'...

Did she not want it to be a shared venture—not want to marry him and make a family with this baby and maybe others?

Because she didn't love him?

Or because of the CF thing?

His heart ached, and he longed to ask, but his fear of her answer was greater than his need to know. So he changed the subject.

'You said, when you told me you were pregnant, "that last time" your morning sickness had begun early. When was "that last time", Sam? Surely I'd have known of it?'

CHAPTER NINE

To tell or not to tell?

Did it really matter after all this time?

Sam studied the dessert menu as she pondered the questions, not seeing any of the options, just trying to think. Then, aware of the tension growing between them, she lifted her head to meet Andy's eyes.

'That was the cause of the argument,' she said, the words blunt and hard as stones. 'Between Nick and me—when we crashed.'

Another pause, the words that had been held in by locked-away memories caused such pain and guilt she could barely speak. Then, slowly, it came out.

'Nick said a baby would interrupt my career trajectory—and to me it was such a stupid thing to say, especially as I so wanted a family. I blew up.'

She studied Andy's face, seeking understanding—compassion even—but in her emotional state saw nothing.

'I hadn't had a family—not a real one. Just me and Mum.

I thought Nick knew how much I wanted children, I'd talked about it often enough.'

Andy nodded, but it was an uncomfortable nod. He'd always known a family hadn't been part of Nick's agenda, although, apparently, Sam, his wife, had not!

But she had a story to tell—a confession to finish.

She took a deep breath, twiddled her dessert spoon, then met Andy's eyes again.

'He said, get rid of it. Those were his first words, then he went on and on about how it would wreck my career and his career, and I lost it, Andy. Said he didn't know me at all—didn't know how much I ached for a family. I was furious with him—I said things I should never have said, things about him having controlled my life for too long. I was so angry—real redhead rage—I was yelling like a madwoman. It was no wonder Nick was speeding.'

'Sam!'

The single word made her blink, and now she *did* see concern and understanding on his face, and as he took her hands in both of his, the hot memories of her anger melted away and she clung to his fingers—a lifeline back to the present...

'You can't keep blaming yourself,' he said, his voice scratchy with emotion. 'I know I was in shock and somehow took that out on you and I'll never forgive myself for that, but you weren't to blame. Yes, the things you said might have upset Nick, but he was a grown man, thirty-five, and reacting by speeding was a stupid thing to do—*his stupid reaction* caused that crash, not your words.'

'But I lost the baby,' Sam said, still trapped in her memories. 'I could have walked away from Nick—divorced him, kept the baby and followed a new career, even though I'd never considered my work as a "career"—never even thought about a bloody career trajectory!'

Andy smiled at her. 'I know that, love,' he said gently, and that one little word, tacked onto a simple reassurance, made her heart leap.

'Dessert?'

She shook her head, hugging the word to her, although she knew it was probably just a casual endearment.

He'd made it very clear he'd taken her in because she was his best friend's widow—love between them had never been mentioned, although she hadn't realised how she'd felt about Andy until...

Well, that had been her reason to move out.

'So, whatever happens, you want to keep this baby?' he said.

Brought back to earth with a thud, she could only shake her head.

'I'll get genetic testing first and let's go from there. CSV sampling will tell us the baby's okay, and after that— Oh, Andy!'

She knew she was probably looking piteously into his eyes, and could hear the plea in her voice, but how the hell did you make that kind of decision? Surely, as a medical practitioner it would be an ethical one, but for her as a person such a very personal one.

'Let's pay the bill and walk,' he said, as she saw the shadows on his face—shadows of the past, reflections of the shadows she'd have had on hers earlier.

'*Two* near marriages?' she probed, as they walked towards the cliff-top in front of the lighthouse, desperately needing to get away from her own problems.

He nodded.

'So tell me,' she said gently.

'The CF thing did raise issues,' he said, sliding his hand out of hers and clasping both hands behind his back, a clear signal to her that this was not a subject he wished to pursue. Because he still felt deeply about the women—or about one of them in particular?

She'd loved Nick, but would have left him in a heartbeat to have the child she'd so longed for. Which kind of answered the question about this baby. Providing she wasn't a carrier, and the baby tested negative for CF, then she'd…

Damn and blast, why did life have to be so difficult?

'Hey, you'll be over the cliff if you don't slow down!'

She should be thinking about Andy, not her own problems, she reminded herself, stopping by the protective railing and looking down.

Andy's voice brought her out of her useless speculation, and she turned back towards him, aware she'd been getting carried away—aware of him.

'There's too much to think about,' she said, walking back and taking his hands in hers as she faced him. 'And I *have* to think about it, Andy.'

'I know, love,' he said, so gently and quietly she thought her heart might break.

She moved closer and put her arms around him, held him—waiting, hoping.

For what?

Words of love?

'Just get the testing done and we'll go from there,' he said, easing her back a little so he could look into her face. But with the moon behind him, his remained in shadow and told her nothing.

They walked back to the car in silence, the magic all around them unnoticed or maybe it had gone completely.

'Just get the testing done, and we'll go from there.'

His words echoed in her head.

Go where? she wanted to ask, but if she proved to be a carrier…

They could have this baby if it tested negative, but other babies—the family she wanted? She could go the IVF route so the fertilised eggs were tested, and only the ones without CF implanted, but…

You are getting far too carried away with yourself You want

a family, but Andy has said nothing about it—might not even want to be part of this one.

Just get the test and go from there!

They drove home in silence, both, she imagined, lost in their own thoughts. And as he pulled the car into the underground car park she knew the silence needed to be broken. It had already grown to something far too big between them.

And any bigger?

Well, there'd be no them.

If there *was* a them to begin with.

Her heart ached at the thought. 'Just for now' hadn't really started, and it was over—or all but over—before it had begun.

'Do you know of a good medical practice nearby? I'll need a referral for the test.'

It wasn't the perfect way to break the silence, but at least it was practical. And Andy grasped at it.

'There's one in the main shopping centre in town, the one behind the hospital.'

The silence resumed, but only for an instant.

'I'll come with you,' he said, and she had to smile.

'Andy, it's only a blood test, or maybe a swab from inside my cheek. I could do it myself and send it to a private testing agency but let's not get too carried away.'

He'd stopped the car and opened his door so they had a little light, and she saw the concern on his face—concern that seemed to be easing towards dread.

She took his hand.

'I'll be fine,' she told him. 'It's a lot to think about, but it's pointless getting too far ahead of ourselves with all the what-ifs. Let's just get this first test done and take it from there.'

'If you're sure you don't want me there...'

The hesitant words made her smile.

'Andy, it's a *blood test*!'

He didn't answer, getting out of the car and coming around

to open her door, which she would normally have done herself, only she was puzzling over why he was so concerned.

Had the last woman he'd asked to take a test broken his heart? Refused, and walked away?

Did he still love her?

She slammed the door on the thoughts sprouting in her brain, and took Andy's offered hand so he helped her out of the car, and then he took her in his arms and held her close.

'Kind of put a dampener on the evening,' he said softly into her ear, and the warmth of his breath against her skin had her body stirring. But she knew she had too much thinking to do to be getting more involved with Andy.

Although as his lips moved to the little hollow beneath her chin she wondered just what harm there'd be in going ahead with 'just for now'.

Heaps, you idiot, her head yelled at her. Your heart's already far too involved, don't make it worse,

'We'd better go before Rod appears and tells us it's a public car park,' she said, easing away from him. She fled, aware she'd been rude, hadn't even thanked him for dinner, but right now she needed solitude, and a space she could call her own in which to think.

Andy watched her disappear through the heavy fire door, and realised he had absolutely no idea where he stood with this woman he was pretty sure he loved.

Had loved, certainly, when he and Nick had first met her.

She'd been an intern, rostered onto the ED for a term, and she'd been so bright, so alive, even on days when she'd worked through the night and stayed on because she was needed.

And he'd stupidly, as it turned out, had his one and only experience of love at first sight. It had been ridiculous, really, as he'd kept telling himself all through Nick's courtship of her and her starry-eyed wedding to his best mate.

But that was a long time ago, and what he felt now—well, this was certainly different, this was like a deep ache in his gut.

As if he was right back in the past again, in the agony of wanting a woman he couldn't have. Loving her?

He shook his head, aware he didn't want to answer that question even to himself.

He'd loved Annabel, but she'd obviously not loved him enough that she could back away at the first mention of CF, refusing even to consider a genetic test because she'd wanted children and wouldn't risk him as a father.

Which left him where?

Forget it, he told himself. He might not need to think about any of this or make any decisions. The next decision would surely be Sam's.

The medical centre had an appointment for her. Port being a holiday centre, they usually employed extra locums at these times. The pathology office was next door, so by midday she was done.

The genetic testing of the foetus would need a specialist, who had offices in the private hospital, where she could also have the sample taken under ultrasound.

While on a roll, she made an appointment to see an obstetrician in a couple of weeks, then, because she'd driven into town, took a detour home so she could get a feel for the place and check out the private hospital.

Aware she was getting far too far ahead of herself but unable to stop herself hoping, she began to think about options.

If she stayed with the obstetrician through her pregnancy, she'd probably have her baby here, although if she stuck with the public system she'd probably have a group of other mothers with her all the way and a midwife she could contact at any time.

And, if anything went wrong—like a premature birth—her baby would end up in the public system anyway, as they had the best neonatal facilities.

But she was impressed by the cottagey look of the private hospital—she'd check it out when she had her specialist appointment.

Following no particular route, she drove through suburb after suburb, most of them fairly new, as if the town's expansion into a city had been recent, but she loved the tree-lined streets—the trees still small but promising shade and privacy in the future.

Her phone rang as she climbed out of her car.

Andy!

'How did it go?'

'The blood test was fine, as easy and straightforward as you imagine. No instant results so we just have to wait. But I've made an appointment for an obstetrician to do the CVS, and I drove past the private hospital where he has his offices and through some new and not quite so new suburbs. It seemed from the amount of building that the town developed rapidly.'

'A new hospital, a university, even a big government science establishment, which could, from all the rumours, be developing robots small enough to be inserted into humans to control bad impulses. Or hamburgers made from insects—that's another school of thought. In truth, no one knows but they've a big establishment on the edge of town and every kind of animal imaginable in paddocks around it, leading to a fair few unlikely rumours about interbreeding between species, so who knows?'

'Don't you know anyone working there that you could ask?' Sam said, intrigued by the ideas.

'I do, and they just smile at me so my imagination has even more lurid fantasies.'

Sam laughed. 'More lurid than mind-controlling bots?' she teased.

'Far more lurid.' He laughed, and asked if they could meet up when he finished work.

'I guess so,' Sam said, but she did wonder if she needed a bit of distance between herself and Andy so she could get her head straightened out.

* * *

But meeting after work didn't eventuate, Andy being kept late by the admission of a two-year-old who had found small button batteries in a jar and swallowed them, thinking they were candy.

An X-ray showed eight still in the stomach but fortunately revealed none in the oesophagus or windpipe.

'We'll do a small procedure called an endoscopy,' he explained to the parents, aware he wouldn't want to leave the hospital until he knew the child was all right.

But this was how life would be for him and Sam, should they ever manage to get together.

He swore inwardly and continued his explanation to the parents.

'He'll be given light anaesthesia and the surgeon will pass a tube down his throat into his stomach to retrieve the batteries, and also check that there's no damage to the lining of his stomach. He'll be very sleepy after it, but it's not a major procedure for him.'

After settling the parents in the waiting room, with tea and biscuits and magazines in an attempt to take their minds from what was happening, he accompanied the surgeon to Theatre. He'd do the anaesthesia, and that way see what was going on inside his patient.

'I can see eight on the X-ray,' the surgeon said. 'Do we know how many he swallowed?'

'The mother didn't have a clue, but the father thought maybe there could have been ten in the bottle.'

'What on earth were they used for?' the assisting nurse asked, and Andy shook his head as he considered how easily such things happened.

'Apparently, one of the parents' elderly grandfathers lives with them, and he wears hearing aids, but he's always taking the batteries out and leaving them all over the place, so they're gathered up as soon as they're seen and put into the bottle, to be used when he loses another pair.'

'Well, I've got eight,' the surgeon said, and peering at the screen Andy could see eight of the tiny batteries now encased in a tiny bag.

'I'll bring them out, but some could have gone further into his digestive tract, so the parents should watch for more appearing in his stools.'

He paused before adding, 'I'd be happier if we'd known the exact number.'

'None appeared in the digestive tract in the X-ray,' Andy reminded him, although they both knew with the folds within the small intestine something so small would appear as little more than a tiny blip.

'We'll just have to hope for the best,' he added, wondering if hoping for the best was all you could do with your own children in many situations.

He was beginning to think like Sam, worrying about possible accidents and illnesses to possible children.

Because now there was a child?

The thought excited him to the extent he smiled, although he knew there was still a long way to go before he and Sam could explore their options further as far as the current possibility went.

He and Sam?

Would there ever be an Andy and Sam?

'All done,' the surgeon said. 'You should keep him up in the PICU for twenty-four hours, but I couldn't see any obvious damage to the lining of his stomach so he should be fine.'

Andy stayed with the boy in Recovery, wanting to assure himself he really *was* all right. And possibly as an excuse not to go home just yet.

He had to talk to Sam—to talk about things other than CF— but he was fairly sure that, at the moment, it was in the forefront of her mind, and the admissions of love he'd like to make to her would go unheard—or, worse, unheeded.

* * *

Sam was sitting on the couch in his living room with bits of paper strewn around her.

'I had to get the CF thing straight in my head and you know what? Even if we're both carriers there's only a one in four chance of our child having CF. Those are pretty good odds, don't you think?'

'Weren't you the one who was saying we wouldn't bother with it until we got the test results?' he teased, although his heart had leapt at Sam's use of the word 'our'.

So he moved closer, stepping cautiously through the mess of paper, to take her hands and haul her to her feet, where he wrapped his arms around her and held her until he felt her body relax against his—slumping in tiredness from her emotional research.

'Come to bed,' he said, and when she began to object, he kissed the words away.

'We don't know anything yet,' he reminded her as he slid kisses down her neck. 'So, just for now...' he added, as his kisses reached the top of her breast, his lips seeking a way in beneath the loose tank top she was wearing.

Now his tongue had reached her nipple, lapped at it, and he felt her quiver, her body pressing closer to his, her lips now against his neck, her fingers tugging at the buttons on his shirt. Now she hauled his head, lips found lips, while their hands took over stripping their clothes off, and as his tongue met hers, felt it slide against his, desire ramped up a notch, and together they fell to the couch, his feet still entangled in his trousers, but nothing mattered but the sensation—the slide of skin on skin, fingers and lips teasing each other, the pressure for release building and building.

His fingers felt her heat and moistness, and her cry of, 'Please, Andy,' broke any restraint he'd managed to hold onto and he slid into her, moving with her, holding her arching body close, until with another cry she went limp in his arms and his own release surged through him, a groan of utter abandonment escaping him.

They lay, bodies slick with sweat, held together by the force of the passion they'd shared, neither moving, neither speaking, their breathing somehow synchronised. Until, after what seemed like for ever, Andy slid his body beneath hers, kicking off his trousers in the process, and looked up into her face.

'Repeat after me: I will forget about everything genetic until I get the test results.'

Sam smiled down at him, hair beautifully tousled around her flushed face, eyes shining with the aftermath of sex.

'Consider it said,' she answered huskily. 'I'm far too pooped to think of anything tonight and should be back to my normal sensible self by morning.'

'Stay the night with me?' he asked, not wanting to let her go. Ever!

But that was a way off yet.

He saw her smile and a sleepy nod, which was more than enough encouragement to slide off the couch and lift her in his arms, carrying her through to the bedroom, where he dropped her on the bed.

Sam looked up at him. She was so tired—pleasantly tired, ready to sleep tired—and yet she wanted more—something more—and as she turned onto her side, already half-asleep, she was aware of Andy pulling a sheet over her naked body, and knew what she'd wanted from him.

Love.

CHAPTER TEN

SAM WOKE TO find Andy gone—sometime in the night, she rather thought, vaguely recalling a phone ringing and Andy's hushed voice.

She stretched luxuriously in the big bed, aware of the musky smell of sex on her body, and pleasantly surprised to find memories of Andy's touch still alive on her nerve endings.

But noises outside the bedroom suggested he was back, his voice calling to her, 'Up, lazybones, breakfast in fifteen minutes!'

She leapt out of bed, heading for the shower, sorry she hadn't kept some clothes—undies at least—in Andy's bedroom. But once showered and clean, she pulled on the previous day's tank top and skirt.

Breakfast was a plate of bacon and eggs with hot rolls and butter, served on the balcony. What could be a better follow-up to a night of passion? The honey pot was on the table, already attracting the interest of flying insects, and a couple of small jars of jam the insects seemed equally interested in.

She sat, at peace with the world for the moment, until the

smell of the bacon had her stomach roiling, and she fled to the bathroom.

'Dry toast?' Andy suggested sympathetically, as she came out.

She nodded.

'Well, go back out onto the balcony—I've removed the other breakfast but left the honey in case you needed something sweet.'

The brisk breeze from the ocean and, Sam suspected, a little air freshener had removed the smell of bacon and she was able to relax into a chair—but only for as long as it took to remember she had to make an appointment with a doctor to get her CF test results later today.

'We haven't talked about what happens if the test is positive,' Sam said, as the thought of finding out was already churning her delicate stomach.

'Because there's no point,' Andy said firmly. 'We could talk—discuss—for hours all the what-ifs, but why waste our breath on that? We'll wait and see then talk about what next, okay, love?'

There was the word again, the word that let hope creep into her heart.

He came and stood behind her, his hand resting on her shoulder, kneading gently, his fingers straying into her hair, lifting tendrils of it and letting them drop, running strands through his fingers...

He sighed and his fingers tugged gently at her hair so she lifted her face to look at him, look into eyes that didn't hide the confusion—despair?—he was feeling.

'I'd already decided—after Annabel—that it was best I didn't marry, didn't father children. Now here we are, and everything is different, Sam. And, anyway, I have to get back to work.'

He bent and kissed her on the lips—making her glad she'd put a bit of toothpaste on her finger and given herself a bit of a tooth clean so at least her breath was sweet.

But what use was that?

And why the kiss?

Hadn't he just told her he didn't want to marry?

But if he loved her...

There it was again—love.

Her mind was going round in circles, so she cleaned up the few dishes she'd used, stacked them in the dishwasher, and headed downstairs. What she needed was a swim to clear her head, keep busy so she didn't have to think about Andy, and the decision he'd made well before she'd happened along—his decision not to marry...

Andy couldn't remember a day at work when his mind hadn't been fully focussed on the job. Over the years he'd learned that even a slight distraction might mean he'd miss a minor change in a patient's status or, worse, forget a test he could have performed to get a better result.

So, to have his mind wandering to Sam, to the feel of her in his arms last night, the sweet musky smell of her, and most frequently of all to the test results she'd get today, was a new distraction.

He'd had enough distractions in the past to know how to retrieve his focus, but keeping it there?

Would she know by now?

His gut twisted at the thought, although he knew the percentages of her *not* being a carrier were far higher than a positive test.

Work—think about work!

But he'd held her in his arms as they'd slept, learned the way her body fitted best into his, and felt her heartbeat against his chest. And had known he loved her...

'Are you sure?' Sam demanded of the doctor, although such a question would have irritated her no end if she'd been working.

The doctor smiled and passed her the second sheet of paper.

'See, they've even sent us pictures!'

He pointed to two strings of figures printed on the page.

'This is the little bugger we want to look at.'

It was typed in red so it was totally obvious.

'See, no mutation in it whatsoever—check for yourself.'

She looked at the two sets of numbers and letters, which were both identical.

Her relief must have shown in her face for the doctor raised an eyebrow.

'Especially good news?' he said, and Sam smiled and nodded at him.

'Very, especially good,' she said, taking the papers from his hand and collecting her little backpack from the floor beside her chair.

'I'm glad,' the doctor told her. 'All the best to you.'

Sam departed, aware she should have been asking questions about the possibility of being one of the rare genetic carriers who didn't show up on tests, or discussing possible referrals to an obstetrician for the foetal test, but she'd sort all that out later. Right now she needed to send a text to Andy.

But that thought stopped her dead on the pavement outside the medical centre. She had absolutely no idea how Andy felt about her pregnancy.

She clutched her hand to her belly, protective of the new life there. There was still the foetal testing to be done but she felt reasonably certain that would be okay.

No! This baby was here to stay, with or without Andy.

With or without Andy?

The joyous bounce in her step slowed—stopped.

Just because *she* was desperate for a family it didn't mean Andy was.

And even if he did want one, did he want one with her?

There'd been no word of love between them—oh, he'd called her 'love'—but in the same way he might have called her 'sweetheart'.

But neither had she mentioned how she felt about him.

Too wary of rejection to lay her feelings bare?

Although early on she really hadn't been sure of love herself, hadn't been sure it wasn't just an overwhelming relief to have someone she knew and liked working with her.

Then slowly he'd crept into her thoughts—worse, into her blood, and bones, and sinews—until a casual touch could send her heart racing, a smile make her whole body sing.

Damn it all, life wasn't meant to be so complicated—she was sure of this. For the past three years she'd lived, if not at first but much more lately, quite happily single, never thinking about a long-term relationship, still living with a doubt that marriage to Nick had been *her* failure rather than his.

And *never* thinking about love...

'So, when should we get married?' Andy asked, walking into his flat where she'd been preparing a meal and handing her a large bunch of blue cornflowers. 'Must have had mainly girls arrive today to have had only blue ones at the hospital florist,' he added with a smile, then he kissed her cheek, and said, 'Well?'

Disturbed in ways she couldn't put in words, Sam thrust the flowers back at him.

'It's your flat—you'll know where you keep vases, if you have such things, and when did marriage come into the equation?'

'But of course, we'll get married. I want to be part of this child's life and isn't marriage the easiest way to achieve that? This is just the start—we can have a family!'

Sam closed the oven door on the chicken and lentil casserole she was making and turned to face him.

'There's more to marriage than having kids,' she said quietly.

'Of course, there is,' Andy said, the bunch of flowers still clutched in his hand. 'There's sharing lives, and hopes, and dreams, and ups and downs, I guess, and being there for each other through good times and bad, and just, well, having each other to lean on.'

Sam sighed. Should she prompt him? Tell him how she felt? But if he didn't love her back, they'd both be embarrassed…

Embarrassed? She'd be downright devastated!

Damn it all, surely, she was old enough now to talk honestly about emotions and not get herself twisted up in knots like a fifteen-year-old.

Well, here goes nothing!

She took a deep breath, looked directly at him, aware there'd be challenge in her eyes.

'And love, Andy? Where does love come into it?'

He stared at her for a moment, then crossed the kitchen, rooting around in a cupboard and finally coming up with a large jar that had presumably held preserved fruit at some time.

He rinsed it then filled it with water, plonking the stems of the flowers into it.

Sam curbed the urge to say he should have trimmed the stalks and cut the string around them, she was far too tense.

Hands free now, he came towards her, put his hands on her shoulders and studied her face, his own concerned—a little wary.

'Sam,' he eventually said, 'I have loved you from the moment I first saw you in that bar. You married Nick, and I was happy for you both, but it didn't stop how I felt, so I kept away. And now you're here, lovelier than ever, carrying my child, and I've still been too…cowardly, I suppose, to tell you how I feel.'

He drew her closer, still speaking.

'You asked the question, Sam—the love question—the one I haven't dared ask you in case you weren't ready to love again, might never want to love again. But *my* love, if you'll accept it, is big enough for both of us.'

Now she was held against his chest, his arms tight around her, her face buried in the curve of his neck.

'You never said,' she muttered against his shirt.

'Cowardly, I know, but to have spoken of it, and been re-jected, would have been almost more than I could bear.'

She moved so she could hold him, tightened her arms, and still talking into his shirt muttered, 'Rejected? Never! Of course I love you! How could I not?'

She leaned back so she could see his face, the smile quirk-ing up one side of his lips.

'You are the kindest, most unselfish man I've ever met. You'd do anything you could to help others—everyone can see that from your doctoring. But you're warm, and protective, and, well, you're Andy, and I love you with all my heart!'

It was some time later that Sam found the words she needed, to ask one final, vital question.

One that she hardly dared to ask…

'Would you have walked away from a relationship if I'd been a carrier?'

He looked at her and shook his head.

'I doubt very much that I could have, Sam, not loving you as much as I do. But we'd have had to have had a serious conver-sation about children and, knowing you want them so much, that might have made things different.'

There was a pause that made her heart stand still.

'*You* might have walked away!' he added.

She moved back into his arms, holding him tightly.

'I couldn't walk away from you, Andy. I love you more than life itself, so you're stuck with me.'

She eased back so she could lay a palm against his cheek.

'And given that I could still be one of the five percent who don't show up as carriers, we'll have this baby, and any other baby, tested, okay?'

And, again, he drew her close.

'I like the sound of other babies,' he murmured, then kissed her on the lips, a kiss that said so much that could never be put into words. A kiss that was a promise and a pledge and a deep declaration of love…love that would last for ever.

EPILOGUE

THEY WERE MARRIED three weeks later, high on the cliff, beneath the lighthouse. With the sparkling sea as a backdrop, innumerable members of Andy's family—who'd been waiting a long time to see this spectacle—and Sam's mother, flown out from the clinic on the Cambodian border, as guests, the two of them repeated their vows, eyes on each other, everyone else melting away.

'I love you,' Andy said as he bent to kiss her lips.

'And I you,' she said on a breath before those lips met hers.

But as they walked into the lighthouse restaurant, she was met by a crowd of men and women, friends from her past, some she'd kept in sporadic touch with and others she'd thought lost for ever.

Andy had found every one of them and had organised for them to come and share their special day.

And suddenly she was home again, among the friends she'd fled three years ago, and home had become a safe haven, a real home, with Andy by her side for ever.

* * * * *

The Right Reason To Marry

Christine Rimmer

Christine Rimmer came to her profession the long way around. She tried everything from acting to teaching to telephone sales. Now she's finally found work that suits her perfectly. She insists she never had a problem keeping a job—she was merely gaining "life experience" for her future as a novelist. Christine lives with her family in Oregon. Visit her at christinerimmer.com.

Books by Christine Rimmer

Harlequin Special Edition

The Bravos of Valentine Bay

The Nanny's Double Trouble
Almost a Bravo
Same Time, Next Christmas
Switched at Birth

The Bravos of Justice Creek

Not Quite Married
The Good Girl's Second Chance
Carter Bravo's Christmas Bride
James Bravo's Shotgun Bride
Ms. Bravo and the Boss
A Bravo for Christmas
The Lawman's Convenient Bride
Garrett Bravo's Runaway Bride
Married Till Christmas

Montana Mavericks: Six Brides for Six Brothers

Her Favorite Maverick

Montana Mavericks: The Lonelyhearts Ranch

A Maverick to (Re)Marry

Visit the Author Profile page
at millsandboon.com.au for more titles.

Dear Reader,

Widowed single mom Karin Killigan got married ten years ago because she was pregnant. The marriage ended in tragedy. She's never doing that again.

But then last Christmas, she threw caution to the winds and began a secret affair with an old high school flame, Liam Bravo. Being with Liam was the perfect occasional escape from her busy life as a hardworking single mother of two—or it was until the impossible happened and she ended up accidentally pregnant. Again.

Liam Bravo has always kind of skated on the surface of life. He owns a successful trucking company, has a big house in Astoria, Oregon, and for those important emotional connections, he has a large, loving family of Bravos in beautiful Valentine Bay.

What more could a guy want?

Well, the truth is, he's always carried a bit of a torch for Karin. And when he finds out she's having his baby, he's all in from day one. How many ways can a man show a woman that's he's the one she should marry? Liam Bravo is determined to discover them all. No matter how she tries to resist him, he won't give up trying to get it right, to claim Karin's heart and a place at her side.

I hope you get as much satisfaction as I did watching Liam come into his own as he learns how to love and be a part of something bigger than himself. We all need to remember not to give up until we get it right—especially when it comes to love.

Have a beautiful holiday season, everyone. May your Hanukkah be rich in tradition, your Christmas glorious and your New Year the happiest yet!

Christine

For MSR, always.

CHAPTER ONE

IT WAS A cloudy Friday afternoon in mid-October when Karin Killigan finally had to face the unsuspecting father of her unborn child.

It happened at Safeway, of all places. He was going in as she went out.

She had her hands full of plastic shopping bags. Her mind was on dinner and the thousand and one things she needed to whip into shape at the office before the baby came. She was staring straight ahead and didn't even see him.

But Liam Bravo saw *her*.

He grabbed her arm. "Karin. My God."

His touch, coupled with the low, rich sound of his voice, set off a chain reaction of emotional explosions inside her. Shock. Guilt. Total embarrassment. A flare of thoroughly inappropriate desire. She let out a ridiculous squeak of surprise and almost dropped a bag full of dairy products as she blinked down at his hand on her arm. Even through the barrier of her coat and the sweater beneath it, she could feel his heat and his strength.

Slowly, she forced her gaze upward to his gorgeous face. The cool autumn wind stirred his dark blond hair and his sun-kissed brows had drawn together over those summer-sky eyes of his.

Somehow, she made herself speak. "Hello, Liam."

"Excuse me." The impatient voice from directly behind her reminded her sharply that they were blocking both doors.

"Come on." Liam tugged her away from the doors and along a short concrete walkway.

She followed numbly, despising herself for never quite working up the nerve to break the big news to him, thus forcing them both to face it now—at Safeway, of all the impossible places.

"Here." He pulled her in close to the brick wall of the building, between a bin full of pumpkins and stacks of bundled kindling. "Let me help you with those." He made a grab for the shopping bags dangling from both of her hands.

"No." She shook her head at him. "I've got them. I'm fine." Total lie. She was very far from fine.

"You sure?"

"Positive," she said way too brightly. "Thanks. I'm, um, really surprised to see you here." Understatement of the decade. He lived in nearby Astoria and somehow, since the last time she'd seen him the previous March, she'd never once run into him in Valentine Bay. Until now. It wasn't that she'd been avoiding him, exactly. But she certainly hadn't sought him out. "I mean, there's a Safeway in Astoria, right?"

"I stopped in to see Percy and Daffy and this store was on my way home." Percy and Daffodil Valentine were brother and sister. Neither had ever married. In their eighties now, Liam's great-uncle and -aunt lived in an ancient Victorian mansion on the edge of Valentine City Park.

"Oh, I see," she said, because he'd fallen silent and it seemed that she ought to say something.

His gaze had wandered downward to her giant belly, only to quickly jerk back up to her face again. "This is awkward." *Oh, no kidding.* "Please don't be offended..."

"No. Of course not." How could she be? She should have told

him months ago, on the night she broke it off with him. But she was a big, fat coward. She hadn't told him then, nor had she managed to work up the courage to call him and ask for a meeting. And now the poor guy had to find out like this. Her cheeks and neck were too hot. They must be flaming red. And her heart? It pounded so hard she couldn't hear herself think.

"You're pregnant," he said.

"How did you guess?" It was a weak joke and neither of them laughed.

Beneath his golden tan, his face seemed to be growing progressively paler. "I'm sorry, but I couldn't help thinking that..." He faltered, which broke her heart a little. Liam Bravo never faltered. He was always so smooth. Even way back in high school, he could make a girl's clothes fall off with just his smile. He wasn't smiling now, though. He drew in a shaky breath. "I have to know. Is it...?"

There really was no putting this off any longer, so she answered the question he couldn't seem to ask. "Yes, Liam. It's your baby."

He flinched and his eyes widened. He started to reach for her again, caught himself and let his arm drop to his side. After that, he just stood there staring at her, his sexy mouth hanging open.

God. What a horrible way to tell him. But at least she'd finally done it.

People bustled by them, going in and out of the store. "We can't do this here," she said. When he only continued to gape at her, she went on, "Tell you what. I'm going straight home..."

A low sound escaped him, kind of a cross between a grunt and sigh, but no actual words came out.

"Home," she repeated. "The house on Sweetheart Cove? I'll be there the rest of the day. Feel free to drop by when you're ready to talk." Carefully, so as not to bump him with her bags of groceries, she turned and made for her car.

He didn't say anything or try to stop her. But she knew that wouldn't last. He was bound to have questions—a million of them. Starting with *why the hell didn't you tell me*? She figured she had an hour, tops, before he appeared at her door.

Probably breaking the land speed record for a hugely pregnant woman on foot, she waddled toward the relative safety of her Chevy Traverse.

Karin lived with her dad, Otto Larson, and her two children, Ben and Coco, on the first floor of a large beach house owned by her brother, Sten. As she pulled the Traverse into the garage beneath the house, her dad came down the inside stairs, seven-year-old Coco close on his heels.

Otto went straight to the hatch in back to get the groceries.

Coco, in blue tights, red shorts, a blue T-shirt and shiny red rain boots, had stopped at the foot of the stairs to spin in a circle. The kid-size red blanket tied around her neck for a cape fluttered as she twirled. "Mommy, I'm Supergirl!" she shouted as Karin carefully lowered herself from behind the wheel. "Don't worry, I will save you! I have *vast* superhuman strength, speed and *stanima*, X-ray vision, super breath and also, I can fly." Arms out, she "flew" at Karin, who laughed in spite of what had just gone down at Safeway.

Coco halted at Karin's big belly. Reaching out her small arms and tipping her head back, she gave both Karin and the unborn baby inside her a hug. "I love you, Mommy, and I love our baby, too!" Coco beamed a smile so big it showed the gap where she'd recently lost two lower baby teeth.

Karin bent to plant a kiss on the top of her curly head. "And I love you. Lots."

Otto shut the hatch. He had all the grocery bags, two in each hand.

"I'll help, Grandpa!" Supergirl proclaimed. She planted her rain boots wide, stuck out her little chest and propped her fists on her hips. Otto set two of the bags on the garage floor, fished out a block of Swiss cheese from one and passed it to her. The cheese in one hand, both arms spread wide, cape rippling, Coco ran back up the stairs and into the house, slamming the door behind her.

"You gotta love that enthusiasm," said Otto as he bent to pick up the bags again. Karin just stood there staring down at his bent head. His hair was all white now and thinning, his pink scalp showing through at the crown. He met her eyes as he stood again. "What happened?" he asked quietly.

She replied in a small voice. "I saw Liam at Safeway."

"You tell him?" Her dad and her brother, Sten, and Sten's wife, Madison, knew that Liam was the baby's father. Sten and Otto had been after Karin for months to tell the man that he was going to be a dad. Madison mostly stayed out of it, though Liam was actually one of her long-lost brothers.

Karin stared into the middle distance, thinking of Madison for no particular reason. Sten's new bride had been switched at birth, of all impossible things. She'd met Sten when she came to Valentine Bay last March to find the family she'd just learned she had.

"Karin. You tell Liam?" her dad asked for the second time.

She blinked and made herself answer the question. "Uh. I did. Yes. I told him."

"And?"

"And I said I was going straight home, that if he wanted to talk about it, I'll be here."

"You're thinking he'll be coming by, then?"

She nodded. "And soon, would be my guess. If you could maybe keep the kids downstairs…?" The house was really two complete houses in one. Karin, her dad and the kids lived on the first floor just above the garage. Sten and Madison had the upper floor when they were in town, which they weren't right now. Madison was a bona fide movie star. Currently, she and Sten spent most of their time in LA or on location wherever she was filming.

"No problem," said Otto. "I'll keep an eye on the kids and send Liam up when he gets here."

* * *

On the top floor of the house, in Sten's quiet kitchen, Karin brewed a cup of raspberry leaf tea. As she waited for it to steep, she stood at the slider that opened onto the wide upper deck and watched the layers of clouds over the water. The waves slid into shore and retreated, leaving the wet sand smooth as glass in their wake.

"Karin." Liam spoke from directly behind her.

She stiffened in surprise and turned to face him. His hair was kind of standing on end and his eyes had a haunted look. "Hey. I, um, didn't hear you come in."

He stared at her for several seconds with a numbly disbelieving expression on his face before he finally said, "Your dad. He told me to just go up."

"That's fine. Great. Let's sit down, why don't we?" She gestured toward the sitting area.

"No, thanks." He blinked at her. "I'd rather stand."

"Maybe some tea or something?"

"No. Nothing." He turned on his heel and strode away from her. When he reached the hallway that led to the bedrooms, he turned again and came back, halting in the same place he'd been before he stalked off. "You're pregnant."

Hadn't they already covered that? "Yes, I am."

"I can't... I don't..." It was just like at Safeway. The poor man seemed incapable of completing a sentence. "I mean, uh, you said it was..."

"Yours, Liam," she gently confirmed again. "Yes. The baby is yours."

"And you're due...?"

"In a week."

"A week." The wild state of his hair made more sense as he put both hands to his head, got two fistfuls of hair and pulled. "Mine. Wow. Mine." And off he went again, his long legs carrying him swiftly past the table, on through the sitting area to the hallway that led to the bedrooms. Next to the hallway, stairs led down to the lower floor. For a moment, he just stood there, his head going back and forth, as though he couldn't decide whether to run down the stairs or set off along the hallway.

Karin didn't know what to do, either, so she just waited by the slider. Eventually, he turned and came toward her again.

"A week," he repeated when he stopped a foot away from her. "I'll be a dad in a week is what you just said."

Excuses weren't going to cut it. She offered them anyway. "I'm so sorry, Liam. I was going to tell you earlier, but I didn't really even know where to start. And there's not much you could do at this point, anyway. So I thought I would just wait until after the birth."

"You thought you would just wait…"

"Yes. Liam, I promise you, there's no pressure. You can think it over, decide how much involvement you want to have." Okay, yeah. No matter what he decided, eventually, she would be after him to spend a little time with his child. And he would have to cough up some child support, too. But it felt beyond rude to hit the poor guy with all that today when he seemed so completely torn up to learn there was a baby on the way.

"No pressure," he echoed blankly.

"That's right. There's no big rush to make decisions. Truly, you can just take your time, figure out what works for you."

He raked his hair back with both hands. "But…married, maybe? We should get—"

"What? Wait." Now she was the one frantically blinking. "Married? Us?"

"Well, uh, yeah."

She needed to nip that terrible idea right in the bud. "No, Liam. Don't be silly. Of course not." No way was she getting married just because there was a baby coming. Been there, done that. Bought the T-shirt, saw the movie. Lived through the heartbreak. Never. Again.

And dear God in heaven, could she have made a bigger mess of this?

"Listen," she said. "After the birth we'll do DNA. You'll have plenty of time to deal with this. You really will—and you know, you look awful. Liam, come on. You need to sit down." She reached for his arm.

He jerked away before she could make contact. "I'll stand." They just stared at each other.

She cast desperately about for something meaningful to say. "Liam, I really am so sorry to—"

"Stop." He actually showed her the hand.

And then he spun on his heel again and paced off toward the stairs, shaking his head as he went, turning right back around and coming toward her once more, halting stock-still a few feet from where she waited. He looked wrecked, ruined, but he held his broad shoulders straight and proud. "Last March, when you broke it off with me, did you know you were pregnant then?"

She wanted to lie to him, make herself look a fraction less like a complete jerk for the way she'd handled the situation. But she didn't lie. "Yeah. I knew then."

His forehead crinkled in a frown. "You broke it off, but you didn't bother to tell me you were having my kid?"

"I felt awful. I couldn't make myself admit to you that we were having a baby. I mean, why me? How many women have you been with?"

He fell back a step. "What's that got to do with anything?"

"Liam. I know you. I grew up with you. We were in the same grade at school. We even went on two dates in high school, remember?"

"Of course, I remember."

"My, um, point is, you're hot and easy to be with. The women have always loved you and you have loved them right back. How many of those women did you get pregnant?"

"Karin." He was pulling his hair again. So strange to see him like this, at a loss. Undone. "Come on, now. Where is this going?"

"The answer is none of them, right—not until me?"

Now he looked worried. "Why do I feel like anything I say right now is going to be wrong?"

"Oh, please. No. You are not wrong. This is not your fault— it's not my fault, either, though. Or at least, that's what I keep telling myself. But I also can't help asking myself, why does the condom fail only for *me*? Why couldn't *I* have sense enough to get back on the pill—or better yet, get a contraceptive implant? But every time you and I got together, I really thought it would be the last time. What was the point, I asked myself? I wouldn't be having sex with anyone again anytime soon. But then I would get a free evening and I would remember how you said to give you a call anytime—I mean, think about it. Four times, we got together."

That first time had been last December, at Christmastime. Then there'd been once in January, once in February and that last time in March. The first time, she'd promised herself it would be the only time. The second time, too. And that was the one where the condom must have failed.

After that, it hadn't mattered anyway, whether she got herself an implant or not.

"Four times together," she muttered, "and *this* happens." She looked down and shook her head at her protruding belly. "What is the matter with me, to do that to you?"

"Uh, Karin, I—"

"No, really. You don't have to answer that. It's not a question that even needs an answer. And I swear I was going to tell you about the baby that last time, in March. I saw that last night as my chance to let you know what was happening…" She ran out of breath. But he only kept on staring.

So she sucked in another breath and babbled on. "When I called you that night in March, I swear it was my plan to tell you. But then, well, you kissed me and I kissed you back and I thought how much I wanted you and how long it was likely to be before I ever had sex with a man again. I thought, *one more time*, you know? I thought, *what can it hurt*?"

Still, he said nothing.

She couldn't bear the awful silence, so she kept right on talking. "I promised myself I would tell you afterward, but then afterward came, and the words? They *wouldn't* come and then I started thinking that you didn't need to know for months. Liam, I messed up, okay? I messed up and then I didn't reach out and the longer I didn't, the harder it got. And now, well..." She lifted her arms out the sides. "Here we are."

He just continued to look at her through disbelieving eyes. For a really long time. She longed to open her mouth again and fill the silence with the desperate sound of her own voice. But she'd already jabbered out that endless and completely unhelpful explanation of essentially nothing. Really, what more was there to add to all the ways she'd screwed up?

He broke the silence. "I have to leave now."

She felt equal parts relieved—and desolate. "Okay."

"But I will be back."

"Of course."

"We'll talk more."

What was she supposed to say to that? "Sure. Whenever you're ready."

"Okay. Soon." And then he was striding away from her for the fourth time.

She watched as he vanished into the stairwell and didn't move so much as a muscle until she heard his car start up outside and drive away. After that, for several grim seconds, she thought she might cry, just bawl her eyes out because she felt so terrible about everything and she'd done such a crap job of telling poor Liam he had a baby on the way.

The tears never came, though. Eventually, she turned around and stared blindly out at the ocean for a while.

By the time she remembered her raspberry leaf tea, it was cold.

CHAPTER TWO

LIAM GOT HALFWAY to the gorgeous house he'd built for himself in nearby Astoria before he realized that he needed to talk to his oldest brother Daniel.

Years ago, when their parents died, Daniel, eighteen at the time, essentially took over as the head of the Bravo family. He became a second father to all of them. Daniel was only four years older than Liam. Didn't matter. When Liam needed fatherly advice, he usually sought out his oldest brother.

He called Daniel's cell from the car.

"Where are you?" Liam demanded when Daniel picked up.

"Hi to you, too. I'm at the office." Daniel ran the family business, Valentine Logging. "What do you need?"

"Long story. I'll be there in ten."

"Good enough."

Valentine Logging had its headquarters on the Warrenton docks between Valentine Bay and Astoria. Liam parked in front of the hangar-like building that housed the offices.

Daniel was waiting. He ushered Liam into his private office, shut the door and gestured toward the sitting area on one side of the room. "You look like hell. What's going on?"

"I need to talk." Liam sank to the leather sofa. "You know Karin Killigan?"

"Of course." Daniel dropped into the club chair.

"Karin and me, we had a thing last winter."

Daniel frowned. "Wait a minute—Karin's pregnant, right?"

"Yeah. How did you know?" Did everyone know but him?

"Keely told me." Keely was Daniel's wife.

"How did Keely know?"

"She hung out a little with Karin at Madison and Sten's wedding. According to Keely, Karin was noticeably pregnant then—but you missed the wedding, right?"

"Right." He'd felt bad to miss it, but he'd had a work conflict in Portland, one he couldn't put off or get out of.

Liam owned Bravo Trucking, which he'd built up from a few rigs that hauled strictly for Valentine Logging into a fleet with over two hundred trucks and two hundred fifty employees. His original terminal was nearby, right there in Warrenton. Last year, he'd opened one in Portland, too.

Daniel was leaning forward again. "Are you saying the baby is yours?"

"Yeah." The word scraped his throat as he said it. "Karin says she's been trying for months to work up the nerve to tell me. I probably still wouldn't know if I hadn't seen her coming out of Safeway a couple of hours ago." And he had that feeling again, like if he sat still, he might just lose his mind. So he jumped up, paced to the door and then paced back again.

Daniel said, "You never mentioned you were dating Karin."

"Dating?" He stopped by Daniel's chair. "I wouldn't call it dating. It was only a few times, whenever she could get away. She wanted it kept just between the two of us. I agreed it would be the way she wanted it and I never told anyone else that we were hooking up."

"Liam," Daniel said quietly. "Sit back down. Come on, man. It's all going to work out."

He dropped to the couch again. "I guess I'm kind of in shock."

Daniel got up. "Scotch or water?"

Liam braced his elbows on his spread knees and put his head in his hands. "Neither. Both." Dropping his hands from his face, he flopped back against the cushions and stared up at the ceiling.

Daniel asked, "Didn't you and Karin date in high school?"

"Briefly." Liam shut his eyes. "I always thought Karin was cute, you know? Senior year, she asked me to a Sadie Hawkins dance. We had a great time. I took her out to a show a couple of weeks later. But when she started hinting that she wanted to be exclusive with me, I told her what I told all the girls, that I didn't do virgins and I wasn't getting serious with anyone. Ever."

"Classy," remarked Daniel wryly. "And I'm guessing that was it for you and Karin in high school."

Liam let out a grunt in the affirmative. "When we met up last December, it was so great to reconnect with her. She's smart. She takes zero crap, you know? A guy can't get ahead of her. Better-looking than ever, too, with those gorgeous eyes that look blue at first glance but are actually swirled with green and gray. Plus, she has all that wild, dark hair. And her attitude is seriously snarky. She's fun." He couldn't help recalling the shock and guilt on her face when he'd stopped her at Safeway. "Not so snarky today, though. She really felt bad, that she'd waited so long to tell me…"

"Here you go."

Liam opened his eyes. Daniel stood over him, a bottle of water in one hand, a glass with two fingers of amber liquid in the other. "Thanks." Liam set down the glass on the side table and took a long drink from the water bottle. "I should go." He drank the rest of the water and set the empty bottle by the untouched glass of Scotch.

"Hold on," said Daniel. "I thought you said you needed to talk."

"I did talk." He rose and clapped his brother on the shoulder. "Thanks for listening."

Liam's new house in Astoria was four thousand square feet and overlooked the Columbia River. He'd had a decorator in to furnish it in a sleek, modern style, lots of geometric patterns and oxidized oak, pops of deep color here and there.

As a rule, coming home made him feel pretty good about everything. He had a thriving business, a fat bank account and a gorgeous house. By just about any standards, he'd made a success of his life so far.

Today, though, a big house and money in the bank didn't feel all that satisfying. He was going to be a dad. Just like that. Out of the blue—at least, that was how it felt to him.

Karin had kept saying that he didn't have to do anything right now.

Wrong.

He needed to do *something*. He just didn't really know what.

Maybe he should call Deke Pasternak. Deke was in family law. A little legal advice couldn't hurt about now, could it?

The lawyer answered on the second ring. "Hey. Liam. Good to hear from you. How've you been?"

"I just found out I'm going to be a father. Baby's due in a week."

Usually a fast talker, Deke took several seconds to reply. "Well. Congratulations?" He said it with a definite question mark at the end.

Two could play that game. "Thanks?"

"So… You want to meet for a drink or something?"

"How about a phone consultation?"

Five slow beats of complete silence, after which Deke asked, "You okay, man?"

"I'm working on it. Just bill me for this call and tell me what you think."

Deke did some throat-clearing. "What I think?"

"Yeah."

"About your being a dad?"

"That's right."

"Are you asking as a friend or do you want my legal opinion?"

"You're billing me, aren't you?"

"Uh, sure. So this isn't anyone you were dating seriously, then?"

Liam thought of Karin again, standing there by the sliding glass door in her brother's empty kitchen, looking miserable. "Why does that matter?"

"Let me put it this way, how did you find out that the baby's yours?"

"She told me."

"Ah. Right there. That could be a problem."

"Well, she should have told me sooner, yeah. She admitted that."

"No, Liam. What I mean is, what she told you proves nothing."

"She's seriously pregnant, man. I saw her with my own eyes."

"Not what I'm getting at. I'm trying to say that before you take *her* word for it, you need to let me arrange for DNA testing. It's best to clear up any doubts right out of the gate. I hate to say it, but it's a possibility that this baby isn't even yours."

Liam had always been an easygoing sort of guy. He never got worked up about anything. But hearing Deke Pasternak imply that Karin Killigan had lied to him about her baby being his? That just pissed him the hell off. "You're way off base there, Deke. She already mentioned a DNA test, as a matter fact. She's a straight-ahead woman and she's not trying to trap me."

"I'm just trying to help you."

"No. Uh-uh. You don't know this woman."

"Well, I—"

"She would never try to trap a man—she's so independent, she called off our relationship before I could figure out a way to convince her that we should even have a relationship. She wasn't even going to *tell* me about the baby until after the birth. I think she would have put off sharing the big news with me forever if that had been an option for her. But she's a good woman and that wouldn't be right. So, no. If she says the baby's mine, it's mine, damn it."

"Liam. Come on. Don't get me wrong. I'm not disrespecting the, her, mother of your child."

"Yeah? Coulda fooled me."

"I only meant that it's important to prove paternity once and for all. You need to get irrefutable proof and proceed from there. You do that, you know where you stand. And when you know where you stand, you can decide what to do next."

Why was he even talking to Deke? The guy had always irritated him. "You just don't get it, do you, Deke? I'm going to be a *father*. Like in a week! I have no clue how to be someone's dad." True, in the past year or so, he *had* been thinking that it was time for him to start considering having a family of his own.

But not in a week, for crying out loud!

"I'm sorry, Liam. But I don't really think it's legal advice you're looking for here."

Liam had to agree with that. "You're right. Gotta go. Have a good one, Deke."

"You, too. Ping me anytime you—" Deke was still talking as Liam hung up.

He dropped his phone on the sofa table, took off his boots and stretched out on the couch. That lasted maybe thirty seconds, at which point he realized that no way could he keep still.

Sitting up again, he put his Timberlands back on.

He needed to…know stuff. A lot was expected of a guy as a dad. Witness Daniel, for example. Married at nineteen with three brothers and four sisters to raise. And now he had twins from his first wife, Lillie, who'd died shortly after the twins' birth. Twins, and a daughter with his second wife, Keely.

The responsibilities never ended for a guy like Daniel. He worked all day and then went home to a wife, a couple of three-year-olds, a nine-month-old baby girl and their youngest sister Grace, who hadn't moved out on her own yet. Daniel made it all look pretty effortless, mostly—or at least, he had since he and Keely got together. He was a happy man now.

Liam could learn a lot from Daniel. He really shouldn't have just jumped up and run out of his brother's office like that. He had a million questions and Daniel would be the one to answer them.

However, to get advice from Daniel, he would be required to sit still and listen. That wasn't happening. Not now, not today.

Grabbing his phone and the jacket he'd shucked off when he entered the house, he headed out again—back to Valentine Bay and Valentine Bay Books down in the historic district, where the fortyish blonde clerk greeted him with a big smile. "How can I help you?"

"I'm having a baby. It's my first and I need to know everything."

"Well, of course you do." She led the way to the baby and childcare section and recommended a few books on first-time fatherhood.

He grabbed those. "I'm just going to look around for a while."

She left him to it. An hour later, he'd chosen more than twenty new-dad and baby books. After all, he had a lot to learn. And that could take a lot of books.

Back at home, he stuck a frozen pizza in the oven and sat down to begin his education in fatherhood.

At two on Saturday morning, he was still reading. Not long after that, he must have dropped off to sleep. He woke to daylight at his breakfast nook table with his head resting on *The Expectant Father: The Ultimate Guide for Dads-to-Be*.

He made coffee, had a shower and called both of his offices, where for once everything seemed to be rolling along right on schedule.

At a little after nine, he was knocking on the door of the house on Sweetheart Cove, a bag of baby books in one hand—just the ones he thought had the most to offer, in case he needed to refer to the experts while discussing his upcoming fatherhood with Karin.

Karin's daughter answered the door. She was a cute little thing with big blue eyes and curly hair in pigtails.

"You came yesterday, didn't you?" the child demanded at the sight of him.

"That's right, I did."

"Grandpa told us to stay in the great room when you came, but I peeked." Her little mouth drew down at the corners in a puzzled frown. "Who *are* you?"

Otto Larson appeared from the living area. He wore a patient smile. "Coco, this is Liam Bravo. Invite him in."

"Come *in*, Liam Bravo." She swept out an arm in the general direction of the arch that led to the downstairs living area.

"Thank you, Coco." He stepped into the foyer.

"You're welcome."

Liam shut the door as Coco darted to her grandfather and tugged on his hand. Otto bent close and she whispered in his ear.

He gave Liam a wink. "Yep. Liam is one of *those* Bravos. Your Aunt Madison is his sister."

"I knew it!" crowed Coco. She aimed a giant smile at Liam, one that showed a gap where she'd lost a couple of lower teeth. "Aunt Madison is my *friend* and we have to be careful and not talk about her to most people because she is a movie star and she needs her *privacy*. But since you're her brother, I can say what I want about Madison to you."

Liam made a noise in the affirmative.

Coco Killigan chattered on. "I'm seven and I go to second grade. I have two best friends in my class and for Halloween, I will be Jewel from *101 Dalmatians*." Coco pointed at the bag of books dangling from his left hand. "You brought books. I like books."

"Coco," said Otto fondly. "I think Liam's here to talk to your mom."

Coco giggled. "Okay!" and skipped away through the arch into the other room.

"Come on," said Otto. "I'll get Karin." He turned and led the way into the first-floor living area, where a boy a couple of years older than Coco sat at the table with a laptop, a paper notepad and a stack of schoolbooks. Otto introduced the boy as Ben, Karin's son.

"Nice to meet you," said Ben, sounding much older than his nine or ten years. He had straight brown hair and serious brown eyes.

As Liam tried to think of what to say to him, Karin spoke from behind him.

"Liam."

He turned to her. She wore jeans and a long, ribbed sweater that clung to the front of her, accentuating her enormous belly. Her wild hair was pinned up in a sloppy little bun. She wore no makeup and the shadows under her eyes made her look tired—tired and soft and huggable, somehow. He wanted to wrap his arms around her and bury his nose in the curve of her neck, find out if she still smelled as good as he remembered.

"I wasn't expecting you." She didn't seem all that happy to see him.

Too bad. He was going to be around. A lot. She would need to get used to that. "I said I'd be back."

She glanced past him, at Otto. "Dad, I'll just take Liam on upstairs?"

"Fine with me," the older man replied.

She focused on Liam again and pasted on a tight smile. "This way…"

Liam followed her back into the foyer and up to the empty top floor, where she offered him a seat in the living area.

He took the sofa and set the bag of books at his feet.

"So, how are you doing?" Karin lowered herself into one of the chairs.

He had so many things to say and no idea where to start. "Uh. Good. Fine. Really. I talked to my lawyer."

"Well, that's good." She gave an uncomfortable little laugh. "I think…"

Now she looked worried—and he didn't blame her.

Seriously? Deke? He had to go and mention Deke? Nothing good was going to come of telling her what Deke had said. "He, um, wasn't helpful, but the point is I'm realizing that everything is workable. You need to know that I will provide child support—and I've read a little about parenting plans. We'll get one of those."

"That's great." She sat with her knees pressed tightly together, like someone waiting for an appointment she wasn't looking forward to.

He leaned in. "I also want you to know I'm here for you, Karin. Whatever you need, I'll make sure that you get it."

She nodded at him, an indulgent sort of nod, like he was her seven-year-old daughter, or something. He felt a flare of annoyance, that she so easily categorized him as someone she didn't have to take too seriously.

The annoyance quickly faded as he realized he missed her—missed the *real* Karin, the woman who kissed him like she couldn't get enough of the taste of him, the one who was always ready with some wiseass remark.

He wanted the real Karin back.

He also wanted her to learn to count on him, to trust him, though he'd never been the sort of guy who was willing to work to gain a woman's trust.

But he'd never been almost a father before, either.

Somehow, impending fatherhood changed everything. She was the mother of his child and he wanted her, wanted to be with her, to take care of her.

One way or another, he would get what he wanted.

* * *

Karin wasn't sure she liked the way Liam was looking at her. It was a thoughtful kind of look, a measuring look. It was also intimate, somehow.

He was a beautiful man, all golden and deep-chested, with hard arms and proud shoulders. It would be so good, to have those arms around her, to rest against that strong chest. Looking at him now, in the gray light of this chilly fall morning, she couldn't help wishing…

No.

Never mind.

Bad idea.

She and Liam weren't a couple and they never would be.

"So," she said to break the lengthening silence between them, "What's with the bag of books?"

"Research." He granted her a proud smile. "You know, first-time fatherhood, pregnancy, labor and delivery. All that. I've got a lot to catch up on and I've been doing my homework. I stayed up late trying to get a handle on all the stuff I need to know."

He was too sweet. He really was.

She'd been awake half the night, too, feeling bad about everything. And now she sat across from him waiting for him to get thoroughly pissed off at her—that she'd gotten pregnant in the first place when he used a condom every time. That she didn't bust to the baby when she broke it off with him and then, for all those months and months, that she'd never once reached out to let him know he was going to be a dad. He probably wondered if she ever *would* have told him.

And frankly, if he hadn't spotted her at the supermarket yesterday, she had no idea when she would have pulled up her big-girl panties and gotten in touch with the guy.

They stared at each other across the endless expanse of Sten's coffee table. Liam looked like he had a million things to tell her—tender things. Kind things. Helpful things.

The man truly wasn't angry. Not yet, anyway. He was sweet

and sincere and he just seemed to want to be there for her and for the baby, to do the right thing.

His kindness reminded her sharply of how much she'd liked him when they met up again last year. In addition to his general charm and hotness, Liam Bravo, high school heartbreaker, had grown up to be a good man.

And right now, that just made her want to cry.

He said, "I was thinking…"

"Yeah?"

"Looking back on that night in March when you broke it off, I knew there was something weighing on your mind. I should have tried harder to get you to open to me."

She couldn't believe he'd just said that. "Liam. You were great. Don't you dare blame yourself."

"Look, I just need to know what *you* need."

"I'm good, I promise. Everything's pretty much ready. We're just waiting for the baby to come."

He frowned in a thoughtful sort of way. "Have you been going to childbirth classes?"

"I took the classes, yes. Like I said, I'm ready."

"A labor coach?" he asked and then clarified, "Do you have one?"

"I have two, as a matter of fact—Naomi and Prim." Naomi Khan Smith and Primrose Hart Danvers had been her best friends since kindergarten. Both women were married now. Naomi had two boys.

"Prim and Naomi. Makes sense." He'd grown up with her BFFs, same as she had. "And even though I get that you're all set and Prim and Naomi will take good care of you, I want to be there, when the baby comes."

She tried not to picture him standing beside her while she sweated and groaned with her legs spread apart. If he wanted to be there, he had the right. "Yes. That's fine. Great."

"So you'll call me, when you go into labor?"

"I will, absolutely."

* * *

Liam had a million more things to discuss with the soon-to-be mother of his child. But sitting here across from her in Sten Larson's too-quiet great room, he couldn't seem to remember a single one of them.

She just looked so brave and uncomfortable—and alone. Beyond being smart and good-looking and self-reliant, there was something that hurt his heart about Karin Killigan, something walled-off and sad.

"What else?" she asked. He knew she was trying not to sound impatient, but it was obvious to him that she couldn't wait for him to leave.

And why stay? She didn't really want him here, there was nothing he could do for her at the moment—and he hated the feeling that he contributed to her sadness.

"Nothing else—not right now, anyway," he heard himself say.

She stood, a surprisingly agile move given the size of her belly. "Well, all right then. Come by anytime. I mean that. Or call. Whatever."

"Thanks." He grabbed his bag of books and followed her down to the lower floor.

Her little girl stuck her curly head into the foyer as Karin was showing him out the door. "Bye, Liam Bravo."

"Bye, Coco."

"Can I call you just Liam?"

When he glanced at the silent woman beside him, she shrugged. "Up to you."

He gave Coco a smile. "Just Liam works for me."

"Okay! Bye, Liam. You can come and see me anytime." Coco waved as Karin ushered him out the door.

Liam went back to Astoria and had breakfast at a homey little diner he liked. From there, he went on to his office at the Warrenton terminal and put in a half day of work.

That evening, he drove the few miles to Valentine Bay and

stopped at the Sea Breeze on Beach Street for a beer. His baby sister Grace was behind the bar. She served him his favorite IPA and asked him if something was bothering him.

"It's all good," he lied and Gracie left him alone except to give him a refill when he signaled for it. He sat there sipping his beer, feeling kind of gloomy, going back and forth over whether or not to just tell his youngest sister that he was about to be a dad. At some point, he would have to break the big news to the whole family.

Soon, actually. The baby would be here in no time at all.

It all felt so strange. Completely unreal. He still had no clue how he was going to do it—be a dad.

But he wasn't giving up. Uh-uh. Karin and her sad eyes weren't keeping him away. He would be there for her and for his kid whether she wanted him around or not.

"Is Liam your boyfriend, Mommy?" Coco took a big sip of her milk and then set the glass carefully down. She picked up her fork and speared a clump of mac and cheese with ham.

Karin and her dad shared a glance across the dinner table. Otto lifted one bushy eyebrow. Karin read that look: *it's as good a time as any.*

She cast a sideways glance at Ben. He was watching her, wearing what she always thought of as his Little Professor look. Serious. Thoughtful. Ben never just burst out with things the way Coco did. He watched. He waited. He made carefully considered, responsible decisions.

"As a matter of fact," Karin said to her daughter, "I've been meaning to talk to both you and Ben about Liam."

"I like Liam!" Coco speared a green bean and stuck it in her mouth.

Dear God. Where to even start? "I like Liam, too," Karin said, trying to sound relaxed and natural and feeling anything but. "And several months ago, I…went out with him."

Ben's forehead scrunched up the way it always did when

some complex math problem didn't compute. "You were dating Liam?"

Not dating, exactly. "Uh, yes. I was. We're not, um, dating anymore, though. But we are friends. And that's a good thing. Because, as it turns out…" Was she blowing this? Most likely. She forged on anyway. "We will all probably be seeing a lot more of Liam because he is the new baby's father."

Ben said nothing.

Coco was incredulous. She set down her fork. "*Our* baby's father?"

"Yes." It was official. She was a terrible mother who needed lessons in how to share awkward, confusing information with her own children. "Liam is our baby's dad."

Coco frowned. "Is he going to come and live in our house?"

"No, honey."

"But doesn't he want to be with the baby?"

"Yes. Yes, he does. And he will be here often to see the baby. And when the baby gets older, the baby will probably stay with Liam some of the time."

"Oh," said Coco, and picked up her fork again. "Okay." She stabbed herself another big bite of mac and cheese.

Karin glanced across at her dad again. He gave her a shrug and a reassuring smile.

Ben, who understood the mechanics of reproduction, asked the question she'd been dreading. "How come you didn't say who the baby's dad was when I asked you before?" He'd asked several months ago, not long after she'd made the announcement that he and Coco would have a new brother or sister.

Because I'm a lily-livered scaredy-cat, she thought. She said, "Well, sweetheart, as I said then, I wanted to talk to the baby's dad first."

"You took a long time to talk to him."

Ouch. "Yes, I did. I'm sorry about that, I really am."

Ben tipped his head to the side, pondering. "Why? Were you nervous, to tell him?"

Understatement of the decade. "I was, yes."

"But now he knows and he's happy that he'll be a dad?"

"I haven't asked him that question. But he seems very determined to be a *good* dad."

Ben was still looking kind of troubled over the whole situation.

But Coco wasn't. "Our baby will like having Liam for a dad," she declared. "Liam's nice—and I finished my dinner. What's for dessert?"

Otto chuckled. "I think there might be a full carton of chocolate ice cream in the freezer."

Karin brushed Ben's arm. "Want to go talk about this in the other room, just the two of us?"

Ben shook his head. "Thanks, Mom. I'd rather just have some dessert."

On Sunday, Karin went in to work at Larson Boatworks, the boat-building and refitting company her dad had started thirty-five years before. Karin ran the office.

That day, her dad kept an eye on the kids at home so she could spend several hours tying up loose ends on the job before the baby came. When she got back to the Cove late that afternoon, her dad reported that Liam had dropped by.

"Should I call him?" she asked.

"He didn't say to ask you to."

"Did he mention what he needed to talk to me about?"

Her dad gave her a look, indulgent and full of wry humor. "I'm not sure he *knows* what he needs to talk to you about."

For the rest of that day and into the evening, she kept thinking that she probably ought to call Liam, check in, ask him if he had any questions or anything. Somehow, though, she never quite got around to picking up the phone.

Monday, her leave from work began. Her dad dropped the kids at the bus stop and then went on to work.

It was nice, having the house to herself. She took a half hour just deciding what to wear and ended up settling on a giant purple T-shirt dress with an asymmetrical hem.

Really, she didn't want jeans or leggings wrapped around her balloon of a belly today, so she settled on thigh-high socks in royal blue with her oldest, comfiest pair of Doc Martens boots on her feet.

Once she was dressed, she felt suddenly energized, so she vacuumed and dusted and rechecked the baby's room for the umpteenth time, making sure everything was ready. Around eleven, just as she finished assembling two large baking dishes of lasagna and sticking them in the freezer to reheat when needed, she heard the doorbell ring.

It was Liam. He had a pink teddy bear in one hand and a blue bear in the other.

"I forgot to ask. What are we having?" He smiled that killer smile of his, and she felt way too glad to see him.

She laughed. "It's a boy."

And just like that, he threw the pink bear over his shoulder and handed her the blue one.

The man was too charming by half. "Thank you—and I think we should save the pink one, too."

"Is there something you aren't telling me?" He pretended to look alarmed. "We're having twins, aren't we?"

"Oh, God, no. I just meant it seems wrong to leave it lying there on the front step."

He went and got the pink bear. "Fine. The baby gets two bears."

It seemed only right to offer, "Would you like to see his ultrasound pictures?"

"I thought you'd never ask."

She ushered him in. As he brushed past her, she got a hint of his cologne, a scent of leather and sandalwood that caused a sudden, stunning remembrance of the two of them all those months ago, naked on tangled sheets.

He paused in the arch to the living area and glanced back at her. "Something wrong?"

"Not a thing." She shut the door and followed him into the first-floor living area.

In the kitchen, she put the blue bear down on the counter. He set the pink one beside it as she went to the double-doored fridge, which was covered with family pictures and artwork created by both Ben and Coco. "Here we are." She took the two ultrasound shots from under a strawberry magnet and handed them over. "These were at eighteen weeks."

He studied them. "Wait. Is that...?" He slanted her a grin.

"What sharp eyes you have, Liam Bravo. Yep. A bona fide penis—and I have a video of that same procedure. Want to see it?"

"Oh, yeah."

She stuck the pictures back on the fridge and led him to the table where she'd left her laptop. He laughed in a sort of startled wonder as he watched his son wave his tiny arms and feet, yawn and suck his thumb.

After he'd seen the whole thing through twice, he glanced up at her. "You said you were all ready for him. Does that mean he has a room and everything?"

She grabbed the two teddy bears and gestured toward the hallway to the bedrooms. "Right this way." He followed her as she explained, "We're lucky this house has so many rooms, including five bedrooms on this level. I had a sort of craft room/home office in one." She led him to the end of the hall where the door stood open. "Ta-da!" She put the bears on the dresser by the door.

"Wow." Liam seemed really pleased.

And out of nowhere, she was recalling one of the depressing fights she'd had with Ben, Sr., before Ben was born.

Bud, as everyone always called him, had kept promising to help her paint the tiny closet of a spare room at the apartment they'd shared back then.

Somehow, though, he never found the time to keep his promise. Bud had loved the life of a commercial fisherman and he was always out on a boat, working the fisheries up and down the Pacific coast, from Southern California to Alaska. He just kept saying "later," every time she tried to pin him down as to when, exactly, he would put in some time on the baby's room.

In the end, she fixed up the room herself, though not until after they'd had a doozy of an argument over it—one in which they both said a lot of things they shouldn't have. It was always like that with her and Bud. They would argue bitterly.

And then Bud would go off to work and be gone for weeks.

In the end, she'd tackled the nursery nook alone. When Bud came home, she showed him the finished product. He'd waved a dismissing hand and said it looked "fine" in a dead voice that communicated way too clearly how trapped he felt.

Liam's voice drew her back to the present. "The mural is amazing."

Covering the whole wall behind the crib, the mural included a snowcapped mountain, a starry night sky, an airplane sailing by the moon and tall evergreens standing sentinel off to one side, everything in grays, greens and silvers.

"Northwest outdoorsy," Liam said. "I like it a lot."

She rubbed her belly. The baby was riding really low and she'd had some contractions.

He was watching her. "You okay?"

"I'm fine. This baby is coming *soon*."

His eyes got bigger and he straightened from his easy slouch in the doorway. "As in now?"

She waved a hand and chuckled, thinking that this visit was going pretty well and she was glad about that. "Relax. Probably not today."

"Whew." He gazed at the mural again. "You paint that wall yourself?"

"More or less. Stencils. You can't beat 'em."

He shifted his gaze to her. He had a way of studying her,

like he was memorizing the lines of her face. He used to do that months ago, sitting across from her at whatever bar they met up in, or later, naked in bed. One night, she'd teased that he should take a picture. He'd promptly grabbed his phone off the table by the bed and aimed it at her, snapping off two shots.

She'd demanded he delete them, because who needs naked pictures of herself on a guy's phone?

He'd handed her the phone. She'd seen then that he'd only taken close-ups of her face. And when she glanced up at him, he gazed back at her so hopefully, like it would just be the greatest thing in the world, to have a couple of shots of her grinning, with total bedhead. She'd agreed he could keep the pictures—and then grabbed him close for a long, smoking-hot kiss.

Liam was still watching her. "Have you chosen a name for this baby boy of ours?"

"No, I have not. I kind of thought you might want input on his name."

Apparently, that was the right answer because he granted her a beautiful smile. "Thanks. I'll be thinking about names. I'll make up a list of ones I like. We can talk it over." Solemnly, he added, "I read all about baby daddies. I don't want to be that guy."

Her heart felt like someone was squeezing it. She hardly knew what to say. "You have *other* children?"

"Huh?" He seemed horrified. "No! Wait. I get it. You mean 'baby daddy' as in a flaky guy who has kids by different women, but I wasn't so much referring to the multiple baby mamas aspect. I meant a flaky guy, yeah. But in this case, a guy with only one baby, a guy who's basically a sperm donor with minimal involvement—that's what I *don't* want to be. I want to be on board with this baby, available, helping out. I want to be *there*, you know? Tell me you know that." He seemed so intense suddenly, as though it really bothered him that she might not understand his sincerity about pitching in.

"Hey, really. It's going to be okay, Liam."

"I hope so."

"It really is. I know I dropped the ball in a big way by not telling you what was going on sooner. I should've pushed past all the crap going on in my head and gotten in touch."

He watched her way too closely. "What crap, exactly?"

Uh-uh. Not going there. "My point is, I promise you that we *will* work together. You don't have to freak out."

"I'm not freaking out," he said vehemently—and a bit freakily.

Was this all going south suddenly?

And just when they'd both seemed to be feeling more at ease around each other.

She kind of wanted to cry, which was probably just hormones. But still. She really did want to get along with him. "Okay. You're right. You're not freaking out and I shouldn't have even hinted that you were and I'm really, um…" Her already weak train of thought went right off the rails as she felt something shift inside her—a gentle shift, yet also a sudden one, a tiny *pop* of sensation deep within.

And then something was dripping along the inside of her thighs.

Frowning, she looked down, which was pointless. Her giant belly blocked her view and whatever was dripping down there, it was only a trickle. So far, her thigh-highs seemed to be absorbing it.

"Okay," said Liam. "Something's happened. What?"

She made herself look straight into his startled blue eyes and she put real effort into speaking calmly. "My water just broke. Would you mind driving me to Memorial Hospital?"

CHAPTER THREE

EVEN MORE STUNNED than he'd been for most of the past few days, Liam croaked out, "Drive you to the hospital? Yes! Yes, I can do that."

"Great." With a low groan, Karin gripped the crib rail and lowered her head.

"Karin, are you…?"

She put up her free hand. "Just a contraction. Hold on…"

He stood there in the doorway waiting, feeling completely useless, as she panted and groaned some more.

Finally, she let go of the crib rail and looked straight at him. "Where's my phone?"

"I think I spotted it on the kitchen counter?"

"Right." One hand under her enormous stomach, she lumbered toward him. He fell back from the doorway so she could get by and then trailed after her as she made for the main room.

In the kitchen, she snatched up the phone. "This'll only take a minute. I've got a group text all set up—to Naomi, Prim and my dad. All I need to do is hit Send." The woman amazed him. Was there anything she wasn't ready for? She poked at the phone. "There. I'll call my doctor on the way—now get me a bath towel. Try the hall bathroom, first door on the left. I'll meet you at the front door."

"A towel?" He just stood there gaping at her because somehow his feet had forgotten how to walk.

"You want me to leak amniotic fluid all over the seats of that fancy blue Supercrew pickup out in front?"

"Uh. No?"

"Then go."

That got him moving. He raced off and returned with the towel. She had a suitcase ready, just waiting in the hallway. He took the suitcase and helped her into her coat. She grabbed her purse from the table by the door and off down the outside stairs they went, pausing midway for her to weather another contraction.

At the truck, he threw the suitcase in back, spread the towel on the seat and helped her in. She was already on the phone with her doctor as he turned the pickup around and headed up the hill behind the house.

At Memorial, he learned that the doctor was on the way and they were ready for Karin. They whisked her into a labor and delivery suite and let Liam tag along.

Luckily, he'd studied up on what the father should do during the birth. He'd learned that his sole mission in the delivery room was to be a source of strength and support, to be as patient and attentive to his baby's mother as he possibly could.

He really tried to be that, even though when her girlfriends showed up, he was mostly relegated to staying out of the way as they stepped up on either side of her to comfort her and coach her through her contractions. They fed her ice chips and helped her to the bathroom when she needed it. The whole thing took hours, with the doctor in and out, the delivery nurses, too.

Once he asked if he could take pictures.

Naomi turned to him and spoke gently, "It's so great that

you're here, Liam, but Karin doesn't want you taking pictures of her lady bits."

"I would never do that," he answered fervently. "Just...maybe of the baby and then maybe of Karin with the baby and then maybe I could hold him, too—I mean, after he gets here, of course?"

On the far side of Karin, Prim was stifling a giggle.

Naomi grabbed him in a hug. "Isn't he adorable?" she asked Karin and Prim as she let him go.

He was trying to decide whether or not his manly dignity had just been impugned when Karin said, "Of course you can take a few pictures with your son." She met his eyes directly and he knew she was remembering that night in February, when he'd snapped a shot of her in his bed and she'd assumed he'd gotten more than just her face.

"Terrific," he replied, suddenly just crazy happy, right there in the delivery room, crazy happy and sure that everything was going to work out fine, though exactly what "fine" entailed he had no clear idea.

Things got messy soon after that. There were fluids and a little blood and Karin's groans started to sound more like screams and angry shouts.

But then the baby's head was crowning and everything sped up. As soon as the little guy's shoulders emerged, it was all over. The rest of him slipped out quick and easy. He was so tiny and wrinkled and red, covered with sticky whitish goo, wailing as the doctor caught him and laid him in Karin's waiting arms. Naomi grabbed Liam and pulled him around to stand in front of her, right next to Karin and the naked infant on her chest.

On Karin's other side, Prim stepped back so the nurse could wipe some of the goo off the baby and the doctor could deal with the umbilical cord. All Liam could do was stand there and stare.

He'd never realized how much he wanted children.

Not until this moment, when he actually had one—yeah, he'd

had vague yearnings in the past year, to get more serious about his life, to get married, start a family.

But only in a generalized sort of way.

Until today.

Today, he knew exactly what he wanted—to be a father to this perfect little miracle he and Karin had made.

"Take a picture, Liam," Karin teased softly as she stroked the baby's shoulder, her hand gliding down the fat little arm to the tiny fist. Instantly, the baby wrapped his itty-bitty fingers around her thumb and held on.

Liam got out his phone and snapped a few shots.

The nurse gave him a towel to put on his shoulder. She let him hold his son for the first time. That was amazing, though it didn't last long.

He passed Naomi his phone and she got a few pictures of him with the baby. Too soon, the nurse took the little guy back and gave him to Karin again and she nursed him for the first time. Liam thought maybe he should turn away, give her some privacy. But she didn't seem concerned and nobody else cared. He watched as his son latched right on and went to work, the fingers of his right hand resting on the upper slope of Karin's breast, opening and closing as he sucked.

Liam watched not only his newborn son, but his son's mother, too. He stared and marveled and thought how, from that first night they'd had together last Christmas, she'd been constantly keeping him at arm's distance, giving in to the attraction between them, yeah. But then, once the hot times were over, pushing him away.

And what about the last few days since he'd found out about the baby? She'd continually reminded him to take his time, think it over, figure out just how *involved* he wanted to be.

As though a man could choose his level of involvement when he became a father.

There was no choosing with something like this. When it came to fatherhood, a man needed to be all in.

And he was. *In* this. Going for it. All the way.

Okay, he got it. He knew he had no idea, really, what the hell he was doing. But he could learn. And he *would* learn. One way or another, he was making it work with Karin. He damn well would create a family with the mother of his child.

Last Friday, that first day he found out she was pregnant, he'd stuttered out a half-assed proposal of marriage. She'd said no before he even really got the words out.

No wasn't going to cut it.

She glanced up from the baby and into his eyes. "Liam?" She seemed alarmed. "What's wrong?"

"Not a thing." He felt so calm, so absolutely determined. He held her gaze, steady on. "Marry me, Karin," he said.

Karin was wasted, completely exhausted.

She'd done this twice before, yes. But experience didn't make having a baby feel any less like pushing out a watermelon. She just wanted to lie there and nurse her newborn and be grateful that labor was over, thank you very much.

But no.

Liam had to go to the marriage place. Hadn't they already agreed that marriage was no solution to anything?

And did he have to be so sweet about it? Sweet and determined and handsome and even-tempered and so damn helpful.

Liam Bravo was a dream.

Someday, he would make some lucky woman very happy.

But that day was not today and that woman was not her. No way was she going to be the one that Liam Bravo married because he felt he had to.

After the ongoing disaster with poor Bud, she'd had this fantasy that someday, maybe, she would actually get it right. In that lovely, impossible illusion, she'd imagined finding a man who would love her just for her, and then fall in love with Ben and Coco, too. That man would marry her for love and love alone. Duty and obligation and doing the right thing wouldn't even enter into it.

Later, they would have a baby or two, maybe. Like normal people do.

As of now, she was reasonably certain her fantasy was never actually going to come true. But that didn't mean she would settle for less.

Liam was still standing right beside the bed, staring down at her and the baby as though he could *will* her to agree to his well-meaning but totally unacceptable proposal.

The doctor had left the room and the nurse and Naomi and Prim had fallen dead silent the moment Liam said the *M* word.

"Would you all give Liam and me a moment alone?" Karin asked her suddenly speechless friends and the too-quiet nurse.

"Of course." The nurse gave her shoulder a pat.

And the three women filed out the door so fast you'd think there was a fire. Or maybe a gas leak.

"Liam…" Karin kissed her baby's head and shifted a fraction so he was settled more firmly at her breast.

The man beside her bent closer. He was so good-looking, with those fine blue eyes and that mouth that made her think of deep, wet kisses. He also just happened to be kind and thoughtful and determined. Everything a woman could ask for in a man.

"Just say yes," he commanded. "It will work out. We'll be happy, you'll see."

Was she even a tiny bit tempted?

Of course. She was a heterosexual single mom. What was *not* to adore about Liam Bravo? The guy was practically perfect—at least right now, as he stared down at his newborn son after the excitement and drama of birth. Blinded by the wonder of new life and eager to do right by his child and his child's mother, marriage would naturally seem like the only choice to him.

The resentment, the growing certainty that she'd trapped him, the longing to be free of her—all that would come later.

Except it wouldn't. Because she wasn't going to marry him. No way. "Liam, we've been over this."

He shook his golden head. "We haven't. The other day, you said no before I even got the question out."

"I'm sorry I didn't hear you out, but my answer wouldn't have changed no matter what you said or how convincing you were or how patiently I waited for you to finish saying it. I'm not getting married just because we have a baby together. I need you to believe me when I tell you that."

"Listen." He straightened and stuck his hands in his pockets. "Don't give me an answer right now. Take your time. Think about it."

"Liam, I've already—"

"Think about it." A thread of steel had crept into his tone.

She had no need to think about it. Zero. Zip. Nada. She'd already given him her answer. Twice now. But he wasn't listening and an argument right now wasn't going to be good for her, for him or, most important, for their baby, who'd just been ejected from the warm, quiet safety of her womb. "All right. We'll talk about it later. If you need to. But my answer won't change."

"Just tell me you'll think about it."

She gave him a nod, though she really shouldn't have. He might construe any positive gesture as encouragement. But right now, she would do just about anything to stop this pointless marriage talk.

"Thank you." Liam bent close again. He brushed her forehead with his big, warm hand and placed a sweet, light kiss where his palm had been. "Thank you for my son and for promising to keep an open mind about marriage."

An open mind? Uh-uh. Her mind was locked down and dead bolted on that subject.

But for right now, he could go ahead and refuse to accept what she'd told him twice. Eventually he'd get the message. She even dared to hope the day would come when he would be grateful to her for not taking advantage of him at this emotional time.

As for the touch of his lips on her skin, she shouldn't have liked that so much, shouldn't have let herself sigh just a little when he bent near.

Really, she shouldn't even have allowed that kiss, should have turned her head away when his fine lips descended. He was a wonderful guy and she needed to begin developing a strong coparenting relationship with him—one that wouldn't include kisses, not even on the forehead.

Today, though, was a special circumstance. She'd just given birth to his baby. Surely, this once, a kiss on the forehead couldn't hurt...

Per hospital policy, Karin stayed the night at Memorial. Her girlfriends left after she was all settled in a regular room in the postpartum unit.

Liam stayed on. Karin suggested more than once that he ought to go home, get some dinner and a good night's rest. He said he wasn't tired.

A nurse came in with the birth certificate forms. They hadn't chosen a name yet, so the nurse helped them fill out everything else and told them where to send the form when the name had been decided. The space for the baby's last name didn't go empty. Liam wrote "Bravo" in there and Karin didn't object. No, she wasn't going to marry the guy, but she was determined to be respectful of his place in their baby's life.

The nurse left and finally, at a little before seven, Liam went off to get something to eat in the cafeteria.

Not five minutes after he went out the door, her dad and the kids arrived to meet the new baby. Apparently, Otto had spoken to them about how to behave in the hospital. Coco was as enthusiastic as ever, but she kept her voice down and sat with her little hands folded in her lap, a wild-haired, blue-eyed, second-grade angel. Ben was just Ben—curious and serious, even more polite than usual.

They each held the baby and seemed to enjoy that.

"He's kind of red," remarked Ben. He looked up. "But that's normal. I read that newborns have thin skin and the red blood vessels can show through."

When Coco's turn to hold her baby brother came, Ben leaned close and gently touched his head. "Soft spots," he declared with a solemn little nod. "They are called fontanels and there is one in front and one in back of the skull so that the baby's head can be flexible when he's coming through the birth canal and also so that the brain can grow quickly, now that he's born."

"He is so cute," Coco said in a carefully controlled whisper. "But his nose is kind of squished."

Ben loftily explained that a flattened nose also tended to happen during birth. "It's a tight squeeze," he said to his sister. "But his nose will assume its normal shape over time."

Coco looked up, frowning. "Mommy, what's our baby's name?"

"We haven't decided yet," Karin answered with a smile. *Note to self—ask Liam if he's made that list.*

Otto took the baby from Coco and declared him absolutely perfect. He'd just returned him to Karin's arms when there was a tap on the half-open door.

Liam had returned. "Hey. Should I come back?"

"Liam!" Coco exclaimed—and then realized she'd almost shouted. She clapped her hand over her mouth briefly and then stage-whispered, "Hi."

"Come on in," said Otto. "I've got to get these kids home, anyway. Homework to do, baths to take."

Liam glanced at her for permission.

What could she say? She waved him forward.

A few minutes later, after Karin's dad had assured her that he'd reached Sten in LA and reported that the newest member of the family had arrived safe and sound, Otto herded the kids out the door.

Liam said, "I'll bet you're tired."

"Oh, maybe just a little…"

"I'll leave you alone. But can I hold him—just for a minute?"

Her heart kind of melted at the longing in his eyes. "Of course."

He came close and she handed the baby over. Liam adjusted the swaddled blanket around his little face.

Karin leaned back against the pillow. "I keep meaning to ask if you've thought about a name yet."

He gently rocked the blanketed bundle from side to side. "I really can't decide."

She shut her weary eyes. "Well, think about it. We need to call him something other than 'the baby'."

"Will do." And he started whispering—to the baby, she assumed. She couldn't hear what he said, but the soft sound of his voice was soothing and she was so tired...

When Karin woke, Liam was gone and the baby was asleep in the plastic bassinet beside her. She didn't learn until breakfast time that he'd spent the night in the waiting room.

"I stayed just in case you might need me," he said when he came in with a sausage and egg sandwich in one hand and a paper cup of coffee in the other. He had bags under his eyes and his hair was slicked back as though he'd used the hospital restroom to splash water on his face. "When will they release you?" he asked.

"Later this morning or this afternoon, after my doctor comes by to check on us and sign us out of here."

"I'll drive you to the Cove."

She shook her head. "My dad's coming. He'll have the baby seat all hooked up in the car, ready to go."

He sipped his coffee. "Right. I need a baby seat."

She couldn't help chuckling. "Most conscientious single dad. Ever. Like in the history of dads."

That gorgeous smile lit up his face. "Thank you." He toasted her with his paper cup. "I do my best."

After he ate, he held the baby again. When he handed the

little boy back, he said regretfully, "I suppose I need to check in at work, maybe even go to my place and take a shower. But I'll see you both later on today."

"Sure. As I said, I don't even know for certain what time they'll release us."

"No problem. I'll see you soon." He kissed the baby on the cheek and left.

As it turned out, the doctor didn't come to release her until the afternoon. Otto got one of the moms to bring Ben home from soccer practice. He picked up Coco from school and brought her to the hospital with him. She chattered away as they put the baby in his car seat and headed home.

At the Cove, the garage beneath the cottage next door was wide open. Karin spotted the back end of Liam's F-150 Raptor parked inside. Back when they were hooking up, he drove a black Audi Q8. The pickup suited him better, she thought, a true guy's guy sort of vehicle.

Not that what car he drove mattered to her in the least. What mattered was that the garage next door was wide open and his pickup was in it. The smaller house was a rental and vacation property. Sten kept it fully furnished, but he hadn't rented it to anyone since Madison had stayed there last spring.

Karin turned to her dad. "Do you have any idea why Liam's truck is parked in the garage next door?"

"I thought you knew," her dad replied. "Liam called Sten and Sten leased him the cottage."

CHAPTER FOUR

IN THE HOUSE, Coco ran to her room. The minute the little girl disappeared down the hall, Karin pitched her voice low and asked her dad, "Would you keep an eye on Coco? I'm just going over to talk to Liam for a minute."

"Kary." Otto spoke gently, like she was made of glass and about to shatter. "He's a great guy."

"Did I once say he wasn't?"

"Just give him a chance, that's all I'm suggesting."

"You're right. He's terrific and I intend to work with him and honor the importance of his place in our child's life. What more do you want from me, Dad?"

"Well, you could open your eyes. You're as bad as Sten was with Madison—pushing a good thing away for all you're worth."

"Not true." Yeah, Sten had been a thickheaded fool about Madison, ridiculously certain for way too long that it couldn't work out for them. But Sten and Madison were a completely different situation than Karin and Liam and her dad really ought to know that. "My eyes are wide open, I promise you."

"That man next door? He is not Bud."

As if she didn't know that—and she felt obligated, as always, to defend her dead husband. "Bud was a good man."

"Never said he wasn't."

The baby, whom she'd carried from the car in his baby seat, gave a questioning cry. "Shh, now. It's okay," she whispered to him. To her dad, she said, "I really can't have this conversation right now. I need to go next door. Will you keep an eye on Coco?"

Otto studied her face for several uncomfortable seconds before finally giving it up. "Sure."

"Thanks, Dad." She gave him a grateful smile and hustled to the baby's room as her newborn fussed in the seat. He quieted as soon as she wrapped him close in the baby sling Prim had given her for a shower gift.

At the cottage, she went in through the open garage door and was halfway up the interior stairs when Liam pulled open the door above that led into the laundry room.

"Hey." He beamed down at her like she was the one person in the whole world he'd been waiting to see. "Come on in." He stepped back and ushered her inside, leading the way to the kitchen that opened onto a deck with stairs down to the beach. The cottage had a similar footprint to the main house, with the entrance facing the hill behind it and the main living area looking out over the ocean.

Liam had all the kitchen cabinets open, with groceries piled on the counters. He gestured at the table by the slider. "Have a seat."

"No, thanks. I won't stay long." She stroked the curve of the baby's back. He wiggled a little, then settled against her.

"I like that sling thing. I need to get one." Liam stood too close, right there at the end of the counter with her—really, did he have to be so tall and broad and manly? "Keely has one," he said. "She uses it constantly. My niece Marie loves it."

"Liam. We need to talk about this." She tried to sound stern— but understanding, too.

He chuckled. "You sound like Mrs. Coolidge. Remember her, fourth grade? She'd get so disappointed if I didn't turn in my homework. *Liam*, she would say. *What am I going to do with you?*"

No way was she getting detoured down memory lane with him. That could be a very long trip. They'd known each other since the beginning of time, after all. "Moving in here, just out of the blue like this, is a little extreme, don't you think?"

"No, I don't think it's extreme in the least." He leaned back against the counter and folded his arms across that hard chest. He wore a lightweight blue sweater. The sleeves were pushed up, revealing forearms with just the right dusting of silky-looking hair and those sexy veins that only served to accentuate his gorgeous, hard muscles. "I'm really glad I thought of it. Lucky for me, it was empty. Sten says he took it off Airbnb and Vrbo because he's in LA most of the time. When he *is* here, well, Madison doesn't really want strangers right next door anyway. People can get intrusive, living next to a movie star—they're going to try to make it home during the holidays, did you know that?"

Karin rubbed the baby's back some more, soothing herself as much as her little boy. "Yeah, I knew that."

"The downstroke is that your brother said this cottage is mine for as long as I need it. He even gave me the go-ahead to fix it up any way I want, including a room for the baby. I'm thinking deep blue and a mural on the crib wall, like the one you did, except not. Maybe a dinosaur mural. Or stars and moons..."

She tried again to get through to him. "Liam, I just don't think it's a good idea, you living here. There are, well, boundaries, you know? We need to observe them."

"And I am observing them."

"No. You're moving in next door."

"Karin, come on. I'm in this house and you're in the other house. We definitely each have our own defined space. It's not like I'm suddenly asking to share a place with you."

"But I would rather that you—"

He cut her off. "Look, I know what our baby needs most now is you. But if I'm living here, he's going to know me as part of his life from the start. That matters to a kid and it matters to me. I can play backup parent from the beginning. Anytime you need help, I'm right next door." He pushed away from the counter and stepped in too close again. She steeled herself against all that charm and hotness. "This is a good thing, me being close by. You have to know that."

She backed away a step and tried another tack. "What about that beautiful house you built in Astoria?"

He gave an easy shrug. "It's too far away from my son. When I get around to it, I'll put it on the market."

"Just like that? But you *love* that house."

"My priorities have changed. But don't worry about it. I'm not selling it right away. If I suddenly decide I can't live without that house, it'll still be there. Right now, though, I need to live *here*, near you and the baby."

Oh, this man. Her heart could melt into a hot puddle of goo just listening to some of the things he said.

And that was the whole point, now wasn't it? *Not* to get a melted mush-ball of a heart just because a good man was trying to do the right thing by his child. She needed to stand strong on her own, be supportive of Liam as a coparent to their son, but remain mindful that he had his life and she had hers and having a baby together did not mean they *were* together.

"You're just going to do this, aren't you?" she demanded. "You're living in this house next door to *my* house no matter how I feel about it."

He took her by the shoulders, his big, warm hands so strong and steady, and he captured her gaze and held it. "You'll see. It's going to be great."

Back at the other house, her daughter greeted her at the front door. Coco had changed clothes. Now, her shorts were blue and her T-shirt was red. Yellow knit arm warmers covered her wrists to her elbows. She had a swatch of gold mesh fabric tied around her head and a red construction-paper star pinned to it in the exact center of her forehead.

"Wonder Woman, how's it going?"

Coco crossed her arms in front of her face. "Just tell me you need help, Mommy, and I will save you." Coco wiggled her eyebrows over the barrier of her arms.

"Whew." Karin made a show of wiping imaginary sweat from her forehead. "That is really good to know."

"I have lots of powers, Mommy." Oh, yes, she did. Coco had an iPad and she knew how to use it. She always did her research, superheroine-wise.

"What powers, exactly?"

"I have superhuman strength and I never get tired. I glide through the air on the wind. I have super speed and *agitally*. I can smell everything and see everything and hear the most smallest sounds."

"I feel safer already."

Coco stood tall. "You're *welcome*, Mommy." And off she flew toward the kitchen.

As for Karin, she went straight to her bedroom, pulled out her phone and called Sten.

He answered on the first ring. "How's my new nephew?"

"He's sweet and beautiful," she said loftily. "You're going to love him."

"I can't wait to meet him. Liam tells me you haven't settled on a name yet."

"No, we haven't—and about Liam…"

"Yeah?" The single word was freighted with challenge. She could just picture Sten drawing his shoulders back, standing a little taller. "What about him?"

Reminding herself that she would stay calm and not yell at her brother—for the sake of the innocent child sleeping next to her heart if for no other reason—Karin paced back and forth at the foot of the bed. "I am really upset with you," she said in a purposely soft, calm voice. "You could have at least discussed it with me before you leased him the cottage."

Sten snort-laughed. "And have you make up a thousand meaningless reasons why I shouldn't rent to him? No, thanks. He's family, Karin, in case you've forgotten. He's my brother-in-law and he wants to be near his kid. There's nothing wrong with that."

"I am actively resisting the powerful need to start shouting mean things at you."

"Go right ahead and shout. I can take it. Because I'm pissed at you, too. You have to give that man a chance, Karin. He wants to be there for your baby and it's part of your job to help him do that."

It was essentially the same thing their dad had said. It had aggravated her the first time she heard it. This time, it made her want to throw back her head and scream. She took a slow, deep breath before replying. "I *am* helping him, Sten. I support him totally as the baby's father."

"And yet you took forever to get around to telling him he was even going to be a dad. Karin, I really was starting to think you never would."

"Sten, okay." She stroked the baby's nearly bald head with one hand and pinched the bridge of her nose with the other because sometimes Sten gave her a headache—and because, yeah, he was right. "I messed that up, I admit it. But at least he knows now. He was there for his son's birth. And now, thanks to you, he's even living in the house next door."

"You're welcome."

She heard the humor in her brother's voice and couldn't help but smile. "I think Liam plans to be the most *involved* dad that has ever existed in the whole of time. And I think it's great, I really do. I am not getting in his way, I promise you. Liam will have every chance to be there for his kid."

"Good," said her brother. "That's how it should be. And now

he's got the cottage, it will be so much easier for him to help you out whenever you need him."

"By that you mean you won't tell him that you've changed your mind and the cottage isn't available after all?"

"Way to go, little sister. I think you're finally getting the picture."

Karin did take her brother's words to heart.

She invited Liam over for dinner that night. He showed up right on time. When the baby cried, she let him do the comforting. A little later, for the first time, Liam changed his son's diaper—a loaded one, too.

Really, her baby's dad was one of the good guys.

And that was the problem. He was a good man and he wanted to do right and it would be oh, so easy to let herself believe that they could share more than a son.

She would just have to keep holding the line against any suggestion that the two of them should get married. Eventually, he'd come to see that her saying no had been the best thing for everyone involved.

Thursday after dinner, she asked her dad to watch the sleeping baby so that she could go over to the cottage and discuss DNA testing with Liam.

He answered the door looking way too handsome in black jeans and a dark sweater with the sleeves pushed up those amazing forearms. Really, it wasn't fair that he looked so good. She, on the other hand, wore the outfit she'd thrown on that morning—a stretched-out gray Henley-style tunic and yoga pants. She'd also run out of the house without bothering to check her hair or freshen her lip gloss.

Had she actually been naked with this gorgeous specimen of a man on four separate and glorious occasions? It seemed so very long ago...

And yet, it really had happened and she had the baby to prove it.

"Hey."

"Hey."

"Where's the baby?"

"Sleeping. My dad'll call if he needs me."

"Come on in." He gave her that smile of his, the magic one that could make a girl's panties combust, and led her to the sitting area.

She took a chair and got down to it. "I came to talk DNA. There's a lab right here in town. We can all three go together, you, me and the baby. Just name a date and time—or I can meet you there, if that works better for you."

"DNA?" He dropped to the sofa. "It's not necessary. I know the baby's mine. I don't need a DNA test and I don't care if we have one."

"*I* care, Liam."

His burnished brows drew together. "Don't do that."

"What?"

"Don't give me that look, Karin. Like you disapprove of me."

Now, she felt awful. "I didn't. I *don't*." She stuck her hands between her knees and leaned toward him across the coffee table. "Not at all. What I meant was, well, proof is so easy to get now. There's no reason *not* to get it. All it takes is a cheek swab and you'll never doubt that our little boy is yours."

He shook his head her. "I already have no doubts. I know you, Karin. You have absolute integrity. If there was a doubt, you would have told me so that day at Safeway." He spoke with total conviction.

Now, her cheeks felt too warm and her tummy all fluttery. "Thank you." Her throat had clutched. She gulped to loosen it up. "That was a beautiful thing to say to me."

He leaned forward, too, so earnest and determined. "I don't need a test, Karin."

"I hear you. But *I* do—and not because I have any doubt you're the baby's dad. It's just, I want that, for you to have objective proof. Even though I accept your word that you don't need it."

He dropped back against the cushions with a hard breath. "Sorry. I don't get it. But if it's what you want—"

"It is. Please."

The following Monday afternoon, together, they took the baby to a lab right there in town to have their cheeks swabbed. Liam, eager to use the new car seat he'd bought, did the driving.

Later, back at the Cove, mindful of her resolution to treat Liam with kindness and consideration, Karin invited him to dinner again. "About six, if you can make it."

He accepted with a wide grin and showed up an hour early. She refused to let herself get annoyed about that. Instead, she reminded herself that the guy planned to stay at the cottage indefinitely and she'd better get used to having him around.

Really, what was not to like about Liam? He was easygoing and also easy on the eyes. He even offered to help in the kitchen.

"I've got this. But you can help the kids with cleanup after if you insist."

He had a beer with her dad and jumped to his feet when the baby cried. "I'll get him." He headed for the bedrooms and she didn't stop him.

When it was time to eat, he carried the blue bundle with him to the dinner table, where Coco fawned all over him and the baby in his big arms.

Coco did have one complaint, though. "Liam. Mommy. Our baby needs a name. Nobody likes to be called just 'the baby.'" Coco wrinkled up her little nose in disapproval.

"He's a newborn," said Ben. "He doesn't know how to talk and he doesn't understand words. That means he has no idea what we're calling him."

Coco tossed her curly head. "Well, *I* care what we call him and I'm his big sister." She smiled sweetly and actually fluttered her eyelashes. "I will be happy to choose a name for him. How about Brecken? There's a boy named Brecken in my class. He talks without raising his hand and chews with his mouth open, but I still like his name. Or how about Kael or Ridge?"

Karin met Liam's gaze across the dinner table as he glanced up from the baby in his arms. His eyes gleamed with humor. The moment tugged at her heartstrings, somehow. She was reminded of the past, of their long history together.

When Karin and Liam were Coco's age, he'd had a big crush on their second-grade teacher, Miss Wu. One morning, he brought Miss Wu a handful of wilted wildflowers he must have picked on the way to school. At recess, a couple of the other boys had razzed him. They'd called him a kiss-ass. Liam had just laughed and walked away.

Karin, flanked by Prim and Naomi, had watched the exchange. She and her friends waited, wide-eyed, for the two bullies to follow him, taunt him some more, maybe even throw a punch or two.

Didn't happen. The boys just stared after him, looking baffled. Liam simply had that way about him, always had. A born charmer, so easy and comfortable in his own skin. Bullies never knew what to make of him.

Really, the only time Karin had seen the man at a loss was recently, in the first few days after he found out about the baby.

Across the table, Liam tipped his head to the side, watching her. He offered, "My dad's name was George. Maybe George for a middle name?"

Coco piped up with, "I like Brecken better."

Otto stepped in. "Excellent suggestion, sweetheart. But I think your mom and Liam will be making this decision."

Coco released a gusty sigh. "Well, o-*kay*. I don't need to be the decider, I guess. Just as long as my baby brother gets a name."

Otto reached over and patted her shoulder as Karin asked Liam, "What do you think of Riley? Riley George Bravo?"

He bent to the baby and whispered something. Then, still

leaning close, he turned his head as though listening for a reply. He straightened in his chair with a nod. "He likes it. Riley George, it is."

Tuesday around nine, after everyone had left the Cove but Karin and Riley, two of Liam's sisters knocked on her door. Harper and Hailey had come to fix up the baby's room over at the cottage.

Hailey said, "But we wanted to stop by, say hi to you and meet Riley first."

Karin invited them in and made them coffee. They took turns holding the baby and filling Karin in on their mutual dream, which involved hosting children's parties and producing community events at an old theater downtown. Both blue-eyed blondes, the sisters were less than a year apart in age. They'd gone off to OU together, majored in theater arts together and graduated together the year before. Now, they both lived in town.

"My new nephew is the cutest guy ever," declared Hailey when it was her turn to hold Riley.

Harper agreed. "He is adorable—and Liam is so happy. All he talks about is the baby."

Hailey asked, "Can you blame him? I mean, look at this little guy." She grinned at Karin. "Liam likes *you* a lot, too."

Karin wasn't sure how to respond to that—mostly because she was constantly reminding herself *not* to like Liam too much. "He's a really good guy." She tried not to wince at how lame that sounded.

Harper said, "Okay, maybe this is out of bounds…"

"But we're just gonna ask," Hailey picked up where her sister left off. "If you don't like the question, tell us to mind our own damn business."

"We won't be offended."

"Fair enough." Karin sipped her tea. She had a pretty good idea where this was going.

Harper scooted closer to the table and wrapped her hands around her coffee mug. "So...what's the story with you and Liam? We didn't even know you guys were a thing."

"Well, we weren't a thing, not really." Karin turned her teacup in a slow circle as she tried to decide how much to say.

"Riley here would beg to differ." Hailey bent close and nuzzled his fat cheek. "There must have been *some*thing."

Karin confessed, "You're right. There was." It really had been terrific, her long-held secret fantasy come true—a few hot, stolen nights with the guy she'd crushed on so hard back in high school.

Harper reached over and gave her arm a reassuring squeeze. "Don't be sad."

Hailey looked concerned. "We didn't mean to upset you."

"You haven't. No way. It just, um, happened, between Liam and me. It started last December, on a girls' night out..."

She'd almost canceled on Naomi and Prim that night. Ben had come down with something and was running a low fever. She'd decided to stay home. But her dad and Sten had ganged up on her. She deserved a break, they said. Ben would be fine, they promised her. And she would only be a phone call away.

So she'd gone. "Believe me, with two kids and the Boatworks to run, I hadn't been getting a lot of nights out. My girls and I met up at Beach Street Brews. Liam just happened to be there that night, too, with some of his trucker buddies. He and I started talking. It was so easy between us. I couldn't get over that—then again, we've known each other all our lives, so why wouldn't we be comfortable with each other, right?" She met Harper's eyes and they shared a smile. "It was a great night. And so were the other nights we got together. But he wasn't looking for a relationship and neither was I. It was just for now and just for fun. And then, well, surprise, surprise. Riley came along."

Harper nodded. "It happens."

"Wedding bells, maybe?" Hailey asked, looking hopeful.

"No," Karin said gently. "He's an amazing guy and I like

him a lot, always have." Maybe too much, but his sisters didn't need to know that. "We're not in love, though." It caused an ache in her heart to say it. But sometimes the truth hurt. She finished softly, "We just want the same thing and that's to do the best we can for Riley."

They left it at that. The sisters stayed for another half hour or so. Before they left for the cottage, Karin gave Hailey the blue teddy bear Liam had brought over that day Riley was born. "I want him to have it for the new room."

That Friday, the DNA results came through.

It was official. Liam was Riley's biological father.

That evening, Karin took Riley over to the cottage to talk to Liam about a parenting plan.

"Hey." He gave her his killer smile. "Come on in."

In the kitchen, he offered her something to drink. "I'm guessing no alcohol, with the nursing and all, but I've got juice and I picked up some of that raspberry tea you like."

"I'm good, thanks."

He let his gaze trail down to the baby, who was attached to the front of her as usual, lately. Karin kind of loved watching his face when he saw his son. His mouth got so soft and his eyes a little dreamy. It was too damn cute by half. "Mind if I hold him?"

She eased Riley out of the sling and handed him over. The baby blinked up at his father and then yawned.

Liam bent his head close and nuzzled Riley's button nose. "Lookin' good, RG." He glanced up and caught her watching him. "What?" But then, before she could answer, he gestured her forward. "First things first. Let me show you his room."

She followed him down the hall to the bedroom next to the master suite. It was all ready for Riley. "Wow. That was fast."

He looked up from whispering to the baby. "Yeah. I got right on it. Lots of online shopping with overnight shipping. I gave Keely a credit card and she ordered most of the blankets and baby clothes, all the baby supplies and a diaper bag. I picked out the furniture myself."

"It looks great." Open shelves over the changing table were stacked with everything a baby might need. The walls were dark blue.

"I love the teddy bears and the tree," she said of the wall mural behind the crib. One bear floated midway up the wall on a couple of heart-shaped pale blue balloons. Three others climbed the tree.

"Harper did that, the mural and the detail stuff. Hailey painted the walls blue. Then the two of them put the furniture where they thought it should go." He gazed at her steadily. "They mentioned you had them over for coffee."

"Yeah. It was great to see them. We had a nice little chat." *About you and me and why we're not getting married. But you don't need to know that, so please don't ask.*

He didn't. He was all about the baby as he circled the room, whispering things in Riley's ear, stopping by the easy chair next to the window and glancing up at Karin. "RG and me, we need to try out this chair."

"Go for it." She leaned in the doorway and folded her arms across her middle.

He sat down. "Check this out." He leaned back and the easy chair became a recliner. "Pretty sweet, huh?"

"Perfect." And it was. *He* was. Totally devoted to his surprise son. It brought her joy to see them together—joy and a bittersweet ache in her chest that Bud had never really been able or willing or whatever to show that kind of steady, doting love to Ben. At least with Coco, Bud had been more affectionate—when he was around.

"What?" Liam was watching her.

She waved the question away with a shrug.

He glanced down at the baby again. For a few minutes, they were quiet. Liam held Riley as Karin leaned in the doorway enjoying the sight of them, the feeling of peace that seemed to fill the blue room.

"He's sound asleep," Liam whispered as he rose. "I want to put him in his crib." It was all fixed up, with cute blue-and-white bedding, including soft bumpers to cushion and protect a newborn. The blue teddy bear was propped in a corner.

"Good idea," she whispered back.

He put the baby down and tucked the blanket around him, bending closer for another kiss.

Rising to his height again, he came to her. She pulled away from the doorway to face him.

And then he was taking her by the upper arms, his big hands so warm and gentle. He caught her gaze and held it, that beautiful smile flirting with the corners of his full mouth.

She just knew he would kiss her and that she would let him.

But he didn't. "Come on," he said. "You know you want that raspberry tea. I haven't taken the baby monitor out of the box yet, but I think we'll hear him if we just leave the door open."

Liam had one of those electric kettles. It heated the water in no time.

As she waited for the tea to steep, he pulled a Boundary Bay IPA from the fridge and popped the cap. "So, what's up?" His strong throat rippled as he took a long drink.

"I thought we should kind of get moving on our parenting plan."

With a slow smile, he shook his head. "Always with the plans."

They stood facing each other on the same side of the counter. She had a strong urge to whirl around, dart over to the table and pull out a chair, put some distance between them. If he came and sat down, too, the table would serve as a barrier to keep her from giving in to the longing inside her.

She felt he was always asking a certain question—he asked it with his eyes and his body language, with his very attentiveness. It was partly *will you marry me?* But it was more, too. He was asking for kisses. And slow, sweet caresses. He was asking for more nights like the ones last winter.

And maybe asking was too weak a word. Maybe he was more...anticipating. Waiting for the moment, the *right* moment to make his move.

What were they talking about?

Parenting plan. Right. "Structure is a good thing." Dear Lord. Could she sound any prissier?

He set his beer on the granite countertop and took a step closer. That brought him right up in her face. She should run for the table—or maybe right on out the door.

But she didn't want to run.

She wanted those kisses his eyes kept promising, wanted to just stand here and suck in the warm, delicious, manly scent of him, to admire the fullness of his lips and the chiseled perfection of his jaw, to drown in the baby blue perfection of those eyes.

"We really don't need a parenting plan, Karin."

"Uh." Her mind felt thick and slow. Warm molasses ran through her veins. "Yes, we do."

"RG is eleven days old. At this point, I just need to be here whenever you want backup or a break. That's my job and we can't put that on a schedule. Not right now. Except when there's something at Bravo Trucking I have to handle ASAP, I'm yours. And RG's. Push comes to shove, you and our son are the priority and my business will just have to get in line."

What he said made perfect sense—not to mention making her feel looked-after, taken-care-of. It would be so very easy to give in, let him have his way about everything.

To let herself fall.

So easy, to love him, to give her heart and soul to him.

Easy and scary and not in her plans. Because it was better, safer, not to start counting on him. Not to let herself give her trust to him and take the chance that eventually he would let her down.

Her poor heart had had enough of that. She just couldn't go through that kind of hurt and disappointment again.

Good men got right behind the idea of stepping up and making a lifetime commitment when a woman needed them. But sometimes, in the long-term execution of that commitment, they started feeling trapped by the very thing they'd sworn they wanted.

Uh-uh. Not going there again.

Liam moved that extra inch closer. She could feel the warmth of him now, smell his clean, manly scent.

Really, he was much too close. She drew in a breath and her breasts met his chest. Her whole body tingled.

She ought to just step back. But she didn't.

He lifted a hand, slowly, the way a person does around a skittish animal, ready to back right off if she gave him the slightest indication she wouldn't welcome his touch.

She could not for the life of her give him that hint. The delicious anticipation was simply too great.

She thought of all the things a woman considers when she's just had a baby and a man looks at her as though he intends to kiss her.

If she ended up with her clothes off, how bad would she look to him? Her belly was too soft and her breasts were blue-veined and swollen, cradled in a nursing bra. Her panties? Plain cotton and not brand-new. How long had it been since she'd washed her hair?

And what did any of that matter?

There was no way she was getting naked with him tonight. She wouldn't get the go-ahead to have sex for weeks yet—not that there weren't a lot of other things short of the main event they could do if they wanted to.

Oh, why was she thinking about sex right now?

Why was she thinking about sex at all?

She wasn't having sex with Liam. Not tonight, not ever. He was her partner in parenting Riley and the last thing they needed was to muck up that important relationship with something as volatile as sex.

"You're blushing." He leaned close and whispered the words into her ear. His breath was so warm, tickling her earlobe and brushing the curve of her cheek. "You smell like heaven, Karin, always did. Now there's a baby lotion and a fresh-baked cookies sort of smell, too." He actually sniffed at her.

"Cookies? Excuse me?"

"Sorry. I smell what I smell and it smells really good." His lips were right there. She felt them, skimming, soft and warm, against her cheek. He nipped at her, gently, like she was an actual cookie and he wanted a taste.

The light pressure of his teeth on her skin made her gasp.

His hand touched her hair, those long fingers gently combing through it, easing out the tangled spots. He used to do that, stroke her hair, when they were in bed together. "I always loved your hair. Since way back when we were kids."

"You didn't." Her voice sounded so odd to her, husky and low.

"Yeah. It's dark as coffee, and shiny, with red glints in sunlight and a blue-black sheen to it by lamplight. And it's always kind of wild, falling every which way. Back when we were kids, I always wanted to stick my fingers in it, to pull on it and bury my face in it."

"I would've punched you out if you'd tried that."

"I kind of thought you might, so I kept my greedy paws to myself—and then in high school, those two dates we had?"

"Don't remind me."

"I wanted more with you, even then."

"Coulda fooled me."

"But we were barely eighteen, much too young to go being exclusive."

She laughed, a husky giggle of a sound that she quickly stifled. "I can't believe I'm standing here whispering with you, and giggling, too, like some brainless fool. I keep telling my-self to step back, step away from you."

He nuzzled her cheek again. "How's that working out for you, Karin?"

"It's not."

"We've got a thing. You know we do."

"Riley is not a thing."

"Karin," he chided. "I'm not talking about RG."

"You *should* be talking about Riley. *We* should be concen-trating on Riley."

His hand left her hair. He trailed a finger down the side of her throat, stirring up a naughty string of hot little shivers as he went. And then he put that finger under her chin to get her to look at him. His eyes burned into hers, the blue color deeper than usual.

"I've missed you," he said, "since you dumped me last March."

"I didn't dump you. How could I dump you? We weren't to-gether."

"Yeah, we were. From that first night, I wasn't with anyone but you. How about you?"

"No. But you know what I mean. It wasn't serious. We weren't even dating."

"Karin."

"What?"

"Shut up." He stole a quick, perfect kiss. Her lips burned at the brief contact. She yearned, she really did. Every molecule in her body hungered for more.

And he knew it, too.

He knew it and he gave her exactly what she couldn't stop herself from wanting. Lowering his amazing mouth, he settled it more firmly over hers.

CHAPTER FIVE

LIAM TOOK CARE to kiss her slowly, with restraint and yet with promise. He knew she was right on the brink of breaking.

And she could break either way—in surrender. Or in flight.

He wanted her surrender, at least as much as he could get of surrender in a kiss.

"I'm not having sex with you," she said breathlessly against his mouth.

"I know." He'd read the damn books, after all.

Framing her boyish, beautiful face between his hands, he broke the kiss to gaze down at her. He'd always loved the way she looked, with those eyes that were blue and then green and then blue again, seeming to change colors in changing light. He admired those high cheekbones, that pointed little chin. And those plump, perfect lips that invited his kiss.

"It's just a kiss," he reminded her.

"Liam," she whispered. He heard longing in that whisper and he swooped in again to give her exactly what she longed for, going deeper this time, urging her to open, to let him in.

She resisted at first, but then, with a tiny groan, she gave it up. His tongue slipped between her softly parted lips and he tasted her fully as he let his hands wander a little, out along her slim shoulders, down her back.

Good. She felt so very good. She was making him ache, making him hurt in the best possible way.

He pulled her closer, pressing his hardness against her, cupping a hand at the back of her head to hold her in place so he could kiss her even more deeply. She was heaven in his arms and he had missed holding her, missed the fire between them, the way they bickered and nipped at each other.

It was really fun, with Karin. She was the girl he'd known forever, and yet the girl who kept changing. He'd lost her in high school because he'd told her right out that he didn't intend to be anyone's boyfriend. Then she'd married Bud Killigan, who was a couple of years older, a guy Liam hardly knew. And then last March, he'd lost her again, lost her before he even got a chance to persuade her she should spend more time with him.

He wouldn't lose her this time. Now they had RG and that made it necessary that they be together. One way or another, he would convince her she belonged with him.

Sometimes he got impatient. It was his nature to be so. But mostly, it didn't matter to him how long it took her to finally realize he was the one for her. Getting there definitely was half the fun.

With a sigh, she pulled away.

"Get back here," he commanded and dipped close to claim her lips again.

She only slid her hands up between them and pressed them flat to his chest, exerting undeniable pressure, the kind a man had no right to ignore. "I have to go, Liam." She gazed up at him, those blue-green eyes so serious. Her soft lips were red and swollen and he was on fire to taste them again.

That wasn't going to happen tonight, though. Reluctantly, he released her.

She stared up at him, looking earnest and adorable and turned on and embarrassed. "I shouldn't have kissed you."

He dared to put a finger against those perfect, swollen lips. "I'm glad you did."

"But we—"

"Karin."

She blew out a hard breath. "What?"

"It was a great kiss. Let it be." He pushed her mug and saucer toward her along the counter.

"Fine." She took the tea bag out of the mug, plopped it on the saucer and took a sip.

He heard a reedy cry from the baby's room.

She heard it, too, and set down the mug. "Time to go."

Could he get her to stay if he tried? Probably not. He'd pushed her enough for one night.

A few minutes later, in the baby's room at the main house, Karin nursed Riley and thought about Liam.

She really shouldn't have kissed him, but she couldn't quite bring herself to regret that she had. That kiss had been amazing. She refused to feel bad about it.

She just needed to make sure it didn't happen again.

That wouldn't be easy. Liam was proving to be a lot more persistent than she'd ever imagined.

Since the day he learned that she was having his baby, he'd gone right to work insinuating himself into every corner of her life. Her brother, her daughter and her dad had definitely fallen under the influence of Liam Bravo's charms.

Sten was all for the guy, lecturing Karin to treat him right, renting him the damn cottage without consulting her. Coco had what amounted to a kiddie crush on the man.

And since the day after Karin and Riley came home from the hospital, Otto and Liam had developed their very own private tradition: morning coffee, the two of them. Her dad would head over there at the crack of dawn. He'd stay for an hour or so and get back to the main house in time for breakfast.

When it wasn't raining, he and Liam would sit out on the mist-shrouded deck of the cottage together. Most mornings, Karin could hear them faintly, talking and laughing, like they were best buds or something.

Ben was the only one who held the line against Liam. Her older son was always polite around any grown-up. But he hadn't really warmed to Liam. He was civil around the baby's father and not much more.

Ben's reserve didn't stop Liam, though. He was always asking about Ben's latest science project and listening with rapt attention when he finally got Ben to open up a little about it. Twice already, he'd picked up Ben and a couple of teammates from soccer practice when Otto was stuck late at the Boatworks.

Okay, yeah. The more she thought it over, the more she came to the simple conclusion that Liam Bravo was amazing. He was amazing and she had a crush on him just like her daughter did.

But really, how long would he be living next door? When would he realize he missed his easy, independent single lifestyle?

Karin just needed to keep herself from counting on him too much. That way, when he finally agreed on a parenting plan and went back to his own life, she wouldn't be brokenhearted, wouldn't miss him too much.

She just needed to watch herself, not let herself start squabbling with him. Squabbling with Liam was far too much fun. And kisses? No more of those. And she really had to avoid any more trips down memory lane. They had far too much history and it made her feel way too fond of him to reminisce with him about stuff that had happened way back when.

No kisses. No reminiscing. No banter.

"I can do that," she said out loud to no one in particular—strongly enough to give Riley a scare. He popped off her breast and blinked up at her, startled.

"Oh, honey, it's okay..." Laughing softly, she guided him back to her nipple. "You've got a good dad and your mama loves you," she whispered to her baby son. "It's all going to work out just beautifully, you'll see."

As a rule, on Halloween, Karin or her dad would take the kids trick-or-treating along the streets above Sweetheart Cove. This year, Ben had declared himself old enough to take Coco without adult supervision and Karin had agreed to that.

But this year, it was raining. Steadily, in buckets. Coco whined all day and Ben looked grim and unhappy.

Around four, Liam showed up at the sliding door that opened onto the deck. Her dad let him in.

"Riley's sleeping," she said to Liam, when the two men joined her in the kitchen area where she was standing at the open fridge trying to decide what to whip up for dinner.

"No problem," Liam replied. "I'm not here to see the baby."

"We need to talk to you." Her dad shot a quick glance around the living area. "Are Coco and Ben still in their rooms?"

"Umm-hmm. I believe Coco is actively sulking because the rain very likely will mess up her Halloween. Ben's not happy about that either. He's focusing his frustration on working out issues with his latest science project, I think."

"As long as they're not in earshot, good." Her dad kept his voice low, just between the three of them. "We need to talk about tonight."

"There's a kids' Halloween party at The Valentine Bay Theater," Liam said. "There'll be games and some skits and a really simple haunted house—nothing too gory. And bags of treats for everyone."

Karin shut the fridge door and turned to face the men. "Right. I saw a flyer somewhere about that."

"It's a Hailey and Harper production, essentially," Liam explained. "Eight bucks a head to get in."

Otto said, "Liam and I were talking about it over coffee this morning, that it might be an option if the rain didn't stop. The kids could wear their costumes and do something a little different this year. Liam and I will take them and you can have the evening to yourself."

"We figured you might not want to take the baby out on a rainy night," added Liam. "And just as another option, if you'd prefer, I can watch RG and you can go with your dad and the kids."

She'd yet to get out her breast pump and she didn't really feel like dealing with that at the moment, anyway. Not to mention, Riley wasn't even two weeks old. She wasn't ready to be away from him for that long.

Liam read her so easily. "Too soon, huh?"

She nodded, though a Halloween party really would cheer the kids up. And to steal a couple of hours for herself?

Talk about a new mom's dream-come-true. "I have to admit, the idea of me and Riley and the second season of *Killing Eve*, that's pretty tempting."

"We thought so." Her dad seemed pleased.

"So we're on?" asked Liam.

She hesitated. Liam made it way too easy for her to say yes to him and his plans.

And come on. What in the world was wrong with that, when his plans inevitably involved ways to help her make life better for herself and her family?

"Thank you," she said to both of them. "I think it's a great idea."

Liam stayed for dinner—it only seemed right to feed the guy, what with him giving up his evening to take her kids out for Halloween.

They set off, the four of them, at a little before six, Coco dressed as Jewel the Dalmatian and Ben, in a light blue jacket and bow tie, as Bill Nye, the Science Guy.

Once they were gone, Karin grabbed a bottle of ginger beer and sat on the sofa. Sipping slowly, she listened to the steady drumming of the rain on the roof and thought that never in the history of women had there been such a perfect moment. Everybody gone except her baby, who was sleeping.

After she finished her pretend beer, she spent an hour on the phone catching up with Prim and Naomi. Then she made popcorn and watched three episodes of *Killing Eve*, only getting up to pee and to feed and change Riley when he cried.

It was after ten when the Science Guy, Jewel the Dalmatian and the two men arrived home. Of course, they'd stopped for ice cream after all the excitement of Harper and Hailey's Halloween extravaganza. Even Ben was jazzed up, sucking on a Starburst from his bag of treats and raving about the cool ways Liam's sisters had used dry ice to make fog.

"Mom. It was sick. That fog, it not only overflowed from the witch's cauldron. They had it pouring out of the mouth of a giant carved pumpkin and rising from the base of a gnarly 'hanging' tree."

Coco was so happy, she pranced in a circle. Her doggy ears bounced as she pawed the air, fake-growling when her grandpa suggested it was time to call it a night.

Otto insisted, though. "Kiss your mom good night and say thank you to Liam."

Ben and Coco dutifully pecked Karin on the cheek and offered up a duet of thank-yous to Liam. Then Otto herded both of them off down the hall to put on their pj's and brush their teeth.

That left Liam on the sofa with Riley in his arms and Karin standing by an easy chair trying to decide whether to sit down or start hinting that it was time for him to go.

He looked up from their son with a lazy, lopsided grin. "Don't worry. I won't stay long."

She couldn't stop herself. She grinned right back at him and then said sincerely, "Thank you. You turned a big disappointment into a memorable event."

"For you. Anything." He said it quietly, kind of tenderly and yet teasingly, too, so that she could tell herself he was only kidding around.

She almost opened her mouth to remind him—teasingly, of course—that they were coparents, not a couple.

But why even say it, jokingly, or otherwise? He hadn't done anything to imply there was more than coparenting going on between them. Not really.

And he looked so relaxed and happy. He'd made her kids happy, too, and given her a precious evening all to herself. How could she keep her walls of emotional safety in place when he wouldn't stop being so damn wonderful?

He got up. "Walk me out?" Still holding the baby, he headed for the entry hall.

She followed along, far too content to be going wherever Liam led her. He turned and passed her the baby when they got to the door.

When she had Riley, though, Liam didn't step back. Uh-uh. He leaned even closer.

And she reminded herself to step back. But she didn't. Anticipation flaring inside her, she stayed right where she was.

Their lips met. Her heart lurched and then kicked into a deeper, hotter rhythm. She sighed against his parted lips.

"Thanksgiving," he said as he broke the tender contact.

Puzzled, and a little annoyed at how much she'd wanted that kiss to last longer, she frowned up at him over their sleeping baby. "Um. What about it?"

"We always have it at Daniel's."

Where was he going with this? "Okay...?"

That mouth she loved kissing way too much curled in a slow, ovulation-inducing smile. "This is an invitation, Karin. I want you and the kids and your dad to join me and the rest of the Bravos for our family Thanksgiving. Rumor has it that Sten and Madison just might be showing up, too."

"Do Daniel and Keely know you're inviting the whole Killigan-Larson crew?"

He did that thing, a lopsided grin coupled with a sexy glint in his sky blue eyes. "Say yes, and they will."

"That just doesn't seem right."

"What do you mean it's not right?" He had that look now, the patient one he gave her whenever she threatened to go off the rails over something he was trying to convince her to do.

"It doesn't seem right for you to just invite all of us without at least warning your brother and his wife first."

"It's a Bravo family thing. The more the better. We love a large group and our Thanksgivings and Christmases just keep getting bigger."

"But think about it. Now, counting Madison, there are nine of you again." A brother, Finn, had vanished years ago. The Bravos still had investigators looking for him.

"Karin." Liam spoke softly, gently, as though she were a not-too-bright child. "I know how many siblings I have."

"Of course you do, but I don't think you realize how many people you could potentially be talking about."

"Sure, I do."

"No. Liam, it could be a *lot* of people."

"Didn't I just say I know that and that it won't be a problem?"

"Think about it. Daniel, Matt, Aislinn and Madison are married, so you have to count their spouses."

"So?"

"So some of those spouses will probably have people *they* want to bring. And let's not forget your great-aunt Daffodil and great-uncle Percy. And Daniel's got three kids."

"Why are you telling me all this stuff I already know? Just FYI, Karin, it's *my* family."

She reminded herself not to raise her voice. She would wake the baby. "Well, I know that," she whispered.

"And guess what? Connor and Aly Santangelo got back together."

That gave her pause. The two had been married and then divorced years ago. "Seriously?"

He nodded. "They're in New York, but they hope to be back for the holidays. They remarried in Manhattan, a courthouse wedding a week and a half ago—the day after Riley was born, as a matter of fact."

"Which only further proves my point. Aly's got that big family of her own here in town. Will *they* all be coming? Liam, do you hear what I'm saying? Maybe there isn't room for four extra guests and a baby."

"It's Daniel's house, the family house. There's *always* room. And who all is coming is not your problem. All you have to say is yes. Just tell me you would love to come and bring the kids. I've already talked to your dad. He's all for it."

"You talked to my dad about it without even checking with me?" She spoke too loudly. Riley squirmed in her arms and let out a cry. She lifted him to her shoulder and rubbed his little back. "Shh," she whispered to him, "it's okay, Mommy's sorry she scared you." She rocked him side-to-side a little and he seemed to settle.

"Karin." Liam reached out.

"Don't." She stepped back to keep him from touching her. She wasn't sure why, exactly, she was so upset about this invitation. It just felt like…a big step. A step she wasn't in any way ready to take. A step she kept telling herself she would never take. "See, Liam. You have your family traditions and we have ours. So, doesn't it just make more sense for you to go ahead and go to your brother's the way you always do for Thanksgiving and we'll just have our family dinner here the way *we* always do."

"No." A muscle twitched in his square jaw. "That makes no sense to me at all. I asked you to come to Daniel's because *that's* what makes sense to me. I want you there, Karin. I want our baby there and your dad and Ben and Coco, too. And Madison and Sten, if they can make it up from LA. I want us all together. That's what Thanksgiving is, all the people you care about the most, together, if at all possible. And it *is* possible, completely possible, if you'll just say yes."

Riley started fussing again. She rubbed his little back, pressed her lips to his warm, silky forehead and said to Liam, "You're being purposely thickheaded."

"*You're* being pointlessly negative and obstinate."

"No, I'm just—"

"Enough." His voice was carefully bland. "Think about it, okay? Let me know what you decide." He pulled open the door and went through, shutting it behind him before she could say another word.

CHAPTER SIX

A WEEK WENT by during which Karin and Liam hardly spoke.

Early most mornings, she heard him laughing with her father out on the deck at the cottage. More than once, she saw him jogging along the sand in a hoodie and track pants, his shoulders so broad, his hips so lean and tight, his long strides carrying him quickly along the shoreline toward the rocks and shallow caves way down the beach. It caused an ache inside her just to watch him, to take in the sheer perfection of him.

Every evening when he returned from Bravo Trucking, he came to the house to visit his son. She would hand the baby over and walk away.

From the kitchen area or down the hall in her room or in the baby's room, she could hear him joking around with Coco and talking to Ben. He would give the baby to her dad when he was ready to leave.

One time, he was still in the great room with Riley in his arms when she wandered back out from her room to check on them. Her dad was nowhere in sight and the kids must've been in their rooms.

"Here's your mama," he said to his son and handed him over. "See you tomorrow, Karin." And he left her standing there by the slider. Turning toward the glass, she stared out at the dark sky. A moment later, she heard the front door open and then close.

Every time she saw Liam, she expected him to ask her if she'd made up her mind about Thanksgiving. She was *waiting* for him to ask, actually. And when he did, she would reply, *Thank you, but no.* She would say that she really had given his invitation serious thought and she appreciated it very much. However, thinking it over hadn't changed her answer; he should go to his family for Thanksgiving and she and her family would have their usual holiday dinner right here at Sweetheart Cove.

But the days went by and Liam didn't ask her, which made her feel edgy and uncomfortable inside her own skin. After all, she knew very well that he didn't *need* to ask again. The ball was in her court. She only had to give him her answer—and that was something she felt ridiculously reluctant to do until he brought it up.

Stalling much? Oh, yes, she was.

On Friday evening, Karin had Riley in the baby sling and had just finished cleaning up the kitchen after dinner when Liam tapped on the slider. She went over and let him in.

He glanced past her shoulder. "Otto okay?" Her dad was conked out, snoring in his favorite chair in front of the TV.

"Just tired. He had a long day rush-retrofitting a fishing boat. As usual, the owner wants the boat back in the water yesterday—sooner if possible."

Liam looked strangely wistful. "The kids?"

"Coco's got a birthday party sleepover. Ben's at a friend's, home at eight."

He came inside, bringing the scent of leather, moist night air and a hint of diesel fuel. "Kind of quiet without them."

"Except for the snoring and the WWE reruns, you mean." She

shut the slider, extricated the baby from the sling and handed him over. "Here you go."

He got Riley settled on one arm and then held out a check.

She took it and saw it was made out to her. "Five hundred dollars? What for?"

"To help out with Riley. Since he's mostly with you at this point, I figure five hundred a month, for now. You need more?"

"Of course not." She had a terrible, hollow feeling in her belly as she realized he must be leaving, moving out of the cottage. Just as she'd expected, he was missing his big house and his no-strings lifestyle, so he was going to throw her some monthly child support and go back to his own life.

He spotted the cloth diaper she'd left on the back of a chair and grabbed it, laying it on one broad shoulder and lifting Riley against his chest. "Okay, Karin. Tell me what's the matter."

"Nothing," she lied.

"Then how come your face is red and your mouth's all pinched up?"

"I don't know what you're talking about."

"You're pissed off."

"No, I'm not." She folded her arms across her middle, realized how defensive the posture must look and made herself drop her hands to her sides. "So. When are you leaving?"

He whispered something to the baby and then frowned down at her. "Leaving?"

"Uh, well, I assume you're going back to your own place?"

"No. I live at the cottage now." He studied her, still frowning. "What gave you the idea I was moving out?"

She held up the check. "Well, I mean. I thought…" What *had* she thought? Now, she just felt foolish. "I don't know. I thought you were, um…"

"Paying you off because I won't be around?"

When he put it that way, it sounded awful—even though that was exactly what she'd thought. She waved the check again. "If you're next door, there's no need for this right now, is there?"

"What's my being next door got to do with paying my share of my son's living expenses?"

Nothing, she realized, and felt even more foolish.

He stroked the baby's head with his big hand. "I get it. The Larson-Killigan family is doing just fine. You're not hurting for cash and all the bills are getting paid."

"You'd best believe it."

"So open an account for him. Get going on his college fund. It's RG's money so save it for when he needs it."

Karin cast an uncomfortable glance at her snoring father. "Let's go talk in Riley's room."

"Sure." He followed her across the great room and down the hall.

She ushered him into the baby's room ahead of her. "Well," she said, after shutting the door. "I just thought we would get a parenting plan—you know, a legal, binding agreement. Whatever support arrangement we would make would happen then."

"Why go to court if we can come to an agreement without dragging the state of Oregon into it?"

It was a valid question. Damn it. "I don't know, I…" She blew out a hard breath and busted herself. "Okay, I'm sorry. I jumped to the conclusion that there was no need to start writing me checks unless you were moving out."

He seemed to relax, a ghost of a smile pulling at the edges of his too-tempting mouth. "Apology accepted—and I'm staying right here at the Cove. Get used to it."

The room was too small and he was too big and solid and masculine, standing there holding their baby in his strong arms, not quite smiling as he gazed down at her.

"Okay, then," she said, her voice aggressively cheerful, totally fake. "I'll leave you with Riley and, um, I'm right down the hall if you need me."

"That's good to know." He said it too softly, but with a slight edge of roughness that played a sexy, hungry tune on every nerve ending she had.

She pulled open the door and got out of there, fast.

* * *

That following Monday Karin went back to work on a part-time basis. Her plan was to go in for a few hours a day and take Riley with her.

But then when Liam showed up at the door Monday night and she mentioned that she was trying to catch up at the Boat-works, he offered to help out. "I can take Riley for you, at least a couple of times a week," he said.

"But what about Bravo Trucking?"

"It's great being the boss. I can pretty much set my own hours."

There was so much to catch up on. She could get a lot more done without the baby there to interrupt her. "You sure?"

"Yeah. We should try it. See how it goes. How 'bout Wednesday, nine to noon, to start?"

It was too good an offer to pass up. "All right, then. You're on."

Two days later, she dropped Riley off at the cottage. Liam had everything he needed right there, all the baby paraphernalia a newborn could ever require. All she had to provide was enough pumped breast milk to keep Riley fed until noon.

She passed Liam the baby and set the bottles on the counter. "The milk can be out of the fridge for four hours. If you put it in the fridge, you want to bring it just to body temperature by running warm water over the bottle or letting it sit in warm water."

He kissed Riley's plump cheek and gave her a smug grin. "I've read all the books, Karin."

She bopped her forehead with the heel of her hand. "That's right. You're an expert."

"Yes, I am. Don't you worry. RG and me, we got it all figured out."

When she returned at noon, Liam handed her the sleeping baby.

"How was he?" she whispered.

"Perfect. I can take him Friday, same time?"

"You're on. Thank you." She started to turn for the stairs.

"Karin." Something in his voice sent a lovely shiver racing down her spine. She stopped and met his eyes again. "You don't have to thank me. I hope you know that."

She cradled Riley closer. It was cold out that day. "I, um, well, I appreciate all you do to help out."

"It's my job," he said and she knew he was going to say more. Stuff she probably didn't want to hear. Maybe he was finally going to ask her for her decision on Thanksgiving...

But then he only gave a slight shake of his golden head. "Go on back to the other house. It's cold out."

Relief and guilt swirling through her in equal measure, she turned and hurried down the stairs.

That Saturday night after the kids were in bed, Karin curled up in her room with a fast-paced thriller on her e-reader.

Her dad appeared and tapped on her open door. "Got a minute?"

"Sure." She set the device aside.

Otto just stood there in the doorway, looking at her.

"Dad. What?"

He stuck his hands in the pockets of his ancient Carhartt work pants. He wore a plain white T-shirt and she found herself staring at his arms. They were strong arms from a lifetime of hard work, strong and scarred, freckled and dusted with reddish hair now gone mostly gray. Otto Larson was a good man, a man who had dedicated his life to taking care of his family.

"I'm just gonna say it, Kary. You need to give Liam Thanksgiving. He wants it, a lot. He's gotten himself all invested in this one simple thing, for our family and his family to celebrate Thanksgiving together."

"Dad—"

"I'm not finished. Liam's been nothing but here for you in every way that you'll let him be. Even if you can't give him all that he wants from you, you can say yes to Thanksgiving, you know you can."

"All that he wants from me? What does that even mean?"

Her father looked smug. "You really want to go there?"

She didn't. No way. "He sent *you* after me?" It came out sour and accusing. Because it was.

"No. He asked me what I thought of the idea and I said I was all for it. That was more than two weeks ago. He said he would ask you and then he didn't say anything more about it for days. So *I* asked *him* where we were on that. He said you were *thinking it over.* How long you planning on thinking about it before you actually give the poor man an answer?"

Her dad rarely annoyed her. But right now, he was definitely rattling her cage. "Liam Bravo is a long way from a 'poor man.'"

"Well, I for one feel sorry for the guy when it comes to you—and no. I'm not saying you should give him more than you're willing to give him. I'm saying it's Thanksgiving. And I know that *I'm* thankful for a man who is turning out to be a real dad to little Riley and who has knocked himself out to help you any way he can and been stepping right up for your other two children, too, showing an interest in who they are and what they're up to, driving them to and from wherever they need to go, even coming up with the perfect alternative when Halloween got rained out."

Everything her dad was saying?

True.

She pulled at a thread on the comforter. "You're right," she muttered reluctantly. "He's a terrific guy."

"So show him you appreciate all he's done. Say yes, we would love to go to Daniel Bravo's house for Thanksgiving."

When he put it like that, how could she say no? "Okay."

"What's that? Speak up."

"Fine, Dad. I'll accept Liam's invitation to Thanksgiving with the Bravos."

"Great. How 'bout doing that right now? All three kids are in bed and the lights are on over at the cottage."

Liam heard the tap on the slider and glanced that way. It was Karin, in flannel pajamas printed with penguins, a pair of Uggs and old Portland State hoodie with the hood pulled up over her hair.

"Got a minute?" she asked when he let her in.

He stared down at her upturned face, at that smart little mouth he couldn't wait to kiss again. "What do you need?"

She pushed the hood off her hair. "That Thanksgiving invitation still on the table?"

He felt a punch to his chest. The good kind, like his heart was reminding him that it was still beating. He could see her answer right there in those beautiful eyes. "You're saying yes?"

She nodded up at him, eyes bright and full of light, her face scrubbed clean of makeup, her dark hair a nimbus of shiny, wild curls. "We would love to come. All of us. You really think Daniel and Keely will be able to handle the crowd?"

"No problem."

"Well, okay, then. I'll, um, let you go..."

He caught her arm. "Just a second."

"Hmm?"

"This." He wrapped his other arm around her and swooped down to claim her lips.

She didn't resist.

On the contrary, she slid those pretty, slim, hardworking hands of hers up his chest and hooked them around his neck. "I didn't come here to kiss you," she said, as she kissed him.

He pulled her even closer. "Sometimes good things happen when you least expect them."

She laughed, her breath sweet with a hint of minty toothpaste, her body soft and warm in his arms.

He'd spent a lot of his life avoiding giving his heart. It was all due, he'd told himself, to the tragedies in his family when he was a kid—the disappearance of a brother, the sudden death of both parents. Loving people hurt so bad when you lost them and he loved too many people already. It was too late for him with his brothers and sisters, with Great-Uncle Percy and Great-Aunt Daffodil. He loved them before he learned the sad lesson that love ended up meaning loss that ripped you up inside.

But at least, his younger self had concluded, he could avoid the awful emotional danger of loving a woman.

His younger self hadn't known squat.

It took the birth of RG to show him the big picture. Karin had always been the one for him. All these years, he'd thought he'd dodged the love bullet. Wrong. He'd just been waiting for the right time to admit the truth to himself: Karin Larson Killigan owned his heart.

Sadly, Karin now seemed as determined as he used to be not to go there. He had a bad feeling that for her, the right time to give her heart to anyone was never.

She would probably mess him over royally. He'd get just what he'd always feared out of this deal: disappointment, hurt and the kind of loss that ripped a man's guts out.

He'd get everything he'd always been afraid of.

And he didn't even care. He wanted her and their baby. He wanted serious Ben, bubbly little Coco and stalwart, big-hearted Otto, too. He wanted to make a family with all of them, his deepest fears be damned.

If only he could find the way to get her to say yes to him.

"Liam." She sighed, her soft lips parting. He tasted her, nice and deep and slow.

Until she pulled back and her eyes fluttered open.

He touched her sweet, pointy chin, guided a wild curl behind the curve of her ear. *I want to marry you, Karin.* It sounded really good inside his head.

He almost went ahead and said it.

But he had a crappy feeling that laying another proposal on her right now would just ruin a great moment.

She'd given him Thanksgiving. He'd kissed her and she'd kissed him back.

For now, he would call it a win and not push his luck.

As it turned out, Sten and Madison couldn't make it home for Thanksgiving. Connor Bravo and his wife Aly didn't come either. They were still in New York, where Aly was training her successor at the advertising firm where she'd worked for the past seven years.

But even with two siblings and their spouses unavailable, Daniel and Keely's big house on Rhinehart Hill overflowed with family on Thanksgiving Day. The rest of the Bravo siblings came, including Matt with his wife, Sabra, and Aislinn with her husband, Jaxon, and also the housekeeper and foreman from Wild River Ranch where they lived. Keely's mom, Ingrid, and Keely's aunt, Gretchen, had arrived at the crack of dawn to help with cooking and general holiday prep. The food looked amazing. They had turkey, a gorgeous ham and a beautiful prime rib. And more sides than Karin could count.

Harper and Hailey, the family event planners, had set up ongoing games of turkey bowling and pin the feather on the turkey for anyone who wanted to play. They had a big pumpkin-shaped jar full of candy corn and made everyone guess how many candy kernels were inside for a possible prize of...a big bag of candy corn.

Daniel's twins, Frannie and Jake, were three now, happy kids who talked nonstop. Keely's baby, Marie, born the previous January, was already learning to walk. Marie staggered around on her fat little legs, constantly falling and dragging herself upright to try again. She was also a big talker, though her endless chatter made sense only to her.

Coco found Marie enchanting and spent a good portion of the afternoon holding the baby's fat little hand, helping her in her shaky efforts to stay on her feet. The attention delighted

Marie to no end. She beamed up at Coco like she'd found a new best friend.

Ben took an interest in the twins. He bundled them up in their winter coats and took them out to the backyard for a long walk around the garden paths. The Bravo family basset hound, Maisey Fae, loped along in their wake.

Everyone made a big deal over Riley. Grace Bravo, the youngest of Liam's siblings, offered Karin her bedroom off the kitchen for a private place to nurse. Gracie suggested that Riley could have her bed if he dropped off to sleep—which he did, about a half hour or so before the big meal. Keely gave Karin a baby monitor to use and she surrounded Riley with pillows and left him to nap.

When they sat down to eat, Great-Uncle Percy and Great-Aunt Daffy each gave a toast. Percy raised his glass to long life. Daffy, to true love. Aunt Gretchen said grace.

Karin, seated next to Liam at one of the two long pushed-together tables, felt his big, warm hand brush hers under the table as Gretchen recited her sweet prayer of thanks.

It was good, Karin thought, to catch up with the Bravos again. She'd put up a lot of resistance to coming here today. And now she found herself grateful that her dad had convinced her she needed to say yes to Liam's invitation.

As amens echoed around the packed table, she gave the man her hand, even opening her fingers a little, lacing them with his at his urging.

He leaned close. "I'm glad you're here."

She met those beautiful eyes and almost wished…

Well, better not even to let herself complete that thought. "Me, too," she replied. "I'm glad you invited us."

He gave her a smile that made the tall white candles in the middle of the table seem to burn even brighter. "So, you're having a good time?"

"I am. Very much so."

A teasing gleam made his eyes look even bluer. "Clearly, you should say yes to me more often."

Should she?

Doubtful. Coparents needed to respect each other's space. However, Liam Bravo was turning out to be a whole lot more than she'd ever bargained for. He was not only hot and tempting, but so persuasively persistent, as well. He was good to her kids and friends with her dad and thoroughly determined to do right by his child. She would be lying if she tried to tell herself she didn't find him extraordinarily attractive on a whole lot of levels.

He leaned a fraction closer. "What is that secretive smile you're giving me?"

"Just thinking that you're a really good dad." And he *was* a good dad, so she'd only told him the truth—only not all of the truth.

He laughed. "Do you give that look to all the good dads?"

And she went ahead and answered honestly. "Only you, Liam."

His thumb slipped in between their joined hands. He stroked her palm. It felt so good, so wonderfully thrilling and deliciously naughty.

And she was probably losing her mind a little what with all this...thankfulness she was feeling. Losing her mind and getting crazy ideas.

Ideas like how maybe she ought to be more open to him, to this attraction she felt for him.

Okay, yeah. She knew very well it would be better, smarter, not to mix their mutual parenting responsibilities with physical intimacy.

However, they were really good together in that way. They had chemistry, an excess of it. She'd always been drawn to him, since way back in high school. And the nights they'd shared at the first of the year still fueled her fantasies all these months and months later.

And now he lived right next door.

With every day that passed in which he was funny and kind and thoughtful, helpful and gentle and patient and so understanding—not to mention superhot—well, it just got harder and harder to remember that keeping a certain distance between them was key. It got harder and harder not to wonder why they shouldn't enjoy themselves a little.

As long as they both went into it with their eyes open, as long as they agreed that it didn't have to go anywhere, that they could be together just for now and just for fun. That if it didn't work out in the long run, they would act like adults, reestablish the boundaries and go on as Riley's parents who weren't together but wanted the best for their son.

Didn't divorced people do that all the time?

Really, if they kept it just between the two of them, didn't let the kids or her dad know, so that no one got unrealistic expectations of how things might turn out...

Well, she couldn't stop asking herself, what could it hurt?

CHAPTER SEVEN

THE LARSON-KILLIGAN family had a tradition.

On the Saturday after Thanksgiving, they all went out together and chopped down their Christmas tree. They brought it home and stood it up in the picture window in the great room. From the attic, they hauled down box after box, each one packed full of Christmas decorations collected over the past three generations.

Then they all worked together decorating the tree, decking the fireplace mantel with boughs and twinkly lights and setting up the crèche that had belonged to Karin's mother's mother.

That morning, Liam appeared on the back deck just as Karin, Otto and the kids were sitting down to breakfast before heading to Oja's Christmas Tree Farm.

Karin glanced up and saw him standing there. She knew what was going on without having to ask, but she turned to her dad, anyway. "Looks like someone invited Liam."

"That's good!" enthused Coco. She bounced from her seat and darted over to the door, the black towel she wore for a cape flopping in her wake.

Otto swallowed a bite of pancake. "He has that Supercrew F-150. The console in front turns into a seat, so there's room in the cab for all of us and the long bed is perfect for hauling the tree home."

"Good thinking," Karin said wryly.

Coco, all in black to match her "cape," shoved the slider wide and threw out her arms to the sides. "Hi, Liam! I'm Raven. I have instant healing for me and for others. I travel to different dimensions. I teleport and *astro projet*—"

"She means 'astral project,'" Ben corrected.

Coco turned and glared at him. "You interrupted me. That's rude."

"Sorry," said Ben and crunched a bite of bacon. "But you might as well get it right."

Coco sighed, the sigh of all sisters put-upon by older brothers. "Now I can't 'member the rest—but come in, Liam. Have some pancakes. We got blueberry syrup and plenty of bacon."

Karin, who found she was not the least annoyed that her dad had invited Liam without consulting her, started to rise. "I'll get you a—"

"Don't get up." He was smiling at her, the smile she somehow felt was only for her. "I know where the plates and coffee mugs are."

"Well, all right." They shared a long look full of humor and promise and banked heat, one of those looks she decided she didn't need to think too deeply about. Not now, not on tree-decorating day.

It was good, what she felt for him. She might as well enjoy that goodness, whatever might or might not happen next.

Bottom line, she was getting used to having Liam in her day-to-day life. He wasn't going away and she could either accept the situation gracefully or grump around like a shrew trying to protect herself from some possible future heartache.

And yeah. Overthinking. She needed to cut that out, too.

Liam poured himself some coffee and carried his full mug

and a place setting to the empty chair across from her. Karin pushed the platter of pancakes his way and he took four. Otto passed him the bacon.

Coco announced, "Here's the butter and the blueberry syrup for you, Liam."

"Thanks." He captured Karin's gaze again. Little zings of fizzy excitement went zipping all through her. "RG?"

"He went back to sleep after I fed him." She tipped her head at the baby monitor perched on the counter. "So far, not a peep."

"Eat up, folks," said Otto. "The tree farm opens at ten."

For once, the weather cooperated. It was cold out, but clear. They bundled up in winter gear and piled into Liam's big pickup. Otto and Ben sat in front with Liam. Karin sat in the middle in back, Riley in his car seat on one side and Coco in hers on the other.

At the farm, they wandered up and down the rows of trees, finally settling on a nine-foot noble fir with gorgeous, thick branches in majestic even tiers.

Back at the Cove, they took a break for hot chocolate with miniature marshmallows. Then Karin cued up her holiday playlist. To the holiday stylings of Bette Midler and Michael Bublé, Weezer and NSync, they brought the tree in and stood it up in the tree stand. After that, they trooped up and down the stairs until every box of tinsel, lights and decorations was stacked in the great room, ready to roll.

Once they had the lights on the tree, they stopped for soup and sandwiches.

Karin was having a ball. She loved getting out all the old decorations, remembering who had made or bought or gifted the family each one, and when. They took turns holding Riley when he wasn't napping. Karin got out her phone and snapped lots of pictures. Liam did, too.

It was great, the perfect family activity, all of them working together to kick off another year of Christmas memories, the house all warm and cozy, full of holiday tunes and the smell of evergreen. Karin missed having Sten there, but Liam fit right in. Everything was perfect.

Or it was until they got around to setting up the crèche and Liam suggested, "The baby Jesus in the manger should be right in the middle, under the star."

And Ben piped up in his coolest, most dismissive Little Professor voice, "We like it a little to the side. And I don't think you even really need to be here, Liam. We've been doing this for years without you and we don't need you now."

Poor Liam, standing there with Riley on one arm and the manger with its glued-in hay bedding in his opposite hand, didn't seem to know what to say.

Otto stepped in. "Liam's here because I invited him," he said in a careful tone.

Ben chewed his lower lip. He looked miserable. Had he been this way all day?

Karin couldn't believe she hadn't noticed till now that her serious, levelheaded older son wasn't his usual agreeable self. She asked gently, "What's going on, Ben?"

He stuck his hands in the pockets of his tan jeans and hunched his thin shoulders. "Well, I just mean, we do Christmas with the family and he's not our family. He's not my dad or Coco's dad. He's just the baby's dad."

Apparently, that was too much for Coco. "Benjamin Killigan, you are not being nice."

Ben scowled at her, defiant at first. But then his face kind of crumpled. "Okay." He set down the star that fit into the steepled roof of the stable and turned to Liam. "I'm sorry. I shouldn't have said that stuff."

"Ben." Liam tried to reassure him. "It's all right."

"No, it's not. It's not all right. It's not all right at all." And he darted around Otto's easy chair and took off down the hall. They heard his bedroom door slam shut.

For a moment, no one spoke. There was just Bette Midler singing "Have a Yule that's cool…"

Liam glanced down at the baby asleep in his arms, and then back up at Karin. "Maybe I should go."

"No, you shouldn't." She held his gaze. "Please stay."

Her dad backed her up. "Yeah. Don't go. Your leaving won't solve anything."

For once, Coco had nothing to add. She stood by the sofa, blue eyes big and sad, glancing from one grown-up to the other as though hoping one of them would do what grown-ups are supposed to do and make it all better.

Karin suggested, "Why don't you guys go ahead and put the crèche together? I'll talk to Ben."

When Karin tapped on her older son's door, he didn't answer. She counted slowly to thirty before trying, "Ben?"

He responded then. "It's open."

She turned the knob and pushed the door inward. Ben sat on his bed hunched over his laptop, looking absolutely miserable and completely not-Ben. Her brilliant oldest child usually took things in stride and never lost his cool.

Karin asked, "May I come in?" She got a shrug for an answer and decided to consider it a yes. When she sat down beside him, the screen of the laptop showed he'd brought up his favorite video game, but hadn't started playing it.

He shut the laptop and set it aside. "What?"

She wrapped an arm around him. He stiffened at first, but then gave in and sagged against her. She dared to drop a kiss on the crown of his head. "I'm not sure where to start. Maybe if you told me what's bothering you?"

He tipped his head back. Their eyes met, but only for a moment. Then he looked down again. "I don't know, really," he muttered in the general direction of the floor. "I miss Uncle Sten. And now there's the baby. It's not Liam's fault, I know that. He's nice, but…" He made a frustrated sound in his throat.

"Look. Everything's just different, okay? Everything's *not* the same." He looked up and their eyes met again. She smoothed his hair. It was one fussy, motherly caress too many. "Mom. Don't." He scooted out from under her arm.

Her heart ached as she let him go. Somehow, she managed to let several seconds of silence elapse before trying again. "Uncle Sten won't be gone forever."

He shot her a look of pure annoyance. "Two years. At least. Until Madison gets through making those movies she already signed up to make." Sten and Madison would settle right here in the Cove once Madison had honored her outstanding contracts. She said she was giving up acting, that she wanted a different kind of life—a family with Sten, a home in Valentine Bay.

"In the meantime, though," Karin reminded her unhappy son, "they'll be back whenever they can—including over Christmas. They both seem pretty sure they'll make it home during the holidays."

"Mom. I know that. And I just told you. It's not the same that they come back to visit. Like they're *guests* or something."

"I'm sorry, honey. It's just…the way life is. Stuff changes, you know? People move away. But the happy news is that, in Uncle Sten and Aunt Madison's case, they eventually will come back."

"I *know*, Mom. And I get that you want to make me feel better, but can you please quit telling me stuff I already know?"

"I'm just trying to find out exactly what has you upset, that's all. You mentioned the baby…"

He lifted one shoulder in a sort of half-hearted shrug, but that was all she got.

She suggested, "So the baby's just more stuff changing and that makes you feel unhappy?"

"Mom?"

"Hmm?"

"Can we just…not be doing this right now? Can I just go back out there and say sorry again to Liam and we can fix up the manger with the baby Jesus in the middle and just have a nice time finishing up the decorations?"

"Of course we can. But I do want you to know that I'm here and ready to listen whenever you want to talk some more about this."

He dropped his head back and groaned at the ceiling. "Mom." He must have stretched that word into at least three syllables. "I *know.* Can we go back out now, please?"

She ought to just leave it at that. But she couldn't stop herself from taking one more stab at making things right for him. "I love you, Ben. I always have and I always will. Having another baby in the family can't change how much I love you or how much Uncle Sten loves you or your grandpa, either. We all love you so much. That's the one thing that is never going to change."

"I know, Mom." He said it kindly that time, with only a hint of exasperation. "I love you, too."

They returned to the great room, where Ben went straight to Liam. "I really am sorry for what I said."

"Apology accepted," Liam answered in that easy way he had. "And you know, I think you're right about baby Jesus. A little to the side is better than directly under the star."

At ten that night, Liam was in the office he'd set up at the cottage. With RG to consider, he wasn't spending as much time at Bravo Trucking as he used to. Having a baby meant rearranging priorities and being more flexible.

He could get a lot done from home, he'd discovered, working at night when RG was with Karin. He liked to watch the fuel situation closely, change his buying strategy whenever better options presented themselves. And he kept on top of the shippers and the brokers he used. Trucking was a cash flow intensive business. If people started paying late, he needed to know and either stop dealing with them or make sure they started paying timely again.

The doorbell rang just as he was thinking he would call it a night.

What do you know? It was Karin—in blue pajamas dotted with snowflakes this time and a green hoodie. Same Uggs as before.

"Is it too late?" she asked.

"For you?" He couldn't stop himself from grinning. "Never."

She held up her phone. "My dad will call if Riley wakes up."

"You should have just brought him over."

"No." She raked the hoodie off her head, revealing all those untamed curls he loved. "It's always best to let sleeping babies lie."

Liam stepped back and ushered her in. "You want a drink or something?" he offered as he shut the door.

She shook her head. And then she took a step forward.

And then, without him having to do anything but open his arms, she was flush against him, all sweet warmth and perfect softness. She surged up. Her mouth met his and clung.

God. She tasted good. He could kiss her forever. No woman had ever felt as right as she did in his arms.

She dropped back to her heels, breaking the kiss, but letting him hold her. "I've been telling myself that we should…" The words petered out. She frowned up at him, her cheeks pink, her breath coming fast. "I don't know how to say this."

"Sure you do." He bent and brushed a kiss between her eyebrows. "Take your time."

"Could we maybe sit down?" She seemed nervous. It was cute. Like they were back in high school again and she wasn't quite sure how to act with a guy.

He took her hand and led her toward the main room. In the sitting area, he turned on the gas fire and pulled her over to sit beside him on the couch. She set her phone on the coffee table. "Okay. It's like this. I was thinking that maybe you and I could kind of see where this thing might go between us."

Satisfaction filled him. At last they were getting somewhere.

He couldn't resist pressing the point a little. "So you're finally admitting that we had a thing—that we *are* a thing?"

She groaned and covered her face with her hands. "Okay. Let's not get caught up in the *thing* controversy again."

"Just admit it's there, between you and me, and I'll let it go."

She dropped her hands, squared her shoulders and drew in a slow breath. "Then yes, okay? It's definitely *there*, between us."

"It never went away."

She pursed up those way-too-kissable lips. "Is this you letting it go?"

He touched her hair—and she didn't duck away. Taking total advantage of this perfect moment in which she was finally saying at least part of what he wanted to hear, he guided a wild curl behind the shell of her ear. "So maybe I want to rub it in a little. Sue me."

She poked him in the side with an elbow. "You're just asking for it, mister."

"You bet I am."

She laughed. And then she sighed. Her cheeks were bright pink. He found her irresistible like this, all shy and kind of awkward. "I was, um, thinking, hoping that we could just have it be between you and me, not say anything to the kids or my dad."

He didn't want to be her secret. He'd *never* wanted to be that. And he especially didn't want to be her secret anymore. But he also didn't want to blow this chance with her. "*Yet*, you mean. Not say anything to anyone *yet*."

"Yes, Liam. I mean, you know, see where it goes."

That didn't sound so bad—scratch that. It sounded damn good. For now, anyway. "Agreed." He took her by the shoulders and pulled her close.

She let him, even tucked her dark head under his chin. They sat quietly, staring into the fire. He stroked her hair some more, kissed the crown of her head and breathed in the citrusy scent of her shampoo. She shifted and let out a sigh.

"What?"

"Nothing." The way she said it, he knew there was definitely something.

"You worried about Ben?"

She didn't answer immediately, but when she did, she told the truth. "Yeah, a little. I think he feels kind of left out. Coco's such a charmer. Her heart is wide open. She's never had a problem demanding what she needs. Ben's the serious one and sometimes he kind of fades into the background. Now there's another boy in the family. Ben's no longer the only son."

Liam stroked a hand down her arm. It felt so good, just to sit here, the two of them, touching. Talking. "And then there's the baby's dad who isn't *his* dad, a guy who moved in next door and is always butting in on all the family events."

"Ben loved the Halloween party," she reminded him. "And he seemed to have a great time at Daniel's on Thanksgiving."

"But then I kind of pushed my luck with baby Jesus, huh?"

She chuckled, the sound both sweet and rueful. "Ben does think you're a good guy, though. He's said so more than once." She tipped her head back and met his eyes. Hers were sea-blue in the firelight, and troubled. "The truth is, Ben didn't really have a great relationship with Bud—I don't mean Bud was abusive or anything. He was a good man, but kind of hard to talk to. He was gone a lot, working. And when he came home, he was distant and distracted. There were money problems. Plus, Bud hardly knew his own dad. His parents got divorced when he was only two and Bud stayed with his mom, and then she died when he was just nineteen. He didn't seem to know where to start trying to be a dad himself. He was better with Coco, but with Ben he just kind of wasn't *there*."

It was a lot, what she was telling him. More than she'd ever said about her husband before. Liam knew he had no right to resent the guy, but he did. For causing Karin pain and making her wary of trying again—because no matter how she tried to be fair to her husband's memory, it was pretty damn clear that Ben, Sr. had not been around as much as he should have.

In a weird, twisted and unacceptably selfish way, Liam resented that Karin had married the other guy in the first place. If she'd only waited until he got his head out of his own ass, he would have had a lot easier time convincing her she belonged with him.

But then, if she'd waited, there would've been no Ben and no Coco. And the more he got to know Karin's kids, the less he could picture a world without them in it.

She pulled away from him and sat up. "I guess that was way more information than you ever needed."

"Get back here." He caught her arm, but gentled his hold—and his attitude. "Please?"

"I did love Bud." She met his gaze, defiant. "But it was young love, you know?"

He didn't, not really. Releasing her arm, he trailed his fingers over the worn, soft fabric of her sleeve until he captured her hand. "The kind you grow out of?" He turned her hand over and bent close to kiss the heart of it.

"The kind that isn't strong enough to weather the rough patches."

He tugged on her fingers until she swayed toward him again. Gathering her in, he tipped up her chin and took her mouth. She opened for him and he sank into the kiss, drawing it out, making it last.

When he finally lifted his head, he eased both hands under her hair, lacing his fingers at the nape of her neck, tipping her face up to him with slow strokes of his thumbs. "I want to ask Ben if he'll come with me to Bravo Trucking. I was thinking tomorrow, just him and me, a drive up to Warrenton in the afternoon."

"You're looking for my permission?"

"I am, yeah."

"What if he turns you down?"

"That's okay. I'm not gonna pressure him. If he says no, I'll say it's an open invitation. If he changes his mind, he just needs to let me know and we'll make it happen."

She dipped her chin in a nod. "It's all right with me—but be prepared for Coco to want to come, too."

"I was more thinking a one-on-one with Ben."

"I get it. Just giving you a heads-up."

He didn't want Coco feeling left out. "I'll take her, too. Just her and me, another time."

"That actually might pacify her. But are you sure you want to be driving my kids back and forth to Warrenton to take the Bravo Trucking tour?"

"I'm sure." He kissed her again. Because she tasted so good and she'd admitted she wanted him. It wasn't enough, what she was offering, to be together, but only in secret. Not nearly enough.

But it was a start.

And from now on, he needed to have his hands and his mouth on her every chance he got.

That kiss led to another. And another after that. He actually had her hoodie unzipped before she called a halt.

"I need to get back." She zipped up again. "Morning comes early when you've got three kids."

"Damn," he said with a smile. "For a minute there, I thought I was about to get lucky."

"You are." She leaned close and caught his earlobe between her teeth. At his groan, she laughed. "Just not tonight."

He asked only half-teasingly, "Do you have your doctor's approval to fool around with me?"

"I will. My checkup's on Monday." She bunched up his shirt in her fist and yanked him close for another smoking kiss. "And this time we're using two forms of birth control."

"I've got the condoms."

"Great. And after Riley was born, I got an implant before I left the hospital."

"Taking no chances, huh?"

"That's right." She kissed him again, but pulled away much too soon. "You'd better come over for breakfast. You can talk to Ben then. I'll help you out with Coco, say I need her at home to get going on the Christmas baking."

"Works for me." He yanked her close again and covered her mouth with his. For a moment, she gave in and let him hold her.

But only a moment. "I mean it." She grabbed her phone. "I need to go home."

Reluctantly, he followed her to the door.

The next morning, as usual, Otto came by the cottage for coffee.

Liam mentioned that he hoped to take Ben up to Warrenton that day to show him around Bravo Trucking.

"Kissing up to my grandson, huh?"

"You'd better believe it."

"You'll make Coco jealous."

"Coco will get an invite of her own."

Otto set his mug down on the table and stared out the slider. It was raining pretty hard, the sound a steady drumming on the roof and the deck. "Is that what Karin needed to talk to you about last night—you taking the kids to Warrenton?"

Liam shook his head. "The tour of Bravo Trucking was my idea."

Otto gave him a long, considering look. "So what *did* my daughter want to talk to you about last night?"

Liam got up, got the coffeepot and refilled their mugs. "Lots of things," he replied, mindful of his promise to Karin that they'd keep their new togetherness just between the two of them for now. "We've got a kid. There's all kinds of stuff we need to deal with, day to day."

Otto Larson was nobody's fool. His mouth curved in a secret smile. "You're saying you'll need to spend time, just the two of you, on a regular basis to discuss RG's care, is that what you're telling me?"

"Pretty much."

Otto stared out the window some more. Dawn was slowly breaking, revealing a gray, overcast sky. "She had a rough time, with Bud—and don't get me wrong. Bud wasn't a bad guy. Just too young, wanting to do the right thing and yet not quite up to the job. You'd better be good to her."

"I'm trying, Otto."

"I know, son. I like that about you."

At breakfast, Liam made his move. "I need to head to Bravo Trucking today for a couple of hours. Ben, would you like to ride along with me?"

Ben looked up from his scrambled eggs. His eyes were wary. "What for?"

"Thought you might get a kick out of a tour of the place." He sent a quick smile in Karin's direction, but didn't let his gaze linger. She looked way too damn pretty in a flannel shirt with her hair escaping every which way from the messy bun she'd put it in. "I already cleared it with your mom."

Karin confirmed that. "Fine with me if you want to go."

"Could be fun." Liam kept his tone offhand. "Check out a diesel engine, maybe go for a ride in a semitruck."

Those serious brown eyes flashed with interest, but Ben played it cool. "Okay, I'll go."

"Good. We'll leave in an hour or so, maybe grab a burger on the way back?"

"Sure. I'll be ready."

Coco had somehow managed to restrain herself till then. But she was not the kind of girl to let a good time pass her by. "'Scuse me, Liam? *I* like trucks. Can I please go with you guys?"

"Not today, honey." Karin eased in gracefully with her interference play. "I really need your help with the Christmas cookies."

"But what about Ben? He always helps, too. We should all help because helping is good."

"I kind of want to see that engine," Ben ruefully confessed.

Karin suggested, "I'm also going to need help next weekend with the fudge and divinity and candy cane bark."

Liam trotted out his perfect solution. "How 'bout this? Ben and I will go this week. Coco, I'll take you with me next week. You can each see the trucks and help your mom with the candy and cookies, too."

"All right!" Coco agreed, beaming. "I like making cookies and I like trucks, too!"

The baby monitor on the counter came to life with a questioning cry. The table quieted. They all knew the drill by then—it was always possible that RG would fuss for a minute and then go back to sleep.

Not this time, though. His cries grew more insistent.

Liam glanced at Karin, who was already looking at him. "Please do," she said with a grin and a wave of her hand.

He pushed back his chair and headed for the baby's room.

The rain had let up by the time Liam and Ben got on the road to Bravo Trucking. It was a little awkward, with just the two of them. They hadn't spent much time alone together up till then and Ben's outburst the day before kind of hung in the cab between them.

Liam cued up a playlist on low, just to have a little noise in the background. He asked about soccer. Ben's team, the Valentine Bay Velociraptors, had just wrapped up their fall season. The boy answered Liam's questions as briefly as possible. The subject of soccer died a quick death.

Next, Liam tried science. Ben said he was working on a special project, studying the temperate rain forest of the Pacific Northwest, which stretched from California to British Columbia and was the largest temperate rain forest on the planet. The science conversation fared better than sports, lasting a good ten minutes.

After that, Liam let the playlist make the noise for a while. It wasn't too bad.

Ben really perked up when they got to Bravo Trucking. He happily trotted along beside Liam, who took him through the corporate office, the fuel island and the shop. Even on a Sunday, Liam had a couple of things he needed to deal with in his office, but the few truckers hanging around the driver's lounge were happy to keep Ben busy, telling him stories of the road, answering his every question.

Liam took him out to get an up close and personal look at that diesel engine as promised, and to get a quick rundown on the different types of trailers—from dry vans, to refrigerated trailers, to flatbeds, step deck trailers and lowboy trailers used to haul freight. And for the big finish, Liam took him for a ride in a Kenworth W900B, the kind he used to drive when he first started out hauling timber for Valentine Logging.

It was way past noon when they headed for home. Ben had more questions about the trucking business and the conversation flowed naturally, Liam thought. Halfway there, he pulled the pickup in at a little roadside diner. It was nothing fancy, just burgers, fries and milkshakes. There was a small, fake Christmas tree by the door strung with tinsel garland, lights and shiny balls. The sound system played Christmas tunes.

They got a booth in the back corner and a waitress brought their food. Liam was trying to come up with a good way to maybe get Ben talking about the baby Jesus incident the day before. But he had nothing, really. Every time he came up with a possible opener, he cringed before he could get the words out.

So what, exactly, was on your mind yesterday when you ran for your room?

Maybe not.

Or *Do you resent having me around, Ben? Can we talk about that?*

Yeah. No. Maybe something less direct: *How's it working out for you, having a new baby brother in the house?*

Ugh. Somehow every conversation starter he considered

sounded like lame psychobabble in his head. He had no clue where to begin.

And Ben was suddenly way too quiet again. They stuffed fries in their mouths and sucked down their milkshakes, avoiding eye contact as much as possible.

Then Ben surprised him.

The kid ate a giant bite of his burger and stared directly across the booth at Liam as he chewed and swallowed. "I kind of want to ask you something," he said when his mouth was finally empty. "It's got nothing to do with trucks."

Liam resisted a sudden urge to squirm in his seat. "Go for it."

Ben dropped his half-eaten burger to his plate and slurped up more milkshake, setting the tall plastic glass down with a definite clunk. "Well, Liam. I mean, you're always so nice. It makes me nervous. What's up with you?"

CHAPTER EIGHT

LIAM HAD TO hand it to the kid. "Way to go, Ben. We might end up having a real conversation, after all." Ben frowned at him. Liam ate a french fry. "Define 'nice.'"

"Hmm." Ben took a moment for another giant bite of his burger. Then he said, "You're just too great about everything. You never get mad and so far, you're always there when my mom needs you. You think Riley is the best thing ever, even when he's pooping his diaper and screaming. And you never seem to get annoyed at Coco—I mean, I love my sister but sometimes when she won't stop talking it's like..." He put his hands to either side of his head and made an exploding sound. "And what about you and Grandpa?"

"I like your grandpa."

"Exactly. You and Grandpa are like best friends all of a sudden. You get along with everybody. It's like you actually believe there's a Santa Claus—big news, Liam. There isn't. Santa is physically impossible and as an adult, you should know that."

"Ben."

"What?"

"I do know there's no Santa Claus. I've known for years and years."

"I didn't say that I think you *believe* in Santa Claus, I said you *act* like you do."

"Point taken. I just felt the need to clarify."

"Liam. Are you messing with me?"

He busted to it. "Yeah. Maybe a little."

"I thought so. And it's okay—but that reminds me. Coco still believes in Santa, so you better not ruin it for her."

"Coco will never hear the truth about Santa from me. I promise you that."

Ben pointed a french fry at him. "Make sure you keep that promise."

"I will—what else makes you nervous about me?"

Ben devoured that fry and two more. "You're always around."

"You sound kind of pissed about that."

"Not pissed, not exactly."

"Then what?" Liam asked. Ben just looked at him, frowning. Liam let the wordless moment stretch out as Bing Crosby warbled "Do You Hear What I Hear?" from the speaker in the corner above their booth.

Ben shook his head. "I don't know. But I'm not pissed at you, okay?"

"Got it. So, you say I'm always around…"

"Because you are."

Liam shrugged and reminded him, "Your grandpa is always around."

Ben gave him that look, the one that said, *grown-ups are so dense*. "Well, yeah. Grandpa lives with us."

"And I live next door. Your brother is my child. It's a good thing, the right thing, for me to be around a lot. Plus, I *like* being around a lot."

Ben stared at him long and hard. "Do you really?"

"Yeah. I do. Really."

"Well, my dad was hardly ever around." Ben said that too

softly, his gaze shifting downward. He said to his plate, "I hardly even knew him. And I don't think he liked me very much."

Pay dirt.

And now Liam was scared to death he would blow it. But he'd signed on for this, so he waded in anyway. "I would bet Bravo Trucking that your dad did love you, Ben."

Ben shot him a sharp glance, then went back to examining the puddle of ketchup on his plate. "You're just saying that because that's what you're supposed to say about a kid's dad."

"Uh-uh. You're the kind of kid any dad would be proud of. You're smart and you put other people first, which believe me, *I* didn't when I was your age. You look after your sister and your mom and your grandpa and RG, too. I've only known you for six weeks and I love you already."

Ben snort-laughed. "Right." But at least he looked up and met Liam's eyes.

"It's true, Ben. I really do love you. A lot." Liam realized how much he meant those words as he said them. He also felt so damn sorry for Bud Killigan. For Bud, it was too late to show his own son anything ever again—and Ben was watching him across the table, brown eyes steady.

Liam forged ahead. "It's also true that I didn't know your dad, but I do know that sometimes grown-ups can get so wrapped up in their own problems that they don't realize they're not giving the right signals to the ones they love."

"Signals?"

"Yeah. I mean, sometimes people fail to show how much they love the ones who matter to them, they get lost in the things that are bothering them. When that happens, they can miss their chance to show their love to the ones who mean the most to them. I would bet that's what happened with your dad."

Ben got that look. Like he was deconstructing his latest science project. "You mean that my dad's dead and how he really felt is not provable, so why not just tell myself he loved me?"

"I meant what I said, Ben. Your father loved you. Maybe he

didn't do the best job of showing it, but that doesn't mean the love wasn't there."

"But it's not *provable*." Ben tapped a fist on the table for emphasis.

"So what? It's a hell of a lot more likely that he did than he didn't—and come on, what did I just say? Who *doesn't* love you? Everybody I know loves you."

Ben's mouth twitched, as though he was trying not to grin. "You're exaggerating."

"Nope. Truth. That's all you'll ever hear from me."

Ben grabbed his milkshake and sucked down the rest of it in silence—until the end, the part kids always loved most. Noisily, he sucked air. "I'm done." He set down the red plastic glass. "Thanks for the lunch."

"You're welcome."

"We should probably get back on the road."

Liam debated whether he should try to keep the man-to-man moment going. But he didn't want to mess with whatever progress he'd made.

He grabbed the check. "All right then. Let's go."

Things were quiet in the pickup as they headed home. Liam didn't fill the silence with music this time. A little quiet never hurt. And maybe Ben would have more to say.

They were five miles from Sweetheart Cove, when Ben asked, "So you're staying, then? You're not going away?"

"I'm staying." His own voice sounded so sure and he wondered, was he promising more than he could deliver?

No. However it worked out with him and Karin, he meant to be there—and not only for RG. "There's nowhere else I would rather be than with you and your mom and RG and Coco."

"And Grandpa." Ben said it more as a reminder than a question.

"And with your grandpa, too."

* * *

Karin rang Liam's doorbell at nine that night.

He opened the door and then just stood there, grinning at her. "God, you're good-lookin'." She wore yoga pants and a giant Welcome to Valentine Bay sweatshirt, her hair in a bun, same as that morning, untamed curls escaping every which way. "No other woman could ever compare."

She put one foot behind her and executed an actual curtsy. "And as you can see, I got dressed up real fancy."

"I've always been a big fan of the natural look."

"Oh, I'll just bet you have." She held up her phone. "No telling how long I'll be here. Riley was kind of fussy today."

"You'd better get in here, then." He took her arm, pulled her inside with him, shut the door and reeled her in close. She melted against him. For several perfect minutes, there was just her mouth and his mouth, the feel of her body pressing close to his, the glide of her eager hands up over his chest and around his neck.

Too soon, she broke away and grabbed his hand. "Come on. We need to talk." And she led him into the main room, turned on the fire, pushed him down on the sofa and sat on his lap.

There was more kissing. On his lap like that, she was rubbing him right where it mattered most. He considered all the things that would be okay for him to do to her without her doctor's approval. There were a lot, now that he thought about it, and all of them tempted him.

But then she pulled away again and slid off his lap to sit next to him. She leaned her head on his shoulder. "So. How'd it go today with Ben?"

"Great. He got a tour of the yard, hung out in the driver's lounge. We went for a ride in one of the trucks. I think he had a good time."

"You, um, get a chance to talk to him?"

He balked. Suddenly it seemed wrong to tell her what her son had said over burgers and fries. "We talked, yeah."

"And?"

He rubbed the back of his neck, stalling. "It turned out to be kind of a man-to-man thing."

"That's good, right?"

"What I'm trying to say is I'm not sure I should betray his confidence, you know?"

She got that look women get, a little angry, a lot superior. "One, he's nine years old. Two, I am his mother. Three, that I am his mother means I need to know what's bothering him. And four, did he ask you not to tell me what he said to you?"

"No, he didn't. It's just..." He sought the right words. They didn't come, so he settled on, "Karin, some things a kid doesn't want to tell his mother."

"He's *nine*," she insisted, those beautiful eyes pleading now. "Just tell me this much. Did he mention his dad?"

Her begging eyes did him in. Screw the bro code. He couldn't keep stonewalling her. "Yeah. Ben said he didn't think his dad liked him."

"That's not true." Frantic color flooded her cheeks.

"Hey." He put up both hands in complete surrender. "I believe you. We argued over it. I tried to get him to see that his dad could love him and not be any good at showing it."

Her pretty mouth trembled. "Do you think you convinced him?"

"Not a clue. But he didn't seem upset, honestly. Just kind of puzzled at the weirdness of adults."

"Yeah. He's like that. My little professor..." Her eyes were fond and dreamy—but then she glanced at Liam and demanded, "What else did he say?"

"He wanted to know if I was going to stick around. I told him that I wasn't going anywhere."

She gave him a slow nod, but her eyes spoke of doubts. "It's better not to make him that kind of a promise."

He disagreed. "It's a promise I intend to keep."

"Liam. You never know how things will turn out. People

think they want one thing and then, as time goes by, they realize they want something else altogether."

"I know what I want. And I told Ben the truth. I live here and I'm not leaving."

She bit the corner of her lip. "Look. I think you just need to know something. When I married Bud, I was pregnant with Ben." She stared at him, apprehensive, as if she expected him to be surprised.

He wasn't. Not in the least. "I kind of figured as much. People do that, you know?"

She scoffed. "Get pregnant accidentally or get married because they're pregnant?"

"Both."

"Well, we *were* in love, Bud and me."

"Yeah. You told me that last night."

"Bud swore he was all in—with me, with the baby. He made a lot of promises. I was young and hopeful and crazy about him. I just knew we were going to be happy together forever and ever. I said yes. We got married…" Her voice faded off. She stared into the middle distance, her eyes far away.

And then she said, "It was mostly downhill from there. Before Ben was even born, Bud had turned angry. Distant. I think he came to realize that what he really loved was life on a boat. He wanted his freedom. I just wanted it to work with us. I wanted it so much.

"For a while after Ben was born, Bud seemed…better, I guess. He even said that he wanted another baby. Looking back, I think he was trying to get behind being a husband and a dad. At the time, I was just ecstatic. I thought we were going to be all right. So we had Coco. And things were okay, for a while. But it didn't last. Finally, on that final night he was home before he died, we had a big fight. He said he wanted a divorce and I said that was just fine with me. I meant it, too. I knew we were done, that what I'd believed was lasting love just…wasn't. We never should have gotten married in the first place. A week later, the salmon troller he was on sank in the Bering Sea."

Liam reached out to her slowly. She'd always seemed so strong to him. Not now, though. Right now, she was fragile as glass. "I'm sorry. So sorry, Karin. For Bud. And for you."

She flinched when he touched her cheek. But then, with a shuddery little sigh, she sagged against him. "I hate that he died. I hate that he didn't have time to... I don't know. Get to know his kids? Figure things out? Find a little happiness, a life that really worked for him."

"Yeah." He pressed his cheek to her hair and wished he had something helpful to say. "People shouldn't be allowed to die until they're at least eighty and they've worked through all their crap and made peace with their loved ones."

She tipped her head up and looked at him, her eyes wet with unshed tears. "Exactly. There oughta be a law."

On the table, her phone lit up and vibrated.

She pulled free of Liam's hold and grabbed it. "Hey, Dad." Liam heard Otto's voice faintly on the other end. "He's probably just hungry. I'll be right there." She hung up. "Gotta go."

Liam wasn't ready for her to leave yet. She needed time, after the tough things she'd said to him. Time for him to hold her and kiss her some more, time for him to ease her fears, to reassure her that things with Ben really were going to be all right. He wished he could just go over to the main house with her, help her with the baby, sleep in the same bed with her.

But already she was pulling her shell of self-reliance back around her. She'd learned all the wrong lessons from her troubled marriage and her husband's sudden death.

Liam considered himself an upbeat guy. He looked on the bright side as much as possible.

But when it came to Karin, sometimes he wondered if he would ever really break through.

Ten minutes later, Karin sat in the comfy chair in Riley's room with her feet up on the fat ottoman and Riley at her breast. She rubbed his velvety cheek with a finger and whispered, "I love you, Riley George. I love you so much…"

She let her head fall back against the cushion and closed her eyes.

Raw. She felt raw and too open, after the things she'd told Liam tonight. It had seemed best, to explain it all, give him the whole truth about poor Bud. He needed to understand why she wasn't willing to give in and give the two of them a real shot.

Why getting serious with him was out of the question.

Liam was such a good guy and surprisingly persistent.

But she needed to keep a realistic perspective on their situation. No way was she letting herself get in too deep with him. He kept saying he wasn't ever leaving, that he wanted to be with her and her family. She was sure he meant it.

But just because he meant it now didn't mean he wouldn't change his mind someday.

She simply couldn't take that risk. Giving herself to him and then losing him, having him look at her the way Bud used to, like he wondered how he'd got himself into this mess—well, that could break her. And she couldn't afford to be broken. She had a family to think about.

After tonight, she was definitely reevaluating her brilliant plan to climb into bed with him again.

Uh-uh. He would be far too easy to fall in love with. Having a secret sexual relationship with him was just begging for trouble.

No. The sex thing couldn't happen. She needed to make it clear to him she'd changed her mind about that.

Liam got up early Monday morning and drove to Portland for some meetings at the office there. He didn't get back to the Cove until seven that night.

After a shower and some takeout he'd picked up from his favorite Italian place in town, he called Karin. She didn't pick up. He debated just heading over there, saying hi to Otto and the kids and getting her promise that she would be over as soon as she got everyone settled for the night.

But their thing was a secret thing. He wasn't supposed to do anything that might clue the family in to what was going on between them.

So he left a message. "I miss you. Come over as soon as you get the kids to bed?"

And then he went to his home office and dealt with email and messages, feeling antsy, distracted and so damn eager to have her with him again.

Finally, at a quarter after nine, the doorbell rang. He raced to the front hall and yanked the door wide, planning to sweep her up in his arms and kiss her hard and long.

The tortured look on her face stopped him cold. "What?"

"I'm sorry," she said. "But I never should have suggested that you and I get something going again."

He gaped at her. "Wait. No. What are you talking about?"

"I'm talking about you and me. Liam, you know it's a bad idea."

"I don't know any such thing."

"Well, you *should* know. Because it *is* a bad idea." She wore a sweater over jeans and a knit shirt. But it was cold out, with a brisk wind. She was shivering, her arms wrapped around her middle, her hair wilder than ever, the wind catching it and blowing the dark curls along her cheek, across her forehead.

"You're freezing." He stepped back and gestured toward the main room. "Just come in. I'll turn on the fire, fix you some of that tea you like. We'll talk this out."

"No."

"Karin—"

"I really can't. I don't know what I was thinking when I suggested we should start in with each other again."

"Look. You're freaking out. It's okay. We can talk about it—just talk, that's all."

"No, Liam. Talking won't change anything."

"You're shivering." He reached for her.

She stepped back before he could touch her. "No. Really. I just wanted to tell you, to let you know where we are on this. We need to focus on Riley, not end up in bed together. Having sex again, you and me, it's not a smart idea and it's not going to happen."

Five minutes ago, he couldn't wait to see her face. Now he just wanted to put his fist through a wall. He had a thousand reasons why she was all wrong about this. He wanted to start spouting them, frantically, one after the other, until he'd changed her mind.

But where was that gonna go? Nowhere. He could tell by the tilt of her head and the set of her mouth that she wasn't going to give him an inch.

So be it. If she didn't want to be with him, screw it. He was done with this noise.

"Well, okay then," he said. "I can take Riley for a few hours Wednesday and Friday, in the morning, same as last week."

"Liam, please don't be—"

"You've made your point, okay? No need to pound it into the ground."

He watched her throat move as she swallowed. A dark curl caught on her lip. She swiped it away. "All right."

"Wednesday. Nine in the morning. I can do eight, if that's better."

"No. Nine is great. Thanks."

"Don't thank me. He's my kid. Good night, Karin." He shut the door.

CHAPTER NINE

KARIN WENT HOME hating herself a little, and yet certain she'd done the best thing for her, for Liam, for Riley. And for Ben and Coco, too. None of them needed Karin and Liam to get into something together and then have it all go to hell. For kids, especially, consistency mattered. Romantic drama between the adults they counted on could scar them for life.

Tuesday morning, Otto went over to the cottage first thing, as usual. When he came back, he didn't say a word about what was or wasn't going on with her and Liam. But he had that look. Like Karin had kicked a puppy or something.

She felt like such a complete jerk.

And it only got worse.

Early that afternoon, she was sitting in the little breakroom at the Boatworks eating a tuna sandwich with Riley snoozing in his carrier on the chair beside her. He made a small sound in his sleep, sort of a cross between a sigh and a gurgle. She glanced down at him.

And she realized that he looked just like Liam—a baby Liam

with fat cheeks and no hair. Riley was going to break a lot of hearts, no doubt about it.

Something happened in her chest, like a pinch and a burn. She ached. For Liam. She wanted…

To talk to Liam. To tell him that their baby looked just like him. She wanted to whisper with him, to laugh with him. She wanted to sit next to him in front of the fire.

She wanted so many things, none of which she was ever going to get. Loving a man entailed risk. And after Bud, she was definitely risk averse.

Plus, Liam was sick and tired of her crap. She didn't blame him, she truly didn't. He probably wouldn't want anything to do with her now, not even if she begged him on hands and knees.

And her dad was still giving her dirty looks.

That night, once all three kids were in bed, she went and stood by her dad's recliner and demanded, "Did Liam say something to you about me?"

He muted the TV and then pointed the remote at her. "Liam didn't say a word to me about you. Not one word."

"Then why do you keep looking at me like you're pissed off at me?"

"Because something's bothering Liam and something is way off with you. My guess is, you two are having problems. And I know Liam well enough now to be reasonably certain he'd do just about anything for you. And that means *he's* not the one at fault."

"First of all, we aren't together, Liam and me. How can we have problems?"

"That's a question you need to answer for yourself."

"And second, you're *my* dad. You're supposed to be on *my* side, and yet you jump right to blaming me."

He grunted. "It's not blame, not really. It's more that I'm frustrated with you."

"Oh, really?"

"Yeah, Kary. Really."

"I'll bet you're not *frustrated* with Liam, now are you?"

Her dad heaved a weary sigh. "I'm so proud of you, Kary. I always have been, and even more so in the last few years. It was awful, what happened with Bud. But you've never been one to whine about how rough you have it. You work hard at the Boatworks. You're an amazing mother and you've created a good life for the kids and for yourself, too."

"Thanks," she said flatly.

"It's only the truth."

"And I know you, Dad. I know what you're doing here. Just hit me with the rest of it."

"All right." He swiped a scarred hand back through his thinning hair and leveled his faded blue eyes on her. "Truthfully, Kary, when you know you've messed up and you don't want to admit it, you're a brat, pure and simple." He pointed the remote at the TV and the sound came back on.

She just stood there, glaring at the side of his head, waiting for him at least to glance her way again. He didn't. "I take it I'm dismissed?"

"I love you, Kary," he muttered, still not looking at her. "I love you and you need to work things out with Liam and that's all I have to say on the subject." He stared at the rerun of *Two and a Half Men* as though he hadn't already seen it ten times before.

Karin fumed. She longed to go full-out drama queen on him right then. But what good would that do—except to prove him right?

Head high and mouth shut, she whirled for her room, where she closed the door, sat on the bed and called Naomi. "My dad's pissed at me and I really can't blame him," she confessed.

"Hold on," said her lifelong friend. "I need quiet for this." A minute later, Karin heard a door shut on Naomi's end. "There. Silence. Such a rare and beautiful thing."

"Naomi, I messed everything up."

"Let me guess. This is about your hot baby daddy, right?"

"Don't call him that. He's so much more than that—and I hate that you know me so well."

"No, you don't, you love it. What happened?"

"Riley looks just like him."

"Kary. Kids do have a tendency to look like their parents."

Whipping a tissue out of the box on the night table, Karin swiped at her suddenly leaking eyes. "My dad called me a brat and I think he might be right."

"Oh, baby. Pretend that I'm hugging you and tell me everything."

That took several minutes and three more tissues.

"So then," said Naomi. "You want to be with Liam, but you're *afraid* to be with Liam."

"Yeah. Completely. On both counts. I want another chance but I still don't want to rush anything. I still want it to be just between him and me, at least for a while, because I have no idea what I'm doing and what if it all goes to hell? That wouldn't be good for anyone, especially my children—oh, and what does it matter what I want, anyway? I've screwed everything up with him six ways to Sunday. He'd be crazy to give me another chance. *I* don't even like me very much right now."

"Well, *I* love you."

Karin fell back across the bed and sniffled at the ceiling. "I love you, too. You're the best, Naomi."

"And what are you going to do now?"

"Try again, anyway?" Karin answered with a little moan.

"That's the way you do it—except minus the question mark. You need to be owning that stuff."

"I'm going to try again, anyway. Period."

"Yeah! Go get him, tiger."

Easier said than done.

Wednesday, she put on her best jeans and a red sweater and took ten whole minutes fiddling with her hair and putting on blusher, lip gloss and mascara before she took Riley to Liam's for the morning.

The extra effort got her nowhere.

Liam hardly even looked at her. "Hey, RG." He reached for Riley.

She handed him over, along with an insulated pack full of bottles of frozen pumped milk.

"Great," he said, and hooked the bag over his big shoulder.

She'd planned to ask him for another chance, she really had. But her throat locked up and the words wouldn't come.

"Noon?" he asked, stroking Riley's back, his blue gaze locked on his son.

"Uh, yeah. Noon is good."

"All right then." And he stepped back and shut the door.

It was the same at noon. She rang the bell and Liam answered with Riley all ready to go. He passed her the baby, confirmed the time she would be dropping him off on Friday—and shut the door.

That night, Prim called. Naomi had told her everything and Prim wanted to know how she was doing. Karin explained her complete failure to get Liam to so much as look directly at her. "Let alone give me a chance to try to reach out."

Prim gave her a pep talk and she hung up sure she would do better on Friday.

Didn't happen. The baby handoff was faster, if possible, than it had been on Wednesday. She found herself standing alone on the step, minus the baby, staring at his shut door. At noon, he passed her Riley—and closed the door. Again.

Her dad got home at two that day to hang the outdoor lights on the porch, the back deck and down the outside stair railings, front and back. An hour later, Karin was straightening up the great room when she glanced out the slider and saw her dad and Liam hanging the lights together.

At four, when the kids got home from school, the men were over at the cottage putting up outdoor lights there, too. She knew because Coco and Ben had stopped over there before showing up at the main house to beg Karin to be allowed to go help.

"We already asked Grandpa and Liam," pleaded Coco.

"It's okay with them if it's okay with you," said Ben.

Karin gave her permission. The two ran out the slider and didn't come back.

By quarter of six, she had dinner all ready. The outside lights looked great. Karin turned on the tree lights and the star in the crèche and the lights on the mantel, too. She bundled Riley up and took him with her to see how the work was going.

They'd finished hanging the lights on the cottage, too. The big, multicolored bulbs lined the eaves, the railings and the stairs, so cheery and festive, pushing back the cold, foggy night. Feeling unsure and way too nervous, she mounted the steps to the deck.

They were all there, inside, in the living area, decorating a tree that stood near the wide picture window. For a long, bittersweet moment, she hung back in the shadows, cradling her baby close, just watching. They already had the lights on. Liam stood on a ladder holding a big, lighted star. He slipped it over the top branch, took a moment to prop it up nice and straight and climbed back down. The kids and her dad were busy hanging ornaments. Nobody had spotted her out there in the darkness, not with every light on inside.

Really, she didn't want to interrupt them. They seemed to be having such a great time. Dinner could wait.

She started to turn—and then stopped herself.

Even if Liam had decided she wasn't worth the trouble relationship-wise, they still had a baby to raise. He got along with her family and he really didn't seem to be going anywhere.

Sneaking around out in the dark, avoiding him, was no way to behave.

Riley made a tender little cooing sound in her ear as she marched to the slider and knocked on it.

"It's Mommy!" Coco's gleeful cry was clear even through

the glass. She hung the ornament in her hand and ran to shove the slider wide. "Come in! We are decorating Liam's tree."

"I see that. It's looking good." She cast an admiring glance at the tree—and her gaze collided with Liam's. Collided and held.

She pasted on a smile. "Just wanted to see if anyone was hungry?"

"We're *starving*," moaned Coco.

Karin was still staring at Liam as he stared right back at her. She suggested, "Why don't you all come on back to the house, have a quick dinner and then you can finish Liam's tree?"

"Good idea," said Otto. He turned for the pile of coats tossed on one of the chairs and handed the top one to Ben. Coco ran over there and grabbed hers.

Liam didn't move.

"I hope you'll come, too." Karin's stomach was all twisted in knots. Riley, picking up her anxiety, had begun to squirm in her arms. "Please."

Liam didn't smile. But his mouth got…softer. And his eyes got deeper somehow. "How could I say no?"

Dinner lasted maybe twenty minutes, max. They shoveled down the stew she'd made and everybody pitched in to make short work of cleaning up.

They were all pulling on their coats again as Karin finished wiping the kitchen counters.

"You coming?" asked Liam. She glanced up from the sponge in her hand as he pulled on his jacket. His eyes were ocean blue, beckoning her down to drowning. "Please." He said it so softly. Just for her.

And she felt…hope, like a bright pulse of sheer happiness, lighting her up inside.

"Yeah," she said. "I'll grab some cookies and the baby and be right over."

Three hours later, Liam's tree was fully decorated. They all agreed that it looked fantastic. Karin plated the cookies she and

Coco had baked and Liam made hot chocolate—with marshmallows—after which he produced a deck of cards and challenged them all to a game of slapjack.

They played for an hour or so. By then, both kids were yawning.

Otto said, "Come on, you two. Time to go home and get ready for bed."

Coco whined, "Not yet…"

Ben tried bargaining. "Just one more game."

Karin shook her head. "Your grandpa's right. It's getting late."

The kids gave it up and grabbed their coats.

Trying for offhand and not really succeeding, Karin said, "I was thinking I would just hang around here with Liam until Riley wakes up." She'd fed him an hour ago and put him in his crib there at the cottage.

"Great idea." Liam gave her a look that sent a sweet shiver up the backs of her knees.

Her dad tried really hard not to smirk. "Come on, Ben. Coco. Kiss your mom good night and let's go."

As soon as her dad and the kids were gone, Karin sat on the sofa and tried to figure out what to say first. Liam, who'd carried the last of the empty cocoa mugs over to the sink, returned and sat beside her.

She felt the cushion shift, but couldn't quite bring herself to look directly at him. Not yet. The great room was suddenly very quiet. Because, sheesh. Where to even begin?

She stared at the tree and considered remarking on the beauty of it. But they'd pretty much covered that subject before the kids left.

Cautiously, she turned her head toward the man beside her.

He was looking right at her, a knowing grin tugging at the corners of that mouth she might actually get to kiss again, after all—maybe even tonight. "You got something to say to me?"

The butterflies in her stomach went wild, bouncing around

in there, fluttering madly. "So much for my dad not figuring out what's going on between us."

"Not much gets by your dad. I like that about Otto." He continued to gaze at her, his eyes low and lazy, like a big, golden timber wolf contemplating his next easy meal. "And did you just admit that there *is* something going on between us, after all?"

She wished he would just grab her and kiss her and they could skip the part where she confessed her own stark terror of this dangerous magic that sizzled between them. "I freaked out, okay? I freaked out and then when you said I was freaking out, I lied and denied it. I'm sorry, Liam. I'm such a coward. I don't want to get hurt again. I don't want my children hurt again. I want to protect myself. But I want to be with you, too. I want it so much."

"Hey." He said it gently and her heart just melted. "I understand. It's okay. And Karin, I would never hurt you."

"I know you wouldn't, not on purpose. And you've been amazing, you really have, with me, with my kids and my dad. And our son is so lucky to have you, Liam. A lucky, lucky little boy."

He reached for her then, slowly, giving her plenty of opportunity to duck away. She didn't. He framed her face between his hands. "I'm not going to hurt you, Karin. I mean that. I just want to be with you."

"Me, too. I do want to be with you." Gladness pulsed through her, simply to feel his touch again. "But I still…" Her chest felt so tight, bursting with emotions that terrified her at the same time as they filled her with hope and yearning. "Just you and me, huh? Nobody else has to know until we see how it goes."

He shook his head. "Didn't you just say that your dad's already on to us?"

"He'll leave it alone if we make it clear we want it that way."

"Fair enough. Not a word to anyone, Otto included."

"Not even in the morning when he comes over here under

cover of darkness and you two drink coffee and talk about... whatever you talk about."

"Manly things."

"Oh, I'll just bet."

"I won't talk about you with him, Karin, not even then. Not until you're ready."

"Thank you," she whispered. He smelled so good, of soap and evergreen and the wind off the ocean at night.

Slowly, he brushed his lips across her mouth, back and forth, setting off sparks, making her ache in the best kind of way. The light caress sent a hot pulse of desire straight to her core.

He eased his fingers back into her hair, combing them through it. "I'm so glad you're here. I hope RG sleeps for hours." He fisted her hair, pulling it a little the way he'd said he'd always wanted to do back when they were kids.

She teased, "Good luck with Riley sleeping for hours..."

"You're right." Liam caught her lower lip between his teeth and bit down with a growl. "We need to get moving here. He could wake up at any time." Slowly, cradling her face in his hands, pulling her with him, kissing her all the way, he stood. Once they were both upright, he pulled her even closer.

They shared another kiss. A deep one that went on forever, until her whole body quivered in eagerness and a pleading groan rose in her throat.

"Time for bed." He took her by the waist and flung her over his shoulder, like a fireman saving her from a burning building.

She would have cried out in mock protest, but the last thing she wanted to do was take a chance of waking the baby, so she settled for playfully kicking and pounding his broad back as he carried her off down the hall.

In the master bedroom, he shut the door, took her to the king-size bed and let her down to the rug—but he didn't let her go. He ran both hands down her arms and then back up over her shoulders. His touch felt so right. He cradled her face again and kissed her some more.

When he lifted his head that time, she gave the room a quick once-over. "The bedroom looks great." It was in grays and tans, with black-and-white prints on the walls.

"Thanks. Let's get naked."

She laughed. "Eager, much?"

"How did you guess?" He plucked at the sleeve of her sweater. "This is in my way."

She grinned up at him. "I got my checkup."

"Yeah?" Oh, those eyes of his. He could make her come with just a look.

"I officially have the all clear to do naughty things with you." She sounded breathless. He made her that way.

"Good." He took the sweater by the hem. "Arms up." She obeyed his command and he swept it up and away.

She frowned at him. "Wait a minute. You shut the door. We won't be able to hear—"

"Yeah, we will—stay right there." He went to the dresser and grabbed the baby monitor she hadn't noticed until then. "I have two receivers, one for out in the living area and this one." He flipped it on. The small screen showed the crib and Riley asleep in it. "Infrared, so I can see him even when the light's off. Cool, huh?" He set it on the nightstand.

"Very cool—but do you have condoms?"

He pulled open the drawer and took out a chain of them, dropping them next to the monitor. "Any more questions?" He didn't wait for her answer, but instantly commanded, "Take off the jeans."

He hooked his fingers into her waistband. She moaned just at the feel of his fingers pressing her belly as he undid the button right below her navel.

"Need some help?" She toed off her Uggs, ripped her fly wide and wiggled the jeans down over her hips.

"God. Karin." He looked at her like she was the most beautiful woman in the world, a look that sent pleasure zipping all through her, a look that banished any leftover nerves about how unsexy her poufy belly and plain white nursing bra must be. He whipped off his thermal shirt. "Finally."

He had one of those universal gyms down in a corner of the garage and he ran on the beach just about every day. Keeping fit really paid off. He was so beautiful, everything sculpted and hard, with that wonderful trail of golden hair leading down to the happy place. And she was so glad—to be here with him, the two of them. Alone in his bedroom.

If they got right on it, they might even manage to have actual sex before Riley woke up.

"Hurry," she begged.

They quickly got rid of the rest of their clothes and he took her by the shoulders and pulled her down across the bed on top of him.

She laughed as she kissed him, bracing her knees to either side of him, rubbing herself shamelessly against his hard belly, reaching back to wrap her fingers around his thick, hard length.

He groaned when she did that, his hands stroking down her back, grabbing the twin globes of her bottom, holding on tight. He felt so good, so solid and strong. The manly scent of him tempted her, promising all the pleasures she remembered so well. She'd missed this, the two of them, naked, together. Missed it so much.

She wanted him all over her, covering every inch of her. "I want you on top of me."

"Done." He rolled them, taking the top position. She wrapped herself around him like a vine.

He kept on kissing her, a kiss so hot it could burn the house down, a kiss that went on forever, his tongue claiming her mouth, his body covering hers.

This. Right now. With him. It just didn't get any better.

He scattered more kisses, across her cheek, down the side of her throat, stopping to nip at her collarbone, sucking her skin against his teeth. She'd have marks there in the morning.

But so what? She had turtlenecks. And every kiss thrilled her. It all felt just perfect. Exactly right.

"I missed you," she cried. It was a confession, one she couldn't hold back.

He caught her face in his hands again. "I'm here. Here to stay."

"Oh, Liam." Better not to talk about it. Better just to grab this moment and squeeze every drop of joy from it.

His palmed her breasts. She moaned at the pleasurable ache. "Fuller," he said, his voice rich with approval.

She winced. "I'm leaking."

He pulled back enough to grin down at her. "Shut up. You're beautiful." And he took her mouth yet again, spearing his tongue in, sweeping along the edges of her teeth, drinking her down.

When he broke that kiss, it was only to press his lips to her chin, her neck, the hollow of her throat. He dropped a chain of kisses between her breasts. Moving lower, he kissed her belly and the soft points of her hip bones.

And then, easing her thighs over his shoulders and settling between them, he kissed her in the most intimate way. He made her crazy with his lips and little nips of his teeth, with his talented tongue, while his clever fingers played her so perfectly.

It felt so good. She tossed her head against the pillow, whispering his name, moaning it out loud more than once, threading her fingers in his hair, pulling him closer, urging him on.

He eased her legs wider, kissed her more deeply, continuing to stroke her with those skilled strong fingers of his, driving her toward the peak until she gave it up to him, gave herself over completely.

She cried his name as she came.

Had she passed out from sheer ecstasy?

It was just possible.

He moved away. She forced her heavy eyes open and saw

he was up on his knees between her wide-open thighs, rolling on one of the condoms.

She reached for him. "Liam. Come here."

He didn't have to be told twice. With care, he lowered himself to her, gathering her into him, taking her mouth again. She tasted her own musky arousal on his lips.

And she was lost again in the glory of it, kissing him hungrily, reaching down between them, taking him—carefully, so as not to rip the condom—in her hand, guiding him to her.

He surged in hard. She rose up to meet him with a deep, needful groan, lifting her legs and wrapping them good and tight around his lean waist.

After that, he took over, hard and fast at first, so that she could only hold on and let it happen, let him sweep her away into a world of pure, perfect sensation. But then he slowed. He rocked her in a steady, thrilling glide, going deep and then pulling back—only to return to her, over and over again, stoking the heat within her, fanning the fire.

She hit the crest so suddenly, chanting his name, pulling him closer, tighter, as another finish rocked her.

There was a lull. She closed her eyes with a sigh.

But then he started moving again and it felt so good, so right. Her body responded instantly. Another fulfillment spun into being from the embers of the last.

Liam stayed with her, whispering encouragements, urging her to take what she needed from him. Sweet bolts of pleasure unfurled within her, spreading out from her core, flowing down her arms, along her legs, bringing hot shivers to the backs of her knees and the soles of her feet. Until every part of her had been swept up, spun around, carried away into complete satisfaction.

And then it was his turn. He thrust in hard and so deep— and stilled. She felt his finish claiming him. Wrapping her arms around him, she cradled him close as his climax rolled through him.

There was stillness. She shut her eyes and sank into the lovely, floating feeling of ease. Of peace.

A few minutes later, he got up to take care of the condom. Returning with a cool, wet cloth, he gently bathed her breasts and down her belly. It felt wonderful, that cloth, cooling and soothing, too.

Her eyes were so heavy. She hadn't realized how tired she was. He left her again. She shook herself awake and started to get up.

But then he was there. He came down to the bed with her and pulled the covers over them, gathering her into him.

"I should get Riley, go home." She kissed the side of his throat.

"Not yet." His lips brushed her ear.

She rested her head on his shoulder, listened to his heart beat deep and steady. So soothing, that sound. "If I don't go, I may never move from this spot."

He stroked her hair, smoothing it away from her cheek. "Stay. Just for a minute or two..."

When she opened her eyes, her baby was crying. She tried to push back the covers.

But the hard, warm arms wrapped around her held her even tighter. He nuzzled a kiss in her hair. "I'll get him, bring him to you."

"I have to go, Liam. What time is it, anyway?"

"A little after one..."

She pushed at his chest. "Gotta go."

He kissed the tip of her nose. "He's going to be hungry. You can feed him. And then you can go."

She looked up to meet his eyes. His white teeth flashed with his grin. "Well, go on, then," she said. "Go get him."

He kissed her nose a second time, slid out from under the covers and turned on the lamp. She squinted against the sudden light and brought up a hand to shield her eyes.

"We'll be right back." Stark naked, he headed for the door.

She shoved the covers away and lowered her bare feet to the rug. Shivering a little, she darted around, snatching up her clothes from the floor, from the chair and from the foot of the bed.

Riley kept crying—in stereo—on the monitor and from the room next-door. "Whoa, buddy." She heard Liam groan. "That's quite a load." She paused after pulling on her sweater to watch the monitor as he carried the yowling infant away from the crib and out of sight.

But she could hear him clearly as he continued to murmur reassurances and promises that everything was going to be fine. Riley wasn't going for it. Every time she thought he might settle down a little, he'd suck in a big breath and start bawling again.

Once she'd thrown on her clothes, she crossed the hall and stood in the doorway of the baby's room. "Thanks for taking on the hazardous waste."

He turned to her with the still-crying Riley cradled against his broad, bare chest. "Hey. It's in the job description."

She held out her arms. "My turn." He passed her the squirming baby and she carried him to the easy chair in the corner. Once she was settled, she put Riley to her breast.

A hearty eater, he latched right on.

She glanced up at the naked man standing over her. "Hear that?"

"Silence," he replied with a nod. "It really is golden." Showing no inclination to go put some clothes on, he studied her face, his gaze moving from her eyes to her lips and back to her eyes again. "I want to lock you in this house and never let you go."

Did she feel a little thrill at that hungry look he wore, at the low roughness of his voice? Absolutely.

But she gave him an easy shrug. "I think they call that kidnapping. It's frowned upon by law enforcement. And people who get kidnapped don't like it much, either."

"Buzzkill," he whispered tenderly. "Next you'll be saying I should go get dressed."

"Never." She gave him a slow once-over. "You look so good naked."

He braced a hand on the back of the chair and bent close for a quick, hard kiss. "I'll leave you alone." He laid his palm gently on Riley's head, cradling it, encompassing it—but just for a moment. And then he turned for the door.

She smiled as she watched him walk away. Not only did he look amazing, he was funny and good to her. And every time he kissed her, she wanted to hold on tight and never, ever let go.

But that would be rushing things, that would be getting all caught up in big emotions, making life-changing decisions without using her head.

Forever was a long, long time. If she ever headed down that road again, she would be 100 percent certain she'd taken the right turn.

CHAPTER TEN

OTTO CAME TO the cottage that morning, as usual, before dawn. Liam turned on the tree lights and the fire. They sat on the hearth with their full mugs of coffee.

"Karin didn't come in until almost two this morning," Otto remarked in a tone so offhand as to be almost humorous.

"What? You stayed awake waiting for her to come home?"

"The habits of a lifetime, my boy. They never die."

Liam sipped his coffee. "I got orders not to talk to you about what is or isn't going on between Karin and me."

"What she doesn't know won't hurt her."

Liam scoffed. "Easy for you to say. You're her dad. She trusts you absolutely. I'm the interloper."

"Just ask her to marry you. It can't be that complicated."

"Otto. You have no idea."

"I'm on your side. So's Coco. And Sten. Madison, too. I think you've even turned Ben around."

He perked up at that. "Ben? Really?"

"Really."

That felt damn good, to think he and Ben were on the right

track now. "And Madison, too, huh? Well, she is my sister. She *should* be on my side—even if we hardly know each other." Liam had only talked to the newfound Bravo briefly, at a couple of family dinners back in the spring when she first came to town to meet the family. "It's not right, that I hardly know my own sister."

Otto raised his mug in a quick salute. "You'll get your chance, soon as she and Sten move home to stay."

"You really think she's giving up her career? I read somewhere that she makes millions a year."

"They say money isn't everything."

"They say a lot of things."

"That's right. Because they're true—and yeah. I think Madison is going to finish out those final projects she couldn't get out of and settle right here on Sweetheart Cove, have a few babies, make a good life with Sten. Just like you and Karin need to do."

Liam stared straight ahead. "Not talking to you about Karin."

"Come over for breakfast, why don't you?"

"For a guy who's supposed to leave it alone, you're damn persistent—and no. Even I'm not *that* pushy."

"Karin said to ask you."

"Stop yanking my chain."

"I'm not. She was up with RG when I headed over here. She said, 'Tell Liam we're having waffles and he's welcome to join us...'"

Liam got up, grabbed his phone from where he'd left it on the coffee table and texted Karin. Your dad says I'm invited for breakfast. He glanced back at Otto. "You want more coffee?"

"Yeah."

Karin answered as he was passing the tree to get the pot from the kitchen. What? You didn't believe him?

Should I?

Liam, please join us for breakfast. Today. Tomorrow. Any morning the mood strikes.

Damn. This was progress. It was going to work out for them. She would get past her fear that he would do her the way Bud had. She was learning to trust again.

He just had to curb his impatience, take it one step at a time.

I'll be there.

She sent back a thumbs-up. He stared at that simple emoji and felt like he'd just won the lottery. Or maybe free soloed up El Capitan and lived to tell about it.

"Told you," said Otto with a self-satisfied smirk. "Now bring that pot over here. I need my caffeine."

At breakfast, he behaved himself. Mostly. Now and then, he would catch himself staring too long at Karin, but he didn't think he was all that obvious.

That night, she came over with Riley as soon as the kids were in bed. She'd nursed him at the other house and when she put him in his crib at the cottage, he didn't even make a peep.

They had a couple of hours, the two of them, in bed. It was so good with her. He got now why some guys never looked at another woman.

Why would he want to look at someone else when he could spend every free moment staring at Karin, talking to Karin, laughing with her, kissing her, having great sex with her?

Sunday morning, he went to breakfast at the main house again. Karin gave him that certain smile, the one that was only for him. After they ate, he helped Coco with cleanup.

She was Batgirl today, rattling off her special powers, leaning in close to ask with completely adorable and uncharacteristic shyness, "Are you still taking me to see the trucks today, Liam?"

"You still want to go?"

"Yes, please!"

"Can you be ready at nine?"

"Yes, I can!"

Karin took him aside to remind him that Coco was only seven and tended to trust everyone she met. She needed closer supervision than nine-year-old, super mature, overly cautious Ben.

"I hear you," he promised. "I won't let her out of my sight."

Coco wore her black tights and yellow rain boots for the trip, but Karin insisted that she switch out her towel cape for a coat and a warm wool hat. The red hat had a border of snowflakes and a big, white pom-pom that bounced all the way to Bravo Trucking. Coco pretty much talked nonstop.

She charmed everyone in the driver's lounge. Liam hung out with her there for half an hour or so, took her for a quick tour of the offices and the fuel island and then out to have a look at the engine of one of the trucks.

He showed her how to pop the hood latches and then how easily the giant hood opened with a tug on the front. When he launched into his spiel about how the engine worked, she stared up at him as though transfixed by his every word.

"Questions?" he asked once he'd given her a quick rundown.

"Um, no." Those blue eyes were so serious. "But I would really like to go for a ride in this truck, Liam."

"Now?"

Her pom-pom bobbed and her smile bloomed wide. "Yes, now, please!" She looked up at him like he'd grabbed her a handful of stars. "I'm glad you're our baby's daddy, Liam."

All of a sudden, he felt kind of choked up. "Me, too."

"I think you should get married to Mommy and we can all live happily ever after like in *The Wild Swans* and *Frozen* and *Beauty and the Beast*."

Me, too! But that time he didn't say it out loud. A guy had to be careful about the promises he made. Especially to children.

Coco had her head tipped to the side now. She stared up at him, frowning a little. "Maybe you should just think about it?"

"I will—now, how 'bout that ride?"

Liam boosted her up into the cab and took the wheel.

They circled the terminal and she pointed out the buildings she'd visited. When they got back where they'd started, she wasn't ready to quit, so he drove her across the Youngs Bay Bridge and into Astoria. They rumbled along Marine Drive, circling back using Commercial.

On the way home to Valentine Bay, they stopped at the same diner he and Ben had eaten at the week before. Coco wanted the works, a burger, chocolate milkshake and fries. She only managed to eat about half of all that before she wiped her mouth with her napkin and gave him one of those looks she was an absolute master at—one of those I'm-the-cutest-little-girl-in-the-universe looks.

"It was really good, Liam, but I'm *really* full. My eyes are bigger than my tummy. That's what Grandpa always says. But Mommy says we have to practice not wasting food."

"We'll take it to go."

"The milkshake will melt."

Was he getting played? It was starting to seem like a definite possibility. "Hmm. Looks like you already ate most of the milkshake."

"It's my favorite." She grinned so wide, he could see the gap on the bottom where she'd lost two baby teeth. The white rims of her grown-up teeth had just begun to show. "I like chocolate milkshakes more than french fries and a *lot* more than a hamburger."

Liam leaned in and lowered his voice to secret-sharing level. "What are you telling me that you're not telling me?"

She giggled. "You're funny, Liam."

"Did you do something you shouldn't have done?"

"Not exac'ly."

"So then, what's going on?"

Her little shoulders sagged. "Well, Mommy usually says if they don't have a mini-burger and a small-size fries, I should just skip the fries. And the milkshake was kind of big, too. I was afraid to ask for a mini-shake because maybe they don't have those and even if they do, I would rather have a big one."

Wouldn't we all? "So you broke the rules about wasting food, is that what you're telling me?"

Those eyes were enormous in that little pixie face with that perfect pointed chin just like her mom's. "Umm-hmm."

How big of a deal was this, really? He had no idea. It was all way above his pay grade, parenting-wise. "I'm not about to make you take the leftovers home."

She brightened. "You're not?"

"I'll just tell your mom that I didn't know the rules and I let you order too much food."

"Liam," she chided. "That's not gonna work with my mom."

"Why not?"

"'Cause my mom knows that *I* know the rules and I'm s'posed to follow them—and you know what? I'll just take the leftovers home."

He kept his expression carefully neutral though a grin was trying really hard to stretch the edges of his mouth. "You sure?"

"Umm-hmm. It's okay if I order too much food as long as I eat the leftovers later."

"Problem solved, then?"

"Yeah, 'cept I have to eat the leftovers."

"Life is full of choices."

She wrinkled her little nose at him. "That's exac'ly what Mommy says."

That night, Karin came over again. She'd left RG sleeping at the other house. Her dad would call when he needed her. "Sorry. I probably won't be staying all that long."

"I'll take you however I can get you." He caught her hand, pulled her into his arms and walked her backward down the hall to the bedroom, kissing her all the way. They made love fast and hard, with no preamble, rolling around on the bed, holding on to each other good and tight. It was great.

And then, when Otto didn't call, they started again, this time making it last, indulging in deep, lazy kisses and slow, sweet caresses. After that second time, they talked.

"Coco can wrap the average adult around her pinkie finger," Karin said. She was lying on her back, the covers pulled up over those breasts he loved to kiss, curling a lock of her hair around one of her fingers. "But you nailed the leftovers issue. Well done."

Feeling contented, happy with the world and everything in it, he scooted a little closer to her side of the bed, braced up on an elbow and just let himself enjoy looking at her, breathing in the sweet scent of her that was a little bit musky from all the fun they'd been having. "I wouldn't say I nailed anything. I just let her talk herself into doing the right thing."

"You're good with kids." She gave him a teasing little smile. "You're going to make some lucky woman the perfect husband."

And just like that, in the space of a few seconds, all his easy contentment vanished. "What the hell is that supposed to mean, Karin?"

"Whoa." She rolled to her side and faced him fully. "What'd I say?"

"You want to see me with another woman?"

"Liam, come on. Of course not." She brushed his shoulder with a tentative hand. He had to consciously hold himself still in order not to jerk away from her. "It was just a figure of speech."

Impatience rose inside him, making his skin feel too tight and his pulse throb like an infected wound. "Sometimes I think you don't take me seriously."

"That's not true." She ran her palm down the outside of his arm, petting him. Soothing him.

It worked. To a degree.

But she'd reopened this can of worms and damned if he was

just going to shove the lid back on and pretend nothing had happened. "I don't want *some* woman, Karin. I want *you*."

She put a finger to his lips. "Liam, come on, don't…"

Gently, he guided her hand away from his mouth. "Marry me."

She just looked at him. Her eyes were a thousand years old.

He said it again. "Marry me."

"Because of Riley," she whispered bleakly.

"Yeah. Because of our son. What's wrong with that? Because of Riley and because I want you and I don't want to be with anyone but you. And because of Coco and Ben. Hell, because of Otto. We can make a good life. We can make it all work."

"Don't." She touched his mouth again. "Please."

"Because I lov—"

"No." She glared at him. "Uh-uh. Don't say it. I really and truly do not want to hear it."

He sat up and swung his legs over the edge of the bed—at which point he realized he was staying right here. Because there was nowhere he wanted to be but with her. Even when he was mad at her, he didn't want to walk away from her.

And she had it right. He shouldn't have started in with this, shouldn't have let himself lose it over some offhand remark of hers.

Behind him, the bed shifted as she rose to her knees.

She touched him. He felt her tentative hand on his shoulder. "Liam." He felt…everything. Her touch, her body behind him, so smooth and soft; her breath caressing the back of his neck. "Liam, I'm sorry. That was a crappy thing I said. I want you, too. I do. I would be so jealous if you went out and found someone else. You're important to me. So much so that it scares me."

"There's nothing for you to be scared of. I'm not Bud. I've had my time to be free, to keep things casual and easy, to answer to no one but myself. I know what I want now and I want to be with you. I want to answer to you, Karin, and to be responsible for you. I want to be the one they have to call if you're in need."

"And I want to be with *you*. So much. But I'm not just jumping into something permanent. I'm never doing that again. I'm not ready to go making promises about forever. I just need to take it one day at a time. And I do love this—you and me, together. Like this. I love how you are with me. And with Riley. With my family. It's only that sometimes it kind of feels like it's too good to be true, you know?"

He shook his head and a humorless chuckle escaped him. "Do you hear yourself? You like everything about me. You just don't believe I'm for real."

"Look, I've got issues, I know it. I'm not blind to myself, to who I am. I'm not the easiest woman to be with. I'm not trusting. I've got…defenses. And I guess I'm always half expecting you to figure out that I'm a pain in the ass and this thing with us just doesn't work for you."

Her hand was still on his shoulder. He reached up and laid his over it, sliding his thumb in under her fingers to rub the soft heart of her palm. "I'm going nowhere. How am I going to convince you of that?"

"Liam…" It was barely a whisper. She moved in closer behind him, pulling her hand out from under his, but not to retreat. To get closer. She pressed her soft breasts against him, wrapped her arms around his belly and rested her cheek on his shoulder. "Liam."

All he had to do was turn his head. Her sweet mouth was right there. She smelled of citrus and rain and baby lotion. She smelled like all the best things, everything he'd ever wanted all wrapped up in one contrary, difficult, big-eyed, wild-haired woman.

I love you, Karin.

No, he didn't say it. She didn't want to hear it. But he thought it, thought it over and over, as he kissed her.

I love you.

He turned and curved his body over her, carrying her down to the bed again, sweeping his hands along her arms, into the silky curve of her waist, down over her smooth thighs, parting her, touching her, so slick and wet, already primed for him.

I love you.

She reached down between them and curled her hand around him, taking command of him. He groaned his pleasure into their kiss as she stroked him, tightly, forcefully. A little bit roughly.

Just the way he liked it.

He reached out, grabbed a condom from the nightstand, managed to get the thing unwrapped. She helped him, taking it from him, rolling it down over his aching length.

I love you.

The words were there, in his head, pulsing with the beat of his heart as he sank into her. As she wrapped herself around him, pulling him tightly to her, so good. So right.

I love you.

As he moved within her, rocking her slowly, taking her higher and higher.

I love you.

As she came apart, chanting his name.

CHAPTER ELEVEN

AFTER THE NIGHT she wouldn't let him say the *L* word, Liam tried to keep his focus on the good things.

Like how Karin couldn't stay away from him. She appeared at his door five or six nights out of seven and she stayed for an hour or two, at least—sometimes much longer.

But she always returned home before the kids woke up. And she continued to insist that they keep their relationship just between the two of them. He hated her restrictions, like she was keeping him in his place, not letting him get too close.

Most Sundays, he went to dinner at Daniel's. It was a Bravo family tradition. He'd tried several times to get her to come with him, to bring the kids and Otto, too. She always had some reason why it just wouldn't work. He asked her again the second Friday in December. Riley was asleep in the crib at the cottage and they were sitting by the fire in the main room.

She sipped the last of her raspberry tea and answered regretfully, "Thanks, but I don't think so, Liam."

"Just one time," he coaxed. "This Sunday."

"Your brother and his wife do not need a bunch of extra people descending on them."

"Yeah, Karin. They do. Especially if it's you and the kids and Otto. You were there at Thanksgiving. They loved having you. You're welcome there anytime."

She set her empty mug down, leaned in and kissed him. "Thanks, but no."

"Then how about Christmas? Come to Daniel's for dinner Christmas Day."

"Liam…"

He pulled her close and kissed the tip of her nose. "Don't answer now. Think about."

"I just don't…"

He covered her lips with his before she could dish out another denial. She seemed only too happy for the distraction. He gathered her closer and deepened the kiss. Then, pulling her up with him, he led her down the hall to his bedroom. As he dragged her down on the bed with him, he reminded himself that he was focusing on the positive, looking for the good things in what he had with her.

Kissing her. Holding her. Having her in his bed…

These were very good things.

And the sex was by no means all of the goodness.

He loved the way she trusted him with Coco and Ben—and seemed to count on him, too. She didn't hesitate to ask him to ferry them around or keep an eye on them when Otto was at the Boatworks and she needed to run over to the store. Who knew he'd ever be the kind of guy who couldn't wait to drive the kids to play dates and sleepovers, to take Coco to her Hip-Hoppin' Dance Class and Ben to Science Club?

The next week, he even managed to get himself an invite to the Valentine Bay Elementary School Christmas show wherein Coco played a singing, dancing snowflake and Ben wore a beard, a yellow robe and a crown as one of the Three Wise Men.

Liam was so proud of them, he was first on his feet to lead the standing ovation when they all came out and took their bows.

Every morning, he showed up at the main house with Otto for breakfast. And every morning, Karin smiled at him like she was glad to see him. He kept waiting for the day when she'd move in close, maybe offer her sweet mouth for a quick kiss, the day when she'd say something soft and low and welcoming, just between the two of them.

But the mornings went by, one by one, and a more intimate breakfast greeting didn't happen. He told himself that it *would* happen. Someday very soon. He just needed to stay positive. She would get over her fear of giving her heart to him.

They would be together. *Really* together. Live in the same house, sleep in the same bed—and not just for a few stolen hours, either. Uh-uh. Same bed.

All. Night. Long.

Negativity crept in, though. Sometimes he couldn't help thinking that all he'd ever had of Karin Killigan were stolen moments. From last Christmas to now, she fit him in when she could manage it—and yeah, she fit him in just about every night as of now. That was progress, definitely.

But she wouldn't simply let it be known that she was with him.

Even if she wouldn't marry him, she could let him be *more*. More than her baby daddy. More than her coparent. More than the helpful guy next door. More than the man who made her cry out his name two or three times a night.

Be patient, he kept telling himself.

And he tried, he really did. But his patience was fraying. No matter how often he reminded himself that he and Karin really hadn't been together all that long and that he needed to chill, back off, let her find her way to him in her own time, he couldn't help feeling frustrated.

He'd finally figured out what he wanted out of life and he didn't want to waste a moment going forward. But he was stuck at the threshold of his own happiness, waiting for Karin to open the damn door and let him in.

The kids had the usual two-week holiday break from school. It started the Friday before Christmas.

Karin needed to wrangle them childcare for when she had to be at the Boatworks. They didn't want to spend their Christmas vacation at a winter break camp and they didn't want to hang around the office at the Boatworks with her, either. Usually, her dad and Sten helped her out. But Sten was in LA. And Otto had a couple of big refitting jobs. He couldn't look after them as much as he usually did.

Liam said he would stay home and watch them a couple of days a week, but she turned him down. He already took Riley every Wednesday and Friday till noon. And he had a business—a busy, successful, demanding one. He needed to spend his workdays running it. He couldn't be hanging around her house looking after the kids.

She had a couple of trusted sitters she'd always used, but both of them were well into their teens now. One had a job flipping burgers and the other was spending her Christmas break at her dad's house in Telluride.

She was kind of at her wit's end with the situation and gearing up to tell Ben and Coco that they were going to have to go to day camp.

And then, Sten and Madison came home.

Sten called on Saturday morning during breakfast to say that Madison had two weeks off from filming the science fiction epic she'd been working on since May. They'd chartered a private jet and would be arriving at Valentine Bay Executive Airport at noon.

At a quarter of one, they showed up at the house in a Lincoln Navigator with Madison's bodyguards, Sergei and Dirk. Everyone was home, including Liam, who'd driven up to Bravo

Trucking for a couple of hours that morning, but returned in time to be there to greet the newlyweds.

When Madison emerged from the back seat, her streaky blond hair piled up in a sloppy bun, wearing old jeans and a giant sweater that hung off one shoulder, Coco shouted, "Madison! Merry Christmas!" and ran straight for her. Madison opened her arms and the two of them hugged it out like the best buddies they'd become back in March when the movie star first came to Sweetheart Cove.

Ben went right to Sten for a slightly more restrained greeting. And then there were hugs all around.

Karin grabbed her brother and whispered mock desperately, "Thank God you're here. I need a kidsitter."

He laughed. "Little sister, whatever you need for the next two weeks, you're gonna get it."

They got the car unloaded and Sten, Madison and the bodyguards settled upstairs in Sten's half of the house. That day, they all mostly just hung out in the downstairs great room around the tree, catching up, taking turns holding Riley and playing board games. Karin kept the Christmas tunes playing in the background. She also cooked a big dinner and they all sat down to eat together.

Once the kids were in bed, Otto headed down to Sten's workshop under the house. He had a few Christmas projects he was working on. Liam invited Madison and Sten over to the cottage for a drink.

"You, too, Karin." He turned those baby blues on her and gave her one of those smiles that melted her midsection. "Bring RG. You can put him to bed over there."

She almost said no, because she didn't want her brother or Madison figuring out how close she and Liam had become—which was a ridiculous excuse, and she knew it. There really was some sense in not letting her kids start to see her and Liam as a couple until they were certain their relationship would last.

But Madison and Sten would be fine no matter what happened in the end between Karin and her baby's father.

Karin put on her coat and bundled up the baby and they all five went next door. One of the bodyguards trailed after them to the cottage but didn't follow them inside.

It was nice, really. Riley went right to sleep in his crib. Liam got everyone something to drink and they sat around the fire. It had started snowing, a light snow, one that wouldn't stick on the ground, but they could see it drifting down beyond the windows, lit by the Christmas lights strung in the eaves and along the deck railing, the white flakes spinning in the cold wind.

Madison was all about getting to know Liam better. "It's another of the many crappy things about being switched at birth," she said. "I feel like I have twenty-seven years to make up for. Liam, we should have grown up together. I should know all your quirks and irritating habits and be constantly ragging on you about them." She snuggled up against Sten, who sat beside her on the sofa. "We should be like Sten and Karin."

"Yeah." Sten gave a wry chuckle. "Karin always knows what's best for me. It's really annoying."

No way Karin could let that remark pass. "I'm very wise, actually. I give excellent advice."

"Oh, really?" Liam had taken the seat beside her in front of the fire. She found herself wishing he would put his arm around her—at the same time as she told herself she appreciated his restraint.

Yeah. No doubt about it. She was kind of a mess over him, longing for it to be the real thing with him and simultaneously terrified that it would all blow up in her face—and what were they talking about?

Right. Her willingness to give her big brother advice. "You'd better believe I've given Sten advice. I've made it my mission to set him straight whenever he needs it."

Sten groaned. "Yeah. Whether I want to be set straight or not."

Karin admitted, "Now and then it's just possible that I've been a tiny bit in your face."

"A *tiny bit*?"

"Come on, Sten. Don't give me attitude. You know I was right about you two." Karin raised her ginger beer in a salute to Madison.

Madison asked eagerly, "What did you say to him?"

"Sorry. I can't give you specifics. It was a private conversation between a thickheaded brother and his brilliant, emotionally sensitive and extremely perceptive sister. Let's just say he was scared to take a chance on what he had with you and I helped him to see that he was all wrong."

Now Madison was grinning at Sten. "You *were* scared." She kissed his cheek.

"But I got over it."

"Oh, yes you did." Her voice was soft and she leaned into him. "And magnificently, too."

"Magnificent. That's me, all right." Sten kissed her.

Karin glanced away from the private moment between her brother and his wife—and into Liam's waiting eyes. At least he didn't get on her for her own reluctance to take a chance on love.

Not right then, anyway.

Later, after Sten and Madison had gone back to the other house, Liam locked the door, turned off the lights and led her down the hall to his room.

"I was afraid you'd run right out the door after them," he teased as he took her red sweater by the hem and pulled it off over her head.

She kissed his beard-scruffy, sculpted jaw. "The baby's still sleeping and I want to be here with you—and my brother and Madison are grown-ups. They can think what they want about me and you." She got to work unbuttoning his flannel shirt.

He interrupted her busy fingers long enough to get rid of her bra. Then he tipped up her chin and kissed her, the sweetest kind of kiss, slow and teasing, as she continued to work her way from one button to the next down the front of his shirt.

She slipped the shirt off his fine, broad shoulders. It dropped to the rug.

He asked, "So you challenged your brother to take a chance on love, huh?"

She was just about to kiss him, but defensiveness curled through her as she met his eyes. "Really, it was a completely different situation with Madison and Sten."

Liam dipped his head and whispered in her ear. "Different than what?"

"You know very well what."

He pulled back enough to look at her again. "You mean, different than you and me."

"That's right."

He traced the line of her jaw with a slow pass of his index finger, making her shiver a little, causing that lovely, hollowed-out feeling low in her belly. And he asked, "Specifically, how are Madison and Sten different from you and me?"

"They were both single, no kids involved. It was simpler for them. Less baggage, you know?"

"Kids or not, everybody's got baggage, Karin."

"You're not hearing me."

"Yes, I am." His fingers eased under the fall of her hair and he cupped the back of her neck, rubbing it a little, easing tension she hadn't even realized was there. "When I took Coco to Bravo Trucking, she said you and I should get married and we'd all live happily ever after like in a Disney movie. And as you already know, Ben only wanted me to promise I wasn't going to go away. RG is just a baby, but I have a really strong feeling he's not going to mind if his parents end up married to each other. So I would say the baggage we're talking about isn't really to do with the kids, is it?"

"Of course it's to do with the kids. They're the top priority—and about Coco saying we ought to get married. How did you answer her?"

He pulled her closer and pressed his lips to the center of her forehead. "Before I could figure out a good answer, she changed her mind and suggested that I just think about it. I said I would. We left it at that."

"Why didn't you tell me this sooner?"

He tipped up her chin so she had to look at him. "Please don't freeze up on me."

"I'm not, I just..." She had no idea what to say next and ended up murmuring weakly, "They're my kids. I don't want them hurt."

"I would never hurt them." He said it sincerely.

And she believed him. "I know." *Not on purpose, anyway.* "And you're right. I do have baggage. Way too much of it."

"You could...let me help you carry it." He gazed down at her so steadily.

She wanted to grab on to him—grab on tight and never let him go.

Because he was so good to her and to her children. Because who did she think she was kidding?

Her heart was already his. And she didn't want to think about that, about how it would all work out in the end, about where they were going and if they would ever actually get there. She just wanted to hold him close and feel his heartbeat next to hers and pretend there was no tomorrow.

Hold him close and lose herself in the glory of right now.

She undid another button. "Liam?"

"Hmm?"

"Kiss me. Now."

His lips touched hers and she slid her hands up to link behind his neck. All her worries flew away. It was just Liam and Karin, holding on tight, keeping each other warm on a cold winter's night.

* * *

"Come with us for Sunday dinner at Daniel's," Madison said the next morning at breakfast. "Let's have the whole family together."

"Yeah." Sten put in his two cents. "Please come."

Coco literally bounced in her chair. "I know I'm not s'posed to interrupt when the grown-ups are deciding things, but just in case you want to know what I think, I think yes! We should go!"

Ben was nodding. "I think so, too," he solemnly intoned.

"I *like* the Bravos," Coco proclaimed. "And I bet they have a big Christmas tree."

Karin slid a glance at Liam. He was looking down, but she knew he was barely hiding a grin. "So Liam. What do you think?"

He glanced up at last and she took the full force of his sky blue gaze. "I'll say it again. I want you all to come to Sunday dinner at Daniel's."

How could she keep saying no when he looked at her that way?

She couldn't. And she didn't.

That afternoon, she packed up plenty of cookies and Christmas candy and the leftover ham from the night before and off they went to the Bravo house on Rhinehart Hill. They took two cars, Liam's F-150 and the Navigator, with one of the bodyguards behind the wheel.

Once they got there, Karin wondered why she'd ever said no. Everyone really did seem happy to see them. She'd always enjoyed hanging out with Liam's sisters, and the giant Christmas tree in the family room was a beautiful sight to behold.

She got to touch base with Connor and Aly Bravo, who'd just returned from New York, where Aly had finished up at her longtime job there, sublet her apartment—and married Connor for the second time.

Aly asked to hold Riley. She sighed when Karin laid him in her arms. "He is just perfect." Connor's bride glanced up with a glowing smile. "Connor and I are expecting in May."

"Wow. Congratulations."

"What can I say? It was unexpected, but we aren't complaining. We both always wanted kids."

Aly had five brothers, one of whom had been born just a couple of months ago. Of her older brothers, two were married with children and Dante, the oldest, was divorced with twin daughters. Aly said that she and Connor would be spending Christmas Day at her parents' house and Christmas Eve right here on Rinehart Hill with the Bravos.

"It's good to be home." Aly smiled dreamily down at Riley. "I love New York. But for me, there's nothing like Christmas in Valentine Bay."

A little later, Keely, Daniel's wife, pulled Karin aside and invited her and the kids and her dad for Christmas dinner. "I'm sure Liam's already asked you, but I just wanted you to know how much we'd all love it if you guys would join us for Christmas Day, too."

Karin shocked the hell out of herself and almost said yes on the spot. After all, Sten and Madison would be coming here to the Bravo house, as would Liam. She and her dad and the kids might as well come, too. But her reluctance to get swept up in too much togetherness with Liam and his family won out. She thanked Keely and promised to talk to Liam about it.

It was after nine when Karin glanced over and saw that Coco had fallen asleep on the floor in front of the tree.

She leaned close to Liam and whispered, "Time to go."

Leaving Sten and Madison and the bodyguards behind, Karin, Liam, Otto and the kids headed for home.

Once they got everyone into the house, Otto said, "Give me that baby."

Karin didn't argue. She passed him the baby carrier in which Riley slept, his chin on his chest, drooling a little.

Her dad said, "I'll put the kids to bed. There's milk in the fridge if RG here gets hungry. You two have a nice night."

"So much for not letting anybody know we're together," she

grumbled to Liam several minutes later. They were already in his bedroom, under the covers, cuddled up close.

"You're the one who's all tied in knots over that," he reminded her.

She used her fingers to comb his hair back off his forehead. "I'm...getting used to it."

He ducked close, pressed his mouth to her neck—and blew a raspberry against the side of her throat. When she laughed and wriggled away, he said, "Good. Because I really am going nowhere—as I've said so many times I've lost count."

She cuddled in close again. "Keely invited us all to Christmas dinner."

He slid an arm under her shoulders and drew her closer still. "And you said...?"

"That I would talk to you about it."

"And...?"

Really, why hold out against having Christmas at Daniel and Keely's house? Her family loved going over there. And so did she. "Sure. Let's spend the afternoon at Daniel's."

He tipped up her chin and stared into her eyes. "Tell me I'm not dreaming. Tell me you just said yes to Christmas dinner with the Bravos."

"Yes, I said yes."

He kissed the tip of her nose. "That wasn't so hard, now was it?"

She laughed. "You are impossible."

"But in the best kind of way, right?"

"Oh, absolutely." She settled her head on his shoulder. "I do like this, Liam. You and me, how it's all kind of working out."

"We're making progress, together." He breathed the words into her hair.

"Umm-hmm." Held safe in his arms, she shut her eyes and let herself relax completely. It really was getting easier, day by day, to put the past behind her, to start letting herself imagine a future with Liam.

Yes, at first it had seemed far too similar to the situation she'd gotten herself into with Bud—a baby on the way and a man just trying to step up and do right. But Liam really did seem to like being a family man. And he really did seem to care for her. Not to mention, she was so completely in love with him.

In love with Liam.

Just thinking those words sent a warning shiver through her, no matter that she'd grown increasingly sure they were true.

It wasn't something she felt entirely ready to deal with yet. And she certainly wouldn't be saying I love you out loud to him.

Not yet. Not until…

Who knew? She didn't. But it was going to take some time yet, before she would be willing to declare her love to Liam. Right now, she couldn't even let *him* say the words.

Right now, what she felt for him was for her to know and no one else to find out. She needed more time to become absolutely certain that what they had together really was as strong and enduring as she had started to let herself hope it might be.

Liam drove down to his Portland offices early the next day for a couple of meetings. He was finished before noon and decided to make a detour into downtown, do a little Christmas shopping at an upscale mall called Pioneer Place.

He picked up a few things for Coco and Ben on the first level and then rode the escalator up to the second. If he remembered correctly, there was a certain jewelry story up there.

Tiffany & Co.

He spotted it right away and a feeling of satisfaction spread through him as he thought of Karin. They were getting it together, him and Karin. They had a happy, healthy baby boy and every day he felt more a part of the Larson-Killigan family.

Her kids and her dad trusted him. And Sten had been on his side from the first, not even hesitating to lease him the cottage all those weeks and weeks ago, when he was a brand-new dad, desperate for a closer connection to his son and to the frustrating, unforgettable woman who was so determined not to let him get near.

Maybe it was a little early to go browsing engagement rings. But hey, how often did he get anywhere near Tiffany & Co.? Pretty much never.

What could it hurt just to look?

Someday soon, he'd be needing the right ring. And when that happened, it would damn well be the best.

Inside the store, there were fancy wreaths on the walls, a tree all decked out with Tiffany-blue lights and white satin bows. Christmas music played, turned down tastefully low, like a hum of holiday cheer in the background. He was greeted by the guard at the door and by a couple of salespeople. A pretty woman with pale blond hair asked if there was something or someone in particular he was shopping for.

He shook his head. "Just looking."

"Ah. Take your time. Let me know if there's anything I can do to help."

He thanked her and browsed the big, gleaming cases of engagement and wedding rings, each one more sparkly and beautiful than the one before it.

It was a little overwhelming—until he saw *the* ring. It was simple and perfect, with a gorgeous square diamond glittering so brightly on a platinum band.

The blonde stepped near again. In a soft, pleasant voice, she began talking about responsible sourcing, about the four C's of diamonds—carat, cut, color and clarity.

He looked up and grinned at her. "I want that one, and the platinum band with the diamonds for the wedding ring..."

Liam left Tiffany & Co. feeling equal parts exhilarated and stunned. He'd just bought a matched pair of sparklers that cost more than his truck.

And he'd honestly only gone in there to look.

But hey. When he finally did get down on one knee and offer

his ring to Karin along with his heart and all his worldly possessions, she was going to love that ring.

And if the impossible happened and the perfect ring wasn't right for her, the nice saleswoman had assured him that he could bring Karin in to choose something else.

So it was nothing to get freaky over. He'd wanted the best for Karin and he'd gotten the best.

And for now, he had a plan: do nothing. Not for a while. He would put the perfect rings away, enjoy the rest of the holiday season and wait for the right moment, no matter how long it took to get there.

Karin was skittish about love, about marriage. He knew that. He *got* that. He honestly did. He understood her fears and her doubts. The catastrophe of her first marriage still haunted her. And she needed a whole lot of time to learn to trust that he was all in with her the way Bud had never really been.

His phone buzzed with a text just as he reached the parking garage a block from the mall. It was Karin.

Pork chops tonight. 6 o'clock. Interested?

He wore a giant grin as he paused on the sidewalk to answer. I'll be there.

Dinner was great. RG was up, so Liam ate with the baby on his lap. Sten and Madison joined them. Afterward, Coco dragged Liam into her room and whipped out a pink plastic pitcher, her Christmas gift for Karin.

"Isn't it beautiful, Liam? Won't Mommy just love it?"

He agreed that it was one fine-looking pitcher and Karin would be so happy to have it. Next, he checked in with Ben to see how he was doing on his latest project for Science Club.

Around eight, he returned to the cottage and headed straight for the wall safe in the bedroom closet to check out his Tiffany purchase. A part of him still didn't quite believe he'd just gone out and done it—bought Karin a ring.

But he had. And it was freaking gorgeous.

He'd just stuck the tiny black velvet box into the blue Tiffany box and then back into the safe and returned to the main room when she showed up at the slider.

He shoved open the door and she came straight into his arms like there was no place on earth she would rather be. "Dad shooed me out again. He promised to look after RG and make sure Ben and Coco get to bed on time."

"Otto's my hero."

"Mine, too." She sighed and tipped up her mouth in an invitation to a kiss. It was an invitation he accepted with enthusiasm.

Damn, she was beautiful. She just seemed to glow with happiness, so easy and comfortable with him, with the world, with the life they were making, day by day, the two of them—even if she hadn't quite gotten to where she would admit that out loud.

They hung out in the main room for a while, enjoying the fire, discussing Christmas Eve, which they would share at the other house with the kids and Otto, Sten and Madison. Christmas morning, he would cook breakfast for everyone here at the cottage. Then they would return to the main house to open presents.

And then, as she'd miraculously agreed the night before, they would head up to Rhinehart Hill for Christmas dinner with his family.

Life didn't get any better than this.

He scooped her up in his arms and headed down the hall to his bedroom, where he made love to her slowly, his mind and heart overflowing with words of love.

Words that he really didn't intend to try to say out loud again. Not yet.

But she was moving beneath him, sighing his name, those blue-green eyes shining as she gazed up at him through the dark, thick fringe of her eyelashes. All that coffee-brown hair was spread out on the pillow, tangled and wild. He wanted to capture the moment, never let it go.

And then she said it, so soft and low he might not have heard it if he hadn't been staring directly down at her beautiful face. "I love you so much, Liam. I love you. I do."

And it was like a dam breaking inside him, the words spilling out of him, the ones she'd never let him say before. "I love you, Karin. You're everything to me..."

Afterward, she seemed kind of quiet, but she tucked herself in nice and close to him. Idly, she traced the shape of his ear, brushed her fingers along his jaw, combed them up into his hair.

He pressed a kiss to the curve of her shoulder and she made a soft little sound in her throat. It sounded like approval. Affection.

Love.

And he just couldn't do it. Couldn't wait another day, another hour, another minute to ask her, to promise her everything, to give her the ring he'd chosen for her.

He kissed her shoulder again and breathed in the incomparable scent of her skin. "Do not move from this spot."

She let out a throaty little moan. "No worries. I don't think I *can* move. I just might be in an after-sex coma."

He chuckled. "Try to stay conscious. I'll be right back." He slid out from under the covers and turned for the closet.

"Liam, what—?"

"Just wait. You'll see." He pulled open the closet door, switched on the light and shoved a row of shirts to the side. Four quick pokes at the keypad and he had the safe open. The blue box was waiting. He took out the black velvet box inside and returned with it to the bed.

She was sitting up by then, clutching the sheet to her chest. "What are you up to?"

He dropped to a knee, held out the tiny box and flipped the lid back.

She stared down at the ring, eyes big as sand dollars. "Liam."

"Marry me, Karin."

She just kept staring, clutching the sheet even tighter. "I, um, that's the most gorgeous ring I've ever seen."

"Say yes."

She winced—she actually winced at him. "Liam. I'm so sorry. I can't do that. You know I can't. Not right now."

CHAPTER TWELVE

KARIN SINCERELY HATED herself at that moment.

Liam stared up at her from where he knelt on the rug, a frown creasing his brow. He flipped the box shut, fisted his hand around it and let his arm drop to his side. "You said you love me."

"I know. And I do, but…" Really, what was he supposed to think? "I'm sorry," she babbled. "I shouldn't have said it. I didn't mean to say it."

He rose and set the magnificent ring in its velvet box on the nightstand. And then he just stood there by the bed, so tall and strong, wearing nothing but a somber expression, his eyes full of shadows and sadness now. "You didn't mean to say you love me?"

"No! I… Well, of course, I…" She stopped, forced herself to take a slow breath, and tried again. "I do love you, even though I tried really hard not to."

He almost smiled, but then his fine mouth flattened out again. "No kidding."

"I fell for you, Liam. I've fallen. I'm just gone on you. I wasn't going to tell you, though. Not until I was ready to, um, move on to the next step. But it's been so good between us lately. And tonight was so perfect and beautiful and true. I got carried away, I guess. The words just slipped out. I'm so sorry."

One golden-brown eyebrow inched upward. "Sorry that you love me?"

Could she *be* more confusing? "Please. No. That's not what I mean." She reached out and took his hand. He didn't exactly give it to her, but he let her have it, he didn't jerk away. "Come back to bed."

He stared at her so strangely, like she'd hurt him so bad, broken something inside him. "Karin. Are you gonna talk to me about this? Tell me, honestly, why you keep refusing to take a chance on us?"

"Please…" She tugged on his hand. "Come here."

He gave in and got back under the covers with her. They propped their pillows against the headboard and sat up, side by side. "Okay," he said. "Talk."

She put her fingers to her temples and rubbed to ease the tension that caused a dull throbbing behind her eyes. "I just have to be sure that we can really make it work before there are rings and promises of forever. I have to be 100 percent certain. I can't take a chance that I'll mess up again. It's just not fair to the kids—or to you, really. Some things, you can't come back from, Liam."

"You have to know that you're never going to get the certainty you say you need. When you love another person, you're always taking a risk. There are no guarantees."

What could she say to that? She knew he was right.

He held her gaze. "So, Karin. Take a chance. On me. On us."

A frustrated cry escaped her. "But horrible things can happen. You have no idea."

"Yeah, I do. When he was only eight years old, my brother disappeared in Siberia, vanished without a trace never to be seen or heard from again. Two years later, my mom and dad died in a Thailand tsunami. Believe me, I know about horrible things."

Shame made her cheeks burn. "Oh, my God. You're right. Of course, you know exactly what I'm talking about. And I am so sorry—about Finn, about your dad and mom. Could I *be* any more insensitive?" She covered her face with her hands.

"Hey. Look at me."

She dropped her hands and made herself face him. "Yeah?"

"Bad shit happens. To everyone. And for you, that means Bud, right? You're trying to tell me that you're not really over his death, that he's always going to be a barrier between us?"

"Not in the way that you think. It's not like I'm in love with his memory or anything. Liam, what haunts me is that I rushed into marriage with him and it all went to hell. Everybody got hurt—my children included. I wish I could make you see."

He regarded her so steadily. "I think I do see. I don't like it. I think you're punishing yourself for something that really isn't your fault. But I get it. I do." He looked so exhausted, suddenly.

And seriously, who would have guessed that sexy, charming, commitment-phobic Liam Bravo would grow up to be such an amazing man?

She reached out a tentative hand and combed his hair back with her fingers. He didn't duck away. She tried to take heart from that. "You look worn-out—worn-out from dealing with me."

He caught her hand, opened her fingers and kissed the center of her palm. His lips were so warm, his breath a caress in itself. "Let's try to get some sleep, okay?"

"Yeah. Okay."

They settled down into the bed. He turned off the light and then pulled her in close. She cuddled against him, grateful for his arms around her.

And all too aware that she was the one holding them back.

* * *

Karin opened her eyes to daylight.

Morning?

It was morning already? She slid her hand across the bottom sheet.

Empty.

Liam had left the bed.

"No!" She popped straight up to a sitting position, her heart going a mile a minute.

The kids would already be up by now. Up and wondering where Mom had gotten off to.

And her dad...

She'd never asked him outright to keep her nighttime visits with Liam a secret. What if he took her staying here till morning as a signal that she and Liam were outing their relationship? What if he just told her son and her daughter that she was over here? What if he sent Coco to summon them to breakfast?

Uh-uh. No way. The kids were not supposed to know about her and Liam. They weren't supposed to get their hopes up, to start counting on him to be there, be a real father to them, as the years went by.

Because no matter how sure Liam seemed now—getting down on one knee, whipping out the most beautiful ring she'd ever seen, telling her he loved her and asking her to marry him...

He could so easily change his mind, move back to his big house in Astoria, come by Sweetheart Cove only to pick up and drop off his son.

Coco and Ben would be devastated.

No. That couldn't happen. Her kids were innocent. They didn't deserve that kind of pain. They'd already suffered enough in their short lives.

"Liam...?" She heard water running.

The door to the master bath stood open.

The shower.

He was taking a shower.

How could he have just left the bed without waking her up? How could he be so thoughtless?

He knew she should have been back at the other house long before now.

Furious, literally shaking with frustration, she jumped from the bed and started grabbing her wrinkled clothes, yanking them on as fast as she got hold of them.

The water shut off. By then, she'd dropped to the bed again to put on her ankle boots. Liam emerged from the bathroom, a towel around his lean hips, a tender smile on his lips. He looked so manly, lean and tall, like every woman's perfect fantasy man, his hard biceps flexing as he rubbed his wet hair with a second towel.

And for some reason, his tender smile, that easy way about him, it all just made her madder than ever.

She tugged on the second boot and jumped up to face him. "What is the matter with you?"

He stopped drying his hair. Endless seconds elapsed before he said quietly, "Nothing. Nothing's the matter with me."

"Why didn't you wake me?"

He tossed the towel on a chair. "You looked tired, so I let you sleep."

She wanted to start shrieking at him, to grab him and shake him until he realized how careless he'd been. "You knew I needed to get back. The kids will be up now. What am I going to say to them?"

"Karin. You don't have to *say* anything to them. They won't be damaged for life just because you spent the night over here." He spoke to her so gently, carefully, like she was a crazy person throwing a fit.

And maybe she kind of was. Somewhere in the back of her mind she knew she was behaving very badly. "You are so irresponsible," she accused, though he wasn't. He was wonderful, always there when she needed him, always patient and thoughtful and ready to help.

She was totally overreacting, her heart aching from his beautiful proposal she couldn't allow herself to accept. She knew, absolutely, that one way or another, she was going to lose him. She just didn't know when it was going to happen.

She wished he would just get it over with and leave her, already.

"Liam, I can't do this. I'm so sorry, but we have to stop this. I want you to please go see your lawyer. I want you to decide what kind of parenting plan works for you. Then we can come to an agreement on custody and all that. We need to move on. We need to settle this once and for all."

He just stood there in his towel, looking handsome and bleak, staring at her.

For Liam, it happened right then, as they stared at each other across a distance of maybe ten feet that suddenly yawned wide as the Grand Canyon. He realized he'd reached his breaking point with her.

He couldn't take anymore. It just wasn't going to work with her. He'd knocked himself out trying to show her how much he loved her and wanted a life with her. But she just would not believe him.

At some point, a guy had to salvage the last of his pride, take the diamond ring back to Tiffany & Co. and get on with his own damn life.

"Fair enough," he said, his own voice dead, flat in his ears. "I'll talk to my lawyer."

She had the nerve to look stricken. Like *he'd* just hurt *her*. "Good," she said, the word breaking a little in the middle. "Talk to your lawyer—and you'll move back to your own house?"

That, he wouldn't do. "I want time with my son and living here is the best way for me to get that. And truthfully, I promised Ben I wouldn't leave. I'm living in this cottage for as long as Sten is willing to keep cashing my checks. If you don't want to be with me, well, that's up to you. But I live here now, Karin. And I'm not going anywhere."

CHAPTER THIRTEEN

KARIN WALKED OUT.

She grabbed her coat from the peg by the front door and went back to the other house. What else could she do? She'd pretty much wrecked everything. Better to just get the hell out.

At the main house, they were all gathered around the breakfast table—the kids, her dad, Sten and Madison. She walked in and they all turned and looked at her.

"Where's Liam?" Ben asked.

She waved a hand, trying to look casual and easy and probably blowing that all to hell. "Oh, he'll be over in a minute, I'm sure." Her gaze collided with Sten's and she *knew* that *he* knew something was terribly wrong. She blinked and looked away—but not far enough to escape the concerned frown on her dad's face.

Right then, the baby monitor on the counter erupted with fussy cries. She had never in her life felt so relieved to hear her baby crying. "I'll, um, just go take care of him…" And she fled for the sanctuary of Riley's room.

After she'd fed and changed the baby and pulled herself together a little, Karin returned to the kitchen. The adults had dispersed, which suited her just fine. Coco and Ben were clearing off the table.

"There's eggs and bacon left for you," said Ben.

"Great. Thanks." She put Riley in his bouncy seat and sat down to eat in spite of the fact that she had zero appetite.

Coco stepped close. She wrapped her arms around Karin's neck, rested her head on Karin's shoulder and said wistfully, "I love you, Mommy."

Kids. They always sensed when things were off with the grown-ups. Karin patted the small hands clasped around her neck. "Love you, too. So much."

Coco pulled away, but then took the seat next to Karin's. "Sten and Madison and Dirk and Sergei are taking us to the ranch where Aislinn lives today." Aislinn was the Bravo sister born to Lloyd and Paula Delaney, the one who'd been switched with Madison the day they were born. Madison was slowly getting to know all her newfound brothers and sisters, but she and Aislinn had hit it off from the first. The two shared a special bond. "We're going to have lunch there," Coco added. "Madison says Aislinn has rabbits that live on her porch and we get to pet them."

"That's great." Karin sincerely hoped she sounded at least a little enthusiastic.

"Liam never came," Ben said too quietly from over by the sink.

Karin turned in her chair to meet her son's serious eyes. "I'm sure he'll be over later." Truthfully, she kind of wished that Liam wouldn't be over at all, though it was both wrong and ridiculous for her to wish such a thing. His son lived here. He was friends with her father. He had actual relationships with her older children.

He'd said it repeatedly himself. He was not going anywhere.

Well, except for as far away from her as he could get. She'd made sure of that.

* * *

Liam spent most of the day at the Warrenton terminal. Around five when he packed it in, he was tempted to take a little detour on the way home to the cottage. There were bars on Beach Street calling his name.

But he intended to be at Karin's for breakfast the next morning, whether she wanted him there or not. No way he was showing up at her table with a hangover.

Uh-uh. He needed a clear head tomorrow. He would see the kids and reach an understanding with their mother that nothing had changed in terms of RG. He would have his son from nine to noon Wednesdays and Fridays, as per their prior agreement. And she would damn well reach out to him if she needed someone to watch the baby any other time.

At the cottage, he had a beer and nuked himself some frozen lasagna. Once he'd shoved down the food, he considered calling Deke Pasternak and making an appointment to talk about custody and a damn parenting plan. He'd told Karin he would.

But later for that. Right now, RG needed him nearby and available. He was both. Problem solved.

Just as he began considering the big question of whether or not to have a second beer, he heard footsteps out on the deck. For about a half a second, his heart bounced toward his throat and hope exploded in his chest.

But it wasn't Karin.

It was Ben, sweet, serious Ben. The kid looked apprehensive and that had Liam pissed off at Karin all over again.

He got up and pushed open the slider. "Come on in."

The wind was blowing, the sky thick with dark clouds, the waves out beyond the beach tossing and foaming. Ben hunched into his down jacket, like a turtle seeking the safety of his shell. "I can't stay very long."

Liam stepped out of the way. "Get in here. It's cold out there." The boy crossed the threshold and Liam shut the glass door. "Want some hot chocolate or something?"

"No, thanks." Ben shoved his hands even deeper into his jacket pockets. "So. You and Mom are fighting?"

Liam saw it all in those serious brown eyes. Ben had lost his father. Now he anticipated losing Liam, too—and right now, the boy was waiting for Liam to say something, to somehow ease his fears. Too bad Liam had nothing all that encouraging to say. "Your mom and I are having some problems, yes."

"What problems?"

"Ben, I can't go into detail about it, but things aren't good between your mom and me right now."

Ben's face started to crumple—but he kept it together, straightening his narrow shoulders, hiking up his chin. "So, you're moving out?"

That, he could answer more emphatically. "Nope. I'll be here. I live here."

"What about breakfast tomorrow?"

"I'll be there."

"Yeah?"

"You have my word on it."

"What about Christmas? You still cooking breakfast for us Christmas morning?"

"That is my plan." If Karin thought differently, well, they would have to discuss it. She would actually have to *talk* to him. That could be good, right?

Or maybe not.

Ben wasn't finished. "And will you be there Christmas Eve and are we all going up to the Bravo house for Christmas dinner?"

In spite of how craptacular he felt at that moment, Liam almost smiled. "How come you didn't ask your mom all these questions?"

Ben gulped. "I kind of had a feeling I would get better answers from you."

Liam wanted to grab the kid and hug him, but he had a suspicion that any sudden moves on his part wouldn't be welcome right now. Ben needed reassurance that the ground was solid under his feet, that the people he'd come to count on and trust wouldn't abandon him, no matter what weird stuff happened between the grown-ups. "I'm not sure about all our specific plans. What I am sure about is that I'm going to be here, just like I said I would. No matter what happens, that's not going to change."

"Not ever?"

"Not for a long while, anyway. You've got my number." Ben had his own phone. They'd exchanged numbers back in October, the first time Liam drove him to soccer practice. "Anytime you need to talk to me, you just call, text or show up at my door."

Ben yanked his right hand from his pocket and stuck it out. Liam shook it.

The hug happened after all when Ben kind of swayed toward him and Liam put his free arm around him.

Ben quickly stepped back. "Okay, then. I just needed to know. See you for breakfast." He turned and shoved the slider wide, stepped through and closed it. With a last, solemn nod at Liam through the glass, he took off across the deck.

"What's going on with you and Liam?" Otto asked Karin that night when the kids were in bed and Sten and Madison had gone upstairs.

"I don't want to talk about it, Dad. I really don't."

"That man's in love with you. And you're in love with him. Whatever it is, you need to work it out with him."

"Stay out of it, Dad."

He narrowed his eyes at her and put on his stern voice. "Fix it."

She knew with absolute certainty that she was about to burst into tears. "Please, Dad…"

His hard expression melted as he reached out his big hands and clasped her shoulders. "Aw, honey."

She sagged against him and whispered, "I messed up. I messed up bad."

He patted her back. "Now, now. You'll work it out, I know you will."

"I don't think so, Dad. I was terrible to him. He's not going to forgive me and I can't say I blame him."

"Love forgives all. Just give it time…"

An hour later, when she couldn't sleep, she put on thermal pants and a heavy sweater, her shearling boots, a winter jacket, mittens and a beanie, grabbed Riley's monitor and went out to sit on the deck. She wasn't the least surprised when Sten, as bundled up as she was, came out the door behind her and took the empty chair at her side.

All the wise advice she'd given him back in April when he screwed things up with Madison seemed to hover in the cold night air between them, taunting her.

"Colder than a polar bear's nose," he said mildly. "At least the wind's died down a little."

She wrapped her arms a little tighter around herself. "Don't start in on me, Sten. Please?"

He gave a wry chuckle. "Talk of the weather really bugs the crap out of you, huh?"

She huffed out a breath. "Okay, fine. Just say it."

"Not sure where to start. I don't know what's wrong between you and Liam, not really."

She tugged her beanie more firmly down over her ears. "I jumped all over him for no reason at all."

"Oh, come on. There had to be a reason."

"Yeah, well, not an *acceptable* reason. He asked me to marry him and that scared me to death—and let me be clear. I did worse than jump all over him. I told him we were done and he should move back to Astoria and come up with a parenting plan."

He made a thoughtful sound. "You're in love with the guy, right?"

She stared out at the restless gray ocean beyond the wide

stretch of sand and found it surprisingly easy to tell her brother the truth. "I am, yeah. I am very much in love with Liam Bravo."

"I used to think you would never marry anyone again, that Bud was your true, forever love, lost tragically at sea, but you'd learned to be happy with the kids, on your own."

She groaned. "So romantic."

"Yeah, well. I never did want to think there might be big issues between you and Bud."

"There were. I never should have married him. He wasn't ready. I wasn't ready. The love we had was…not that strong."

"This love you have with Liam, is it *that* strong?"

She didn't even have to think about it. "Yeah—but what if I'm wrong? So far, I've kept him at a distance by making him promise that what we have would stay just between the two of us. When he asked me to marry him last night, I turned him down. Then I drummed up a fake reason to break it off between us. I love my children, and you and Dad. But my track record at loving a man? We should face it. It's not good."

"Someone very wise once told me that I shouldn't let getting my heart broken by the wrong person keep me from giving the right person a fighting chance. Take your own advice. Give the *right* man a chance."

"How did I know you were going to say that?"

He grinned. "Super painful, isn't it? When your own words come back to bite you in the ass…"

The next morning, Liam showed up for breakfast. Coco ran and hugged him. Everyone else played it cool and subdued.

Karin ached all over just to see him sitting there at the table with Riley asleep in a sling strapped to the front of him.

So close.

But no longer *hers*.

The plans for Christmas Eve and Christmas Day were brought up and reconfirmed. Karin didn't make a peep when that happened. Liam didn't have to be hers to be part of the family. He was Madison's brother and Riley's dad. And even if he wasn't *hers*, Coco and Ben had definitely come to think of him as *theirs*.

When he got up to go, he still had Riley hooked to the front of him. "So, Karin, how about if I just take RG with me now? You can pick him up at noon, or whatever. Just take your time."

"Um, that would be great." She smiled at him. It was more of a grimace, really. But hey, at least she tried. She filled an insulated pack with bottles of breast milk to replenish the stash at his place and sent him on his way.

And then, somehow, she got through her morning and showed up at Liam's door at noon on the nose. He had Riley all ready to go. The handoff took maybe a minute. She tried not to look directly at Liam. She had this feeling that if she actually met his eyes, she would drop to her knees and start pleading with him to give her one more chance.

In a way, dropping to her knees kind of seemed like a viable approach to this huge problem she'd created. But she was so afraid he'd turn her down, that he'd realized he'd been all wrong to want to build a life with her. He would say no.

And she would have to know for certain it was over.

She just couldn't face that. Not yet.

Liam planned to go up to the Warrenton terminal as soon as Karin came for RG. But the sight of her just kind of broke him. She was trying so hard to be civil, even kind. He'd expected her to give him dirty looks when he showed up for breakfast, to put up a fight about what to do for Christmas, to insist that really, the plans they'd made earlier needed to change.

Those things didn't happen. She nodded when the rest of them agreed that the Christmas schedule would stay the same. And then, at noon, when she came to pick up RG, he'd been sure she would start in about the damn parenting plan.

Nope. She thanked him, forced a smile, took the baby and left.

If she'd only been a jerk to him, he would have found it at

least a little easier to hold on to his anger with her. Instead, he missed her, *ached* for her, wished he could find a way to heal the breach between them.

Not thirty-six hours after he'd lost her, he was already trying to figure out how to find his way back to her.

Yesterday, he'd had some vague idea that he'd head down to Portland today after Karin came for RG, that he would check in at his offices there and take the ring back to Tiffany & Co.

But now he realized that what he really needed was someone he could trust to talk to.

He thought of Otto first. He really did trust Karin's dad and the man was older, much wiser and good at heart, with that understanding way about him.

But Otto was Karin's dad. And dragging Otto into this, putting him in a position where he might feel he had to take sides...

Uh-uh. That wouldn't be right.

Liam called Daniel. It turned out his oldest brother was spending the day before Christmas Eve at home with his family.

At a little after one, Liam was sitting on the sofa in Daniel's study at the house on Rinehart Hill.

"Scotch?" asked his older brother as he poured two fingers for himself. Daniel inevitably brought out the good Scotch for man-to-man talks.

"Thanks, but no."

"So, what's going on?" Daniel carried his drink over to the chair across from Liam.

And Liam laid it on him. "I'm in love with Karin—completely. It's deep, Daniel, what I feel for her. And it's real. I bought a ring and then night-before-last I asked her to marry me. She said she loves me, too, but she put the brakes on, turned me down." He recounted in detail the story of the fight and the breakup that had occurred early yesterday morning.

When he finally fell silent, Daniel said, "And then you realized you were wrong and you don't love her after all?"

Suddenly, Liam wished he'd taken that drink. "What the hell, Daniel? No. Uh-uh. I do love her. She's everything to me."

Daniel sipped his Scotch. "You still want to marry her, then?"

"You bet your ass I do. I just, well, what did I do wrong and how can I make it right?"

"Judging by what you've just told me, you didn't do anything wrong."

"I didn't…? Daniel, if I didn't do anything wrong, then there is no way for me to make it right."

"Not by yourself. At some point, she's going to need to meet you halfway."

"I don't know. It's really hard for her. She had a bad experience with Bud Killigan."

"Not your fault. But you said that *she* said she loves you, right?"

"She did, yeah."

"So stay steady. Don't let her fear scare you away."

Easier said than done. "You know how I am. I get enthusiastic. And that makes me impatient. I *knew* I should've waited. I *planned* to wait until she was more sure of me, of *us*. But then she said she loved me and I completely lost my head. I grabbed the ring and got down on my knees."

"That's okay. You got a right to be you, man."

"I just don't know how you do it, Daniel. How you've done it for all these years, the way you've put up with all of us, *been there* for all of us, even with all the crap we've laid on you, all the challenges we've thrown at you."

Daniel gave a slow, pensive shake of his head. "I've made some giant mistakes along the way."

"Maybe, but you hung in. You always found a way to make it right. No matter how bad things got, you kept stepping up."

Daniel set down his drink and leaned forward in his chair. "And that—what you just said. That's how you do it. That's how you make it work. You have to be there when you're needed— you have to be there just *in case* you're needed. And don't even try to kid yourself, you will always wonder if you're doing it right, if you're messing something up that's going to make it harder for someone you love down the line. No matter what, though, you do the best you can. And sometimes you screw it up. And then you scramble to try to make it right again. But you can never get it right if you don't keep putting yourself out there in the first place."

Bolstered by his big brother's advice, Liam decided that he would reach out to Karin again.

This time though, he would be reasonable and careful. He would make it crystal clear to her that he didn't want to push her, he just wanted to be with her—yeah, he wanted to marry her. He wanted her for today and tomorrow and the rest of their lives.

But if one day at a time was the only way she could do it, one day at a time was just fine with him.

And if she still needed to keep what they had together a secret from Ben and Coco, he would respect her wishes and make certain she got back to the main house every morning before dawn.

At first, he was thinking he couldn't wait. That he needed to try to make things right with her immediately.

But that was just his impatient nature taking over again.

He ordered himself to slow down, to think it through more carefully. It was the day before Christmas Eve. He didn't want to mess up the fragile peace between them. Coco and Ben were counting on their Christmas plans. He couldn't take the chance that Karin would not only turn him down, but decide she just wasn't comfortable having breakfast at the cottage Christmas morning or going to Daniel's for Christmas Day.

No. He needed to wait at least until the day after Christmas to try to make things right with her.

Instead of heading back to the Cove and pounding on her door or blowing up her phone with calls and texts, he went into downtown Valentine Bay.

He loved his hometown at Christmas. All the shop windows

had Christmas displays and the streetlamps were wrapped in garland and hung with lighted wreathes. He dropped some bills into a couple of Salvation Army pots and did some last-minute Christmas shopping, more gifts for Ben and Coco, Otto and Sten and his nieces and nephew.

At some point, he started thinking about all the families who couldn't afford piles of presents under their trees. So he bought even more toys and made a quick run by Safeway and Walgreens to help fill the Toys for Tots donation boxes. Before he went home, he stopped at a diner he liked for a quick dinner.

Back at the cottage by seven, he turned on the Christmas lights inside and out, cued up the holiday tunes and spent a couple of hours wrapping the gifts he'd found on his impromptu shopping spree.

It was snowing at nine fifteen when he stuck a bow on the last package and got up to put it under the tree. He heard footsteps on the deck and glanced up to see Karin standing on the far side of the sliding door.

For a moment, he almost didn't believe his own eyes.

But then she raised a hand and gave him a sheepish wave.

Real. She was real.

His blood racing through his veins and his breath all tangled and hot in his chest, he went to let her in.

CHAPTER FOURTEEN

SNOWFLAKES GLITTERED IN her hair and her cheeks were pink from the cold. She gave him a beautiful, wobbly little smile. "Dad's got Riley. I was hoping we could talk." The look in her eyes? It promised him everything.

He wanted to grab her, wrap her up tight in his arms and never, ever let go.

But then he reminded himself that she'd only said she wanted to talk. The thing *not* to do right now was make wild assumptions.

"Yes," he said. "I would love to talk."

"So then, may I come in?"

Feeling foolish for keeping her standing out in the cold, he stepped clear of the doorway. "Please."

She entered the kitchen and he shut and locked the slider.

"Here. Give me your coat." He moved behind her. She let him slip it off her shoulders. He laid it over the back of a kitchen chair. "Tea? Hot chocolate?"

"No. I just want to talk."

He ushered her over to the fire. They sat on the hearth side by side.

"You're busy," she said nervously, gesturing at the coffee table, where he'd left the rolls of bright wrapping paper and the big bag of ready-made bows.

"Nope. I'm all done." He turned and stared directly at her then—like a gift in itself, just looking at her. "I have wrapped the last present." And damn it, he couldn't wait another second to touch her. He reached for her hand.

And she gave it, her slim fingers sliding between his, weaving them together.

It was everything he'd ever wanted, her hand in his. He was so glad he'd waited, given her time to come back to him when she was ready—and was he jumping the gun again? Assuming more than she was offering?

"Talk to me," he said.

Her eyes were dark with shadows. "If I talk about the past... is that okay?"

"Anything, Karin. Everything. I want to understand. I want to be the one you come to—for the good things. And for the tough things, too."

"I, um..." She hesitated. He made himself be quiet, made himself simply wait as she blew out a slow breath and tried again. "I didn't love Bud—I mean, I didn't love him enough. Not the way a woman needs to love a man she builds a life with. I married him because he said he loved *me*, because I was pregnant and worried about the future. Saying yes to him seemed like the answer to a bunch of questions I didn't even really know how to ask. It was not the best choice. It was, in the end, a pretty bad choice, to marry Bud. And when he died, I swear I felt like I had killed him."

He couldn't let that stand. "No. What happened to him wasn't your fault."

She leaned her head on his shoulder. "You're right. I know

that I didn't *really* kill him. But for a long time, I blamed myself for his death."

"But not anymore?"

"No. Bud really was like those songs you hear and those books you read about sailors. He was married to the sea. He loved the life on a fishing boat. And he died doing what he loved. I can't say I take comfort from that, exactly, but it is what it is and at least I'm no longer telling myself it was all my fault. I've made a lot of progress with that."

He kind of wanted to scold her for ever having blamed herself. But this was *her* story she was sharing. He had no right to tell her how to feel about her part in it.

She lifted her head from his shoulder and grinned at him. "Look at you. So restrained."

"I'm trying." He pressed their joined hands to his heart. "Go on."

She drew in a slow breath. "So, I got over blaming myself for Bud's death. However, I have remained absolutely determined never to make the same mistake I made with Bud. I have sworn to myself that I will never again marry a man for the wrong reason." She gazed directly into his eyes. "But what is the wrong reason? *That's* what I didn't really understand—not until the last couple of days. Not until I felt I had lost you. Only since then have I started to see that the wrong reason wasn't about the baby I was going to have. It had nothing to do with being pregnant. It was about the love. I didn't love Bud enough. And for that reason and that reason alone, I had no right to marry him." Her eyes gleamed so bright. A tear escaped and slid down her cheek.

"Don't cry, sweetheart." Liam leaned in and kissed the wetness away. "I love you. I want you. I want a life with you. I love you way more than enough."

She touched his cheek with her free hand, a quick brush of a touch, too quickly gone. "When I put off telling you I was having your baby, it was because I knew you were a stand-up guy, and I was dreading that you might ask me to marry you for the same reason Bud had, because you felt obligated."

His laugh sounded pained to his own ears. "Okay, yeah. In the beginning, that day I spotted you at Safeway and the truth came out, I honestly didn't know my ass from up. I was only trying really hard to do the right thing."

She sniffled a little, smiling at him through her tears. "And I knew that."

"But doing the right thing isn't the reason I want to marry you now. Not anymore. Everything's changed now. Now I've figured out what I had no damn clue about for way too long. Not back in high school. Not last winter, in those amazing nights you gave me before you broke it off. And not that day in October when I finally found out I was going to be a dad."

She searched his face. "What? Tell me."

"I've figured out why I could never really get you out of my mind. I understand now why I was pissed off when I heard you'd married Bud, why, through all the years since high school, I've always felt this pinch in my chest whenever I thought of you. It's because you're the one. The one for me. I do love you, Karin. I will always love you. More than I'm ever going to know how to say."

Karin just stared at him.

He squeezed her hand. "What did I do?"

"Liam, you said exactly what I needed to hear."

"But are you okay?"

She drew a slow, shaky breath. "Never better. And I mean that sincerely."

Holding hands was not enough. He pulled her into his arms. She lifted her beautiful face to him.

And he kissed her, deep and slow and infinitely sweet.

"I love you, Liam Bravo," she said when he lifted his head. "So much. Way more than enough to last through the hard times. I love you enough to be with you forever."

"So then, it's good that I didn't take the ring back?"

"Yes." She kissed him again, hard and quick. "Yes, to everything. To that amazing, perfect ring you chose for me. To the future. To our wedding. To me staying right here with you all night long and then the two of us going to the other house together for breakfast tomorrow, where we will break the big news to the family that we're getting married."

Maybe his mouth was hanging open. A little. "You mean that?"

"I do. Every word."

He pressed his lips to the velvety skin at her temple. "Well, all right then. Count me in." He claimed her mouth again, a kiss that melted into another kiss and another after that.

A while later, they turned off the fire and switched off the lights. He led her down the hall to his room.

"I should probably be patient," he said, "but I'm going for it anyway. I don't want to wait. I want to get married right away. If that doesn't work for you, just say so right now."

"Yes."

He blinked down at her. "Yes, you agree to getting married right away?"

Her grin was slow and full of equal parts joy and mischief. "Maybe at New Year's?"

He couldn't stop himself. He pushed his luck some more. "Matt and Sabra got married last New Year's. It was just the family and close friends, at Daniel's house."

She didn't balk, didn't even ask for time to think it over. "I would love that."

It was stacking up to be the best Christmas ever. "We can discuss the idea with Keely and Daniel on Christmas Day."

"Totally works for me."

Had he ever been this happy? He couldn't remember when. "Wait right here?"

"Yes."

He was back with her in under thirty seconds. She gave him her hand and he slipped on the ring he'd chosen for her. It fit perfectly. The saleswoman at Tiffany & Co. had helped him guesstimate the size.

"I love it," she said and reached up to frame his face in her two soft hands. "I love *you*."

"I love you, Karin Killigan. And I will be loving you every single day for the rest of our lives."

"We did it all backward," she whispered. "This shouldn't be possible. But somehow, it's all come out absolutely right."

They were married on New Year's Day at the house on Rhinehart Hill. A trucker friend of Liam's who also happened to be an ordained minister officiated. Karin had no bridesmaids and Liam skipped the groomsmen.

The bride and groom stood up together in a room full of family and friends, with Ben on Liam's side and Coco next to Karin. Riley George slept through the brief ceremony, held close in his father's loving arms.

They settled in together at the main house on Sweetheart Cove. Sten sold Liam the cottage for a bargain price and Liam had the cottage rebuilt to accommodate a growing family. By the time Sten and a very pregnant Madison returned to Valentine Bay to make their home in the main house, the cottage was ready for Liam, Karin, the kids and Otto.

A year later, Karin gave birth to another boy. They named him Aiden at Coco's request.

* * * * *

Making Room For
The Rancher
Christy Jeffries

Christy Jeffries graduated from the University of California, Irvine, with a degree in criminology and received her Juris Doctor from California Western School of Law. But drafting court documents and working in law enforcement was merely an apprenticeship for her current career in the dynamic field of mommyhood and romance writing. She lives in Southern California with her patient husband, two energetic sons and one sassy grandmother. Follow her online at christyjeffries.com.

Books by Christy Jeffries

Harlequin Special Edition

Twin Kings Ranch

What Happens at the Ranch...

Sugar Falls, Idaho

The Firefighter's Christmas Reunion
The SEAL's Secret Daughter

Furever Yours

It Started with a Pregnancy

Montana Mavericks

The Maverick's Bridal Bargain

Montana Mavericks: The Lonelyhearts Ranch

The Maverick's Christmas to Remember

Montana Mavericks: What Happened to Beatrix

His Christmas Cinderella

Visit the Author Profile page at
millsandboon.com.au.

Dear Reader,

It's true what they say: it takes a village to raise a child. I remember before I became a mother that I was never going to let my kids watch too much TV or eat junk food or talk back to me. Then I gave birth and soon learned that we get the children we're meant to have—which sometimes means the exact opposite of what we were expecting. This is why parents need support systems... especially now during times of global pandemics and virtual learning.

I come from a blended family and my parents always set a great example for us on how to get along well with exes and anyone else in the community who had their child's best interests at heart. We're all doing this thing called life together and, in the process, we're raising the future generation of scientists and lawyers and teachers and health care professionals—the very people who will be taking care of us in our old age.

In *Making Room for the Rancher*, Dahlia Deacon King is coparenting her precocious five-year-old daughter with her ex-husband, and local rancher Connor Remington has some opinions on how she should be doing things. Sparks fly, boundaries get fuzzy, and in the center of it all is a smart and compassionate little girl with a stray dog and a determination to bring everyone together.

For more information on my other books, visit my website at christyjeffries.com, or chat with me on Twitter, @christyjeffries. You can also find me on Facebook and Instagram. I'd love to hear from you.

Enjoy,

Christy Jeffries

Facebook.com/AuthorChristyJeffries

Twitter.com/ChristyJeffries (@ChristyJeffries)

Instagram.com/Christy_Jeffries/

PROLOGUE

GOOD EVENING, WYOMING, we are reporting live from the Twin Kings Ranch following the funeral of United States Vice President Roper King, who was born and raised right here in the small town of Teton Ridge, in the heart of Ridgecrest County.

As many of you know, Roper King was a well-respected war hero and successful cattle rancher who started out in local politics, then served two terms as the governor of Wyoming before becoming vice president. The guest list of attendees read like a star-studded who's who of celebrities, foreign dignitaries and politicians, including the president of the United States and her husband.

The service began as a somber and dignified celebration of life, then took an unexpected turn when political analyst Tessa King, one of Roper King's daughters, collapsed on the front steps of the church and was quickly spirited away by the Secret Service. While we don't have an update on Tessa's condition, there are reports that she was later seen at the private graveside service along with her five siblings.

Hold on, I'm getting word that one of the Kings is driving this way through the gates and it might be... No, it's just one of the other family members. Possibly one of Roper's less famous daughters.

We will update you with all new developments. Now, back to our news desk for more highlights from today's event...

CHAPTER ONE

"WILL GRANDPA ROPER have any friends in Heaven?" five-year-old Amelia asked as they took a right onto Ridgecrest Highway, which wasn't so much a highway as it was a two-lane road that cut through the middle of downtown Teton Ridge, Wyoming.

"Mmm-hmm," Dahlia King Deacon murmured in response.

In fact, all of Dahlia's answers since her father's death were either nods, shoulder shrugs or noncommittal mumbles. Although, to be fair, her daughter hadn't ceased her rapid-fire questions since they'd said goodbye to the rest of the family and driven away from the Twin Kings Ranch ten minutes ago.

"Do you think Gan Gan is gonna move to Heaven, too?" Amelia asked next.

"Someday, but not anytime soon." Dahlia put her elbow on the windowsill of her truck, using one hand to prop up her pounding head while the other hand steered them down the familiar route. Normally, she would encourage her only child's inquisitive mind and happily engage in the back-and-forth. But today had been emotionally draining, and she was trying to hold it together as best she could.

Plus, Dahlia's twin sister, Finn, had already answered most of Amelia's questions when they'd been in the back seat of the limo, going from the church service to the family cemetery, and then back to the main house for the somber reception.

So far, Amelia's questions today included:

Did Grandpa Roper really know all these people?

Why are there so many movie cameras outside?

Do all those policemans work for Uncle Marcus?

Is it okay if I ask the President for one of her candies?

Can I be the president when I grow up?

When can we go home?

The last question had been exactly what Dahlia needed to hear to snap her back to reality.

Instead of saying goodbye to her mother, Dahlia had made a quick excuse to one of the Secret Service agents on protective detail before taking Amelia's hand in her own and sneaking out through the kitchen, past the catering staff who were hauling the leftover food to the matching bunkhouses behind the stables.

As soon as she'd gotten Amelia buckled into her booster seat, Dahlia had driven home on autopilot. She hadn't expected so many news vans to still be parked outside the front gates of her family's cattle ranch, and breathed a sigh of relief when none of them followed her.

Nobody ever expected the daughter of the third richest man in Wyoming to be driving a fifteen-year-old Ford F-150 crew cab with a cow-sized dent in the front grill and a Follow Me To Big Millie's sticker on the back bumper. They especially didn't expect it when that same man was Roper King, vice president of the United States.

Make that the former vice president of the United States.

To everyone else, Roper had been larger than life—war hero, politician, billionaire, national icon. But to Dahlia, he'd simply been Dad.

And now he was gone.

A ribbon of pain curled around Dahlia's throat, all the pent-up emotion of the day's orchestrated funeral threatening to suffocate her. She choked down a rising sob, telling herself it was only a twenty-minute drive to their little apartment in town. Twenty minutes before she could put on a Disney movie for her daughter, and then go have a good cry in the shower where nobody would be able to see her. Or ask her if all mommies got red-faced and snot-nosed when they cried.

The dark sunglasses she'd been hiding behind all day were no match for glare reflecting off the snow-covered Grand Tetons as the bright sun lowered along the opposite end of the sky. Dahlia was so busy adjusting her sun visor she almost didn't see the ball of white fur dart across the road in front of her.

Slamming on the brakes, she yanked the steering wheel to the right, keeping her grip on the worn leather as the truck skid off the road and shimmied to a stop. She threw the gearshift into Park and turned around before she could unbuckle her seat belt.

"Are you okay, Peanut?" she asked Amelia, hoping her daughter couldn't tell that Dahlia was still trying to catch her breath.

"Why did that doggy run into the road like that?" Amelia replied, whipping her neck around for a glimpse of the white ball of fur who'd nearly caused them to career into the ditch. "Where is his mommy? Is it a boy doggy or a girl doggy?"

"Amelia." Dahlia reached between the seats and put a hand on her daughter's bouncing leg. Other than a sagging black hair bow and matching snags across both knees of the white tights (which had come courtesy of the child's earlier visit to the stables with her twin cousins), Amelia appeared none the worse for wear. "Focus over here. Are you hurt at all?"

"I'm fine." Her high energy daughter barely glanced her way before unbuckling herself from her seat. "Can I go pet the doggy?"

"We don't pet strange do—" Dahlia started, but Amelia already had the back door open.

"Is that the doggy's daddy?"

Dahlia fumbled out of her own seat and dove into the back,

trying to snatch the corner of Amelia's black velvet skirt before her daughter could climb out the door that should have been set to childproof lock. She had no idea who her daughter was talking about, nor would she unless she could get her hips unstuck between the driver's and passenger seats and follow after the girl.

Could this day get any worse?

Dahlia had to simultaneously wiggle at the waist while doing an elbow crawl over the discarded patent leather shoes on the floorboard before she could pull her legs the rest of the way through. By the time she was able to use the armrest of the wide-open door to pull herself upright, Amelia had already made her way to the front of the hood and was talking to someone.

A man.

"Is that your doggy? What happened to his leash? What's his name? Is it a boy? Why aren't your shoes tied?" The steady stream of questions didn't provide the man with any opportunity to respond. But it did buy Dahlia a little bit of time to get her bearings, allowing her to push her sunglasses back in place and adjust the pencil skirt that had twisted up like a corkscrew during her ungraceful descent from the truck.

It also gave her a second to study this irresponsible dog owner, who was now holding his palm cupped against his forehead like a visor as he scanned the dense trees lining the road.

And really, a second was all she needed to make a snap judgment. Dahlia owned the only bar in town and could read a person the second they walked through the door. Five bucks said this guy was just another hipster tourist lost on his way to nearby Jackson Hole.

The man was over six feet tall, lean but muscular. He wasn't completely winded by the recent chase of his dog, so he must work out somewhat regularly. His faded Aerosmith T-shirt could've been well-worn, or it could've been one of those hundred-dollar designer shirts that people paid extra to achieve the same look. His stiff jeans still had the fold creases down the leg, and a pair of high-top basketball sneakers were in fact, as Amelia had just pointed out, untied.

"You want us to help you find your doggy?" her daughter asked before Dahlia could stop her. "Mommy is the bestest at finding my shoes and my crayons and my grandpa's glasses. Gan Gan says that Mommy could find trouble in a haystack without even looking."

The stranger turned toward her, his eyes shaded behind his hand. Dahlia forgot about searching for the runaway dog, and instead concentrated on finding a deep enough hole that she could hide in.

It was a mistake to stay quiet for any length of time around Amelia, because that only encouraged the child to continue talking. As if to prove her point, her daughter added, "But Grandpa doesn't need to look for his glasses no more because he went to Heaven."

Amelia's voice had gone softer with the last sentence, the young child's sadness creeping into her normally exuberant tone. Dahlia's throat did that constricting thing again, and she didn't trust herself not to start bawling in front of a perfect stranger. Instead, she sucked in her cheeks, trying to take a few steadying breaths through her nose.

The man finally parted his lips, opening and then closing them before kneeling down so that he was eye level with Amelia. "I'm very sorry for your loss."

"That's what everyone keeps saying to us. But we didn't *lose* Grandpa. He went to sleep and didn't wake up. Right, Mommy?"

Two curious gazes turned up to Dahlia. One set was the same blue as her own, full of curiosity. The other set was an unfamiliar golden brown with flecks of green, full of uncertainty and maybe a hint of pity. Or maybe the guy just wanted them to think he was some stranded motorist in order to lure them into a false sense of security.

Crap. Getting abducted would be the green olive garnish to this four-martini day.

"That's one way to put it." Dahlia used her trembling fingers to push a fallen strand of hair behind her ear. She stepped closer to Amelia, putting her arm around her daughter's shoulder while simultaneously easing the five-year-old back a few paces so that she wasn't within snatching distance of a potential kidnapper.

Maybe Dahlia had been a little too quick to refuse the Secret Service's offer of an escort home. She'd always felt perfectly safe in her small hometown, well-known by the locals, yet pleasantly anonymous to most outsiders. Now, though, she'd broken all of her own rules about talking to strangers. Sure, there might not be a windowless panel van parked nearby or lollipops falling out of the man's pockets, but helping a random guy find his "lost dog" was supposedly one of the oldest tricks in the book.

The stranger in question rose to his full height, which was still several inches taller than her—even in her uncomfortable high heels. Stepping backward again, she glanced down at his large hands and the skin on the back of her neck prickled. He wasn't holding any sort of weapon, but he also wasn't holding a leash.

If she could get Amelia anywhere close to the rear door of the truck, Dahlia might have a better chance of making a run for it and locking them both in the cab. She spoke without taking her eyes of the man. "Peanut, go back to the truck and get your shoes on so we can help look for this man's lost dog."

Luckily, Amelia's need to ask a million questions was usually only superseded by her need to help an unfortunate animal, and she quickly obeyed.

"No." The man lifted up those same hands, palms out. "It's not *my* dog. He was on my property and I thought he might be lost. So I was tracking him, trying to get close enough to see if he had a collar. I almost had him, but then he heard your truck and took off running across the highway."

She noted the golden skin of his uncovered forearms. Nobody who lived in Wyoming this time of year had a sun-kissed tan like that.

"So you're saying you live in Teton Ridge?" she asked, knowing full well that if anyone new had moved to town, she would've heard about it. Amelia was now by the passenger side door, and Dahlia took another step in retreat.

"Lady, if you want to run back to your truck and lock the doors, I'm not going to stop you. I get it that you're out here on this road in the middle of nowhere and you think I'm some sort of madman chasing after a dog that clearly doesn't want to be caught. I'll just head on back to my ranch and everyone can go about their business."

"How?"

"How what?" He tilted his head, his dark copper hair cropped short, almost military-length.

"How are you going to get back to your ranch?" she asked, sounding like Amelia, who was now sitting on the loose gravel buckling her patent leather shoes onto the wrong feet.

He rocked back on the heels of his untied sneakers. "The same way I got here, I guess."

She didn't mean to let out a disbelieving snort, but the only ranches between the Twin Kings and the heart of town were the abandoned Rocking D Ranch, which was at least another eight miles south, and the Ochoa family's Establos del Rio. Most of the Ochoas had been at her dad's funeral, though, and they certainly hadn't been wearing Air Jordans and an Aerosmith T-shirt.

"I'm Connor Remington. The new owner of the Rocking D." He glanced at the sun sinking behind the trees, but didn't seem especially concerned by the fact that, in less than twenty minutes, it would probably be pitch-black outside and at least twenty degrees colder.

His story was at least plausible, considering the owner of the neighboring ranch had recently passed away. Besides, if the man was going to pretend to be a local rancher in order to flag down a passing motorist, he would've at least tried to dress and act the part. Which meant he wasn't pretending.

Lord, save her from dumb city boys who had absolutely zero sense of direction. Dahlia sighed in resignation. "Hop in the truck. I'll give you a ride."

Connor Remington hadn't been planning to meet any of his neighbors on his first day in town, but here he sat. In the front seat of an older truck, next to a quiet woman whose face was obscured by the largest sunglasses he'd ever seen, and fielding questions from a magpie of a little girl who was making her mother's white knuckles—no wedding ring on the left hand—grip the steering wheel tighter every time she asked a question.

"So I take it you live nearby?" he asked, trying to be polite.

The woman gave a tense nod. Her hair was a dark blond and twisted into a tight knot on top of her head. Her somber black outfit, coupled with the little girl's comments about her dead grandfather, suggested they'd just come from a funeral.

"We live in town" the little girl offered. "Gan Gan wants us to live at the big house on the ranch, but Mommy says she'd rather live in Siberia. Have you ever lived in Siberia?"

"Actually, I've stayed in a tent there once." Connor turned in his seat to smile at the child in the back seat. "It was summer, though, so it wasn't as cold as you'd think."

"You don't have to play along," the woman murmured out the side of her mouth. "It'll only make her ask more questions."

"I don't mind," Connor answered honestly. Besides, he was getting a free ride back to his ghost town of a ranch. The least he could do was be hospitable. Even if only one of the other occupants in this vehicle felt like engaging in conversation. "So since you're the first neighbors I've met, what else do I need to know about living in Teton Ridge?"

"Well, my Mommy's name is Dahlia but my aunts and uncles call her Dia. 'Cept Grandpa. He was the only one allowed to call her Dolly."

Connor caught a slight tightening of the muscles along the woman's already rigid jaw line and again felt the need to apologize for their loss. However, when his own father had passed away all those years ago, Connor hadn't been comfortable being on the receiving end of condolences for a man most people never really knew. It had felt forced and overly polite. So instead, he remained silent as she took a right onto the road that led to the Rocking D. Clearly, she'd been here before.

The adults' awkward silence, though, didn't stop the little girl in the back seat from continuing. "All of Mommy's brothers and sisters have nicknames. 'Cept Uncle Marcus. But he kinda has a nickname because everyone calls him Sheriff. Do you have a nickname?"

"Some of my friends at my old job call me by my last name," he replied, but the child squinted at him as though she were about to tell him that didn't count. "My dad used to call me Con."

Whoa. Now that wasn't something he'd thought about in a long time. Maybe it was being here in Wyoming, fulfilling a promise his dad broke, that had Connor thinking so much about the old man. Or maybe it was all this talk about dead fathers and their unique names for their kids.

"Well, I'm Amelia, but my friends call me Bindi."

Dahlia whipped her head around, a line creasing the smooth area right above her sunglasses. "No, Peanut, nobody calls you that."

"They will. When I go to school, I'm gonna ask Miss Walker to tell all the kids to call me Bindi Irwin from now on because I love kangaroos and doggies and owls and hamsters and someday I'm gonna be a zookeeper for all the animals and be on TV like my aunt—"

"Here's the Rocking D," Dahlia loudly cut off her daughter. The truck hit a huge pothole in the rutted-out dirt driveway, but the woman didn't seem to notice as she murmured again to

Connor, "They were having a *Crocodile Hunter* marathon on the Animal Planet channel last week."

"Where's your chicken coop?" Amelia asked, her head on a swivel as they pulled into the driveway between the farmhouse and the barn. "Where are all the cows and horses?"

"Well, I just moved here today so I don't have any animals yet. At least none that I know of." Hell, he'd only had one real conversation with his great-aunt before she'd passed away. At the time, he'd been so busy trying to absorb the shock of having a long lost relative that he hadn't thought to ask her about the livestock. "In fact, I haven't even gone inside the house yet. All my stuff is still in the car over there."

"That car's just like the one in the Princess Dream House commercial. It's even white like Princess Dream's."

"It's actually a rental," Connor explained when Dahlia parked behind it. He wasn't the flashy sports car type, but when his plane was diverted to Rock Springs late this morning, the white convertible had been the only option available. Having lived on military bases the past twelve years, Connor was in a hurry to finally settle into a place of his very own and gladly took the keys to the last vehicle in the lot.

Plus, in his one and only conversation with his great-aunt, he'd promised her that he'd take care of her ranch and make her proud. He didn't have much experience with fulfilling dying wishes, but from what he'd learned from her probate attorney about the state of things out here, Connor was already way behind.

Amelia burst out of the truck before either of the adults, but luckily didn't go too far. Dahlia was quick to follow and caught up with the little girl by the overgrown bushes that were blocking the path leading to the house.

"So you bought the old Daniels ranch? Sight unseen?" Dahlia finally removed her sunglasses, and Connor was rendered almost speechless at the clear blue depths. They were slightly red-rimmed—from crying?—but that didn't take away from her beauty.

"Actually—" his own eyes followed hers and he saw what she saw "—I inherited it. My great-aunt was Constance Daniels."

"So you're the one she always talked about?" she asked, her words crashing into him like a wave of guilt. Before he could explain the unusual family connection, she added, "The one who was supposedly going to bring her ranch back to life?"

Something about the sarcasm in her tone immediately put him on the defensive. "That's the plan."

"Let me guess." She glanced down at the creased jeans he'd bought at the mercantile on his way into town. "You've just moved here from the big city, but you've always dreamed of being a cowboy."

"The way you say it makes me sound like a cliché who is destined to fail." He was repeating the same words his own mother had used when he'd told her about the Rocking D and his promise to his dying great-aunt. Connor narrowed his eyes slightly, practically daring this woman to doubt him, as well.

She returned his challenging stare, her expression completely unapologetic as she boldly sized him up. "*Destined* might not have been the word I would have used. But tougher men than you have tried their hand at making a name for themselves out here in the wilds of Teton Ridge and most of them gave up before their first full winter."

Fortunately, Connor had a history of proving people wrong. He crossed his arms in front of his chest, his biceps muscles flexing on their own accord. "How do you know how tough I am?"

Dahlia's lashes flickered ever so slightly as her pupils dilated, but she didn't break eye contact. Her full lips pursed ever so slightly, as though she were holding back the perfect retort, and his eyes dared her to say it out loud.

"So where is the white doggy now?" Amelia interrupted the adults' intense but unspoken staring competition. "Do you think it'll come back here? Do you have food for him? Where will he sleep if it snows?"

"Amelia," Dahlia sighed and finally looked down at her daughter. "Let Mr. Remington settle into the place before you start bombarding him with all your questions."

It was a little too late for that. The corner of Connor's lip tugged up in a smirk. Not that her mom's warning would do any good. The child hadn't stopped asking questions in the entire thirty minutes he'd known her.

He bent down because he could see that the girl was genuinely worried about the lost dog. Hell, Connor had been worried about the scruffy thing himself, otherwise he wouldn't have tracked it on foot for almost seven miles. He guessed he was like Amelia that way, too. Once he got on a trail, he didn't like to veer off course until he had all the answers. "I'll leave a little bowl of water and some blankets outside on the porch for him in case he comes back. Hopefully, he's at home now, all cozy in front of the fire and dreaming about his next adventure tomorrow."

The child nodded, but the concern didn't entirely leave her face. She tilted her head and started a new line of questioning. "Why is there still a sticker on your leg?"

"Because the boots and jeans I was wearing when I first got here were all muddy." He didn't mention the abandoned well he'd nearly fallen into when he'd been exploring earlier. That would've only given Dahlia more ammo for her claim that he had no business owning a ranch. "But then I saw the little white dog and these new pants were the closest thing I could put on before the dog ran off."

"You mean you took your pants off outside?" she asked, her round eyes growing even rounder.

He dared a glance at Dahlia, whose cheeks had gone a charming shade of pink. "Well, nobody was out here to see me."

"One time, Mommy went into the river because my pet salmon was stuck on a rock. She had to take off all her clothes so she didn't catch the new-moan-yah. Aunt Finn said cowgirls gotta do what cowgirls gotta do. But Gan Gan says a lady never knows who could be watching."

Connor really needed to hear more about this pet salmon, he thought, smothering a laugh. Although, it wouldn't be appropriate for him to ask for any more details about a naked and soaking wet Dahlia while her daughter was standing between them.

Instead of offering an explanation, the supposed fish rescuer rubbed her temples, which didn't lessen the rosy color now staining her cheeks.

"Okay, Peanut, we really need to get back on the road. We can look for the dog on our way into town." The promise did the trick because Amelia waved goodbye and skipped toward the truck. Dahlia stuck out a hand. "Good luck with the Rocking D, Mr. Remington."

"Thanks again for the ride home." He took the smooth but firm palm in his own and an unexpected current of electricity shot through him. The jolt must've made its way to his brain because before he could stop himself, he added, "Maybe I'll see you in town some time and can repay the favor?"

She jerked her hand back quickly, but her face went perfectly neutral, as though she'd used the same thanks-but-no-thanks expression a thousand times before.

"I'm sure you'll be far too busy out here." She gave a pointed look to the broken wood slats in a fence that might've been a corral at one point. Then she glanced at his favorite basketball shoes, which felt about as out of place on this rundown ranch as her black high heels. "A city boy like you is going to have his work cut out for him."

As she and her daughter drove away, Connor recalled his aunt's probate attorney making a similar comment when she'd offered to sell the property for him. The lawyer had warned him that it was going to take a lot of determination and a hell of a lot more money to get the place operational again.

Yet, he was just as undeterred then as he was now.

Clearly, Dahlia wasn't going to be the only skeptical local who doubted his ability to make this ranch a success. The prettiest, maybe, but not the only one.

Good thing he hadn't come to Wyoming to make friends.

CHAPTER TWO

CONNOR SLEPT LIKE crap in the musty-smelling, knickknack-filled three-bedroom house his great-aunt had bequeathed him. Thank goodness some thoughtful neighbor had cleaned out the fridge and shut off the gas and water pipes long ago. At least he hadn't arrived last night to a flooded living room and the smell of rotting food.

Growing up, his old man had told plenty of stories about spending his summers on a ranch in Wyoming, but never once mentioned the woman who'd owned the place. Even if he had spoken about his aunt Constance, Connor's mom wouldn't have believed a word Steve Remington said.

That was why nobody was more surprised than Linda Remington when Connor got a call from an assisted living facility in Wyoming. Because of Steve's transient lifestyle—bouncing in and out of different correctional facilities in between his occasional visits to his son and wife in Boston—followed by Connor's numerous military deployments, it had taken a dedicated social worker and a wily trusts-and-estates attorney nearly three years to help a determined Constance Daniels track down her next of kin.

Connor had only met his great-aunt a few weeks ago—via video chat and a spotty satellite connection onboard an aircraft carrier in the Pacific Ocean. She'd passed away before he'd returned from his final deployment. However, her probate attorney informed him over the phone that the ranch had been abandoned since Connie's first stroke, nearly three years ago.

So it wasn't as though Connor had been expecting anything fancy when he'd arrived at the Rocking D yesterday afternoon. Besides, he'd slept in worse conditions when he'd been on assignment with his scouting unit in the desolate regions of the Altai Mountains between Kazakhstan and Russia. He hadn't been lying to Amelia when he'd said he'd once been to Siberia.

He was no longer in the business of tracking people, though. Which was why Connor tried not to look for the little girl and her mother as he drove into downtown Teton Ridge the following morning. Actually, *downtown* was a generous name for the center of a city with a population of less than two thousand. So he was sure that if he wanted to find them, it wouldn't be too difficult.

There were a handful of restaurants and shops, a sheriff's station attached to a county courthouse that likely housed all the local government offices, a giant feed-and-grain store, and a small nondescript hardware store. If residents needed anything more than that, they'd either have to order it online or drive into Jackson Hole or Pinedale to get it.

Most of the buildings appeared to have been built in the heyday of the Wild West, a combination of wood and brick structures constructed so close together only a horse could pass between them.

His first order of business would be to go to the hardware store with the long list he'd made last night in Great-Aunt Connie's empty kitchen. Then he'd go to the market down the street for some groceries.

Scratch that. He needed a hot coffee and an even hotter breakfast before he did anything. He slowed his rental car and pulled into a parking space in front of a place called Biscuit Betty's. The smell of bacon hit him as soon as he climbed out of the convertible and his stomach growled. He was halfway to the front entrance of the restaurant when he caught sight of a blond girl skipping out of the bakery next door.

Amelia.

His skin itched in recognition, and then tightened when he saw Dahlia exit behind her, a stack of pink bakery boxes stacked so high in her arms he could only see the top of her bouncing ponytail.

Connor jogged over and took the top three boxes before she could object. "Let me help you carry these."

Dahlia's smile faded when she realized who'd relieved her of her load. Was she expecting someone else? A boyfriend, perhaps?

"I can get them," she insisted, her face now slightly pinched in annoyance.

"Oh, hi, Mr. Rem-ton." Amelia smiled brightly, the opposite reaction of her mother. "Mommy said we wouldn't see you again for a long time 'cause you'd be too busy working on your old junky ranch."

"I didn't say junky," Dahlia interjected a bit more quickly than she had yesterday when Amelia had made similar candid comments. She must've gotten a good night's sleep last night because she gave her daughter a discreet but pointed look rather than a resigned sigh. "I said run-down."

"It's both run-down *and* junky," Connor admitted, holding back a smile at their honesty. "And I plan to get busy on it as soon as I buy some supplies."

"Mommy told Ms. Burnworth at the bakery that the inside of your house was probably worse than the outside and that—"

"Here, Peanut." Dahlia shoved a pink box into Amelia's arms right before she could get to the good part. "Carry this for me and you can have one of the apple spice muffins when you get inside."

The little girl tipped the box sideways, the flimsy lid threatening to spill the contents, as she ran down the sidewalk.

Connor smothered his grin when Dahlia darted a glance his way. "Sorry about that. I should remember to watch what I say around her. I never know what she's going to blurt out."

"Like I told you yesterday, I really don't mind talking to her. She's a smart girl and..." Connor's voice trailed off as he saw Amelia rush inside a wide door below a wooden sign that read Saloon. He had a sudden flashback to his own childhood and his old man taking a way-too-young Connor to some of the less finer drinking establishments in Dorchester, Massachusetts. "Did she just go inside that bar?"

"Oh, yeah." Dahlia began walking that way, but not with any sense of urgency. As though it were totally natural for a five-year-old to hang out inside the local pub. "I should probably get in there."

"Isn't it a little early in the day for a drink?" He heard the judgment in his own voice and tried not to wince. He didn't know this woman. Who was he to project his own childhood insecurities on her daughter? "Sorry, I guess it's none of my business."

"You're right." Dahlia turned to him, her shoulders thrown back and her eyes almost a violet shade as they filled with anger. "It's *not* your business or my mom's business or anyone else's business where and how I choose to raise my daughter."

Wow. The woman had been quiet yesterday, letting her five-year-old do most of the talking. But clearly, she wasn't shy about choosing her battles and speaking up when she felt threatened.

"I didn't mean to imply that it was. I was just making an observation based on my own experience—"

"Can I make myself a drink, Mommy?" Amelia used her little body to prop open the thick wooden door. She had a half-eaten muffin in one hand and a smear of cinnamon crumbs across one cheek. "I promise not to put too many cherries in it this time."

"Sure, Peanut," she replied, but it wasn't in the same dismissive way as when she'd given in to her daughter yesterday. Dahlia put one hand on her hip and lifted her brow at Connor, all but challenging him to make another comment about her parenting decisions.

She'd been attractive before when her eyes had been redrimmed and tired after the funeral yesterday. But her razorsharp focus and the firm set of her sculpted jaw made her damn right sexy. Both intrigue and desire weaved through his gut, and Connor knew that if he didn't voice his concerns now, he would get blinded by her pretty face. Just like he'd gotten blinded by his dad's pretty words all those years ago.

"Anyway, I drove by a library on my way into town earlier and a smart girl like Amelia would probably love to, you know, go there instead of a saloon..." Connor stopped talking when Dahlia's eyes narrowed and her mouth hardened. Maybe he'd gone too far.

"Don't stop now, Mr. Big City Rancher." Dahlia put her other hand to her hip and leaned slightly forward. "I'm sure you have so many more words of wisdom to impart. I'd especially love to hear your advice about family matters, considering you never even met your great-aunt Connie—who was a wonderful woman, by the way, and didn't deserve to die all alone in an assisted living facility without so much as a visit from a single relative."

Ouch. Not that Connor didn't already feel guilty about that last part.

"Technically, I *did* meet her," he said. FaceTime counted, right? "And I would've visited her sooner if I'd known that she existed."

"Well, you were certainly eager to meet your inheritance," Dahlia shot back.

They were faced off on the sidewalk and he could practically see the steam rising from her. Maybe it was more recognizable, considering he was equally angry about the assumptions she'd automatically jumped to concerning *his* decisions. He'd never asked for an inheritance or anything else in his life. In fact, he seriously doubted—

"There's the doggy!" a voice called out and broke his concentration. He turned just in time to see Amelia race into the street, her muffin still clutched in her grip.

Connor had already dropped the pink bakery boxes and was running after her when he heard the horn of a big truck.

The scream of warning froze in Dahlia's throat just as Connor swept Amelia into his arms, yanking the child into the center median with him just before the orange big rig could smash into them both.

Dahlia, whose response was only a few seconds behind Connor's, almost got hit by a red compact car in the oncoming lane after she sprinted into the middle of the street to ensure her daughter was unharmed. Her voice returned just in time to yell some choice words at the taillights of Jay Grover's flatbed truck. The damn fool had been repeatedly warned to slow down whenever he drove through town, but warnings only made the contrary jerk want to drive faster.

"Is she all right?" Dahlia asked Connor between adrenaline-fueled breaths. The three of them were now standing in the center of Stampede Boulevard. Well, technically, only two of them were standing there. Her daughter was still in the man's arms.

"How come it's okay for you to say the *F* word, but not me?" Amelia asked, and Dahlia let out a shaky breath.

"I think she's fine," Connor replied, a smooth spot on his neck jumped visibly with his pulse, which was apparently pumping equally as fast as Dahlia's.

As much as she wanted to tear into him just a few moments ago, she couldn't stay mad at the guy for his earlier judgments.

When it came to looking out for her daughter's safety, he'd actually put his money where his mouth was, and had been the first to run into the street to save her.

"Where's the doggy?" Amelia squirmed in his arms as her head twisted to search for the scruffy white mutt that had been the cause of yet another near accident.

"Oh, Peanut, let's get you inside right now. We can come back and look for the dog later." Preferably when Dahlia's nerves were more settled. And after she scolded her daughter for running into the street without looking for cars. Unfortunately, neither of those events would likely happen if Connor was hanging around.

"But what about school? I can't be late again."

Dahlia checked her watch and saw that it was nearly 7:30 a.m. Amelia made it sound like she was chronically tardy, when in fact her daughter simply liked to be the first kid to arrive so she could be the one to feed the class hamsters.

"Well, I might need a few minutes." Dahlia shoved her still shaky hands into the pockets of her jeans, not relishing the thought of hopping behind the wheel of her truck until she was a little less rattled.

"But I promised Miss Walker we'd bring the muffins for the bake sale."

"I can drive you guys." He hefted the child higher, the muscles in his biceps flexing under a plaid work shirt. His jaw was set in a rigid line and his soft tone suggested he was well aware of the fact that Dahlia was still shaken by her daughter's near fatal encounter with a speeding madman.

"Fine," Dahlia said, almost a little relieved to have someone else there with her. Being a single mother meant she didn't always have someone sharing the physical burden. Micah, Amelia's father, was financially supportive and rarely missed his nightly calls with his daughter to talk about her day. But it wasn't the same. Even with most of her family living nearby, there were still times when Dahlia felt like she was going at it alone. Right now, she was still shaky enough to appreciate Connor's steady voice and quick reflexes. "I need to run inside and get something real quick, though. Can you salvage what's left of those muffins?"

She waited for a motorcycle to pass before leading them back to the sidewalk and toward the building she'd bought and lovingly restored. She saw Connor's eyes dart up to the second floor and stare at the freshly painted blue sign that was at least a century old, the gold block letters large and unmistakable: Big Millie's.

To his credit, though, he didn't ask any questions. Probably because the pink bakery boxes were upside down and Amelia was already talking his ear off about the little white dog. Dahlia slipped inside and grabbed the Safari Park lunch box and her daughter's pug-shaped backpack, then followed him to his rental car parked in front of Biscuit Betty's.

By the time they got to the drop-off line at Teton Ridge Elementary School, both Dahlia and Connor had made several assurances to Amelia that they'd keep their eyes open for the stray and try to help it if they could.

Several sets of curious eyes turned toward them as Dahlia climbed out of the convertible—which was thankfully closed this cold morning—to help her daughter unbuckle.

"Can I help you with the boxes?" Connor asked.

"Yes," Amelia said as Dahlia practically yelled, "No!" The last thing she needed were the other parents asking her what she was doing with some wannabe cowboy nobody in town knew. "The crossing guard will yell at you if you don't keep traffic moving. Just park over there and I'll run her inside the building."

"Don't forget to take care of our dog," Amelia shouted from the sidewalk before she waved goodbye to Connor.

"What dog?" Marcus King, dressed in his county sheriff's uniform, asked before the car door was even closed.

"Jeez, Marcus. You scared me half to death," Dahlia told her big brother, who was walking his twin sons, Jack and Jordan, to the flagpole.

"The dog me and my new friend, Connor, found and then lost again. Bye, Mommy," Amelia waved before running to catch up to her cousins.

Marcus wasn't the least bit subtle as he studied the license plate of Connor's rental car as it pulled into a parking spot. "Who's that?"

"Connie Daniel's nephew who just inherited the Rocking D. I'll fill you in later. But right now—" Dahlia pushed the pink bakery boxes into her brother's arms "—I need you to take these to the bake sale table before Melissa Parker comes over and invites you to the monthly mingle happy hour at the bar tonight."

The threat of having to actually socialize with other single parents was enough to get her nosy brother moving along without asking any more questions.

When Dahlia climbed back into Connor's convertible, she adjusted her dark sunglasses and slid low in the seat until he drove out of the parking lot.

"Careful, or I might think you're embarrassed to be seen with me," he said as he pulled out onto Stampede Boulevard.

"I just don't want to have to answer any questions."

"Like from the cop back there?" Connor asked. "He seemed pretty interested in committing my license plate number and physical description to memory."

Was that a note of jealousy she detected in his tone? History had taught her to be wary of insecure men. Not that she wasn't already wary of Connor Remington. Annoyance prickled her skin. "That's my brother. He's the sheriff and he's very protective."

"Cool," Connor said.

"Why is that cool?" She felt her eyes narrow behind her sunglasses.

"I guess because I always thought it would be neat to have a protective older brother or sister. Someone to look out for me when I was young."

Her heart softened, but only slightly. "Did you get picked on a lot as a kid?"

"Not any more than anyone else. But my dad was gone a lot and my mom worked two jobs. So I was on my own for the most part. I'd always wanted siblings."

Dahlia thought about the other five King siblings and relaxed against the leather seat. "Trust me. It's not all it's cracked up to be. They're always up in my business or arguing with each other. If you think my daughter is a talker, just wait until you meet the rest of the—"

She caught herself before she revealed too much about her family.

"Anyway, thanks for getting to Amelia just in time this morning. And for the ride to the school."

"No problem." He turned his eyes away from the road long enough to smile at her, and something in her tummy went all topsy-turvy. Connor Remington might be completely out of place in a town like Teton Ridge, but he was still a damn good-looking man. And it had been a while since Dahlia had been alone in a car with a man she hadn't known since childhood, good-looking or otherwise.

"Where should I drop you off? Burnworth's? It's kind of an odd name for a bakery."

"Just pull in here." She pointed to the open parking spots near the old-fashioned hitching post in front of Big Millie's.

He surprised her by exiting the car when she did.

"You don't have to walk me inside," she told him when he followed her to the wood-planked walkway that lined this side of the street.

"Actually, I was on my way to get some breakfast earlier." He stared at the overhanging cedar awning she'd replaced three years ago, keeping it as authentic to the historical building as possible. "So do you work at this place?"

His earlier words criticizing her for letting her daughter hang out in a bar hovered between them. Defiance made her square her shoulders. "I *own* this place."

"There you are, Dahlia." Ms. Burnworth, the older woman who was a co-owner of the bakery next door, made her way toward them so quickly, her apron with the words Taste The Burn stenciled across the front flapped in the breeze. "Another one of your daughter's critters is hanging out in the back alley again. Kenny is in a foul mood, complaining about the allergies he doesn't even have. But I wanted to get out here first and warn you that he's threatening to report you guys to the health department this time if you try and sneak it upstairs."

"Is it a scruffy white dog?" Connor asked.

Ms. Burnworth eyed him over her bright pink reading glasses. "Are you with Animal Control?"

"No, I'm—"

Just then, a yelp sounded from somewhere behind the building and Dahlia unlocked the heavy oak door and rushed through the bar and toward the back entrance, the quickest way to get to the alley. She'd no more than gotten the heavy screen security door open when a dirty ball of fur dashed straight through the kitchen and launched itself right up into Connor's arms.

Kenny Burnworth, Ms. Burnworth's brother and one of the biggest hypochondriacs in town, was giving chase with a rubber spatula as his only weapon of defense. Dahlia had to quickly put up her hand to stop the cranky old man from coming inside. "I'll take care of it from here, Mr. Burnworth."

The dog, now huddled safely in Connor's arms, let out a small whimper, and the baker let out an obnoxiously fake sneeze. "You better, Dahlia. This is the second one this month. Say, are you with Animal Control?"

She followed the older man's gaze toward Connor, who cradled the dog protectively. "No, sir, I'm not."

"Too bad." Mr. Burnworth fake sneezed again. "I would rather this place was still a brothel rather than a damn halfway house for every stray animal wandering around town."

When her neighbor left, Dahlia closed the screen door before finding a small stainless-steel bowl that she could use as a makeshift water dish. Connor followed her out of the kitchen and into the refurbished saloon.

He set the dog on the recently sanded hardwood floor so it could drink, then stayed down on one knee near the scared animal. Dahlia's heart gave a little jump at his tender concern and she distracted herself by trying to find the dog something to eat. Right in the middle of the massive twenty-foot-long oak panel bar, she spied half a glass of orange juice and one of Amelia's leftover muffins and broke it into smaller pieces.

The animal took the offered piece and gulped it down in one swallow. When the pup gobbled up a second chunk without so much as a growl, Connor slowly stood up and began studying the open floor plan of the high-ceilinged room. He lifted one copper brow and asked, "Was this place really a brothel?"

Normally, Dahlia got a kick out of her not-so-well-known family legacy and being related to a self-reliant woman who'd made quite a name for herself at the turn of the last century. After Connor's earlier unsolicited advice, she hesitated for a second before remembering that she was raising her daughter to be just as strong as the rest of the women in their family.

Dahlia straightened her spine. "Yes, it was. Back in the 1890s, women didn't have a lot of options when it came to supporting themselves. They had even less when their husbands took off and left them with a small child to raise. So my great-great-grandmother did the best she could."

"Your great-great grandma is Big Millie? Is that her?" Connor zeroed in on the sepia-toned photograph framed above the antique cash register. "She doesn't look all that big."

"Well, her daughter was also named Amelia and the townspeople referred to them as Big Millie and Little Millie. Her portrait is..." Dahlia tried to think of the most polite way to describe the less attractive and downright intimidating woman who was rumored to have strong opinions and a supernatural sense about her neighbors. "It's a bit less inviting and currently on display somewhere else."

Actually, the life-sized portrait of the not-so-little woman hung above the mantel at the main house on Twin Kings Ranch where Dahlia's father insisted she was able to watch over the family. Her mother hated it, which was all the more reason for Dahlia to insist Grandma Millie the Second stay put.

"And did Little Millie, your great-grandmother, take over the family business?"

"Yes, right before prohibition. By then, they were making so much money as the only speakeasy between Casper and Idaho Falls, the bootleggers couldn't keep up with the high demand. They closed down the upstairs business and started manufacturing their own booze."

Connor's mouth formed a small O of surprise, and Dahlia bit back a smile. If he was so easily shocked by her deceased relatives, just wait until he met some of her living ones—like her sister Finn or her aunt Freckles. Now there were a couple of women who weren't afraid to make a grown man blush.

Not that she had any intention of introducing Connor to them anytime soon. Or at all. Her jaw tightened and she tried not to stare at him as he appraised the saloon, not bothering to hide his curiosity. Especially when she was equally as curious about him.

Before she could ask him something about himself, though, he nodded at the walls covered in shiplap and the huge antique gilt-edged mirror hanging behind the bar. "Is this what it looked like back then?"

"I tried to keep as much of it as original as I could." What had once started out as a fixer-upper project soon became Dahlia's refuge, a place to invest in herself after her divorce. "Except I converted the smaller…ah…*rooms* upstairs into one big apartment."

"And you're not allowed to have any pets in your own apartment?" Connor was now eyeing the very shaggy dog who was currently stretched out on its back in front of his cowboy boots, exposing its matted belly for a rub. In that revealing position, it was easy to see that the dog was in fact male.

Sure, they probably could keep the animal since she did own the building and the living quarters were separate from the commercial area. However, if Dahlia didn't draw a line somewhere, they'd have every dog and cat for miles around sheltered at Big Millie's.

Today, it was time to draw that line again. Her daughter had a way of bringing home strays, Dahlia thought as she studied the newcomer who had bent down again to rub the dog's belly. If she gave in now, she'd likely have two unwanted strays on her hands.

She sighed. "Even if my neighbor didn't make a big stink about it, we just don't have the room for another animal. A sweet pup like this needs room to wander and explore. He'd probably do great out on a ranch. A place with plenty of land and an owner who needs the company…"

She let her suggestion hang in the air, but Connor immediately shook his head. "Nice try, but I'm not in the market for a fluffy white ball of mischief."

"That's weird. I thought you wanted him." Dahlia tried a different tactic. If Amelia were here, she would've fluttered her eyelashes several times in confusion. Her daughter couldn't imagine anyone *not* wanting an animal—or ten. "You followed him from your ranch all the way to the street."

"Yeah, I was trying to see if he had a collar or needed help."

There it was. His admission that he'd gone after the animal first. Finders keepers and all that.

"That must be why he's already so attached to you." Okay, so maybe she was laying it on a little too thick. But the dog seemed to be in agreement with Dahlia's assessment because it chose that exact moment to stick out its small pink tongue and lick Connor's hand. She could tell by the softening of Connor's lower lip into a near smile that he was already a goner.

Feeling relieved, Dahlia knelt down to scratch the tangled and dirty fur between the mutt's ears. Unfortunately, her lowered position put her face only a few inches from his, and that rip current of awareness shot through her again. He must've felt it too because his hand froze just before it could graze hers.

His hazel eyes locked onto hers and Dahlia couldn't have looked away if she'd wanted to. His voice was deep and low as he lifted one side of his mouth. "Fine, I'll help. Just so we're clear, though, I'm only doing this because I promised Amelia I would. I have no intention of actually taking on a responsibility that belongs to someone else."

"Of course." Dahlia immediately stood back up, not entirely sure he was only referring to the dog. "Dr. Roman has a microchip scanner at her office over on Frontier Avenue. I'm sure she can help you find the owner."

"Dr. Roman, huh?" He easily scooped the dog into his arms as he rose to his full height. "Why do I get the feeling that you and Amelia are used to passing off stray animals to unsuspecting strangers?"

"Who else would we pass them off to?" She walked behind the bar, needing to put some distance between them. "Everyone else in town knows better than to get within a twenty-foot radius of my daughter when she's got an animal in her sights."

Plus, if Connor wanted to be a real rancher, he needed to get used to caring for all types of animals. Really, she was doing the good-looking city boy a favor. Maybe giving the man a little bit of responsibility of his own would teach him not to offer up his unwelcome opinions about Dahlia's responsibilities.

And if she could keep him from interfering in her personal business, then it would be a hell of a lot easier for her to stop thinking about his.

CHAPTER THREE

"LET ME GUESS." Dr. Roman chuckled to herself after Connor had explained to the vet how the scruffy white pooch ended up in his care. "Amelia Deacon was the little girl who talked you into adopting a stray?"

So Deacon was their last name. Connor tucked that tidbit of information into his mental file in case he needed it later on. "I'm guessing you know Amelia and her mom?"

"Yeah, my oldest son went to school with Dahlia and Finn." The veterinarian removed her reading glasses from the top of her black corkscrew curls, setting them on her nose before turning most of her attention to the new patient. "That family sends me more business than I can handle."

Finn. Another name, another breadcrumb. Connor collected clues the way Amelia Deacon apparently collected stray animals. Only he didn't know where this particular trail would lead or why he was on it in the first place. He had his hands full with getting the Rocking D running again. He shouldn't be out chasing after dogs *or* single moms. No matter how beautiful they were.

The single mom, not the dog.

The scared mutt was anything but beautiful, and smelled even worse than he looked. He watched the vet make soothing noises as she examined the little ball of white and mud-stained fur crouched low on the stainless-steel table. Connor was going to have to pay the car rental company an extra cleaning fee just to get rid of the stench from the short drive over here from Big Millie's. And if they ever found the owner, he was also going to have a serious talk with whoever had neglected the most basic of their pet responsibilities. This scrappy little guy deserved better than whoever had let him get this bad.

When Dr. Roman finished her exam, she pulled a small treat out of the pocket of her lab coat and fed it to the dog. "I'm not seeing anything out of the ordinary, but one of my vet techs is going to need to get him cleaned up a little before we can be sure. His hair is so matted our microchip scanner might have missed something."

Connor had never been a big spender and rarely took paid leave, which meant he still had a few paychecks coming his way before his official discharge paperwork got finalized. Unfortunately, he needed most of that money to get the ranch operational again. He had no idea how much this vet bill was going to cost.

Growing up, his mom had never let him have a pet because she'd said they were too expensive and too much work. Was it more or less than what the military paid for the horses in their Calvary units? During his first day of training at the Marine Corps Mountain Warfare Training Center, one of the instructors told them how much the hay and grain alone cost, and Connor had almost fallen out of his saddle.

"Don't worry," Dr. Roman said, probably seeing the color drain from his face as he tried to add up how much money this would set him back. "Dahlia will want me to bill her for the exam and grooming and any necessary medications."

Having a single mom covering the cost didn't sit well with Connor. Especially because owning a saloon in a small Wyoming cattle town—no matter how authentically refurbished Big Millie's was—probably didn't generate a huge amount of extra cash. "No, I'll pay for whatever the dog needs."

Connor seriously regretted those words two hours later.

He'd gone to breakfast, the hardware store and the grocery store before returning to Dr. Roman's clinic to pay the final bill—which, thankfully, was a lot less than what it would have cost for a horse. The receptionist had him sign some papers and was swiping his credit card when the vet tech handed him a leash attached to a clean, freshly trimmed white dog that looked nothing like the dingy mutt he'd dropped off.

"What am I supposed to do with him?" Connor asked, staring at the colorfully striped bandanna jauntily tied around the dog's neck.

The man whose purple scrubs matched his dyed Mohawk gave him a sideways look. "Take him home, bro. Feed him. Play with him. Go on walks with him. You know? All the normal things people do with their pets?"

"But he's not *my* pet," Connor tried to explain as the receptionist handed him his credit card receipt. "Isn't there a shelter or a humane society or something that could take him?"

"Bro. You signed the form and paid the bill, so that kinda *does* mean he's your pet now. Or at least your responsibility. If you want to—" the tech lowered his voice and spelled out the next word, "—R-E-L-I-N-Q-U-I-S-H him, the nearest shelter is in Pinedale. About an hour away."

Connor, though, had a trunk full of frozen dinners and rocky road ice cream he had no intention of wasting. And that was how, less than twenty-four hours after arriving in Teton Ridge, he ended up with a little white dog riding shotgun in his sporty convertible, both of them appearing about as citified and un-cowboy-like as they could get. If he wanted any of the other ranchers in town to take him seriously, his next order of business would be to find the keys to the old Chevrolet truck he'd seen in the barn this morning.

How had one attractive woman and one little girl so thoroughly put a wrench in his carefully constructed plans? And how had he let them? His old man had always said that when Remingtons found "the one" they knew it. That was why his dad was always so determined to come back to his wife and son time and again and promise to change. But it didn't explain why his mom had kept taking Steve back.

In fact, Connor's disappointing experiences with his father had made him reluctant to form attachments, emotional or physical. As an adult, he'd been trained to get a job done and move on to the next. So settling down on the Rocking D, investing in the property and his future, was already putting the unfamiliar concept of permanency in his mind.

Then he'd met Amelia, who was open and honest and had such pure intentions, Connor already knew he'd be unable to tell the child no. His reaction to her mom, though, was a whole other thing. Not that he believed his dad's claims of his genetic ability to know when he'd met "the one." Hell, Connor learned early on not to believe most of his father's outlandish claims.

Still.

There was something intriguing about Dahlia, and if he had more downtime on his hands, he might have looked for answers.

He meant to take the dog to the shelter in Pinedale the following day, but then one thing after the next happened and he was too busy to do much of anything that first week on the ranch.

First, he had to find a nearby auto parts store to get a replacement battery and a new fuel pump before he could even get to work on the truck. Then Tomas Ochoa, who owned the ranch just north of him, paid him a call about the broken fence between their properties. Connor offered to pay half the costs and Tomas offered to have his son and a school buddy help with the labor so they could get the railing in place before calving season. The teens did such a great job, Connor hired them to come over the following weekend and help him rebuild the corral.

One of his great-aunt Connie's friends from the community church showed up with a casserole and the name of a local woman who did some housekeeping. While Connor had learned how to make hospital corners on his bunk in boot camp, having someone do a deep clean on the house while he saw to everything else that needed fixing on the ranch might be worth the expense.

The delivery guy from the hardware store gave him the names of some local ranch hands who might be looking for some extra work, but Connor still didn't have horses, let alone the money to pay someone else to care for them. One of the sheriff's deputies, not Dahlia's brother, saw him grabbing dinner to go at Biscuit Betty's one night and invited him to the rec center to join a game of pickup basketball if he ever found the time.

Everyone he met was warm and welcoming and they all asked about the white pup, who by now wouldn't leave Connor's side, following him around as if his pockets were full of Dr. Roman's dog treats. When he explained how he'd ended up with the stray, everyone would laugh and make a reference to Dahlia Deacon and her daughter. He'd yet to come across anyone who didn't know them. But any time Connor would ask about the woman—no matter how casually—the trail would go cold and the townspeople would essentially close ranks and not say another word about her.

Having moved from place to place all his life, Connor was accustomed to feeling like the new kid on the block. However, this small town was different from any of the heavily populated neighborhoods he'd lived in growing up. The inhabitants of Teton Ridge were as nosy as he'd expected, but also extremely friendly (except for Mr. Burnworth at the bakery who never threw an extra muffin in the bag for the dog like his generous sister and co-owner did). Everyone was free with words of advice and recommendations, but they were also strangely protective. There was no way to blend in, nor was there a way to keep his head down and mind his own business. He stood out everywhere he went.

Which was why two weeks later, when he was at Fredrickson's Feed and Grain pricing galvanized steel troughs and controlled aeration storage bins for hay oats, he was approached by yet another new face.

An older gentleman with a bushy gray mustache and a set of wiry eyebrows shooting out below the brim of his straw cowboy hat moseyed up beside Connor. The man's shiny belt buckle might've been a rodeo prize at one point, but it was hard to tell since his barrel chest and rounded belly shadowed the waistband of his jeans.

"Are you that kid who inherited Connie Daniels's old place?"

Connor was thirty-two and a decorated military veteran. But even he knew that when a bristly old cowboy called you *kid*, you didn't correct him. Especially when Connor was shaking his work-roughened hand, which had a grip likely earned from decades of wrestling steers. "Yes, sir. I'm Connor Remington."

"Name's Rider. I remember your dad, Steve. Used to get himself in pretty deep with those Saturday night poker games over at Big Millie's. I was there the night he lost the Rocking D's prize longhorn while holding nothin' but a pair of nines. Ol' Connie finally put her boot down after that." Rider made a tsking sound, but before Connor could offer his standard apology for his father's lack of control around whiskey and card games—the older man went on. "I heard you were looking to breed some Morgan horses on your great-aunt's ranch."

Yep, there was no such thing as minding one's business in Teton Ridge. Not that Connor had anything to keep private. In fact, with his own memories of his old man already fading, it might be pretty informative to befriend the people around here who could give him a bit more insight into Steve Remington, and more importantly, his great-aunt Connie. "Yes, sir. That's my plan."

Rider crossed his arms over his massive chest and planted his boots a few feet apart, as though he was going to be standing there awhile. "What are you starting with?"

Connor told Rider about the three-year-old untried stallion he'd bought at an auction in Cody after he'd returned his rental car to Jackson last week. The stud would be delivered in a few days and Connor was in a hurry to make sure the small stables were ready. The conversation shot off from there and the two men stood in the aisle for a good twenty minutes or so discussing the safety of in-hand breeding versus pasture breeding as well as MHC proteins playing a role in genetic differences and horse compatibility.

When the old cowboy seemed convinced that Connor actually knew what he was talking about, Rider said, "I have a couple of mares that'll need to be covered at the end of the month. Why don't you bring your new stallion to my ranch? We can see how he does with the ladies, and if any of them take a liking to him, we can work out the stud fees."

Connor's chest suddenly didn't feel so heavy. It was the break he didn't know he'd been hoping for. He'd planned to invest in a few broodmares himself, but he also needed extra cash to pump into the infrastructure at the Rocking D while he waited for his investment to produce several—or hopefully more—foals.

"Sounds like a plan." Connor again shook the man's hand. "Where is your ranch?"

Rider's wiry eyebrows dipped low and he took off his cowboy hat to scratch the steel bristly hair underneath. "A few miles down the road from yours?"

Connor had the feeling that the older cowboy expected him to know every single ranch and cowpoke in Ridgecrest County. Sure, he'd heard of some of the bigger outfits nearby, like the Twin Kings and Fallow's Crossing, but it wasn't as though Connor'd had a ton of downtime to figure out who worked where yet. He'd rather remain quiet than ask an obvious question. Or worse, make a wrong assumption.

A few seconds of silence hovered between them before Rider finally replaced his hat. "By the way, I know the sins of the father don't always pass to the sins of the son. But just in case you're lookin' for a good poker game, you won't find that at Big Millie's anymore. My niece runs a respectable establishment nowadays."

Connor's ears shot to attention and his pulse spiked. "So Dahlia is your niece?"

"That's right." One side of Rider's gray mustache hitched upward. "I heard you'd been askin' about her around town."

Okay, so apparently Connor's horse breeding plan wasn't the only thing folks in Teton Ridge were talking about. He hoped his gulp wasn't noticeable. "I don't suppose you'd buy the excuse that I was just being neighborly?"

"Ha!" The old man's laugh was loud enough to draw the attention of several customers and Freddie Fredrickson behind the register. "If I had an acre of property for every young buck who wanted to be *neighborly* with my nieces, I'd have the biggest spread in Wyoming."

A woman wearing denim overalls and a cap embroidered with the words Crazy Chicken Lady made a sniggering sound as she pushed her cart full of organic scratch grains past them.

"Sir, with all due respect, Dahlia Deacon seems like a perfectly nice lady and a great mom. And yes, I can see how many men would be interested in getting to know her better. But I assure you, all of my energy is focused on getting the Rocking D up and running. I don't have time to be pursuing anyone, let alone someone who so clearly doesn't want to be pursued."

"Did Dahlia tell you she didn't want to be pursued?" Rider asked.

"The subject never came up." And it likely never would.

Rider leaned in closer and lowered his voice. "Can I give you a word of advice, son?"

Nobody had called Connor *son* since his dad had died, and he didn't know how to feel about it. While he could use all the advice he could get, a warm sensation bloomed at the nape of his neck and all he could manage in response was a gruff "Hmm?"

"Dahlia will never raise that particular subject. She has good reason to keep her business to herself. But when the right guy comes along, Amelia will let her know." With that, Rider walked to the opposite end of the aisle, and then to the cash register up front.

Remingtons always know when they've found "the one."

Connor shook off the eerie sensation of his own father's words echoing back to him. All this talk of his old man was putting strange ideas in his head.

Not to mention the fact that Connor didn't believe a mom would actually take relationship advice from her five-year-old. Especially when Amelia hadn't proven herself to be the most discerning when it came to liking every person and animal that came along.

Sure, the little girl could outtalk anyone he'd ever met, and even *he* had already given in to the child's appeals once. But Connor had lived through too many of his own parents' battles to ever feel the need to win someone over. Besides, he hadn't been blowing smoke when he'd said his sole focus was on his ranch. It had to be. If Connor failed at this unexpected shot to fulfill his lifelong dream—as well as his promise to his great-aunt on her deathbed—then, like his old man, he wouldn't have anyone to blame but himself.

"C'mon, Mommy. We gotta check on him. It's been a whole month."

"It's barely been two weeks," Dahlia corrected Amelia way too early on a Saturday morning. "I'm sure Mr. Remington is taking wonderful care of the dog."

"But I don't even know if it has a name." Her daughter's eyes filled with that infamous King determination. Finn, Dahlia's twin sister, had once given her niece a book entitled *Girls Can Do Anything They Want*. Ever since she'd first read it, Amelia had taken the words to heart. It was a great motto for empowering young women, but only when it didn't undermine the mothers of those same women.

Nobody could always get what he or she wanted. In fact, just a few days ago, Amelia *wanted* to eat a bowl of chocolate chip ice cream for breakfast before school. But Dahlia *wanted* her to eat a bowl of oatmeal. Neither of them got what they wanted after *that* particular standoff.

Dahlia quickly weighed her options. She could say no and hold her ground—which was what every parenting advice guru would probably tell her to do. Or she could say no, and then later in the day when the negotiations continued—because they would always continue with a determined Amelia—Dahlia might be tempted to give in, thereby becoming a pushover.

Which left a third option. Instead of simply giving in, she could make Amelia think it was Dahlia's idea to go and visit Connor all along.

And that was why forty-five minutes and a quick shower later, Dahlia and her daughter were pulling into the driveway of the Rocking D with a box of doughnuts and a bag of squeaky toys.

Putting the truck in Park, she fought the urge to check her reflection in the review mirror. Why should she care how she looked when Connor saw her?

Maybe because she and her daughter were barging in on someone, unannounced, at eight thirty on a Saturday morning. Or maybe because the man walking out of the stables carrying a bundle of wood planks under one strong arm and a ladder in the other sent an unexpected thrill down her spine.

"There he is!" Amelia exclaimed as she unbuckled herself from her booster seat before Dahlia had even switched off the ignition. She really needed to remember to get that childproof lock fixed on the back-seat doors.

Hurrying after her daughter meant there was no time for Dahlia to give a second thought to her appearance. Luckily, instead of running straight to Connor, Amelia ran straight for the dog, who'd cleaned up even better than his new owner. Not that Connor needed to clean up. But at least he'd traded in those sneakers and that stiff denim for worn cowboy boots and a pair of faded jeans that settled low on his narrow waist.

Whoa.

Wait a minute. What was that all about? Why was she even paying attention to his jeans?

"Sorry for showing up unannounced." Dahlia slid her palms in her back pockets.

Connor's only reply was to set the bundle of wood down on the ground, his broad chest stretching against the fabric of his chambray work shirt. Her mouth went dry and, even though he hadn't asked what they were doing there, she swallowed before pouring out an explanation.

"I had the morning off and Amelia was really insistent about checking on the dog. She wanted to find out if you'd named him yet. I told her I was sure you had, but with her being in school during the week and me working in the evenings, the weekends are pretty valuable as far as quality time goes and I didn't feel like wasting a whole Saturday arguing with a five-year-old. I didn't have your number or I would've given you a heads-up. Or just sent you a text asking about the dog. Not that I'm fishing for your number or anything. Because I really don't need it and I'm sure that this is a onetime thing. I promise that my daughter and I don't make a habit of showing up at strangers' houses unannounced. Especially because you're probably super busy getting the ranch working again. The new roof on the stables looks great, by the way. Oh, we brought doughnuts."

What had gotten into her? She was talking even more than Amelia usually did. Dahlia squeezed her eyes shut, took a deep breath and counted to three before she embarrassed herself any further. When she dared a peek at the reaction on his face, she realized he was smirking at her.

"That sounds great," Connor said simply. Almost too simply.

"Which part?" Dahlia asked, pretending that her cheeks weren't the same color of pink as the strawberry smoothie she'd downed on the way over here.

"All of it." His smirk turned into a knowing smile. "But especially the doughnuts part. I worked through breakfast this morning."

He turned to Amelia, who was sitting in the dirt with the white pup licking the smeared glaze frosting and sprinkles off her face. "I have some chocolate milk in the kitchen."

That was it? Dahlia thought as she walked around to the passenger side of the truck to retrieve the pink bakery box and bag of dog toys. She'd just rambled on and on, talking more to Connor in the past thirty seconds than she had the entire first two times she'd met him. And all he could offer her in return was some chocolate milk and a *that sounds great*?

She bit her lip as she approached the man, who was kneeling next to her daughter and the dog, discussing the possible breeds in the little white stray's ancestry.

"Maybe he's part poodle," Amelia suggested.

Connor shrugged. "It's possible. The vet thought he might be part terrier. He definitely knows how to pick up a scent and track the badgers that keep trying to build their home under the old henhouse over there."

"Are there any roosters in there? Uncle Rider has a rooster that's meaner than lizard poop, 'cept Uncle Rider doesn't really say the word *poop*. He says the other one that I'm not allowed to use. His rooster is called Diablo and pecks at people when they hafta collect the eggs. 'Cept for me. Diablo likes me 'cause I have a sweet tem-pre-mint 'round animals. That's what my aunt Finn says." Instead of waiting for an answer, Amelia took off running toward the dilapidated chicken coop that looked like a razed tree fort and was apparently the last item on Connor's fix-up list.

"I actually met your uncle Rider the other day at the feed store," Connor said casually, and Dahlia felt the hairs on the back of her neck stand at attention. As soon as the man found out who her family was, she'd never get rid of him. Men and women alike loved hitching their lassos to the Kings. Or at least to their money and prestige.

She'd been dealing with it her whole life, and it was one of the reasons she'd never really dated much after her divorce. She could never tell who genuinely liked her, or who simply wanted to get closer to one of the wealthiest and most successful families in Wyoming. But Connor's next question convinced Dahlia that he still hadn't put all the pieces together yet.

"He took down my number and when my new stallion arrives, I'm going to bring it out to his ranch to see if any of his mares are compatible. He said his place is close to here, but I've met so many people in town, I don't really know who lives where."

Rider never felt the need to tell people his last name, let alone his address. He might not be as world famous as his twin brother, former Vice President Roper King, but as an old rodeo star and the co-owner of the second largest ranch in Wyoming, he was notorious in his own right.

"How'd you know Rider was my uncle?"

"He mentioned meeting my father once at Big Millie's. He wanted me to know that you run a respectable establishment and warned me that if I was anything like my old man, I should stay far away."

Dahlia tilted her head as she studied him. "And are you?"

"Staying far away?" Connor shrugged. "I've tried to, but you keep finding me."

"I meant are you anything like your father." Not that she had any idea who his father was or what that would prove. "Wait. Did you just say you've been trying to avoid me?"

"I meant that in a good way," he said quickly, but she was already rocking back on her boot heels.

That was certainly a first for Dahlia. Not that she thought the man—or any man—was dying to spend time with her, but she was usually the one to do the avoiding. The unexpected disappointment kind of stung. "So I should be flattered that you don't want to be around me?"

"I never said that I don't *want* to be around you, Dahlia. Obviously, I do. That's why it's been a struggle."

His insinuation, along with his use of her name, turned that disappointed sting into a warm tingle. She knew why she'd been keeping *her* distance from Connor, but now she was intensely curious about why he'd felt the need to do the same. Before she could ask him, though, Amelia and the rather adorable mutt were running back toward them.

"Hey, Mr. Rem'ton. Look at him following me everywhere I go with no leash. Aunt Finn says that if you got the goods, you can get 'em to follow you anywhere you want. That means I have the goods. Just like Mommy."

"Oh, jeez, Amelia." Dahlia would've covered her blushing face, but Connor was already covering his, his broad shoulders shaking. "Please don't repeat what Aunt Finn says."

"Is your uncle Rider married to your aunt Finn?" Connor asked Amelia when he finished laughing. He clearly was still trying to piece it all together and Dahlia wasn't going to make it any easier for him. Especially when she should be more focused on watching what her sister was saying in front of her daughter.

Amelia giggled. "No, silly. Uncle Rider is married to Aunt Freckles but they don't live together 'cause Aunt Freckles said she's too old for that nonsense. Aunt Finn is Mommy's age so they're only kinda old. They're twins. I wish I was a twin, but it's just me. Mommy said she's done having babies, but Aunt Freckles told Mommy not to count her chickens afore they hatch. When do your chickens get here?"

And just like that, Amelia spun the conversation right back to her favorite topic—animals. Thank goodness, because her daughter had just delivered a mouthful of information, potentially providing Connor with all types of details about their family if he could've gotten a word in edgewise to ask for clarification.

"I don't have any roosters or chickens yet. But I do have my very first stallion being delivered this afternoon."

"I can't wait to see your new horse. What color is he? What's his name? Where are you gonna put him? Do you have a saddle? Aunt Finn said all cowgirls need their own saddles. Can I go see his stable?" Amelia shot off toward the large outbuilding sporting a fresh coat of red paint.

For the next thirty minutes, Connor patiently showed Amelia around the stalls, which were empty, the tack room, which was only half-empty, and a feed storage area, which was stocked completely full. Dahlia and the white dog both trailed behind them obediently—except Dahlia was the sucker still holding the doughnut box.

Or maybe Connor was the sucker, since he was the one stuck answering all of Amelia's constant rapid-fire questions. She loved her daughter's curious nature, but sometimes Dahlia's own brain felt as though she were trapped in a perpetual game of fast-paced trivia and she had to know all the answers all the time.

Dahlia's mother, the former first lady of Wyoming and second lady of the United States, was the opposite. Sherilee King would prefer to host a head-of-state dinner for a thousand of her closest friends rather than enjoy a quiet meal at home. She often cautioned Dahlia about being overshadowed by anyone—especially a five-year-old. However, being the King who didn't fit the mold made Dahlia want to encourage her daughter's natural personality all the more.

Of all her siblings, Dahlia was the least like her parents. She was the reserved one, the one who preferred staying behind the scenes. Marcus was the Sheriff of Ridgecrest County. Duke had been a football hero before becoming a highly decorated pilot in the Navy. Tessa was a political analyst with her own show on a cable news channel. Finn ran their family's multi-million-dollar ranch and was responsible for several dozen employees and some of the best livestock in the state. MJ, the baby of the family, had gotten into some trouble recently, but Dahlia was sure the eighteen-year-old would get his act together and come out on top. Because that was what Kings did. They excelled.

Except for Dahlia. She'd been the one who dropped out of college one semester shy of earning her interior design degree. She'd been the one who'd ended up pregnant after a one-night stand during the height of her dad's hard-fought election campaign. She'd also been the one who'd insisted on marrying that same guy, knowing full well the improbability of a lasting marriage with a famous musician who was always gone on tour.

Not that she regretted her very brief relationship with Micah Deacon. After all, she'd gotten Amelia out of the whole deal. Plus, she and Micah got along pretty well, and Amelia loved her regular video chats with her daddy and spending time with him whenever he got a break in his schedule.

While Dahlia was happy and fulfilled with the life she'd made for herself here in Teton Ridge, there was always the unspoken expectation that she could have been so much more than a mother and a bar owner. She was a King, after all. Yet, nobody seemed to care that in reality, she'd never wanted anything more than what she already had.

She was perfectly content being herself and living life on her own terms. Just as she was content allowing Amelia to be *herself.* Even if that meant the little girl repeated things at the worst times or came up with the most inappropriate questions.

"But how does the baby get *inside* the girl horse's tummy?" her daughter asked Connor, who suddenly tugged at the collar of his shirt.

Instead of focusing on the smooth sun-kissed skin along his neck, Dahlia jumped into the conversation in the nick of time. "Peanut, why don't we let Mr. Remington get back to work?"

"Fine." Amelia gave a dramatic sigh. "Aunt Finn promised

to let me watch a horse baby get borned next time they have one at the ranch. So I'll just ask her."

Heat spread across Dahlia's cheeks and she made a mental note to talk to her sister about how much exposure to the natural mechanics of animal procreation a five-year-old should have. Even one as precocious as Amelia.

"Thank Mr. Remington for giving us a tour of his ranch," Dahlia instructed her daughter, who immediately obeyed.

"You're very welcome." Connor's smile was directed at Amelia, but Dahlia's insides quivered at its charming effects all the same.

She shook her head quickly, reminding herself not to get drawn in. "And tell... Sorry, what's the dog's name again?"

Connor took off his ball cap and scratched his head. His close-cropped hair had grown at least half an inch since they'd first met. Not that Dahlia was paying attention to such things. He sucked in one of his lightly stubbled cheeks before admitting, "I haven't exactly given him a name yet."

Amelia gasped. "But he hasta have a name."

"What about Casper?" Connor asked. "Because he's white and follows me around everywhere like a friendly ghost."

"No. You can't name a dog after a ghost. All the other animals will be scared of him. Even though ghosts aren't scary to me anymore because I'm a big girl and met one once." Amelia tapped her chin, thoughtfully and Dahlia pretended like her daughter's fanciful imagination about ghosts was totally normal. "How about I think about it tonight and we can come back tomorrow with a perfect name."

"Peanut, we can't keep bugging Mr. Remington."

"Please, call me Connor." This time when Connor smiled, he looked directly into Dahlia's eyes. The earlier quivering was nothing compared to the ripple now coursing through her rib cage and settling in her tummy. "You both are welcome to come visit the Rocking D anytime."

"Woo-hoo!" Amelia did a little jump and then skipped to the truck.

"Be careful, Connor," Dahlia told him. "Amelia will hold you to that."

"I never offer something unless I mean it." He took a step closer to Dahlia and her breath caught in her throat. This wasn't good. "I was hoping that if I gave you some time and space, you'd eventually figure out that I'm a decent guy. So earlier when I said I was trying to stay away from you, I didn't mean to imply that you have to stay away from me."

"Nice to know." She shoved the doughnut box at him, quickly putting a stop to any flirtatious thoughts he might be harboring. "Now you won't be surprised if my daughter turns your ranch into a full-blown refuge for stray and injured animals."

"I have a feeling both you and your daughter are always going to keep me on my toes with your surprises." He took a maple bar out of the pink box and held it up like a salute. "Thanks for the warning, though. And thanks again for stopping by with breakfast, Amelia!"

Her daughter heard only the last sentence and waved enthusiastically out the back window. "See you next time!"

"Looking forward to it." Connor winked at Dahlia before taking a big bite of his doughnut. When he licked the corner of his mouth, she knew she had to get out of there. Fast.

She mumbled a goodbye and turned to retreat to the truck before she started licking her own lips.

Driving away, Dahlia kept herself from looking in the rearview mirror. Obviously, she had no intention of showing up unannounced again and dumping any more of Amelia's lost causes on the unsuspecting rancher. But somebody needed to tell him not to get his hopes up, thinking there might be something to this spark between them.

Clearly, nobody else in town had bothered to warn Connor Remington that Dahlia King Deacon and her family would always be a whole lot more than he bargained for.

CHAPTER FOUR

"SO WHAT'S UP with you and this new guy who inherited the Rocking D?" Dauphine "Finn" King asked her twin sister as they sat on the top ledge of the smaller indoor corral, watching Amelia's riding lesson.

"Nothing is up with us." Dahlia hadn't gone back to Connor's ranch the following day like Amelia had wanted to. Nor did she have any intention of returning. Ever. Instead, she focused on her daughter sitting high and proud in the tiny custom-made saddle as her uncle led the five-year-old in slow circles. "Remember when Dad taught us how to ride? It's weird to think he's gone now and our kids won't get to know him like we did."

"One, I'm never going to have kids. And two, Dad didn't teach me. Uncle Rider did. Probably because I didn't need as many lessons as you." Finn, who was an accomplished horsewoman, gave Dahlia a light shove. "And don't change the subject. I heard this new guy was asking about you around town."

Out of all the siblings, Finn was probably taking the loss of Roper King the hardest. But she was the most stubborn and refused to talk about her feelings. So Dahlia didn't push. Her tough-as-nails sister would talk about it in her own time and under her own terms.

Instead, Dahlia sighed and answered, "He's probably only asking about me because he was there when Amelia spied a stray dog and talked him into keeping it."

"Amelia could sell a drowning man a glass of water." Finn laughed. "I heard about the stray. I also heard that the mutt follows him everywhere. He was sitting outside on the patio at Biscuit Betty's with the thing. And nobody sits on the patio at Biscuit Betty's before March."

"Foolish man. The guy is a total goat roper," Dahlia said, using the slang term for a wannabe cowboy. "He has no business trying to play rancher out here in the middle of Wyoming."

"Look at me, Aunt Finn." Amelia waved as she rode by. "I'm doing it all by myself."

"Stop waving and keep both hands on her reins, Peanut," Finn coached. "Gray Goose will be more comfortable if you're in charge."

Dahlia shook her head. "I can't believe you have my daughter riding a pony named after vodka."

"I can't believe you would mind, considering y'all live at a brothel."

"It's a saloon," Dahlia replied. Finn was always teasing someone about something. So Dahlia indulged her by engaging in yet another argument about her choice of profession just so she could distract her sister from the real topic she wanted to avoid: Connor Remington.

"So what's his story?" Her twin must've sensed the one thing Dahlia didn't want to talk about. "Why's he here? Is there a Mrs. Goat Roper?"

Good question. The guy had to be single, right? He certainly acted as though he was, with that sexy smirk and those heat-filled stares. Besides, Dahlia could usually spy a married man a mile away. Still, she chose to ignore the second part of Finn's question. "Judging by his tan, I think he's from California, maybe? Or some big city. I'm pretty sure he was in the military at some point because he stands like he's constantly in the 'at ease' position. He never knew about his great-aunt Connie until just a bit before she passed away. From what I could tell, he was pretty shocked about inheriting the ranch, but he's intent on making it work. Which tells me he probably has all his savings riding on this and nothing else to fall back on. Oh, and I did find out that he was an only child. But I didn't pry into his personal business because it's personal."

"Yet, you felt comfortable foisting one of your daughter's strays off on him?" Finn asked, one eyebrow lifted.

"It was either *I* take the dog or *he* takes it. Have you met Mr. Burnworth?"

"Mr. Burnworth is a cranky pile of bones who told me I smelled like I'd been rolling around in manure last time I was in the bakery. How does such a skinny and bitter old man manage to make the best damn pies around? His baking skill is the only thing that's kept him in business all these years. It certainly isn't because of his customer service."

"Well, his baking and his sweet sister. She deserves a medal for putting up with him for so long."

"That's the same thing people say about you." Finn made her voice high-pitched as she mimicked most of their elementary school teachers. "Dahlia's so chill and gets along with everyone. What in the world happened to Finn?"

"Oh, please." Dahlia playfully shoved her sister. "Deep down, you're the softest one of all of us Kings. You just have the toughest exterior. And the hardest head."

"Take it back. I am not soft." Finn's boot swiped at Dahlia's, but she dodged the kick just in time. Her sister stuck out her tongue in response, then added, "I'm certainly not soft enough to let you and your sweet-talking daughter pawn off any more animals on me. Unlike that so-called cowboy of yours."

An image quickly appeared in Dahlia's mind—of the wannabe rancher's broad chest and flat stomach in that snug T-shirt he'd been wearing the day they'd first met. There was certainly nothing soft about Connor Remington. Except maybe his lips…

"Whoa, that's a look I haven't seen in a while," Finn interrupted her thoughts. "You're interested in this new guy."

"No I'm not. I merely took pity on him because he has a decent-sized ranch without a single animal on it."

"So you've been spending time at his ranch?" Finn raised an eyebrow.

"Only twice. You make it sound like I'm stalking the man. I dropped him off the first time we met." She told her sister the story about how he was out on the road looking for the stray in a T-shirt—*don't think about the shirt*—crisp new jeans and sneakers. "And then a few days ago when Amelia wanted to check in on the dog."

"But he's getting more animals, right? I heard Uncle Rider wants him to bring his new stallion out here to see how he does in the breeding stalls. Rider actually got a kick out of the fact that the man had no idea who he was when he ran into him at the feed and grain."

"See. That's my point," Dahlia told her sister. "How can any legitimate rancher in a thousand-mile radius *not* know who Rider King is?"

"Fair enough. At least you can be assured that he isn't using you to get closer to the Kings." This time, Finn's voice was more solemn than playful. Both sisters unfortunately learned at a young age to be wary of men wanting to lasso themselves to their family's ranching connections. "Speaking of which, what's the latest on the donkey's behind, anyway?"

"I'm assuming you're referring to the father of my child?" For some reason, Dahlia's twin had never really taken to Micah Deacon, even though there was never any animosity between Dahlia and her ex. Besides, Micah was a good dad and would drop anything for Amelia if she needed it. "You know full well that Micah was never using me to get close to the Kings. That was the drummer in his college band. Remember, you had him in your Intro to Animal Science class our freshman year at UW?"

"Oh, yeah. That guy who tried to move in on you before the divorce papers were even signed, then tried to get his name on the deed for Big Millie's."

"It didn't go quite that far." Dahlia's lower spine stiffened at the reminder. "I had a lot going on at the time."

"Speaking of staying busy, I heard Micah was going to be doing another tour this summer. Does Amelia ever get to see her dad?"

Dahlia straightened her shoulders. "They FaceTime on the phone a few nights a week and he bought her that iPad to make the video calls easier and so she could text him whenever she wants. And, of course, so she can play her favorite games. He might be able to fly in from Nashville for spring break. Everyone's doing their best to make it work."

She often got tired of explaining her unique co-parenting situation to people, including her own family. Someone always wanted there to be a bad guy when a relationship ended, but the truth was that she and Micah were both the good guys, they just weren't good together.

"Lil' Amelia looks like a natural up there," Aunt Freckles called from a few feet away. Technically, Freckles was no longer their aunt since she'd been separated from Rider longer than she'd ever been married to him. But she loved the King children like her own and when Roper died, she'd dropped everything and came out to Wyoming to help.

"She's sure got it, all right." Finn hopped off the fence and walked over to Freckles.

"That reminds me." Dahlia jumped down and followed. "When you teach my daughter expressions like that, she usually repeats them at the most inopportune times."

"Expressions like what?" Freckles asked.

"The other day she told some random man that her aunt says when *you got it*, the guys will follow you."

"Got what?" Freckles narrowed a teal-shadowed eye and put her hand on one leopard-printed spandex covered hip. The older woman had to be pushing eighty, but she wore more makeup, hairspray and Lycra than four twenty-year-old beauty queens. Combined.

"Itttt," Dahlia repeated, pointedly sounding it out. Although, Amelia had no idea what she was even referencing at the time. And to be honest, now Dahlia wasn't quite sure, either.

"Oh." Freckles nodded. "*Itttt*. Well, the girl ain't wrong. Men are easily led around by their—"

"She was trying to explain why the guy's dog was following her," Dahlia quickly cut off Freckles. "So she was repeating a phrase she'd heard from Finn."

Finn shrugged. "Sounds like the phrase works in both situations."

Freckles smiled, revealing a bright red streak of lipstick on her front tooth. "Any chance this *random man* with the dog is that new rancher in town who's been asking about you?"

"My guess is yes," Finn replied. "Otherwise, Dahlia wouldn't be so embarrassed about it. She has a thing for him."

"Who do you have a thing for, Mommy?" Amelia asked as she led the gray pony out of the corral.

"No one," Dahlia said a little too quickly and the women beside her shared a knowing look. Finn and Freckles might not be related by blood or fashion sense, but they were definitely two birds of a feather.

Everyone was reading way too much into Dahlia's nonexistent dating life. There was nothing going on between her and Connor. But if she protested, they'd only become more suspicious.

So Dahlia shoved her sunglasses higher on her nose and quietly vowed to stay away from the man before the rumors really started to spread.

* * *

When Amelia and Dahlia didn't show up on the ranch the following day, Connor told the dog, "I should still call you Casper."

Of course, as soon as he settled on a name, he'd likely run into the adorable and persuasive child who'd insist on renaming the mutt, anyway. After all, it wasn't a matter of *if*, but *when* he'd see Amelia and her mom again. He'd learned a lot since he'd moved to Teton Ridge, but the one thing that still kept him on his toes was the small-town rumor mill. He might be able to physically avoid seeing the co-rescuers of his new pet, but he wouldn't be able to avoid hearing about them. Or vice versa.

So he spent the following week the same as the past two weeks, working on the ranch, meeting more townspeople and not referring to the dog by any name. Oh, and thinking about Dahlia when he wasn't busy with everything else.

It helped that his new stallion arrived on Monday and he didn't have as much time on his hands to think about anything but his ranch. By Friday, though, he needed to go back into town for a specialty feed Dr. Roman had recommended for Private Peppercorn.

The three-year-old stallion's grand sire was a proven Morgan stud who successfully covered more than fifty mares a season. Technically, he'd been registered as Colonel Peppercorn on his official papers, but Connor gave the untried stallion a demotion until he proved himself and earned his rank.

"Well, boy, if we go now, we can grab you a muffin before the feed store opens." He held open the truck door as the shorter dog defied gravity and easily launched himself into the cab of the truck.

When he parked outside Burnworth's—which had to be the worst name for a bakery ever—he cracked the window. The dog's ears perked up and he bounced across the bench seat, but Connor held up his hand, using the command signal he'd used in the Marine Corps when they'd had to silently post up outside a suspicious location.

"Stay," he told the dog before shutting the truck door. The animal's ears fell and its eyes blinked in confusion. "Come on. Don't look at me like that. Mr. Burnworth threatened to cut us both off if I brought you into the bakery again. Just wait for me here. I'll be right back."

But Connor was no more than halfway across the sidewalk when he heard an excited yip and turned around in time to see the scrappy white mutt wiggle out of the opening in the window. Instead of running toward Connor, though, the animal ran straight for Amelia who dropped to her knees just in time to be greeted by a wet nose and an even wetter puppy tongue.

"Hi, Goatee! I've missed you, too. How's my best boy?" As Amelia rambled on, the dog responded with more licking and tail wagging. "I've been wanting to come visit you at the ranch again, but Mommy said we should let you get settled and... Oh, hi, Mr. Rem'ton. Look, Mommy, Mr. Rem'ton and Goatee are here."

"I see that," Dahlia said as she balanced a travel mug of coffee in one hand and a red backpack in the other. She was bundled into a coat and scarf, her honey-blond hair hanging in loose curls under a Dorsey Tractor Supply ball cap. "Hi, Mr. Remington."

"Connor," he reminded her. "And apparently, this is my dog, Goatee? Is that what we're calling him?"

"Yeah. Don't you love it?" the little girl asked.

Connor squinted at the animal who, despite his recent grooming, still had a slight patch of longer hair that the clippers must've missed. "I'm guessing because that fur on his chin makes him look like he has a little beard?"

"No. Because Mommy and Aunt Finn were talking about you being a goat roper, even though you don't got no goats on your ranch."

"What's a goat roper?" he asked. But he could tell by the pink staining Dahlia's cheeks that the term wasn't complimentary.

"Amelia, how did you even hear that? You were supposed to

be paying attention to your riding... Never mind." Dahlia turned toward him, but seemed to have trouble making eye contact. "It just means you're new to ranching."

"When I talked to Daddy on FaceTime last night, I had to ask him what it meant, too," Amelia reassured Connor. "He said that if I heard it from Aunt Finn, it couldn't be good. But I told him it was Mommy who called you that and then he just laughed and laughed and said Mommy has lots of experience with goat ropers."

Dahlia's face was now so red she almost matched the kid-sized backpack, which was sliding off her shoulder. "Peanut, why don't you go ask Ms. Burnworth for a muffin for both you and Mr. Remington. I mean for you and *Connor*," she amended with a bit too much emphasis. It was almost as though she wanted to remind everyone that he actually had a real name and not the unexplained nickname.

Feeling a mischievous grin tugging on the corners of his mouth, Connor reached into his pocket for a twenty-dollar bill and handed it to the girl. He wasn't about to let Dahlia off the hook with this one.

"And will you get something for *Goatee*, too?" Just in case Dahlia didn't hear him emphasizing the goat reference, he repeated it. "*Goatee* likes the banana muffins best."

"What about for you, Connor?" Amelia asked. His name had never sounded so innocent or so endearing. "What kind do you want?"

"Oh, surprise me." As the dog started to follow the girl, Connor swooped him into his arms. "Not you, Goatee. You're staying here with us. Even if your name is the result of someone's trash-talking session about your owner."

"It wasn't trash-talking so much as me voicing concern that perhaps the Rocking D is a bit more than you can handle." Dahlia lifted her own chin proudly before petting the dog under his. "Besides, he *does* look like he has a little goatee."

"How do you know what I can handle?"

With the dog still secured in his arms, Dahlia stood only inches away. The tip of her tongue darted out to touch her lips before she cleared her throat. "I don't. I really don't know you at all."

"Exactly. So maybe you should get to know me a little better." Even to his own ears, the words sounded like an invitation. A dare. "I mean, before you jump to any more conclusions."

"Just because you figured out how to dress the part—" her eyes slowly traveled the length of his body to his boots and then back up again. The tilt of her mouth suggested she appreciated what she saw and his jeans suddenly felt tighter "—that doesn't make you a real cowboy."

Now he was the one whose skin was heated. Except, instead of blushing from embarrassment, his blood was pumping from arousal. He returned her earlier appraisal of him, allowing his eyes to scan just as slowly from her bulky jacket to her long legs encased in fitted denim. As he lifted his eyes back to her, he took a step closer. "I've never pretended otherwise."

"Have you ever worked at a ranch before, Connor?" Was it his imagination, or did she step closer, as well? Her face was tilted at an angle to look up at him while his head was lowered close enough that the brims of their hats threatened to collide.

He opened his mouth leisurely, taking his time with a single-word response. "No."

He was rewarded with the thrill of satisfaction when Dahlia's gaze dropped to his lips. And stayed there as she asked her next question. "Ever been in the saddle before?"

Oh, if she only knew.

Before he could tell her exactly how experienced he was, though, Amelia returned and Goatee reminded the two adults that he was the only thing wedged between them and full-body contact. The girl must not have noticed her mother jumping away as though she'd been startled.

Amelia pulled a muffin out for the dog before handing the white bag to Connor. "I got you blueberry. That's my daddy's favorite kind. He eats them all the time when he's on his tour bus and then his fingers turn all blue and so does his guitar strings."

Tour bus. Guitar. Deacon. Everything suddenly clicked together as he watched the girl feed the dog still balanced in the crook of Connor's arm. "Is your dad—"

Dahlia quickly interrupted. "We need to get to school, Amelia. You don't want anyone feeding the hamsters before you."

"Wait," he said to Dahlia, but her expression had gone blank, her mask already back in place. "Are you married to Micah Deacon?"

The last thing Connor wanted to be doing was standing on a public sidewalk in the middle of his newly adopted hometown publicly lusting over a famous musician's wife. Or anyone's wife, really.

"No, I'm not." Dahlia pulled her hat lower on her brow.

"Mommy and Daddy got dee-vorced when I was a baby." Amelia's casual response was the exact opposite of her mother's tense one. "We do co-parenting. Just like Peyton's family. Except Mommy and Daddy don't ever yell at each other like Peyton's parents do."

Dahlia stiffened and took a step back. "Okay, well, on that note, Amelia, we really do have to be off to school." She managed a polite wave at Connor, but it didn't take a psychic to know that the whole dynamic between them had shifted.

Amelia gave him a fluttery little wave, too. "Bye, Connor. Bye, Goatee."

As Connor watched the duo walk away, he wasn't sure whether to feel relief or confusion. If Amelia's assessment was correct, it was great that Dahlia and her ex got along so well. For their daughter's sake. But if they did, in fact, get along so well, then why hadn't they stayed married?

Not that any of it was his business. But if there was still some unsettled business between them, it did explain the woman's standoffishness. She probably didn't want people speculating about her and her famous ex-husband. Then again, maybe she was holding out hope of reuniting with the man and keeping her family intact. She certainly wouldn't be the first woman to do so.

Speaking of which, Connor probably should call his mother this afternoon and check in. His mom loved to remind him of how many times she'd given his father a chance to prove that he'd changed, that things could be different for the three of them once Steve sobered up. His mom also loved to remind him of how wrong she'd been to believe in such a pipe dream.

Connor had grown up determined to be a better man than his father, which meant he wasn't about to make a promise he couldn't keep. He'd also grown up determined not to be like his mother and fall for someone who couldn't love him back.

He wasn't sure exactly what was going on between him and Dahlia, but whatever it was, he'd better walk a fine line of not breaking either of his childhood resolutions.

CHAPTER FIVE

DAHLIA USUALLY WORKED the lunch shift at the bar, then flipped the closed sign at two o'clock so she could pick up Amelia from school. As business had steadily grown over the past year, she'd hired another bartender to cover more of the evening shifts. However, Dahlia usually liked to be downstairs when the weekend manager clocked in to go over any details that needed her attention.

Since Fridays were paydays for most ranch hands, Dahlia was currently adding more beer mugs to the custom-made glass chiller installed under the old-fashioned bar—right next to the very modern ice machine. Amelia sat on a bar stool across from her, her iPad propped open against her Shirley Temple as she FaceTimed with her dad.

"And then Miss Violet pushed Uncle Marcus into the pool while he was still wearing his policeman's uniform and everything. Aunt Finn said he needed to cool off, anyway, and me and the twins laughed and laughed because he looked so silly, Daddy."

"Aw, man, I wish I could've been there to see it. Did you

practice your backstroke while you were at the pool?" Micah asked his daughter. He'd taught her to swim over the summer and had been instrumental—both vocally and financially—in getting the city council to add an indoor pool when the town voted to renovate the old rec center.

"Yep," Amelia replied. "I practiced real good. Even after I got water up my nose. Aunt Finn got me some new goggles. Hold on, I'm gonna go upstairs and get them. Talk to Mommy while I'm gone."

Her daughter quickly angled the device toward Dahlia before rushing up the stairs to their apartment. "Hey, Micah," she said as she straightened the screen so that her ex-husband was vertical.

"Oh, wow, Dia, the new shelves turned out nice." Micah nodded toward the thick halves of reclaimed pine logs holding up the colorful bottles of premium liquor.

"Thanks. It was touch and go with the install, but you were right about using the iron brackets. Anyway, did you see that email from the school about how they printed the wrong Spring Break dates on the upcoming calendar?"

"Yeah, I forwarded the correct dates to our tour manager so she doesn't schedule anything for the band that week. Listen, I have to run into a doctor's appointment right now. Tell Amelia to text me a pic of her in those new goggles. I'll call her after her riding lesson tonight."

Dahlia gave Micah a thumbs-up before disconnecting the call.

"I can't believe how well you guys get along," Rena, her weekend manager, said as she breezed in from the swinging kitchen door. Rena was the same age as Dahlia, but she was petite and outgoing and had way more experience when it came to dating. She was also enrolled in the online program at UW working on her masters in hospitality, so Dahlia valued her professional opinions even more than her relationship advice.

"Really?" Dahlia shrugged. She couldn't imagine not getting along with Micah. Probably because there weren't any unresolved feelings lingering between them. Just mutual respect and a common goal—to make sure their daughter was happy.

"Does he know you have a new man?" Rena asked. "'Cause things might change when the old guy finds out about the new guy."

Dahlia's stomach dropped and she tried to sound as casual as possible when she asked, "Who says I have a new man?"

Rena double knotted a short black apron around her tiny waist. "Everyone is talking about you and that dude from the Rocking D and how you guys can't take your eyes off each other when you see him in town."

"Pfshh." Dahlia picked up a discarded white dishrag and twisted it in her hands. "I barely know the guy. We've only met a handful of times."

"Uh-huh," Rena said, her tone full of doubt. "We'll see how long that lasts."

As if to prove Rena right, though, Dahlia ran into Connor four more times the following week and then five the week after that. Not that she was keeping count. Fortunately, Amelia was always with her, which prevented another close encounter like the morning in front of the bakery when she'd gotten so close to the man she could smell the minty toothpaste on his breath and the woodsy sage-scented soap on his skin. On the other hand, having her daughter there as a de facto chaperone meant Dahlia couldn't keep her personal business from spilling out of Amelia's mouth, either. And right there on the public sidewalk for anyone to hear.

Whether it was at the market or the hardware store or even once in front of the vet's office, Amelia and Goatee seemed to have a second sense about each other, zeroing in on each other before the adults could take cover and hide. Not that Dahlia would actually hide from anyone. But she'd been known to slip into the bank or the post office or even the sheriff's station if she saw someone coming her way and wasn't up for conversation.

Not that Connor seemed to be the type to hide, either. He always appeared happy to see Amelia and patiently listened to everything she said, no matter how embarrassing it might be. However, two nights ago, when they ran into him picking up one of the famous chicken pot pies at Biscuit Betty's, Amelia had invited him to join them for dinner and he'd been especially quick to make an excuse about having to run off and do whatever it was he normally did in the evenings.

What did he do with his free time when it got dark on the ranch? Did he call his girlfriend back home? Did he watch sports on TV or sappy Lifetime movies? Did he go for a jog or lift weights? Dahlia imagined him shirtless, tan, perspiration trickling along the ridges of his muscles as he did biceps curls—

"Can't we just stop by for a second?" Amelia interrupted Dahlia's inappropriate thoughts from the back seat as they passed the turnoff for the Rocking D the following Friday afternoon.

"Not today, Peanut. We're already late for your riding lesson as it is. Last time we were late, Uncle Rider made us muck the stall, remember?" And frankly, Dahlia was much too old to relive her least favorite childhood chore, even if it supposedly built character. In fact, she was seldom late for that very reason. While growing up, the only saving grace was that Finn often got the same punishment for talking back, which meant her twin sister shoveled a lot more manure than she had. Dahlia still grinned at the memory.

"But Connor said Goatee has been getting too close to Private Peppercorn lately and isn't allowed in the corral no more when they're working. He probably could use an extra cuddle so he doesn't feel left out."

Left out. It was exactly how Dahlia felt right that second. She didn't remember hearing Connor say any of that the last few times they'd seen him in town. In fact, she didn't even know that he'd hired anyone else to work with him on the ranch. "Who's Private Peppercorn?"

"His new horse. Mr. Connor said when he got him, the paperwork said Colonel Peppercorn but he hadta give the horse a dee-mo…a dee-mo…"

"A demotion?" Dahlia prompted.

"Yeah, a demotion 'cause Peppercorn is too young. Connor said that when he was a Marine, only the old people were colonels and they hadta work real hard for it."

When did he say any of that? Dahlia was sure she would've remembered it. Especially since the military reference confirmed her earlier suspicion that he'd served in the armed forces. "Was I there when he was telling you about Peppercorn?"

"I think so. But you were busy talking to Mr. Thompson about beer."

Woodrow Thompson, better known around town as Woody, had gone to high school with Duke, Dahlia's favorite brother. He used to say that Woody would've easily beat him out as the class valedictorian if he'd actually shown up for classes. Micah used to love it when Woody would randomly stop by and jam with the band who practiced in Micah's garage. He could play any instrument he picked up, but would never show when they were hired to play at an actual venue. In fact, Woody had kept the same part-time job at the Pepperoni Stampede for the past thirteen years and lived in an old Airstream behind his grandma's house off Moonlight Drive. He volunteered once a month at the vet's office, but otherwise didn't do much of anything. Nobody understood how someone so smart and so talented could be such an underachiever.

When Dahlia took Amelia to the library after school yesterday, she'd seen Woody checking out books about yeast and hops, and he mentioned that he'd been brewing his own beer in a kettle on his cookstove. For some reason, Dahlia had always felt an odd kinship with Woody. Maybe because people seemed to expect more of out of guys like him when they were perfectly content with their lives as they were. So she'd asked him to bring a few bottles by Big Millie's and he'd left. When she'd caught up with Amelia, she was giving Connor and Goatee a tour of the new audiobook listening center in the children's section.

It was also the same time that the no-nonsense librarian whispered a stern reminder to Connor that only service animals were allowed inside the building. Dahlia never even got the chance to ask him why he'd been in the library in the first place. Probably looking for a copy of *Horseback Riding for Dummies*.

Okay, that was mean. But seriously. What was the man always doing in town with his funny-looking dog, casually running into Dahlia and charming Amelia? He should be spending more time on that ranch of his. And she needed to find a hobby of her own to get her mind off him. Maybe Finn would let her redecorate one of the bunkhouses. Again.

Dahlia kept her foot on the accelerator as they continued past the spot on Ridgecrest Highway where they'd first met Connor. Her daughter was being unusually tight-lipped today, probably because she hadn't given in for once. But since this wasn't Dahlia's first rodeo with Amelia, she made a mental note to start thinking of excuses for why they couldn't stop at the Rocking D on their way home. Because there was no way her daughter would simply give up on asking.

Up ahead, she spotted several black SUVs stationed along the road just inside the entry gates to the Twin Kings. But seeing Secret Service units parked on the grounds was just as common as seeing work trucks and delivery vehicles lately. In fact, a couple of weeks ago when she'd brought Amelia, there'd been a sleek black helicopter lifting into the air and Amelia hadn't even blinked twice.

That was what it was like growing up as a King, the daughter of one of the wealthiest families in Wyoming. The children had all been raised to expect the unexpected. Whether it meant entertaining a last-minute royal guest or foreign dignitary, or their father canceling all of his campaign events spontaneously to hop aboard the private jet and fly the entire family out to Albuquerque to visit one of his buddies from Vietnam.

So fifteen minutes later when she saw the reverse lights on a horse trailer backing into the stables, she didn't think anything of it. In fact, it took Amelia shouting, "He's here!" before Dahlia felt that shiver of awareness she got every time—

No. Her stomach sank when she recognized the distinctive red truck in front of the horse trailer. Not everything in her body sank, though. Her nerve endings betrayed her by zipping to life.

"What's he doing here?" Dahlia mumbled, but Amelia had already abandoned the pony to go running toward Goatee, who'd let out an excited yip the moment the driver's-side door opened.

Connor's jaw was set and his expression was schooled, probably because Rider and Mr. Truong, the stable foreman, were already approaching his trailer, saying something about the stallion in the back. But she could tell by the slight widening of his eyes that he was definitely confused. When he saw Amelia, he blinked several times before his smile finally softened his face.

Was it because he was genuinely happy to see her daughter? Or had he just figured out exactly who her uncle was? A horse breeder trying to make a name for himself was certainly going to appreciate landing the Twin Kings as one of his clients. But Rider King, and more importantly Finn King, wouldn't do business with the man if he couldn't deliver.

Connor might've been trained as a tracker for one of the world's most elite fighting forces in the world, but as soon as he pulled up to the address on his GPS, he was sure he'd made a wrong turn.

This was the Twin Kings? Connor had only done some preliminary research about the local ranches, and while he'd known this one was the biggest on this side of the state, the owner was listed as King Enterprises, LLC. Was Rider the foreman here?

The overly official-looking guard at the front gate asked him for his name and then checked his ID. He said something into the clear wire attached to his earpiece, a military-grade communications system, then instructed Connor to take the *main road*—because apparently there were non-main roads—to the *big stables*—because apparently there were multiple smaller stables—and then someone would show him where to back in his trailer.

"This place is a far cry from the Rocking D," he muttered to Goatee as he crested the hill where an enormous house sat at least a football field away from a matching stone-and-timber building that had to be the Big Stables. The dog only barked in agreement, then peeked out the window.

A man in a straw cowboy hat came outside and made the universal hand signal to roll down the window. When Connor complied, the man introduced himself.

"I'm Mike Truong, the stable foreman. Rider and Finn were hoping we could unload your stallion directly into the southwest chute. We have several mares separated in the adjacent stalls, but they're not twitched yet. We like to have all our gals comfortable in their familiar surroundings so we can keep things as natural as possible for them. Two of my best handlers are with them to watch for aggressiveness and compatibility. Usually, with untried studs like yours, we have them stay overnight and act as a teaser of sorts to confirm which mares would be receptive. But we can wait and see how the courtships go. Now, if you want to back in, my guys will guide you."

Connor might be good with horses, but he'd never had to tow them in a trailer until recently. The transportation unit had always done that for him. It took him several attempts to navigate the trailer into the wide-open doors of the stables and then line it up perfectly with the gate to the southwest chute where someone had hung a wood-carved sign that read Tunnel of Love.

"Feels like we're both under some serious pressure, Pep," Connor said to the horse who couldn't hear him, anyway. To say he was already overwhelmed by the time he caught sight of Rider in his rearview mirror, arms crossed over that distinctive barrel chest, was an understatement. He wanted to yell out the window that he was way better with a horse than he was with a trailer, but he'd show them soon enough.

Shoving the stiff truck gear into Park, Connor gulped in a deep breath before opening the door to exit. It took every ounce of control he possessed to stand there and pretend that he always drove up to multi-million-dollar cattle ranches and wasn't completely starstruck by the vastness of the successful operation. Hell, even the *stable* was more like an indoor arena, with several corrals and hundreds of paddocks. It was tough to act like any of this was normal. Especially when he couldn't even keep his own dog from leaping out excitedly.

Instead of one of the nearby stable hands catching Goatee, though, it was little Amelia Deacon who lifted the dog in her arms and rubbed her face against its scratchy white fur. Connor could feel his eyes widening in surprise at seeing the child here, but there was also something about her familiar face and excited greeting that made him feel as if he were on his own turf. As though he weren't a complete fish out of water. But then his eyes landed on Dahlia holding on to the lead of a gray pony and suddenly it all snapped into place.

The funeral Dahlia and Amelia had been coming home from the night they'd met on the side of the highway.

The ranch security detail, who dressed like Secret Service agents.

Twin *Kings* Ranch.

Holy crap.

Dahlia's father was Roper King, the former vice president of the United States.

Which meant her uncle was Rider King.

Connor hadn't followed the news much since his discharge, but how'd he miss something this big? He was a neighbor to one of the most powerful political and cattle families in the world.

His forehead broke out in a sweat and he quickly slammed the felt brim of his Stetson lower on his brow as Rider approached the window of the horse trailer first. The stallion's impatient snorts coming from inside grounded Connor, immediately returning his pulse to a steady rate. Being around horses always made things simpler. And this was just a job, same as any other.

"So you're Private Peppercorn, huh?" The older man lifted a weathered hand between the bars and stroked the horse's silky black forelock. "Lil' Amelia tells me you got a demotion, young fella."

"That's true," Connor admitted, watching Dahlia as carefully as she was watching his meeting with her uncle. A tingle traveled up the back of his neck. She was probably too far away to hear them, which likely explained the crease in her forehead. Clearly, she didn't trust him around anyone in her family. "His previous owner gave him a rank he hadn't earned yet."

"Smart decision. What branch were you in, son?" Rider asked, and it took Connor a moment to pull his eyes away from where Dahlia was directing Amelia to stop giving Goatee chunks of carrots she had in her pocket—no doubt for the pony.

"The Corps."

"I knew I liked you," Rider replied, his beefy hand slapping Connor on the back. "I was Third Recon Battalion. From '67 to '71."

Amelia approached with the gray pony. Goatee was now in Dahlia's arms, looking perfectly content to be carried around as if he were the emperor of the stables.

"Sorry to do this to you, son, but I accidentally double-booked this afternoon." Rider's bushy gray brows and mustache made it difficult to determine whether or not he was truly remorseful. Or if it was in fact an accident. The glint of satisfaction in the older man's blue eyes—the same shade as Dahlia's and Amelia's—seemed almost scheming. "I've got a riding lesson with this fine cowgirl right now. But Lil' Amelia's mom will keep you company while you introduce your stallion to the ladies over there."

"I'll what?" Dahlia blinked several times and Connor

would've laughed at her trying to contain both her surprise and annoyance at the assignment her uncle had just dealt her.

Rider threw a heavy arm around Connor's shoulder. "Now Dahlia, we can't keep this young stud in the prime of his life pinned up when there are plenty of gals practically lined up to meet him."

"You better be talking about the stud in the back of the trailer." The look she shot her uncle would've broken lesser men. But apparently the older man wasn't the least bit fazed.

"Who else would I be talking about?" Rider's hearty laughter rang out as he squeezed Connor's shoulder with enough force to practically steer him toward Dahlia. "Look at those fillies over there just waiting to be neighborly. Love is in the air, all right."

"What does *be neighborly* mean?" Amelia asked, and Dahlia shot her uncle another withering look.

Rider cleared his throat before giving the child a leg up into her small pink saddle. "Never mind all that, Peanut. Now take the reins like I showed you…"

The older cowboy quickly led Amelia and her pony to a smaller corral inside the stables. Which left Connor and Dahlia alone near the horse trailer.

"Sorry you got ditched like that," she said to him. "I'm sure you were pretty excited to score the Twin Kings as a potential client, but, well, my uncle takes his family responsibilities pretty seriously."

"I would've been excited to have anyone as a potential client." Although, there definitely was the potential for some professional recognition if one of the most successful ranches in the state recommended him. "But I never got a chance to get excited because I was still processing it all when I finally put two and two together. I'm guessing there's a reason why you didn't want to give me the heads-up?"

"Yes. Millions of reasons." She didn't expound, but he guessed that she was referring to the financial ones. "Men tend to act differently around me when they know my last name."

He lifted a brow. "Only men?"

"No, but they're typically the ones who are bold enough to actually think that if they can get into my pants, then they can get into my family."

Whoa. Connor's fingers flexed impulsively at her candor. He didn't like the idea of anyone using Dahlia. Or getting into her pants. "If it makes you feel any better, I didn't know you were related to the Kings until right now. But it certainly explains why you were so standoffish before. And why everyone in town clammed up the second I asked about you."

"First, I'm not standoffish. Second, you were asking people in town about me?"

Should he deny it? Connor might not have time to invest in a full-fledged relationship, but he also didn't have time to play games.

"Of course I asked around. I'm not going to pretend that I wasn't interested in you. I still am, even though I'm way more cautious now that I know how it might be perceived." Hearing a whinny and the stomp of an impatient hoof reminded Connor that he wasn't here to flirt with the single mom. "But right now, I need to see to my horse."

Connor hadn't asked Dahlia to keep Goatee in her arms as he unhitched the trailer, but it gave her something to do instead of standing there awkwardly and thinking about his admission that he was in fact interested in her.

Her knees had gone a little wobbly and if more people hadn't been standing around the stables staring at them, she might've made a similar admission. Of course, it didn't help that some smart aleck, probably Finn, had hung up a sign over the entrance to the breeding chute that read Tunnel of Love.

It must be all the equestrian pheromones in the air that were throwing her off balance. Since she had no intention of following her uncle's request to walk him into the enclosure where the waiting mares had already caught Peppercorn's scent, she made her way to the cab of the truck and found a leash for the dog.

The stallion was young and, from the looks of things, eager to strut its stuff in front of his female audience. Connor had to circle the animal around several times to get it calm enough to lead the animal into the enclosure. Mr. Truong and several other experienced handlers watched Connor and the stallion intently, probably in case they needed to jump in and help control the reins.

Dahlia held her breath for a few seconds when Peppercorn reared back on his hind legs, but Connor proved to be more than capable of redirecting the horse. A warmth spread to her lower extremities as she watched him maintain control with a steady hand on the bridle and gentle words in the horse's ear. His command over the situation in the stables suddenly made her wonder if he'd just as easily take charge in other places. Like the bedroom.

Oh, Lord. Dahlia quickly clipped the leash to Goatee's collar and decided to go get some fresh air and cool down before someone confused her for one of the mares in heat.

When she returned an hour later from her walk, Finn had finally arrived and Rider was balancing Amelia on his shoulders as they watched Connor loading a very reluctant stallion into his trailer.

Her family wasn't only sizing up Private Peppercorn, they were sizing up Connor, as well. Seeing how he handled himself. And apparently, they must've approved of something because when Amelia caught sight of her and the dog returning to the stable, she yelled, "Hey, Mommy, Private Peppercorn picked Rita Margarita to be his new girlfriend. Connor's gonna bring him back tomorrow morning to visit again, but Aunt Finn says I don't get to be here for that."

"Aunt Finn is right," Dahlia replied loudly, before murmuring to Goatee. "For once."

"Aunt Finn says that Connor and Goatee can stay and have dinner with us, though."

"As long as Gan Gan doesn't mind," Dahlia replied as she kept her expression neutral. If she hinted at the slightest protest, her family would know something was up. But if she acted happy to have him stay, then he'd get the wrong impression.

"Actually, I should probably get Private Peppercorn home," Connor replied, saving both of them. "He's had a bigger day than I was expecting and needs his rest before he meets Rita Margarita's friends tomorrow."

"Speaking of military ranks, son," Rider said. "What was your MOS when you were in the Corps?"

"Here comes the inquisition," Dahlia murmured to Goatee, while a small part of her hoped the man passed her family's test with flying colors. "Let's see if your owner holds up to the spotlight."

"Initially, I was Infantry. After my three years were up, though, I had a buddy from boot camp who talked me into applying to MARSOC."

"What's MARSOC?" Finn asked.

Rider answered before Connor could. "It stands for Marine Forces Special Operations Command."

"Wait." Dahlia narrowed her eyes. "You didn't tell me you were Special Forces."

"You never asked." He smirked, before returning his attention to her uncle. "I was selected for the Marine Raider Regiment."

Rider let out a whistle. "So you were a Raider. Pretty impressive. Almost as impressive as Private Peppercorn's charm with those mares over there."

"Let me ask you this, Mr. Remington." Finn winked at Dahlia and she knew exactly what was about to come next.

"Please don't…" Dahlia said despite the already sinking sensation in her stomach. But her twin ignored her.

"My sister told me you were new to owning a ranch."

Connor was now staring directly at Dahlia, his knowing

smirk making her go weak the knees. She suddenly felt the need to sit down. "I believe the exact term she used was *goat roper*?"

Finn laughed. "Her words. Not mine. But what I wanna know is how does a newbie cowboy who grew up in... Where did you grow up?"

"Primarily Dorchester. We moved around a lot."

"So how does a kid from one of the toughest neighborhoods in Boston know so much about quality horseflesh? Clearly, you picked a winner with your first stud over there."

"When I was an operator, my company commander made us attend a course at the Mountain Warfare Training Center. He wanted us to learn how to hump our supplies into some rough desert terrains we couldn't get to with a Humvee. Turned out I was pretty good with the pack animals and outdoor tracking. Several of us from my unit were integrated with various Army Operational Detachment Alpha teams. As one of the intelligence sergeants, I spent the last two years of my career tracking enemy combatants on horseback."

"Dang," Finn replied. "I knew Dahlia had you all wrong."

Crap. Dahlia usually prided herself on her ability to read people, yet she'd totally missed the mark on him. Although, in her defense, the man didn't really dress like a cowboy. And how was she supposed to know that the military still used horses?

As if the embarrassment and awkwardness coursing through her wasn't enough to make her want to hop in her own truck and take off, the well-dressed and overly protective Sherilee King appeared at the stable doors.

"Dinner was ready ten minutes ago," Dahlia's mother scolded the group still standing around the trailer before her eyes landed on Connor. "Are you who I think you are?"

"Jeez, Mom," Finn chastised the former socialite who was normally well-known for her diplomatic hostessing skills. "Is that any way to greet our new neighbor?"

"Is this Dahlia's new man?" Aunt Freckles appeared behind Sherilee.

"He's not my new—" Dahlia started at the same time Amelia replied. "Yes. This is our new friend Connor and his dog, Goatee. Mommy said they could stay for dinner if it was all right with you, Gan Gan."

"That's not exactly what I said," Dahlia pointed out, not daring so much as a glance in Connor's direction. Her family was overwhelming enough under normal circumstances.

"You might as well join us, Mr. Remington." Sherilee sighed, a rare sign that the perfectly composed King matriarch was at her wits' end. "I mean, why *wouldn't* you want to sit at our table and bear witness to my oldest son arguing legal defenses with his ex-girlfriend. Or enjoy the hospitality of my youngest son pouting while he spends the whole evening texting with his underage drinking buddies about how the Secret Service is trying to ruin his life? Unless, that is, you care at all about your arteries. My *former* sister-in-law made enough fried chicken and country gravy to clog even the healthiest of hearts."

"And *my* former sister-in-law," Freckles countered, "already ate enough biscuits and freshly whipped honey butter to choke a small horse."

"I had half a biscuit, maybe two." Sherliee began launching an intense argument about how stress eating actually burned calories.

Finn, who usually loved watching a good verbal sparring match, used an elbow to nudge Dahlia in the rib cage. "They really know how to sell the King family dining experience, huh?"

Dahlia shook her head, then dared a glance at Connor, whose face was pivoting back and forth as though he were watching a tennis match between the two older women who had never really gotten along.

Pushing through her own growing headache, Dahlia said, "Please don't feel like you have to accept my mother's not-so-tempting invitation. Our family dynamics are a little...off... since my dad passed away, and I'm sure you have more important things going on tonight."

It was a weekend, when most single men in town showed up at Big Millie's. Her manager Rena would've said something if Connor had so much as stepped foot inside the bar. So maybe he was finding his weekend entertainment elsewhere. Not that it was any of Dahlia's business.

"What's more important than getting to know your new neighbors?" Finn asked Connor, although she didn't do that obnoxious wink in Dahlia's direction this time. "You can pull the trailer up to the house and Private Peppercorn should be fine thinking about his fruitful endeavors."

"Plus…" Dahlia's uncle lifted Amelia off his shoulders and easily transferred her onto Connor's before he could object. "My wife makes a mean fried chicken and uses real cream in her mashed potatoes."

Freckles paused mid-argument with Sherilee to point a long acrylic fingernail at Rider. "I'm not your wife anymore, you addle-brained cowboy."

"That's not what you said last night when you snuck out to my cabin."

Dahlia groaned at the implication, Finn covered her ears and made a gagging sound, while Sherilee pinched the bridge of her surgically-enhanced nose.

"Everyone get up to the house before dinner gets cold," her mother finally snapped. Then she smiled sweetly at Connor. "You, too, son. That's an order."

"Yes, ma'am." Connor did a mock salute, then winked at Dahlia. "How can I refuse an order?"

CHAPTER SIX

HOW COULD CONNOR refuse the order, indeed?

The main house was unlike anything he'd ever seen. He'd entered through the massive kitchen, which was fancy enough to be in one of those magazines his mom used to subscribe to. The formal dining room had a table big enough for thirty and the living room looked like the lobby of a five-star hotel. That is, if five-star hotel lobbies had six-foot tall portraits of a fearsome King ancestor creepily staring down her hawkish nose at him from over the fireplace.

Dahlia's aunt, who insisted he call her Freckles, set up a little cushion beside a water bowl for Goatee. And then she gave Amelia an apple to take outside to Private Peppercorn in the trailer.

Rider had been right. The fried chicken really was amazing. And Mrs. King had also been right in asking what was one more person added to the mix. Besides Dahlia mouthing the word *sorry* to him several times, he wondered if anyone else noticed his presence. But that didn't stop him from enjoying the teasing and bickering and liveliness of it all. Having eaten most of his meals the past few weeks with just Goatee, Connor sat back and took it all in.

There was so much going on at the table and not even all of the family was here. Nor did everyone present make it through the entire meal. When Amelia and Marcus's twin sons went into the kitchen to help Freckles with dessert, Mrs. King declared she had a headache and excused herself. Not wanting to wear out his welcome, Connor said, "I should be getting my horse home."

"I'll walk you out." Dahlia rose from her seat so quickly she nearly knocked over her upholstered chair. Judging by the way her eyes had alternated between rolling in annoyance at the upscale but rustic-looking chandelier above and glancing at the clock on the mantel all throughout dinner, she had to be eager to see his taillights disappear.

For a second, he thought Goatee would prefer to stay on as a house dog at the Twin Kings, lounging on his plush pillow and eating the table scraps Amelia kept sneaking him. But the dog proved to be slightly loyal when he stretched before reluctantly following Connor toward the open entryway and the monstrosity of a front door.

They were on the front porch before Dahlia exhaled a ragged breath. "Sorry for all the drama tonight. My family can be pretty overwhelming. And that's if you know them. I can only imagine how we must look to outsiders."

"I actually enjoyed it," Connor said honestly. "One of my favorite things about living in the barracks was going to the mess hall to eat with everyone. For the most part, when I was growing up, it was just me and my mom. And on the nights she worked, I only had the TV to keep me company."

"What about your dad?" she asked. "Did he ever visit?"

Connor didn't like talking about his father's criminal record under normal circumstances. And standing on the front porch of a prosperous cattle ranch surrounded by Secret Service agents was anything but normal. "He was in and out of the picture.

Out of it more often than not. Whenever he'd get released, he'd make all the usual promises about changing for the better, but it never lasted more than a few weeks."

Her full mouth opened, then closed again. He could tell that she wanted to ask him all the questions, and maybe he owed her that, considering many of her family secrets had pretty much been revealed now.

Since he wasn't quite ready to say goodbye, he asked her a question instead. "So Rider and Freckles are divorced, I take it?"

"Correct. Freckles owns a café over in Sugar Falls, Idaho, but she came out for my dad's funeral. We all adore her, but as you witnessed, she and my mom don't get along very well. They never have. I once asked my dad if it was a power struggle thing, with both of them being married to twins, and he told me that they each wished they could be more like the other. I know," she added when Connor tilted his head in confusion. "It's crazy since they're complete opposites. But my dad and Rider were complete opposites, too. Kind of like me and Finn."

"Finn definitely takes after your aunt more." He chuckled, thinking about both women's colorful personalities and irreverent humor.

Dahlia crossed her arms over her chest, which served to lift her breasts higher against her soft gray sweater. "Does that mean you think *I* take after my mom?"

She looked so adorable when her eyes narrowed at him like that, he couldn't help the chuckle escaping his lips. "Not exactly. Your mom seems very... How do I say this tactfully?"

"Controlling?" Dahlia prompted. "Overly concerned about appearances? Calculating? Almost mob boss–like in her ruthless attempts to keep everyone under her thumb?"

This time Connor did laugh. Loudly. "No, she just seems very intent on holding her family together no matter what."

"She is." Dahlia sighed before running her fingers along her scalp and shaking out the curls. "None of us will admit it, but she's usually pretty good at it, too. It's just that her methods can be incredibly frustrating at times. You saw how she was with Marcus and Violet tonight, right? How she finds ways to force them to interact?"

"Yeah, what's the story with them? Were they also married?" This family certainly kept in touch with their exes more than usual. Including Dahlia, who was currently co-parenting with Amelia's father.

"They never married, although I think they came close. Violet was in town for the funeral, which was the same night one of Marcus's deputies arrested MJ for underage drinking." This was the conversation that had dominated the family discussion tonight. "Marcus thinks our eighteen-year-old brother needs to learn a lesson, but my mom hired Violet to represent him in court. So that's why Marcus was in such a bad mood tonight. Although, to be honest, he's been in a bad mood for the past few years."

"And you have another sister? Tessa? Is she that famous news anchor?"

"She's a political analyst. She had a little moment with a Secret Service agent at our father's funeral. It's been all over the news, so she was hiding out here for a while. I'm guessing you haven't been on the internet lately?"

"Only if it involves horse testosterone levels, roof leaks or pasture enclosures." Connor scratched the stubble covering his chin. "Looking back, I should've at least done a simple Google search of your name. Or even Rider's. I mean, obviously I knew who Roper King was and that he was from Wyoming. But I guess I just assumed he'd be buried at Arlington National Cemetery. And that his children would be older. I guess it never registered that the funeral you'd attended the day we met was for the vice president. Although, I'm still kicking myself that I hadn't put two and two together sooner."

"To be honest, it was actually quite refreshing to have someone not know who I was. Or who I was related to." She smiled halfheartedly. "Oh, well. It was nice while it lasted."

"Don't worry. I won't hold all of this—" he gestured at the grand house and the even grander cattle ranch surrounding him "—against you."

"How accepting of you." She lifted one brow and he winked to let her know he was teasing.

Then he counted off on his fingers. "So that's four siblings?"

"Five. My brother Duke had to return to his ship the week after the funeral. He's a pilot in the Navy and the perfect son. Ask any of my siblings whom they're closest to and they will all say Duke. Probably because he's the most like my dad."

Roper King had been a legend—a war hero and a well-loved leader. "I knew you'd lost your father recently, but I hadn't imagined *that* type of loss."

Now it was Dahlia's turn to tilt her head. "Didn't you tell me your dad had also passed away?"

Connor lifted his face to the clear night sky sprinkled with bright stars. "Yeah, but it wasn't nearly as big of a deal."

"I'm sure it was a big deal to you, Connor. I don't feel my father's loss any more than someone else just because of who he was."

Connor's throat grew heavy, but he swallowed the emotion. "Except I was used to my father leaving and never knowing if he'd return. So when he died, it was almost as though I'd been preparing for it my whole life."

"That's tough." Dahlia nodded knowingly and for a moment, he could almost believe that she hadn't grown up with a life of wealth and privilege. She had such a sympathetic expression as she listened intently. It probably made her a great bartender. "How old were you when your parents split up?"

"Which time?" Connor shoved his hands in his pocket. "The first time I remember him leaving was when I was about Amelia's age. The last time was when I was sixteen."

Right before Steve Remington had died.

"Divorce is so hard on kids." Dahlia exhaled deeply, bringing his attention to the condensation of her breath as it expelled in a long silky cloud from her lips. "I was blessed to have an amazing father. When I ended up pregnant a bit sooner than I—or anyone else—anticipated, it was my bond with my dad that made me vow that I'd never deny Amelia the same opportunity to have a relationship with hers."

The cool night air was thick and heavy between them and he felt like he should say something, but for some reason he held back. He'd already told her more than he'd ever shared with anyone else and she seemed to be lost in her own memories, looking off at the moon in the distance. Besides, his parents had never technically divorced—nor had they valued a healthy relationship with him over the dysfunctional one they shared with each other.

He cleared his throat. "I should probably get back to the Rocking D. Tell your aunt that her fried chicken was the best I've ever had."

"Yeah. I bet you didn't think you'd be getting both dinner and a show tonight. Everyone always expects the Kings to be this perfect version of the all-American family. But when they're behind closed doors, they're usually more than most people bargain for."

Connor grinned. "Once I realized none of the wisecracks or arguments were at my expense, I actually enjoyed your family."

"I'm glad someone did," she replied with a little wave before going back inside.

Connor hadn't been lying. Dinner with the Kings had started off overwhelming, but in the end he'd become mildly entertained and almost flattered that they were comfortable being themselves in front of him.

So much so that he'd felt totally comfortable opening up to Dahlia on the porch about his father. In fact, the only time he'd been uncomfortable all evening was the unexpected uneasiness he'd felt when she'd briefly mentioned her ex-husband. Probably because he didn't know the man and, therefore, couldn't separate the guy from his own experience with having a father so far away. Silently, though, he hoped Micah Deacon was worthy of Amelia's love and Dahlia's dedication to co-parenting.

From where he was standing, though, the man had to be a fool. Because if Connor would have been lucky enough to have Dahlia as his wife, or Amelia as his daughter, he couldn't imagine ever leaving them.

Dahlia had a love-hate relationship with the Spring Fling Festival that took place in the nearby town of Fling Rock every year on the first weekend of March.

As a child, she'd loved the bright lights of the Ferris wheel, the thrill of the carnival games and the towers of fluffy cotton candy she and Finn would mash into balls before shoving the quickly dissolving wads of sugar into their mouths.

As a parent, though, she hated the rickety nuts and bolts of the quickly assembled rides, as well as the money losing odds of the carnival games. But she still loved the cotton candy. So much that she'd invented a signature cocktail at Big Millie's called the Sweet Circus, a sugar-rimmed martini glass with a pink candy-flavored vodka. Finn was usually the only one who ever ordered it.

In fact, it was Finn who'd insisted they bring Amelia to the festival tonight and promised to go on all the world-tilting, hair-whipping, nausea-inducing rides with her. But then her sister had an issue with an employee's workers comp claim and canceled at the last minute. Amelia begged to go anyway, and that was why Dahlia was currently walking down the midway, trying to patiently explain why they didn't need to go to the livestock auction scheduled to start in thirty minutes.

That was also a new development in the love-hate equation Dahlia now had with the Spring Fling. She would love seeing the animals with her daughter, but she would hate telling Amelia no when the child would inevitably insist they take one home.

"Peanut, where would we even put a sheep?" she asked her daughter when those blue eyes threatened to produce a few tears. It was tough to use rational logic with a five-year-old who thought about everything emotionally.

Amelia stopped in her tracks. "How about the parking lot behind Big Millie's? We can build a sheep pen there."

Dahlia was about to look up toward the sky for some sort of divine intervention, but her eyes landed on the cowboy who was waiting for them to move out of the middle of the midway.

"Excuse me, ladies, do you know where I could find a good sheep for my ranch?"

"Connor!" Amelia squealed with joy. Then she quickly scanned the area around his feet. "Where's Goatee?"

"I had to leave him at home. The organizers of the Spring Fling are pretty clear about no pets allowed at the fairgrounds. So I left him with a new squeaky toy and promised to bring him back something."

"Are you really looking for a sheep?" Amelia asked hopefully. "Because they're gonna have an auction and you can buy one right there inside that big red barn."

"I'm thinking about it. But I'm still doing my research." He winked at Dahlia and she was reminded of their conversation on the Twin Kings porch exactly a week ago. Had he finally done an internet search on her family? Her stomach felt like she was back on the Tilt-a-Whirl until he added, "I have several acres of pasture full of weeds that need to be chomped down before Private Peppercorn can get out there and graze on the grass. But then again, Dorsey Tractor Supply has a display of lawn mowers over in the home and garden sec—"

"You don't need a lawn mower." Her daughter jumped up and down before tugging his hand toward the arena. "I know where you can get a sheep instead."

Ha, Dahlia thought as she followed along. Connor might've proven himself when it came to horses, but there was no way he knew what he was about to get himself into. Within ten minutes, Amelia had fallen in love with three potbellied pigs, six dairy calves, two pygmy goats, an angry bighorn ram who Amelia insisted *just needed a hug*, and a forty-five pound turkey who most definitely did not need or want a hug.

"Don't look now." Connor moved behind Dahlia and spoke so low and so close she could feel his warm breath against her ear. A spiral of heat swirled its way from her jaw line to her toes. "But there's a Radical Reptiles snake exhibit just through those open doors. Do you want me to distract her when we go by so she doesn't add a boa constrictor to her list of animals to take home?"

Dahlia threw back her head to laugh, but Connor was so close behind her that her ponytail brushed against his shoulder. She took a step forward too quickly, and her boot heel caught on something in the straw, causing her to stumble.

Connor's firm arm snaked around her waist and hauled her against him. Drawing her in the opposite direction of where she was trying to go. Before she'd lost her footing, she'd been trying to avoid feeling the rounded muscles of his chest against her shoulder blades. But now that she was in this position, she was having a tough time pulling herself away.

He didn't seem to be in any hurry to yank his arm back, either.

Her daughter's eyes were glued to a pair of playful goats inside the pen in front of them, so maybe it wouldn't hurt for Dahlia to lean against Connor for just a few more seconds.

Ever since she saw him interacting with her family on the Twin Kings, she'd been allowing herself to consider Connor Remington in a different light. Not that his admission about being interested in her was some sort of big revelation. It was no secret that they were both attracted to each other. Although, it did make her pulse spike pleasantly when he'd said the words aloud.

No, the change came when he revealed that he had prior experience with horses. As much as Dahlia hated being wrong about her earlier assessment of him, there was something comforting about the fact that he might actually have a shot at running the Rocking D. And if he was successful, then he might actually stick around. And if he stuck around, perhaps it wouldn't be such a bad thing for Dahlia to get to know him better. For them to explore exactly how deep this mutual attraction of theirs went. For them to get a little closer...

"Mommy," Amelia interrupted her thoughts. "Were you trying to climb into the turkey stall?"

"Huh?" Dahlia blinked several times to clear the confusion. "No, why?"

"Because Connor hadta pull me down, too, when I was getting a closer look at that big sheep with the horns." Her daughter's eyes flicked down to where Dahlia's hand now rested on top of Connor's, which was firmly planted above Dahlia's belt buckle.

When had their fingers gotten intertwined like that?

Connor's thumb lightly stroked another circle over the fabric of her shirt, making the sensitive skin underneath tingle with a delicious heat just before he slowly slid his hand away. "No, your mom was following the rules perfectly. She just tripped on that half-eaten corn dog someone dropped on the ground."

"Oh, no," Amelia gasped. Before Dahlia could stop her, the girl swooped in to grab the discarded heap of deep-fried batter covered in mustard and bits of straw. "Littering is bad. An animal coulda tried to eat that and would've gotten the broken stick stuck in his throat."

"You're right." Connor deftly retrieved a dark disposable green bag from his back pocket. "I always keep these handy for Goatee. Let me take that and we can go find a trash can."

While Dahlia had been rooted to the ground, letting the panic at being caught in a semi-embrace wash over her, Connor once again sprang into action. Not only had he reacted calmly and quickly, he'd wisely led her daughter in the opposite direction of the Radical Reptile display.

By the time Dahlia caught up with them, she was relieved to see him already helping Amelia get a healthy dollop of hand sanitizer from the complimentary dispenser. As Dahlia watched them, a memory popped in her head of her own dad at the Spring Fling years ago. Dahlia and Finn had made a mess of their cotton candy and their hands were sticking to everything they touched. Roper had picked them up in both arms, walked them over to the open door of the men's room and called out, "Females on deck!"

Their dad had held them for what seemed like forever before several men trickled outside, then he took them into the empty restroom and helped both of the girls scrub all the stickiness from their hands and faces.

Dahlia had always assumed that her dad was so good with kids because he'd already had three of them by the time she and Finn came along. But the more she watched Connor's natural and easy interaction with Amelia, she had to wonder how a man with no kids, who'd only known her daughter for almost two months, could act so...well...fatherly toward her.

No. Amelia already had a father. Micah would've happily taken the messy half-eaten corn dog from their child and then helped her wash her hands. But Micah wasn't here, which made Amelia more susceptible to wanting to fill that void. It was one thing for Dahlia to get physically close to Connor. It was another to let her daughter develop an emotional attachment to him.

"Are you ready to go pick out Connor's sheep now, Mommy?"

Nope, Dahlia wanted to shake her head frantically. She wasn't ready to pick out a sheep and she certainly wasn't ready to encourage any sort of bond between him and her daughter, even a seemingly innocent bond over farm animals. But how did Dahlia explain her adult concerns to a small child?

She couldn't.

So Dahlia did what she always did, she distracted. "How about we get some kettle corn instead?"

And Amelia did what *she* always did. "How about we do both?"

"I think I saw a concession stand by the bidder registration table." Connor wiggled his eyebrows at Dahlia and her pulse skipped a beat when he lowered his mouth next to her ear again. "Not only did your daughter just call your bluff, she followed it up with some double or nothing."

The corners of Dahlia's lips couldn't resist smirking upward. "Oh, we'll see whose bluff gets called when she talks you into buying that ram with anger-management issues."

By the time the three of them made their way to the auction stage with a large bag of popcorn, three lemonades and two candy apples, the surrounding wooden bleachers were completely filled with potential buyers and spectators. In fact, it was so crowded that they had to make their way up the stands to the very back row, and even then Amelia had to sit on Connor's lap because there was only enough space for the two adults.

Luckily, she hadn't recognized anyone from Teton Ridge yet. Not that it should matter.

Dahlia's hip was wedged against Connor's and it took an act of supreme concentration to keep the rest of her thigh and her knee from touching his. Especially since there was barely any space on the narrow foot riser below after they set down their cups of icy lemonade. With the way her daughter was leaning forward excitedly, it would only be so long before the adults' entire bodies were pivoted together to keep Amelia's limbs from bumping into the people around them.

"Oooh, I like that one, Connor." Amelia tried to raise the bidding paddle, but Connor deftly switched it to his other hand, and hid it between his upper leg and Dahlia's. She shivered at the feel of his wrist grazing against her jeans.

If he was equally fazed by the contact, he didn't show it. Instead, he casually explained to her squirming daughter, "That's a pig. We're only interested in the sheep, remember?"

Five minutes later, Amelia tried again. "What about a baby pig? Like a really, really small one?"

"The small ones usually grow up to be big ones. Plus, horses and pigs don't always get along. Private Peppercorn already gets annoyed with Goatee's new obsession with his carrot treats. We don't want to have him fighting with a pig, too."

This prompted a discussion about whether or not the sheep would get along and where everyone would sleep in the barn. Her chatter would only stop each time a new animal came on stage, with Amelia avidly watching the bidding until the auctioneer yelled, "Sold!" Then she'd launch a different discussion.

Each time her daughter asked a new question—which had to be every thirty seconds—Amelia's tiny body would shift, which would cause Connor to bump into Dahlia, which would set off another alarm of sensations throughout her body. After a while, it seemed pointless to hold herself so rigid to avoid making contact with the man. Maybe if she relaxed and let the laws of physics run its course, her body would stop having such an intense reaction to his.

After the pigs paraded through, the goats came next and then the alpacas had their turn on the stage. By the time they got to the cows, Dahlia noticed that Amelia's questions were coming with less frequency and her posture was drooping. When the auctioneer finally announced the first lamb, her daughter was sound asleep, a fistful of buttery popcorn still clutched in her tiny hand and her sticky candy apple–smeared face pressed into the curve between Connor's shoulder and neck.

Dahlia's lungs felt like balloons inflating with way too much helium. It was too late to keep emotions out of it. The damage was done. She didn't think there could possibly be any sweeter sight in the world than her daughter happily exhausted and nestled comfortably in Connor Remington's strong arms.

He must've known the exact minute her carefully built walls began to crack because he caught Dahlia's gaze and whispered, "Should I wake her?"

She shook her head. "No, let her sleep. Unless she's too heavy for you."

Connor smiled. "Not at all. Although, it might help my balance to readjust just a little." His biceps, which up until now had been wedged against hers, eased behind her lower back. "There. That's better."

She gave a pointed look to where his hand casually rested on her opposite hip, then suppressed her own smile. "That was a pretty smooth maneuver."

Pressed against his side like this, she could feel his chest rumble as he chuckled lightly. "Thanks. I've been waiting to do that since they brought out the first goat."

"Only since then?" Dahlia asked, unused to hearing the flirtatious tone in her own voice.

"Okay, so maybe since that first time you and Amelia stopped at my ranch with doughnuts." That magical thumb of his traced a circle on her hip and it felt as though the denim fabric separating their skin would catch on fire. "I mean, I thought about it way before that., But I hadn't really hoped I might have a shot at it until that day."

She lifted her chin, bringing their faces closer together. "And is it everything you'd been hoping for?"

"Yes," he said, then swallowed. "And no. Hold that thought."

The couple who'd been sitting beside them had left and since the crowd had lessened as more and more animals were purchased, she watched him carefully ease Amelia's sleeping form along the bench, the kid-sized puffy blue jacket a pillow under her head and the backrest of the bleachers preventing her from rolling off.

When he turned back to Dahlia, she knew what was coming next. Anticipation rippled through her and she tilted her head up right as he lowered his.

"This is what I was really hoping for."

As soon as he kissed her, there was no denying that was the exact thing she'd been waiting for, as well. And oh, man, her expectations were definitely exceeded. Connor's mouth was firm and agile and tasted like sweet lemonade. When his tongue traced along her lower lip, she eagerly opened up to quench a thirst she hadn't known she had.

Her arms wrapped around his neck to keep her from completely falling into him as her body ached to get closer to his. His fingers splayed along her rib cage, holding her in place as his mouth thoroughly explored hers. When she tilted her head to allow him a deeper angle, he tightened his grip on her waist and yanked her against to him.

They were like two love-starved teenagers making out on the bleachers for all the world to see and Dahlia couldn't remember the last time she'd felt so reckless. So alive. So intoxicated. She couldn't be bothered to think that someone from their town might've been there to see them. All she could think about was how right all of this felt.

"Ladies and gentlemen," the auctioneer's voice rang out on the speakers above them. "This is the last animal of the night."

Connor pulled away and blinked several times before realizing the stands around them were empty. "Oh, no. I missed the sheep I'd wanted to bid on."

"Wait. You really were going to buy a sheep?"

"Yeah. Why wouldn't I?"

She resisted the urge to tap her swollen lips, which still felt as though they were on fire. "I thought you were just trying to make Amelia happy."

"Well, I was. But then I kinda talked myself into it along the way."

"So maybe you could go to one of the livestock auctions in Riverton," she suggested. "They have them once a month."

"That won't work. When Amelia wakes up, she'll ask why we didn't get one here. And do you want me to answer honestly and say it was because I couldn't keep my hands or my mouth off her hot mom?"

His tongue was skilled in more ways than one. Her heart was already skipping beats from his kisses. Now it threatened to shut down completely at his smooth words. Nobody had ever called her a *hot mom*, at least not to her face. And they certainly had never been equally as passionate about their commitments to her daughter.

Connor didn't release her hip as he leaned forward and squinted at the stage. "Now which one is left?"

CHAPTER SEVEN

"SO HOW'D YOU end up with this feathered friend?" Dr. Roman asked when she made a house call on Monday to check on Peppercorn after his busy week at the Twin Kings. "I thought you were only setting up for horses out here."

Connor was still kicking himself over that acquisition. He hadn't been in the market for a sheep, let alone a damn turkey. In fact, the only reason he'd gone to the Spring Fling Festival was because Finn King said it would be a great opportunity to network with other ranchers from western Wyoming and eastern Idaho who'd traveled there every year for the event. She'd been right, although he now had a feeling that she'd also had ulterior motives.

Connor had met several other horse breeders at the rodeo exhibit and was about to drive back to the ranch when he caught sight of Amelia and Dahlia getting off the Tilt-a-Whirl. Sure, he'd run into them around the town of Teton Ridge before so running into them there wasn't shocking in and of itself. What had made his own heart tilt and whirl, though, was the realization that seeing them *away* from town had—for the first time in his life—made him feel as if he was finally home. As if he was finally ready to put down even more roots and invest himself into the ranch both physically and emotionally.

Buying a sheep seemed like a good way to further develop his holdings here at the Rocking D while simultaneously making Amelia happy. But unlike his adoption of Goatee, he couldn't totally blame the King-Deacon women for suckering him into this unexpected and very unnecessary acquisition.

He took off his hat and scratched his head before answering the vet. "I picked him up at the livestock auction at the Spring Fling Festival in Fling Rock."

"I love that festival. We take our grandkids every year." The vet jerked a thumb toward the chicken coop, which Connor had spent the rest of the weekend repairing. "And every year we see the same Bourbon Red that never gets a single bid. I think he's getting bigger with age."

Great. Now Connor was the sucker who'd brought home a turkey nobody else wanted. Although it hadn't taken him long to figure out why the auctioneer had been so surprised to see his paddle in the air.

"Not only does the thing poop all over the place, he squawks and pecks at any human or animal that comes within a five-foot radius." Connor held up his bandaged left hand. "He did this when I was trying to let him out of his transportation cage."

Yet, the look on Amelia's face when she found out that Connor had *rescued* one of her favorite animals made the injury and the headache from the bird's nightly serenade of angry gobbles worth it.

And that amazing kiss he'd shared with Dahlia on the bleachers had been worth at least three more turkeys just like this one.

"How's his diet?" the vet asked.

"He eats anything he can get his beak on. Goatee was sniffing around a little too close to the chicken wire yesterday afternoon and now I can't find the little metal name tag that used to hang on his collar."

"Uh-oh. That might explain why he's so cranky."

"No, he was cranky well before he got here."

"Mind if I give him a sedative and try to do a quick examination?" the vet asked, but she was already pulling on a pair of latex gloves.

Connor couldn't help but wonder if there'd be an extra charge for that since this would be the second animal on his ranch she'd be seeing today. He'd already dropped a hundred bucks on the turkey and another three hundred on feed and fencing supplies to repair the coop when it became apparent that Peppercorn would kick out his stall door if he had to share the barn with the hot-tempered turkey on the opposite side of the stables.

Connor said a silent prayer of thanks that Peppercorn had several more live covers booked for this week and he was starting to see a return on his investment. Then he told Dr. Roman, "Knock yourself out. But I've got a load of hay arriving right now so I hope you brought some tranquilizer darts."

"I always come locked and loaded," she replied as she walked to the small mobile clinic trailer she towed behind her SUV.

The delivery truck from the feed store pulled up beside them and when the young driver climbed out, Dr. Roman asked, "No practice today, Keyshawn?"

"Nope. We didn't even make the playoffs this year. So my dad is having me do deliveries after school until baseball starts up next week."

Keyshawn Fredrickson was tall and muscular and, according to his dad Freddie, had recently gotten a full academic scholarship to Howard University. He'd also been one of the teenagers who'd come over with Luis Ochoa, Tomas's son, to help repair the fence. In addition to getting a sturdy enclosure for his pasture, Connor also got to hear about the drama surrounding the Teton Ridge High School basketball coach being fired during the back half of the season.

Connor might've only been in town six weeks, but he already knew all the local gossip. Unless it had to do with the Kings. Nobody had bothered to fill him in on any of that. He picked up a pair of hay hooks to help Keyshawn unload the bales of alfalfa.

"Whoa, is that the mean old turkey from Spring Fling?" The teenager paused with only one hook under the bale wire as he gaped in surprise at the vet entering the chicken coop.

Connor felt a resigned groan vibrate against the back of his throat before admitting, "That's the one. I'm guessing you're familiar with him, too."

"I won my girlfriend a goldfish at the Sink-A-Hoop game and as we're walking through the livestock arena, that crazy dude poked his wrinkly bald head between the slats and ate my girlfriend's goldfish. Tore right through the plastic bag and swallowed the thing whole. Then he almost ripped my thumb off when I tried to wrestle the bag away from him."

Connor again held up his bandaged hand. "Tell me about it."

The squawking started immediately and was followed by intense wing flapping. Connor was about to sprint over to the coop when he saw the flash of a syringe in the vet's hand and then the large bird flopped over in a heap of reddish brown feathers.

"He's a bit heavier than I was expecting," the vet called over to them. "If one of you can help me get him into the trailer, I have an ultrasound machine that might give me a better idea of what's going on."

"Man, Doc Roman is a badass," Keyshawn said after Connor helped her load the turkey onto the stainless-steel table in her tricked-out mobile clinic. "There's no way you could pay me to go into an enclosed space with that thing. Even if it's passed out cold."

"Who's passed out cold?" a little voice said and Goatee ran off the porch with an excited yip.

Connor had been so focused on getting the turkey into the mobile clinic without accidentally waking it that he hadn't heard Dahlia's truck pull into the drive.

"This crazy bird Mr. Remington found at the Spring Fling." Keyshawn answered.

"Oh, you mean Gobster?" Amelia smiled to reveal a new missing tooth. "Connor won him 'cause he was the highest bidder."

"Wait, you actually paid money for that thing?" Keyshawn's head whipped around to Connor, who would've felt suitably embarrassed if he wasn't feeling a rush of excitement at seeing Dahlia walking toward them. "And what kind of name is Gobster, anyway?"

"It's short for Gobble Monster," Amelia said. "I wanted to name him General Gobble 'cause Connor's horse has a soldier name, too. But Connor said he definitely didn't earn *that* rank. Look, we got him a silver ID tag to match Goatee's, but we haven't found a collar small enough for him."

Connor winced. He was *not* looking forward to the moment when Amelia noticed that Goatee's ID tag was now missing. As the girl continued talking to Keyshawn while he unloaded the hay, Connor used the opportunity to talk to Dahlia alone.

"Hey," he said. Because they weren't truly alone.

"Hi. Sorry for dropping in on you again like this, but I still don't have your number. Not that you need to give it to me. I mean, I know we, uh, you know, on Saturday night. But I don't want you thinking that *I'm* thinking that totally changes things between us or that I'm expecting you to give it to me. It's just that if I had it, I could've warned you that Amelia was insisting we stop by on our way to her riding lesson and check on the turkey."

"Dahlia," he replied when she took a short pause from her adorably sweet and nervous rambling. "We kissed on Saturday night."

Her eyes darted to where Keyshawn was telling Amelia about the biggest chicken he'd ever seen. But the blush that stole up her cheeks made her pretty pink lips seem that much more kissable. "Yes. That's what I said."

"No. You said we *uh, you know.* And I just wanted it to be super clear that we kissed and that I enjoyed it and that I would even like to do it again. Right this second, in fact. But I have a feeling you might not think now is the best time, what with the town veterinarian and the feed store owner's teenage son here to see us. So, please take my number and maybe we can find another time to make that happen. Soon."

"Well, I think I found the problem." Dr. Roman came out of the back of her trailer, and Keyshawn took a few steps closer to Connor. "It appears that the turkey has what looks to be a broken piece of wood lodged in its upper intestine. Almost looks like half of a Popsicle stick."

"The missing part of the corn dog!" Amelia shouted. Then her face went pale. "Is Gobster gonna die?"

"We should only be so lucky," Keyshawn mumbled, which Amelia thankfully did not hear. Connor nudged the teen with his elbow, and the young man scrunched his face. "What? You don't celebrate Thanksgiving?"

"I don't think he'll die," Dr. Roman said. "I can give him some medicine to help him pass the stick."

"You mean like poop it out?" Amelia asked rather loudly. Keyshawn laughed and Dahlia pinched the bridge of her nose.

"Exactly," Dr. Roman told the child. "If he can't pass it by himself, then I can do a surgical procedure to retrieve it."

"Will it hurt him?" Amelia asked, her eyes full of alarm.

"Not as much as pooping it out would," Keyshawn answered.

"Then we should do it," Amelia declared.

Dahlia sighed. "Peanut, Gobster is Connor's turkey. He gets to make the decision about what's best for the animal."

Connor wasn't prepared to make this kind of decision. His eyes sought Dahlia's, but her only response was to lift one of her shoulders in doubt. Did he really want to shell out more money for the opportunity to keep a mean turkey around to continue wreaking havoc on his ranch?

"What's the success rate on an operation like this?" Connor asked.

Dr. Roman's lips pressed together in a crooked line, as though she were trying to keep a straight face. Finally, she said, "Well, I don't usually do surgery on a turkey. Why don't I give him some medicine for his digestive tract and see if that takes care of the problem naturally."

"As much as I'd like to hang around and see that," Keyshawn said, his face scrunched into a look of disgust. "I've got one more delivery to make."

The teen drove off, and Amelia followed the vet into the back of her mobile clinic, asking a million questions a minute.

By the time Gobster was returned to the coop—still sleeping, thankfully—and Dahlia was done putting away instruments and sterilizing everything Amelia had touched in the mobile clinic, Dr. Roman seemed more than eager to be on her way.

The dust was still settling on the driveway that led from the Rocking D to the highway when Amelia slipped her tiny palm into Connor's hand and said, "I hope Gobster is all better by Friday."

"Why Friday?" Connor asked, thinking there was no way it could take that long.

"That's the day of the father-daughter dance at my school and I want you to take me."

Dahlia's stomach felt as though someone had dropped a bale of hay on her midsection. And it didn't help that Connor's normally suntanned face had gone slightly pale.

"Amelia," Dahlia chided, her breath rushing out of her chest. "That's probably not something Connor would be comfortable doing."

"Oh. You don't know how to dance?" Amelia blinked at him. "I could teach you."

Connor knelt down to her daughter's eye level, and Dahlia braced herself for Amelia's impending disappointment, no matter how polite the man was when he declined.

"I'm flattered that you invited me," he started before his eyes flicked up to Dahlia's, as though seeking her approval to break her child's heart. All Dahlia could do was nod. After all, she'd brought Amelia out here unannounced, putting them both in this uncomfortable situation. Connor continued, "Wouldn't you rather your dad take you to the dance?"

"Daddy is working and can't come. Besides, Miss Walker said it doesn't have to be a dad that comes with us. We can bring any grown-up we want and I wanna bring you."

This wasn't the first time Micah couldn't be here for an important event and Dahlia and Amelia were no strangers to making the best of it. "Peanut, why don't you ask Uncle Marcus or Uncle Rider to go with you?"

"'Cause Uncle Marcus has been grumpy since Grandpa's funeral. Jack and Jordan said it's 'cause he's secretly in love with Miss Violet. And last time Uncle Rider came to my school, Peyton said he looked like Santa Claus and then all the kids ran over to him and he didn't even get to hear the holiday song our class worked so hard on."

Connor lifted an eyebrow in Dahlia's direction and she nodded. "It's true. Rider showed up for the Winter Wonderland performance last December wearing a red flannel shirt and the kindergarteners mobbed him. It was quite the scene."

"But Connor is the same years old as the other dads at my school." Amelia pointed to the Def Leppard T-shirt. "And he wears the same shirts like *my* daddy."

Dahlia would be lying if she hadn't also noted the similar tastes in classic rock fashion between the rancher and her ex-husband. But none of the other fathers at Teton Ridge Elementary—including Micah Deacon—were as good-looking as Connor.

"Come back, Goatee." Amelia took off running toward the

dog who'd mustered up the courage to cautiously approach the chicken coop. "Gobster can't play right now. He's sleeping so he can go poop before Connor takes me to the father-daughter dance."

"Sounds like she isn't going to take no for an answer." Connor stood and ran his hand through his close-cut auburn hair.

"She usually doesn't. But don't worry. I'll talk to her tonight and find someone else to go with her."

"Like your little brother, MJ?" Connor asked.

Dahlia tipped back her head to stare at the clouds forming in the sky, as though an answer would fall down and land on her like a raindrop. "No, not him. You know how MJ got arrested and charged with drunk and disorderly? He happened to be with Kendra Broman at the time of his arrest, and her father, Deputy Broman, will most likely be at the dance with his younger girls. He still hasn't forgiven MJ for resisting arrest. I'd ask Mike Truong to take her, but he'll be going with his daughter." Now Dahlia was just thinking out loud. "Maybe one of the Secret Service agents still assigned at the ranch could take her."

"Or perhaps the friendly and personable Mr. Burnworth from the bakery," Connor suggested sarcastically—or at least she hoped he was being sarcastic—before shoving his hands in his pockets. "Anyone but me, huh?"

Great, now she'd insulted him again. "I'm trying to get you off the hook here, Connor. You've already done enough for Amelia with the stray dog and then the turkey. You don't need to take this on, as well."

"What if I want to go?"

Her heart caught in her throat, but then her brain shoved it back down as her senses went on high alert. *What's in it for you?* she almost asked. Instead, she narrowed her eyes. "Why would you offer?"

"Because I grew up knowing what it was like to be the only Cub Scout without an old man at the pinewood derby, or the third wheel with some other father-son team on the annual jamboree camping trip."

The red flag warnings inside her head immediately turned to white in surrender. A second ago, she'd been willing to send Amelia to the dance with a Secret Service agent, just so her daughter wouldn't feel left out. But that would only make them all stand out. Maybe going with Connor wasn't such a bad idea.

Amelia adored him and talked about him so much that people in town were already making assumptions about them. Hell, the guy had bought a stupid turkey at a livestock auction just to make her daughter happy. Then he'd paid to have the veterinarian come out to his ranch to examine the thing instead of ringing its neck, plucking it and turning it into his Sunday supper.

And Dr. Roman wasn't cheap. Dahlia had certainly paid more than her fair share of vet bills with all of Amelia's strays. So maybe Connor really was doing this out of the goodness of his heart.

Still. She had to give him one more opportunity to back out gracefully. "I should warn you that there will be lots of over-sweetened punch and pink cupcakes and Taylor Swift songs at this event."

"Doesn't sound much different from my usual Friday night." Connor smiled. "What time should I pick her up?"

Maybe there really was something about Remingtons knowing when they'd found "the one." Or the ones plural where the Deacon-King women were concerned. Because Connor was getting to a point where he couldn't explain this persisting connection he felt with both of them.

"How did you get yourself into this mess?" he asked his reflection in the dusty mirror above Aunt Connie's antique dresser as he knotted, undid, and then re-knotted the only non-military issued tie he owned. One minute, he'd been warning himself not to get too attached to Dahlia, and the next minute he'd practically jumped at the chance to take Amelia to the father-daughter dance.

A couple of hours later, Connor realized he wasn't the only man in town who was questioning how he'd landed himself in this situation.

"Got roped into playing rent-a-dad, I see," Deputy Broman said, raising his voice over the sound of a dance floor full of giggles and the latest Katy Perry song blasting out of the hired DJ's speakers.

Connor had met the man at Biscuit Betty's the first week he'd been in town. The deputy had been polite enough at the time, expressing his condolences about the loss of Aunt Connie and asking how Connor was settling in at the Rocking D. Then, after noticing Connor's Air Jordans, he'd made a not-so-subtle suggestion to stop by the new rec center in town to play a few games of pickup basketball.

But now the man's words were more insulting than challenging.

"Looks like your eye has healed up nicely," Connor replied, purposely referencing the shiner young MJ had landed when he'd resisted arrest.

"Humph. Kid's lucky his big brother is my boss. Or else he would've had more than a dislocated shoulder after getting my daughter drunk like that. The whole damn family is nuts if you ask me."

Connor hadn't asked him. But that didn't stop him from standing there silently and gathering intel. The dance had reached the point in the evening when most of the men were gathering on the sidelines, looking at their watches and asking their buddies the score of the UW game. Most of the girls were still swirling around the gym floor in big groups with their friends, their sugar highs peaking from all the buttercream frosting and fruit punch.

"Here, Connor, can you hold these for me?" Amelia shoved her glitter-encrusted silver shoes at him before running barefoot back to the center of the dance floor where a pile of pink and white balloons were being used as an impromptu trampoline. He added the shoes to the purple cardigan, white-sequined headband and rainbow unicorn purse already shoved under his left arm.

"She's a cute kid," the deputy continued. "Looks just like her dad, too. My cousin went to high school with Micah and played some jam sessions with him back in the day. I mean, I get that he has this big career and stuff, but it's just weird, you know."

Connor hated that his interest was piqued. But that didn't stop him from asking, "What's weird?"

"That he would've just taken off for Nashville and left his wife and kid here."

Wife? Connor swallowed the bitterness in the back of his throat. "I thought he and Dahlia were divorced?"

"Only because the rest of the Kings pushed so hard for it. If it had been me, I would've stayed here and fought for my kid. I mean, not to the level of Jay Grover over there." Broman jerked his chin at Amelia's friend Peyton's dad, who'd spent half the evening arguing on the phone with his divorce attorney and the other half complaining about his bitter custody case with any unsuspecting dad who walked by the punch bowl. "But I certainly wouldn't be riding around the country in a tour bus while some guy off the street waltzes in and takes over my parental role."

"I'm not taking over any role." Connor's shoulders jerked back instinctively, but he maintained his grip on his colorful collection of discarded accessories. "Amelia still has a father. He just isn't here right now."

"Don't get so defensive." Broman held up his palms. "You see a hot single mom and a kid who's so desperate for attention she talks to every stray animal who comes along. I don't blame you for wanting to step up and do the right thing. Plenty of guys would love to be in your shoes right now. Or at least they think they would until they find out what they're getting into."

Connor was seriously starting to get annoyed with people in this town making assumptions about him. His voice was tense when he asked, "Is this the part of the conversation where you tell me what I'm getting into?"

"Look, man," the deputy said right as the last song of the night ended. "I'm just trying to help."

"Help what?" Amelia asked from just a few feet away. The balloon in her hands was sagging almost as much as her eyelids, the sugar rush finally wearing off.

"Carry you to the truck," Connor said before using his free arm to scoop her up onto his hip. She immediately let her cheek fall on his shoulder.

"You don't need any help carrying me, Connor." Amelia yawned. "You're stronger than Gray Goose. And he's the biggest pony at the Twin Kings."

They were halfway across the parking lot when Deputy Broman and three of his daughters pulled up beside them in the Ridgecrest County patrol unit.

"Hey, kid," Broman called out his window, causing Amelia to sleepily lift her head. "Next time you talk to your *dad*, tell him I said hi."

Connor's fists clenched at the man's purposeful tone when he'd said the word *dad*. He had to practically shake out his knuckles before he started acting like angry Jay Grover back inside the gymnasium.

Instead of agreeing to pass along the message, Amelia just nuzzled against Connor's shoulder and mumbled, "I don't like that policeman. I wish Uncle MJ was allowed to punch him again."

Connor's chest shook from the laughter he tried to hold in. Apparently, Amelia wasn't that starved for attention, because she certainly recognized an antagonistic jerk when she saw one. As his smile faded, though, he wondered if she also recognized an envious jerk when she saw one, too. Not that Connor was actually jealous of Micah—a man he'd never even met.

But something about Broman's words had stirred to life an overwhelming sense of protectiveness toward the child. Connor had never experienced a paternal instinct like he had back inside that dance.

He wanted to be the one to protect Amelia, and he wanted everyone else in town to know it.

CHAPTER EIGHT

"LOOKS LIKE THE night was a success," Dahlia said as Connor carried a sleeping Amelia through her front door.

"I hope so," he whispered, following her down the hall to the bedrooms. "We all made it out in one piece, although the last time I saw my tie it was being used as the pole for the limbo contest."

Her heart melted at the tender way he carefully tucked her daughter into the twin-sized bed. When he returned from his second trip from his truck downstairs, everything inside her turned into a complete puddle of sappy mush.

"It's so loud downstairs at the saloon right now. How do you guys get any sleep on weekends?" Connor asked as he crossed the threshold. Amelia's zebra-print booster seat was secured in one of his arms while the strap of the rainbow unicorn purse was falling off the opposite muscular shoulder. He dropped the sparkly shoes, hair bow and purple cardigan in a pile on the entry table and Dahlia thought her knees were going drop, as well.

"Like this." She closed the thick front door behind him. "I paid a fortune to soundproof the floor and walls. Can I offer you a drink? I have beer and wine or even fruit punch if you haven't gotten enough of that tonight."

"I would love a beer," he said, looking much more rumpled than when he'd arrived on their doorstep a few hours ago. His hair was barely mussed, but the sleeves on his now-wrinkled white dress shirt were rolled up and his gray slacks sported a pink frosting stain down the front. "In fact, I was surprised that the booster club at the school wasn't selling adult beverages at the dance. They could've raised so much money."

She retrieved two bottles of Snake River Pale Ale from her kitchen fridge before meeting him in the living room. "Plenty of other dads have suggested the same thing."

His eyes flashed with something—anger, frustration, annoyance...she wasn't sure—before he quickly blinked the emotion back and schooled his features. He took the beer from her hand and slumped onto her sofa. "Then I'll leave it to the *other dads* to bring it up to the booster club."

Dahlia could've sat in one of the custom upholstered chairs opposite him, but after making out with the guy on some bleachers and sending her daughter to a school dance with him, purposely distancing herself from him would've seemed entirely too formal at this point. She chose the corner of the sofa beside him and asked, "Why did you say it like that?"

"Because I'm just a rent-a-dad, as someone pointed out tonight. So I don't really get a vote in the matter."

The muscles recoiled in Dahlia's shoulders. "Who would say something like that? Did Amelia hear them?"

"No. I would've probably given him another black eye if he'd said it in front of her." Connor tilted the beer to his mouth, and even though his frame was casually lounging against the decorative throw pillows, his knuckles were white from clenching the bottle so hard. "Maybe I still will if I ever play against him on the basketball court and he has his uniform off."

Realization crossed her expression, and Dahlia pulled her

legs onto the sofa and tucked her bare feet under her. "Deputy Broman is such an ass."

"But he wasn't wrong." Connor's head fell to the side as he turned his face to her. "I'm not a dad or even a relative. Which is fine. I'm not looking to replace anyone. But something about the way he said it just didn't sit well, you know? Like he was trying to put me in my place."

"Broman has had a chip on his shoulder ever since Marcus beat him in the election for sheriff. How does he know what your place is?"

"What *is* my place, Dahlia?" Connor shifted his torso, extending his arm to drape along the back cushions of the couch as he studied her.

She wasn't going to pretend like she didn't know exactly what he was asking. She'd spent the entire week since their kiss at the Spring Fling asking herself the same question. "I haven't figured that out yet. What do you want it to be?"

"I like spending time with you and Amelia. In fact, I'd like to spend even more time with you. But if things don't work out, it could be complicated."

"If things *do* work out, it could be just as complicated." Dahlia bit her lower lip, surprised she was open to the possibility in the first place. She'd only dated once since her divorce and that had been a disaster.

"How complicated?" he asked, dropping his hand so that the tips of his fingers were resting on her shoulder. A shiver radiated through her at his slight touch.

"I'm not just a single mom, Connor, all on my own. Amelia and I might be a package deal, but my ex-husband is still a big part of our lives, and he always will be. Then there's my family. You might think that going to dinner at the ranch every once in a while is a fun spot of entertainment, but they actually can be a lot to handle."

He leaned forward to set his empty bottle of beer on the coffee table. "It's true that I don't need any extra complications right now."

Instead of getting up and leaving, though, he slid his body closer to hers. Dahlia's breath suspended while her pulse picked up speed.

"But you've seen my ranch. I don't know how to back down from a challenge. When I'm hot on the trail of something…" his voice was low and direct and sent a thrill all the way to her toes "…the twists and turns and roadblocks along the path aren't a deterrent for me. Only an enhancement on the way to my goal."

His lips lowered to hers, his mouth capturing Dahlia's breathy exhale.

Connor had only intended to kiss Dahlia briefly, just to confirm that after everything that had happened tonight with Deputy Broman, their attraction was still strong enough to steer them both down this trail together.

But this kiss was even hotter and more intense than the previous one. He'd barely begun exploring Dahlia's mouth when she shifted her back against the arm of the sofa, sinking lower into a reclined position as her lips slanted over his, her tongue inviting him to delve deeper. Her hands slid across his shoulders until they were firmly planted on his upper back, encouraging him to follow her lead and lower himself until he was balanced on his elbows over her.

She brought one knee up alongside his waist, moaning deeply as his hips settled between her legs. His arousal pressed against the confines of his zipper as she arched against him and groaned.

Finding the hem of her shirt, Connor eased his hand underneath, the heat of her silky smooth skin skimming his palm as he maneuvered the snug fabric higher until he could cup her breast. Dahlia's moans turned into little pants as he used his thumb to trace circles around her tightened nipple.

When Connor had kissed Dahlia at the livestock auction, he'd been limited by the narrow bleachers and the public venue. Now, though, fully stretched out on her living room sofa, there was nothing stopping them from taking things to the next level. His body was already thrumming with anticipation.

Except, just like last time, Amelia was still asleep nearby. The realization made him lift his head and pull back slightly. Dahlia's lips were swollen and her lashes slowly fluttered open. "What's wrong?"

"Amelia could wake up at any moment and come in here and see us."

Dahlia's face lost some of its rosy glow. "If we go to my room, you could sneak out before she gets up in the morning."

"You have no idea how much I want to carry you to your bed right now." He groaned as he dragged himself away from her and plopped onto his side of the sofa. "But if we sleep together, I don't want there to be any sneaking around."

"That's fair," she replied, pulling her top down, which only emphasized the erect state of her nipples. His own chest swelled with pride that he'd been the cause of her arousal. Then it quickly grew hollow when he realized she wasn't going to insist that they didn't have to sneak around. Instead, she asked, "So we just go back to running into each other around town and pretending none of this happened?"

"Only until you realize that you want something more." His hand shot through his hair, trying to smooth it into place after the way she'd run her fingers over it.

"You seem pretty confident that I'm going to come to that realization." Her eyes traveled down the length of him, and Connor stood still, holding back a smile as she boldly assessed him. She would've had him questioning himself if her pink lips weren't so puffy and her pupils weren't still dilated.

"A man can hope, can't he?" He bent down to give her a quick parting kiss. He couldn't risk letting his mouth linger and still walk out of her apartment with full control of his libido.

If he was going to sleep with Dahlia, he needed her to be absolutely sure. Because once Amelia found out about them, there'd be no going back.

Dahlia stayed awake long after Connor left on Friday night, wondering if she should've convinced him to stay the night. In the end, though, he'd done the honorable thing by leaving. Plus, she'd never been very good at sneaking around. That had been Finn's specialty growing up. Dahlia had always been afraid of getting caught.

She'd barely fallen asleep before dawn when the theme song from *Top Gun* jarred her awake. She recognized the ringtone and reached for her smartphone.

Before she could say hello, her brother Duke asked, "Permission to buzz the flight tower?"

The phrase from their favorite movie was their inside joke and they used it instead of saying, "Brace yourself for this." Dahlia groaned and pulled the down comforter over her head. Last time Duke had asked to buzz the flight tower, it was to tell her that Uncle Rider had invited Aunt Freckles to the Twin Kings for their dad's funeral.

It had only been a couple of months since then, and the King family had been even more turned upside down since Tessa had been stranded at the ranch with that sexy Secret Service agent. Her sister had been so secretive about things before she'd left, Dahlia still had no idea if she'd decided to pursue anything with the guy. Then there was MJ's arrest and Marcus dealing with his ex-girlfriend staying in town to defend their baby brother. Dahlia didn't think she could handle any more King family drama. She pushed her hair out of her sleepy eyes before replying, "Negative, Ghostrider. The pattern is full."

Duke chuckled. "Well, I hope you have a huge cup of coffee because the controls are out of my hands on this one."

"Who messed up this time? Finn? Mom? Certainly not you."

"Of course not me," Duke snorted. "I'm the golden child, remember?"

"You never let us forget." Although, last time Duke had left town, something had been going on between him and his husband, Tom. Even Tessa, who'd been dealing with her own relationship issues, had commented on Tom leaving the Twin Kings a week before Duke had. But their brother was the family mediator and was always too busy working through everyone else's problems to bring any attention to his own. "So what's the latest gossip?"

"I got an email from Kenneth P. Burnworth about an hour ago."

"Mr. Burnworth?" Dahlia shot up in bed. "Since when does my annoying and grouchy neighbor from the bakery email you?"

"Since Tom and I hired him to do our wedding cake a few years back. Anyway, seeing as how I'm his favorite King at the moment, he thought I should know that Jay Grover was in the bakery this morning telling everyone that some hotshot new rancher out at the Rocking D took Amelia to the father-daughter dance last night."

"Well, he did." It wasn't like Dahlia expected it to be kept a secret. Nothing traveled faster than the news posted to the Teton Ridge Elementary Booster Club social media page. "And his name's Connor, by the way."

"Yeah, Uncle Rider told me about him last month. What's his deal?"

"Connor inherited the Rocking D from his great-aunt Connie. He's a horse breeder and Rider asked him to bring his stallion out to Twin Kings."

"I meant what's his deal as far as it relates to my niece? And to you, I guess. But especially to my niece."

"It's so nice to be loved, big brother." Dahlia rolled her eyes. "Anyway, you know about the white stray dog and how we met, right?"

"Yeah, that all happened before I had to return to my ship. I remember being at Big Millie's that night with Tessa and her Secret Service agent when you told everyone you weren't interested in the guy."

Dahlia collapsed on the fluffy pillows. "Well, he's starting to grow on me."

"You know who he's not growing on?" Duke asked, but didn't wait for a response. "Mr. Burnworth. Your neighbor doesn't think it's natural for a grown man to be bringing a dog all around town with him. He thinks Connor is using the mutt to win favor with Amelia, which will in turn win favor with you, which will in turn get him one step closer to your trust fund and the deed to Big Millie's. Mr. Burnworth doesn't like having you as a neighbor, but…how did he phrase it… He'd rather trust the devil he knows than the one he doesn't."

That sounded like something her neighbor would've said. Despite their businesses running on completely different schedules, the older man's chief concern was that she'd expand the saloon into something bigger and drive away his customers. "So what did you reply to Mr. Burnworth?"

"I told him that I'd like to order five dozen of his famous chocolate chip muffins to be shipped to my squadron. I'm not going to argue with the best baker in Wyoming."

"You don't argue with anyone, Duke."

Her brother's pause was longer than she expected—even with him using the spotty reception onboard the aircraft carrier. Finally, he sighed before saying, "Depends on who you ask."

"Talk to me, Goose," Dahlia said, using another line from their favorite movie. "Is everything okay with you and Tom?"

Duke cleared his throat. "Yeah, we've just had some challenges with my latest deployment. It's what we signed up for, though, right? Look, I've got to meet my squadron in the ready room for a briefing. I just wanted to give you the heads-up that people are talking. Give Amelia a kiss from her favorite uncle."

The call disconnected, and Dahlia burrowed under her covers for a few more minutes before hearing the unmistakable clanging of pots and pans tumbling out of the kitchen cupboard.

"I'm okay," Amelia called down the hallway, but Dahlia was already out of bed.

"I hope you're not using the stove without permission," she said to her daughter as she trudged barefoot into the kitchen on the cold hardwood floors.

"No, Mommy. I'm just getting everything ready to make you and Connor pancakes."

Dahlia had to do a double take around the living room and entryway to make sure she hadn't missed something. Namely, an early-morning visit from an unexpected rancher. "Peanut, Connor's not here."

Amelia's lower lip curled downward. "But I thought he was gonna sleep over."

"Why would you think that?"

"Because Peyton's mom has a boyfriend and sometimes he spends the night at their house. Peyton's dad got real mad at her mom's boyfriend at the bake sale and dumped a tray of fudgy bars right over his head. But I don't think my daddy would dump fudgy bars on Connor's head."

"No, I don't think he would, either," Dahlia agreed, hoping she wasn't lying. But how was she supposed to know what would happen if Micah and Connor ever met? How they would react to each other. She'd like to think they'd get along, but she'd owned a bar long enough to see what happened to men when they got competitive or when their heated emotions got the best of them.

It was one of those unknown complications she'd mentioned to Connor last night. If they took their relationship to the next level and then things didn't work out, how would Amelia react?

It was why Dahlia hadn't seriously dated anyone since her divorce. Sure, there was Seth, the drummer from Tectonic Shift who'd tried to *comfort her* after she and Micah first split. But Amelia had still been a baby and Dahlia had soon realized what

Seth's real intentions were. In hindsight, the experience had been a wake-up call for her. It had also cemented in the fact that Micah, despite their amicable divorce, would always put Dahlia and Amelia first. Even over his own band. Which made it that much easier for Dahlia to get along with her ex-husband and foster that bond between him and his child.

But this was different. Amelia was older and Connor's intentions—judging by his reoccurring thoughtfulness for her daughter, as well as his restraint last night—might actually be honorable. If things didn't work out with Connor, though, she wouldn't have the same compelling reason keep him in Amelia's life. Her daughter didn't necessarily need another father figure.

Dahlia bit her lower lip. Would it be worth the risk? Only time would tell.

Damn.

Sometimes being a grown-up sucked.

CHAPTER NINE

"WITH TESSA AND DUKE both gone now," Freckles told Dahlia that Saturday evening, "having the kids all spend the night here will help distract your mom from worrying about MJ's upcoming court case."

Normally, Dahlia loved the fact that Amelia got along so well with her cousins and that her family's ranch was close enough that someone was always willing to keep Amelia overnight when Dahlia needed a little time to herself. But after that make-out session with Connor last night, and then her talk with Duke this morning, she didn't quite trust herself to be alone long enough to think.

"What does Mom have planned for them?" Dahlia asked, thinking about the last cousin sleepover when Sherilee King, who was constantly relapsing in her battle to be a vegan, tried to teach the kids how to make butterless carob chip kale cookies. After that failure, MJ ended up sneaking the kids into the bunkhouse's deep freezer where Gan Gan kept her secret stash of *emotional support* ice cream for an all-you-can-eat sundae party. Amelia had called home in the middle of the night with a bellyache.

"A tofu burger bar, but don't worry. I already have some ground sirloin patties pre-grilled and sitting in the oven warmer and that new cartoon movie cued up on Netflix. You know the one where the animals all sing 'Jolene' and '9 to 5'?" Aunt Freckles pointed to the extra-small T-shirt barely covering her extra-large bosom. It was lime green with the words I Beg Your Parton bedazzled above a picture of the famous country singer. "Can't ever go wrong with a little bit of Dolly."

"Maybe I should stick around?" Dahlia suggested, already envisioning the future conversation where she'd have to explain to her daughter why a chorus line of dancing giraffes would be singing the words *please don't take my man*.

"No way," Finn said as she entered the kitchen, the mud still on her boots from where she'd been working in the outer corrals. "No kids want their parents ruining the fun of a sleepover. Could you imagine if Mom would've shown up at Kelly Gladstone's house when she had her slumber party in tenth grade?"

"She *did* show up, Finn." Dahlia threw a piece of popcorn at her twin. "But you and Kelly had snuck out to watch Micah and Woody playing with their garage band at Big Millie's. I had to cover for you and say you were in the bathroom because you ate too much cheese on your pizza."

"Is that what got Mom started on her lactose-free kick?" Finn tilted her head. "I was wondering why she always watches me like a hawk whenever Mr. Truong gets the Pepperoni Stampede to cater lunch for the ranch hands. You've always been the worst at covering for people, Dia."

Dahlia immediately flashed to Connor's words last night about not being willing to sneak around. He was right. Even if it wasn't a small town and she wasn't from one of the higher profile families, she would no doubt get caught.

"You should bring back live bands now that you own Big Millie's," Finn suggested, snapping Dahlia back to the present moment. "In fact, I was going to meet Violet in town to have a drink tonight. Join us and we can figure out where to set up a stage."

"That wouldn't exactly be relaxing for me since the only place to have a drink in town is Big Millie's and it's supposed to be my night off." As a business owner who lived above her place of livelihood, it had been too tempting in those early months when she was just getting started to not spend every waking moment at the bar being a helicopter boss. She'd had to make a conscious decision that if she and her daughter were going to live upstairs, Dahlia would designate two days a week to completely distance herself from her work. Originally, that had been on Sundays and Mondays, when there was the least amount of business. But when Amelia had started school and Dahlia'd hired two trustworthy college students as part-time bartenders, it worked out better for everyone's schedule for her to take the weekends off.

Freckles wiggled her penciled-in eyebrows. "Maybe you should see if Connor Remington wants to take you out on a date tonight."

"Yeah, I heard he went with Amelia to the father-daughter dance," Finn replied, making Dahlia wish she could be anywhere else but her family's kitchen right now. See, there was no point in her and Connor trying to sneak around. Not when everyone was already trying to push the narrative of them being a couple. Oh, sure, right now, she could still pass him off as a family friend. But it wouldn't be long before someone said something in front of Amelia.

"Yes." Dahlia straightened her shoulders defensively. As soon as she exhibited any sign of doubt or remorse, her family would take that as an open invitation to pounce. Hell, they'd jump in with their opinions no matter how she responded. But it was always safest to hold her ground. "Amelia invited him and you know how insistent she can be."

"I also know how cautious her mother can be." Finn tapped her chin. "How did Micah feel about all of this?"

"Of course, he'd rather have been here himself, but he's used to his daughter having to attend things with her uncles."

"Yeah, but Connor Remington isn't exactly her uncle. Has he spent the night yet?"

Dahlia blushed, not from embarrassment but from guilt. Because the man almost *had* stayed over last night. She kept her voice resolved, though, when she answered, "Of course not."

"Why not?" Finn asked. "I saw the way you two were checking each other out when he was here with his stallion a couple of weeks ago and stayed for dinner. Couldn't tell the difference between you and the stall of pent-up broodmares panting after Private Peppercorn."

Dahlia's eyes threatened to pop out of her head and she had to snap her mouth closed before she could respond to her sister. "That's a real flattering comparison."

"It's also an accurate one. Come on, Dia. There's no shame in being attracted to a guy or even acting on that attraction. You're a single mom, not a nun."

"I can second that," Freckles said as she peeled the potatoes for her fresh-cut fries. "I may not be married to your uncle, but that doesn't stop me from slipping into his bed every few nights. It ain't a crime for a woman to enjoy a good roll—"

"Eww, Aunt Freckles!" Finn interrupted just in time. "We really need you to stop giving us those kinds of visuals."

"Finally, something I can agree with my youngest daughter on," Sherliee King said as she breezed into the kitchen in her expensive yoga clothes, not a drop of sweat threatening her professionally applied makeup. "Just because you're traumatizing our bodies with all that unhealthy cooking of yours, Freckles, doesn't mean you have to traumatize our minds, as well."

"Your mind could do with a little more dirtying if you ask me, Sherilee." Freckles pointed her potato peeler at their mother. "Don't forget, you and Roper stayed in the original cabin with us that first year before the big house was built. Your bedroom was right above mine and Rider's and when that headboard would get going, it sounded like a team of Clydesdales were storming through the roof."

Finn made a gagging sound, but Dahlia turned to her mom in shock.

Sherilee was the epitome of grace and class and everything one would expect from a famous politician's wife. Plus, Roper had always been surrounded by aides and friends wanting favors. Dahlia knew her parents had loved each other, but they never seemed to have much time together unless it was a formal event when there were walls of news cameras capturing their every move. "Really? You and Dad barely used to hold hands in front of us when we were kids."

"That's because they couldn't just stop with the hands," Freckles chuckled. "Why do you think your dad's campaign bus was nicknamed Ol' Faithful?"

"Because we lived near Yellowstone?" Dahlia asked and Finn covered her ears as though she already knew the answer was going to be something they wouldn't want to hear.

"Yes." Sherilee nodded earnestly at the same time Freckles shouted, "No! It was because the tiny bedroom in the back of the bus would spring to life at the same time every day. Just like clockwork."

Dahlia's jaw dropped in amazement. And slight aversion at the sullying of her childhood innocence.

"Your father was the love of my life." Sherilee held up her chin. "And what happened in our own private bedroom—"

"Or in the back of the campaign bus," Finn interjected.

"—was nobody's business but ours," their mother finished, narrowing one eye in her signature stern expression as she addressed all of them.

"See, Dia." Finn nudged her. "Even Mom agrees. What you and Connor Remington do out at his ranch is nobody's business but your own."

"Whoa." Sherilee held up a slim manicured hand displaying the fat diamond ring she never took off. "Who said anything about Dahlia and Connor Remington?"

"The whole town, Sherilee." Freckles rolled her eyes. "You've been so focused on MJ's arrest and Tessa getting tangled up with that agent, you haven't been paying attention to the latest romance brewing over at Big Millie's."

"I knew that saloon was gonna be the death of me." Sherilee opened the door of the hulking stainless-steel refrigerator. "Freckles, what have you got to eat in here?"

Uh-oh. Sherilee King was truly stressed if she was looking for her sister-in-law's calorie-filled cooking.

Dahlia braced her hand on the marble counter. "Actually, you guys, Connor has only been to the bar once—and we weren't even open at the time. So you can't blame my business. If anything, you can blame Amelia. She's the one who keeps me running into him."

"Amelia likes him that much?" Sherilee said around a mouthful of bacon Freckles had already precooked and hidden under a plate of foil for the burger bar. "Why didn't you say so? She's usually a pretty good judge of character, you know."

"She's five, Mom," Dahlia said, thinking this was another aftershock of the earlier confusion that had rattled her world. "She collects stray animals like other kids her age collect Pokémon cards."

"Yeah, but she has a second sense about these things. Your dad was the same way. He could read people."

"Can we go look at the ponies?" Amelia ran into the kitchen just then. Jack and Jordan, her two older cousins, followed behind her.

"Yes," Finn said to her niece. "But give your mom a kiss goodbye. She has to go see a man about a horse."

"Like a real horse?" Amelia asked with hopeful eyes.

"No, Finn is using one of her funny expressions again. Now,

be good for Aunt Freckles and Gan Gan. I'll see you in the morning."

As Dahlia drove down the Twin Kings driveway leading to the highway, she couldn't stop thinking about Connor or the fact that *both* her mom and Finn seemed to be fine with the relationship. It wasn't that she needed her family's permission, or even their approval, to get involved with a man. In fact, the King women were very seldom in agreement on anything, and she couldn't help but think this was some elaborate plan of using reverse psychology to steer her in a different direction.

It wouldn't be the first time.

As she approached the turnoff for the Rocking D, a spike of rebelliousness caused her to jerk the steering wheel to the left. Like everyone else in her family, Dahlia had nothing to be ashamed of. She was tired of fighting this attraction between her and Connor. They needed to address it and deal with it once and for all.

She would simply stop by his ranch and explain that their relationship couldn't really go anywhere. Except, when she pulled into his driveway, she saw him sitting tall in his saddle as he rode Peppercorn along the fence line. He gave her a wave and then kicked his legs in the stirrups and set his horse on a furious pace, as though he was racing her back to the stables.

Dahlia was so impressed with his riding ability she pushed her foot down harder on the accelerator of her truck to match his pace so she could keep him in her sight. In fact, even after she parked, Dahlia was struck with a consuming need to continue watching Connor work with his horse that she told him, "Go ahead and finish up with him. I can hang out here with Goatee."

Connor removed Peppercorn's saddle and checked the horse's legs and hooves for injuries as the stallion drank from the water trough. As anxious as Dahlia was to talk with the man, she appreciated the fact that he took his time caring for his horse.

Dahlia sat beside Goatee on the porch steps, who was also breathing heavily as they both studied Connor. Of course, the dog had a good excuse for his panting. He'd just run like crazy to keep up with his owner.

Gobster, on the other hand, seemed to be the only living species on the ranch who wasn't staring adoringly at the man. In fact, the turkey ignored all of them as he roosted in his tree, poking his beak into a branch as he searched for bug snacks.

"I need to be more like that feathery one over there," she said absently to the dog as she scratched the wiry white hair between its ears. "He gets what he wants and then does his own thing. What do you think, Goatee? If I sleep with Connor once and for all, I should be able to get him out of my system, right?"

Instead of talking her out of the idea, the animal's response was to lower its furry chin onto its paws. But it didn't matter what Dahlia told the dog or told herself after Connor walked the horse into the stables and then emerged a few minutes later. His hat was gone and he was bare from the waist up, shooting a spiral of heat directly to her core. She would've gulped but her mouth had immediately gone dry.

His jeans hung low along his hips and his wet hair was dripping water onto the muscular ridges of his shoulders and chest. "Hope you don't mind, but I needed to wash some of the dust off me and I just got that old sink in the stables working."

Yep. Dahlia was totally going to sleep with him. She'd just have to deal with the what-ifs later.

Connor had braved colder water than what came out of the porcelain chipped utility sink inside the stables. But he'd needed some cooling down if he was going to have a civilized conversation with Dahlia, especially after the way she'd been studying him from the porch steps for the past ten minutes.

The woman had the ability to observe everything, without letting on that she was even paying attention. Like she was multitasking in her brain and filing everything away for later. She was usually very casual in her assessments, but she rarely missed anything. So when she directed the full scope of her attention on him, it was piercing.

His plan had been to wash up out here and then go inside the house to grab a clean shirt. Yet when she rose from the steps, her bottom lip clenched between her straight white teeth, Connor was pretty sure he felt the remaining droplets of water on his skin evaporate from the heat of her stare.

He opened his mouth to ask if she wanted to go inside, but before he could get the words out her lips were on his. Unlike their past two kisses, which were more leisurely and exploratory, this coupling of their mouths was frantic, intense. He backed her up the stairs and her arms clung to his neck as he felt around behind her for the front door.

Connor had won medals and commendations for his situational awareness, but he couldn't say how they'd gotten from the entryway to the bedroom. One minute he was unbuttoning her shirt and the next she was arching on the bed below him, her tight budded nipple in his mouth. He needed to slow down, to savor every second of having Dahlia in his arms, but all he could hear were her breathy moans encouraging him to go faster.

At least it *was* the only thing he could hear until the excited bark came from the furry bundle of energy who'd just jumped onto the bed with them.

"Sorry," Connor sighed.

Dahlia chuckled, the sound raspy. "He thinks its playtime."

"Not for you, though, boy," he told Goatee before scooping the dog off the quilt. "Let me take him to the other room. I'll be right back."

He hoped Dahlia didn't change her mind in the time it took him to find a long-lasting rawhide bone for the dog and then stop by his bathroom to get a pack of condoms out of the medicine cabinet. When he returned to the room, though, she'd pulled back the sheets and was propped up with her elbows behind her, wearing nothing but a pair of blue lacy panties and an inviting smile.

His heart stopped in its tracks, then resumed pounding at an uncontrollable pace.

Standing beside the bed, he began to unbutton his jeans, but her fingers stopped him. "Let me do that."

Despite the need vibrating through him, he held himself perfectly still as her fingers skimmed the sensitive skin below his fly. When his arousal sprang free, he closed his eyes and groaned. She took the condom from his palm and rolled it onto his hardened length, while he returned the favor, sliding the soft fabric of her panties downward and over her hips.

Yesterday, he'd told her that he wanted her to be sure about them before they took their relationship to this level. So far, her body's response to his indicated that she was more than sure. But he still needed to hear the words. As he settled himself between her thighs, he said, "There's no going back after this."

Her hands cupped his face as she pulled him closer. "Good," she replied before capturing his mouth with her own.

He entered her swiftly and she gasped. Holding the rest of himself completely still, he pulled back his head and asked, "Are you okay?"

"Yes. I just… It's been a long time and I don't remember it feeling this good. This right. Please, Connor…don't stop."

His heart thumped behind his rib cage as he resolved to make each sensation last for her. He retreated slightly before filling her again, yet with each thrust her hips arched to meet him. As her breathing hitched higher, he felt himself growing closer to his own climax. Next time he would make it last for both of them, but for now he needed to take care of her needs first. He reached between their interlocked bodies and used his thumb to brush against the sensitive bud centered just above her entrance.

It only took a few strokes before Dahlia threw back her head and called his name, her constricting muscles pulling him deeper inside her. She was still shuddering under him when Connor shouted with his own release.

* * *

The sun was barely rising when Dahlia heard the unmistakable gobble from outside the window. Stretching with a soreness and contentedness she hadn't expected, she rolled over in the bed to find Connor sitting up with just the sheet covering him from the waist down.

He was watching her intently, but she couldn't muster up so much as a single blush. Instead, she smiled deeply, feeling the happiness all the way to her toes, which had been properly curled a couple of times throughout the night. "I thought only roosters crowed at the crack of dawn."

"Gobster already thinks he's part peacock and part garbage disposal. So why not add alarm clock to his list of charming qualities?"

"I noticed Goatee won't go near him. Maybe Gobster needs a turkey friend to keep him company?"

"Tell that to the poor bird who'd be stuck in the cage with him. He'd probably peck it to death."

She smiled, then tucked her body against his side. His fingers brushed her hair away from her face and she thought she could certainly get used to waking up like this. Turkey noises and all.

She let her own fingers trail along the light dusting of copper-colored hair highlighting Connor's chest, following the curls as they narrowed across his abdomen and then lower. Lifting her face to his, she teased, "I hope you don't mind that I can't seem to get enough of you."

His arm flexed around her as he brought her closer. "Last night, when we were making love, you made a comment about it being a long time for you."

Now, Dahlia did blush. But only slightly. She remembered adding on the part about never feeling this way before, but thankfully Connor hadn't been arrogant enough to gloat over that bit. "It has."

"Am I the first guy you've dated since your ex-husband?"

Would this be considered dating? She and Connor had never

really gone out together just the two of them. Also, was this a conversation she should sit up for? It felt better to talk about something like this while she wasn't making eye contact.

She laid her head on his shoulder and let out a deep breath. "Actually, there was a guy named Seth, one of Micah's band mates at the time. It was after we split up, and it only lasted for a few weeks."

"Why?"

"When the rest of the band moved to Nashville, Seth said that he was staying behind to help me with Big Millie's. Amelia was barely walking and I'd taken on this huge project partly because I loved the idea of owning and redecorating a historic saloon, and partly because I needed to prove to myself that I had my own life besides being Roper King's daughter or Finn King's twin sister or Micah Deacon's wife or Amelia's mom."

Connor didn't reply, but his hand continued a soothing circular pattern, tracing pleasantly along her lower spine.

"Seth would meet with the contractors if I was busy with Amelia, and it wasn't long before he started trying to make decisions that weren't his to make. And throwing around my family's name to build up his own list of people who would owe him favors. Turns out Micah had kicked him out of the band at the airport. He hadn't told me because he knew I had enough to worry about without adding his own career drama to the mix. When he found out Seth was still in Teton Ridge trying to cash in on his ex-wife's name, Micah wanted to kick his ass."

"Good," Connor said. "He should have."

"Except Micah had to get in line behind my mother, my siblings, and most importantly me. But not as much as I wanted to kick my own ass for letting the guy *help* me out in the first place. My dad told me not to beat myself up over it, but I'd never failed at anything in my life and I'd already dropped out of my interior design program and gotten a divorce in the same year. It sucked to have someone try to take advantage of me when I was already dealing with so much."

"I bet it did." Connor used his free hand to lift her chin so she was looking at his face. "Micah's leaving must've been rough on you."

"Not really," she said, then saw his eyes widen. "Okay, that sounds super shallow. I mean, the *idea* of divorce was a tough pill to swallow because it felt like I was admitting defeat. But it wasn't as if I really loved Micah in that way."

"Wait. You married someone you didn't love?" Connor shifted and his sheet dropped a bit lower, revealing the patch of bronze hair just above his... Dahlia had to shake her head to get back on subject.

"I should probably start at the beginning. When I was in my senior year at UW, Finn talked me into going to a bar nearby because Micah would be playing there. See, I knew Micah from school, but he was in the same grade as my brother Duke and normally played at some local places around Ridgecrest County. But Finn was the one who followed his music career and dragged me to this honky-tonk in Laramie. To be honest, I was more impressed with the old bar than I was with the band. In my defense, though, I was an interior design major and the saloon was a classic study in Wild West motif. It had stretched cowhides pinned up over the dark wood paneling and there were these antique red glass chandeliers hanging from the ceilings. And don't even get me started on all the polished brass and the exquisite ironwork..." She trailed off when she realized he was holding back a grin. "What's so funny?"

"Of course, you would be more impressed with the saloon decor than with a Grammy award–winning guitarist."

"Well, he hadn't won any Grammys at that time. But I'll stand by my original statement. The bar really was the perfect mixture of kitschy cowboy charm and old world elegance. Anyway, after their set, Finn and I were sitting with the guys in the band and Micah and I got to talking about Duke and Teton Ridge and our shared love of exposed log beams and brick facade architecture.

"We slept together and the following day it soon became apparent that the only thing we had in common was being from the same small town and our mutual love of interior design elements. When I found out I was pregnant, Finn—without my knowledge—paid him a visit and convinced him that the honorable thing to do would be to marry me. See, I was always the rule follower, while Finn was the rebellious twin. So to have her pushing for us to get married made it seem all the more reasonable. I remember thinking that if Finn, who could talk her way out of anything, thought this is the only way out of this mess, then that was my best option. Plus, my father was about to be announced as President Rosales's running mate and it just seemed like something we should do."

"How did the rest of your family react?" Connor asked.

"My mom said she would've expected something like this from Finn but not from me. So that stung. But my dad told me not to make any rash decisions. That I should do what feels best. It was actually his advice that made me think I should try to make a marriage with Micah work. I adored my dad and I wanted my child to have the kind of father I had growing up."

"But things didn't work out with you and Micah?"

Dahlia shrugged. "Up until the night I'd slept with him, I'd never really done anything impulsive or shocking. Looking back, it wasn't even all that reckless considering I'd known Micah all my life and he got along so well with everyone in my family. I figured it was a safe way to get a little rebellion out of my system, and then he and I could move on to being friends. But we just wanted different things out of life. He wanted to be famous and move to Nashville and I wanted to stay in Teton Ridge and carve out a quiet life for myself. So now we both live the lives we want and we make it work for Amelia."

"And you remain friends?" Connor prompted.

"I mean, we remain friendly with each other. We're co-parents, which means we have the same ultimate goal in mind and we have to work together to achieve it. But it's not like I'm confiding all my deep dark secrets to him."

"And what about me, Dahlia?" he asked, his finger now tracing along her arm, over her shoulder and down to her collarbone. "Am I a secret?"

"Not exactly," she said, giving an involuntary shiver at his caress. "Nobody can really keep a secret in this town. But…"

"But?" he prompted.

"I'd rather Amelia not know all the details."

"You don't think she's going to ask questions?"

"Of course, she'll ask questions." Dahlia rolled her eyes as she collapsed on her back. "Have you *met* my daughter?"

"So then what's your plan?" he asked before replacing his tracing fingers with his mouth, which now had full access to both her breasts.

She sighed from the scratchy texture of the stubble along his chin as it grazed her aching nipples and braced her hands on his shoulders. Then she pivoted her torso and pushed him until he was the one on his back. She deftly planted one of her legs on the other side of his hip in order to straddle him.

"Right now, my plan is to have my way with you one more time before I have to go pick her up and deal with those questions." Seeing his eyebrow raised at her avoidance of his question, she knew he wasn't going to drop the subject. So she smiled down at him and added, "Depending on how that goes, my next plan will be to casually run into you on occasion and act like I'm not imagining you walking out of your barn wearing just your jeans and cowboy boots."

He planted his hands firmly on each of her hips and pulled her against his hardened manhood. "Does that mean I have to act like I'm not imagining *you* in just those little blue panties laid out on my bed all ready for me?"

When that magical thumb of his moved from her hip to her inner thigh and then higher, Dahlia threw back her head to draw more air into her lungs. "Only until we get each other out of our systems and can move on to just being regular friends."

His thumb paused mid-flick and if she hadn't been so intent on finishing what they'd just started, she would've realized that Connor Remington had his own reservations about that plan.

CHAPTER TEN

CONNOR WAS FINALLY getting a handle on being a rancher and, for the first time in his life, he felt as though the seeds of permanency he'd planted were coming to fruition. He'd bought himself a new flat-screen TV—Aunt Connie's old twenty-two incher still had the turn knobs for channels two to thirteen and wasn't compatible with an updated cable box—and even a new set of pots and pans that were from this century. In fact, he'd planned to pull them out of the box this morning and make Dahlia some pancakes. Another first for him, since he'd never cooked breakfast for a woman.

Then he'd been hit with the reality that they weren't exactly on the same page about taking their casual relationship to the next level. Emotional attachments normally weren't his thing and just when he'd finally convinced himself that his growing connection with Dahlia would be worth the risk, she'd thrown out that offhand comment about moving on to being friends. He understood that she'd experienced that kind of one-and-done relationship with her ex-husband, but Connor didn't want to be lumped into the same boat as Micah Deacon.

He, unlike Micah, planned to stay in Teton Ridge—indefinitely. It was one thing to sleep with someone and then go about your business when you lived thousands of miles away. It was different when he was going to be running into her regularly at the bakery or the grocery store or even at her family's ranch.

In fact, tomorrow he was supposed to take Peppercorn to the Twin Kings for another group of mares whose cycles hadn't been ready the previous week. At this rate, his stallion's stud fees were bringing in enough money that he'd be able to buy a couple of broodmares himself so he could start his own program.

That reminded him that he needed to get the horse out later this afternoon for a good run so he'd be primed for tomorrow. Connor checked the time on his phone and saw that it was already noon. His mom always expected him to call on Sundays and she should be out of church by now. The phone rang three times before Linda Remington picked up.

"Connor? Is that you?" his mom asked, as though anyone else ever called her from this area code.

"Hey, Ma. How was your week?"

"Same as it always is. Except half the ladies in my bunco group came down with food poisoning after Carla DiAngelo brought something called bourbon-laced meatballs to the potluck on Thursday night. I didn't touch the things, obviously, because you know Carla has a heavy hand with the measuring cup and doesn't cook all the alcohol out." Connor's mom refused to go near an open liquor bottle, let alone partake in so much as a drop. Probably because her husband had such a problem avoiding the stuff. He wondered what his mother would think about Connor dating a bar owner. "And Dr. Ahmad is still trying to get me to see that dermatologist about the mole on my shoulder, but I told her it's always been that color since I can remember."

"Maybe you should have it checked out, Ma, just in case?" He made the suggestion, knowing it was futile.

"Bridget Shaw once saw someone about that little ol' sunspot she has on the tip of her nose and they talked her into getting something called a microdermabrasion peel. Her face looked like a scalded lobster for a whole month and her insurance didn't even cover it."

"That's because Mrs. Shaw went to her daughter's best friend's unlicensed beauty shop, not a dermatologist."

"Humph." His mother had some serious trust issues, not that Connor could blame her after dealing with his old man for so long. But her skepticism was getting worse lately. Thankfully, she changed the subject. "Father Brannigan asked about you at mass today. I told him to pray for you."

"Good. I'll take all the prayers I can get."

"So you're still planning to stay out there in Wyoming?"

And so it began. The same conversation they had every week. Where his mother forgot that she was talking to her son and began channeling some of the old conversations she used to have with her unreliable and untrustworthy husband.

"Yes, I'm still staying in Wyoming. The ranch is coming along nicely and I already have three animals now." He didn't admit that two of them weren't going to make him any money and one would end up being more of a headache than it was worth. "I plan to get another horse next week."

"Things always go well at first," she said, the cynicism heavy in her tone. "Then something'll happen to change your mind."

"If something goes wrong, then I'll stay here and deal with it. I made a promise to Aunt Connie, remember?"

"I'm sure your father used to make all kinds of promises to her. Then he named you after her and started making the same sorts of promises to you. We all saw how that turned out. I doubt she really expected you to keep your word."

"Well, *I* expect me to keep it. I'm not Steve Remington, remember?"

His mom exhaled loudly. "I know you're not. But as his son, it doesn't stop me from worrying that you'll fall into the same path eventually."

"I'm also *your* son. Give us both a little credit, Ma." Connor didn't like to brag about his accomplishments, but it would be nice if she could at least acknowledge that Connor was almost the same age his dad had been when he'd died. And Connor had yet to be arrested. Or fired from a job. Or in debt to any bookies. In fact, the medals on his dress blues (which had just arrived from storage last week) proved that Connor was more than capable of handling himself under pressure and not taking the easy way out of things.

"I just liked it better when you were in the military." His mom sighed. "I didn't worry about you so much."

"You know that most parents worry *more* about their kids when they're deployed to combat zones?"

"Yeah, but you were with other soldiers and officers and you guys had people watching over you." *Not always*, Connor wanted to correct her, but she was determined to see things her own way. "What kind of support system do you have in Wyoming? Have you even made any friends?"

"Yes, I have friends," Connor replied, trying not to think of Dahlia using that word to describe them. "And I have good neighbors and several of the business owners in town know me whenever I come in. It's a small town, Ma. Why don't you let me buy you a plane ticket so you can fly out and see for yourself?"

"I'll think about it," she offered, but Connor doubted that she would truly consider it. His father had had them moving around so much during their marriage, trying to escape his mistakes, his mother turned into a homebody in her older age. She rarely left her neighborhood now, let alone traveled out of state. At least she had a few dependable friends, even if they brought bourbon-laced meatballs to bunco night and got facials in the back room of someone's house.

By the time he hung up, Connor felt like he'd just finished a weekly chore. He loved his mom and appreciated the sacrifices she'd made working multiple jobs to keep a roof over his head and food on the table. But sometimes he felt as though he were more of a burden to her, a constant reminder of his old man. Sure, she loved him in her own way, but they'd never been especially close—probably because she'd built up so many of her own emotional walls. He couldn't imagine her patiently answering his questions the way Dahlia did with Amelia. Or her insisting on a family dinner every Friday night, the way Sherilee King did with her kids.

Maybe that was why he was hoping for something more with Dahlia. He wanted to feel that family connection. He looked at Goatee, who was taking the long way around the chicken coop to avoid Gobster. "It certainly would explain why I'm spoiling the both of you."

Connor saw Dahlia on Monday afternoon when he was getting ready to leave Twin Kings following a successful booking session with Peppercorn. She and Amelia were just arriving for the after-school riding lesson and he expected there to be some awkwardness because of Saturday night, but there was none. In fact, Dahlia even greeted him first and laughed along as Amelia told him all about how Peyton lost one of the class hamsters on the playground at recess and Mr. Tasaki, the PE teacher, found it scampering across the pull-up bars. Then, when nobody was watching, Dahlia walked him to his truck and gave him a kiss goodbye.

Clearly, she hadn't moved on from the physical attraction stage to the just friends stage yet. Which was perfectly fine with Connor.

On Tuesday morning, he ran into her at the grocery store and they ended up walking down the narrow aisles together, discussing the best flavors of cereal and Amelia's favorite lunch meat—ham, but not smoked or honey ham, just plain regular ham. Dahlia didn't seem to mind that Lupe Ochoa, Tomas's wife, kept giving them the side-eye when they were all standing in front of the dairy section at the same time. She kept right on talking about Greek yogurt versus Icelandic yogurt (Connor

didn't know there was a difference), and he had the sudden realization that she could be nearly as chatty as her daughter. Dahlia
didn't kiss him goodbye in the parking lot, though, because
Lupe had followed them outside and wanted to say hi to Goatee, who was still having a hard time understanding why he'd
had to stay tied up to the picnic table outside while his owner
had gone into the market. But Dahlia had texted him later that
night and told him that she'd wanted to kiss him goodbye. He'd
almost driven into town to give her the opportunity to make
good on her offer, but he knew she was working.

On Wednesday afternoon, the latch on the back of his horse
trailer broke and he needed to run to the hardware store before
they closed. He was coming out just as Dahlia and Amelia came
walking past the door.

"Mommy and I are going to the Pepperoni Stampede for
dinner because she doesn't feel like cooking." Amelia smiled
as she pulled on his hand. "Come on. You can come with us."

He lifted his brow at Dahlia to ask if that was okay. Again,
she surprised him with a wide smile and said, "It's all-you-can-
eat salad bar night."

"There's my favorite air hockey player," Woody said to Amelia
when it was their turn to order at the counter. "I built a couple
of wooden step stools in my workshop since the last time you
were in. The manager was worried about the liability, but all
the kids love them because they can reach the pucks better."

Amelia let out a whoop and immediately ran to the arcade
section of the pizza parlor to check out the games. Woody jerked
his chin at Connor and said, "Are you that new rancher in town
that everyone's been talking about?"

Woody, with his purple Mohawk, multiple piercings and
sleeveless Pepperoni Stampede tee displaying an array of colorful tattoos, didn't fit the mold of what one might expect a
typical small-town Wyomingian to look like. But he was just as

much a part of Teton Ridge as Dahlia was and she watched Connor closely to see his reaction to Woody's unique appearance.

"Connor Remington." Connor smiled as he reached his hand across the counter to shake Woody's. "I think we met before, though, when I brought my dog into Dr. Roman's office?"

"That's right." Woody nodded in recognition. "White terrier mixed with maltese. I remember animals better than I remember faces, bro. Did you end up taking it to that shelter in Pinedale?"

"Nope. He's most likely curled up at the foot of my bed right now or sitting in my kitchen tearing apart one of the million squeaky toys Amelia keeps giving him."

"Right on. Brenda, the receptionist at Doc D's office didn't think you'd keep him, but I knew you'd make the right call. You gotta be careful with those toys, though, bro. Some of the squeakers are super tiny and can get stuck in their throats when you're not watching."

"Yeah, I learned that the hard way." Connor leaned an arm on the counter between them. "So what I did is buy a box of tennis ball–sized squeakers online, right? Then I cut open the toys, replaced the small squeak with the bigger one and sewed them back up. It's loud as hell, but at least I don't have to do the Heimlich maneuver on my dog again."

"Now that's a genius idea." Woody pointed, his fingernail covered in chipped black polish. "If I wasn't already working ten hours a week here and volunteering at Doc D's one day a month *and* making my own brew on the side, I might want in on that business model. Do they hold up pretty well after you cut into them?"

"The trick is you've gotta do a zigzag backstitch, then run it in the reverse direction to really lock it in there. Takes Goatee at least three hours to get the thing apart."

"Right on." Woody nodded, but Dahlia stared at Connor with a sense of awe.

"You sew?"

"Yeah. My mom couldn't really afford to replace my jeans

every time I got a hole in the knee so our neighbor, who worked at a dry cleaners, taught me how to fix it myself. Aunt Connie had the same kind of machine in that back room at the Rocking D."

"That was her quilting room." Woody nodded wistfully. "Connie Daniels used to make the best quilts in town. She tried to teach me some of her techniques, but I didn't have the patience, bro."

A pointed cough came from someone in line behind them.

"Speaking of patience," Mr. Burnworth grumbled before raising his voice. "I'd like to order before Mayor Alastair over there makes his third trip to the salad bar. He always takes all the cherry tomatoes."

Dahlia asked Woody for their usual and Connor added a second pizza and a pitcher of beer, however, there was another delay as she and Connor argued briefly over who was going to pay. She ended up letting him because she didn't want to draw any more attention to the fact that they were having their first meal in public together.

When they finally got settled in a smaller booth in the corner, Amelia reappeared and asked for quarters for the arcade. Before Dahlia could pull out her wallet, Connor was handing her a five-dollar bill. "Do they have a change machine?"

"Yes. Peyton is here with her dad, too, so can I share with her? She's real good at sharing because she and her dad only get one salad plate and one soda when they come here and they hafta take turns."

"Of course." Connor pulled out another five-dollar bill.

When Amelia ran off to rejoin her friend, Dahlia rolled her eyes. "You didn't have to do that."

Connor shrugged, looking a little uncomfortable. "I used to be the kid at the team pizza parties after baseball practice who didn't have any extra money for the games. My mom used to tell me that it would build character, but there was usually a generous parent who'd slip me a few quarters when nobody was looking."

Dahlia felt something tug low in her belly. His mom was probably right about it building character because Connor Remington had to be one of the most compassionate men she knew when it came to animals and children. Then she realized how shallow she must've sounded by casually dismissing his generosity to another child. "I only meant that Jay, Peyton's dad, is a notorious cheapskate when it comes to his daughter because he doesn't want his ex-wife coming after him for more child support. However, the guy is in Big Millie's at least once a week and easily runs up a hundred-dollar bar tab each time. Usually only on the weekend when I'm not working because he knows I'll call him out on it. Someone needs to build *his* character."

A server delivered a red plastic cup full of lemonade for Amelia and a pitcher of beer for her and Connor to split.

"Plates are already by the salad bar when you're ready." The young woman jerked her thumb toward Mayor Alastair and Mr. Burnworth who were fighting over the same pair of plastic tongs. "But you might want to wait until those two get through the line. Heather Walker got hit in the eye with a slice of cucumber last week when she tried to get between them."

Connor poured the beer into the frosted mug in front of Dahlia. "Yeah, I was at Biscuit Betty's last month when she officially called off Dollar Waffle Day half an hour after it started. Syrup is surprisingly tough to clean off leather cowboy boots."

The server shook her head and muttered, "I hate all-you-can-eat Wednesdays," before walking away.

"So, you seem to be learning the *Who's Who* of Teton Ridge pretty quickly." Dahlia took a sip of the icy cold pale ale.

"I'm trying. It helps being known as *the new guy with the little white dog who is dating Dahlia King Deacon*." He used his fingers in air quotes for the last part.

Dahlia dipped her head nervously. "Someone already asked you if we were dating?"

"They didn't ask so much as assumed. I guess enough people have seen us together that they figure it's a safe assumption."

"Does that bother you?" she asked.

"Not if it doesn't bother you." He brought his beer glass to his lips, his eyes refusing to break contact with hers as he drank deeply.

She felt the blood rush to her brain. It was true, she wanted to keep whatever this was between them a secret, mostly for Amelia's sake. But Dahlia couldn't deny the way her body reacted every time she saw Connor around town. She should've been more guarded after they'd slept together, but she couldn't hide the fact that she was legitimately happy to see him. They talked about nothing, but everything, and there wasn't any sort of pressure to avoid him now that they'd already let the cow out of the barn so to speak.

"I think I am okay with it. I mean, as long as we take things—"

"Mommy, look what we won from the claw machine," Amelia interrupted, pointing to a stuffed panda bear in Peyton's arms. "If we can't win another one, then we're gonna co-parent this one together."

Peyton's dad chose that moment to suddenly stop scrolling on his smartphone and walk across the restaurant to check on his daughter. "Who won it, though? Whoever won it should get to take it home."

Amelia narrowed her eyes at the man. "Peyton won it, but with *my* quarters."

The other girl's lips curled down and she looked like she was about to cry. "Amelia, how 'bout you just keep it at your house?"

"No, it's both of ours and we're gonna share it," Amelia insisted and Dahlia's chest burst with pride.

"Come on, Peyton, don't be so quick to back down," Jay Grover told his daughter. "You gotta stand up for yourself."

Dahlia opened her mouth to tell Jay exactly what she thought about him and his inability to back down. But Connor beat her to it. "Buddy, why don't I buy you a drink and we let the children work this out for themselves."

Connor put his hand on the man's shoulder rather firmly—judging from the way Jay winced—then steered the man toward the front counter where Woody was still working. Dahlia had three brothers, grew up on a working cattle ranch with some of the best bronc busters in the business and she owned a bar. She knew how to break up a fight if she needed to. But right now, her priority was the two little girls in front of her.

"So what are you guys going to name the panda?" she asked them.

Neither child answered, though. In fact, Peyton was chewing on the end of her braid, her eyes huge as she watched Connor speak to her father. Dahlia wished she could hear what they were saying, but she understood why he was keeping his voice so low. The server brought out two pizzas and Dahlia, using the mouthwatering distraction to her advantage said, "Girls, I'll walk you to the bathroom so you guys can wash your hands. Then, Peyton, you can join us for dinner."

Amelia was having a difficult time peeling her curious eyes away from Connor—probably because she feared a repeat of the fudgy bar bake sale incident. Dahlia had to nudge her daughter toward the tiny ladies' room that barely had enough room for one person at the pedestal sink. She waited outside the door for the girls, watching as Jay nodded grudgingly at Connor, his mouth clamped shut in an angry line.

Woody went to the drink station himself to retrieve a red plastic cup, filled it with soda, then handed it to Jay. Dahlia let out the breath she hadn't realized she'd been holding as the man returned to his table, slumped lower in his seat and picked up his phone to continue his scrolling.

The girls came out and she led them back to their booth just as Connor returned. The muscles in his shoulders seemed more relaxed and he smiled, even though she could tell he was keeping Jay in his field of vision. "You ready to hit the salad bar?"

Dahlia nodded and followed him to the other side of the restaurant. When he handed her a chilled plate, she asked under her breath, "What'd you say to him?"

"I reminded him that his daughter was watching his behavior and that he didn't want to set the example that grown men fighting with women or arguing with young kids was ever acceptable." Connor settled a heaping pile of romaine lettuce on his plate. "I might have suggested that he doesn't want her marrying a guy who treats her that way or even dating someone who is too cheap to buy her a soda."

"That's all?" she asked as she followed him down the row of cut vegetables. The conversation would've been a lot quicker if that was the only thing Connor had said to Jay.

The cherry tomato bowl was completely depleted so he added a carrot stick to her plate. "I told him that if he didn't agree to let the girls share the panda, then we were going to be stepping outside to discuss the matter more thoroughly."

Dahlia shuddered. Her uncle Rider had talked enough about his elite Special Forces training and how the Marine Corps had taught him to *discuss the matter more thoroughly.*

Amelia and Peyton sat together on one side of the booth with the stuffed animal between them. Which meant Dahlia got to enjoy the warmth of Connor's long leg pressed against hers all through the meal. The girls finished their pizza and were just about to take Andy Pandy, as they'd named him, to visit the arcade again when Jay shuffled over to their table to tell Peyton it was time to go.

Amelia's bubbly smile quickly turned into a frown when her friend gave a last longing glance at the panda before walking out the door. Her daughter sniffed and said, "But we didn't get to decide how we would share Andy Pandy."

"Why don't we take him to the Frozen Frontier next door?" Connor nodded at the toy bear. "Maybe we can distract him with an ice cream sundae while we come up with a visitation schedule for you and Peyton."

Dahlia could kiss the man for once again having the perfect suggestion where her daughter was concerned. In fact, she barely waited until they were outside on the sidewalk, then quickly planted her lips on his when Amelia skipped off ahead of them.

"You're so good with her," she whispered as she pulled away before they could be caught kissing.

Amelia was already to the corner and holding open the door to the ice cream parlor when they caught up to her. Connor swung the girl into his arms so she could see the all the flavors in the glass case before placing their order, and Dahlia didn't think her heart could handle the cuteness overload.

They had just squeezed into wrought-iron chairs crammed tightly around a minuscule table when Dahlia's cell phone shot to life with the opening bars of Foreigner's "Jukebox Hero."

"That's Daddy's ringtone," Amelia said excitedly, reaching for the phone and pushing the speakerphone button before Dahlia could stop her. She glanced at Connor to see how he would react to her taking a call from her ex-husband while they were in public. But he was biting into his homemade chocolate dipped waffle cone as though he didn't have a care in the world. "Hi, Daddy! We're at the Frozen Frontier with Andy Pandy."

"Hi, Andy and Pandy," Micah said. "Are those the class hamsters you get to take home for spring break?"

"No, Daddy. We can't bring hamsters inside the ice cream place. We came here with Mommy's new boyfriend, Connor."

Dahlia gasped and Connor nearly choked on his mouthful of Rocky Road. But Micah didn't comment on their daughter's awkward announcement before he started talking about something else. In fact, Dahlia couldn't even focus on what he was saying because she was mentally calculating how long Amelia had known about her and Connor. Clearly, they hadn't been as stealthy as she'd hoped.

"Did you hear me, Dia?" Micah asked from the speaker on

her phone. He and her siblings were the only ones who called her by the nickname.

"Sorry, I missed that."

"I said that the orthopedic specialist thinks I'm going to need to do that wrist surgery after all. It's an outpatient procedure, but the rehab is pretty intense and I won't be able to play for a while. So I'm going to have to miss both the European and Asia legs of the world tour."

"Ms. Betty at the diner said her husband went to rehab, but it didn't work. Will your rehab work, Daddy?"

"It should, baby doll. It's not the same kind of rehab. Plus, I'm planning on doing it out there in Teton Ridge. There's a therapist in Jackson Hole who does home visits for…uh…clients who prefer to keep a low profile."

Dahlia knew she should reply—should say *something*. But for some reason, her ears weren't quite processing Micah's words. Maybe it was because of the way Connor was now sitting like a stiff wall of tense muscle beside her. Was he mad about having to listen to Amelia's conversation with her father?

"How long will you be here, Daddy?" Amelia asked. Okay, so Dahlia must've heard right. Micah *was* coming to visit.

"Two to three months depending on my physical therapy. I was hoping to plan it for summer break when you're out of school and we can spend more time together, baby doll. But the doctor says I already waited too long. He had a spot open up tomorrow, so as long as the procedure goes well, I should be on a plane to Wyoming by this weekend."

"Yay!" Amelia was now sitting on her knees, her hot fudge sundae threatening to topple over in her excitement. Connor's face was completely devoid of emotion, but his whole body was rigid. He was clearly way less thrilled than her daughter, who eagerly asked, "Are you gonna stay with us this time? You can sleep in my room."

Dahlia gulped, but resisted the urge to look at Connor to see how he was reacting to the suggestion that she and her ex-husband sleep under the same roof. She immediately set the record straight. "No, Peanut. You know Daddy never stays with us because our apartment is too small."

"But he can't sleep at Grandpa Tony's no more." Amelia pointed out. Micah's dad had sold his house a few months ago and moved to a retirement community in Tennessee to be closer to his son. The nearest hotel was in Fling Rock, and Micah wasn't really a nondescript motor inn kind of guy anymore.

"My publicist is working on lining up a place for me," Micah replied. "I told him there are usually vacation rentals available near Jackson Hole now that the ski season is winding down."

"But Jackson Hole is so far away," Amelia moaned as she propped her elbows on the table in defeat. "Like almost a whole hour."

Then her daughter's eyes landed on Connor's stoic face and suddenly lit up. Dahlia knew exactly what the girl was thinking and shook her head in warning. But Amelia shared her ill-fated idea, anyway.

"Hey, maybe my daddy can stay on the Rocking D with you, Connor!"

CHAPTER ELEVEN

"No!" CONNOR SAID a bit too quickly, only to hear Micah Deacon on the other end of the line echoing the exact same word. And just as emphatically.

Amelia's face fell, Dahlia dropped the spoon she'd been clutching, and the teen employee of Frozen Frontier chose that exact moment to wipe down the other tables nearby that were already cleaned.

Connor cleared his throat, feeling as though he'd just thrown Andy Pandy out of a moving car window. He'd just finished giving Jay Grover a lecture about putting his daughter's needs first, so how did it look now for Connor to refuse to host Amelia's father out on his ranch?

But seriously, he and the man weren't friends. They didn't even know each other. Clearly, Micah knew how awkward it would be to stay with the guy who was sleeping with his ex-wife because he'd had the exact same response as Connor. Even Dahlia looked like she would rather be any place but here, having this exact conversation.

"But why not?" Amelia asked, looking at the only two adults

who were physically present and had to actually witness the disappointment crossing her sweet face.

"Because, baby girl," Micah finally said via speakerphone. "That would be kinda awkward."

"But why?" Amelia insisted.

"Well, because I've never even met Connor in person. What if we don't like each other?"

Don't like each other? The ice cream cone in Connor's hand cracked under the pressure of his tense grip. Broman had made that comment about jealous dads at the dance, but Dahlia had brushed it off as the deputy being bitter. Obviously, though, Micah already had his own reservations and wasn't afraid to voice them.

"But why wouldn't you like each other?"

Good question, Connor thought. Unless Micah was hoping to get back together with Dahlia, what reason would he have to not like the man currently dating her?

Now Micah cleared his throat. "Who knows? Maybe he'll think my cooking is terrible. Or maybe I'll think that he snores."

"I don't snore," Connor said, surprising himself with his defensive tone.

Amelia turned to Dahlia who'd managed to find a new spoon and was now shoveling ice cream into her mouth so quickly, it was a wonder she didn't have brain freeze. "Mommy, does Connor snore?"

He lifted a brow at her, daring to admit in front of her exhusband and the eavesdropping teenaged ice cream scooper that she'd already spent the night with him.

"Okay, everyone," Dahlia said after she swallowed a final gulp of mint chip. "Here's what's going to happen. Connor is going to stay at his house on the Rocking D. Amelia is going to stay our apartment above Big Millie's. And Micah is going to stay...wherever he finds a place to stay that isn't the Rocking D or Big Millie's. And I am going to go home right now before I keep stress eating ice cream and barking orders like my mother usually does."

"Don't let Sherilee hear you saying that," Micah said, then chuckled. Because of course he was already privy to all the inside jokes about the King family. "Alright, I'll talk to you tomorrow, baby girl."

Amelia grudgingly told her father good-night and when Dahlia disconnected the phone, she shoved it into her jacket pocket. As though she was shoving from her mind all the drama the little device had just conveyed.

"So I guess this is what you meant by complicated?" Connor offered, trying to make light of the situation.

"What's complicated?" Amelia asked.

"Life, Peanut," Dahlia answered truthfully, then shook her head as if to clear it. "Anyway, tell Connor thanks for the pizza and the ice cream. Let's get Andy Pandy home so you can read him a book before bed."

Amelia picked up the stuffed bear and gave a dejected sigh. "Thanks for the pizza, Connor."

He walked them home, which was only a block away, and then spent the next twelve hours trying not to think about how one phone call had steered him so thoroughly off course.

The following morning, his phone vibrated in his back pocket and his senses went on full alert when he saw his mother's contact info on the screen.

They usually only talked on Sundays, so it was pretty out of character for her to be calling him in the middle of the week. "Hey, Ma. Is everything okay?"

"Well, I guess that depends. I went to see the dermatologist and he removed the mole to test it for cancer."

"Did you get the biopsy results already?"

"No. But that's not why I'm calling. When I was in the waiting room, I ran into someone."

Connor put the call on speaker and set the phone down on the workbench so he could talk while repairing the sliding mechanism on the trailer door latch. When his mom didn't continue talking, he asked, "You still there?"

"Do you remember when we lived in that apartment off Melville?"

"I remember living in a couple of places off Melville."

"The one by the park where you played Little League?"

"Oh…yeah, sure."

"Do you remember playing on that baseball team with the coach named Greg? He…uh…he and I went out a few times?"

"Of course. I loved Coach Greg. He had all those cool stories about being a Marine. He was probably the biggest influence on me enlisting."

What Connor didn't say was that the months his mom had dated Greg had been the best of his childhood. The guy had been easygoing and treated his mom right and would've made a great stepdad.

Of course, his parents weren't divorced at the time, which posed a problem. Whenever Connor's dad would be in jail, his mom would swear she was going to leave him for good. That year, he'd hoped that she would keep her promise because he really liked Coach Greg. But then Steve got released, and just like every other time when his old man was fresh out of jail, he'd sworn he was going to stay sober, and his mom had gone back to him.

"Well, that's who I saw at the doctor's office. I guess he had a few sunspots he was getting checked out. But we started talking and one thing led to another and, well, he asked me out to dinner this weekend."

"That's great, Ma. What's the problem?"

"I wasn't sure if you would approve or not. You were pretty mad at me when I broke up with him."

"I was twelve back then. I'm thirty-two now. You don't need my approval to date anyone."

"It probably won't work out, anyway. I can't believe he even recognized me with all my gray hair. Maybe I should just call the whole thing off."

"Ma," Connor said, pinching the bridge of his nose. "Stop being so cynical all the time. What do you have to lose by going out with Greg? You deserve to be with a nice guy."

There was a long pause on the other end of the phone before she finally sighed. "Okay. Then I'll meet him for dinner. He asked about you, you know? You should've seen him smile when I told you you'd joined the Marines. He said he'd always known you'd do big things."

Hearing his mom repeat Greg's words made Connor's rib cage ache with the gratification he'd never gotten to hear from his own father. How could a man who'd only been in his life for six short months have made such a big impact on him?

After he hung up with his mom, he sat on the stool and stared emptily at the workbench. Wow. How much different would his life have been if she'd stayed with Greg instead of going back to Steve?

How much different would Amelia's life be if Dahlia dated Connor instead of going back to Micah?

Not that she was going back to her ex. Just because the man was coming to town for a few months didn't mean that Dahlia would throw Connor over for him. Or that Micah didn't deserve a chance to win his family back.

Great. Now he was sounding like his mom, focusing on everything that could go wrong. Still. He knew all the signs of what was coming and he didn't want to influence what was ultimately Dahlia's decision. She alone needed to figure out what would be best for Amelia. In the meantime, maybe he should distance himself a little while they sorted out what Micah's return might mean to all of them.

Dahlia was foolish to think she could simply get Connor out of her system after just one night together. If seeing him with her daughter these past couple of months wasn't enough to make her fall for him, seeing him sharing common interests with Woody and then putting Jay Grover in his place would've cemented things for her. In fact, she'd wanted to invite him back to her apartment instead of going to the Frozen Frontier with him. Amelia already referred to him as her boyfriend, so would it be a stretch to explain that Connor wanted to have breakfast with them when her daughter saw him at the kitchen table the following morning?

She'd been hoping to ease everyone into the idea of Connor becoming a part of their lives, but then Micah announced he was returning to Teton Ridge, which immediately threw them all into a tense discussion she hadn't been ready for. Then Micah made that stupid crack about the possibility of them not getting along and Connor had snapped back, and Dahlia wasn't entirely sure she wanted to take on the role of mediator.

When she saw Connor at the bank on Thursday, Dahlia asked if he wanted to grab some lunch at Biscuit Betty's or even take a sandwich over to the park. She'd hoped that spending a few minutes alone together would help her get a feel for how he was handling the recent development. Although he was friendly, his eyes didn't quite meet hers when he said he had Goatee in the truck and needed to get him home. Everyone knew that he took his dog to "socialization" classes at the dog park at least once a week.

She couldn't read his mind, but it didn't take a fortune-teller to see the writing on the wall. While she had no intention of getting back together with her ex-husband, they were also navigating what had become a multi-pronged relationship. Micah was the father of her child, and if that wasn't enough, he was also good friends with several members of her family—Duke and Marcus, not Finn—and they'd grown up in the same town. Hell, they were friends with many of the same people. Of course, Connor would have doubts about where that left him.

Maybe he was pulling back to protect himself. And maybe she should let him.

As Dahlia was finishing the inventory in the stock room on Friday morning, a task she always did before taking off for the weekend, the motion sensor at the front door of Big Millie's chimed. When she went to see if it was a delivery, she was shocked to see Sherliee King standing right inside the door, her knit suit and Italian leather pumps looking completely out of place in the Wild West–styled bar.

Aunt Freckles slammed into the back of her sister-in-law. "Something wrong with your legs, Sherilee? You're holding up traffic here."

Now, *there* was a woman who looked completely at home in a honky-tonk. Freckles's jeans were painted on legs that weren't quite as slim as they had been thirty years ago, and her black leather jacket boasted a motorcycle club patch that was probably as authentic as she was.

"Well, I'd move, Freckles," her mom snapped, "but your tacky rhinestone belt buckle is now stuck to the back of my knit jacket. You should be more careful. I mean, this is St. John, for God's sake."

Dahlia sprang into action and came around the bar to help her mother disentangle the tiny crystals snagged between the delicate knitted fibers of the silk. "What are you doing here, Mom?"

"I figured it was finally time I come check out this place for myself." Her mother had never been shy letting Dahlia know exactly what she thought about the family heritage behind Big Millie's. Sherilee nodded at the ornate staircase that led to a remodeled balcony with only five feet of the original railing remaining. "I see you got rid of all those doors upstairs where the former residents used to entertain their customers."

"Not totally rid of them. I just walled off everything past the balcony and turned them into our private apartment."

Her mom's cosmetically sculpted nose barely quivered as she sucked in a deep breath of indignation. "Really, Dahlia. You're as bad as Finn sometimes."

Freckles winked at her as she bit back her smile. It was a

King family pastime to shock the normally unflappable and tightly reserved Sherilee King. Dahlia was glad to know she hadn't lost her touch since moving off the ranch.

"Since you're here, can I get you a glass of wine or a vodka soda or something?"

"I'll take a margarita if it's no trouble," Freckles replied.

"It's ten o'clock in the morning," her mom said. "What kind of self-respecting establishment sells liquor at this time of day?"

"Luckily, I know the owner," Dahlia replied as she walked behind the bar. "And if you're real nice, I'll give you the family discount."

Her mother rubbed at a nonexistent crease on her Botox-enhanced forehead. "Fine. I'll take a vodka martini. Extra dirty."

"Ooh, change my margarita to one of those." Freckles snapped her fingers, the long nails painted the same shade of coral as her lipstick. "We might need the big guns to get through this."

Dahlia grabbed the stainless-steel shaker from the shelf under the bar. "What happened?"

"I found out I'm receiving the Presidential Medal of Freedom this weekend," Sherilee said the same way one might say that they found out the Easter Bunny wasn't real. "Several of the representatives from the charities I've worked with will be there."

"Wow!" Dahlia blinked. "That's an incredible honor, Mom. Why are you so worried about it?"

"Because we've got a lot riding on this plan."

Dahlia was afraid to ask, but couldn't help herself. "What plan?"

Freckles then went into detail about an elaborate scheme she and Sherilee had plotted to get Tessa to the White House, where they'd have Grayson Wyatt, the Secret Service agent her sister had fallen in love with, waiting there to propose.

"Yeah, I can see why you'd think that something like that could totally backfire on you." Dahlia was tempted to pour herself a martini, as well. "So you came here to have me talk you out of it, right?"

Her mother and aunt exchanged a look before her mom shook her head. "No, the plan is in place. But we need all you kids there so Tessa doesn't get suspicious."

"*This* Sunday? As in less than forty-eight hours?"

"Actually, we would need to take the Gulfstream over to DC tomorrow so we can get everything in place."

Dahlia shook her head. "No can do. Micah is supposed to arrive first thing tomorrow morning. Amelia is spending the day with him."

"Perfect." Her mom clapped her hands together. "That means you're free to go with us."

"You want me to leave my child behind?"

"No, I want you to leave her with her father. Micah Deacon is perfectly capable of taking care of his daughter for one night. Possibly two if things go sideways and we have to chase after Tessa."

"But she's never stayed anywhere without me, other than at the Twin Kings with you guys. Even when I take her to visit Micah in Nashville, we usually stay together in the guesthouse on his property." Oh, jeez. Hearing the words coming out of her own mouth, Dahlia realized she sounded exactly as controlling as Sherilee. Was she really that much of a helicopter mom?

"You could have Micah stay with her here. I mean upstairs." Sherilee shuddered as she said the word. "Where she'll have her own bed and toys and everything is familiar to her."

"No, Mom. I don't want my ex-husband sleeping in my bedroom."

"You only have the two bedrooms upstairs now?" Freckles looked up at the ceiling. "I could've sworn there used to be at least eight of them up there back in the day."

Her mother threw back the rest of her martini. "Then have Micah stay with her out at the ranch. Only the staff and a small security detail will be there since we'll all be in DC. Amelia'll be comfortable and it has a ton of extra bedrooms that were never used for illicit purposes."

"Not as far as you know," Freckles murmured into the rim of her glass. She swallowed, then added, "Honestly, darlin', I don't think lil' Amelia is gonna want to go to DC. Could you imagine having to sit through that boring presentation and all the ridiculous speeches?"

"Hey!" Her mom shot her aunt a pointed look. "I'm *making* one of those ridiculous speeches."

"My point exactly." Freckles made a saluting motion with her martini glass. "Let her stay in Teton Ridge with her daddy and enjoy some one-on-one time with him."

Dahlia slowly felt her resolve slipping. Then Sherilee played her final hand. "Even Duke will be flying into DC for the occasion. Hopefully, Tom won't have any surgeries scheduled and can drive over from Walter Reed to meet us."

Not only did Dahlia miss her big brother, she needed to find out what was going on between him and his husband. "Fine. I'll ask Micah if he's okay with it when I talk to him tonight. But you better not let Finn know he's staying at the Twin Kings."

"You don't have to tell me twice." Her mom held up her empty glass. "This was one of the best I've ever had. And for what it's worth, I really do like what you've done with the place. It's got both charm and that bit of Western rustic chic that probably makes it a big draw for all those people on social media trying to post whimsical old-timey pictures. In fact, you know what would look great right there on the wall by that picture of Big Millie? That portrait of your dad's grandma. I'm thinking of redecorating and, needless to say, it really doesn't go with my vision."

"You mean the portrait of Little Millie?" Dahlia scrunched her face. Her great-grandmother might've been an excellent businesswoman and gambler, but the painting of her hanging over the fireplace at the Twin Kings was equal parts gawdy and intimidating. She always seemed to be watching everyone.

"No, thanks. Aunt Freckles, maybe you and Uncle Rider would want it for the cabin?"

"Are you kidding?" Freckles shook her head so hard the loose skin around her neck jiggled like Gobster's. "That woman scared the hell out of me when she was alive. I don't want her mean, judgy face looking over me and Rider when we're getting naked on the bear skin rug in front of his fireplace."

"For the love of God, Freckles!" Sherilee slapped both of her palms over her eyes like a blindfold. "I'll never be able to unsee that image."

"I'm serious, though," Freckles said. "Ol' Grandma Millie gives me the creeps. Did you know that Rider once told me she still talks to him? Gives him advice and such?"

"That's ridiculous," Sherilee scoffed, right before she shoved three blue cheese–stuffed olives in her mouth in quick succession. "She's been dead for fifty years now. If the talking portrait of a dead woman was giving advice in my home, don't you think I'd know it?"

Freckles tsked. "She probably doesn't talk to you because she knows you wouldn't listen, anyway."

Dahlia was still chuckling when her mother and aunt walked out of the bar a few minutes later, bickering as much as they had been when they'd first arrived. She finished her inventory, then spoke to Micah after his procedure. Even though he was still a bit loopy from the anesthesia, he was looking forward to having Amelia with him for the whole night. He'd also suggested that Finn not know he would be staying at the Twin Kings, but that could've just been the aftereffects of the pain meds talking.

That night, even though things were still awkward between her and Connor, she didn't feel right leaving town without talking to him. She dialed his number, and he answered on the second ring.

"Hey, is everything okay?"

"Yes, why?" she asked, pulling her small suitcase out of the closet and hefting it onto her bed.

"Because you've never called me before."

That was true. They'd texted a few times, but usually, they talked in person...like when they ran into each other in town. "I just wanted to let you know that I'm going to be out of town this weekend."

"Oh." He paused, and she wondered if she was making a bigger deal out of this than it was. For all she knew, he couldn't care less that she'd be gone. He probably wouldn't have even noticed. Then he asked, "Are you taking Amelia to stay with her dad after his surgery?"

"I wish," she quickly replied then heard his sharp intake of breath. "I mean, that would be way easier than what my mom and aunt talked me into."

Connor actually chuckled at that, which made Dalia smile in relief. But he didn't ask for any details, which made her determined to continue talking and keep the conversation going.

"Anyway, Amelia is going to be staying out at the ranch with Micah. I've never really left her overnight so I'm kind of worried, even though I know her dad will take good care of her. But it's weird knowing that I'm going to be so far gone and not actually in control of the situation." Dahlia hadn't noticed that she was piling way more clothes into her suitcase than she'd ever need for an overnight trip. But it kept her hands busy as she continued to talk and talk and talk. "You probably think I'm acting like a helicopter mom, which is totally a fair assessment given how neurotic I must sound. God, I'm turning into my own mother who is right this second interfering in her grown-up daughter's love life. Tessa's love life, not mine. Our love life is going fine, I hope. Don't you think it's going fine between us? Oh, jeez, now I sound like my mother again putting you on the spot. Except, I'm not nearly as crazy as her, I promise. Speaking of crazy, did I tell you how she's talked all of us into going to DC, even though, it's a horrible plan that's never going to work—"

A bark thankfully cut her off before she could keep rambling on. "Is that Goatee?"

"Yeah, he's mad at me because I stopped throwing the squeaky toy for him so I could answer the phone."

"Oh, I didn't mean to interrupt you guys," she said, finally drawing in a long breath.

"You can always interrupt me, Dahlia." When he said her name like that, his voice equal parts silky and husky, her legs threatened to give out. "Besides, I like listening to you when you do your nervous talking thing. I always wonder how long you'll go before you finally run out of something to say."

"Well, I'm glad one of us enjoys it." She collapsed onto the bed, thankful he couldn't see her do a nosedive into the pillows to drown out her embarrassment. When she came up for air, she heard her phone beep and said, "Listen, my aunt is calling through on the other line and I have to answer it or she'll tell my mom and *she* will send my brother over here to check on me. Maybe we can talk more when I get back?"

"I'll be here," Connor said.

It wasn't until Dahlia was trying to fall asleep later that she realized he hadn't assured her that their love life was, in fact, fine.

Saturday morning, she and Amelia pulled into the nearby airfield, her daughter as excited as Dahlia was nervous. Micah's chartered plane arrived just before the Twin Kings jet was scheduled to depart for DC. Amelia ran to her father, who easily lifted her up into his arms, despite the fact that he had a cast on one hand and a guitar strapped to his back.

All of her family was already waiting onboard the private jet for her and she saw her sister glaring out the oval window at her ex-husband and then tapping impatiently at her watch to indicate that they were already late.

"Okay, so Amelia's suitcase is packed and in my truck. Can

you drive with your hand and wrist like that?" Dahlia asked before handing over her keys to Micah.

"Of course," Micah said. "There's still only that one stoplight in town, right?"

"No, there's two now. We're quite the metropolis. Anyway, Amelia has a duffel bag packed with her favorite stuffed animals. And she still uses that green blanket at night and won't fall asleep without it. Aunt Freckles said the kitchen at the ranch is already stocked with premade meals that can be microwaved." She bit her lip. "I feel like I'm forgetting something."

"Don't worry, Dia. We'll be fine." Micah bounced Amelia higher on his hip and she giggled. "Tell your mom congratulations on her medal and try to talk Duke into coming back here afterward for a jam session. Maybe we can get Woody to join us."

"You could ask Connor to play with you guys, too." Amelia said, and Dahlia rolled her eyes behind her sunglasses.

"Oh, yeah?" Micah wiggled his eyebrows at Dahlia before returning his attention to his daughter. "What does Connor play?"

Dahlia frowned because she hadn't seen an instrument at his house when she'd stayed the night last weekend. Of course, she hadn't seen the sewing machine, either. Was there something else she'd missed about him?

"I don't know," Amelia said. "But Miss Walker says everyone gets an instrument when we do Music Mondays. She has extra triangles and maracas and even a tambourine he could probably use."

"Let's worry about that when Mommy gets home tomorrow," Dahlia said, then gave her daughter one last hug and kiss goodbye.

She gave a final wave at the top of the steps before stepping onto the plane and taking her seat. And just because it seemed like the right thing to do, she sent Connor a text letting him know that her flight was leaving. That way, she couldn't be held responsible for anything that happened while she was gone.

Such as her persuasive daughter talking her dad into stopping by the Rocking D unannounced with a pair of maracas.

CHAPTER TWELVE

CONNOR SAW DAHLIA'S truck spitting up dust in the distance as she pulled onto the driveway leading to his ranch. No, that couldn't be Dahlia. She'd sent him a text less than an hour ago saying her flight was leaving, but nothing else to indicate she would be missing him while she was gone. So then who was driving her Ford to the Rocking D and why?

A twinge of jealousy spun itself into a rock-sized lump when he saw who was behind the wheel. Micah Deacon hadn't shut off the engine before Amelia unbuckled herself and jumped out the door.

Goatee came tearing across the yard with a chorus of excited barks to greet her.

"Hi, boy." She dropped to her knees, giggling at the slobbery kisses. "I brought my daddy over to meet you and Connor and Peppercorn and Gobster."

"Man, she's fast," the man said as he came around the front of the truck. "I'm Micah. I'd shake your hand but…" He held up his right hand covered in a white cast-like bandage. Only his fingers were exposed. "Sorry for barging in on you like this."

"No problem," Connor said, a tenseness in his stomach as he sized up Dahlia's ex-husband while pretending any of this was normal. "I'm starting to get used to it."

Both men fell in step behind Amelia and Goatee as she led the tour to the chicken coop first to meet Gobster, who was flapping his wings and making threatening caw sounds. As soon as the turkey's caws turned into screeches, Goatee made a detour straight to the safety of the porch.

"Whoa. That's one angry looking bird." Micah kept his good hand on Amelia's shoulder to prevent her from getting too close to the wire fencing. Seeing the man's quick instinct to protect his daughter eased some of the heaviness in Connor's stomach.

"Tell me about it. I went into the coop this morning to feed him and he took a bite out of my favorite shirt." Connor held out the cotton tee with what used to be an image of the Beatle's *Abbey Road* album. "Tore a hole right through Ringo Starr."

"At least he didn't go after Paul or John," Micah replied. "That would've been a one-way ticket on the stuffing express."

"What's the stuffing express, Daddy?" Amelia asked.

Micah winced like a preacher's kid who'd just gotten busted saying a curse word. "Oh, just one of those weird farm terms I heard your aunt Finn use once. Now where's this horse I've been hearing all about?"

"He's in the stables!" Amelia grabbed Micah's unbandaged hand in one of hers and then reached back for Connor's. "Let's go."

If Micah Deacon thought it was odd having his five-year-old daughter literally forming a link between him and his ex-wife's boyfriend, the man didn't say. And if he wasn't going to complain, then Connor certainly wasn't going to bring it up.

But he had to think it was weird, right? Even the most easygoing guy on the planet would know that the situation could go sideways pretty quickly. Just as it had on the phone call earlier this week.

They made their way to the stables. Just a trio of two men

and a little girl who had no idea how awkward this was. As they stood in front of the stall, Micah stared at the hand-carved sign hanging from the fence that read Sergeant Peppercorn.

"I thought you said his name was Private Peppercorn?" Micah asked his daughter.

"It was. But then Aunt Finn said that he earned a promotion and made him that sign. Did you know that he has eighteen girlfriends right now? Aunt Finn said it's fine for stallions to have that many but if a *man* does it, we can kick him in the—"

"How about we show your dad where I'm going to put the new mare when she gets here?" Connor interrupted just in time. Then he forced himself not to make eye contact with Micah, who was clearly having a tough time keeping a straight face.

"It's over here, Daddy," Amelia said, happily skipping ahead of them. Goatee returned now that they were out of Gobster's field of vision and he jumped up onto one of the straw bales, yipping until Amelia followed him.

As the little girl and the dog played hide-and-seek in the barn, Micah turned to him. *Here it comes*, Connor thought. The real reason for this visit.

"Just in case you're wondering—" Micah rocked back on his heels "—this whole thing is awkward for me, too."

Connor's only response was a single nod of acknowledgment. Although, he did resist the urge to fold his arms defensively over his chest. Instead, he assumed the military at ease position, clasping his hands behind his back.

"You probably think I'm a deadbeat dad who ditched my kid to run off and become famous."

"Actually, I never really thought that," Connor admitted. "Dahlia is pretty clear about your co-parenting situation and I know that you're active in Amelia's life, even when you're out of town."

Micah shrugged. "Well, I think that about myself sometimes. Back when she was a baby, it was easy to tell myself that Dahlia could handle things. That Amelia was too young to even notice that I wasn't around. But now she's getting older and more aware of everything. Man, she's so damn smart, you know? It's a trip talking to her on FaceTime and hearing about her day and it's starting to eat at me that I can't be with her all the time. Sometimes I regret not staying here and making things work."

Connor felt his last statement like a swift kick to the chest and dragged a deep breath in through his nose. Micah must've seen his reaction because he held up his unbandaged palm.

"No, man, not like that. It never would've worked between me and Dahlia. She figured I was safe because we'd known each other forever and a lot of the guys she'd met in college didn't make it a secret that they were mostly interested in her family name. Anyway, we both knew it was hopeless before we even walked down the aisle. What I meant was that I regret not making things work by staying here in Teton Ridge, staying closer to my daughter. Don't get me wrong, Dahlia's done an amazing job. She's such a great mom, and I appreciate the way all of the Kings have stepped in and helped while I've been away on tour. And I can't even begin to thank *you* for being involved and taking her to that dance and just, you know, being good to her mom and…crap…this is starting to sound really weird." Micah scratched his head. "Anyway, what I'm trying to say is that I'm glad Dahlia has you and I don't want you to feel threatened in any way now that I'm moving back to town. Unless I find out you're not the man they think you are."

Connor blinked twice, but chose not to focus on Micah's last sentence. "*Moving* back to town? Or just staying here for a couple of months for physical therapy?"

"Here's the thing. I haven't told anybody this, not even the guys in my band. But the surgeon says my wrist is pretty messed up." He sighed, finally appearing as though he might actually be stressed. "It's going to be a long time before I can pick up a guitar again and even then, it probably won't be at the same level I was playing before. So it kind of seemed like the universe was telling me that it was okay to take a break. To return to Teton Ridge and be a normal dad again."

Connor didn't want to think about what this new development would mean as far as his relationship with Dahlia. Or the bond he'd established with Amelia. But then he saw a little blond ponytail poke out from behind a hay bale and knew how he *should* feel. He cleared his throat. "Yeah, well, that'll be great for Amelia."

"I hope so." Micah was also watching Amelia, a determined look in his eyes. "I guess we'll all just have to figure out how to make things work."

Connor hoped it would be just that simple. But there were a lot of lives and personalities at play here. Things had been complicated enough before her ex-husband returned full-time.

If his past training had taught him anything, he knew that once he made the decision to go down this trail, he'd have to stay the course and keep his senses on high alert. Because his emotions weren't the only ones at risk of getting lost.

"Hey, man." Micah's voice was rushed when Connor answered his phone later that evening. "I hope you don't mind, but I got your number from Mike Truong, the stable foreman."

Connor gripped the rope he'd been coiling tighter. "Is something wrong with one of the mares?"

"No. I wish it were that simple." That was when he heard Amelia's hiccupping sobs in the background.

"Is she okay?"

"Physically, yes. But I can't get her to stop crying. Something about a panda and Peyton, and I can't really understand the rest through all the tears. I was gonna call Dahlia and ask her to interpret for me, but I don't want her thinking I can't handle my own daughter for the night. So I called you."

Connor didn't know whether to be flattered or confused. But then he heard Amelia do that hiccupping sob again and it no longer mattered how Connor felt. "Can you put the phone on speaker so I can ask her?"

"There," Micah said. "Amelia, can you tell Connor what's wrong?"

"Tonight is s'pose to be my night to co-parent Andy Pandy." Hiccup. "But when I used my tablet to talk to Peyton, she said she forgot him at her dad's house." Hiccup. "And her dad won't bring him to her mom's 'cause they're fighting." Hiccup. "And now Andy Pandy won't know that I love him." Two hiccups.

"Did you catch all that?" Micah asked.

"I think so. Do you know Jay Grover?"

"Unfortunately. Let me take you off speakerphone so you can fill me in."

Connor explained about the claw machine at the Pepperoni Stampede and the co-parenting agreement between the girls and his subsequent conversation with Jay.

Micah snorted. "Did you really tell him you were gonna kick his butt if he couldn't get on board with the co-parenting plan?"

"I might've used more colorful language at the time. But he shouldn't be such a crappy dad just to get back at his ex-wife. And I didn't like the way he spoke to Amelia, either. Tell her I'll drive over to Jay's to pick up Andy Pandy and bring him out to the ranch for her."

"I'll come with you," Micah said, but before Connor could protest, he added, "Not that you couldn't take him. From what I remember, he lost every single wrestling match his sophomore year before Coach Plains cut him from the team. But the guy is a yeller and knows how to cause a scene. You don't want to risk having Deputy Broman responding to a disturbing-the-peace call. With Marcus out of town, Broman is probably looking for an excuse to lock up someone else important to the Kings."

Connor shoved down the thought that he was actually significant enough to be considered as someone important to the Kings and instead asked, "But I thought you and Broman were good friends? At least that's what he said at the father-daughter dance."

"A lot of people think they're my friends," Micah replied. "They're usually full of it. I'll be by to pick you up in fifteen minutes."

The line disconnected and Connor thought about taking off on his own and going to Jay's without Micah. However, by the time he fed Peppercorn and Gobster—he didn't want to risk delaying their dinnertimes and have the turkey try to eat a hole through the chicken wire again—Micah was bouncing up the drive in Dahlia's truck.

Connor whistled for Goatee before he opened the back door. The dog sprang onto the back seat beside Amelia. Micah squinted at the small white dog, who was in need of another haircut. There was no mistaking the sarcasm in his voice when he asked, "Do you really think we need to bring the attack dog?"

Connor climbed into the front seat. "I figured he'd be a good distraction to keep Amelia occupied in the car so she doesn't hear us talking to Jay."

Micah nodded as though any of this made sense. "So just to be clear. We're two grown men, taking a five-year-old and a white fluffy dog with us to possibly go kick another guy's ass over a doll?"

"Andy's a panda bear," Amelia corrected from the back seat. "And Mommy said A-S-S is a bad word."

"Mommy's right," Connor told the girl before lowering his voice to talk to Micah. "Let's hope things don't escalate that far. But if they do, you take care of Amelia. I'll deal with Jay."

"I know I'm not Special Forces," Micah said, surprising Connor with his intel. Not that he blamed the man for doing his research. "But I got my start playing in some of the roughest honky-tonks and dive bars on the rodeo circuit. I can throw a mean right hook."

"Not with your wrist like that, you can't." Connor pointed to the street ahead. "Turn here."

"Crap. I guess I'll have to use my left hand."

"Look, if one of us goes to jail for hitting him, it should probably be me since you have Amelia tonight."

"I can probably afford a better attorney, though," Micah replied, then shot him a sheepish smile. "No offense."

"Maybe we should focus on a plan that doesn't involve either of us getting into a fight or getting arrested?"

"Peyton says Andy Pandy sleeps on her bed," Amelia said, clearly listening to every word from the back seat. "Maybe we can just sneak in the window and get him."

"No," both Connor and Micah said at the same time.

"Baby doll, you can't just sneak into someone's house," Micah said as he turned onto Jay's street. "Your mom would be so mad at us if we let you do that."

"But I know which window is hers."

Connor turned around in his seat. "Amelia, I need you to stay here and keep Goatee from barking or getting out of the truck, okay? He doesn't know this neighborhood and we wouldn't want him running away again and getting lost."

"Maybe you're right." The little girl nodded solemnly as she stroked the dog's back.

"Besides, I'm sure if we just knock on the door and talk to Peyton's dad, he'll be happy to give us Andy Pandy," Micah said, and Connor almost believed him.

Of course, Jay's flatbed truck wasn't in the driveway and his house was dark when they parked at the curb. When nobody answered the door, Amelia rolled down her window and yelled, "Oh, no! Andy Pandy is all alone in there. We can't just leave him here. It's *my* night."

"Hey, baby doll, which room is Peyton's?" Micah called back to Amelia.

"You can't be serious," Connor said, looking up and down the darkened street. "That's breaking and entering."

"Are you going to go back to the truck and tell her that we

can't get her doll? Because I'm not gonna break her heart like that."

"It's a bear," Connor corrected absently. But one look at Amelia's tear-stained face was all it took to agree to something so ridiculous. "Okay, you go into the room. I'll stay out here as the lookout."

After all, Connor had done way more dangerous missions than this in enemy combat zones. In fact, he was the third wheel in this situation. His role was secondary to Amelia's actual father's. How bad could it be?

"Can you say that again, Peanut?" Dahlia asked her daughter, thinking the cell phone might've cut out. "Where's Daddy?"

"The deputy put him in the back of the police car."

Dahlia's stomach dropped. "What deputy?"

"The deputy that Uncle MJ punched."

Oh, hell. Dahlia needed to go get Marcus. She walked out the door of her hotel room and, trying to keep her daughter talking, asked, "What are you doing right now?"

"Eating an ice cream with Keyshawn. Did you know he lives next door to Peyton's dad's house?"

Dahlia had to breathe through her nose. "Why are you at the Fredricksons' house?"

"I'm not. I'm in the truck. No, Goatee, dogs can't have chocolate ice cream."

Dahlia stopped in the middle of the long hallway between her and Marcus's room. "Goatee is with you?"

"Yeah, he got in the car when we picked Connor up."

They picked Connor up? What in the world was going on? "Can you put Connor on the phone?"

"I don't think he can talk right now."

"Why not?"

"'Cause he's in the front seat of the police car."

"Oh, my gosh," Dahlia said, then caught herself. *Stay calm.* "Amelia, I need you to tell me what happened."

"Nothing really. We just came to get—" The call cut out for a second. When her daughter's voice returned to the line she heard "...that's all."

It sounded like a lot more was going on. "Is Keyshawn still there with you? Can I talk to him at least?"

"Hold on a second," Amelia told her, then forgot to move the phone away from her mouth before yelling, "Hey, Keyshawn! My mommy wants to know if you can come talk to her." There was a pause and then Amelia said, "He said he'll be right over when he finishes giving his witness statement."

Dahlia slid down the wall of the hotel hallway until she was sitting on the plush carpeting. Thankfully, Marcus came out of his room at that exact second and saw her. "Dia! I was just coming to find you."

"Keep eating your ice cream, Peanut. I'm going to stay here on the phone with you and wait," she told her daughter in the calmest voice she could muster. Then she covered the mouthpiece on her phone and asked her oldest brother, "What in the hell is going on back in Teton Ridge?"

"Apparently, Micah was breaking into Jay Grover's house with the intent to remove an item from the premises. Connor was in the front yard, acting as the lookout."

"Wait, back up. They took Amelia with them? My daughter was an accomplice to a burglary and my truck was the escape vehicle? I knew I shouldn't have left. Please tell me Jay wasn't there. The last thing I need is for that guy to try to sue me."

"They're still getting witness statements, but it sounds like Amelia wanted to let Goatee out of the car to pee. Then Amelia had to pee, so Connor walked her over to the Fredricksons' and asked if she could use their restroom." Marcus put his hand over his mouth and his shoulders shook several times before he could continue.

Dahlia wanted to shake her brother by the front of his shirt. "I'm glad you think this is funny."

"No, no. It gets better." His mouth twitched several times and he had to look away briefly. "So Amelia had just gone inside the Fredricksons' to use the bathroom when Connor heard Jay's truck coming down the street. He tried to run back to the house to give Micah the signal, but Micah had gone in the wrong room and was wandering around the house in search of a—" Marcus paused to wipe the back of his hand across his eyes, but the tears of laughter were already escaping "—a panda bear. Apparently, they'd broken into Jay's house to steal a stuffed animal."

Dahlia gasped. "Not Andy Pandy?"

"That'd be the one. When Jay pulled up, Connor tried to waylay him in the yard so Micah could make his escape. Except Micah, not knowing Jay had returned, throws the panda out the window and it lands in the boxwood shrubs below. According to witnesses—"

"Oh, great. There's witnesses?"

"Whole damn block. At this point, Jay starts yelling, 'Thieves, thieves,' at the top of his lungs and races to the bushes. Connor is faster, though, and beats him there, getting the bear first. Jay attempts to sucker punch Connor, but his fist glances off his cheek. So Connor returns the hit and lays Jay flat. Now Jay is out for the count and Micah is trying to shimmy himself down the trellis, but he only has one good hand so he slips right before he lands in the bushes by Jay. His elbow lands in Jay's solar plexus, which wakes the man up and he starts yelling again and raising holy hell. Broman and a junior deputy are now on scene and an ambulance is there on standby."

"So did Amelia see any of it?" Dahlia asked and didn't realize she'd dropped her hand from the mouthpiece of the phone until she heard her daughter's response.

"No, me and Goatee missed the whole thing 'cause the Fredricksons have a cat and Goatee wanted to chase it. Mr. Freddie said that maybe Goatee should sit in the truck and give his cat a break, so he gave me an ice cream and asked Keyshawn to watch me until the policemen decide what to do with Daddy and Connor. Oh, here they come now. And they have Andy Pandy with them!"

"Here, you better talk to them." Dahlia passed the phone to Marcus. "I don't trust myself not to completely lose my cool, and my daughter doesn't need to hear that."

She rubbed her temples as her brother spoke to her ex-husband, wincing every time he'd have to pause to recover from his sudden bouts of laughter. When he hung up, he told Dahlia, "Everyone is fine. Micah's taking Connor home and then he and Amelia will head straight to Twin Kings."

"Thank God." Dahlia sagged against the wall. "I can't believe Broman didn't arrest them."

"Oh, he still plans on it. But I told him to hold off on filing the official charges until we get back. Mom will kill you if you leave early and ruin her surprise for Tessa tomorrow."

CHAPTER THIRTEEN

DAHLIA STOOD OUTSIDE the county courthouse steps on Monday morning when Connor and Micah came out of the adjacent sheriff's building.

Connor's lips were pressed in a firm line, looking suitably embarrassed by the whole affair. As he should. However, Micah had the audacity to smile and wave at her. "Thanks for posting bail for us, Dia."

"I didn't do it for you. I did it so my daughter doesn't have to come visit you guys behind bars. Can you even imagine how awful a jailhouse visit is for a kid?" As soon as she saw Connor flinch, she knew she'd said the wrong thing. "Oh, my gosh, Connor. I'm so sorry. Of course you know exactly what that would be like."

"You're only speaking the truth." Connor rubbed the back of his neck. "Funny thing is I spent my whole life trying not to be like my dad and the one time I actually do something I think is fatherly, this happens. I promise, Dahlia, I'm not the kind of guy who normally gets into brawls and gets arrested."

"Technically, you weren't arrested. You just had to appear

for an arraignment and then post bond," Violet Cortez-Hill said as she broke away from where she'd been huddled in discussion with the district attorney. "And you didn't get charged with the battery since all the witness statements reflected that you acted in self-defense."

"Thank God for that," Dahlia said, not only relieved but also touched by his admission that he felt "fatherly" toward her daughter. "I appreciate you always wanting to do what's best for Amelia, but what were you guys thinking? Now you have a burglary charge on your record."

Micah raised his bandaged hand. "I'm the one with the burglary charge. Connor just got accessory to burglary. For a former military scout, you're a real crappy lookout, man."

"I was taking your daughter to the bathroom. Besides, I told you which window to go in and you picked the wrong—"

"Hey," Violet quickly cut off Connor. "The DA is going to be walking by any second. Let's not admit to the crime in front of him, shall we?"

Marcus came out the door marked Sheriff, took one look at Violet, then almost turned around and went back inside. Then he saw Dahlia and asked, "Seriously, Dia? You hired my ex-girlfriend as their defense attorney, too? Is my entire family suddenly getting a group rate?"

"Good morning, Sheriff." Violet's smile was so bright and taunting that Dahlia nearly laughed. "I was on my way to your office next to ask you about the alleged victim in my clients' case. Jay Grover?"

"What about him?"

"A little birdie told me that Mr. Grover was doing a little breaking and entering of his own right before he confronted my clients and accosted one of them."

"Is it considered an accost if he couldn't even land the punch?" Micah asked Connor, who lifted one shoulder.

Marcus didn't bother looking in their direction he was so

focused on his ex-girlfriend. "Does this little birdie happen to work in my office?"

"You know I won't reveal my sources. But I've already gotten the DA to agree to reduce the charges from burglary to trespassing. As soon as he watches the video footage I obtained of his star witness, I have a feeling Mr. Grover is going to be so embarrassed, he'll want to drop the charges altogether."

"She's good," Micah said to Marcus, who only clenched his jaw tighter. "Violet, any chance you do contract negotiations?"

"As mind-numbingly boring as that sounds," Violet replied to Micah despite the fact that her eyes were locked onto Marcus's stern face. "I've got a big case coming up this week and need to get through that before I can focus on my next career path."

"That's right. MJ's trial starts in a few days. Are you going to be at the family dinner tomorrow, then?" Micah asked, and Connor's eyes immediately shot to Dahlia's.

"Probably not," Marcus said at the same time Violet nodded and said, "Yes, I'm bringing a pie from Burnworth's."

After a couple more seconds of intense glaring, her brother stomped back to his office and Violet headed down the steps.

"Okay, then I'll catch everyone there," Micah said more to himself before addressing Dahlia and Connor. "I've got to run to my physical therapy appointment, but I should be done in time to grab Amelia after school. I'll call you."

And just like that, Dahlia and Connor were left standing alone on the courthouse steps. If he was going to tell her that he needed a break from her and all the trouble she and her family had caused him, now would be an opportune time. She swayed slightly before bracing herself for the inevitable.

"So you've got a big family dinner going on?" he asked, catching her off guard.

"Oh. Um. Yeah. My mom has this annoying PR person who wants us all to meet before MJ's hearing so we can best plan our strategy for a public show of support. Duke flew back with us from DC and invited Micah to stay on at the ranch. They were friends all through school and the best men at each other's weddings."

"You mean the wedding to you?"

Maybe Dahlia shouldn't have reminded him of that fact. But the past was there. It happened. She couldn't erase it. "Yes, Micah's wedding to me. The one we had before we got a divorce. Is that a problem for you?"

"I want to say it is. I even want to be jealous of the guy or find something to dislike about him. But I can't. It just might take me some time to get used to it, I guess."

An unexpected and very tiny drop of hope blossomed inside her. "I don't know if any of us will get used to it. I know you've been pulling away lately and I'm not sure if it's because of your own stuff you have going on. Or if it's because the attraction isn't there anymore..." She paused, letting her words hang in the air in the hopes that he'd fill in the rest for her.

Connor's head shook firmly. "It's definitely not because of you."

That blossom of hope got a little bigger before she realized that he hadn't denied the fact that he'd been pulling away. Dahlia was too invested at this point, though, to keep fishing for answers. Seeing Tessa and Grayson find their own happiness this weekend was all the encouragement Dahlia needed to be like her strong female ancestors and take matters into her own hands.

"Then it must be because of the situation," she said with more confidence than she felt. "If it's weird for you to be around my ex, I get it. I probably wouldn't enjoy being around your ex, either. But if you truly do want to give things a shot between us, then it's something you're going to have to get used to. And there's nothing like a King family dinner to get your feet wet."

For the first time in several days, she finally got a genuine smile out of the man. "Is that an invite?"

She leaned up on her toes and dropped a light kiss on his lips. "No, it's a warning. If you still want to run after that, then I won't stop you."

* * *

Connor sat in the living room at the main house on the Twin Kings Ranch, trying not to feel like the wannabe cowboy that Amelia had adopted like one of her strays. But everyone in this room had known each other for decades and he was clearly the newcomer. He would've been way more comfortable eating in the bunkhouse with the rest of the ranch hands, or even in the kitchen with Freckles as she finished cooking the dinner that Sherilee King was already complaining about.

The condensation on his glass of iced tea dripped down his hand before splattering on his jeans. He would've set it down on the end table beside his silk upholstered chair, but the wood finish probably cost more than his last pay stub.

Dahlia threw him the occasional smile, but she was sitting with Violet, Finn and Tessa, all looking overwhelmed at the stack of glossy bridal magazines Mrs. King had just dropped in front of them. Marcus and Grayson, the Secret Service agent who was now engaged to Tessa, were discussing law-enforcement training tactics. That conversation might've been more appealing to join if Connor wasn't awaiting a possible trial for trespassing and hoping not to draw any more attention to his potential criminal record. Duke and Micah were discussing their glory days playing high school football, and though Connor had played kick returner on his own varsity team, he didn't know most of the names they were referencing.

Normally, Amelia was the one who put him at ease in big situations like this, keeping him talking by asking him a million questions a minute. But she'd gone out for a ride on her pony with Rider and Marcus's twin boys. Connor had been tempted to join them, but then it might seem as though he were steering clear of Micah or running away from interacting with Dahlia's overwhelming family.

And Dahlia was right. If he wanted to be in a relationship with her, he'd have to eventually learn to deal with all of this. For years, this was the exact type of emotional attachment he'd been trying to avoid. Yet, now, he found himself wanting the one thing he'd always wanted as a child. A family.

He was also on the edge of losing it, though.

"I'm gonna go check and see if Rider and the kids are back yet," Micah told Duke before leaving Connor sitting alone by everyone's favorite King sibling.

"It's a lot to take in, huh?" Duke's voice was calm and knowing. "Even for someone who used to be Special Forces and probably saw a lot of action on his deployments."

"Am I that obvious?" Connor asked.

"If it makes you feel any better, Grayson over there was once a sniper on the Counter Assault Team. After nearly a month of being assigned to Twin Kings full-time and getting the full vetting and approval of my eagle-eyed mother, he still can't stop peeling the wrapper off that beer in his hand."

The words were probably supposed to be comforting, but only put Connor slightly more ill at ease. "So, you're saying it won't get any easier?"

"Nah, it'll definitely get easier. Tom does just fine with all the chaos and drama. Of course, he has ten brothers and sisters of his own, so he's used to it."

"Ten? Wow. I was an only child."

"I know. I saw the briefing file in the Secret Service bunkhouse."

Connor gulped. "They have a file on me? Already?"

"Don't worry. It's pretty basic. They screen everyone who comes in and out of the Twin Kings. Once MJ's hearing wraps up, though, they'll be shutting down their operation and returning to DC."

That's right. Dahlia had explained to Connor that after the vice president's funeral, a few agents had stayed on at the ranch due to Tessa's recent media storm and MJ's arrest. Now that the new vice president was sworn in, though, the protective detail would be reassigned.

"I'm sorry to hear about your father, by the way," Connor offered. "He once visited the troops when I was still a grunt stationed at Camp Dwyer and he was larger than life. I didn't even know he was from this part of Wyoming before I moved here."

Duke's pleasant smile slipped and his brief nod was his only acknowledgment of the condolences. Damn. Maybe Connor shouldn't have brought that up. And here he thought he was doing so well and finally relaxing a bit.

Before he could change the subject, Micah burst into the room. "Hey, Rider and the kids aren't back yet. Mike Truong expected them over thirty minutes ago."

Dahlia sprang to her feet and, instead of running to her ex-husband, she turned her wide pleading eyes to Connor. He walked to her and kissed her temple. "I'll go looking for them."

"We'll all come," Finn said, but Connor was already heading out the door.

Mike had two trail horses saddled and was buckling a bridle onto a third.

"Do you know what direction they went in?" Connor asked the foreman.

"They took off toward the west, but the trail forks several ways from there. Two of the agents went out in an ATV, but there's a number of paths out there that are way too narrow for anything but horses."

"Can I take this one?" Connor pointed at the pale palomino whose saddlebags were already packed.

"She's all yours. Grab one of the red first-aid backpacks and a walkie-talkie from the tack room. They should all be charged."

Connor already had his foot in the stirrup when Finn grabbed his horse's bridle. He expected Dahlia's twin to question him about his abilities. Instead, she said, "Stick to the area south of the main trail. I'll take the north side. Hopefully, Rider kept everyone together."

Connor hadn't been past the stables on his prior visits to the Twin Kings, but he set the palomino on a dead run along the dirt road heading west. A two-seater ATV raced past him and he saw

Marcus and Micah inside. Maybe they should've formed a better plan or at least assigned designated search areas so they weren't all covering the same areas. But it was an eighty-year-old man and three kids on ponies. How far could they have gone?

The Twin Kings was a working cattle ranch and it hadn't rained in at least two weeks, so there were hoofprints everywhere he looked. But as he passed a smaller trail, he noticed a different set of prints. Rabbit. Several sets, including two tiny ones that likely belonged to a couple of babies. And they were relatively fresh. If Amelia had seen the bunnies, there was no doubt she'd followed.

Connor slowed the horse and scanned the shrubs and overgrown grass surrounding the trail for more clues. Then he saw it. One random leaf on a sagebrush had a damp dark spot on it. Keeping the reins in his hands, he slipped off the horse to get a closer look. His nose knew what it was before his eyes did. Chewing tobacco. Rider once offered him a dip when they were in the stables. He said he never chewed in front of Freckles or Sherilee and could only sneak it when he was out of the house.

Getting back into the saddle, Connor followed the trail as it narrowed. The sun had already gone down behind the Teton Mountain Range in the distance and there would only be about fifteen more minutes of natural light before he'd start wishing for his old pair of military-issued night-vision goggles.

After a quarter of a mile, he saw the thin trail again split into two smaller paths. There was a scrap of pink fabric sticking out of a rotted stump just past the fork, but Connor knew Amelia never wore pink. In fact, today she'd been wearing a beige long-sleeved sweatshirt with the bright green Australia Zoo logo on the front. Using his heels to nudge the horse's sides, he continued down the opposite path. He paused briefly at a creek, but didn't cross. He remembered Amelia telling him that Gray Goose, the pony Amelia had likely been riding, hated water and refused to set foot in it. Instead, Connor followed the river rocks along the creek bed north before finding a rabbit den.

Bingo. There were three sets of smaller pony-sized tracks in the dirt near the burrowed entrance. A few feet back were a set of larger horse prints; the hoof marks were sunk deeper into the ground and likely the result of Rider's heavier weight. So, the group had probably followed the bunnies here, but then where'd they go?

His radio crackled to life and he held his breath, hoping someone had found them. But it was Duke advising them that the rescue helicopter from the nearby airfield had just landed at the King's helipad and he and Dahlia would be flying overhead with a search light.

Just thinking about the terror on Dahlia's face back in the living room made Connor pick up speed.

After at least five more minutes, the walkie-talkie again sounded and he heard Finn say, "I have the boys. They were southwest of the Peabody Trail. They're tired and thirsty, but still in their saddles."

Relief washed over Connor before quickly fizzling out. Two people were still missing.

"Where's Amelia?" Micah demanded, the engine of his ATV revving in the background of the radio transmission.

"The boys say Rider got hurt and couldn't ride," Finn advised. "Amelia stayed to watch over him while the boys rode back to the stables to get help. But they got lost."

"Do they know where they left Amelia and Rider?" Dahlia asked over the radio and Connor could hear the strain in her voice. Determination kept him moving forward.

"Negative," Finn said. "I'll get these two back to Violet at the main house. You guys keep looking."

Connor wanted to relay his position and update them with what he'd found so far. But he didn't want to give anyone false hope. Of course, he only had a couple more minutes before he was going to need that search light. He held the walkie-talkie up to his mouth and just as he depressed the button, he heard something behind a wall of fir trees.

Was that…? A shot of adrenaline spiked through his already tense muscles and he tried to listen over the pounding of his heart.

He took a few more steps, then heard Amelia's voice clear as day. "Miss Walker said her Paw Paw once had a heart attack and it felt like a herd of buffalo were stomping around on his chest."

Connor charged through a narrow opening in the branches covered in pine needles just in time to hear Rider groan. "Right now, it feels like a herd of buffalo are stomping around my ears, Peanut. Do you think you could ask a few less—"

"Connor!" Amelia cried and ran straight for him. He was off the horse just in time to catch her jumping into his arms. Relief pulsed through him, causing him to crush her against his chest as he fought back the tears of joy. Amelia giggled, then squirmed until he loosened his hold. "I knew you'd find us, Connor. I told Uncle Rider you're the best tracker there is. Didn't I tell you, Uncle Rider?"

Connor's eyes fell to the older man who was sprawled out on the cold ground, his head propped up under a saddle blanket. "You sure did, Peanut. About a million times."

He carried the girl over to Rider and knelt down. "What happened?"

"Horse got spooked by a damn lizard of all things and reared back. When he came down, I lost my balance and landed on that boulder over there. I think I busted one of my ribs," the older man said, and even in the growing darkness, Connor could see that his face was nearly white under that bushy gray mustache. His breathing was definitely strained. "I used to break a different one every month back in my bull-riding days and then get back in the saddle. I should be fine as soon as I catch my breath."

Rider tried to sit up and cursed.

"Take it easy. There's already a rescue helicopter en route. You should probably keep still until a medic can check you out." Connor reached for the radio clipped to the back of his belt. "I've got Amelia and Rider," he relayed and could only imagine the cries of relief on the end. "Amelia is doing great and Rider is alert and feisty as hell. But he's going to need a medic and possible transport."

Connor transmitted their GPS coordinates, then went to his saddle to get the first-aid bag. He wrapped Amelia in his jacket before tearing open the emergency blanket to throw over Rider in case he went into shock.

Someone had already secured the reins of Gray Goose and Rider's stallion to a nearby branch, but judging by the loose knots, it had been one of the kids. Connor tightened them just as the helicopter made its first pass over the area.

"We're down here!" Amelia jumped up and down, waving as if she were on a parade float, having the time of her life. "We're down here!"

The headlights of the ATV with Marcus and Micah came crashing through a line in the fir trees on the opposite trail just as the helicopter began its descent. Micah was using his good hand to yank the harness-like straps off him as he climbed out of the off-road vehicle.

"Daddy!" Amelia cried with the same level of excitement she'd had when Connor first found them. Then she leaped up into her father's arms to hug him. And the weird thing was, Connor wasn't the least bit envious. In fact, seeing the raw emotion and relief on Micah's face almost made him tear up. Micah might share DNA with the girl, but there had been nothing less intense about Connor's own response just a few minutes ago. It was almost as though he were watching himself, reliving that same adrenaline rush and feeling of euphoria.

Then Micah made the moment even more emotional by turning toward Connor and pulling him into the embrace, as well.

"Thank you for finding her, man," Micah said, his voice scratchy and almost trembling. "I was so damn scared."

"Me, too," Connor admitted, patting Micah on the back. "But we've got her now."

"Okay, you two," Rider huffed as Marcus checked his pulse.

"Don't make it all about yourselves. Leave some drama for everyone else."

"Mommy!" Amelia said, wiggling out of their arms before running toward Dahlia who'd had to make her way to them from the open clearing where the helicopter landed. "Connor found us."

"I know, Peanut." Dahlia dropped to her knees as she squeezed Amelia to her. There were tears in her eyes and when she lifted her face to Connor's, it was probably the most beautiful sight he'd ever seen in his life. "I'm so proud of him."

"Maybe we should buy him a muffin tomorrow to thank him," Amelia suggested.

Dahlia threw back her head, her laugh throaty and raw. When she made eye contact with Connor again, there was a fierce determination that sent heat ricocheting through him. "Oh, I think I owe Connor a lot more than a muffin."

"Come on. Now it's *really* getting dramatic," Rider said before passing out.

Dahlia sat on a sofa in the hospital waiting room with Amelia asleep on her lap, the rest of her family surrounding her as they argued among themselves. Freckles and Sherilee exchanged insults. Micah and Finn exchanged dirty looks. MJ and Tessa exchanged conflicting viewpoints about politics (although, it was honestly refreshing to see her baby brother get fired up about anything since he'd been so sullen and despondent lately). And Duke's frown and jabbing thumbs on his phone keypad suggested he was exchanging angry texts with someone. In fact, the only family members who weren't currently arguing in her presence were Marcus and Violet, but that was because they were together in the emergency room, likely arguing about what color of cast Jordan should get on his arm.

But tonight none of that bothered Dahlia in the least because she had her baby girl safe and sound in her arms.

The bickering stopped long enough for Grayson and Connor to carry in a tray full of coffees in to-go cups.

"Which one is the sugar-free hazelnut soy latte?" her mom asked. Dahlia almost giggled at the way Connor and Grayson stared helplessly at each other, neither one wanting to be the one to tell the formidable Sherilee King that they'd failed in their mission.

"You think there's a fancy espresso bar nearby open this time of night?" Freckles's plastic bangle bracelets jingled as she reached for the nearest cup. "They're from a vending machine downstairs, Sherilee. Stop being such a snob and thank your future son-in-laws for their efforts."

"Well, the cease fire was nice while it lasted," Dahlia sighed, then shifted Amelia's feet off the cushion so Connor could return to his seat beside them.

Connor leaned closer and asked, "Did your aunt just say son-in-*laws*? Plural?"

"Yep," Dahlia said. "And you didn't correct her. So now everyone is going to have expectations about the future of our relationship. If that doesn't scare you, ask Grayson what it's like having Sherilee King and Aunt Freckles plan and orchestrate your engagement and wedding."

"I don't know. Grayson seems pretty happy with Tessa if you ask me." Connor rested his arm along the back of the sofa. "Besides, I don't care about anyone else's expectations or plans for me. I only care about yours."

Two doctors in blue surgical scrubs kept Dahlia from having to answer.

"Mr. King is out of surgery and stabilized," the doctor spoke to the entire room. "One of the broken ribs punctured his lung, so we have him in ICU to keep a close eye on him. Only one of you can go back at a time to visit."

Freckles rose from her chair and nobody else even bothered standing up or objected to her going first.

"That." Dahlia lifted her chin at Freckles as the older woman quietly followed the surgeons down the stark white hallway alone. Then she faced Connor. "That's what I expect. I want you to be my Freckles. She's not related to any of us by blood—or even marriage, legally—and she and my mother can barely stand each other. But when it comes to Rider, there's no question that she's the one who is going to go to him first. I want you to be the person I call when my whole world gets thrown for a loop. I want you to be the one I turn to when my daughter doesn't come back on her pony or when I have to find a way to explain to her that we can't take on another stray. I purposely built my life here in Teton Ridge because I wanted to keep things simple. I wanted to keep my daughter's life simple, away from the spotlight that I grew up in. But there is nothing simple about Amelia. There's certainly nothing simple about being a King. My family is messy and my life is complicated, no matter how straightforward I try to make it."

"Your family is just a tiny bit messy," he said before kissing her forehead. "And your life doesn't seem all that complicated to me."

"Connor. I'm a single mom who owns a bar in a former brothel."

"Well, I'm potentially a convicted felon and an alleged goat roper who owns a ranch that is barely turning a profit."

"Trespassing isn't a felony," Micah said out of nowhere, and Finn sent him a sharp elbow to his rib cage.

Dahlia rolled her eyes. "I also have an ex-husband who married the wrong twin and a daughter that will tell everybody anything that pops into her mind and only stops talking when she's sound asleep."

"I have a dog with codependency issues and a psychotic turkey I bought to impress the woman I love and her daughter."

"Goatee isn't codependent, he just… Wait." Dahlia's knees went wobbly and Amelia almost slid from her lap. "Did you just say you love me?"

"Of course, I love you. I know you have a lot going on and

you were hoping to get me out of your system so we could go back to being friends. But I want to be your Rider, Dahlia King Deacon. I want to be the one you turn to first. Whether it's finding your lost daughter or finding a missing panda bear, I want to live in that complicated, messy world with you and enjoy every second of it together."

Then he kissed her, right there under the harsh fluorescent lights of the hospital waiting room with all of her family members looking on. His hands cupped the sides of her face as his lips sealed his commitment. When he pulled away, Dahlia's insides spiraled with a dizzying happiness that threatened to lift her out of her seat.

Pressing her forehead against his to keep her soaring emotions in place, Dahlia smiled. "I love you, too, Connor Remington."

The waiting room at the Ridgecrest County Hospital clearly wasn't the way Connor had envisioned hearing Dahlia utter those words to him. In fact, twenty-four hours ago, he'd doubted that he'd ever hear them at all. But when she declared her love for him, he knew that he couldn't go another day of his life without hearing them again.

Amelia lifted her head drowsily, her eyes still half-shut. "What's going on? Are we having a party?"

"Not yet," Sherilee King told her granddaughter. "But we're going to when your mom and Connor get married."

"Mom!" all five King siblings in the room yelled at once.

"They barely told each other *I love you*," Finn chastised her mother. "Why don't you give them a little time to get used to the feeling before you have them walking down the aisle. Especially before you say something in front of you-know-who."

Dahlia's twin gave a not-so-subtle pointed look at Amelia, who just shrugged. "I already know they're gonna get married."

Connor brushed the child's hair out of her face. "How'd you know that?"

"Grandma Millie told me."

"You mean the scary old lady in the painting above our fireplace?" MJ asked, the look of disbelief on his face matching everyone else's in the room. "She told you this?"

"Yeah. She talks to me all the time. I'm named after her, you know."

Dahlia's eyebrows slammed together. "Peanut, Grandma Millie passed away a long time ago. Before I was even born."

"I know. Uncle Rider says she talks to him, too. He heard her tell me to find a good one for my Mommy. So I did."

Connor had never believed in the supernatural, but his very first conversation with Rider King came floating back to his mind and sent a shiver down his back.

"Did she say anything else?" MJ asked. "Like if the judge was going to find me guilty?"

Amelia scrunched her nose and forehead. "I don't think so. But she did say Uncle Marcus was too sad all the time and that Uncle Duke needed to be more trusting."

Duke's head jerked up. "What does *that* mean?"

"I don't know." Amelia shrugged. "Ask Uncle Rider. Oh, I almost forgot. She also said Aunt Finn was being way too mean to Daddy."

"Ha!" Micah shouted triumphantly.

"I am *not* mean to your father," Finn argued just as loudly.

"She didn't even mention me?" Sherilee King asked. "I'm the one who's had to live with her up on my fireplace for over thirty years, staring down her judgy nose at me."

Then Tessa asked Duke who he didn't trust, and as several arguments broke out around them, Dahlia put her head on Connor's shoulder. "Remember when you said my family wasn't messy?"

"I think I admitted they were a little bit messy."

"Was that before or after you found out my daughter talks to my dead ancestors and tells fortunes?"

"You know, the first time I ever met your uncle Rider, he

said that Amelia would tell you when you found the right one. I thought he was crazy at the time, and I'm still not convinced he isn't. But maybe Amelia's onto something."

"Did I find you or did you find me?" she asked, a smile playing at the corners of her lips.

Connor kissed her tenderly, then said, "I'm pretty sure we found each other."

Amelia snuggled in between them and nodded to the duffel bag under Micah's feet, which the man kept shushing every time a scruffy white head popped out. "And me and Goatee found two daddies."

* * * * *

Hill Country Cupid
Tanya Michaels

Dear Reader,

As a writer, I always enjoy sharing my stories—but some projects are even more fun than others! I particularly love this Valentine collection because I'm being included with fantastic author Jane Porter and because I got to create a happy ending for Tess Fitzpatrick (one of my favorite secondary characters from my Hill Country Heroes series).

Ballet instructor Tess Fitzpatrick has never been able to resist meddling for a good cause. Single father Nick Calhoun devotes all his time to raising his six-year-old daughter, Bailey, and working on his family's ranch. He leaves the dating scene to his more outgoing brothers. But Tess knows just how much Bailey wants a mom and can't understand why more women haven't noticed how hot Nick is. When she decides to play matchmaker for the quiet cowboy, plans quickly go awry—especially when Nick realizes who he really wants as his Valentine.

Happy reading,

Tanya

My heartfelt thanks to all the wonderful readers
who've let me know how much they enjoy the
Hill Country Heroes series.

CHAPTER ONE

ALTHOUGH IT HAD taken years—and repeated motherly lectures—for Tess Fitzpatrick to accept that she'd never be a prima ballerina, she had to admit she loved her life. She enjoyed her career as a dance instructor at the small studio, and she adored her students. Unlike people trapped in offices, watching their computer clocks and counting the minutes until they could go home, Tess was actually a bit disappointed to be ending the day's lessons. She was in no real hurry to go home and eat dinner by herself. But parents were waiting on the other side of the large observation window.

"Class dismissed," Tess told the roomful of bubbly kindergarten-aged girls. Several of them, including star pupil Josie Winchester, ran up to hug Tess before exiting into the lobby.

There was a flurry of activity as students exchanged tap shoes for sneakers and mothers bundled kids into coats to ward off the late January chill. Within moments, the crowd had dwindled to single mom Farrah Landon, texting while she waited for her daughter to emerge from the restroom, and six-year-old

Bailey Calhoun, who sat in a folding metal chair with a glum expression.

Was the girl disappointed not to be chosen as a soloist? Several classes were combining to put on a special performance for parents during the studio's upcoming Valentine's party at the high school. Bailey had been in consideration for a part that ultimately went to Josie Winchester. It was a minor role in a brief presentation, but Tess understood the sting of being passed over for a chance at the spotlight.

She pulled a piece of chocolate from the jar she kept on the reception desk and went to Bailey's side. "Nice job today." She held out the candy. "I was impressed with how quickly you picked up the new combo steps."

"Thanks, Miss Tess." But neither the chocolate nor the compliment garnered a smile.

Tess ruffled the girl's dark hair. "I'm sure your dad will be here any minute."

Sure enough, the door swung open and in walked Nick Calhoun, Tess's favorite of the three Calhoun brothers. She was used to seeing him in the jeans and boots appropriate for outdoor work at his family's horse ranch, but today he wore a suit. He would have looked downright dashing if he hadn't seemed so ill at ease. As he walked, he tugged his tie loose.

"Daddy!" Bailey's face lit up like the annual Fourth of July fireworks.

Nick looked equally happy to see his daughter, affection obvious in his clear gray eyes. "Sorry I'm late, Bay." He was making a beeline toward them when he drew up short, belatedly noticing blond, willowy Farrah. "Hi."

"Hey, Rick," she said absently, not glancing up from her cell phone.

"Um, Nick. Nick Calhoun?"

That got her attention. "Oh, right! Your brother is Wyatt Calhoun."

He nodded.

"Tell him Farrah Landon said hi." She dropped her voice to a not-quite-whisper as her daughter returned to the lobby. "And remind him that I got divorced last year."

Platinum-haired mother and child exited the studio as Nick waved halfheartedly in their wake. Then he whipped his head around, features flushed. Was he feeling guilty that he'd gotten sidetracked en route to his daughter or was he embarrassed to be caught watching Farrah?

He closed the distance between himself and Bailey, scooping her into his arms as if she weighed nothing, then apologized to Tess. "I had a meeting that took longer than expected."

"Not a problem." She grinned. "I'm guessing from the fancy duds it was important?"

"Discussing some plans for expansion with a loan officer. Dad should have sent Wyatt or Kevin. My brothers are better with…people." His self-deprecating tone made Tess wonder if the loan officer was a woman. Nick darted a glance over his shoulder, in the direction Farrah and her daughter had gone, and sighed. Then he shook his head, smiling once again at his daughter. "You hungry?"

"Starving!"

"Guess we'd better track you down some dinner before you waste away to nothing," he teased.

They were headed for the door when Bailey suddenly swiveled around. "Miss Tess? Did I really do good today?"

"Didn't I say so?" Tess winked at the little girl. "I never say anything I don't mean."

Once the studio was empty, Tess used the time to finalize the choreography for the Valentine's performance. As she locked up for the night, she recalled Nick's wistful expression. No secret who he wanted for his valentine. But Farrah had seemed oblivious. It didn't look as if Nick had a shot—although this *was* the season for romance. Maybe Cupid would decide to intervene on his behalf.

* * *

Tess silently chanted positive thoughts as she entered the bridal boutique Saturday morning. *I am excited for my friend. I am happy for my friend.* After all, it had been Tess who encouraged Lorelei Keller to get romantically involved with Sam Travis in the first place. Tess was thrilled Sam and Lorelei were getting married during Frederick-Fest, the weeklong event that had helped bring them together last spring. So what if their March wedding meant Tess would be wearing her third bridesmaid dress in two years? Prior to this, she'd been in the bridal party for her elegant, swanlike sister, Regina, as well as newly married Heather Winchester.

"Tess! You're here!" Lorelei, not typically a hugger, rushed forward to embrace her. Then she drew back, abashed. "Sorry, didn't mean to tackle you."

"No problem. It's nice to feel so welcome," Tess quipped.

"I couldn't do this without you! You'd think such a small wedding would be easier to manage." Since neither bride nor groom had much family, the ceremony would be an intimate affair in the heart of town with Tess as maid of honor and an old rodeo buddy of Sam's as best man. The reception afterward would be held at the B and B Lorelei and Sam ran together.

Lorelei's dark eyes shimmered with unshed tears. "Usually, I'm great with details, but I'm turning into an emotional basket case. I miss Mom."

The one-year anniversary of Wanda Keller's death was only a couple of weeks away; as much as Tess's own family drove her nuts, she couldn't imagine getting married without either of her parents being alive to see it. "Wanda would have been so happy for you," Tess said. "You know how she adored Sam."

Lorelei nodded. "We've been trying to decide how to honor her during the ceremony. One of her friends suggested I wear Mom's 'lucky pig' jewelry, but I'm not sold on the idea."

Tess chuckled at the mental image of whimsical pigs paired

with her friend's simple strapless gown. "Don't worry, you still have a month to brainstorm."

The two women joined the boutique manager, who led them to luxurious changing rooms for their fittings. Of all the bridesmaid dresses Tess had worn so far, the deep red gown Lorelei had picked was her favorite. There was something about the cut that made Tess feel taller (she'd always been dwarfed by her lithe mother and sister) and the cleavage revealed by the scooped neckline was flattering. She looked curvy rather than chubby. Tess wasn't exactly overweight—not by more than five or ten pounds—but she was by far the most solidly built of the Fitzpatrick women.

Slender Lorelei was even taller than Tess's sister. Tess dreaded the wedding photos of the bride and maid of honor alone. *Vera Wang Meets Abbott and Costello.* Maybe Tess could lose a few pounds before the ceremony. And wear very high heels.

Through the partition separating them, she called to Lorelei, "You have a great eye for color." Conventional wisdom suggested the red might clash with Tess's hair, but the color was so dark it somehow toned down her curls, making them appear more burnished-gold than orange. "This dress is terrific."

A few minutes later, Tess breathed, "I stand corrected. *That* dress is terrific." Lorelei stood on a dais while the seamstress checked her hem. The bride-to-be looked phenomenal, her dark hair and eyes a dramatic contrast to the beaded white dress. "Sam is one lucky guy."

Lorelei grinned wryly. "Yeah, if you overlook the fact that he's saddling himself with an increasingly unstable woman and her demon cat." There had been jokes about putting a little pouch around Oberon's feline neck and letting him be the ring bearer, but Sam had insisted the temperamental pet would get revenge.

After they'd changed back into their regular clothes, Tess invited her friend to lunch. "I'm craving The Twisted Jalapeño. Wanna join me?"

"I never pass up an opportunity to eat Grace's food! And the menu's gotten even more amazing since she partnered with that hunky co-owner. Should I follow you, or do you want to ride together?"

They decided it would be more fun to go in the same car and come back for Lorelei's. As Tess drove, they discussed business at the ballet studio, recent movies and Valentine's Day being only a few weeks away. Since their romantic B and B was a popular destination for lovers, Lorelei and Sam would be working over the holiday but planned to make up the time over their honeymoon. For her part, Tess figured she'd stick with the tradition of attending the big town Valentine dance.

Discussing the romantic holiday made Tess think of Nick and his yearning expression yesterday evening. "Hey, Lor, wouldn't you say Nick Calhoun is attractive?"

Lorelei looked at her blankly from the passenger seat. "Who?"

"I forgot, the only man you ever notice is the one you're engaged to," Tess teased. "He's the youngest of the three Calhoun brothers. You know, the family who owns the Galloping C Ranch?"

"Oh, right. Sam's done some work for them." Lorelei straightened in her seat. "Wait, are you asking because *you're* attracted to Nick? Even though we're keeping the guest list small, you can still bring a 'plus one' to the wedding."

"I'm not asking for me. I just meant…in general." If gorgeous Lorelei saw his appeal, perhaps it wouldn't be far-fetched that Farrah could appreciate him, too.

"'In general?'" Lorelei sounded baffled. But she pursed her lips and considered the question.

"He's the brother with darker hair," Tess supplied helpfully. Wyatt and Kevin both had sandy-brown hair, just a few shades past blond. The color of Nick's hair was richer, as dark as undiluted coffee.

"I think I remember Nick now. He's the short one, right?"

"He's six feet! Maybe he's not as tall as his brothers, but we can't all be Amazons." Tess stopped, chagrined by how defensive she sounded. "Sorry. Personal hot button."

People rarely realized how tall Nick was because he was so often in the company of his brothers and father. Plus, he'd grown up with a tendency to shrink into himself when embarrassed. Back in elementary school, where he'd only been a grade ahead of Tess, he'd slouched when other kids made fun of his stutter.

But he'd grown into perfect articulation and a deep voice with a pleasant hint of raspiness. What Nick needed—and Farrah, too, for that matter—was a wake-up call. The six-foot cowboy bore no resemblance to the awkward, stammering boy he'd once been.

Tess drummed her fingers on the steering wheel. All he needed was a blast of confidence. And possibly a haircut.

"Uh-oh," Lorelei said suddenly.

Tess blinked. "What? What is it?"

"You have That Look. You're planning on interfering with some unsuspecting citizen's life, aren't you? That's the same look you got when you decided enough was enough and gave Asha Macpherson a piece of your mind about the way she talks to her daughter in public."

"Someone needed to! All that 'constructive criticism' was humiliating the hell out of Juliet. Far as I can tell, my chat worked. No one's seen Juliet break down and cry lately. They were at the movies last Saturday and looked like they were having a very nice mother-daughter outing."

"And of course," Lorelei continued, "you used to get that same gleam in your eye when you harangued me about seducing Sam."

"Which, you must admit, worked out pretty well," Tess said with a grin.

"No complaints here. Actually, I admire your instincts. I'm great at understanding numbers, but your gift is people."

One could only hope Nick would be as admiring of Tess's gift. Because her friend was right—Tess had officially decided to interfere.

CHAPTER TWO

THOUGH IT WAS barely noon, Nick felt as if he'd already put in a full day's work. Since his mom had taken Bailey to visit relatives in San Antonio, he was making the most of a free Saturday. He and ranch hand Tim Mullins were trying to catch up on routine maintenance before the busy spring season. Now they could cross "Replace cracked tractor seat" off the to-do list.

Handing the wrench back to Tim, a Texas A&M graduate the Calhouns had hired two years ago, Nick got to his feet. He dusted his hands across his faded jeans. "Everything else I plan to accomplish requires a trip into town for supplies. Want to come with me, maybe grab some lunch after I clean up?"

Tim's grin flashed white against his dark skin. "See, *that's* what you need to do."

"What the hell are you talking about?"

"You, casually inviting someone to join you for a meal. And by someone, I mean Farrah Landon."

"I rescind the invitation," Nick grumbled. "I'll just run to town by myself."

Tim fell into step with him, undeterred. "I realize your ex

was before my time—maybe if I'd met her, I'd get why you're still hung up—but don't you think it's time to move on?"

"You think I still have feelings for Marla?" Nick asked in disbelief. His wife had left him four years ago for a wealthy real-estate developer in Galveston. She rarely crossed Nick's mind unless Bailey mentioned her.

"Um... I may have heard it somewhere."

Mom. It was the responsibility of Nick's dad to worry about the horses and land; it was the responsibility of Erin Calhoun to fret over their sons. She'd always been extraprotective of her youngest.

"Trust me, Marla is ancient history," Nick said. "I'm better off without her."

"So why don't you date? In all the time I've known you, I can count on one hand—"

"I'm a single dad," Nick interrupted, feeling a little guilty for playing the Bailey card. It was true she kept him busy and also true that his being a father added pressure to potential relationships. But there were other issues, too. Half the women in his social circle had known him as a stuttering adolescent, the other half were busy drooling over his brothers. The easiest time he'd ever had talking to members of the opposite sex had been away at college, where he'd met Marla.

"Doesn't Farrah have a kid?" Tim countered.

"Two," Nick admitted. "One Bay's age and one a few years older."

"Then she'd probably consider your parenting experience a good thing. C'mon, I've noticed you noticing her."

"Didn't anyone ever tell you harassing your boss about his personal life is bad for job security?"

"All right, all right. I'll drop it." Tim relented. "For now."

"Speak of the devil." Lorelei paused, her chip halfway to the salsa verde. "You know that guy you were telling me about?"

"Nick?" Tess asked.

"Isn't that him?" Lorelei gestured with her chin toward the hostess podium. "Just walking in now?"

Tess glanced over her shoulder to see Nick Calhoun, once again in his customary jeans, with a handsome guy who looked as if he could be actor Morris Chestnut's younger brother.

"Huh." Lorelei swung her gaze back to Tess, her expression surprised. "I never really paid attention before, but Nick *is* good-looking. Are you sure he even needs help getting a valentine?"

"You should know better than anyone that sometimes people could use a nudge in the right direction."

"And you are going to be that nudge."

Tess gave her a beatific smile. "Precisely." She hoped the hostess would pass their way while leading the men to a table, but the trio went toward the opposite side of the restaurant. Moments later, a waitress brought Tess and Lorelei their food.

At the end of the meal, when Lorelei excused herself to the ladies' room, Tess decided it was time to act. Her short trip across the restaurant was lengthened by the number of people who called out greetings and wanted to chat with her. Tess had lived here her entire life and had been just as outgoing a child as she was an adult. She knew almost everyone, though she couldn't recall the name of Nick's lunch companion.

The man gave her a warm smile as she approached. "Well, hello."

"Hi," Tess said. "I don't believe we've met."

Nick made the introductions. "Tim Mullins, Tess Fitzpatrick. Tim's our most recent hire at the Galloping C, but he lives out closer to Luckenbach. Tess is Bailey's dance teacher. Bay adores her."

"The feeling's mutual," Tess said fondly. "I don't mean to interrupt y'all's lunch, but could I steal Nick for a second?"

"Steal away," Tim said approvingly. "In fact, I just realized I left my cell phone in the truck. I should get it. In case anyone, um, tries to reach me." With that, he was out of his chair in one fluid movement and headed for the exit.

Tess blinked. "He's certainly accommodating."

"He's a lot of things." Nick sounded exasperated. He shook it off, returning his gaze to her as she slid into Tim's vacated seat. "What's up? Is there something we need to discuss about Bailey? I really am sorry I was late getting her last night. Was she worried I forgot about her?"

"Bailey is a joy to have in class and if she was bothered by your tardiness, she forgave you the minute you came through the door. I actually wanted to discuss...you."

He leaned back in his chair, looking confused. "Me? Are you recruiting parent volunteers for the Valentine party? Decorations and homemade cookies aren't really—"

"Nick, we've known each other a long time, right?" Not that they were close, but they'd gone to school together, they saw each other on a weekly basis and they always stopped to exchange pleasantries when they encountered each other in town.

"Sure."

"Then I hope you'll forgive me for being blunt." Tess had realized early in life that she was never going to be the refined, demure Fitzpatrick sister and had embraced her brashness. "I couldn't help notice that when you ran into Farrah yesterday—"

"Not you, too!" Nick groaned. "I've been getting this from Tim all morning. Apparently I have the world's worst poker face."

"Think of it as being expressive and sincere," Tess suggested. "Qualities women like. In fact, I think any woman would be lucky to go out with you."

"Thanks, but I'm not sure past experience bears out that opinion."

"Those experiences are behind you, Nick. It's a brand-new day! Consider me your guardian angel. Your fairy godmother. Or, not to put too fine a point on it, your much-needed swift kick in the ass."

CHAPTER THREE

"I BEG YOUR PARDON?" Nick couldn't quite wrap his mind around what Tess was saying. She'd always struck him as boisterous, possibly unpredictable, but never mentally unstable. Until now. Normal people didn't go around offering to be winged, wand-toting guardians for casual acquaintances. She was right that they'd known each other for years, but he couldn't recall their ever having such a personal conversation. "What brought this on? Did you lose a bet or something?" *I swear to God, if my brothers put her up to this...*

"It's almost Valentine's Day. I'm getting in touch with my inner Cupid. Besides, anyone in town can tell you I'm incapable of minding my own business."

"Are *you* seeing anyone? I was under the impression you're single."

Her pale cheeks flushed rose. "Not relevant."

"Why not play Cupid for yourself?"

She surprised him with a sassy grin, already recovered from her nanosecond of embarrassment. "That's not how it works, genius. Cupid doesn't shoot himself in the butt with his own arrows. Or, in my case, her arrows. However, if there was someone I was seriously interested in, you can bet I wouldn't be too shy to let him know."

"Fair point. You are clearly not the shy type."

"Whereas *you*... You just need a few pointers, a hit of confidence, some practice."

He was almost afraid to ask what kind of practice. "Tess, this is, uh, nice of you." Damned odd, yet nice in a misguided sort of way. "It's not necessary, though. I admit, I find Farrah attractive. I always have." He'd had a huge crush on her for most of high school. He hadn't thought about her much while away at college, but now that they were both single again... "If a relationship's meant to be between us, shouldn't it happen naturally?"

She made a dismissive *pffft* sound. "That's ridiculous. Everything in life that's worth anything takes work."

Where the heck was Tim? As long as the man was taking, he could have walked all the way back to the ranch for his cell phone. Nick glanced around, hoping for an excuse to end this conversation quickly without being rude. He spotted the ranch hand at the bar, chatting amiably with the bartender. *Traitor.*

"Take my dancing," Tess continued blithely. "Was I born with some natural aptitude and a love for ballet? You betcha. But it still required hours and hours of practice and fine-tuning. And what about the Galloping C? When it comes to breeding the horses you sell, are you telling me you just turn them loose in the pasture and hope for the best?"

He stared, dumbfounded by her comparison. "That's, uh, not exactly..."

"Right. Of course not." She waved a hand. "I wasn't saying you and Farrah are like horses. Look, Nick, I know I've caught you off guard. You don't have to give me an answer right now. But my offer stands. When you decide to take me up on it, call me."

* * *

The tiny two-bedroom house on the edge of the Galloping C property was nearly identical to the bungalows the Calhouns rented to guests. What set Nick's place apart, what truly made it home for him, were the accumulated pictures and mementos of Bailey's first six years and the frequent ring of her laughter echoing through the rooms.

Sunday evening found him sitting cross-legged on the floor of his daughter's bedroom, pretending to sip from a plastic teacup. To his left, Bailey's favorite teddy bear perched in one of the dainty chairs that matched the plastic table.

"How's your tea?" he asked his daughter. She brewed the best imaginary pot this side of the Rio Grande.

"Oh, no!" She clutched a hand to her throat. "Mine wasn't tea. It was *potion.*"

He wasn't sure if she meant the magical variety or if she'd mistaken the word for *poison,* so he simply waited, ever-ready to play along.

"The ninjas must be trying to get me again!" She reached beneath the small table to pull out a long cardboard tube that had once held a roll of paper towels. "Here's your sword, Daddy! Fight off those ninjas."

"Aye, aye, Captain." He wasn't sure the naval terminology was strictly logical for a ninja-infested tea party, but his daughter beamed encouragingly, adopting the pirate theme and running with it.

"If you capture all the ninjas, Teddy can make them walk the plank."

"We have a plank?" he inquired. "Since when?"

Bailey hopped onto her bed, extending a pillow over the floor. "This is the plank. But now…everything is…" She gurgled dramatically. "Going black." She fell straight backward, shooting her legs up into the air.

Nick went to her side and dropped a kiss on her forehead. "I am so glad you're my daughter. I bet other little girls' tea parties aren't half as exciting."

"I'm glad you're my daddy." She hugged him. "Because you love me *so much* you even let me stay up late."

"Nice try, Bay, but you have school tomorrow. Time to brush your teeth."

She huffed out her breath in disappointment and trudged toward the bathroom. His strong-willed, highly inventive daughter reminded him of Tess Fitzpatrick and her out-of-the-blue proposal yesterday. It was easy to imagine Bailey growing up to be like the pretty dance teacher, outrageous enough to accost people with unsolicited advice.

Outrageous, but good-hearted.

When he'd been a kid, often too embarrassed to speak to anyone, Tess would say hi to him on the playground, asking if he wanted to swing with her or play catch. She'd been happy to babble and monopolize conversation, so he had little reason to worry about his own articulation.

But was he grateful enough for past kindnesses to let her play matchmaker? What exactly was she envisioning—that she'd stand off to the side texting him suggested dialogue like some kind of modern-day Cyrano? He shuddered.

He didn't want any games or forced awkwardness. And if that meant Farrah never saw him as anything other than Wyatt Calhoun's younger brother... His lip curled. Actually, the idea of Farrah never seeing him for himself sucked.

By the time Bailey returned to the room, she'd regained the bounce in her step.

"Am I still the best daddy even though I'm making you go to bed?" Nick teased.

She nodded, yawning. "I have the best daddy. But Cousin Amber has the best mommy. I want a mommy, too."

"You have a mother, Bay. And she loves you very much." The words were like sawdust in his mouth. Would it be so difficult for Marla to call her daughter once in a while? Maybe send a freaking card? "She just doesn't live here."

The gray eyes Bailey had inherited from him took on a steely determination. "Suzie in my class has two moms. Her old mom moved away, but then her dad got married. Suzie got to carry flowers in the wedding and wear a dress like a princess. Now she has a new mom who lives at her house. Why don't you do that?"

So many reasons, kid. "It's getting late." He gave a melodramatically exaggerated yawn that made her giggle. "How about we discuss this in the morning?"

Nick made sure her night-light was turned on, said bedtime prayer with her, then wandered back to the kitchen. Bailey had come home from dance class Friday with the February newsletter, and he'd stuck it to the refrigerator with a magnet. As always, Tess had included a note at the bottom with her cell number, urging parents to phone her if they ever had any questions or concerns. He scowled at the digits printed on the paper. Was he really considering calling her?

What about the philosophy of relationships developing naturally? The idea that he'd meet a woman someday and that events would unfold artlessly sounded good. But that strategy had gotten him nowhere in the past four years. He pulled the newsletter off the fridge and sighed.

Time to consider a new strategy.

CHAPTER FOUR

STANDING IN THE middle of his kitchen, Nick dialed quickly, knowing that if he hesitated, he'd talk himself out of this.

"Hello?" Tess caught him off guard by answering midway through the first ring. A person practically had to be psychic to answer the phone that fast.

"Oh. Hi. This is Nick." Not sure how to proceed, he added, "Calhoun."

She chuckled softly. "I knew which Nick."

"Well, it *is* a pretty common name."

"True. But you're the only Nick I was waiting to hear from."

"You were really that confident I'd call?" Because he was still surprised by his own actions.

"I have the innate ability to wear people down. But this is actually sooner than I anticipated. I thought it would require further stalking."

Her completely unrepentant tone tugged a half grin from him. However unorthodox Tess might be, she was likable.

"So expecting my call wasn't why you pounced on the phone, then?"

"No, that was a maid-of-honor thing," Tess said. "Lorelei and I have been playing phone tag all night. I'd barely hung up from leaving her a voice mail when it rang again. I assumed it was her. I'm glad it's you."

"That makes one of us," he grumbled. Aware of how ungrateful he sounded, he added, "It's embarrassing to ask for help in this area."

"You didn't ask, I offered."

"Even worse." He reached into the fridge and pulled out a beer. But instead of opening the can, he held it to his temple. He'd been fighting a headache since his daughter's announcement that Suzie had a new mommy. "That means it was obvious that I *needed* help. I must be missing some Calhoun gene. My brothers have never asked anyone for dating advice."

"Last I checked, neither of your brothers is in a happy, stable relationship, either."

Huh. He hadn't really thought of it that way, but she was right. Kevin drifted aimlessly from one woman to the next while Wyatt seemed stuck in a destructive on-again, off-again cycle with a professional barrel racer.

"What changed your mind?" Tess prompted.

"My kid. I was hoping, since we're surrounded by family, including my mom, who bakes birthday cakes and braids hair for ballet recitals, that Bailey didn't feel like there was a big mother-shaped hole in her life. But I was kidding myself. She wants me to remarry. There was talk of being a flower girl and wearing a fancy dress." *Thanks a lot, Suzie, you troublemaker.*

"Not that I would propose to anyone on the whim of a six-year-old," he added wryly. "But maybe I should be more open to possibilities."

"Possibilities like Farrah Landon?" she said knowingly.

He laughed. "That's aiming pretty high. I decided at fourteen she was my dream girl—and haven't managed to speak to her coherently since." He was surprised to have admitted that. But what could he possibly say to Tess to make the situation any more awkward than it already was? Which, in a way, was liberating.

"Ironic that Bay wants a mom," he said. "The cliché is every girl wants a pony—"

"Not every little girl!"

"—and I could give her a herd of ponies. A mom, on the other hand…" He belatedly registered her adamant tone. "You don't like horses?"

"I like them just fine. From a distance."

"I didn't think anything intimidated the Brash and Fearless Tess Fitzpatrick."

"It's not like I'm phobic or anything," she said, trying too hard to sound casual about it. "I just don't have much practice on horseback."

"How 'bout I make you a deal? You step outside *your* comfort zone and go riding with me, and I'll step outside mine and accept your help when it comes to the ladies. It'll be character-building for both of us."

A long moment passed before she grudgingly agreed. "Fine. But only because you really need my help."

Tess was about to accept Tim's offer to walk her to the barn when Kevin, the middle Calhoun brother, stepped out of the trailer that served as a small administrative office.

"I'll take her." Kevin's mouth curved into the automatic grin he gave all women, and he treated her to a lingering once-over that made her skin itch. She was tempted to kick him in the shin with one of her not-quite-broken-in boots. "It'll give Contessa and me a chance to catch up on old times."

Instead of glaring at the use of her hated full name, Tess smiled sweetly. "Which old times? The month when you tried unsuccessfully to get my sister to go out with you or when you never called my cousin again after three dates? She had some *really* interesting things to say about you."

Kevin's self-assured expression faltered. "You know what? I

forgot I promised to help Dad this afternoon. I guess Tim should show you the way after all."

"Well, shoot." Tess's mock disappointment earned a stifled guffaw from Tim.

"So what brings you here in the middle of a Tuesday?" the ranch hand asked as they started down a smooth dirt path. "I know Nick's expecting you, but he was…sort of weird about it."

"Ha! Nick's the most normal of the bunch. *That* one is weird." Tess jerked a thumb over her shoulder, back where they'd left Kevin. It eluded her how anyone could think the smarmy man was more attractive than Nick. "Does he really expect women to fall at his feet? Any female who's lived around here more than a month knows what an unreliable hound he is. The only ones who think his full-court press is genuine are the tourists." Poor things. Maybe Tess should talk to the city council about posting warnings.

Tim peered at her. "Miss Fitzpatrick, did you just duck my question?"

"About why I'm here? Nick's doing me a favor. I'm uncomfortable around horses, and he offered to help." More like *blackmailed,* but she could respect that.

"Ah. Well, here we are."

In the shade of the barn, the crispness of the air became downright frosty. Nick emerged from the barn into the sunshine, smiling his welcome.

"Good to see you, Tess. Glad you didn't change your mind."

"I considered it, but I think it's so important for people to leave their comfort zones and take some risks. Don't you?"

He smirked at her. "Maybe I should have saddled a more spirited ride for you than Ambling Aimee."

"Oh, I'm sure Aimee will be just fine." She prided herself on not sounding shaky as she thanked Tim and bade him goodbye.

He tipped his weathered straw hat. "Good luck, ma'am."

Once she and Nick were alone, she scolded him for the gleam

in his silvery eyes. "It's not chivalrous to look delighted by my terror."

"Oh, please," he retorted skeptically. "I know you're apprehensive, but 'terror'? How scared of horses can you be? You were born and raised in Texas."

"Believe it or not, being an accomplished equestrienne isn't technically a requirement to live here."

"But...hell, Bailey's been riding since she was practically a toddler."

"I don't suppose she has a pony I could borrow?" On second thought, Tess might break it. When she'd pulled on her old pair of jeans that morning, she'd been dismayed they fit so snugly.

Nick led her inside the barn. The scents of leather and hay would have been pleasant if they weren't also accompanied by the earthier—and more foreboding—smell of horses. Whinnies and snorts came from the shadowed recesses of the stalls. "Did something happen to make you scared of horses?" he asked sympathetically. "Bad fall? One of them kick you?"

She grimaced. "No, but thanks for highlighting those possibilities. The worst summer of my adolescence was spent at a camp I didn't want to attend in the first place. The counselors were determined to help me love horses, but each stab at riding went worse than the last."

At the time, it had felt as though all the other campers were reveling in her humiliation. "The final straw was a mean-spirited devil who deemed me unworthy as soon as I got in the saddle. He tried for fifteen minutes to unseat me. After a dead run at a low branch, I decided decapitation wasn't worth the activity points I could earn for my cabin. That was my last time on horseback."

Nick clucked his tongue. "Haven't you heard the saying about getting back in the saddle? You have to try again."

"Said the pot to the kettle. It's been what, four years since your divorce?" She softened her observation with a cajoling smile. "Womankind needs you. There has to be an alternative to guys like your obnoxious brother. He's lucky I didn't kick him."

His eyes narrowed. "Tell me Kevin did not hit on you."

"Worse, he called me *Contessa.* Everyone knows I hate my full name."

"You shouldn't. It's unique, which certainly fits you. And isn't *contessa* nobility or royalty somewhere? That fits, too. You have subjects who love you—well, students—and an innate talent for telling people what to do."

"I'd be annoyed that you just called me bossy except it's totally true."

"Enough stalling." He tugged lightly on her hand. "C'mon, Contessa. It's my turn to give the orders now."

After laughing at Tess's refusal to feed the horse a carrot—the pale gold beast might be gentle natured, but she had *huge* teeth—Nick helped her onto the mare and had her practice in the ring they used for children's birthday parties. Unlike the monster she'd previously ridden, the one who'd tried to behead her, Ambling Aimee accepted Tess with an air of melancholy resignation. *Not unlike my mother, actually.*

Nick excused himself to saddle his own horse so they could ride out in the pasture. Tess had reminded him that this had to be a brief ride—she had a dance class to teach later. He returned quickly, leading a dark red horse whose black saddle matched its mane and tail.

"This is North Star. She's often the lead horse on our trail rides. If you nodded off and slept for the next twenty minutes, Aimee would still follow along with no problem. You don't have to worry about her going rogue." He opened the gate to the ring, clucking his tongue at Aimee. "Ready to really stretch your legs, girl?"

Tess made a concerted effort not to tighten her grip on the reins. Acres and acres of pastureland spread out beneath the blue sky. Lots of space for something to go wrong.

Nick met her gaze. "You're doing great."

"So are you. You say your brothers are the naturals when it comes to talking to women, but you've been charming and funny and patient." She seized the chance to think about something other than how far away the ground looked. "Show Farrah this side of you, and she'll be putty in your hands."

He flushed. "Trying to start a conversation with her is a lot different than this."

Right. Because Tess was more the nonintimidating buddy type than the leggy femme fatale.

She had a sudden flash to her freshman year in high school, to a crush on an older member of the debate team. A crush she'd foolishly believed to be mutual. It hadn't been until he'd finally worked up the nerve to ask her sister to prom that Tess realized why he'd been finding so many excuses to spend time at the Fitzpatrick house.

After Regina shot him down, he and Tess had gone together, as friends. "This will probably be more fun anyway," he'd said as they left her house on prom night. "You're not someone a guy has to worry about impressing." Prom made many young ladies in their glamorous dresses feel like princesses for the evening—Cinderella at the ball. For Tess, it had been like a jarring realization that she was actually the short, squat stepsister. She flinched at the memory, apparently jerking on the reins because Aimee came to an obedient, if unexpected, halt.

"Everything okay?" Nick asked.

"Sure. We're, uh, just waiting for you."

He pulled himself up into the saddle with such easy grace that Tess stared. She'd worked for countless hours to cultivate poise on stage; Nick's rugged elegance was simply who he was.

"My family's owned this ranch my entire life," Nick said as their horses fell in step. "We get tourists, especially in the spring and summer, and I'm used to dealing with them. If I'm saddling a horse for someone, I know how to make small talk.

When I'm on the trail, I can discuss the plants in bloom or facts about livestock. None of that's the same as asking a woman out."

A moment later, he added, "It's not even the asking I mind, really."

"Is it fear they'll say no?" Seeing his strong profile beneath the brim of his hat, the way he effortlessly commanded a thousand-pound animal, she couldn't imagine what idiot woman would refuse him.

"Sometimes it's worse when they say yes. I have had a few dates in the last couple of years, you know. Nothing ruins a perfectly good dinner like awkward conversation. Or the awkward lack thereof. With one girl, I skipped the dinner fiasco entirely and just took her to the movies." He brightened. "That night ended pretty well."

Tess did not want details. "You can't base a relationship on just movies and…other activities that don't require talking. Eventually you'd have to speak to her. All you need is practice. You've been riding horses your whole life, right?" At his prompt nod, she continued, "But your parents didn't send you off at a full gallop your first time out of the gate. We just need to start small. And maybe…"

"What?"

She hesitated. On the drive over here, she'd planned to ask him how he'd feel about a slight change in image. A haircut, some new shirts—just a few minor tweaks that might help Farrah see him in a different light. But Tess was abruptly reluctant. He looked pretty damn good already.

"Tess?"

"I, uh…" She swallowed. "Sorry. Lost my train of thought."

His expression turned sympathetic. "Nerves? We can turn back to the barn if you want."

"What? Oh, no. Aimee and I are doing just fine." Tess had momentarily forgotten she was even on horseback. She'd been too caught up in Nick. *You mean, caught up in how to help him.* That's why she was here, after all. "Do you see many movies?

If this were a romantic comedy, we'd be coming up on a make-over sequence, complete with musical montage."

"Makeover?" He eyed her suspiciously. "The movies I like have shoot-outs, not manicures."

"Which would be helpful if you wanted to kill a guy at high noon. Not so helpful in winning you a valentine. Don't worry, I'm not talking about a full-on makeover. No one's suggesting highlights or a spray tan—"

"I should hope the hell not!"

"But a haircut couldn't hurt, perhaps some new clothes. All of which we can get at a mall. Know what else is at the mall?"

"A bunch of overpriced stuff I don't need?"

"Women. Female salesclerks, stylists, shoppers. Lots of chances for you to practice nonranching small talk."

"Sounds like a blast," he said grimly.

"There's a teacher planning day at the end of the week—my students are all excited about a day off school. We can take Bailey and make an outing of it, hit the food court for lunch, let her ride the big merry-go-round. How bad could it be, a full day of shopping and my shoving you into constant conversation with total strangers?"

"This is payback for making you get on a horse, isn't it?"

No, that was just an added bonus. She gave him a sunny smile. "Why, Mr. Calhoun, I hope you don't think I'm vindictive."

He chuckled. "What I think is, it would be a mistake to ever underestimate you."

That cinched it—he was not only the good-looking Calhoun brother, he was the smart one, too.

CHAPTER FIVE

TESS PUSHED AWAY her empty salad bowl and resisted the urge to steal one of Nick's heavenly-smelling French fries. A few yards away, Bailey waited her turn to go down the spiral slide that dominated the indoor playground. Nick had made the mistake of telling her she could play as soon as she'd finished her food; she'd inhaled her chicken nuggets and macaroni so quickly it was a wonder she hadn't choked.

Now that the two adults were alone, Tess could dispense advice freely. It had seemed wrong to give Nick tips on picking up women in front of his six-year-old. "I know I said you need practice talking to women, but it's not all about what you say. Being a good listener is a *very* sexy trait. And a smile can be just as effective as words. Especially a smile like yours."

He tilted his head, regarding her with a mixture of chagrin and amusement. "I appreciate your trying to inspire confidence, but you don't have to resort to flattery."

"I never say anything I don't mean!" She fixed him with a reproving look. "You know better than that."

He thought she'd been exaggerating the truth to bolster him?

The man must not own a mirror. He wasn't like his brother Kevin, a sly grin always at the ready, but Nick's smiles were infinitely more appealing. Ever since Nick and Bailey had picked her up at her house that morning, Tess had watched him joke with his daughter, particularly enjoying the way his eyes gleamed silver when he laughed.

Nick pressed the heel of his hand to his forehead. "You want me to chat up a bunch of strangers when I can't even talk to *you* without putting my foot in my mouth?"

"People say things that come out wrong all the time. Just say you're sorry and move on."

"That easy, huh?"

"Yep, that easy." Honesty compelled her to add, "More or less."

If Nick was ambivalent about entering the expensive-looking salon on the second floor of the mall, his daughter was out-right hostile.

"Why do I hafta get my bangs cut?" she asked, thrusting her lower lip out so far it was in a different zip code than the rest of her face.

"Because I miss seeing your pretty eyes," Nick said, signing both their names on the waiting list. "I've forgotten what you look like. If your bangs get any longer, you're gonna start walking into walls."

From behind the wild fringe that hung halfway to her nose, Bailey glared. At least, that's the impression he got. But she kept any further complaints to herself, leaving his side to peruse a children's magazine rack.

Nick dropped into the chair next to Tess, imitating his daughter's melodramatic whine. "Do I *hafta* get my hair cut? It's not fairrr."

Giggling, Tess shoved his shoulder. "Cowboy up. Set a good example for your kid." A moment later, she bit her lip. "You won't let them cut too much, though, will you?"

"I thought the point was to make me less shaggy."

"Yeah, but… You look good exactly as you are. It's just that, after people have known each other a long time, sometimes it takes kind of a lightbulb moment to get them to think of each other differently. You're not a stammering fourteen-year-old kid anymore. You only need enough of a change to make Farrah do a double take, to really *see* you."

It sounded good in theory, but given Farrah's seeming disinterest when he'd said hi to her at the studio last Friday, earning a double take might require something drastic. Like a mohawk. Or an Afro. "How do you think I'd look with a buzz cut?"

"Don't even joke about that!" Tess lifted a hand, sifting her fingers through his hair. It felt far better than it should. His scalp tingled beneath her touch, and he had the urge to lean closer.

"Miss Tess, can you help me?" Bay crawled into her ballet teacher's lap. "I'm looking for hidden pictures."

"Then you're in luck," Tess said. "Because I excel at finding those. It's one of my five-hundred-and-thirteen talents."

Bailey's eyes widened. "That's a lot. What are the other five hundred and…" She trailed off, her lips moving silently as she calculated. "Twelve? Is one of them fighting ninjas? Daddy and I do that at our tea parties. Maybe you could help us."

The two females were discussing what style hat one wore to a formal gathering that included kung-fu combat when a woman with purple hair called Nick's name. "Mr. Calhoun?"

Tess slid Bailey to Nick's now-unoccupied chair and walked toward the stylist, giving cheerful instructions.

The woman nodded. "Got it. Don't worry, your husband is in good hands with me. He'll look even hotter when I'm through."

Tess's face flushed. "Oh, no, we're not… He isn't…"

"Sorry." The stylist ducked her magenta-tinged head. "I saw the three of you sitting together and assumed… My bad."

Nick followed her to a chair at the back of the salon, thinking that he could understand her error. Anyone who'd watched Tess with Bailey today could easily conclude the two were mother and daughter. They'd been holding hands through the mall, playing guessing games and singing nonsensical songs. On the isolated occasions Tess had reprimanded the little girl for something, Bailey had immediately corrected her behavior. They didn't look alike physically, but Bay didn't much resemble Marla, either, having inherited Nick's coloring.

Still, Tess and Bailey shared some sort of indefinable inner light, the same enthusiastic natures. Nick's parents were good people; they'd tried their best to do right by their sons but there'd never been a sense of playfulness in his home. Until Bailey was born, the closest anyone in the family had come to a sense of humor was Kevin, but his "wit" centered far too much on his supposed prowess with women. There were few things Nick enjoyed more than laughing with his daughter. Before today, he hadn't given much thought to how rarely he laughed with other adults.

The stylist dampened his hair with a spray bottle. "So if you two aren't married, are you at least dating? Usually my instincts about couples are spot-on."

"Sorry to end your streak, but no."

"Platonic acquaintances don't get that intense about each other's haircuts. And did you see how she blushed? She likes you."

Yeah, she's so crazy about me that she's going out of her way to throw me at other women. Nick returned the stylist's smile in the mirror but didn't bother responding.

What would Tess see in him? He was a horse-raising cowboy who occasionally found it difficult to articulate consecutive sentences; he had little time to date and the only dance performance he'd been to in his entire life was Bailey's recital last spring. Tess's two favorite things in life seemed to be ballet and conversation, and she wasn't fond of horses. All they had in common were ancient playground history and affection for his daughter. Tess Fitzpatrick was exactly what she'd always been, an outspoken yet supportive friend.

Nothing more.

* * *

Tess stopped just inside the department store, next to a pair of mannequins Nick found unsettling. Their features were vaguely alien—and sinister, as if they spent the hours after closing plotting the downfall of humankind.

"This is where we part ways," Tess announced cheerfully.

"It is?" Nick was confused. She'd had a very definite opinion about his hair, yet didn't care what clothes he selected? "I thought this was the montage where I try on outfits for your approval while some cheesy pop song is playing."

Tess shook her head. "Nope. Bailey and I are going to check out that merry-go-round at the other end of the mall. If you want a second opinion on clothes, there are friendly sales associates I bet would be eager to help."

"Ah." So he was being ditched because Tess wanted him to practice flirting, which would be tough with an audience of his daughter and a woman mistaken for his significant other.

"Text me when you're done here," Tess said, "but take your time."

"You say that now." He cocked his head toward his daughter. "Someone can be a real handful."

Tess laughed. "You're talking to the original 'unruly handful.' According to my mother, at least. Trust me, I can keep up."

While Nick had always been grateful for the help his mother gave him with Bailey, Erin Calhoun was the first to admit she was no longer the young woman who'd raised three boys. Her granddaughter wore her out quickly. After a few hours in Tess's exuberant company, he was developing a finer appreciation for the reasons Bay wanted a mom. Renewed determination surged through him. He was going to follow whatever instructions Tess gave him and brave the dating world. Whether Farrah fell for him or not, Bailey wouldn't grow up motherless simply because her father was too skittish to speak to women.

He met Tess's gaze. "Got any last-minute advice?"

"Be yourself, just not *yourself*."

"I should have been more specific. Got any advice that makes sense?"

Intrigued, Bailey stopped turning circles at Tess's side. "You give me advice in ballet class. Are you teaching Daddy about dancing?"

"No, this is different advice." Tess lifted her chin, doing her best to look somber. "I am a woman of much wisdom."

Bailey frowned, her small forehead crinkled in confusion. Nick laughed outright.

"Hey!" Tess jabbed him in the shoulder. "Show some respect for the wise woman."

He grinned down at her. "Aren't wise women usually old and wrinkled? You're…" His gaze slid over her, from her warm brown eyes to her wraparound navy dress, and his words evaporated.

It wasn't a complete shock that she had such a delectably curvy little body—most of the times he saw her she was wearing a leotard and tights, after all. But he was usually in a hurry, ready to spend time with his daughter after a long day and often preoccupied with formulating dinner plans. And Tess was frequently talking to other parents or students, flashing him a smile from across the studio lobby. Though he saw her every single week, he now realized he hadn't truly been looking at her. Suddenly, it—

Oh, hell. He was having one of those, what had she called it earlier? *A lightbulb moment.*

"Nick?" Her voice was soft, more tentative than he'd ever heard it, and her cheeks were scarlet.

Words failed him, as they so often did. He wished he knew how to express how lovely she was without insulting her by sounding stunned. He didn't want to offend her. Nor did he want to sound like his slick, skirt-chasing brother, doling out compliments to any woman who crossed his path.

He cleared his throat. "You… You were going to explain your cryptic statement? About being me but not?"

"Right. While you want to step outside your comfort zone—"

"I do?" he asked wryly.

"Yes. It builds character." Her smile was wide enough to show off her dimples, and he was glad to see her relaxed again, the unwanted tension between them dispelled. "You need clothes that aren't your usual chambray button-downs or shirts with the Galloping C logo. But you don't want to go *so* far outside your norm that you're self-conscious. A man at ease is an attractive man."

"What's attractive?" Bailey interrupted.

"It means women will like him."

"Oh, good!" Bailey clapped her hands together. "If a grown-up lady really, *really* likes him, I might get a new mommy like Suzie."

Nick groaned, eager to change the subject. "Don't you two have a merry-go-round to find?"

"We're leaving," Tess said, her expression apologetic.

Alone, he wandered farther down the tiled path that segmented accessories from appliances. A sharply dressed sales-clerk in head-to-toe black appeared from nowhere, like a coyote who'd scented an injured calf.

"Can I interest you in our new signature fragrance?" Without waiting for an answer, she misted him with cologne.

Blehhh. He coughed, enveloped in a cloyingly sweet cloud. What self-respecting man wanted to smell like this?

"Not for me," he managed, lengthening his stride while she tried to convince him to buy the four-piece collection. Shower gel, deodorant *and* aftershave, all matching the cologne? In Nick's opinion, if a man stunk bad enough to need four combined products to fix it, he should just live in seclusion and not inflict himself on folks.

He slowed once he found himself amid racks of clothes with no idea where to start.

"May I help you, sir?"

Turning warily, he checked to ensure that the auburn-haired woman wasn't wielding a spray bottle. "Umm…"

Tess had encouraged him to be himself. *What I am is a retail-averse cowboy with less than no interest in fashion and vague hopes of impressing a woman.* Well, he could work with that.

"Lord, I hope so." He gave her the most winning smile he could muster; she looked dazed for a second, then smiled back. "I'm not real sure what I'm doin' and I'd love to get your opinion. I'd like to find something appropriate for, say, a first date with a special lady."

"Oh." The woman peered up at him from beneath her lashes. "Lucky girl."

By the time Nick rejoined Tess and Bailey, he had two new shirts, a pair of slacks and a grudging appreciation for the mall. Granted, it would never be his favorite place in the world, but the past hour hadn't been nearly the painful experience he'd anticipated. Janette, the auburn-haired salesclerk, had been a huge help. Maybe the friendly smiles she'd showered on him and the way she batted her eyelashes were because she worked on commission, but she'd seemed genuinely drawn to him. Then there'd been the woman who stopped him on his way out to ask if he'd shrug into a jacket she was considering as a gift.

"For my brother," she'd been quick to add. "Not a husband. I'm single." She was trying to get an idea of fit and said he was tall like her brother.

Perspective was everything. As the shortest male in his family, Nick rarely viewed himself as tall. *You are when you're with Tess.* At her height, she would only barely be able to rest her head against his shoulder. Not that she had any reason to do so, Nick reminded himself, blinking the image away.

Tess and Bailey had finished with the merry-go-round and he'd received a text that they'd moved on to the children's arcade across from the movie theater. They were playing air hockey as he approached, and Bailey spotted him first.

"Daddy!" She rushed toward him, colliding into him with one of her patented tackle-hugs, chatting a mile a minute about all of the things they'd done and seen. "I love the mall."

"It's not half-bad," he conceded.

"Does that mean you're glad we came?" Tess asked.

"It's certainly been a productive day," he said. And the ego boost hadn't sucked. "We accomplished everything on our list. Plus, this place sells cinnamon rolls the size of small planets. Who wouldn't enjoy that? But we should probably head home now," he told his daughter.

Her face fell. "I don't wanna leave. Besides, you said you'd take me to the movie."

"What movie?" Nick didn't recall making any such promise.

She pointed toward the opposite wall, at a poster for an animated movie about a cowboy cat and his adventures with his talking horse. "We saw a commercial on TV and I asked if we could see it and you said you'd take me."

"And I will, eventually. That doesn't mean today. Miss Tess probably has dance classes to teach this evening."

"Actually," Tess interjected, "I follow the school district's calendar. On teacher in-service days like today, I close the studio since some families use the opportunity for a miniholiday."

"And you really want to spend your day off watching a cartoon cat?" Nick asked.

Her smile was sheepish. "I was planning to see it anyway. At least with a kid in tow, I don't feel so silly about it."

Backed by an ally, Bailey pushed her advantage. "So can we, Daddy? Please, please, *please!*"

Why not? After all, he himself was in no real hurry to end their day. He met Tess's gaze. "Are you sure about this?"

"I never say anything I don't mean, remember?"

"Yes!" Bailey pumped her small fist into the air.

Worried his excited daughter might run headlong through pedestrian traffic in her enthusiasm, Nick scooped her up with his free arm. "We still have to check showtimes," he said.

"Okay." Bailey snugged against him then pulled back in surprise. "Daddy, why do you smell like apples?"

"I was spotted by the enemy," he said. "A woman all in black ambushed me—an honest-to-goodness perfume-counter ninja."

"That's nothing," Tess deadpanned, her sparkling eyes at odds with her solemn expression. "You should see the ruthless samurai warriors who work in Swimwear."

CHAPTER SIX

LAUGHTER ERUPTED THROUGH the theater, making Tess realize that the on-screen feline in spurs and a cowboy hat must have drawled something funny. She'd missed it, too distracted by Nick's proximity. Somewhere between now and the "coming soon" previews, part of her brain had forgotten this wasn't a date. It had been too long since Tess had sat in the cool, dark intimacy of a movie theater with a good-looking man's arm around her.

It's not around you. It's just casually draped over the back of your seat. Which was apparently close enough for her pinging hormones.

Tess tried telling herself that the fluttery sensation in the pit of her stomach was simple biology, caused by the total lack of space between seats. Nick's thigh grazed hers every time he moved. And since he was trying to see over his kindergarten daughter, who was incapable of being still, he moved a lot. Bailey had abandoned her own chair ten minutes into the movie, seeking comfort from her father when the movie's menacing villain had burned down a town.

Nick had obligingly cuddled his daughter against his chest. "Don't worry, kiddo, justice will prevail."

One might think the presence of a six-year-old chaperone would help keep the mood platonic. Tess, however, had always adored children and considered being good with kids a very desirable trait in a man. Watching Nick with his little girl made her feel all gooey inside.

At least he was wearing pretentious cologne. It wasn't nearly as heady as the masculine combination of sunshine and leather, the way he'd smelled when he'd helped her dismount from her horse the other day. His hands had grazed over her denim-clad hips, and she'd nearly shivered. Sternly reminding herself it was no more than he did for dozens of tourists every year, she'd squelched her inappropriate reaction.

At the moment, it was proving unsquelchable.

Nick leaned in close, his voice a whisper. "Not having a good time?" His breath feathered over her sensitive ear, intangible contact that nonetheless rippled through her body.

She inhaled sharply. "I'm having... This is, um, great. Really."

"You seem subdued. Highly unlike you." His gaze went back to the screen, and he grinned with boyish enthusiasm. "Shoot-out scene! My kind of movie."

Tess forced herself to focus on the climactic showdown instead of the fleeting and completely foolish dizziness she'd felt when Nick had been so near. Near enough to kiss. She blinked, distracted all over again. The next thing she knew, credits were rolling and Bailey was tugging on her hand.

"This was the best day ever," the little girl announced. "And guess what?"

"What?" Tess asked, hoping for more whimsical conversation about ninjas, something silly to lighten her mood.

Bailey beamed at her. "I've decided *you* should be my new mommy."

* * *

Nick wasn't surprised by Tess's hasty goodbye when they pulled up in her driveway. She was clearly embarrassed by his daughter's earlier suggestion. Rather than respond to Bailey's outlandish idea at the theater, Tess had excused herself by saying she needed the ladies' room. Then she'd sprinted away from them with the speed of a Thoroughbred racehorse. Nick had opted to table the discussion until later.

In the truck, Tess had asked Bailey lots of questions about kindergarten and the ranch, keeping the girl engaged while clearly directing conversation away from marriage. Nick suspected Tess hadn't wanted to say anything that would hurt Bay's feelings. But now that he and his daughter were alone, it was his parental duty to make sure she understood reality.

He glanced in the rearview mirror at his daughter. Her face was wreathed in utter contentment after her day of fun.

"I had a good time today," he began. "I always have fun when I'm with you. You're the most important person in my life, Bailey. I want you to be happy. I know you'd like me to get married, but that might not happen."

Trying to head off the scowl he saw forming, he added quickly, "It *might* happen. But not for a long time. Sometimes men and women date for years before they decide to get married. It's a very serious decision, and before I could ever take a step like that, I'd have to make sure the woman in question loved you as much as I do."

"Miss Tess loves me," Bailey said confidently.

"True, but Miss Tess isn't my girlfriend. You know that, right? I'm not dating her."

Bay shot him that look all kids got when exasperated by the idiocy of adults. "Why not?"

Because... As he thought about the beautiful redhead who'd been making him smile all day, he was suddenly hard-pressed for an answer.

* * *

On Saturday mornings, Tess worked the studio's reception desk while a nineteen-year-old taught a hip-hop class to preteens. For half an hour, the phone rang steadily, but then it got quiet. Tess had just accepted a late tuition payment from an apologetic Parker Casteel when she realized she was all caught up on emails and messages. She decided to hit the vending machine for some caffeine. Tess hadn't been sleeping as well as usual and was fighting the unprofessional urge to take a nap at her desk.

When she returned with a cold can of soda, she noticed that Farrah Landon had joined the other two moms waiting in the lobby, both of whom were silently reading books. The conversation Farrah was having on her cell phone carried.

"I desperately need a night out," Farrah was saying. "Saturday nights should be fun! Do you think your husband would let me borrow you for the evening if I can find a sitter?"

Obviously, Tess wasn't the only one engaged in benign eavesdropping. As soon as Farrah disconnected her call, one of the other moms cleared her throat. "I couldn't help overhearing...are you looking for a sitter? We've been using Eden Winchester—the Ranger's daughter? She's saving up for a car and usually jumps at the chance to earn some money. I don't know if she'll be available on such short notice, but I can give you her number."

"That would be super! I love my girls, but the youngest needs so much one-on-one attention and the oldest is hitting that moody stage. They're exhausting. And my ex is completely useless," she added bitterly.

As time moved closer to class dismissal, more parents and guardians filed into the studio. Despite the increased buzz of noise and activity, Tess heard most of Farrah's follow-up call to her friend, confirming a girls' night at a locally owned beer-and-burger joint that featured pool tables and darts. It was like the universe was giving Tess a sign. She'd planned to nudge Nick and Farrah together at the Valentine's performance—maybe pairing them up to help with the lights or set out refreshments together—and this was a golden opportunity for her to lay some groundwork.

Impatience simmered inside her, but she knew she couldn't call Nick from the studio. She needed to wait until lunch, when she could dial his cell phone from the privacy of her car. He didn't know it yet, but he was taking her out tonight.

The sight of Tess's name and number had Nick smiling as he stripped off his work gloves to answer the touch-screen phone. "Hello?" He leaned against the section of fence he'd just finished repairing, glad neither of his brothers were here to catch him grinning like an idiot.

"It's time to implement Phase Two!"

"Of what, your plan for world domination?"

"Don't be ridiculous. My plan to take over the world is already *well* past the second stage. I'm talking about your courtship of one Ms. Farrah Landon."

Right. He should have guessed that immediately. After all, the only phone conversations he and Tess had ever shared stemmed from his interest in Farrah. "Dare I ask what Phase Two entails?"

"You remember when you told me asking a woman to go out with you isn't as difficult as sustaining conversation through the whole date? You proved yourself capable of casual chatting at the mall. That was like an animated short. Now it's time for the full-length film—dinner with a woman. Specifically, me."

Before he had a chance to process her unexpected declaration, she added, "I happen to know where Farrah will be tonight."

"Oh, Lord. Are you stalking her? I'm having unsettling mental images of you shadowing her to her car and digging through her trash for clues."

"Okay, first, *ew*. And second, maybe you should watch more nature documentaries and fewer police procedurals. I'm not stalking anyone!" Indignation sharpened her tone. "She was broadcasting a private conversation in public. I've never seen her when she didn't have that phone in hand. Honestly, she's probably one of those women who even takes calls in the— Sorry. Not the point."

"I get why a practice dinner might be a good idea. But why does it matter where Farrah is?"

"Because one way for a woman to notice a man is attractive is to see him attracting someone else."

"We're trying to make her jealous?"

"Not exactly. It's more like… Say you walk by a horse in a stable. It doesn't really catch your attention. It's a perfectly fine horse, but nothing about it jumps out at you on first glance. But later, you see someone riding the same horse and realize how much spirit and grace it has. Suddenly, you're intrigued. I know it's short notice, but can you find a sitter for Bailey tonight?"

"Almost definitely." He didn't think his mom had plans but, given her frequent hints about his dating life or lack thereof, he suspected she'd rearrange her entire social calendar if necessary.

"Wonderful. Pick me up at seven. Wear one of your new shirts."

He grinned, already looking forward to the evening. "You're very bossy, Contessa."

"Try to think of it as an endearing quirk."

"Yes, ma'am."

"Wow." Heather Winchester stood on Tess's front porch, beaming. "You look incredible."

"Crap."

"Um…did I say something wrong?"

"I feel like I'm trying too hard." Tess reached out to take the box of altered ballet costumes from her friend. Heather's full-time job was at an art gallery, but she did steady side business as a seamstress. "I don't want to look *too* nice."

"Oh." Heather followed her inside. "Then you missed the mark, because you've never been more beautiful."

"Some help you are," Tess groused. "If you really loved me, you'd tell me I look mediocre at best."

"No can do. Given our past, I promised Zane—and myself—that I'd never lie again. Not even little white lies."

Tess had never been completely clear on the details but she knew that when Heather had first met her Texas Ranger husband, she'd had to deceive him about who she was to protect her daughter Josie from some unsavory people. "You want a glass of wine while I go change?" *Again.*

"Tempting. I can't stay long, though. How about half a glass?"

"Perfect. I'll drink the other half."

Tess's kitchen was tiny, but the sunlight spilling through the large picture window created an airy illusion of space. She pulled down two blue-stemmed wineglasses and retrieved a mellow pinot grigio from the fridge, leaving her friend to pour while she darted back to her room and swapped the deceptively simple black dress for a dark denim skirt and turquoise peasant blouse.

She hurried back into the kitchen, the tile floor cool against the soles of her feet. "Better?" she demanded. "By which I mean, worse?"

Heather leaned back in her chair, considering. "The blouse is a great color for you and the skirt shows off legs honed by years of ballet. I think you're just gonna have to accept that you're gorgeous. You could try another outfit, but it's not really the clothes. There's something…" She stared hard at Tess's face. "Who's the mystery guy who put that sparkle in your eyes, the one you're hoping to impress without being too obvious?"

"No guy!" Tess took the seat opposite her friend. "Well, technically, there is a guy, but not like you're suggesting. I'm having dinner with Nick Calhoun to discuss a…project we're working on."

"Farrah Landon?"

Tess nearly spilled her wine. "How'd you know?" Nick was a private person. If he thought other people were gossiping about their arrangement...

"Lorelei mentioned it. But only because you and I are so close! The way she brought it up, I think she assumed you'd already told me. After all, I know firsthand what a matchmaker you are."

"I didn't do a thing to introduce you to Zane," Tess said, temporarily diverted. "I didn't have to—you were living right next door to him!"

"True, but you pushed me to give him a chance every darn time you talked to me."

"And now you're happily married." Tess raised her glass in a salute to the happy couple. "I am great at figuring out who people belong with."

"If you say so."

Tess bristled. "When have I ever been wrong?"

"Maybe you're not, but... Never mind. You've lived here your entire life, and it's only been a year for me. I don't know Farrah very well. I wouldn't have an impression of her at all except that her youngest was in class with Josie at the beginning of the year. Then they hired that new teacher and shuffled some—"

"What is your impression? Of Farrah?"

Heather bit her lip. "She's very flashy. Take that two-door sports car she drives. It's sleek and sexy but when I see her in the carpool line, it just seems impractical. You should have seen her older daughter trying to climb out of the backseat with her science-fair project. Not that you have to drive a minivan to be a good mom! I don't think she's evil or anything."

"It's okay," Tess said. "I asked for your opinion, remember?"

A moment later, Heather continued. "Her clothes are all name brand. And, correct me if I'm wrong, but I think she lives in the most expensive subdivision in town. Isn't Nick more subdued? I guess I just have trouble imagining her being drawn to him. Seems like she'd be instinctively attracted to the 'hot' brother."

"Nick *is* the hot Calhoun brother!"

At Tess's fervent tone, Heather's eyebrows shot up.

Tess could feel her cheeks blazing. "You know how protective I get of my friends," she mumbled.

"Uh-huh." Heather rose, her expression amused. "I should be going. One last piece of unsolicited advice on your appearance tonight?"

"Sure."

"Wear some of that kiss-proof lipstick that won't smear. Just in case."

CHAPTER SEVEN

EVEN THOUGH TESS had suggested Nick wear some of his new clothes, she must have subconsciously been expecting a pair of his regular jeans and a Western shirt with a small Galloping C logo above the pocket. Because the sight of him in black slacks, a tightly woven hunter-green shirt and lightweight leather jacket was staggering. Clean shaven and with his hair recently cut, he was like an alternate version of himself. Everything she'd found desirable about him was still there but now combined with a new air of sophistication, mystery.

Tess swallowed, her greeting forgotten.

At her silence, Nick's smile faded. "Am I late? Early?"

"You're perfect. Um, right on time."

His voice lowered, taking on a husky familiarity. "You look fantastic."

Their eyes met, and Tess struggled to find a response. Speechlessness was not typically a problem for her. By the time common sense kicked in and she realized the logical reply was "thank you," too many moments had passed, rendering the answer awkward. Crud. Would he think her rude now, unappreciative of the compliment? She was supposed to be encouraging him! Busy second-guessing herself, she didn't quite register his question until he repeated it.

"Ready to go?" he asked for the second time.

Lord. Two minutes into the evening and she was already wishing for a do-over. Was this how Nick often felt, uncertain of what to say and how others might react to him? It was an awful sensation, something that squirmed in her abdomen as if she'd swallowed a bucket of live tadpoles.

"I am definitely ready to get out of here," she said. Having him stand on her front porch was too intimate somehow, as if she might invite him in at any moment. Once they were at the pool hall, she'd regain her equilibrium.

She used her key to lock the dead bolt, trying not to notice how close he was standing. But it was impossible to ignore the warmth from his body, the smell of his skin, something indefinable and entirely Nick beneath the manufactured fragrances of soap and shampoo. Tess inhaled deeply. Then, deciding it was tacky to be sniffing her date, she spun on the heel of her sandal and marched toward his truck.

He followed, reaching to open the door for her at the exact moment she gripped the handle. His hand was strong and callused over hers. A tingling warmth coursed through her, and her mouth went dry.

"Doesn't a gentleman get the door for his date?" he asked softly.

"Absolutely." She flashed him a bright smile, making an effort to relax. "So far, A-plus on your test run. Phase Two, all systems go."

He grinned. "I feel like we need a code name."

By the time he rounded the truck to get in on the driver's side, she'd regained her composure. "Operation Cupid?" she suggested. "Count yourself lucky the only arrows we'll be using are metaphorical. My limited experience with archery was pure disaster. I'm pretty sure there's a picture of me in the administrative offices of Camp Falcon Rock, Most Failed Camper Ever to Pass Through."

"Would this be the same camp of your much-lamented riding experiences?"

"Falcon Rock's the official name. To me, it'll always be a little piece of Hell on Earth. I didn't want to go in the first place, but my parents insisted. They were trying to get my mind off—" She stopped abruptly.

Tess was by no means an introvert, nor was she shy about expressing her opinion—whether asked for or not. But she never discussed this with anyone. She'd never figured out a way to talk about it that didn't make her sound self-pitying or resentful of her sister.

Braking for the stop sign at the top of her street, Nick slid her a questioning glance. "My parents used to force me into activities in an effort to 'get me out of my shell.' I doubt *your* folks had to worry about that."

"No, my being sentenced to camp was an attempt to distract me from ballet. My sister and I had both auditioned for a prestigious summer company. Regina got into her age class. I didn't." She tried to sound nonchalant about ancient history, completely unbothered that her sister had gone on to a successful career in Tess's chosen field. "I'd been psyching myself up for months. Being accepted into that company would have been like Christmas and my birthday and Mardi Gras all rolled into one. Regina only decided to try out at the last minute, after she and her boyfriend broke up, freeing up a lot of her time."

Nick made a sympathetic noise. After a moment, he offered, "Siblings can be real jackasses, can't they?"

His observation startled a laugh from her. "I refuse to answer that on the grounds it may incriminate me."

"Don't get me wrong," he said. "I love my brothers. But it was difficult being the 'runt of the litter.' The youngest, the one with the speech impairment, the one who came last in school. With every teacher I ever had, I felt as if I were either trying to live up to Wyatt's reputation or live down Kevin's. He was more of a troublemaker, although he was always able to talk himself out of the worst scrapes. I don't think he's been at a loss for words a day in his life. Can I admit something awful?"

"Oh, please do."

"I think proposing to Marla was even more exciting because I knew neither of my brothers had ever popped the question. Obviously, that's not the driving reason I wanted to marry her, but it was an added rush. I was doing something first, succeeding in an area they hadn't. Of course, then she left me," he added ruefully, "which restored the natural order of the universe. Or, at least, the Calhoun family."

"What exactly happened between the two of you?" Tess probably shouldn't pry, but when had she ever let that stop her?

He considered his words carefully. "Marla grew up poor in an Oklahoma trailer park. She got to college on scholarships and worked multiple part-time jobs so that she could live with some style. Much as she was infatuated with the idea of my family's ranch and that we owned so much land, she tired of the reality pretty quickly. She was cut out more for country clubs than country living. Her leaving made me wonder…"

If he should have done something differently? "You can't blame yourself for her choices," Tess said. Granted, she didn't know what kind of husband Nick had been, but she felt as if she knew enough about him as a person and a father to make an educated guess.

"That's not what I meant, but thanks."

He was about to make the last turn before they reached their destination, and Tess sensed he'd be less forthcoming with personal details once they were surrounded by a crowd. This was her best opportunity for learning more about Nick and his ex-wife. Not that she cared much about the woman she'd only seen a couple of times in passing, but she definitely cared about Nick Calhoun. Far more than she'd realized.

"What did you mean?" she blurted. "What did you wonder after the divorce?"

"I wonder if I ever should have married her in the first place." He sighed. "If she was truly The One, I probably should have missed her more once she was gone. I would have been faithful, would have honored my vows. But did I really love her enough to justify a lifelong commitment? We met first day on campus, when neither of us knew anyone yet. We were neighbors and ended up with classes together. There was a certain degree of convenience to our relationship. No, that sounds cold. I did care about her, very much."

"You were comfortable with her," Tess translated.

He nodded. "I felt at ease around her. For me, that was a big deal. But if I was so in love with her, shouldn't it have been harder to get over her? I rarely even think about her, except to wish she made more effort to contact Bay. I was angry she abandoned us, but never really grief-stricken. Does that make me shallow?"

"It makes you someone who married young and is functioning as best you can as a single dad. I don't see any crime in that."

"Thanks." He eased the truck into a parking spot, then shot her a look of pure gratitude. "You're a really good friend, you know that?"

"Yeah." A wave of irrational gloom washed over her. "I know."

Nick seemed endearingly nervous once they'd been shown to a booth by the hostess, almost as if this were a real date. Or, perhaps, Tess realized as the waiter wrote down their drink choices, his nerves were caused by Farrah Landon. She sat with a friend at a table on the far side of the dining room.

After the waiter had left to get their beverages, Nick scanned the menu. "Should I try to order for both of us?"

"Do you have any idea what I want?"

"Not really."

She arched a brow, her lips twitching. "And do I seem incapable of making decisions for myself?"

He chuckled. "Not at all."

"Then it would be pretty dumb for you to order for me," she chided lightly. "I'm not sure how that myth got started, that it's macho for a man to pick out what the little lady will have. It's more effective—and sometimes downright sexy—to ask a woman what she likes."

His gaze locked with hers. "Are we still talking about dinner?"

"Um…" Tess was grateful that the waiter returned with her glass of wine, interrupting conversation.

After they'd both ordered, Nick asked, "So, what *do* you like? In a guy, I mean. What do you want in a relationship?"

His question caught her off guard.

"C'mon," he coaxed. "We've spent a lot of time talking about my love life. It's only fair that I ask about yours, right?"

She couldn't fault his logic. Stalling, she sipped her wine. "It's not like groceries. I haven't made a list."

"So make one now," he invited. "You have to have some idea. If ever there was a woman who knew her own mind…"

What was she looking for in a man? Draining her glass, she pondered some of the couples she knew. She skipped over her parents' own unbalanced marriage, where her mother announced decisions as if they were royal decrees and her father mostly kept his head down and tried to stay clear of any female drama. Tess wanted a true partnership, like some of her friends had found.

Sam Travis looked at Lorelei as if she were the most gorgeous woman alive, which was close to true; she had to at least be in the top twenty. Newlyweds Zane and Heather Winchester, who'd each learned from failed first marriages, shared a deep bond, an understanding that would lead outsiders to assume they'd been together for decades. Then there was Tess's sister. In addition to synchronized life goals, Regina and her choreographer husband were an exquisitely matched set. Seeing them together made Tess think of priceless bookends, but they were so unerringly dignified that she secretly found them a bit creepy. Did they ever laugh together?

"Someone I can have fun with," she said decisively. "But a good listener, too, someone who can be playful but intuit when it's time to take what I'm saying seriously. A man who makes my toes curl whenever we…kiss. Someone who believes I'm worth the trouble of pursuing." She recalled men she'd seen court her sister. Tess wasn't the type to play hard to get—she either liked a guy or she didn't—but it would be nice to know he thought her worth proving himself.

"Oh, and he has to be good with kids, obviously." She bit the inside of her lip, wishing she could take back the words. Did they sound like a come-on, given that Nick was absolutely wonderful with his daughter? "I—I've always wanted children. When Regina got married, I hoped I'd soon have nieces and nephews to spoil, but she's adamant about waiting. She doesn't want motherhood to interfere with her dancing career."

Nick swirled his drink around, not meeting her eyes. "Speaking of kids… I should apologize about what Bailey said the other day. About you being her new mother?"

Mortification stung her cheeks. "No apology necessary." She didn't want to sit through a mutual affirmation of there being nothing romantic between her and Nick. Knowing he didn't see her "that way" was fine; trying to smile across the table as he voiced it aloud would be humiliating.

The waiter appeared with their salads. "Anyone want grated cheese? Freshly ground pepper? Another glass of wine, ma'am?"

"Yes, please."

Blessedly, once the waiter had bustled off, Nick didn't resume the topic of Bailey and her impulsive announcement. Instead, he returned to the subject of Tess's list.

"You have a good handle on relationships," he said admiringly. "Some people have unreasonable expectations—they look for perfection and are doomed to be unhappy. Other people are just grateful for any tenderness and settle for less than they deserve. You won't do that."

"I won't?" She certainly had no intentions of doing so, but she was nonplussed by the ringing conviction in his voice.

"Hell, no. You're direct and brave enough to follow your heart." He frowned, glancing toward the table where Farrah sat.

Was he wishing he'd had the gumption to ask her out before now? Was he realizing that, if he had, he could even now be seated across from the woman he'd dreamed of going out with for more than a decade, instead of getting advice from a busybody who hadn't even been in a relationship since...

Her mind blanked as she tried to calculate how long it had been. Lord, was that depressing.

Midway through her second glass of wine, Tess began to feel slightly less depressed. How bad could her social life be if she was sitting here with one of the hottest guys in town, a man who kept nodding at her as if her every word was a pearl? A pleasant buzz stole through her, subtly blurring her thoughts until they were like an alluring watercolor.

She was enjoying her delicious steak and once again feeling her buoyant self when Nick asked suddenly, "What makes a great kiss, one that would curl your toes?"

"I— What now?"

"Your hypothetical criteria was that he be an incredible... kisser." Nick's slight pause and smirk made it clear he knew her thoughts had gone further than that, even if she'd only given him the PG version.

Knowing how easily she blushed, Tess tried very hard not to dwell on what qualities made a man an incredible lover—and tried equally hard not to wonder just how many of those qualities Nick Calhoun possessed. "Um, some things aren't easily captured in words," she demurred.

Mischief glimmered in his eyes. "Are you saying it would be easier to demonstrate than to explain?"

She froze, the idea of him kissing her all too vivid.

"Don't worry, I was teasing," he assured her. "That would go above and beyond the call of duty."

"Not like it would be a hardship," she muttered.

He learned forward in his chair, the earlier humor in his gaze replaced by a more predatory gleam. "Are you saying you'd want me to kiss you?"

"It's crossed my mind." The errant words were out before she could censor herself—not that she'd ever employed much of a verbal filter. "Ignore me. I'm on my second glass of wine."

He shook a finger at her. "You never say anything you don't mean. Isn't that your mantra?"

She could flirt with him, tell herself it was in the name of "coaching" him. Farrah could look over at any moment and see the two of them smiling together, Nick showing a seductive side of himself. But the idea of playacting the truth scraped Tess raw. She felt exposed and queasy.

"I think the smart thing for me to do is shut up," she said firmly. "Radio silence."

"An impulse I can understand, but aren't we supposed to be practicing the art of conversation?"

"Think of this as a disaster drill," she instructed. "What if you're on a date and the discussion goes south? Do you have a contingency plan?"

He considered her challenge, then startled her by scooting his chair back. Standing, he extended one hand toward her.

"What are you doing?"

"This is my plan B." He tilted his head toward the live band and small dance floor through the archway. "I figure we can let the music do the talking for us. Dance with me."

"But…" She'd been aiming for strategic retreat, a little distance between them. Sliding into his embrace was *not* what she had in mind. "We haven't finished dinner yet."

He signaled to the waiter, summarizing the situation in quick pantomime. "Our plates will be safe for five minutes. C'mon, you're the best dancer in town. Are you really going to leave me hanging here? People are watching." He gave her a lopsided smile that was somehow both cocky and lovable. It was the smile Kevin had been attempting his entire life yet never quite capturing. "What will it do to my reputation if everyone sees you reject me? All your hard work reinventing me, undone."

"Oh, fine!" Her acceptance came out in a soft snarl that belied the flutter of anticipation she felt. Dancing was as natural to her as breathing, and the idea of swirling around the floor, her limbs tangled with Nick's, was damned exhilarating.

And the song the band had just started was fast, not one of those sappy love ballads that caused "dancers" to just sway in place. Some claimed slow dances were the most romantic, but Tess found them to be awkward and pointless. Dancing was meant for bodies to *move,* to feel, to push limits.

On the floor, Nick took her hand in his, splaying his other hand against her back. "Keep up now, Contessa." Then he gave her the most devastating grin she'd ever seen. It liquefied her; only years of discipline kept her steady on her feet.

He spun her into a brisk modified polka. Her heart raced, and heat coursed through her. *Left, right, left. Right, left, right.* All while whirring in tightly controlled circles that kept her curves pressed to his broad body, hard with muscles carved from hours of manual labor. One of his legs was between hers, as much as the denim of her skirt would allow, and she felt the briefest twinge of embarrassment that he might guess how the contact affected her. But there was no chance for embarrassment to take root. Not when Tess was having the time of her life.

She was flying, tethered to the world only by the hold of the most attractive man she knew. When she'd seen him on horseback, she'd thought him in his element. But that was before she'd seen him on a dance floor. His body worked in perfect choreography with hers, their inherent rhythm superseding the notes produced by the band. They moved in a pulse and tempo no longer dictated by the music, and she never wanted to stop. Her lungs burned as they spun faster, the need to catch her breath secondary to the harmony of two sublimely attuned bodies completing one motion.

When the song stopped, Nick led her in one last spin for good measure, then dipped her dramatically. Years of accumulated skill allowed her to bend nearly to the floor without overbalancing them. Spontaneous applause surrounded them, and Tess straightened. She'd never been intimidated by performing in front of an audience but suddenly she felt an unfamiliar stab of shyness. Probably because what she and Nick had just publicly shared felt far more intimate than simple dancing, as if they'd done something illicit in front of their neighbors.

Easily a dozen people were staring at them—including Farrah Landon, whose eyes were wide. It was commonplace to see Wyatt or Kevin Calhoun cut a rug with a date but watching Nick masterfully navigate the dance floor was a rare sight. Tess had never needed to offer him advice about women or drag him to the mall in the next county. All it had taken was three minutes and an up-tempo song.

"Plan B, huh?" She forced herself to move away from him, breathing hard. "More like your secret weapon."

CHAPTER EIGHT

NICK TRIED TO focus on what Tess had just said to him, but he couldn't think. *Liar.* He was thinking plenty—about the feel of Tess's lush body, the temptation of what her mouth might taste like, the desire to sink into her. He was shell-shocked, watching her mouth move but not really hearing her words over the dull roar in his ears. What were the odds she'd just said, "Take me, Nick"?

He cleared his throat. "Wh-what?"

"I said, why didn't you tell me you could dance like that?"

"I don't. Usually." Not like that.

He knew how to dance. With all the town festivals and outdoor concerts, it was difficult to grow up here without learning the fundamentals, plus Erin had given all three of her boys some pointers. But he'd wondered if he would be out of practice.

Instead, everything he'd ever known had come rushing back to him the moment Tess stepped into his arms...along with a few things he wasn't sure he'd known in the first place. She was living inspiration, motivation for a man to do his level best.

They returned to their table. Neither of them showed any interest in their food, but they both gulped down glasses of water. Nick flagged down the waiter to request more.

The waiter smiled at Tess. "Bravo! I feel like I should ask you for your autographs after that performance."

Tess ducked her head. "Just letting off some steam."

Nick bit his tongue, battling back suggestions of other ways they could release some steam if she was interested. *Was* she interested? Tess was so naturally outgoing and friendly that a man with limited dating experience might misread her. Had he imagined the sudden huskiness of her voice earlier when she'd said kissing him wouldn't be a hardship? He'd put himself on the line by asking if that meant she wanted to kiss him.

It's crossed my mind.

That wasn't specifically a yes, but it sure wasn't a denial. He cast an involuntary glance at Farrah Landon, recalling just why Tess had invited him out tonight. Catching his eye, Farrah gave him a coy little finger wave that left him bemused.

It was difficult to recall why he'd felt so drawn to Farrah. Nostalgia, combined with their bond as two single parents who had survived divorce and were each raising daughters? He'd asked Tess tonight for specific qualities she would require in a relationship. Why had he never thought to ask himself that question? Hell, Bailey probably had a clearer idea of who he should date than he did.

Which brought him back to Tess.

He turned his gaze back to her, finding her expression shadowed. "Everything okay?"

"Long day," she said weakly. "I was at the studio all day, now this."

He felt his disappointment clear to the pit of his stomach. "So no chance of my talking you into another dance?"

"Actually, I think I'd rather leave now, unless you want to stay for dessert." She rallied, flashing him a smile. "But don't worry. I think we already accomplished our goal in coming here tonight."

Nick didn't answer. He wasn't sure how to explain that they were no longer working toward the same goal.

I am happy for my friend. I am truly and genuinely happy for my friend. Staring out the passenger window even though it was too dark to see the Texas landscape, Tess grappled with déjà vu. Why did it seem as if lately she'd had to give herself these pep talks often, as if she had to compel herself to be glad for others' good fortune? Was she becoming bitter and jealous? Just because everyone was pairing up as decisively as the animals boarding Noah's Ark and she was standing out in the flood with a pair of flippers and a snorkel...

Get a grip, Fitzpatrick. No one likes a whiner.

She turned toward Nick, forcing cheer into her voice the same way she'd doggedly forced her hips into those old jeans to go riding. "In case I forgot to say so earlier, I had fun tonight. Did you see the way Farrah was looking at you when we left the dance floor? She wasn't the only one, either."

"That's...great."

Wow, even *she* had sounded more convincing than that. "What's wrong? You know I'm serious about Farrah seeming interested, right?"

"I know. You mean what you say."

"And that's what you wanted, isn't it? To break the ice, build up to finally asking her out after all these years?" She held her breath, wondering how she'd react if he said no, that he'd been wrong.

I was a fool, Tess, for thinking I wanted a lissome blonde with parenting experience and a hot car. I'd much rather be with a round redhead who has madly untamed curls and a tendency to act without thinking. Yeah. She could just imagine what her long-suffering patrician mother would have to say about *that* flight of fancy.

"Don't think I'm ungrateful for all the help you've given me," he said a few seconds later. "I'm glad she noticed me. It just occurs to me that liking the way I dance isn't a basis for anything real. I should be more analytical about this, like you."

"Me?"

"You were very insightful when you talked about the qualities you consider important."

Her innate sense of honesty forced her to point out, "Those were traits I came up with spur of the moment. Subconsciously, you probably have a list like that, too. Even if you've never itemized it, you have an idea of what's important to you and who you like."

He was quiet as they pulled into her neighborhood. Was he having second thoughts about his feelings for Farrah? Or was he just psyching himself out? After all, he'd had a lot of time to build her up in his mind as his Dream Girl. He'd said himself the first time he spoke with Tess on the phone that Farrah might be aiming too high.

Tess was surprised when he parked the truck in her driveway, cut the ignition and removed the key. Her heart leaped in her chest as if it were trying to execute a *grand jeté*. "You're getting out, too?"

He hitched a brow, disgruntled by her surprise. "What self-respecting man doesn't walk his date to the door at the end of the night?"

It wasn't a real date. But she couldn't quite voice the objection because it was difficult to remember which part hadn't been real. The breathless rush she'd experienced in his arms had certainly been genuine. Her nerves before he came to pick her up, as she'd changed clothes six times and fortified herself with wine, had been one hundred percent sincere. And the way she'd felt tonight whenever she glanced across the table and fell into his gaze...

There went her heart again, leaping around like a crazed soloist in search of a spotlight.

Nick opened her door, offering her a hand to climb down from the height of the truck. His fingers rasped against hers, and she inhaled a shaky breath. She quickly drew her hand away on the pretext of fishing her keys from her purse. They walked up the steps together, and she unlocked the door. Should she invite him in for a cup of decaf coffee? Point out that it was a nice evening and ask him to sit on the porch with her, enjoying the song of crickets and the sparkling canvas of stars overhead?

"Tess?" Despite his velvety tone of voice, she jumped as if she'd heard gunfire.

She tried to camouflage her reflex by turning the knob and opening the door with more force than required. "Yes?"

"I think you're right. Maybe deep down, I do know what I want."

"And?" She swallowed.

As if they were on the dance floor again, he pulled her against him, moving to a song only he could hear. Spearing one hand through her wayward curls, he cupped the back of her head and tilted her face toward his. He captured her mouth in a coaxing kiss that bloomed from gentle to searing in the space of a heartbeat. Heat flooded her body. They explored each other with a frenzied thoroughness. Thought became sensation and movement. His thumb skimmed the edge of her breast through the filmy material of her blouse, jolting a sharp current of need through her.

He moved his mouth from hers long enough to trace feathery kisses up the curve of her neck. "We shouldn't be standing in your doorway like this."

Right, because she'd hate for the neighbors to see the hottest guy in town crazed with desire over her. She tugged him into the dimly lit interior of her house and had just slammed the door when she found herself pressed between Nick and the wall. One of his firmly muscled legs was between hers, pushing the edge of her skirt upward. Cool air teased her thighs, and she trembled.

Nick noticed, backing off immediately. He still had one hand curved at the nape of her neck, but he'd put several inches between them when before there'd only been a few thin layers of fabric. "I'm rushing you, aren't I?"

No! Except…now that he'd paused long enough for her to get oxygen to her lust-addled brain, she admitted to herself they were rushing. Was she subconsciously hurrying because she knew that, if she stopped to think, she'd come to her senses?

She exhaled heavily, managing an apologetic half smile. "We shouldn't be doing this."

"Damn." He shoved a hand through his hair, no longer resembling the polished, urbane version of himself who'd shown up here at the beginning of the evening. "I was so hoping you wouldn't say that."

"Me, too," she admitted. "But it's true."

"Tess, I—"

She held up a hand, halting his words. "You can call me tomorrow. Or later in the week. We can talk then." If she didn't do the sensible and honorable thing by kicking him out now, she might yet lose her head. And no amount of physical bliss tonight would be worth the world of regret and misgivings tomorrow.

Starting out the evening, Nick hadn't had any idea what to expect. And now that the night had concluded…well, he wasn't sure what in the hell had just happened. Shifting uncomfortably in the driver's seat, he tried to ignore the lingering demands of his body and focus on driving safely back to the Galloping C.

Had he screwed up by kissing Tess? As he'd told his daughter, he and Tess weren't romantically involved. And only a couple of hours ago, Tess had referred to their date as a "test run." Instead of adhering to reality, he'd gone with sheer instinct and grabbed her.

He couldn't remember the last time he'd blindly followed his instincts with a woman. Ironically, the person he most wanted to turn to for advice now was probably the last one he should ask. Even though only a week had passed since Tess first approached him, he'd quickly fallen into the habit of considering her his romance coach. No, it was more than that. She was a friend.

No. It was more than *that,* too.

When he pulled up to the ranch's main house, lights spilled from various windows. He could see his brothers and father in the living room. Upstairs, softer light shone from behind the pale green curtains of his parents' room. Then there was a telltale gleam in the tiny window of the bathroom. If he was seeking guidance, there was no shortage of people inside he could ask. But Nick had always been the most private of the Calhoun brothers. Kevin had been bragging about his exploits since middle school, and while Wyatt wasn't as obnoxious as their brother, he also didn't hesitate to kiss a girl—or argue with her—in full view of a crowded bar. The idea of holding his relationship with Tess up for their speculation...

The familiar creak of the front door heralded his arrival. None of the three Calhoun men seated looked away from the sports highlights on the big-screen television.

"Your mama just took Little Bit upstairs to brush her teeth," his father informed him. "There's beer in the fridge if you want to stay for a few minutes. And leftovers, too. Erin made her famous chicken dumplings."

Nick crossed the dark kitchen and filled a glass with cold water. "I had dinner in town. That's why I needed y'all to babysit, remember?"

"Oh, right." Wyatt turned in his recliner. "Big date. How'd it go?"

Kevin snorted. "How do you *think?* He's here with us, isn't he? If it had gone halfway decent, he'd be doing the mattress mambo with— Who were you with?"

"None of your damn business," Nick said matter-of-factly.

Their father jabbed a finger at Kevin. "Watch your mouth. You know your mama doesn't like you talking about the union between man and woman with such disregard."

It warmed Nick's heart to see his towering brother blush like a ten-year-old who'd just been given his first detention. "I'm going upstairs to get Bailey." His parents had assured him she could spend the night here if need be. Since that was sadly not the case, he might as well take her home where she could sleep in her own bed.

Bay sat propped against the headboard of his parents' bed, dressed in a pair of glaringly mismatched pajamas—a pink top printed with neon cowboy boots and green pants, striped in yellow and blue. Amid the boots was a splotch that looked suspiciously like chocolate ice cream. "Daddy! Gramma was about to read me a story. You can listen with us."

His mother was less effusive about his presence. "We didn't expect you this early."

He laughed wryly. "Should I leave and come back?"

"Of course not. It isn't that I'm unhappy to see you. I guess I just hoped you'd take me up on my offer to let Bailey stay the night. In case you and your friend decided to…have a tea party," she improvised.

Nick spluttered, choking on his water. "A tea party?" he wheezed. Was that what they were calling it these days? "Mother, it was a first date! And it wasn't exactly a date, anyway. Although there were dinner and dancing."

"What about a k-i-s-s good-night?" Erin prompted, her eyes twinkling.

"*Mom.* Honestly, you're worse than Kevin."

"Don't be absurd, dear. No one is worse than Kevin. Between his inability to go out with a nice girl twice in a row and Wyatt's holding pattern with that rodeo woman, you may be my only shot at grandchildren. Poor Bailey wants brothers and sisters. She told me."

Nick rolled his eyes. "Now it's siblings, too? Last I heard, the wish list stopped with being a flower girl and having a new mommy come live with us."

"I thought Miss Tess was gonna help you find someone to

be my mommy," Bailey piped up. "But I still think it should be her! She said you were tractor...um, tractive?"

"Attractive," Nick said. Definitely time to change the subject. "So what did you do this evening, kiddo?"

She beamed. "Grandad and I saw a poisonous snake out by the pond and Uncle Wyatt said maybe next time he helps babysit, he'll teach me to shoot a rifle."

"Like hel—" At the piercing look from his mother, Nick quickly amended his word choice. "Heck. You're not old enough for that."

Venomous snakes and guns? Bailey definitely needed more feminine influence in her life. It was becoming easier and easier to adjust to the idea of someday remarrying. Perhaps because he'd met someone he could see himself falling in love with.

"This is awful." Tess lay sprawled across the sofa in the main room of the B and B, an arm thrown over her eyes. Although there were two couples checked in to the establishment, they were currently on a trail ride with Sam. Tess and Lorelei had the place to themselves, leaving Tess free to vent about her wanton behavior the previous night. "Can you believe I made out with him?"

"I'm not seeing the problem." Lorelei sat in a nearby chair, feet tucked beneath her while Oberon the cat stalked in circles around her, still deciding whether he would deign to let her cuddle him. "You kissed the hot cowboy. Yippee, I say. Did I mention you're entitled to a 'plus one' at the wedding?"

Tess glared from beneath her arm. "Many times." She sat suddenly, swinging her legs to the floor. "You're forgetting his long-running interest in Farrah Landon."

"Yet he wasn't kissing *her*."

"Well, no. She wasn't the one convenient. She wasn't the one standing in front of him, undressing him with her eyes. If she had been..." Would he have kissed Farrah with the same passion he'd shown Tess? Would he have bothered to stop if it had been Farrah in his arms, or would the two of them have made love through the night—the way Tess had dreamed of once she'd finally fallen into a fitful sleep?

Tess sighed. "I think I'll take you up on that offer of coffee if it still stands."

When she'd first arrived at the B and B, Lorelei had volunteered to get her a beverage and a breakfast pastry; Tess had felt too miserable to enjoy either. Instead, she'd flung herself onto the couch and into her recriminations. But given her lack of rest, if she didn't get some caffeine in her system soon, she could become a hazard to herself and others.

The two women went to the kitchen, Oberon following them in case there were treats to be had.

Lorelei poured two steaming mugs. "Okay, Nick liked Farrah at some point. They were never a couple, though. He is allowed to change his mind and develop feelings for someone else." She leaned across the counter and lightly bopped Tess on the head. "This means you."

"Over her already? He seems…steadier than that. He's not his brother, chasing after a different woman every week. He can commit. Nick's the only one among them who's been married." *And speaking of his marriage…* The confession he'd made about his feelings for Marla plagued her.

"I know he wouldn't appreciate my talking about him," Tess began, dumping sugar in her coffee. "But you're one of my best friends and if I can't discuss—"

"My lips are sealed. Tell me anything you want, and it'll go no further," Lorelei promised.

"You mean like when you told Heather I was trying to fix him up with Farrah?"

Lorelei winced. "Okay, that was unfortunate. But I really thought she knew. From here on out, no more mistakes like that."

"He confided to me that one of the reasons he proposed to his ex was because he was so comfortable with her."

"Makes sense. You certainly wouldn't want to marry some-one who makes you *un*comfortable on a daily basis."

"Yeah, but… When Sam walks into a room, there's that zing between the two of you. Your first thought is *not* that he's as comfortable as a broken-in pair of sneakers. To some degree, Nick found her safe and convenient. What if he's ducking his feelings for Farrah because they aren't so safe?" Taking the easy way out, as it were.

"And what about you?" Lorelei reproached softly. "Did you come here hoping I'd talk you out of a discomfiting emotional risk? No one gets it more than me, how unpleasant it can be to make yourself vulnerable. But trust me, the rewards of loving and letting yourself be loved back…" She trailed off, fiddling with her engagement ring. Her expression as she contemplated life with Sam was more eloquent than any words she could have used.

Tess stared through the kitchen window at the picturesque flower garden, not wanting to face her slim, accomplished, genius-with-numbers friend as she made this admission. "You know what an understudy is, right? The alternate who learns all the steps for those times the show must go on but the *real* star isn't able to take the stage? I've felt like that so many times, Lor. The perennial bridesmaid, the younger sister who never fully earned her parents' respect, the dancer who was good enough for corps but never solos. I'm waiting for my chance to shine, to star in my own life. I've never let my pride make decisions for me, but I can't budge on this one principle. I can't be any-one's backup plan."

Tess wasn't a kid anymore, content to go to prom with her crush because his first choice couldn't make it. She'd rather never see Nick again than see more of him because he found her easier to talk to and less intimidating than the woman he *really* wanted.

CHAPTER NINE

STANDING BEHIND THE microphone at the front of the school cafeteria, the PTA president clasped her hands in front of her ample boson. "Why, Mr. Calhoun! Thank you for your willingness to help. I thought it would take more wheedling on my part to talk someone into chairing the committee."

Committee? What? He looked around the room at some of the other parents' expressions. Amusement and pity were the chief responses; one single mother whose twins had once celebrated their birthday at the Galloping C mimed a phone with her fingers. *Call me.*

Okay, so, going forward, he now knew to be very careful about standing up at PTA meetings. But the reason he'd bolted to his feet was because he'd spotted Heather Winchester in the hallway, speaking with the music teacher. He knew Heather had helped with costuming the children for the performance that would start once the PTA meeting ended.

He wanted to speak with Heather because she was close friends with Tess Fitzpatrick—the same Tess Fitzpatrick who seemed to be avoiding him. When she'd ushered him out of her house Saturday night, she'd told him to call her later. *Ha!* It was now Tuesday, and she'd yet to return any of his three messages.

Trying to cause as little disturbance as possible, he sidled to the edge of the cafeteria, then quickly exited the room.

"Mrs. Winchester?" He strode toward Heather.

Her friendly smile didn't mask the confusion in her gaze; they'd never spoken before and she was clearly surprised at being sought out. "What can I do for you?"

"Nick Calhoun." He shook her hand. "Our daughters are in the same dance class."

She nodded slowly. "Yes."

Now what? He'd been full of conviction when he'd hurried from his seat, but it wasn't as if he could demand to know why her friend had stopped speaking to him. He could understand that maybe he'd made a mistake in kissing Tess, but she wasn't a shrinking violet. He would have assumed she'd simply tell a guy he screwed up and move on from there. *He* was the one uncomfortable having conversations, not her.

Stalling as he tried to decide on a strategy, he said, "I understand your daughter Josie is one of the best in the class. Will she be doing a solo at next week's performance?"

At the mention of her daughter, Heather immediately softened, her quizzical expression replaced with maternal pride. "Yes, she is. She's so excited about it. She loves dance class."

"My girl's the same way. And no wonder—they have a great teacher, don't you think? I wanted to ask you about Tess. She specifically asked me to call her over the weekend, but she hasn't answered her phone. Have you seen her or talked to her? I'm starting to get a little worried."

Heather bit her lip, apparently unwilling to divulge whether she'd spoken to Tess. Was she afraid he'd press to know what her friend might have confided? "I'm sure she's fine. Probably spending extra time in the studio to get ready for the party next week."

"Probably. But would you do me a favor?" He flashed her the

most charming smile he could muster. "If you see her, remind her to call me? Or, I guess I could just stop by the studio to check on her…" He trailed off, pleased with his stroke of ingenuity.

Judging by the way Heather's eyes had widened, she would no doubt pass along his words. He suspected he would hear from Tess very soon.

"I thought this guy had difficulty talking to women?" Heather said disbelievingly.

"What guy?" Lean, rugged Zane Winchester strolled into his kitchen, his cowboy hat in hand. His voice was a playful mock growl as he put his arm around his wife's waist. "Should I be jealous?" After he'd kissed her cheek, he turned to smile at Tess, who was rinsing lettuce at the sink. "Hey, Tess, staying for dinner?"

Heather nodded. "I insisted."

Truthfully, Tess was grateful not to be at home. As long as she was busy, she had a legitimate excuse for not calling Nick yet. She did plan to call him, truly—she just hadn't figured out what to say. Also, she rationalized that by not being available, she was taking away his crutch. Maybe he'd work up the gumption to call Farrah instead.

"Well, we're glad to have you." Zane snagged a piece of the cucumber his wife had just sliced for the salad. "I know the girls will be thrilled. Josie worships you and ever since you helped Eden with her hair and makeup for the homecoming dance, she definitely thinks you're cooler than me."

Heather laughed. "She's sixteen, and you're her dad. She thinks pretty much the entire world is cooler than you."

He narrowed his eyes. "Watch it. You're still under suspicion because you haven't told me who this mysterious 'guy' is and I know all the places you're most ticklish." He glanced around as if suddenly realizing how quiet the house was. "Where are the girls?"

"Josie spent the afternoon at the Hollingers' playing with

their daughter. Eden just walked over to bring her home for supper. Go wash up. We'll be ready to eat in about fifteen minutes."

Zane grinned. "Is 'go wash up' code for 'get the heck out of the kitchen so Tess and I can talk privately'?"

"You Rangers don't miss a clue, do you? Now, shoo."

"I'm going, I'm going."

Not for the first time, Tess thought how perfect the Winchesters were together. The fact that they'd overcome secrets and difficult odds to find happiness was uplifting. *I will find the right man for me. Eventually.* And when she did, he wouldn't be smitten with someone else.

Heather swept all the chopped vegetables from the cutting board into the salad bowl. "I thought he'd never leave! We've only got a few minutes before the girls get back, so we have to talk fast. Josie's got radar ears, so it's impossible to have a private conversation with her in the house, and if Eden catches on that we're talking about a boy, she'll want in on the conversation, too."

Tess thought of the intense way Nick had kissed her Saturday. "I don't think 'boy' applies." He was all man. She picked up the conversation from where Zane had interrupted. "So explain to me what happened at this PTA meeting?"

"He cornered me in the hall to ask about you. He was charming and determined, not a shy bone in his body." Heather gave her a teasing smile. "I think you cured him. But I don't understand why you haven't called him. What gives, Fitzpatrick? When I was fighting my feelings for Zane early on, you were constantly nagging me to go ring his doorbell and make a move, lay it all on the line."

"This is different."

Heather put her hands on her hips, her expression the same one she used whenever Josie sneaked cookies she wasn't supposed to have or petted a strange dog without first asking an adult's permission. "How?"

"Because…it's *my* heart on the line," Tess said weakly. Oh, hell. She sounded pitiful even to herself. "I'll call him. Tonight after dinner, I promise. Unless I'm here late. That would be rude. He works such long hours at the ranch, and I wouldn't want to wake Bai—"

"You'll be leaving early."

"And to think I believed you were a friend," Tess groused, crossing the kitchen to pull salad dressing out of the refrigerator.

Heather laughed. "As *someone* I know frequently says, people often need a nudge in the right direction. Consider yourself officially nudged."

"Got any pointers on what to say to him?"

"Just be honest. If I've learned anything over the last year, it's the importance of telling the truth, no matter how bad it is." Her tone turned sympathetic. "And, unless I'm way off base, I'd say you've got it pretty bad."

Tess sighed. "I even like it when he calls me Contessa."

"But you hate your full name!"

"Not the way Nick says it." She didn't hate anything about Nick—except how insecure he suddenly made her feel.

From the moment she'd kissed him, she hadn't been behaving like herself. It was time to talk, to tell him he'd officially graduated Romance 101 and send him on his way. Then she'd be free to start getting over him.

When Nick saw Tess's number on his cell phone, he wanted to pump his fist in victory. "It was the threat of my tracking you down in person, wasn't it?" he gloated.

"Polite people say 'hello,'" she retorted, sounding miffed. "I might even accept 'hey' or, under limited circumstances, 'whazzzzup?'"

He reached for the remote and muted his television. Tess got his full attention. "You've been avoiding me."

"Very true." Instead of denying it, she simply owned it. That was his Tess.

"Why?" Hadn't she missed him at all? He'd been going nuts thinking about her.

"I needed to think—"

"Because I kissed you? Should I apologize for that?"

Her breath hitched, a soft, vulnerable sound. "I needed to think about Operation Cupid."

"That's over." He hadn't thought about Farrah in days. He could not care less who she went with to the town's Valentine dance.

"I agree. I think you're ready—you don't need me anymore."

"I do! Not for asking out Farrah—I don't even want to do that. But because…" *Damn it.* Now was not the time to get tongue-tied!

"You should ask her to coffee, at the very least, to prove to yourself that you can. Spend a few hours with her, see if there are sparks. You owe it to yourself to find out." The false cheer in her voice faded as she added softly, "No woman wants to be second choice."

His free hand tightened into a fist. What could he say? Words bounced around his skull, useless in their disjointed state. In a warped way, she was right. It had taken him longer to notice her, to *know* her. But now that he had… What would soothe her without sounding like manipulative flattery? What would convince her of his feelings without scaring her off? He still didn't know if she felt the same way.

"Goodbye, Nick."

Apparently not.

At the end of Friday's dance class, Tess's gaze caught on her own reflection in the mirror that ran the length of the studio wall. *Jeez. I look like hell.* No doubt caused by her lack of sleep lately. On the upside, she was also experiencing a marked lack of appetite, so maybe she really would lose five pounds before Lorelei's wedding. There you go, a silver lining.

She forced a smile for the girls. "That's it for today. I'll see you all next week for our special Valentine's Day performance!" She doled out hugs, squeezing Bailey with extra affection.

"When are you coming over for ninja tea party?" the little girl asked.

"Um…" *When I start dating some hunky fireman who heals my heart and makes it possible for me to be in the same room with your daddy without aching.* "Not sure."

If the universe was kind, Nick wouldn't be the one to pick up Bailey after class. Some evenings, it was Erin who came to get her granddaughter. Tess was glad when Mrs. Showalter asked for a registration form for the special dance camp Tess would be holding during spring break. It gave Tess a reason to go into the little storage room where the file cabinet sat. Whoever was picking up Bailey could come and go without Tess even noticing at all.

"Contessa?"

She resisted the urge to bang her head repeatedly on the cabinet. "You know, there are stalking laws…" She turned, freezing when she came face-to-face with a dozen red roses. "What are those?"

"Flowers," Nick said. "For you."

"Have you lost your mind?" Aware that her studio was full of parents who wouldn't want their daughters taught by a shrieking psychopath, she lowered her voice to an angry hiss. "I told you I wasn't interested! And you know darn well that Bailey is already emotionally attached to me. This isn't fair to her. Did she see those? She'll misunderstand."

"Or she'll understand perfectly. I want to be with you, Tess."

She squeezed her eyes shut, unprepared to deal with this full-court press. Why was it that hearing something part of her so desperately wanted made her want to cry? "You've obviously forgotten what I'm looking for in a guy. I need to be with someone who *listens,* remember? Someone who takes what I'm saying seriously?"

"You also want to be with someone who thinks you're 'worth the trouble of pursuing.'" He gave her a wolfish grin. "See? I listen."

Nick sat through dinner at The Twisted Jalapeño distracted, only half hearing his brother lean out of his side of the booth to flirt with owner Grace Torres when she walked by.

"When are you going to realize you're crazy about me," Kevin drawled, "and leave that pretty-boy chef?"

The beautiful brunette shot him a look so disdainful it could wither crops. "I think the phrase you were looking for is 'Greek god.' And, FYI, not only does my husband have a possessive streak, I'm pretty sure he could come up with twenty different ways to poison you and make it look like an accident." Then she gave the four of them the gracious smile she was known for. "Y'all enjoy your meal now."

Tim laughed out loud while Kevin eyed his burrito plate suspiciously.

"Miss Grace wouldn't really let her husband poison us, would she?" Bailey asked, sounding more excited than alarmed by the idea.

"Definitely not," Nick said. "Miss Grace worked too hard to keep this restaurant open to risk it being investigated by the police or closed by the Health Department. So, no worries. Eat up."

"Eat what? I'm all done," Bailey said.

"Already?" To cover the fact that he hadn't been paying attention, he added, "That was fast."

From across the table, Kevin stared at him as if he were crazy. "We've been here forty-five minutes. How long do you think it should take her to eat a taco?"

"Daddy, can I be 'scused to say hi to my friend Ashlee?"

Two tables away, a little girl from Bailey's kindergarten class sat with her parents.

"Sure." Nick rose from the bench seat to allow her to pass. "Tell her folks I said hi. And ask her mom if she'd like to help on a PTA committee," he said as an afterthought. When he sat back down, he noticed that Tim and Kevin were both giving him speculative looks.

"What?" he asked defensively.

"You tell us," Tim said. "Your mind's been elsewhere since you and Bailey met us here after her dance class. But you were focused when we were working with that new horse this afternoon. What happened between now and then?"

Kevin smirked. "I'm betting he ran into a certain blonde."

No, a redhead, you know-it-all.

"That's right!" Tim snapped his fingers. "Doesn't Farrah have a little ballerina, too?"

"What the hell is everyone's preoccupation with Farrah Landon?"

Kevin and Tim exchanged glances. For a moment, neither spoke, then Kevin ventured, "I can't speak for 'everyone,' but I can tell you what stays on my mind. Her—"

"Oh, stop being an ass for ten seconds," Nick interrupted. "What are you going to do when you've annoyed all the females in a hundred-mile radius and none of them will date you?"

"Grow old alone," Tim said at the exact same time Kevin answered, "Relocate."

"It *is* a woman who's got you this riled," Tim clarified. "Right?"

"Yes. But it's not Farrah Landon. I barely remember what I liked about her."

"Well," Kevin began. "She's got—"

Nick brandished his fork menacingly. "Don't make me stab you." Vowing to ignore his brother, he looked back at Tim. "I think I liked the idea of Farrah. I had a crush on her as a teenager, and it resurfaced now that we're both divorced single parents. But I don't really *know* her, Farrah the adult. Tess, on the other hand—"

"Tess Fitzpatrick? The curvy redhead?" Kevin asked with interest. At Nick's glare, Kevin stood suddenly. "Service is a little slow tonight. Think I'll mosey over to the bar to get my beer refilled."

"Tess, huh?" Tim gave his boss an assessing look. "Good choice. I like her."

"Yeah. Me, too." Understatement of the year. The question now was, how did he get her to accept his feelings? To admit that she returned them? He didn't want to come on too strong—the world had Kevin for that—but he didn't want to give up easily on something his gut told him could be so perfect. Even Bailey saw how good he and Tess could be together and she was only six!

Staring into space as he pondered his next move, his gaze caught on Sam Travis and Lorelei Keller. There were two people who understood what it took to make a relationship work. Would they be willing to give him advice? He remembered that not so long ago, he wouldn't have wanted to discuss his emotions for a woman or admit that he could use a hand. But everything was different now. Tess had changed his outlook.

She'd changed him.

"Be right back, Tim." He walked over to Sam and Lorelei's table, surprised when Lorelei smiled brightly.

"Is it my turn?" she asked.

"What?" His step faltered.

"Well, you've already accosted Heather. I'm the next logical choice."

Sam's eyebrows rose. "You've been accosting married women?"

"He's trying to enlist allies," Lorelei said, seeming very cheerful about his predicament. "To woo Tess."

"Ah." Sam shook his head in sympathy. "Good luck. It's a joy to have a woman in your life, but they can be hell to figure out."

"Hey!" Lorelei objected, looking not at all annoyed.

Sam grinned at her. "Whatever hell you might've caused me, you were worth it, darlin'."

"I know your loyalties are to Tess," Nick said, "but I'm striking out here."

"What is it you want from me, to put in a good word? Because I've already done that," Lorelei assured him. "Personally, I think she's crazy about you."

The surge of pure joy was staggering. It was an unimaginable relief to hear the words, even if they weren't from Tess herself. "I'm crazy about her, too."

"So what's the problem?" Sam asked. "Why aren't you off somewhere with Tess telling *her* how you feel, instead of interrupting date night?"

"I've tried. She doesn't want to listen." His gaze narrowed on Lorelei. "Do you know why? Is it really the Farrah thing? My crush on her dates back to adolescence. I'm sure Tess had plenty of crushes, too."

Lorelei squirmed under the invisible weight of confidences she felt bound to keep. Loyalty and discretion were admirable traits, but, oh, what Nick wouldn't give right now for loose-lipped women eager to spill secrets.

When she finally spoke, her words were disappointingly unhelpful. "Do you have a perfect relationship with your older brothers?"

"If you think that's a valid question, you're obviously an only child."

"True. But Tess isn't. Maybe you should ask her sometime what it was like to grow up in the same house as her stunning, blonde, prima-ballerina sister. That's all I can give you without betraying a friend. You'll have to take it from there."

"Thanks." He wasn't sure yet how she'd helped him, but he appreciated the effort.

"You're welcome." She grinned. "Now get lost. It's date night."

CHAPTER TEN

IT WAS THE type of Friday night perfect for eating frozen yogurt straight out of the carton and watching a DVD she'd seen so many times she'd memorized all the lines. Wearing a dark green tank top with plaid flannel pajama bottoms, Tess crossed her kitchen, refusing to look at the vase of flowers on the counter. Why had she even brought them home?

She'd tried to avoid taking them from Nick at the studio, glad when Mrs. Showalter had impatiently poked her head into the storage room to ask if Tess had found those registration forms yet. Between Tess helping other parents and Bailey declaring that her stomach was making "funny hungry noises," Nick had gone peacefully. But he'd left the roses on her desk.

When was the last time a man had brought her flowers? It was difficult not to be moved by the gesture. *Maybe you should just go out with him.* Of course, if things didn't work out between them—if he one day realized he'd settled for something comfortable and wanted more—his daughter would be crushed. *She's not the only one.*

Tess rubbed her forehead. Behind her eye, there was a stress knot so big she was considering naming it. But she'd cured many a bad mood before with help from *The Princess Bride*. Grabbing her fro-yo and a spoon, she headed to the living room where Westley and Buttercup awaited. The knock at the door just as she was passing startled her enough that the spoon hit the floor with a metallic clatter.

"I'm not home," she called, her voice unapologetically cranky.

"Open the door," Nick said. "It's me."

I know it's you. That's why I don't want to open the door! She swung it wide. "Look—"

"This isn't stalking. It's a final appeal. Hear me out, and if you want me to go, this will be the last time I darken your doorstep."

"You can come in," she said guardedly. "But I am not sharing the cookie-dough yogurt."

"Tough terms, but I accept."

As soon as he stepped inside, she had a memory of the last time he'd been here, so vivid it was almost physical. Her body burned at the mental replay of how he'd backed her against the wall and seduced her mouth with a kiss hotter than—

"Tess." His voice had gone hoarse, and his eyes sparked with desire. "This is ridiculous. If we both want each other so badly—"

"You're calling me ridiculous? Not a good start, Romeo."

She retreated into the living room, partly to put down the cold carton in her hand but more to put distance between them. Nick rarely asked out a woman. And when he did, by his own admission, he half hoped they'd say no. So what did it say about him that he was here now, after she'd already pushed him away?

Rather than come any closer, he sat on the edge of her couch. She paced, too edgy to get comfortable in a chair.

"It wasn't my brothers' fault that I had a speech impediment," he said out of the blue. "But they certainly didn't make it any easier. They picked on me until Dad threatened to tan their hides, but even if they hadn't been openly mocking, it still would have been difficult. Everything always came so damn easily to them. Junior-rodeo trophies, girlfriends, 4-H ribbons, touchdowns on the football team. Was that how it was with your sister?"

"Regina didn't play football."

"I'm opening up to you over here. Can't you meet me half-way?"

Her fingers curled into fists at her sides. "What do you want me to say, that it sucks being the ugly duckling when your sister's the boyfriend-stealing swan? Not that he was actually my boyfriend and, technically, he liked her first…"

Thick anger clogged Nick's mind—not anger at her, but for her. How could she ever have seen herself as "ugly" anything? How could her family have allowed that? And how was he going to trump an insecurity that had been building throughout her life?

"You've been lying, Tess, to me and to yourself. You act like, if I don't go out with Farrah, I'll always wonder what would have happened. But *you're* the one who would wonder. How can you worry that I'd rather be with her when I'm right here, telling you I want to be with you?"

"Nick, you said yourself that when you proposed to your wife, you thought it was the right thing to do at the time. Is that how you feel about it now?"

"She gave me Bailey." He would always be grateful for that. "I don't regret my marriage."

"Will you regret cowardice?" she flung at him. "Settling for someone instead of taking a chance with your 'dream girl'?"

"When I was fourteen! Her cheerleading uniform was probably a strong factor. But I'm not fourteen anymore."

"Neither am I," she said stubbornly. "When I was younger, I would have gone along with a guy who'd seen me as a buddy, who was comfortable and had fun with me, and thought that was enough for a relationship. I deserve more."

His jaw clenched. "People think I'm the one who lacks confidence, but *you're* the one about to throw away the chance at something truly special. I thought you were braver."

A small sob caught in her throat. "Which just proves what I've been saying, Nick. You're wrong about me."

Although she had a standing invitation to join her parents for supper on Sunday evenings, Tess usually declined. She wasn't sure whether her showing up now stemmed from the need to be around people after a miserable Saturday night alone reliving Nick's words, or if joining her parents was some sort of self-imposed penance for hurting him. He'd mostly looked furious when he stormed out of her house the other night, but, beneath that, she'd glimpsed the wounded expression in his steely gaze.

That had haunted her. If she had the power to hurt him, then he obviously cared for her. The question was, how much?

It had been so tempting to give in to him, but she'd resisted. Shouldn't she be proud of the discipline it had taken to stand by her decision? The easy thing, the weaker thing, would have been to drag him into her bedroom and let herself pretend that he'd chosen her out of preference, rather than default.

"Contessa! There you are." Gillian Fitzpatrick leaned in to give her a quick peck on the cheek before ushering her into the pot-roast-scented house. "Why don't you give your father your coat to hang up? Howard, take the girl's coat!"

As Tess shrugged out of the jacket, she felt the prickle of her mother's critical gaze. *What now?* She didn't have to wait long to discover the source of Gillian's dissatisfaction.

"Do you ever use that flatiron I gave you at Christmas?"

"No, I returned it and got an electric ice-cream maker," Tess said defiantly.

Her mother gasped. "What has gotten into you? I didn't raise you to be rude."

Says the woman who usually starts pointing out my flaws within fifteen seconds of my walking through the door. Since Tess couldn't quite bring herself to apologize sincerely, she simply said, "I didn't sleep well last night." *Or the past six consecutive nights.* "I may not be fit company." Was it too late to turn around and go home?

Gillian pressed her lips into a thin line. "Let's just focus on what's important—family. At least I have one of my daughters here. Lord knows when your sister will be able to visit again! Regina is dancing *Giselle* to sold-out houses and as soon as that wraps, she'll have to start rehearsals on *Romeo and Juliet.*"

"Well, I'm glad you have me as a backup between her visits," Tess said.

Her mother either missed or chose to overlook the sarcasm. "We should eat before the roast gets cold. Why hasn't your father come back? It doesn't take that long to hang up a coat. Howard!"

Tess followed her mother to the back of the house. Growing up, the hallway had been decorated with family photos—the Fitzpatricks' wedding portrait, the girls' school pictures. But Gillian Fitzpatrick had redecorated to spotlight a common theme. Silver frames contained large black-and-white prints of Regina; most of them were ballet shots but there were also several of her in her wedding dress. In none of them did her hair have the bad manners to frizz or curl. Tess had sometimes wondered where the other pictures had gone, but she never asked. She wasn't sure she was ready to hear that her high-school graduation photo now lived in the attic.

The food smelled divine, but by the time they reached the kitchen, Tess had no appetite left. Why, on a day when she needed comfort, had she chosen to come here? *Must have confused my family with someone else's.*

Gillian's heels clicked sharply across the Spanish tile as she carried dishes to the table. "Your father's sulky because I didn't make dessert, but I knew you'd appreciate my restraint. How's the weight loss going for your friend's wedding?"

"Swell. In fact, don't be surprised if I barely eat anything," Tess said.

Her father said the blessing. No sooner had they all said,

"Amen" than Gillian said, "When you called to tell me you were coming for dinner, I half expected you to bring a guest."

"You did? Why?" Tess had never once subjected anyone else to one of these strained meals.

"Bitsy Harper said she saw you out last weekend on a date. She seemed to think it looked..." Gillian shot a glance toward her husband before dropping her voice. "Passionate. I do hope you were comporting yourself with decorum?"

"Oh, for crying out... I danced with him. Once. That was all." But, Lord, what a dance. Tess stabbed at her mashed potatoes. She wished she were somewhere with Nick now. "Bitsy Harper has an overactive imagination. Nick and I—"

"Nicholas Pfeffer?" her mother asked, her eyes gleaming. "The lawyer?"

"No, Nick Calhoun. The cowboy," Tess added with relish.

Gillian frowned. "The one who stutters?"

Right, because heaven forbid one of Gillian's daughters date someone with a defect. Would it do any good if Tess pointed out that he hadn't stuttered in *years* but that even if he did, he was a kind, loyal, sexy man with an adorable daughter and a gift with horses? "Yes, the one who stuttered. But it could be worse, right? He could have *frizzy hair!*"

"Why are you raising your voice to me?" Gillian looked genuinely shocked. "Howard, tell her not to raise her voice at the table."

Tess stood. "I shouldn't have come." Not when she was apparently spoiling for a fight. She'd spent her teenage years arguing with her mother and it had accomplished nothing. What was the point in wasting her breath now and ruining her parents' dinner?

"Contessa Gretchen Fitzpatrick, you sit down and finish your meal." Her mother pointed at the chair. "Honestly. You know, your sister would never behave like this."

"Trust me, I am aware. If I knew how to be more like Regina, Mom... Don't you think I would have loved the solos, the boyfriends, the approval from my parents?" Tears blurred her vision, and Tess hurried to the kitchen, wanting to be alone when they finally fell.

She leaned over the counter, pressing her hands to her eyes in a futile attempt to stem the flow. The *click, click* of Gillian's heels wrung a damp groan from her.

"Not now, Mom."

"Shush. Mothers know best." Her mom stood beside her and, for a brief second, put her arm around Tess's shoulders and squeezed. It wasn't much as hugs went, but Gillian had never been demonstratively affectionate. "Now, what's this really about?"

Because a lifetime of resentment at being a second-class citizen in her own family wasn't enough of a reason to snap?

"You've always been outspoken, but you're not typically this emotional," Gillian said. "So what's changed? Is it this Nick?"

Yes. "Despite whatever Bitsy told you, he and I are not a couple. I am single." Utterly and spectacularly single.

"Well, you've always been a very independent person. Not everyone is meant to be in a relationship."

"Jeez, Mom! You don't have to make it sound as if I'll die alone. I *want* to be in a relationship. Regina's not the only one who's dreamed of a big white wedding and her day in the sun as a beautiful bride. I deserve happiness, too." Her voice broke. "Don't I?"

"Tessie."

Both women turned in surprise to find Howard Fitzpatrick standing in the doorway of the kitchen. He locked gazes with his daughter, his eyes full of compassion, and simply opened his arms. Tess threw herself into the bear hug, letting her father soothe her as if she were a little girl. She sniffed, trying not to cry all over his polo shirt.

He held her silently, proving what she'd told Nick once. Sometimes, the words didn't matter. It was okay if you didn't know what to say. Actions were more important anyway.

Hypocrite. If actions were so important, why was she cling-ing to Nick's words, hiding behind them as if they were a shield? Yes, he'd said his feelings for Farrah dated back years. Yes, he'd made it sound as if he'd once considered her the Holy Grail of girlfriends. But those were statements, not actions.

His dance with Tess—that had been an action. Kissing her. Coming to her house the other night. Bringing her flowers.

Was she letting her own insecurities and a few words stand in the way of the happiness she claimed to deserve?

It was strange for Nick to enter the high school Monday evening. He himself had graduated from this school, but that seemed like an alternate universe. There was a disconnect between the kid he'd been and the man escorting his nervous daughter to the auditorium. Her hair was tamed into a sleek dark bun and she wore a red leotard with white tights. He was supposed to deliver her backstage so she could get her tutu and some light makeup. Tess was using this as a way to prepare some of the younger dancers for the much-more-complicated spring recital.

Nick had to admit, he wasn't particularly in a Valentine's mood, but he looked forward to watching his daughter dance. "You are going to be great!"

"My tummy feels funny," she admitted.

His, too. This would be the first time he'd seen Tess since his ill-advised plan of showing up at her house.

If the backstage area was a piece of artwork, it would have been titled "Pandemonium in Pink." Girls were giggling and crying and looking for a missing ballet slipper. Mothers were lacing tutus and applying makeup to little faces. Younger sib-lings were zipping around, ducking between the curtain panels despite repeated reminders that there was no running.

"Miss Tess!" Without waiting for Nick, Bailey ran up to the woman in the center of the chaos, hugging her beloved ballet teacher.

Nick actually experienced a moment's envy that she was allowed to express her affection so unreservedly. He settled for a crisp nod. "Miss Fitzpatrick."

Her gaze was surprisingly warm, like melting chocolate. "Actually, I prefer Contessa."

It wasn't so much her words that threw him as the timbre of her voice. Something had changed, but this probably wasn't the time or place to ask her what.

She swallowed. "Nick, I—"

"Tess, I can't get the music to work!" A teenager with a frantic expression and pink streaks in her blond hair approached Tess. "And Mom asked if we've got any more of those sequined bows?"

"Okay, be right there." Tess looked at Nick. "Can we talk after the performance? Please?"

He wasn't sure what she wanted to say, but he instinctively recognized the vulnerability in her voice. It echoed how he'd felt for the past week. Was there still a chance that she would believe what he'd been trying to tell her? "Absolutely. Anything I can do to help in the meantime?"

"Would you be willing to handle the door-prize announcements and take over raffle tickets? Heather was selling them, but we need her for last-minute costume emergencies. Unless you're handy with a needle and thread?" Tess's dimple appeared unexpectedly, and he badly wanted to kiss her.

"Raffle tickets it is."

A few minutes later, Heather had handed him the roll of tickets and the zipped pouch of cash. "Make sure people know it's for a good cause," she said. For each class at the dance studio, Tess held slots for a couple of students from lower-income families, girls who showed promise and a real love of dance but whose parents couldn't quite afford lessons. The raffle was to help with a fund that allowed those students to buy shoes and costumes.

Determined to make Tess proud and raise money for something important to her, he approached everyone—mothers, fathers, grandparents—and poured on as much charm as he could.

"I'll take ten," a female cooed.

When he turned, he saw Farrah smiling up at him. "That's great. It's for a worthy cause."

She laid a hand on his arm. "You are *such* a good father, getting involved like this. My ex probably won't even bother to show up and support his daughters, yet here you are. Volunteering backstage, getting involved at PTA meetings… I'm a little hurt, you know."

He blinked, having no idea what she was talking about. "You are?"

"I thought maybe you'd ask me to help with your committee." She flipped her blond hair over her shoulder. "I guess since you never asked me, I'll have to take matters into my own hands. Let me give you my number. I've chaired lots of committees. I could give you some pointers. Maybe over dinner?"

"That's nice, Farrah, but—" Looking past her, he spotted Tess. Even from this distance, the naked doubt was clear on her face. Just as he was sure that, from where she stood, Farrah's body language was clear. He doubted people on packed subways stood as close as Farrah was to him. He shuffled back a step. "I appreciate the offer, but my committee's pretty well staffed. I think they need some help with the science fair, though."

As the last strains of music faded softly, thunderous applause filled the high-school auditorium. Tess was so proud. Her girls had all done such a wonderful job today. And, frankly, she was proud of herself, too. Earlier, when she'd glanced across the room and seen Farrah blatantly hitting on Nick… It would have been easy to panic, to tell herself they made a stunning couple, that he should have a chance with Farrah to see if they were well suited.

She'd felt that way for exactly ten seconds. Then she'd realized, *Hell with that. He's mine.* Other women had had their chances. If they hadn't been able to see all the qualities Tess had always known Nick possessed, they didn't deserve him. She couldn't wait to dismiss everyone to the cafeteria, where Eden and some of her friends had set up refreshments, so that she could finally talk to Nick alone. But first, there was one last thing to take care of.

She stepped up to the microphone. "Thank you all so much for coming this evening. I know it means a lot to the girls. I also want to thank you for your support of the studio, which comes in many forms. Volunteer hours, bringing your daughters to extra rehearsals the month of recital, and even the simple act of buying raffle tickets so that we can give the gift of dance to even more girls in our community. I know many of you have bought tickets today and are waiting anxiously to find out if you're a winner. So, without any further ado, I'll turn this over to Nick Calhoun."

He came up the side steps of the stage, and Tess tried not to stare. How was it possible that she'd missed him so much in such a short period of time? She backed farther into the shadows, hoping the parents in the audience couldn't read her hungry expression when she looked at him. Nick stood a few feet in front of her, calling out the names of the winners. Tess realized that in addition to being proud of her students and herself, she was darn proud of him, too. It was difficult to believe that the man making jokes and reading off names was the same boy who'd stammered through childhood, speaking as little as possible and trying not to draw attention to himself.

The total opposite of me. She'd craved the spotlight since she was born. It was funny, how alike they truly were for all their seeming differences. Lost in her thoughts, she wasn't completely paying attention to Nick's words as he concluded.

"How about one last round of applause for the woman who made this all possible, Tess Fitzpatrick, the woman I love."

What? Her heartbeat rocketed. Without making a conscious

decision to move, she bolted to his side, keeping her voice to a whisper. "What did you just say?"

He didn't bother lowering his own voice. "That I love you."

There were murmurs and a few chuckles in the audience. Tess heard a couple of *awww*s. She suspected Heather was among them.

Tess cupped her hand over the microphone, ignoring the screeched blare of feedback. "I…" She couldn't believe he thought this was an appropriate venue to share his feelings, but she was too ecstatic over what he'd said to object.

"Kiss him!" That was *definitely* Heather.

Nick's eyes twinkled. "I'm in favor of that suggestion."

"There are children in the room," Tess pointed out breathlessly.

He gently lifted her hand from the microphone. "Folks, there are food and drinks in the cafeteria. Go enjoy them." Then he led Tess backstage.

"Why did you say that?" she whispered, stunned that this once reticent man had publicly proclaimed his feelings for her.

"Because it's true." Nick pulled her against him. "And I wanted you to know it, beyond a shadow of a doubt. No one else holds a candle to you. I may have called someone my dream girl, but that's what it was—a long-ago, insubstantial dream. What I feel for you is reality. In a lot of ways you woke me up. It's gotten easier to talk to people. I laugh more. Except for when you pushed me away. Don't do that again."

"Definitely not," she promised. She stretched up on her toes to kiss him, stopping at the very last second. "You really love me? Even after I nearly made a mess of this?"

"I love you." He brushed his thumb over her lower lip. It was amazing how such a slight touch could stoke such powerful desire. "And I never say anything I don't mean."

There was suddenly a flurry of motion—Bailey burst through the other side of the curtain, Heather hot on her heels.

"Sorry!" Heather exclaimed. "She got away from me."

Bailey launched herself in the middle of their embrace for a group hug. "Is Miss Tess going to be my new mommy?"

"Um..." Nick looked sheepish, as if only just realizing the consequences of his public declaration. "Let's not put Tess on the spot, kiddo. Maybe we should start with an easier question. Contessa, will you be my valentine?"

"*Our* valentine," Bailey said.

Tess smiled, so full of emotion it was difficult to speak. "Yes." Always.

* * * * *

Subscribe and fall in love with a Mills & Boon series today!

You'll be among the first to read stories delivered to your door monthly and enjoy great savings.

WE SIMPLY LOVE ROMANCE

NEW RELEASES!

**Four sisters. One surprise will.
One year to wed.**

Don't miss these two volumes of
Wed In The Outback!

When Holt Waverly leaves his flourishing outback estate to his four daughters, it comes to pass that without an eldest son to inherit, the farm will be entailed to someone else…unless all his daughters are married within the year!

May 2024

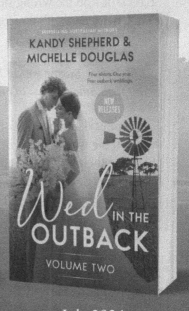

July 2024

Keep reading for an excerpt of
Gift-Wrapped In Her Wedding Dress
by Kandy Shepherd.
Find it in the
Sydney Brides anthology,
out now!

CHAPTER ONE

So HE'D GOT on the wrong side of the media. Again. Dominic's words, twisted out of all recognition, were all over newspapers, television and social media.

Billionaire businessman Dominic Hunt refuses to sleep out with other CEOs in charity event for homeless.

Dominic slammed his fist on his desk so hard the pain juddered all the way up his arm. He hadn't *refused* to support the charity in their Christmas appeal, just refused the invitation to publicly bed down for the night in a cardboard box on the forecourt of the Sydney Opera House. His donation to the worthy cause had been significant—but anonymous. *Why wasn't that enough?*

He buried his head in his hands. For a harrowing time in his life there had been no choice for him but to sleep rough for real, a cardboard box his only bed. He couldn't go there again—not even for a charity stunt, no matter how worthy. There could be no explanation—he would not share the secrets of his past. *Ever.*

With a sick feeling of dread he continued to read onscreen the highlights of the recent flurry of negative press about him and his company, thoughtfully compiled in a report by his Director of Marketing.

Predictably, the reporters had then gone on to rehash his well-known aversion to Christmas. Again he'd been misquoted. It was true he loathed the whole idea of celebrating Christmas. But not for the reasons the media had so fancifully contrived. Not because he was a *Scrooge*. How he hated that label and the erroneous aspersions that he didn't ever give to charity. Despaired that he was included in a round-up of Australia's Multi-Million-Dollar Misers. *It couldn't be further from the truth.*

He strongly believed that giving money to worthy causes should be conducted in private—not for public acclaim. But this time he couldn't ignore the name-calling and innuendo. He was near to closing a game-changing deal on a joint venture with a family-owned American corporation run by a man with a strict moral code that included obvious displays of philanthropy.

Dominic could not be seen to be a Scrooge. He had to publicly prove that he was not a miser. But he did not want to reveal the extent of his charitable support because to do so would blow away the smokescreen he had carefully constructed over his past.

He'd been in a bind. Until his marketing director had suggested he would attract positive press if he opened his harbourside home for a lavish fund-raising event for charity. 'Get your name in the newspaper for the right reasons,' he had been advised.

Dominic hated the idea of his privacy being invaded but he had reluctantly agreed. He wanted the joint venture to happen. If a party was what it took, he was prepared to put his qualms aside and commit to it.

The party would be too big an event for it to be organised in-house. His marketing people had got outside companies involved. Trouble was the three so-called 'party planners' he'd been sent so far had been incompetent and he'd shown them the door within minutes of meeting. Now there was a fourth. He glanced down at the eye-catching card on the desk in front of

him. Andrea Newman from a company called Party Queens—
No party too big or too small the card boasted.

Party Queens. It was an interesting choice for a business
name. Not nearly as stitched up as the other companies that had
pitched for this business. But did it have the gravitas required?
After all, this event could be the deciding factor in a deal that
would extend his business interests internationally.

He glanced at his watch. This morning he was working from
his home office. Ms Newman was due to meet with him right
now, here at his house where the party was to take place. Despite
the attention-grabbing name of the business, he had no reason
to expect Party Planner Number Four to be any more impressive than the other three he'd sent packing. But he would give
her twenty minutes—that was only fair and he made a point
of always being fair.

On cue, the doorbell rang. Punctuality, at least, was a point
in Andrea Newman's favour. He headed down the wide marble
stairs to the front door.

His first impression of the woman who stood on his porch
was that she was attractive, not in a conventionally pretty way
but something rather more interesting—an angular face framed
by a tangle of streaked blonde hair, a wide generous mouth, unusual green eyes. So attractive he found himself looking at her
for a moment longer than was required to sum up a possible
contractor. And the almost imperceptible curve of her mouth
let him know she'd noticed.

'Good morning, Mr Hunt—Andie Newman from Party
Queens,' she said. 'Thank you for the pass code that got me
through the gate. Your security is formidable, like an eastern
suburbs fortress.' Was that a hint of challenge underscoring her
warm, husky voice? If so, he wasn't going to bite.

'The pass code expires after one use, Ms Newman,' he said,
not attempting to hide a note of warning. The three party planners before her were never going to get a new pass code. But
none of them had been remotely like her—in looks or manner.

She was tall and wore a boldly patterned skirt of some silky fine fabric that fell below her knees in uneven layers, topped by a snug-fitting rust-coloured jacket and high heeled shoes that laced all the way up her calf. A soft leather satchel was slung casually across her shoulder. She presented as smart but more unconventional than the corporate dark suits and rigid brief-cases of the other three—whose ideas had been as pedestrian as their appearances.

'Andie,' she replied and started to say something else about his security system. But, as she did, a sudden gust of balmy spring breeze whipped up her skirt, revealing long slender legs and a tantalising hint of red underwear. Dominic tried to do the gentlemanly thing and look elsewhere—difficult when she was standing so near to him and her legs were so attention-worthy.

'Oh,' she gasped, and fought with the skirt to hold it down, but no sooner did she get the front of the skirt in place, the back whipped upwards and she had to twist around to hold it down. The back view of her legs was equally as impressive as the front. He balled his hands into fists by his sides so he did not give into the temptation to help her with the flyaway fabric.

She flushed high on elegant cheekbones, blonde hair tou-sled around her face, and laughed a husky, uninhibited laugh as she battled to preserve her modesty. The breeze died down as quickly as it had sprung up and her skirt floated back into place. Still, he noticed she continued to keep it in check with a hand on her thigh.

'That's made a wonderful first impression, hasn't it?' she said, looking up at him with a rueful smile. For a long moment their eyes connected and he was the first to look away. *She was beautiful.*

As she spoke, the breeze gave a final last sigh that ruffled her hair across her face. Dominic wasn't a fanciful man, but it seemed as though the wind was ushering her into his house.

'There are worse ways of making an impression,' he said gruffly. 'I'm interested to see what you follow up with.'

* * *

Andie wasn't sure what to reply. She stood at the threshold of Dominic Hunt's multi-million-dollar mansion and knew for the first time in her career she was in serious danger of losing the professional cool in which she took such pride.

Not because of the incident with the wind and her skirt. Or because she was awestruck by the magnificence of the house and the postcard-worthy panorama of Sydney Harbour that stretched out in front of it. No. It was the man who towered above her who was making her feel so inordinately flustered. Too tongue-tied to come back with a quick quip or clever retort.

'Th…thank you,' she managed to stutter as she pushed the breeze-swept hair back from across her face.

During her career as a stylist for both magazines and advertising agencies, and now as a party planner, she had acquired the reputation of being able to manage difficult people. Which was why her two partners in their fledgling business had voted for her to be the one to deal with Dominic Hunt. Party Queens desperately needed a high-profile booking like this to help them get established. Winning it was now on her shoulders.

She had come to his mansion forewarned that he could be a demanding client. The gossip was that he had been scathing to three other planners from other companies much bigger than theirs before giving them the boot. Then there was his wider reputation as a Scrooge—a man who did not share his multitude of money with others less fortunate. He was everything she did not admire in a person.

Despite that, she been blithely confident Dominic Hunt wouldn't be more than she could handle. Until he had answered that door. Her reaction to him had her stupefied.

She had seen the photos, watched the interviews of the billionaire businessman, had recognised he was good-looking in a dark, brooding way. But no amount of research had prepared her for the pulse-raising reality of this man—tall, broad-shouldered, powerful muscles apparent even in his sleek tailored grey suit. He wasn't pretty-boy handsome. Not with that strong jaw, the crooked nose that looked as though it had been broken by a viciously aimed punch, the full, sensual mouth with the faded white scar on the corner, the spiky black hair. And then there was the almost palpable emanation of power.

She had to call on every bit of her professional savvy to ignore the warm flush that rose up her neck and onto her cheeks, the way her heart thudded into unwilling awareness of Dominic Hunt, not as a client but as a man.

She could not allow that to happen. This job was too important to her and her friends in their new business. *Anyway, dark and brooding wasn't her type.* Her ideal man was sensitive and sunny-natured, like her first lost love, for whom she felt she would always grieve.

She extended her hand, willing it to stay steady, and forced a smile. 'Mr Hunt, let's start again. Andie Newman from Party Queens.'

His grip in return was firm and warm and he nodded acknowledgement of her greeting. If a mere handshake could send shivers of awareness through her, she could be in trouble here.

Keep it businesslike. She took a deep breath, tilted back her head to meet his gaze full-on. 'I believe I'm the fourth party planner you've seen and I don't want there to be a fifth. I should be the person to plan your event.'

If he was surprised at her boldness, it didn't show in his scrutiny; his grey eyes remained cool and assessing.

'You'd better come inside and convince me why that should be the case,' he said. Even his voice was attractive—deep and measured and utterly masculine.

'I welcome the opportunity,' she said in the most confident voice she could muster.

She followed him into the entrance hall of the restored nineteen-twenties house, all dark stained wood floors and cream marble. A grand central marble staircase with wrought-iron balustrades split into two sides to climb to the next floor. This wasn't the first grand home she'd been in during the course of her work but it was so impressive she had to suppress an impulse to gawk.

'Wow,' she said, looking around her, forgetting all about how disconcerted Dominic Hunt made her feel. 'The staircase. It's amazing. I can just see a choir there, with a chorister on each step greeting your guests with Christmas carols as they step into the house.' Her thoughts raced ahead of her. Choristers' robes in red and white? Each chorister holding a scrolled parchment printed with the words to the carol? What about the music? A string quartet? A harpsichord?

'What do you mean?' he said, breaking into her reverie.

Andie blinked to bring herself back to earth and turned to look up at him. She smiled. 'Sorry. I'm getting ahead of myself. It was just an idea. Of course I realise I still need to convince you I'm the right person for your job.'

'I meant about the Christmas carols.'

So he would be that kind of pernickety client, pressing her for details before they'd even decided on the bigger picture. Did she need to spell out the message of 'Deck the Halls with Boughs of Holly'?

She shook her head in a don't-worry-about-it way. 'It was just a top-of-mind thought. But a choir would be an amazing use of the staircase. Maybe a children's choir. Get your guests into the Christmas spirit straight away, without being too cheesy about it.'

'It isn't going to be a Christmas party.' He virtually spat the word *Christmas*.

'But a party in December? I thought—'

He frowned and she could see where his reputation came from as his thick brows drew together and his eyes darkened. 'Truth be told, I don't want a party here at all. But it's a necessary evil—necessary to my business, that is.'

'Really?' she said, struggling not to jump in and say the wrong thing. A client who didn't actually want a party? This she hadn't anticipated. Her certainty that she knew how to handle this situation—this man—started to seep away.

She gritted her teeth, forced her voice to sound as conciliatory as possible. 'I understood from your brief that you wanted a big event benefiting a charity in the weeks leading up to Christmas on a date that will give you maximum publicity.'

'All that,' he said. 'Except it's not to be a Christmas party. Just a party that happens to be held around that time.'

Difficult and demanding didn't begin to describe this. But had she been guilty of assuming December translated into Christmas? Had it actually stated that in the brief? She didn't think she'd misread it.

She drew in a calming breath. 'There seems to have been a misunderstanding and I apologise for that,' she said. 'I have the official briefing from your marketing department here.' She patted her satchel. 'But I'd rather hear your thoughts, your ideas for the event in your own words. A successful party plan comes from the heart. Can we sit down and discuss this?'

He looked pointedly at his watch. Her heart sank to the level of the first lacing on her shoes. She did not want to be the fourth party planner he fired before she'd even started her pitch. 'I'll give you ten minutes,' he said.

He led her into a living room that ran across the entire front of the house and looked out to the blue waters of the harbour and its icons of the Sydney Harbour Bridge and the Opera House. Glass doors opened out to a large terrace. *A perfect summer party terrace.*

Immediately she recognised the work of one of Sydney's most fashionable high-end interior designers—a guy who only worked with budgets that started with six zeros after them. The room worked neutral tones and metallics in a nod to the art deco era of the original house. The result was masculine but very, very stylish.

What an awesome space for a party. But she forced thoughts of the party out of her head. She had ten minutes to win this business. Ten minutes to convince Dominic Hunt she was the one he needed.

deal. Those shoulders. That smile. I wanted to crawl onto his lap and see if he's as good a kisser as I think he'd be."

"So why didn't you?"

"Because he's interested in you, and anyway, I'm with Richard."

"He isn't interested in me. He's a player, the sort who can't let a woman walk past without making a move."

"Honey, he could hardly keep his hands off you at the lunch table. He almost burst a blood vessel holding back the caveman inside. You should think about it." Sky spoke in a soft voice. "It's time you went to bed with something other than a good book."

She had thought about it, and thinking about it had caused a thrill of excitement low in her belly. "Thinking about it is all I intend to do."

"At least you've thought about it. If you hadn't admitted that, I would have phoned for medical help. Why aren't you going to do anything about it?"

"Because everything about this situation is unreal."

"He looked pretty real to me."

"I have to think of Lizzy."

"Having Lizzy doesn't mean giving up sex. You can't live in isolation, especially in a place like this. You need adult company. For what it's worth, I like him. I think you can trust him."

"I hope so, since he knows the truth." She'd told Sky what had happened. "Did Alec upset you?"

"A little." Skylar slid sunglasses onto her nose. "Personality clash. No biggie."

"I thought you and he seemed—"

"What?"

"Nothing. Ignore me."

"Like I said, I'm with Richard. And even if I wasn't, I don't have a thing for damaged men, and Alec Hunter is definitely damaged, not to mention rude." Her friend stared into the distance. "Insanely good-looking, of course, but that's not enough to compensate for his other deficiencies."

"Ryan mentioned that he's coming out of a bad divorce."

"If yesterday was an indication of his usual level of charm, the surprise is that someone married him in the first place, not that they divorced him."

"He's very successful. And he makes history accessible. I've watched him in a few different things. Type 'Shipwreck Hunter' into a search engine and you can find a video of him in action, kayaking the Colorado River. And last year he helped build and sail a Viking ship. Don't you watch TV?"

"Not much." Skylar watched as the plane approached. "I wish I didn't have to leave. I love this place. All I want to do is curl up here for the summer, walk on the cliffs and make jewelry, instead of which I have to smile and make polite small talk with people who bore me. My feet are going to be screaming by the weekend, and then we're going to The Hamptons to see Richard's family. Pity me."

"You're staying with his family? Are you being vetted?"

"I've already been vetted. Richard never wastes time dating anyone who doesn't have the right credentials. Just in case the relationship goes somewhere. My bloodline has been studied along with anything in my past that might cause embarrassment."

It sounded so unlike free-spirited Skylar that Emily felt another ripple of concern. "Do you want the relationship to go somewhere?"

"You know me. I think about the journey, not the destination. You can waste your whole life thinking about where you're going, and then one day you wake up and realize you missed today because you were thinking about tomorrow. I like to live in the moment."

And yet Richard was the opposite of that. As far as Emily could see, he'd spent his life working toward a single destination, and everything he did was designed to turbo-boost him along that path. "What are you doing with him, Sky?"

"When he isn't focused on the future, he can be charming. And he genuinely wants to do good and change the world. He knows what he wants. He has a goal. That's why he gets frustrated when things don't go the way he wants them to, and people don't feel the same way he does."

Emily felt another flicker of unease. "Be careful." She didn't know why she said it, except that something didn't feel right. "And don't forget I'm here if you need me."

"Hey, I'm the one supporting you." Skylar watched as the plane executed a perfect landing. "One day they'll arrange a direct flight to New York."

"Then this place would lose its charm."

"Maybe. I wish I'd bought one of those blueberry pies to take home. I could really—" Skylar's jaw dropped as the pilot emerged from the plane. "Holy crap, is that—? Tell me I'm hallucinating."

Emily squinted into the sun. "You're not hallucinating. It's Zach."

"What the hell is he doing here? Do you think Brittany knows?"

"I doubt it."

"Should we tell her?"

Emily thought about it. "No. She's in Crete. She's happy. He might be gone by the time she gets back."

"You're right. I can't remember the last time she even mentioned her ex-husband. Did you know he was here?"

"No. Last thing I heard, he was working as a pilot in Alaska. Should we kill him for her?"

"No. It was years ago, and she wouldn't want him to know he hurt her that badly."

"She hasn't been serious about a man since."

"I know. Apparently ten days of marriage to him cured her of commitment forever." Skylar stared at the man standing on the tarmac. Even from this distance there was no missing the power of his physique. He stood, legs spread, eyes hidden behind shades as he talked to an official. "It's wrong that he should look so attractive. It distracts from the fact he's a bastard. I hope he's as good a pilot as that arrogant smile suggests, given that he's going to be responsible for my life. How do I play this? Do I pretend I don't know he broke Brittany's heart?"

"That's probably best as he's in charge of the aircraft. I don't want him to dump you in the ocean."

"Good point. Instead of wanting to kill him, I'll be grateful. After all, if he hadn't acted the way he did, we never would have bonded that first night at college. Do you remember?"

"Of course. I remember all of it."

"I remember Brittany sticking a photo of him on the wall so that we could draw on it. I gave him a nose ring and pink hair." Skylar walked back to the car and hugged Lizzy. "See you soon, Tinker Bell. Make me a necklace. And make Emily throw out everything she owns that is black."

Emily watched her friend leave and then slid back into the car.

She wondered briefly why Zach would be flying for Island Air, and then decided that as Brittany wasn't here anyway, it didn't matter. Neither of them stayed in the same place for long. He'd be gone long before Brittany returned.

Keen to get home as fast as possible, she drove back along the coast road to Castaway Cottage. Today there was no blue sky, and the wind whipped the sea into a foaming, boiling cauldron, toying with boats and keeping swimmers out of the water. Surf crashed over the rocks, exploding in a burst of white froth.

Emily kept her eyes on the road.

If she worked really hard at it, she could just about pretend the sea wasn't there.

Two decades had passed, but she could still remember the moment when the water had closed over her head and dragged her down, hungry for an innocent victim.

Sweat formed on her brow.

Pulling up outside the cottage, she saw that Lizzy had fallen asleep.

Absolved of responsibility for a brief, blissful moment, she closed her eyes.

Only when the child slept did she manage to shake off the tension.

OUT IN THE BAY, Ryan made use of that wind as he hauled the sail and turned the boat. "So, your charm with women is something I aspire to emulate."

Alec ducked under the boom. "I wasn't trying to charm anyone."

"That's good to know." But he could tell that his friend's black mood had lifted and was glad he'd suggested making the most of the wind and the tide.

Work could wait until darkness fell over the water.

In the meantime, he was going to make the most of living next to some of the best sailing waters on the planet.

Penobscot Bay was peppered with hundreds of small uninhabited islands, many with secluded anchorages. A few of the larger islands, like Puffin, had working harbors and communities that swelled to ten times the size during the summer months.

They sailed along the coast, past beautiful old estates of weathered clapboard and wooded enclaves, rocky coves where forest met the sea, inlets, harbors and fishing villages dependent on lobstering and commercial fishing. Ducks and gulls bobbed on the surface of the water, and in the distance he could see the ferry making one of its three times a day trips back to the mainland.

With the wind in their sails, they sped across the water to Fisherman's Creek, past rocky outcrops, nesting birds and seal colonies, finally returning to the island as the sun set.

Ryan pulled his hat low over his eyes as they approached the harbor. "So, what did you think of her?"

"She should come with a warning. Marry this woman and your investments could go down as well as up."

"I was talking about Emily."

"Oh," Alec shrugged. "She looked tense. Jumpy. And she has a kid. Kids mean responsibility. Never mess with a single mother. There is never any question of a casual relationship. They're testing you out to see if you're marriage material."

Ryan decided not to disclose Lizzy's parentage. Not because he didn't trust Alec, but because he respected Emily too much to reveal her secrets. "Did you notice she sat with her back to the water?"

"She had no choice. You picked a table that wasn't big enough for five. I notice you squashed yourself next to her."

"She picked the same seat the day before, and the table was plenty big enough."

"What are you saying? That she doesn't like water?"

"I don't know what I'm saying, but there's something there." Ryan gauged the distance and guided the yacht skillfully against the dock.

"You're showing a lot of interest in her."

"Just being supportive. That's what we islanders do."

"How supportive? Are you planning on tucking her in and kissing her good-night?"

Ryan thought about it. "I might, except I have a feeling I wouldn't be welcome."

"Women always welcome you."

"I think there's more to her than meets the eye."

"There's more to every woman than meets the eye." Alec sprang off the boat. "That's the problem."

RESPONSIBILITY SHARED THE bed with her and kept her awake.

She'd locked the doors and checked the windows, but still the endless possibility for risk swirled through Emily's brain, tormenting her. Next to her, Lizzy slept deeply, curled under the pretty patchwork quilt, her arms clutching the bear.

It was a sight to soften the hardest heart, except that Emily had locked hers away years before and had no idea how to access it. And she didn't want to.

Numb, she closed her eyes and rolled over, but still sleep stayed just out of her reach.

She thought about Ryan, about the way his fingers had felt brushing over hers, the way he'd looked at her with that intense focus that caused the world around them to melt away. Her relationship with Neil had been comfortable and nonthreatening. He'd done nothing to disturb her equilibrium or threaten her sense of safety.

Ryan did both. He made her feel things she'd never felt before. But she had no intention of allowing herself to explore those feelings in greater depth.

She knew she had issues with attachment, and she was perfectly fine with that.

For all his sophisticated charm, Ryan Cooper represented danger. The kind of danger she was keen to avoid.

She finally succumbed to exhaustion as dawn sent sunlight pouring through the window and then woke later, much later, knowing she'd slept too long. The sun beamed strong rays through the glass, adding a warm glow to the white and muted blues of the bedroom.

Daylight and silence made an uneasy combination.

Feeling a powerful sense that something wasn't right, Emily turned her head to check on Lizzy and saw she was alone in the bed.

"Lizzy?" Her stomach cramped, and panic mingled with self-recrimination.

She should have stayed awake.

She shouldn't have taken her eyes off her for a moment.

Telling herself that the girl had probably gone to find breakfast, she sprinted downstairs on legs that felt as useless as cooked spaghetti.

"Lizzy?" The kitchen was empty, but a chair had been dragged in front of the shelves.

Something about the position of that chair seemed all wrong, and Emily looked up and saw the glittery pink bucket was missing.

Her stomach dropped away. It was like losing your footing and tumbling into a dark chasm.

She shot into the hallway and saw that the front door was open.

Please, no, not that. Anything but that.

She should have been more careful. She should have hidden the key. She should have—

Her heart stopped because as she looked past the porch she saw the child on her knees on the beach shoveling sand into the pink bucket.

Her heart crashed against her ribs like waves on the rocks.

"Lizzy!" Forgetting that she was dressed only in flimsy pajamas, she ran. She ran faster than should have been physically possible, but it seemed the body was capable of unusual feats when driven by fear. Stones and tiny pieces of shell ripped at her bare feet, but she didn't even notice, and then she hit the soft sand and it acted like brakes, slowing her strides and throwing her off balance.

She stumbled, regained her balance, dragging air into her screaming lungs as she tried to reach Lizzy. She could smell the sea, hear the crash of the surf and the shriek of gulls, all of it combining to unleash dark memories that merged the past with the present.

The world closed in. She saw the child through a tunnel and knew she had to reach her.

And then she grabbed her, holding her tightly, vowing that this time nothing was going to make her let go. "Don't ever, *ever* do that again." Her legs shaking, she dropped to her knees in the sand with the child against her. "Never, do you hear me? Tell me you hear me. *Tell me!*"

"I hear you. I wanted to see the sea." Lizzy's voice was muffled, and Emily squeezed her eyes shut because she wouldn't care if she never saw the sea again.

Her limbs were shaking, and a horrible queasy feeling gnawed at her stomach.

"You must *never* go to the beach without asking me."

"You didn't want to."

"Beaches are dangerous places, do you understand me?" She released Lizzy enough to look into her face, and it was only when she saw the girl's eyes widen and fill with tears that she realized she was shouting.

Shouting and shaking.

Oh, God, she was losing it.

She should never have come to Puffin Island. She could have been anonymous in a city. A city would have been a better choice.

"Emily." Through a mist of panic she heard Ryan's deep baritone, calm and steady. "Emily? What happened?"

She couldn't answer. There was a weight on her chest, and she couldn't breathe. Was she having a heart attack? Something terrible was happening to her. Through the mists of panic she felt his hand, firm and reassuring on her shoulder, and he was easing her away from Lizzy, telling her that everything was fine, that everything was going to be all right, that she had nothing to worry about.

Which showed how little he knew.

She had everything to worry about.

She shouldn't be here, doing this. She was the wrong person.

Now that she was sure Lizzy was safe, she tried to stand up, but her legs were wobbly and unfit for their purpose. Fortunately Ryan must have realized because he drew her into his arms and held her, enveloping her with his strength as his body absorbed her shudders.

"She's safe. Everything is fine." It was all about the tone, not the words. His voice was deep and level, designed to reduce her panic. Except that her panic had gone too far to be reduced so easily. Her heart was pounding, and her breaths were coming in ragged gasps. She felt dizzy and detached, as if she were falling into a deep, dark hole. The loss of control terrified her.

"Ryan—"

"I know. I want you to stop taking those big gulping breaths because they're making you dizzy. Close your mouth, pretend you're blowing out a candle. That's it. Just like that." His hand moved up and down her spine, long, slow gentle strokes that soothed and calmed. "I'm here. I won't let anything happen to you."

She clung to his shoulders, to hard muscle and warm strength. He was the only solid, safe thing in her world, and she held on like a climber about to fall from a rock face. "Lizzy—"

"She's safe, right here. You're both safe."

From somewhere in the darkness she heard Lizzy's voice. "Is she sick? Is she going to die?"

She didn't hear his response because the sky and his face started to spin together, and she realized with horrible clarity that she was going to pass out. And if she passed out she wouldn't be there for the child. "She can't go in the sea. She mustn't go in the sea. Promise me."

"No one is going in the sea." His voice was strong and sure. "You need to relax."

She tried to say something. Tried to tell him she couldn't relax. She wanted to warn him he needed to take care of Lizzy, but then darkness poured in where there should have been light, and the last thing she remembered were powerful arms catching her as she fell.

HE'D NEVER SEEN anyone so pale. Lying on the sofa back in Castaway Cottage, Emily's cheeks were as white as a Maine winter, the only color in her face the dark shadow of her lashes and the soft pink of her mouth. Still shaken by the moment she'd crumpled in front of him, Ryan reached for his phone and was about to call the medical center when she opened her eyes.

"Thank God." He put the phone down so that he could have both hands free if she passed out on him again. "You had me seriously worried." He'd handled panic attacks before, but none as acute and inexplicable as the one he'd just witnessed. He wanted to understand the cause. A glance at their surroundings had revealed nothing obvious, and gentle questioning of Lizzy had revealed no clues.

Emily struggled to sit up, but he pushed her flat and then wished he hadn't. For the first time since he'd first met her, she had left her hair loose, but even those tumbling curls failed to hide the shape of her breasts clearly visible through the fabric of her pajamas. He'd found himself wishing that whatever had triggered the panic had occurred after she'd dressed.

He wondered what it said about him that she was lying there dazed and vulnerable, and he was thinking about sex.

"Stay there." He shifted slightly, but his attempts to stop her sitting up had shifted her pajama top, giving him a perfect view of the swell and dip of her breasts. "Don't move." He spoke between his teeth, and she looked confused.

"Are you all right?" Emily asked.

"You scared the shit out of me."

Her eyes were soft and dazed. "I'm sorry."

Nowhere near as sorry as he was going to be if he didn't get himself under control. "I'm calling a doctor."

"That's not necessary."

"Emily, you passed out."

"I'm fine now."

"Has it ever happened before?"

She gave a brief shake of her head. "No."

"I'm taking you to the medical clinic." Somewhere he wouldn't be able to lay a finger on her, preferably with a large expanse of water between them. "Or maybe the mainland. You should have tests."

"I don't need tests."

"One moment you were sprinting across the sand as if you were trying to break records, and the next you collapsed."

Aware that Lizzy had been watching, scared, he'd tried to look as if this was normal behavior. As if having a panic attack on a beach was nothing out of the ordinary.

He'd held her, calmed her, breathed in the summer scent of her and tried to forget she was built like Venus. He was fairly sure she'd forgotten she was wearing nothing but thin silk pajamas.

"Where's Lizzy?" Her voice was urgent, and he could see she was about to drag herself from the sofa and prove to herself that the child was safe.

"She's fine. She's in the garden with Cocoa."

"The front door—"

"I locked it."

"She—"

"I know. She told me she stood on the chair to get the bucket. She told me you'd forbidden her from going to the beach." And he wanted to know why. In fact, he had so many damn questions, it was a struggle to hold them back. He intended to ask them later, but first he needed to be sure she wasn't going to pass out again. "Are you feeling dizzy?"

"No. You must think I'm crazy."

"What I think," he said slowly, "is that something scared you. Do you want to tell me what?"

"I woke up and found her gone. Saw the door open. I thought—"

"What? That the press had found you? That she'd been taken? Are you worried about kidnappers?"

"No. Not that." Before she could say anything else, Lizzy came back into the room with Cocoa at her heels. She stopped in the doorway when she saw Emily sitting up.

"You're awake."

"Yeah, she's awake." Ryan rocked back on his heels, knowing that whatever it was Emily had been about to tell him was going to have to wait. "Come and say hi." He knew children denied the truth would often imagine something far worse. It was important for her to see that nothing bad had happened.

Lizzy slid onto the sofa and looked anxiously at Emily. "Are you still mad at me?"

"I was never mad at you."

"You were screaming. You squeezed me hard."

"I was scared. I was mad at myself for falling asleep and not watching you properly. I—I was worried something might happen to you—" Her throat worked as she swallowed. "I'm sorry if I scared you. We'll talk about it properly, but not right now."

"You fell and I thought you'd died."

"Oh, honey, I'm sorry I gave you a fright." The guilt in her eyes told him just how seriously she took the role of guardian.

Lizzy crawled closer. "Ryan said you weren't dead, just sleeping. I guess you were really tired."

"That's right." Her voice sounded husky. "Tired. And worried, because the door was open and you were gone."

"I wanted to dig in the sand. I wanted to use my pink bucket."

"I know. I should have done it with you, then you wouldn't have felt as if you had to do it on your own. Next time I want you to ask me." She looked exhausted, drained, and Ryan could see the effort it took her to put her own feelings second and reassure the child.

He encouraged Lizzy to go back into the garden with Cocoa. The resilience of children never ceased to amaze him. He knew it would be a long time until he forgot the raw fear in Emily's face as she'd sprinted across the sand to grab Lizzy. He could still feel the way her body had trembled against his, the way her fingers had dug into his shoulders.

Guilt chafed, like sand in a shoe. "I never should have bought that damn bucket."

"It's not your fault. It's all me."

"Tell me what happened."

"I had a bad night. Slept late." She lay against the cushions, pale and exhausted. "When I woke, the house was quiet. And then I came downstairs and saw the chair by the shelves."

"Yeah, I saw that. I assumed you'd done it."

"No. I put the bucket out of reach because I was afraid she might grab it and take it to the beach."

"And she did."

"I saw the front door open. All I saw was the sea and I thought—I thought—" Anxious, she shot to her feet and swayed. "You're *sure* the front door is locked?"

"Yes, and the key is in my pocket." He wondered if she knew her pajamas were virtually see-through when she stood in front of the light. He could see the fluid curves of her body through the thin fabric. "Sit down, Emily."

"I'm fine."

He wasn't. He wanted to peel off those pajamas and explore every inch of that creamy skin with his mouth. "Sit down before you fall."

She sank back onto the sofa and closed her eyes. "I should have hidden the key. I put her at risk."

"Risk of what?"

"She's six years old, Ryan."

"I sense this isn't a generic risk we're talking about. I'd like to understand what sent you flying across the sand like a champion sprinter."

"I was trying to reach her. Trying to stop her going in the water. It's my job to protect her."

"Why would she have gone into the water?" He cast his mind back. "She was digging. She wasn't interested in the water."

"Children love the water."

And he knew from her bloodless cheeks that the issue here wasn't the bucket or even the fact that Lizzy had left the house. It was the sea. The sea was the reason she spent her time in the kitchen. The reason she sat with her back to the water and didn't want to go out in his boat.

"Talk to me." He kept his voice gentle. "Tell me what that was all about, because we both know it wasn't about Lizzy."

She curled her legs under her. "You're right, it isn't about her. It's about me. I'm not the right person."

"The right person for what?"

"To be looking after a child."

He remembered feeling the same way, even though in his case the real burden had fallen on his grandmother. "I know all this has come as a shock to you. You haven't had time to get used to the idea that you're her guardian, but you will."

"You don't understand."

"I remember staring at my sister who was asleep in the middle of my bed, and my grandmother telling me we were all she had. I wanted to run like hell in the opposite direction before I could screw it up, because I knew I would. There were a million ways to do things wrong, and I didn't know how to do them right. Trust me when I say I know it feels like an overwhelming responsibility you're not qualified for, but you're going to be fine. You muddle through, twelve hours at a time."

"No, you really don't understand. I'm not the right person." Her fierce tone caught his attention.

"Why aren't you the right person?"

She stared at a point on his chest, her fingers clenched in her lap and then finally lifted her head and looked at him. "Because I killed my sister. She died because of me."

CHAPTER SEVEN

"SHE'S ASLEEP," RYAN SAID, standing in the doorway. He'd spent the whole day and the whole evening taking care of things, and judging from the absence of complaint from Lizzy, he'd handled bedtime with the same cool competence he'd displayed on the beach.

"I usually read to her."

"She told me. *Green Eggs and Ham.*" He gave a short laugh. "It's been a while, but I'm still word perfect. And she recognized quite a few words, so whatever you've been doing has made a difference even in a short time. She's asleep now. She's exhausted."

And she knew she had him to thank for that.

He'd distracted Lizzy with a game in the garden that involved so much running with the ball and the dog she'd worn herself out. When she was almost falling asleep on the spot he'd made supper, enrolling Lizzy in helping him. He'd stood her on a chair at the scrubbed kitchen table and shown her how to break eggs into a bowl.

From her position on the sofa, Emily had watched through the open door as Lizzy had smacked each egg on the side of the bowl and paused as golden yoke and slippery white had slid and pooled in the center. There had been two accidents, and each time he'd cleaned up and let her try again. Plenty of adults would have opted to do the job themselves. Not Ryan. He'd stood, infinitely patient, and let her master the task until the carton of eggs was empty and the bowl filled with yolks that floated like small suns on the translucent liquid.

Then he'd handed Lizzy a whisk and demonstrated the movement. When it had proven too hard, he'd covered her small hand with his and did it with her until they had a frothy mixture. It didn't seem to bother him that he could have done it himself in a quarter of the time.

The part that involved heat, he'd done himself.

He'd stood in front of the stove in Kathleen's sunny kitchen, sleeves rolled back to reveal powerful forearms as he poured the mixture into a pan and produced a perfect omelet.

She'd wondered how she could be noticing he was sexy at a time like this. Apparently she was more vulnerable to the appeal of the strong protective type than she'd thought.

She felt dizzy and strange, as if a healing wound had suddenly been wrenched open, leaving her bleeding and weak. Her mind was flooded with thoughts she'd worked hard to block out for most of her life. At some point she must have slept because she woke to find herself covered with the patchwork quilt.

And now he was standing there, no doubt wondering how soon he could reasonably leave.

"I've taken up so much of your time—"

"It's my time. My choice how I spend it. How are you feeling?"

"Better. Did you leave the door open so we can hear her?"

"Cocoa is lying at the bottom of her bed. If she wakes, we'll know."

"The dog is on her bed?"

"The two of them seemed happy with that arrangement. Is it a problem?"

"No." Emily slumped back against the sofa, thinking that of

all the problems she had, that one didn't even register. "I can't believe you looked after her all afternoon."

He eased himself away from the door frame and strolled into the room, a smile playing around his mouth. "You owe me. And I'll be collecting."

She didn't know whether it was his words or the look in his eyes, but something sent her pulse hammering like rain on a roof. The air simmered with a heat that made it difficult to breathe. She had no defenses against his brand of raw sexuality. She felt out of control, as if she needed to fasten a seat belt or anchor herself to an immovable object. It was like tiptoeing around the rim of an active volcano, knowing that one wrong step would send you plunging into a fiery furnace.

"What do you usually charge for babysitting services?"

"I don't offer babysitting services. This was an exclusive, one-off deal. Don't ever mention it." His eyes gleamed with humor. "I wouldn't want word to get around."

"In that case I'm especially grateful for your sacrifice."

He gave her a long look that brought the blood rushing back to her cheeks more effectively than any medical intervention. "You finally have some color."

And he was responsible for the color.

"I owe you an apology."

"For what?"

"For drowning you in emotion." Now that the sharp edge of fear had passed, she felt deeply embarrassed. First she'd had a meltdown, and then she'd spilled confidences she usually kept locked deep inside. "Most men hate emotion like they hate throw pillows and scented candles."

"I'm not a lover of throw pillows, but I'm not afraid of emotions. They tell you more about a person than hours of conversation."

"If that's true, then by now you're thinking I'm a hysterical neurotic."

"If I told you what I really thought, you'd kick me out." Leaving her to ponder on that, he walked into the kitchen and returned a moment later carrying a bottle of wine and two glasses.

She wanted to ask him what he really thought but wasn't sure she wanted to hear the answer. "Don't you have somewhere to be?"

"I'm where I want to be." He sat on the sofa next to her and put the bottle and the glasses on the floor. "Talk to me."

"Sorry?"

"Tell me what happened."

The breath left her lungs in a rush. "I don't talk about it."

"Maybe not usually, but tonight you're going to talk about it." He poured wine into a glass and handed it to her. "Tell me about your sister." Another man would have tiptoed around the subject. Not him.

"That isn't a very sensitive question."

"This morning you had a full-blown panic attack. I virtually had to peel you off the ground. It would help me to know what happened, so that I can help make sure it doesn't happen again."

"I was with Neil for three years and he never asked for the details."

Sympathy turned to incredulous disbelief. "Never?"

"He respected boundaries."

"I'm starting to understand why you don't feel the need for rebound sex. You can only rebound from something with substance. And I'm not respecting boundaries, so talk to me."

Her hand shook, and the wine almost sloshed over the top of the glass. "What do you want to know?"

"Everything." He eased the glass out of her hand and set it down on the floor. Polished floorboards gleamed in the late evening sun, and through the open window she could hear the relentless sound of the waves breaking on the shore.

"Why?"

"Because I'm absolutely sure you didn't kill her." He reached out and pulled her into the curve of his arm so that her body was pressed against the hardness of his.

She didn't consider herself a tactile person. She and Neil had often sat on separate sofas, facing each other, disconnected, as if occupying different worlds. In some ways they'd lived parallel lives.

It was true that she'd never talked to Neil about her past, but it was also true that he'd never asked. And she realized now that he hadn't wanted to know. He'd talked about respecting boundaries, but what he'd really meant was that he didn't want to deal with emotion.

If Neil had found himself in this position, he would have floundered, both with her emotions and with the child. Ryan had handled both without missing a beat.

"There isn't a happy ending to this, Ryan."

"Yeah, well, we both know life is full of messy endings. Tell me about your sister."

"I was four when she was born. My earliest memory was holding her because my mother was drunk on the sofa. I remember looking down at her and promising that I was always going to take care of her."

"Why weren't the authorities involved?"

"I don't really know. My mother was good at doing just enough, I guess. We slipped through the cracks. By the time my sister was six months old, I was doing almost everything for her. I went from being the loneliest child on the planet to the happiest. I loved her. And she loved me back. The first word she spoke was *Em*, and she used to follow me everywhere and sleep in my bed."

"Sounds like Rachel." His voice was low. "Drove me crazy. It was like trying to shake off a burr that had stuck to your clothes."

"Yes." Her whole body ached with remembering. "I loved it. I loved holding her. Most of all I loved being outdoors with her. I hated our apartment so much. It was cramped, airless, and everything bad happened there. I was the one who begged my mother to take us to the beach. We lived close, but we never went. Spent our days cooped up in one room while she drank her way through whatever money she could scrounge from men." She breathed. "She wasn't a prostitute, not officially, but she'd discovered early on that men liked her body, and sleeping with them was a useful way to get what she wanted. It took me years to see that she had a low opinion of herself. That she didn't think she had anything to offer except a pair of breasts that made men stupid."

"This is why you dress in black and wear your shirts buttoned up to the neck?"

"Sometimes my curves are all men see. Or they see them first, and make judgments. I discovered it was best to take them out of the equation."

"Honey, I hate to be the one to break this to you, but buttoning your shirt up to the neck doesn't hide the fact you have an incredible body—but we'll come to that part later." He tightened his grip on her shoulders. "Finish your story."

"On that particular day she agreed to take us. I don't know why. Parenting wasn't her thing, but it was sunny, and by then she was very pregnant with Lana. I guess she thought she could sleep on the beach as easily as she could sleep at home. I remember pulling a blanket from the bed to sit on. Katy had just started walking, and I thought the sand would be a soft landing."

"The moment we got there, my mother fell asleep." She felt his arm tighten, as if he knew she was getting to the bad part. "I was pleased. She was always angry and I thought we'd have more fun together with her asleep. Katy and I played in the sand, and then Mom woke up and went for a walk."

"She left you?"

"Technically she was never looking after us, but at least until that point she was there. I remember feeling anxious. We lived a short bus ride away, and I didn't know how to get home. And then I saw her sitting in a bar with some guy I'd never seen before. She was nine months pregnant. Can you believe that?"

"He approached her?"

"Maybe. Or maybe she saw him sitting there and thought he looked like someone she could easily part from the contents of his wallet. I carried on playing and next time I looked I couldn't see her anywhere."

His arm was still around her, and he moved his thumb up and down her arm, the gesture soothing and sympathetic. "That must have been terrifying."

"Not at first. You're forgetting, that was my normal. I was used to being unsupervised."

"Didn't anyone on the beach notice that you were on your own?"

"Yes. A woman with a child about the same age as Katy came over to me and asked if we were all right and where our mother was. I'd been watching their family, copying some of the things they were doing. The dad kept lifting the child in the air and swinging her around until she was helpless with giggles. I tried to do it with Katy, but she was too heavy and I couldn't swing her high enough to make it fun."

"Did you tell her you were on your own?"

"No. My mother had told me over and over again that if I was ever asked, I was to say everything was fine. She said that if I didn't do that, they might take Katy away."

His hand stilled. "They might have taken you away, too."

She swallowed. "I wish they had. I've thought about it over and over again. I wish I'd said to that woman, 'I don't know where my mother is.' I wish they'd taken Katy, even if it meant I never saw her again, because at least I'd know she was alive. That was the day I first realized my situation was unusual. I remember looking around the beach at the families and thinking that although those families all looked different, they had one thing in common. There was an adult in charge. Until that moment, I hadn't been aware that we weren't normal. 'Normal' is the life you're living, isn't it? This was how it was for us, so I assumed this was how it was for everyone."

"Your mother didn't come back?"

"Not right then. Katy was bored and she kept trying to eat the sand. I had to find a way of occupying her, so I carried her to the sea. I thought I'd put her toes in the water. I didn't intend to go in deeper, but she loved it so much and she was squealing and wanting more, so I carried her in until I was up to my knees."

"There were other people around you?"

"Yes. It was busy. We splashed for a while, and then we went a little deeper and—" Her heart was pumping hard. "I don't know what happened next. Maybe the beach shelved sharply, or maybe someone had dug a deep hole. Either way I stepped and there was nothing under my feet. I felt the water rush into my nose and ears, and I tried to find the bottom but it wasn't there, so then I tried to push Katy up so that she could breathe, but she was too heavy and my arms couldn't hold her." She felt it again, the rush of the water and the feeling of panic and utter helplessness. "I kicked and struggled, but I could feel the water pulling me. It was so powerful."

"You were caught in a rip current."

"I don't remember anything else until I came around on the beach. I remember being sick, and all these adults crowded around me. I looked around for Katy, but she wasn't there. I must have let go of her when I lost consciousness. They mounted a search and found her—"

She felt his arms come around her, heard him murmur *I'm so sorry*, and *you poor baby*, against her hair, while he held her tightly.

"Then my mother reappeared. She was hysterical, but looking back on it, I don't think it was because of Katy. I think it was because she was afraid she might be charged with neglect."

"Was she?"

"No. The authorities got involved, but in the end they decided it was a terrible accident. I don't know what she said to them and I think we were followed up for a while, but nothing ever happened."

"Did anyone question you?"

"They tried to, but I couldn't speak."

"You were in shock."

Emily felt the ache deep in her chest. "Katy was the only thing in my life I'd ever loved. When I realized she'd gone, nothing mattered. I didn't care what my mother did or didn't do. I was catatonic. Without Katy I didn't care about anything. Five days later my mother had Lana. She expected me to look after her the way I had for Katy, but I couldn't." She breathed, wondering how honest to be. How much to confess. "From the moment Lana was born, I didn't feel anything. I didn't want anything to do with her. My mother told me I was cold. Unfeeling."

"That's horseshit."

"She told me this was my chance to make up for having killed my sister."

"Jesus, Emily, please, tell me you knew that wasn't true."

"When you're a child you believe what grown-ups tell you."

"At least tell me you don't believe it now."

She breathed. "Part of me does, because it's true. I did take her into the water. I did let go of her."

"It was an accident. As you say, you were a child. You shouldn't have been given responsibility for her. A tragic, terrible accident, but still an accident. Did you ever talk to anyone about it?"

"Brittany and Skylar. And Kathleen. They're the only people who know. Talking about it doesn't help, and anyway, it's in the past."

"You sit with your back to the water and you don't go near the sea. I assume that's why you stayed in the cottage with Kathleen while your friends were on the beach. That sounds as if it's in your present, not your past."

"I'm scared of the water, that's true. And I'm scared of having responsibility for a child. I loved Katy with every part of me and losing her ripped my heart out from the roots. I can't love like that again. I choose not to."

His thumb moved gently on her arm. "You think love is something you can switch on and off?"

"I know it is. I don't feel deeply. That's why Neil ended it."

His thumb stopped moving. "Neil ended it because he was a dick."

Emily gave a shocked laugh. "You've never even met him."

"Thank God. I already have enough evidence to know he's a dick. For a start, he was with you for three years and didn't once take the time to explore why you were too scared to open up to him. What the hell was wrong with the guy?"

"Not everybody wants to spill their innermost secrets."

"It's called intimacy, Emily, and it's a basic requirement for a successful, healthy relationship. What you two had sounds more like roommates or first cousins."

She flushed, because hadn't she had that same thought herself? "You can't judge a relationship from the outside. There is no right and wrong. Just what works for that couple."

"I agree, but that's not the only reason I know he's a dick."

Emily sighed. "What's the other reason?"

"He let you go."

Heat rushed through her. She was aware of his arm, locking her securely against him. Of the brush of his hard thigh against hers. "It wasn't his fault. I've shut down that part of myself. I don't want to feel anything."

"If you were mine, I would have made you feel." He spoke with quiet emphasis, his thumb moving in a gentle rhythm over her arm. "I wouldn't have let you hide away."

And that, she thought, was why being with him both excited and terrified her. "Ryan—"

"Who cared for Lana when she was born?"

"My mother had to. It helped that Lana was very pretty. My mother discovered it got her attention and she liked that. Used it. I've often wondered if her childhood contributed to the person Lana became. She was insecure. She learned early how to make her looks work for her. When Lana was about seven, my mother met someone. He was older, no kids of his own. He owned a nice house in a good neighborhood and we moved in."

Ryan stilled. "Is this going to end badly? Because if so, I might need to top up my wineglass."

"No. He was a good man. And that's the weird part because I never understood what he saw in my mother. I think it was complicated. Something to do with having lost his own daughter to drugs and wishing he'd done more. I don't know. At the time, I didn't question it. For the first time in my life I had a room of my own, plenty to eat and access to all the books I could read. Those books saved me. I spent my time lost in worlds that didn't look anything like the one I was living in. I studied hard because I didn't want a life like my mother's. It was because of him I went to college and met Brittany and Sky. When he died, he left me money. I think he knew if he didn't give it directly to me, my mother would drink her way through it."

"And Lana?"

"She was scouted on the subway one day. She worked a short time as a model, then turned to acting and loved it. I think because it gave her the perfect way of avoiding reality. Each film represented a new fake reality. That's why she fell in love with her leading men. To her it was real. And when the filming ended, so did the relationship. Every time."

"Do you think she meant to have Lizzy?"

"I doubt it. Lana wasn't the sort who would be prepared to share the stage with a child. She wanted to be the center of attention. I don't think she saw much of Lizzy."

"So in that way she was like your mother."

"I hadn't thought of it like that."

"And the two of you weren't in touch?"

"I hadn't heard from her in years. That was my fault." It was painful to admit it. "I made no effort to bond with her."

"Because you'd already lost one sister. She could have made an effort, too. She didn't have your reasons for keeping her distance." He leaned forward, picked up the bottle and filled her glass. "Drink."

"You're the one who should be drinking. I can't believe I dumped all that on you. I bet you're just dying to run screaming through that door."

He didn't budge. "Now I understand why Brittany told me you were in trouble. She was the one who suggested you come here?"

"When we were at college, we made this pact that we'd help each other if we ever needed it. My friends gave me something my family never had. A sense of security. I know that, no matter what happens, Brit and Sky will always be there for me. And I for them. When I first heard I was Lizzy's guardian, the priority was to find somewhere safe to stay. The press had been crawling all over the house. I was told that she needed to be kept away from everyone so that she could just process her grief and learn to live life a little. We talked about having security, but I couldn't see how that would do anything but draw attention. No one knew I existed, so the safest thing seemed to be for me to take her and disappear. But of course the first thing a child wants to do when they see Shell Bay is dig in the sand." She breathed. "I should have stayed in New York."

"But you wouldn't have had help in New York." He was silent for a minute. "Emily, it wouldn't take much for the press to find out Lana had a half sister."

"But if they find that out, they will also find out Lana and I hadn't seen each other for years. They're not likely to link us."

"They could."

It wasn't what she wanted to hear, and she felt a ripple of unease. "Even if they did, they wouldn't look for me here, would they? There's no trail."

"No." He turned his head and gave her a smile that was probably meant to reassure her but didn't.

"You're speaking as if you have knowledge. Have you ever been targeted by the press?"

"No." He eased his arm away from her and rose to his feet. "But I know how they operate."

"The lawyers thought the story would probably die. That if I lay low, the journalists would get bored. I paid cash for my ferry ticket, so they shouldn't be able to trace me, and no one is going to be looking for the daughter of a movie star in rural Maine."

"That's true, and even if they come, you'll be protected. The islanders are a close community. We protect our own. If the press arrive, then we'll be ready for them." He turned to look at her. "Thank you for telling me. Now I understand why you don't feel you're the right person to care for Lizzy."

She sagged against the sofa. "You do?"

"Yes, and for the record, I think you're the perfect person."

"You're wrong. I know the same thing won't happen again because I won't let her go near the water, but this is about more than her personal safety. It's about not being able to give her what she needs. Bringing up a child requires more than just accident prevention. To flourish and grow, a child needs to be loved. They need a parent, or parent substitute, who cares about them. It was only when I saw Kathleen with Brittany that I discovered how love could look. I can't do that. I can't give her what she needs. I can't love another child. I won't."

"So why didn't you say no? She could have been put in foster care."

Emily felt something twist inside her. "I couldn't do that."

"Of course you couldn't. Because you already care, Emily. You wouldn't have taken her if you didn't care. But you're scared shitless."

"That part I'm not arguing with." She felt a stinging in her throat. "A child deserves to be loved and I can't love her. I just can't." She heard the shake in her voice and knew he heard it, too. "I won't let that happen to me again."

"And what if you can't stop it happening?"

"I can. I've been this way for so long I can't change. Neil always told me I was cold. That I needed to be 'thawed out.'"

He made a sound in his throat that resembled a growl and flexed his fingers. "Emily, honey, do me a favor—no more talk about Neil for a while."

She thought he was joking, but then she looked at his face and saw the hard set of his mouth and the icy glint in his eyes.

His gaze stayed fixed to her face for a long moment, and then he scooped up the jacket he'd thrown over the chair hours earlier. "I should go." His voice was thickened. "If you need me, call."

The abruptness of his departure shocked her. "Wait—what about Cocoa?"

"Keep her overnight. As long as you push her into the garden by six in the morning, you shouldn't have any accidents. I'll call my grandmother and explain."

She stood up, too, and saw him straighten his shoulders as if he was warding her off. "Thank you for everything you did today. I apologize for drowning you in emotion."

"I'm not leaving because of what you told me, Emily."

"Then why are you sprinting out of the door?"

He let out a long breath. "Because I'm not Neil."

It was her turn to stare. "But—I don't understand."

"I have spent the last few hours trying manfully to ignore the fact you're wearing nothing but a pair of very sexy pajamas." His voice was husky. "I never thought I'd want to put you back into one of those shirts that button to the neck, but right now I'm thinking that would be a good choice of clothing."

"You're leaving because of my breasts?"

"No, not just because of your breasts." He gave a crooked smile. "All of you. The shape of your face, the curve of your shoulder, the dimple in the corner of your mouth—you name it, I'm noticing it. But because you've had a crappy day and you're vulnerable I am making a supreme effort to keep my hands off you and not do what I'm burning to do. Right now, that means walking out that door."

Her heart was beating so hard she thought he must be able to hear it.

She should have just nodded.

Or maybe opened the door for him.

Instead, she asked a question.

"What are you burning to do?"

CHAPTER EIGHT

THIS WAS THE moment to leave.

He knew a mistake when he saw one, and he was definitely looking at one right now.

No single mothers. Wasn't that his rule?

And not only was Emily vulnerable, but there were still things about him she didn't know. Things that made it more likely she'd push him out of her house than invite him to kiss her. There was no way he was leaving her without support, and not just because Brittany would fire an arrow into his butt.

Now he knew what she was going through, he was determined to help her. And helping her didn't involve stripping off those pajamas and pinning her to the kitchen table.

"What I'm burning to do is irrelevant."

"I've been honest with you. I want you to be honest with me." Her voice was soft and smoky, and it slid into his senses like a drug.

Shit.

"Emily, I can tell you that the last thing you want right now is for me to be honest."

"Please."

The right thing would have been to make an excuse, but she

was wearing those damn pajamas, a confection of silk and sin, and she was looking at him with those wide eyes, her mouth was right there and—

With a soft curse, he took her face in his hands. He felt the softness of her skin under his fingers and heard her breathing grow shallow. "You want to know what I'm burning to do? I want to strip off those pajamas and smash down every boundary you've ever created. I want to explore all those places you've never let anyone go, and I'm talking about your mind as well as your body. I'm not like Neil. I don't respect your boundaries. I want you open to me."

Her eyes widened with shock, and her lips parted. "That will never happen."

"If I wasn't about to leave, I'd make it happen." He lowered his head but kept his mouth just clear of hers. She was so close he could almost taste her, feel the short shallow breaths she snatched into her lungs.

"You wouldn't, because—" Her face suffused with color. "The truth is, I'm not that crazy about sex."

For a moment he thought he must have misheard. "You don't like sex?"

"It's fine. Nice." With a whimper of embarrassment, she eased away from him. "I can't believe we're having this conversation. You're right. You should go. And I never should have asked."

"Wait a minute—" He caught her around the waist and pulled her back to him. "Did you say 'nice'? You think sex is 'nice'?"

Her face was on fire. "Yes. What's wrong with that?"

He drew in a deep breath. "Honey, 'nice' sex is for people in retirement homes with dodgy hips and a heart condition. At your age you should be having clothes-ripping, mind-blowing, animal sex that leaves you unable to walk or think."

"All right, you should *definitely* go now." She was deliciously flustered, and he dragged her back to him and slid his hands into her hair, feeling it tumble and curl over his fingers in a slide of soft silk. She smelled like blossoms and sunshine. Her lips reminded him of the strawberries that grew wild in Kathleen's tumbling coastal garden.

"You have gorgeous hair. Is wearing it up part of your disguise, too?"

"I don't have a disguise. Just because I choose to dress in a certain way doesn't make it a disguise. And wearing my hair up is the practical option. It's always breezy on Puffin Island. It stops it blowing into my eyes."

"So, in New York you wore it loose?"

She hesitated. "No."

"Like I said. A disguise. You've created a persona, because you're afraid someone is going to see who you really are. But I see you, Emily Donovan. I'm standing here, looking right at you, so you can damn well stop hiding." His hand was still in her hair, his mouth a breath from hers.

"You don't see me. And I can tell you I've never had clothes-ripping, mind-blowing, animal sex. I'm not like that."

"You mean you weren't like that with *him*. You'd be like it with me, Emily."

"I don't—"

He kissed her. He parted her lips with his, licked into her mouth and felt her go weak against him. Those full breasts pressed against his chest, and he hauled her close, holding her with the flat of his hand while the other stayed buried deep in her hair. He deepened the kiss until white heat snaked across his skin, until rampant hunger and raw sexual need tore through him. Her mouth was eager and sweet, and the softness of her breasts pushed against his chest. He'd intended the kiss to be brief, but now he'd started there was no stopping. Instead of letting her go, he backed her against the wall of Kathleen's hallway and caged her, planting an arm on either side of her and holding her there with the weight of his body. He knew he should probably say something, but he was so turned on he could barely stand upright, let alone speak, and she didn't speak, either. He felt her trembling against him, felt her fingers slide up to his shoulders and hold on as if she were afraid she might collapse without his support.

He dragged his mouth over her jaw and down to her throat, heard her soft gasp as he slid his hands down her ribs, his thumbs brushing the underside of her breasts.

The single button holding the front of her pajamas together slid out of its silky mooring, exposing luscious curves of creamy white flesh tipped with dusky pink.

Ryan had to force himself to breathe. He was so aroused he felt disoriented. Slowly, he slid his thumb over the tortured peak and heard her moan. He stroked, licked, tasted while she whimpered, squirmed and arched against him, those full lush breasts pushing into his hands.

Drunk on her body he slid his hands lower, down the silk of her back inside her pajama bottoms to cup warm, bare flesh. Everything about her was soft and inviting. He could have drowned in her and died happy.

The only sound was the soft murmurs that came from her throat and the steady thrum of his own heartbeat. The tension in the air was syrupy thick, coating both of them in a heavy, suffocating warmth. And then he took her mouth again, kissing her deeply while his fingers slid between her trembling thighs. He parted her gently and slid his finger into that slippery warmth, feeling velvety softness open for him as her body allowed him intimate access. He held still for a moment, stroked his other hand over her jaw and felt her shift against him with restless need. Gently he stroked and teased, paying attention to every gasp and murmur until he felt the pleasure roll through her. She cried out as she came, her body clamping down on his fingers so that he felt every throb, every contraction.

He held her, murmured soft words against her hair, breathed in the scent of her until the last pulse died away and she lay limp against him.

Ryan tried to steady his own breathing.

He was rock-hard. So aroused he was ready to take her there and then, but he forced himself to slowly withdraw his hand and smooth her pajamas back into place.

Her head was dipped forward, so all he could see was the shimmer of her hair and the shadow of thick, dark eyelashes.

"Emily, look at me." His voice sounded raspy and rough, but he was impressed he'd managed to form a coherent sentence, so he wasn't about to apologize for that.

Her hands were locked in the front of his shirt, as if he was the one solid, reliable thing in a collapsing world.

"This is embarrassing. You need to go now."

"Why is it embarrassing?"

"Because you—and I—damn it, Ryan, you know why. We lost control." Her voice was muffled against his chest, and he clenched his jaw.

"I didn't lose control."

Slowly, she lifted her face to his. "You didn't?"

"If I'd lost control, I would have undressed you, not dressed you. If I'd lost control, you'd be naked now and flat on your back on the sofa instead of standing there in your pajamas." And he was starting to question that decision. "You're right, I need to go, but not because this is embarrassing."

"Why, then?"

Because he wanted to undo his good work, rip off those silk pajamas, spread her legs and taste all of her, not just her mouth.

Deciding she wasn't ready to hear that, he smoothed her hair, tilting her face to his. "Because it's getting late, you had a shitty day and you need to get some sleep."

Her eyes were glazed and confused, her cheeks flushed and her mouth damp from his kisses. "I didn't—" Her voice was low and husky. "I wasn't expecting— I can't believe you did that. Or that I— I didn't know it was going to be like that."

"I did." Reluctantly, he released her. "I knew it would be exactly like that."

She stepped back, traced her lower lip with the tip of her

tongue as if she couldn't believe what had just happened, and then sent him a glance that almost had him flattening her back against the wall again.

Her gaze was on his mouth. "Lizzy is upstairs. She could have woken."

"Cocoa would have barked."

She bit her lip. "I don't want her waking up to find me naked with a man. When you're six, it's unsettling."

It had obviously happened to her. Subduing the rush of anger, he focused on the practical. "Could you drop Cocoa back with my grandmother in the morning? She lives in Harbor House. It's the big white one overlooking the bay."

"Of course." She blinked, as if she'd been asleep and woken up on a different planet. "And thank you."

"For proving that a kiss can be more than nice?"

There was a long, pulsing silence. "For listening. For helping me out with Lizzy. As for the other—" her voice cracked slightly "—we won't mention it again. That's the end of it."

He watched her for a long moment and then strolled toward the door.

"It's not the end, Emily. It's the beginning."

AGNES COOPER LIVED a fifteen-minute walk from the harbor and the Ocean Club in a pretty white clapboard house with a shingle roof that pitched steeply at the front. Overlooking the rocks at Puffin Point and the bay beyond that, it had been built on a large plot of land and was protected by mature trees and a well-nurtured garden. Emily was immediately charmed, and the feeling stayed with her as she walked with Lizzy up to the wooden door bracketed by lanterns.

It was the sort of house she'd always pictured when she'd escaped into stories about homesteads and large happy families. The sort of house a child would have drawn, with clean lines and pleasing symmetry.

As she waited for Agnes to answer the door, she smoothed

her hair and tried not to think about Ryan. Hours had passed, and yet she could still feel the roughness of his jaw against her cheek, taste the heat of his mouth and remember the delicious explosion of pleasure he'd drawn from her with each skillful, intimate stroke of his clever fingers. Most of all she remembered the way he'd focused on her, as if she were the only thing in his world. The roof could have fallen in on the cottage, and neither of them would have noticed.

Never in her life had she felt as if she were the focus of anyone's world. In the three years she'd spent with Neil, not once had she lost control. Sex had been a choice, not a need, and it had always followed a predictable pattern. She'd always had the feeling that either of them could have walked away at any point, and it wouldn't have mattered. After Ryan had walked away, she'd felt so wound up and frustrated she'd almost chased after him and begged him to finish what he'd started.

Lizzy tugged at her arm. "Your face is red."

"It's the sun."

She was wondering how she was ever going to look Ryan in the eye again, when the door opened. Any awkwardness she might have felt from the knowledge she'd spent the previous night physically welded to this woman's grandson melted away under the warmth of the welcome.

As for Agnes and Lizzy, it was love at first sight.

Some friendships, Emily knew, were instant, and this was one of those.

Within five minutes of knocking at the door, Lizzy was sitting at the kitchen table eating freshly baked chocolate cookies as if it were something she'd done hundreds of times in her life before.

"Handsome bear." Agnes slid her glasses onto her nose and took a closer look at the toy clutched tightly in the child's fingers. "Ryan's sister Rachel had a bear just like him. He's upstairs somewhere. I had to mend him a few times. Looks like yours could do with mending, too. Would you like me to do that for you?"

Lizzy glanced at Emily and then slid the bear across the table.

Understanding the trust implicit in that gesture, Agnes examined it carefully and then produced a sewing box from a cupboard. "It's nothing serious. Just something that happens when a bear is very loved. Emily, could you thread the needle for me, honey? My eyes aren't what they used to be."

Emily dutifully obliged and then glanced around the sunny kitchen as Agnes settled down to mend the bear. This, she thought, was how she'd imagined a kitchen should look. The countertops gleamed, pots of fresh herbs were lined up along the windowsill, and delicious smells wafted from the stove. Through the windows she could see butterflies flitting through the colorful blooms that crowded the lush, leafy sanctuary.

"You have a beautiful home."

"It's too big for one person. I rattle around like a bean in a jar." Agnes glanced up from her emergency repair and saw Emily looking at the herbs. "I love to grow my own food, but it's harder now I can't tend the garden myself. So, Ryan bought me herbs I could grow on the windowsill."

Having finished the cookie, Lizzy slid off the chair and wandered after Cocoa, leaving Emily with Agnes.

"Thank you for letting us borrow Cocoa."

"I call her my therapy dog because having her around makes everyone feel better." Agnes tilted the bear toward the light and sewed, each stitch minute and carefully aligned. "Did she make Lizzy feel better? Ryan said she hasn't been sleeping well."

"He told you that?"

"Not the detail." She glanced over the top of her glasses, and there was a sharpness to her gaze that hadn't been dimmed by failing vision. "He told me you were looking after your niece." She snipped the thread and handed the mended bear back to Emily. "It's always challenging when life sends you a responsibility you weren't expecting."

"It happened to you."

"Yes." Agnes stared at the garden for a moment, a faraway expression on her face. Then she smiled. "Why don't you make us both a cup of tea, and we'll take it through to the living room. I love early summer, and I don't want to waste a moment of the sunshine. I can't sail any longer, but I love to watch the boats. Ryan is the same. It's in his blood. His father spent every moment of his time on the water."

Suppressing an impulse to ask a million questions, Emily followed Agnes's directions and made tea, added cookies to a plate and carried it all through to the living room at the front of the house.

It was a room full of warmth and charm, flooded with natural light. A large bay window overlooked the sloping garden, and she could see a narrow path winding down to the small rocky cove below.

"This house is perfect."

Agnes gestured to the window seat. "That's my favorite spot. On a clear day you can see right across the bay to the mainland. Do you like sailing?"

Emily put the tray down on the table. "I've always been afraid of the sea." And under that quiet, sympathetic gaze it all came tumbling out, all of it, right up to the point where Ryan had kissed her.

That small detail she omitted, although she knew that at some point she was going to have to think about it, to work out what to say next time their paths crossed.

That time arrived sooner than expected. She turned her head to take another look at the view and saw him striding toward the house, talking on the phone. He took the steps two at a time and then paused, staring across the water as he continued the conversation.

Agnes watched and then shook her head. "There are times when I could drop that phone into the cookie jar and put the lid on it. Technology has a lot to answer for. Still, I suppose it means he can join me for lunch occasionally and isn't tied to his desk."

"Lunch? Oh, my goodness, I hadn't realized it was so late." Flustered by the knowledge that her next encounter with Ryan was going to be so soon, Emily scrambled to her feet. "We just called to drop off Cocoa. We've taken up too much of your time."

"The one thing I have far too much of is time, so someone taking some of it is my idea of a good turn. I enjoyed talking to you. I hope you'll come again."

"We will. And thank you for mending Andrew." Emily glanced out of the window again and saw that Ryan was standing with his back to them. Eyeing those broad, powerful shoulders, she wondered if she could make her escape out of the back door so she didn't have to face him.

The last time she'd seen him he'd—

And she'd—

Holy crap.

Scrambling for her shoes and her purse, she called for Lizzy.

"Is there a fire?" Agnes's tone was mild. "I get the distinct impression you're not happy to see my grandson."

"He's been very kind, but he's already done enough."

More than enough. He'd made her feel things she'd never felt before, and right now she wasn't in the mood to confront that.

"Kind?" Agnes looked at her curiously. "I've heard him described as selfish, ambitious, focused and damn nosy—most frequently by his youngest sister. *Kind* isn't a word I hear too often."

She wasn't sure what word she'd use to describe the man who had been ruthlessly focused on nothing but her pleasure the night before.

Thinking about it made her cheeks heat, so that by the time Ryan strolled into the house, she looked as if she'd been sunbathing without protection.

"Ryan." Agnes brushed the crumbs from her lap. "You missed the cookies."

"My loss." He stooped to kiss his grandmother on her cheek, and Emily felt her throat close as she witnessed the genuine affection between them.

His childhood must have been hard and his loss overwhelming, but he'd grown up surrounded by this easy warmth and love.

"Lizzy and I were just leaving."

He straightened, squeezed Agnes's shoulder and turned to look at Emily. For a moment his gaze lingered on hers, and then he smiled. "I've rearranged my afternoon so I can take you out for lunch."

"Lizzy had a large breakfast, and—"

"Alone."

"Alone?"

The air was heated by a tension that was only present when he walked into a room.

"Good idea. Everyone needs a little adult time." Agnes was brisk. "Lizzy and I will sit here and sort through Rachel's old books and toys. It's a job I should have done a decade ago, but I've been putting it off."

Lizzy appeared in the doorway, Cocoa at her heels. "Can we play?"

"With the toys? Of course. You will decide what we keep and what we give away. Do you like books?"

Lizzy nodded slowly. "Emily has been reading to me."

"Good. Because I have more books than the library."

It was one thing to let Lizzy play in a different room, something else entirely to leave her alone with someone. Emily shook her head. "I can't."

"She's safe here with me." Agnes spoke quietly. "We're not going to leave the house."

Lizzy was holding Andrew tightly. "I'm not allowed to go to the beach."

Emily bit her lip. "Lizzy—"

"I'm too old for the beach," Agnes said calmly. "I'm too old to be brushing sand out of my shoes and out of the house. We are going to stay indoors and have fun. It's been a long time since I've had the pleasure of young company."

To refuse would be insulting to Agnes, but to accept would mean being alone with Ryan.

"She isn't used to strangers." She realized how ridiculous that was as an excuse, when Lizzy had virtually been raised by strangers.

Lizzy must have thought it, too, because she climbed onto the sofa next to Agnes. "I want to stay."

Deprived of excuses by the excuse herself, Emily gave a helpless shrug.

"If you're sure—"

Agnes smiled. "I can't think of anything I'd like more. Don't rush. We'll still be here when you get back, and nothing is going to happen."

Lizzy inched closer to Agnes. "Sometimes there are men with cameras."

Agnes's mouth tightened. "Not on my property, pumpkin."

As she left the house, Emily felt Ryan's hand on her back.

"You told my grandmother the truth?"

"Yes. Was that a mistake?"

"No. And you have no reason to worry about her safety. If Puffin Island were ever invaded, Agnes would lead the defense. She raised two children of her own and then took on three grandchildren. Lizzy is in good hands."

She tried to ignore the warmth of his hand. Tried to forget how those hands had felt as they'd moved over her body. "Four. You're forgetting to include yourself."

"I was part of the management team." His smile made her heart beat faster.

Her level of awareness was a constant hum beneath the anxiety about being responsible for Lizzy. "It's the first time I've left her."

"I know." He stopped and eased her to one side so that a family loaded down with beach gear could pass them. "Raising a child isn't about locking them away until they're eighteen and then pushing them out of the door. It's about giving them the tools to be independent. You should be pleased she was happy to stay with Agnes. She could have been clinging to you, especially after what happened. But we both know that this isn't all about Lizzy. You're looking for an excuse to avoid me."

"That isn't true."

"No? So look me in the eye."

"We're in public."

"I know and I promise not to rip your clothes off. Now look at me."

"What happens when people don't do what you want them to do?"

"If it's something that matters to me, I'm persistent."

Was he implying that she mattered to him? The thought of it made the blood rush from her head. Normally she was a calm, logical thinker, but whenever she was this close to him her thoughts scattered. "You have to back off, Ryan. I can't think when you say things like that."

"Good. You need to think less, not more." He took her arm and guided her across the street away from the bustle of the busy harbor, to the relative calm of Main Street with its attractive buildings and colorful storefronts. They walked past several sea and surf shops and a few high-end boutiques catering to the wealthy set who had fallen in love with the beauty and relative seclusion of Puffin Island. Emily had seen the lavish summer houses dotted around the island, from colonial homes to elaborate beach houses. Despite that, or perhaps because of it, the place had an eclectic, cosmopolitan feel.

"Where are we going?"

"I'm going to buy you an ice cream."

"A—what?"

"You said you'd eaten breakfast and didn't want lunch, so I'll buy you an ice cream instead. Simple pleasures. If you're going to teach Lizzy how to live, you need to start doing it yourself. The next thing I'm going to do is get you out of those clothes."

She felt as if she were trapped in an airless room. "You mean you don't want me to wear so much black?"

He gave her a wicked smile. "Take it any way you like." Without giving her a chance to respond, he pushed open the door of Summer Scoop and smiled at the young woman behind the counter. "Hi, Lisa, how's it going?"

"Good, thanks." The woman used that overly bright tone that people adopted when things were totally crap.

The place was empty.

"I'm treating Emily to ice cream." Ryan put his hand on the small of her back and eased her forward. "Something smooth, creamy and indulgent."

Lisa reached for the scoop. "Kirsti thinks there's an ice cream for every mood. How would you describe your mood today, Emily?"

She felt the pressure of Ryan's hand on her back. The slow deliberate stroke of his palm through the thin fabric of her shirt.

Was "sexually frustrated" a mood or a physical condition? She turned her head, saw the amused gleam in Ryan's eyes and glared at him. "I can't find the words to describe my mood."

"Then tell me your favorite flavor."

Trying to escape the dizzying, distracting stroke of his fingers, Emily stepped forward to examine the various options. "It all looks delicious. What do you recommend?" She was so hot she wanted to jump into the freezer with the ice cream.

"Children love Banana Buttermilk, but for adult first-timers I usually recommend Blueberry Booster or Smuggler's Tipple."

"Smuggler's Tipple?"

"Chocolate and rum." Lisa picked up a small pot. "I can do you a small taster?"

"No need. You said the word *blueberry*, so I'm sold."

Ryan chose Caramel Sea Salt. "Lisa moved here last summer from the mainland. She has six-year-old twins, Summer and Harry."

"Summer?" Emily glanced at the sign over the counter, but Lisa shook her head.

"Just a coincidence. Would you believe that was the name of the place?"

Ryan smiled. "Kirsti would say it was fate."

"Kirsti is an incurable optimist." Lisa's tired smile suggested she didn't suffer from the same affliction. "We arrived here last Easter for a holiday. We needed a fresh start— Well, this seemed like a good place. We used to come in here for a treat, and one day the owner told us she was moving to Florida because she didn't like the winters here. My daughter decided it was named for her." She handed Emily a pretty waffle cone topped with creamy blueberry ice cream.

"Owning an ice cream business must be every child's dream."

"I wanted them to grow up surrounded by fresh air and a community of people who knew one another, so it seemed like my dream, too."

"But it isn't?"

Lisa kept her head down as she dipped into the salted caramel ice cream. Emily could tell she was reluctant to discuss her problems with a customer.

"We're fine. But if a few more tourists chose to buy our ice cream, I wouldn't be sorry." She handed the cone to Ryan. "Eat it in the sunshine because we all know that by tomorrow the sun might have gone into hiding. Enjoy."

Emily licked around the melting edges and moaned. "This is the best thing I've ever tasted." She saw Ryan's gaze drop to her mouth. The heat in that look was enough to melt all the ice cream in Maine.

"I agree with Lisa." His voice was husky, and there was a shimmer of something dangerous in his eyes. "Let's eat this outside."

Emily left the shop, flushed from head to toe. She kept her gaze fixed on the harbor. "Lisa seems worried."

"Does she? The moment you started licking that ice cream, my mind went blank. I was thinking about your tongue and all the things I could do with that ice cream. All of them involved your naked body." He spoke in a low voice and then cleared his throat. "Good morning, Hilda. I didn't see you there."

"Ryan. Emily. It's a beautiful day. Have you caught the sun?" She peered at Emily. "You're looking red. This may not be the Caribbean, but don't make the mistake of thinking you can't burn here. Water intensifies the sun's rays."

"She has fair skin," Ryan said smoothly, "but I'll make sure she buys sunscreen later." He turned and winked at Emily who knew she was the color of a tomato.

"Sunscreen. Great idea." She tried desperately to change the subject. "You were right about the ice cream, Hilda. It's delicious."

"Best ice cream in Maine. Breaks my heart to see the girl struggling, especially with those two young children. In my opinion it was unfair of May Newton to sell her the business in the first place." Hilda's mouth flattened into a thin line of disapproval. "She knew it was in trouble. No one can make the place pay. It's had five owners in as many years."

Emily frowned. "Five owners?"

"You can't sell enough ice cream in the summer months to keep a family going over the winter." Hilda waved at someone on the other side of the harbor. "I'll leave you two to finish your ice cream." She moved away, and Emily sagged against the wall of the shop.

"Do you think she knew?"

"That I was talking dirty to you five seconds before she arrived? Probably. She doesn't miss much."

"I'm going to have to move back to the mainland."

"Hilda had six children of her own, so I doubt that sex is a mystery to her. You have ice cream at the corner of your mouth. Am I allowed to lick it away?"

"Only if you don't mind being punched in public."

"I never object to a physical relationship, and it would do you good to rediscover some of those emotions you've been blocking out." His eyes were hooded, his voice low, and she felt her insides melt faster than the ice cream.

Flirting was as alien to her as all the other emotions swirling inside her. She tried desperately to change the subject. "Is it true that Summer Scoop is in trouble? That the place has had five owners in as many years?"

His smile told her he knew exactly what she was doing. "Yeah, that part is true."

"So you think Lisa made a mistake buying the business?"

He shrugged. "One person's mistake is another person's adventure."

She wondered if that comment was aimed at her. "But with two children to support, the stakes are different."

"True." He finished his ice cream and licked his fingers. "Children have a habit of killing adventure."

She thought of the way Lisa had talked about her kids. Even in that brief encounter, she could see they were everything to her. "I think to some people kids *are* the adventure."

"They can also be too much reality." His tone was dry. "How is your ice cream?"

"The ice cream is delicious. The place should be packed."

"It should be, but it never is. I'm probably a tiny bit to blame for that. The Ocean Club pulls in a lot of casual lunchtime and evening business."

"But it's a different market."

"Maybe, but we're all competing for the same tourist dollars."

Emily glanced at the pretty ice cream parlor. "There should be room for both of you. Do you stock her product?"

"Sorry?"

"Do you serve her products at the Ocean Club?"

"I have no idea. I don't micromanage. I leave that to the chef. I think he makes his own."

"This ice cream is good. And it's homemade on the island from the Warrens' organic dairy herd."

"How do you know that?"

"It says so on the poster. Makes me imagine green pastures and everything healthy, which is ironic given the fat content." She finished her ice cream regretfully. "That was good. It wouldn't hurt you to put in an order."

"That's what I have to do to gain approval?" There was humor in his eyes. "I'll talk to Anton."

"Anton? Seriously?" Emily laughed. "You have a chef called Anton?"

"I do."

"Is he French?"

"No. Born and bred in Maine. The things he can do with a lobster would make you cry. Can those shoes of yours cope with a walk?" He glanced down at her feet. "There's a view I want to show you."

And suddenly she realized that she was standing in the street, laughing with a man as if this was her life. As if she were free to follow her instincts and impulses.

Just for a moment, with the sun on her face and Ryan by her side, she'd forgotten everything.

"I should get back."

"Coward."

"I'm thinking of Lizzy. I haven't left her before."

"She'll be fine with my grandmother." His voice was soft. "Walk with me."

"Why?"

"Because it's midday and half the residents of Puffin Island are going about their business in Main Street. As you're keen to avoid attention, I'm suggesting we get out of here."

"You could just stop looking at me," Emily muttered. "That would do it."

"That isn't an option." He took her hand and drew her into the narrow street that ran between the bakery and the hardware store. It wound away from the main harbor area and was a shortcut to the Ocean Club.

"I might be able to help her."

"Who?"

"Lisa. I might be able to give her business advice. I'm a management consultant. It's what I do. It's what I'm good at."

They took the path that led up past the Ocean Club and turned inland. This side of the island was thickly wooded, with steep trails zigzagging through dense forest. On the other side was farmland, with rolling pastures leading down to the sea.

Shaded from sunshine, breathing in the smell of pine, Emily made a mental note to bring Lizzy here.

"It's pretty." And quiet. The only sound was the call of the birds and the snap of twigs under their feet. "I can see why Lisa would have chosen to live here."

"Here—" he handed her a bottle of insect repellent "—better use this on the areas that aren't covered. We have mosquitoes the size of small birds, and they love black. Tell me about your job."

"My expertise was strategy and operations. I worked mostly in the consumer goods industry."

"You know about ice cream?"

"Not specifically, but that doesn't matter. I'm a problem solver. I look at product, pricing, positioning, supply chains—" She broke off. "This is boring. You don't want to hear the detail."

"All those long words are turning me on, but I confess I zoned out when you said 'positioning.'" He grinned at her. "Clearly I have a thing for management consultants. Who knew?"

"We're in a competitive market. Companies need to stay agile."

He groaned. "Honey, you are killing me. Just don't start talking about growth or I'll be arrested."

Because everything about him unsettled her, she chose to ignore the innuendo. "We apply lean principles—"

"That's going to be a challenge given the amount of fat in Summer Scoop ice cream. I assume you decided to be a management consultant because it requires not a shred of emotion."

"I like the logic and predictability of figures, that's true, but there is emotion attached to what I do. Companies expand and contract depending on the advice my company gives."

"But it isn't personal."

"No," she conceded. "It isn't personal. It suits the way my brain works."

"So, what are you going to do with that brain of yours now?"

"I don't know. I have enough money saved to support both of us for a little while, so I'm still taking it twelve hours at a time." Sun filtered through spruce and pine, and Emily realized they'd walked quite a distance from the harbor. "I never knew it was this densely wooded."

"Maine isn't called the Pine Tree State for nothing. It takes a couple of hours to walk to the top, but the views are incredible. I'll take you one day."

"And Lizzy."

His hesitation was so brief it would have been easy to miss. "And Lizzy." His tone was deceptively light. "If that's what you want."

The way he said it left her in no doubt as to the way he saw their relationship.

For him, it was all about exploring the physical connection and nothing else.

As for her—she had no idea how she saw things.

Confused by her own feelings, she changed the subject. "Would she want help, do you think?"

"Lisa? I don't know her that well, but given that this was her dream, I'm guessing the answer to that would be yes. No one wants to give up a dream, do they? It gets a little steep here." He held out his hand, and she hesitated and then took it. Immediately those strong fingers curled around hers, and she remembered the night before, the way they'd felt locked in her hair, stroking her breasts, buried deep—

"I'm not dressed for hiking." Her face was hot, and she tried to ignore the feel of his hand on hers.

"Are you too hot? Unfasten a button on that shirt. Don't worry about insects, I'll keep my eyes on you."

"I'm cool, thank you." She sent him a look designed to wither, but he merely smiled.

"Really? I'm hot as hell, but that may be because I'm marinating in my own sinful thoughts about last night." Twigs snapped under his feet as he walked. "Have you ever had forest sex?"

Emily almost stumbled. His hand tightened on hers, and she kept her eyes on the ground, picking her way along the trail. "I've lived in cities all my life."

"You've never had outdoor sex?"

"You mean apart from all the sex I had in the middle of Times Square?" Her sarcasm drew a smile.

"You never had sex in Times Square." Swift and sure, he backed her against a tree, caged her. "You never had sex anywhere you might be caught. With you it's all locked doors and the lights off. I bet you've only ever had sex in a bed." A smile flickered at the corners of his mouth, and she felt her tummy tumble.

"You don't know that."

"I do." His gaze dropped to her mouth, and his voice was rough. "Because you've only ever had 'nice' sex. And 'nice' sex isn't the sort that happens with your back against a tree and your skirt around your waist."

"I'm not wearing a skirt, and I don't see anything exciting about bark burn."

Eyes gleaming, he lowered his head toward hers. "Want me to show you?"

Yes. She, for whom sex had been all the things he'd described. Locked door and lights out. "I have to get back to Lizzy." The only sound was the birds in the trees and the pounding of her own heart. "Seriously, Ryan." She tried to evade him, but she was trapped between the tree and the hard power of his thighs.

His hand came up to her face, his fingers gentle. "Am I scaring you?"

She didn't answer because her heart was in her mouth. Her stomach squirmed with a twist of intense desire. Even the smell of fresh air and the sound of the sea hadn't been enough to cool the memories of what he'd made her feel.

"Not scare exactly. But my life is already complicated enough."

"I'm not offering you complicated." His voice husky, he lowered his head and trailed his mouth along the line of her jaw. "In fact, right now I've been reduced to man in its most basic form. What I'm offering is simple."

"You're talking about sex." Her eyes closed and her heart raced. She felt the erotic drag of his mouth move down to her neck and linger on the pulse just above her collarbone. "Sex is never simple."

"It can be."

Dizzy with the intensity of wanting, she placed her hand on his chest "Ryan—"

"Yeah, I know." Reluctantly he eased away from her. "I'm pushing my luck for a first date."

"This isn't a date."

"Ice cream followed by a walk in the woods? On Puffin Island that counts as serious." He tucked a strand of hair behind her ear with a gentle hand. "We'll go back now. You don't have the right footwear for a long walk. If you're going to be living on Puffin Island, you might want to do something about that. Unless you have a secret stash of outdoor gear?"

"Most of my clothes are like the ones I'm wearing."

"That's what I figured. This is an outdoor paradise. We'll have you hiking, mountain biking and kayaking in no time. Better buy some equipment. We have a great selection in the

Ocean Club. And I'm going to take you out on my yacht. The best way to see the island is from the sea." They started walking back down the trail, with sunlight beaming through the trees and the sounds of the forest in the background.

"I will walk in the forest, but I'm never going on a yacht."

"Penobscot Bay has some of the best sailing in the world."

"Maybe, but that doesn't mean I have to experience it first-hand. I don't like the idea of all that water underneath me, and—" she hesitated "—I don't swim."

He stopped. "You never learned?"

"I haven't been in the water since that day."

Shock spread across his face. "I assumed—that should have been the first thing your mother did for you."

"She didn't, and I'm glad she didn't."

"Everyone should be able to swim."

"Not me. I don't need to because I'm never going in the water." She tried to pull away, but he tightened his grip and pulled her back toward him.

"I'm going to teach you."

She closed her hands over his arms to steady herself, her fingers biting into the rock-hard muscle of his biceps. "I don't want to learn."

"I'll teach you in the Ocean Club pool. There's a shallow end."

"I don't care if you're offering to teach me in your tub—I'm not interested in learning to swim. I am happy to hike and ride a mountain bike, but you will not persuade me to go on a boat of any sort, and you certainly won't persuade me to swim."

"Not even if I promise to keep you safe?"

She looked into those eyes and felt her center of balance shift. "A woman might be many things with you, Ryan Cooper. But I don't think 'safe' is one of them."

CHAPTER NINE

AT LIZZY'S INSISTENCE, they called at Agnes's every morning to walk Cocoa. Resigned to her new role as dog walker, Emily paid a trip to the Outdoor Store, equipped them both with hiking boots, rain slickers, insect repellent and a small rucksack, and each day they took the dog and explored a different part of the island. On the first day they followed the road out of the harbor and along the trail that wound its way through overgrown fields to the south of the island, accompanied by song sparrows and butterflies. The trail skirted the edge of the Warrens' farm, sixty-five acres of mixed hardwood, pasture and hay fields. They stopped to admire the herd of dairy cows who provided the organic milk for the ice cream at Summer Scoop, and walked on through meadows crowded with Queen Anne's lace and goldenrod.

On another day they walked the coastal path around to the east of the island. Emily chose the route that went a little way inland, rather than the path that clung to the rocks and rose up over the bluff. Here, the mossy woods crowded the shoreline, sending dark shadows across rocky coves. Gulls bobbed in the water, and seals played hide-and-seek in the surf around the rocks. Cocoa strained at her leash, desperate to explore, but the one place Emily refused to walk was on the beach itself.

She tried to retrace the walk she'd done with Ryan into the woods, but Lizzy was nervous and Emily was afraid of getting lost. She insisted Lizzy wear her hat whenever they were outdoors, but the people she passed were either tourists or locals and none of them showed any interest in a young woman and her daughter. Gradually the acute fear of discovery faded to a dull, background throb.

They returned from their walks at lunchtime, and Emily called into the delicatessen to pick up something for lunch. They then took it back to Agnes's and ate it picnic style, either on the covered porch overlooking her garden or, if mist had blown in, at her kitchen table.

Occasionally Emily left Lizzy with Agnes while she went and bought provisions, but otherwise she kept the child close.

"Do you think I'm overprotective?"

Lizzy had fallen asleep on the sofa after an exhausting morning with Cocoa, and Agnes and Emily were drinking iced tea in the light-filled living room.

"I think you had a bad experience, and you haven't had to rebuild your confidence." Agnes was sorting through another box of children's books for Lizzy. "You lived a life that didn't include the sea or young children, so you didn't have a reason to challenge your fear or push yourself out of your comfort zone. But you will, now you're living here. You can't live on Puffin Island and ignore the sea. It's essential to island life. It feeds us, and it keeps us connected to the mainland."

"I think I preferred the mainland. There was no chance of drowning in Manhattan, and I never went near the Hudson."

"But Manhattan has other dangers."

Emily sipped her tea. "I didn't really think about them."

"That's because we're all a product of our experiences. Someone who had a bad experience in a city might think differently."

"Do you think I can change?"

"You already are. Look where you're sitting." Agnes added another book to the pile. "A week ago you sat with your back to the window, but now you're in my favorite spot on the window seat, looking at the boats on the water. It's a pretty sight, isn't it?"

Emily turned her head. "There's glass between me and the water."

"But you're looking at it. That's progress. And I've made progress, too. Lizzy and I have cleared four boxes of books this week."

"Most of them are now in Castaway Cottage. Thank you. It's generous of you. And I love books." Books were almost all she'd brought with her from her old life. Old battered copies and first editions she'd collected over the years. "Whenever I had something to celebrate, I bought a book."

"I need to reduce all the clutter, but I'm not good at parting with anything." Agnes reached for another box. "This is something else I can't bring myself to clear out."

"What is it?"

"All of Ryan's stories. Of course, a lot of it is online, but I'm not good with the internet, so he used to send me the paper versions." She opened the box, and Emily saw neatly sorted stacks of newspaper clippings.

"There were stories about him in the press?"

"He wasn't the subject of the story, he *wrote* the story. He didn't tell you that? He's so modest. He won a Pulitzer Prize, you know, for news reporting."

No, she didn't know. Emily's mouth dried. "Are you saying he's a journalist?"

"Was." Agnes leafed through the clippings, pride on her face. "The best. He had a way of getting to the emotion of a story. He's a good listener. People tell him things. Things they would never tell other people."

I'm not afraid of emotions.

Emily stood up, feeling as if she were sleepwalking. She'd

told him things. Things she'd never told other people. She'd done things with him she hadn't done with anyone else. "Would you look after Lizzy for a while? There's something I need to do."

"Of course." Agnes glanced up from her news clippings. "She's perfectly safe here with me."

It took Emily less than five minutes to walk the short distance to the Ocean Club.

She strode through the door and into the crowded Bar and Grill where Kirsti was circulating.

"Hi, Emily." Kirsti gave her a friendly smile. "No Lizzy today?"

"She's with Agnes." Her voice sounded robotic. "I need to see Ryan."

"Of course you do." Kirsti behaved as if Emily's unplanned visit was the most natural thing in the world. "He's in his office. He's had a hell of a morning, so I know he's going to be pleased to see you."

No, Emily thought grimly as she walked to the back of the Ocean Club. *He most definitely wouldn't be.*

Ryan's office faced the water, and he was on the phone with his feet on the desk, when she walked in.

"He was supposed to fix the pump. I told him we'd—" He broke off as he saw Emily. "I'll call you back, Pete. Go check it out. Don't delegate this one. If necessary I'll dig out the tools and do it myself." He hung up the phone and smiled.

That assured smile was the final straw. "I need to talk to you."

"Just when I thought a bad day wasn't going to turn good, you walk in." He lifted his eyebrows as she slammed the door shut. "Is this about sex in public places? Because—"

"You lied to me." The anger was like a burning coal inside her. Later there would be other emotions, but right now fury overrode everything else. Fury and a deep sense of betrayal.

Ryan removed his feet from the desk. "Calm down."

"I'm calm. Just angry."

"I'm not sure it's possible to be calm and angry."

She paced across his office and stood in front of him. "I won't ask why you didn't tell me, because that part is obvious, but I will ask what your intentions are. I have a right to know that." She needed to know whether she was going to have to leave the island. The thought made her stomach churn because she had no idea where she'd go.

"My intentions?"

"You lied to me. You sat there and talked to me about how the press wouldn't be interested. You reassured me. You sat in my kitchen and acted as if you were my friend. As if you were someone I could trust. You bought Lizzy a *hat*, for God's sake, to hide her from prying eyes and all the time you're—you're—"

"Wait a minute. Slow down. We're talking about Lizzy? I thought you were talking about this thing we have." The look he gave her could have singed the edges of her hair. "The chemistry. I thought it unsettled you. That's why I backed off. I was giving you space."

Her gaze met his, and for a moment she was knocked off balance. "I'm talking about the fact you're a journalist, Ryan. When were you going to tell me? After a piece on Lizzy came out with your byline?"

He stilled. "How did you find out?"

"I'd like to say I looked you up on the internet because anyone in my position with a shred of common sense would have done that, but I didn't." After they'd had waffles on the deck that first morning she'd looked up the Ocean Club and spent half an hour on their slick website. She'd read his bio and been impressed. She hadn't thought to put his name alone into a search engine. "Agnes was sorting through a file of all the stories you've written. She's proud of you. She didn't seem to know you'd conveniently kept that part of your life from me."

His gaze didn't shift from hers. "Did you look at the stories?"

"No. I wasn't in the mood to mull over your career success. I was too busy wondering why you'd chosen to keep it from me. And the answer is pretty obvious."

"Emily, listen—"

"I listened when you suggested Lizzy and I join you for lunch. I listened when you said I could trust you. I told you everything. And you're such a good listener, aren't you, Ryan? So good at parting people from their secrets. For a while I thought you had a gift with people, but now I realize it's one of the tools of your trade. You even won a prize for it. Tell me, is sex another part of your superior technique to get people to tell you everything?"

His face was blank of expression. "You know it isn't."

"I don't know anything." She felt an ache deep in her gut because even now part of her wanted to believe that what had happened between them was real. "All I know is that you lied."

"I was going to tell you. I was waiting for the right moment."

"And when was that going to be? When you'd told everyone the whereabouts of Juliet Elizabeth Fox?" She saw the brief flare of anger in his eyes.

"Do you really think I would do that?" He stood up so suddenly the chair scraped on the floor. "Hell, Emily. I've been doing everything I can to make the two of you feel safe here."

"For what purpose? So that you can tip off a journalist as to exactly where Lana Fox's child is living and get the credit? Is this what you journalists call an exclusive? You deliberately withheld information about yourself. If your past had no impact on the present, then why didn't you tell me the truth? You told me about your childhood, about your brothers and sisters, your parents, Agnes—but not once did you mention that you used to be a journalist."

He swore under his breath and ran his hand over the back of his neck. "Listen—" He broke off and scowled as the door to his office opened, and Kirsti put her head around. "Not now—"

"Sorry, boss." Kirsti slunk away, closing the door behind her again, and Emily turned and walked toward it.

"You didn't need to send her away. I've said all I have to say."

"Good. So now it's my turn. Sit down."

"There is nothing you have to say that I can possibly want to hear." She reached the door at the same time he did, and he stretched past her and pushed it shut with the flat of his hand.

"Except the truth. You don't have to believe me, but you'll at least listen." He was standing so close to her she could smell that elusive male scent that made her knees weaken.

"Why are you suddenly so keen to tell me the truth?"

"Look around you, Emily. What you see is a man who has plowed every last dollar and cent into this business and this is-land. I'm not a journalist. I haven't worked as a journalist for four years, and even when I did I wasn't reporting the sort of story you're describing." There was a hardness to his jaw and shadows in his eyes that she hadn't seen before.

Or maybe she hadn't been looking.

"So why didn't you mention what you used to do?"

"Because it isn't part of my life now, and once I discovered why you were here, I knew I couldn't talk about it. You needed someone to trust, and if I'd told you, you wouldn't have trusted me."

"You're right, I wouldn't have. But that should have been my choice to make."

"Brittany trusts me. Isn't that enough for you?"

"She should have told me the truth instead of telling me you were a friend."

"I am a friend. And the reason she didn't tell you is because she didn't think it was relevant."

"You were a journalist! How can that not be relevant? And whatever has happened before, I need you to be honest with me now, for Lizzy's sake, if not for mine. Should I be worried? Have you told anyone she's here?"

He hesitated for a second too long. "I made one call after that day you saw the photo in the newspaper, but only to try and get a sense of how interested people were."

Her heart started to race. "You *called* someone?"

"An old friend. And he didn't know why I was calling."

"How do you know? What if he guesses? They could come here."

"The media is losing interest. Lana was the story, not her child. They're not going to come."

"If they do—if they find her and scare her—there is no quick way off the island. If they come, where do I run to?"

"You won't need to run. They won't come."

"That first day when you came knocking on my door—" it was painful to ask the question because she was afraid of the answer "—it wasn't because you were looking for Lizzy?"

"I've told you. Brittany asked me to keep an eye on you."

"Why would you agree? I've known you long enough to know you don't do anything that doesn't suit you. What is this relationship you have with Brittany that you're willing to put your life on hold to keep an eye on a stranger? What do you gain from this if it isn't a story you can sell? She told me that you owe her."

He gave a tired smile. "That's a private joke."

"I've had enough of private. Exactly *what* do you owe her?"

He turned and paced across to the window of his office to stare out over the water. "I was best man at Brittany's wedding."

Of all the things she'd expected him to say, it hadn't been that. "Her wedding? *The* wedding? So you're friends with the bastard who walked out on her at the end of their honeymoon? Oh, my God." A suspicion formed in her mind. "We saw him. He was flying the plane Skylar took last weekend. I recognized him. The first thing Brittany did when she arrived at college was pin a large photo of him on the wall to remind her never to be stupid about a man again. I stared at his face long enough to be able to recognize him when I saw him in person. Did you know he was back here?"

"Yeah, I knew. Zach is the best pilot you'll ever meet. He owns his own plane now and flies the mega-rich to their yachts and beach cottages. The rest of the time he does his own thing, and it so happens he's chosen to base himself on Puffin Island."

"He was flying for Maine Island Air."

"He helps them out sometimes. I didn't think it was something that needed mentioning as Brittany isn't here anyway, and their marriage was over before it started."

"You are the master at withholding information."

"Whereas you clearly support the principle of full disclosure, so by all means go ahead and tell her he's here if you think that's going to make her day and lift her mood."

She knew it wouldn't. "If you were best man, then you must know him well. Are you two still friends?"

"Yes." He didn't hesitate. "Friendship isn't something you throw away just because someone makes a bad decision."

"Bad decision? You don't think he should have left Brittany?" She saw tension ripple across those wide shoulders and he turned to look at her.

"What I think," he said slowly, "is that he should never have married her in the first place. That was the bad decision."

"So why does Brittany blame you?"

He gave a humorless smile. "Because I knew it was a match made in hell. He got cold feet and wanted to ditch her on her wedding day, and I drove him to the wedding instead of the airport because I knew she'd be devastated. I didn't want him to hurt her. Turned out he did that anyway, and I made it worse. Ditching her at the altar would have been a hell of a lot less complicated than ditching her at the end of the honeymoon."

It was a lot to take in.

"What about the rest of it?" She forced herself to ask one more question. "Did Brittany tell you to kiss me? Was that part of the deal?"

His eyes darkened. "You know it wasn't."

"I don't know anything, Ryan. And I don't know you." With those quiet words she turned and left the room.

HE WAITED UNTIL he knew Lizzy would be in bed and then knocked on the door of Castaway Cottage, unsure whether she'd even open it.

The island was folded in mist and darkness, and behind him he could hear the rush of the sea against the shore. He was thinking how much courage it must have taken to choose this place as a refuge, when the door opened.

Emily's feet were bare, and her hair fell soft and loose around her face.

She didn't look pleased to see him, but he'd braced himself for that.

"I need to talk to you."

"We've said all there is to say."

"I want to show you something. Give me five minutes. If you still want me to leave after that, I'll leave." The thought of what he was about to do made him feel as shaky as an alcoholic who hadn't had a drink in a month.

She stared at the box in his arms and opened the door a little wider. "Lizzy is asleep."

"Good, because this is between us." He carried the box through to the kitchen. Given the choice, he would have destroyed it long ago, but he knew keeping it meant a lot to his grandmother.

He put it down on the table next to one of Lizzy's paintings, a classic child's drawing of a house with smoke coming from the chimney. There was a garden, drawn with careful strokes of green, and a curve of custard yellow sand next to an ocean bluer than anything he'd seen in Maine. It was obvious to him that this was his grandmother's house. The innocent charm of the picture jarred uncomfortably with the dark reality he'd placed next to it.

He stood for a moment with his hands on the box.

He'd chosen to live life looking forward, not back, and he didn't relish what he was about to do.

"That's Agnes's box." She stood next to him, waiting. "I already know what's in it."

No, he thought. *You don't.* "I want you to take a look. Read."

"I don't need to read."

"You wanted to know about my past." He felt distant and detached, as if someone else had climbed into his body. "This is my past."

"Which you try and forget. Why? Do you regret the stories you wrote?"

"No. But they stay with you." He flipped open the top and gripped the back of the chair until his knuckles were white. "Especially that one."

She stared at his face and then down at the file. In slow motion, she picked up the clipping on top. Award-Winning Photojournalist Killed in Kabul?

"We worked with a translator and a driver. Together we made two trips into Iraq and four into Afghanistan. Me as foreign correspondent, Finn as a photojournalist."

There was a long silence. "You were a war reporter?"

"I met Finn on my first day in Baghdad, and we hit it off right away. We had an ongoing argument about which was the better medium for telling a story—words or images. He said that I wrote about the truth whereas he showed it. Neither of us wanted to be embedded with the troops. We wanted to be free to tell the stories we wanted to tell. The ones other people weren't telling."

She sank down onto one of the kitchen chairs. "Ryan—"

"After a British journalist was killed, Finn decided he'd had enough. He said we'd ceased to see beauty in the world, only the bad and the ugly. Everything we saw was distorted and discolored by conflict. He wanted to take photographs that didn't involve human suffering. I talked about this place all the time, and we were always making plans. I was going to run a sailing school, and he was going to use his photographic skills to raise awareness of the importance of marine conservation. On really bad days we decided we'd open a bar together and drink our way through the profits." He stopped and heard the scrape of the chair on the floor as she rose to her feet.

A moment later a glass of water appeared by his hand.

He took a sip, embarrassed by how much his hand was shaking.

"We were about to fly home, but I wanted to do one more story, so we went with our translator and fixer to a local village. Finn was joking that he was going to sail my yacht while I did the work when our vehicle was hit." Just for a moment he felt it again, the blinding flash and then the white and the lack of sound. "We were close to a military base. A helicopter pilot risked his life to get us out of there, but it was too late for Finn. He was killed instantly."

Her hand reached across and covered his, slim warm fingers sliding between his.

"I'm sorry."

"I was the one who was sorry. If it hadn't been for me, we would have been on our way home. I was the one who pushed for one more story." Even now, four years later, the knowledge left a bitter taste in his mouth and the gnawing agony of guilt. He reached into the file and pulled out a photograph. "This was one of his last photographs."

She removed her hand from his and took the photograph. "It's very powerful." She stared at it for a long moment and then placed it carefully back in the box and closed the lid. "You were badly injured?"

"Bad enough. I had serious internal injuries and my shoulder was messed up. I was in and out of hospital for four months. I had eight rounds of surgery. And I was a difficult patient. Ask Agnes and Rachel. They took the brunt of it." He stared at the file. "Rachel was home from college for the summer and she virtually moved into my hospital room and stayed there with me until I was discharged. The first day back on the island, she forced me to get dressed, and I managed to walk as far as the harbor before having to sit down. My legs wouldn't hold me and my shoulder was agony. Every day she made me get up and walk a little farther until eventually I was walking as far as the lighthouse. I had no idea my little sister could be such a bully. When I was strong enough to walk as far as Shell Cove, she decided I should start swimming. I remember the day she and Alec forced me to go sailing. It was a perfect day, and I felt the wind fill the sails and knew this was where I wanted to stay."

"So the sea healed you."

"In a way, but I think it was more about the people. Before I left the island I couldn't wait to get away. I felt trapped, I was going crazy. I thought anywhere in the world had to be better than this place, living among people who know everything from how much you weighed when you were born to what you liked to eat for dinner. Then I discovered differently." He licked his lips, not sure whether by being economical with his words he was sparing her the detail or himself. "I guess you could say my priorities changed. An honest person would probably say it was a shame I had to be blown up to discover something I should have known all along."

"I think we don't always see things clearly when we're living in the middle of something." There was a long silence. "I owe you an apology."

"No. I'm the one who owes you an apology for not being honest, but I was afraid you wouldn't trust me. And I wanted you to trust me."

"Because you feel you owe Brittany."

He could have told her the truth. He could have told her that the reason he couldn't stay away from her had nothing to do with Brittany, but that would have led the relationship in a direction he suspected she wasn't ready for it to go. And he wasn't sure he wanted it to go there, either.

Whatever she thought about her suitability for the role of

parent, she'd shown herself to be fiercely protective of Lizzy. That fact alone meant he should stay the hell away from her.

"That's right." He kept his face blank. "I owed a friend a favor."

"The other night—"

"You had a bad experience. Neither of us was thinking straight." Finding willpower he didn't known he possessed, he stepped back and reached for the file. "I should go. I have a pile of paperwork waiting for me before I turn in. If you need anything, you know where I am."

He saw something flicker in her eyes. Hurt? Confusion? Either way, he saw her register the dismissal and draw the conclusion that his attentions had all been driven by nothing more than a Good Samaritan inclination and a debt owed to a friend.

It was a measure of her inexperience that she believed his words over her own instincts.

If she'd looked into his eyes, she might have questioned it because he was pretty sure that the words coming out of his mouth were not backed up by the expression on his face.

He wanted to drive her back against the wall and kiss her until she could no longer articulate her own name. He wanted to strip off those clothes and fill his hands with those voluptuous curves.

Instead, he ground his teeth and walked to the door.

CHAPTER TEN

A SPELL OF hot weather brought tourists flocking to Puffin Island. They spilled off the ferry, a riot of color and smiles, overloaded with bags, children, strollers and equipment for all weather. Some came by car, some as foot passengers, and most of them headed for the beaches close to the harbor. The waterfront was crowded, the restaurants full and the locals talked about how this was the best start to a summer season they could remember in a long time.

The bay was busy, the water dotted with boats of all shapes and sizes, from the majestic schooners that Lizzy called pirate ships to sleek racing boats and small pleasure crafts.

"Can we see the puffins?" Lizzy paused on the harbor, watching as a crowd of people queued to board one of the many trips around the island to Puffin Rock. "Ryan said he'd take us."

"He's very busy." It had been over a week since she'd seen him, and she'd been trying desperately to put him out of her mind. It was hard, just as it was hard to think up excuses to stay away from the water.

Emily looked at the boat bobbing in the waves and felt sick. She was getting a little more confident each day, but was still a long way from taking Lizzy on a boat trip. "Is there anything else you'd like to do?"

"Waffles and chocolate milk?"

Everything Lizzy suggested involved Ryan.

After he'd left that night, Emily had switched on her laptop and done what she should have done right from the start. Typed his name into the search engine.

She'd clicked on article after article, and when she'd finally shut down, hours later, her cheeks had been wet from all the tears she'd shed.

He'd told her he wasn't afraid of emotion, and that was backed up by everything she'd read. His writing was full of emotion. He didn't just report the facts, he reported the effect on those who were suffering until the reader ceased to be an outside observer and slid into the story. She'd felt the heat, tasted the dust, cried with the mother who had lost a child to a roadside bomb. And she'd read the reports written by others on the accident that had wounded him and killed his friend. And they were glowing reports. As a journalist he'd been respected both by his own profession and the military.

The explosion had been global news.

Exhausted, she'd taken herself to bed and lain awake for hours, thinking about how hard his recovery must have been. Clues to just how hard had been in everything he hadn't said.

But he'd built a new life. The life he and his friend had planned together.

And that life didn't include children. It was a responsibility he'd made it clear he didn't want.

He'd helped her because he owed Brittany. There was nothing more to it than that, and she wasn't going to do that horribly needy thing of looking for more. A few steamy kisses didn't mean anything to a man like him. Even without knowing his background, there was a raw physicality to him that told her that a simple sexual relationship was familiar territory to him.

And no doubt none of those relationships had included sex with the lights out.

She needed to move on.

Pushing it out of her mind, she dragged herself back to the present.

"How about ice cream?" Trying to do something that would reduce the likelihood of bumping into Ryan, she made an alternative suggestion. "Let's go to Summer Scoop."

Visiting the shop had become a routine, and not just because Lizzy loved the ice cream. Emily was keen to support the struggling business. She liked Lisa and sympathized with her situation.

"Chocolate is still my favorite." Five minutes later Lizzy was licking her cone, the ice cream sliding down her chin. "Can we live in a place that sells ice cream?"

Lisa handed her a napkin. "It's not the dream it seems, sugar."

Because it was Saturday, both the twins were hovering. They alternated between "helping" in the store and reading, playing or watching a DVD in the little cottage attached to the business premises while Lisa supervised through an open door.

Knowing how hard it was to keep Lizzy entertained, Emily wondered how she managed it. "It must be hard work."

Lisa pushed blueberry ice cream into a crisp waffle cone. "The irony is that I came here because I wanted a better life for the kids. I wanted them to live close to nature. I saw us spending time together as a family. But I spend less time with them now than I did when I was living with my mother in Boston." She handed the cone to Emily. "I'm working, and they're doing their own thing through that door in the living room. At weekends they 'help' in here, but they get bored with that pretty quickly. They entertain each other, but I can't afford to close, so that I can have a day out with them."

"Could you employ someone one day a week?"

"We don't make enough money to pay anyone. One of the freezers broke last week, and that used the last chunk of my savings. You don't want to hear about this. It's boring." Lisa opened a drawer and put a fresh pile of napkins on the counter.

"It's not boring to me. I'm just sorry your dream isn't working out the way you wanted it to."

"I have no one to blame but myself. I had my head in the clouds. No one before me has been able to make this place work, but I thought I'd be different. I like to call it optimism, but my mother says it's blind stupidity." That confession came with a smile, but Emily heard the thickening in her voice.

It was that, together with the hint of weary resignation, that made up her mind.

She dropped into a crouch next to her niece. "How would you like to watch a DVD with Summer and Harry?"

Lizzy stared at her. "Now?"

"Yes. They're just through that door." She felt a flutter of anxiety and suppressed it. She reminded herself of what Ryan had said about the importance of Lizzy becoming independent. "I'll be right here, talking to Lisa. We'll leave the door open." She could see the halo of Summer's blond hair through a crack in the door, hear laughter as the twins watched a cartoon.

Lisa looked surprised, but she pushed open the door to the cottage, and moments later Lizzy was happily settled with the twins and a bowl of popcorn.

"Have you noticed how similar Lizzy is to the twins? They could almost be triplets!"

"It's the hair." Satisfied that Lizzy was safe, Emily turned back to Lisa. "Tell me the truth. How bad is it?"

Lisa gave a tired shrug. "Bad enough to make me want to eat a vat of chocolate ice cream by myself. I stayed up most of the night looking at the numbers, but they were still the same this morning. Looking at them doesn't change the fact this dream is over for me."

"You're sure?"

"Yes. I keep hoping and putting off the decision, but I'm not going to make it through another winter. It will take me a while to sell this place, and I can't afford two places. I don't know which is worse—giving up on my dream or moving back home with my mother and hearing her say 'I told you so.' She makes me feel about the same age as the kids."

"Is there no alternative?"

"Not that I can see." Lisa's eyes filled, and she pressed her fingers to her mouth. "Sorry. I can't believe I'm telling you this. You came in for an ice cream, and instead of a blob of blueberry I give you a dollop of self-pity topped off with liquid misery. I don't charge for that, by the way. It's on the house."

"I asked the question." Emily grabbed a handful of napkins and handed them over. "Here. Blow."

"I don't want the kids to see me like this. You know what it's like." Lisa blew her nose hard. "You try and keep a bright smile on your face, no matter how bad things are. And when I tuck them in at night I realize that none of it matters really as long as I have them. They're the best thing in my life." She gave a faint smile. "Thanks for listening."

"I can do more than listen. I might be able to help, if you'd like me to." Emily glanced around the store, looking at all the unused space. "You say that no one has been able to make this business pay. Did anyone ever try doing anything different with it?"

"Different? You mean apart from sell ice cream?"

"There's more than one way of selling ice cream." Emily walked to the door and stared through the glass to the busy harbor. "There are plenty of people out there. The island is busy."

"But the tourists don't always come in here, so that doesn't help me."

Emily watched the flow of people. "Because they walk straight off the ferry and turn left to the beach."

"On a hot day, yes. And to walk past Summer Scoop, they need to turn right. They sometimes call in at Swim and Sail or visit the Lobster Hatchery, but they don't come down this far." Lisa's shoulders sagged. "I'm doomed."

"You're not doomed. Every tourist that arrives on that ferry is a potential customer. We just need to think about how to tempt people in."

"I was thinking of taking my clothes off." Lisa gave another weak smile. "Just kidding. That would scare them away. I did think of putting a sign up by the ferry if they'd let me, but then I decided it wouldn't help. Folks just want to head to the beach. And you know what the weather is like in this place—it's sunny now, but we get our share of fog and rain, and then people are thinking about shelter, not ice cream. They want something to do with fractious children."

Still thinking, Emily turned. "Fractious children?"

"Yes. You're stuck in a rental property or a hotel watching the rain sheet down or trying to see through mist thicker than the steam from a kettle. You put on the same DVD and then the kids start fighting, and it's all 'Mom, I'm bored.' Puffin Island is an outdoor place. There's stuff you can do in the rain, but drying clothes every day can be exhausting."

Emily strolled across the room, her mind exploring various options. Usually she worked as part of a team of people, and the businesses were large corporations. Her contribution merged with those of others, like a single drop of rain blending with the ocean, unidentifiable and yet still part of the whole. "You have plenty of space."

"It needs redecorating, but I don't have the funds for it and I can't afford to close while it's done."

"Maybe we could do something imaginative with the space. Something that encourages people to come in when it's raining. Offer something they can't get anywhere else on the island."

"I don't have the cash to invest in a new venture."

"It won't be a new venture. Just a few additions to the old one. Tell me about the business itself. Who do you rent the building from?"

"Someone who knows how to bleed a person dry."

"And how many different types of ice cream do you stock?"

"Thirty, but not all of them sell well."

"Thirty?" It sounded like a lot to Emily. Her head was crowded with ideas and questions. "We need to start at the beginning. Those figures that kept you up all night. Would you share them with me?" Back in her comfort zone, she knew what was needed. Here, finally, was something she knew how to do. "If you're willing to share it, I'd like everything you can give me on your business. Turnover, profit, loss—any information you have."

Lisa blinked. "If you give me your email address I'll send some spreadsheets to you. There isn't much profit."

"Yet." Emily scribbled down her email. "We're going to change that."

"Do you really think you might be able to help?"

"I hope so. Helping businesses used to be my job." She didn't add that most of the businesses she'd worked for had been faceless, multinational corporations.

If anything, the small, personal nature of the business made success all the more imperative.

If this business failed, it directly affected a family.

Lisa looked uncomfortable. "I can't afford to pay you, unless you call free ice cream payment."

"If it's blueberry, then the answer is yes. And no payment is necessary, but if it makes you feel more comfortable you can pay me in advice."

"Advice?"

"I have no idea how to raise a six-year-old," Emily said frankly. "You have two of them, and they seem healthy and happy, so you must be doing a lot right. And you seem to do it without turning into a ball of anxiety, so any tips would be welcome."

Lisa gave a disbelieving laugh. "Seriously? That's what you want in exchange for saving my business? You've been a mother as long as I have."

Emily hesitated. "No," she said finally, "I haven't. Lizzy is my niece." She looked around for somewhere to sit. "Do you know what you need in here? Some stools and a little bar where people can sit indoors if they want to." But in the absence of seating, she leaned against the wall, and ten minutes later she'd told Lisa an abbreviated version of the story. All she left out was Lizzy's true identity. That, she hadn't trusted to anyone except Ryan and Agnes.

"So you'd never even *met* Lizzy until a couple of weeks ago?"

"That's right. And I am messing it up."

"I'm sure you're not."

Emily thought about the incident on the beach. Of the number of times Lizzy had asked if they could go and see the puffins and she'd refused. "Trust me, I am."

Lisa was about to say something when the door opened, and Ryan strolled in.

Emily felt her legs melt beneath her. The sensation of control left her. One glance and she was like a teenager with a serious infatuation, except that she'd never felt anything as intense as this as a teenager.

It was the first time they'd seen each other since that evening at her house.

She knew she owed him an apology but had been too much of a coward to seek him out and say what needed to be said.

He paused on the threshold, his gaze locked on hers. She felt a rush of hunger, an awareness so sharp it made her stomach knot, that same white heat that came when he touched her. It felt as if they were the only two people in the room.

Except that they weren't.

"Ryan!" Lisa walked across to him, apparently oblivious to the electric atmosphere. "Emily is going to help me think of ways to boost the business."

"That's good to know." He pushed the door shut. "And it relates to why I'm here."

Emily wondered if he had the same effect on all women and then noticed Lisa's pink cheeks and decided that, yes, of course he did. Ryan Cooper was a sexy guy. No woman was likely to miss that.

She wiped her fingers on the napkin. "I'll leave the two of you to talk."

"Don't go." Ryan strolled across to the freezer and scanned the rows of ice cream. "I have a business proposition for you, Lisa. We'd like to start using your ice creams at the Ocean Club."

Emily felt a rush of gratitude. Without looking at Lisa's finances, she had a feeling that it might not make enough of a difference to keep Summer Scoop afloat, but at least it was a positive step. And he'd taken it.

Lisa's face suggested that any good news was worth celebrating. "Seriously?"

"It's good ice cream. You'll need to talk to Anton about flavors and quantities."

"I'll do that. And thank you." Lisa looked as if she was about to hug him. "Could I offer you a celebratory scoop?"

"Thanks, but after six o'clock my preference is for a cold beer. I'm meeting Alec in ten minutes at the Ocean Bar. That's not the only reason I'm here." His gaze slid to Emily. "We're having a lobster bake on South Beach next Saturday."

"I know." Lisa brightened. "I've booked tickets for the three of us. The twins really enjoyed it last year, and the weather is promising to be lovely. Emily, you should come. Lizzy will love it."

A beach party? She couldn't think of anything worse. People. Distractions. Everyone so busy having fun that they failed to notice when a young child was in trouble. "I can't. Skylar is coming for the weekend."

"Bring her, too." Ryan's tone told her he knew exactly what she was thinking, and his next words confirmed it. "We always employ a couple of lifeguards for our beach parties, and not that many people venture into the water once the sun goes down.

Too cold." He and Lisa discussed a few more details, and then he gave Emily a nod and strolled out of the shop.

Lisa sighed. "With twins, aged six, I don't think about sex much, and then a guy like him walks in, and suddenly I can't help my mind from drifting."

Emily was about to say "who wouldn't" and stopped herself. There were some things she still wasn't willing to share. "I'm glad he's going to stock your ice cream."

"Me, too, although what I'd really like to do is to serve it on his naked body. Not that I want a relationship," Lisa added hastily, "but a few hours of mind-blowing sex with Ryan Cooper would make me forget my troubles."

Or add to your troubles, Emily thought.

She owed him an apology, and the longer she left it, the harder it would be.

Making a decision, she turned to Lisa. "Would you watch Lizzy for just five minutes? There's something I need to do."

RYAN HAD WALKED as far as the harbor when he heard her calling his name.

"Ryan, wait!" There was an urgency to her voice, and he turned quickly, forgetting his intention to keep his distance. The moment he saw her he wanted to drag her against him and kiss her until both of them forgot the time of day. To make sure he didn't touch her, he thrust his hands into the pockets of his jeans.

"Is something wrong?"

"Nothing is wrong." She was slightly breathless. "I owe you an apology."

"For what?"

"For the things I said. For accusing you of deceiving me. I—I overreacted. I understand why you did what you did." She was building bridges while he was trying to widen the gulf between them.

"You were protecting your child."

"You've been nothing but kind to me since I arrived here, and I should have trusted you."

She'd asked for honesty, so he decided to give it to her. "I'm not kind, Emily. Don't make that mistake. My sister will tell you I'm a selfish, stubborn s—" He caught himself and then gave a short laugh. "I was editing it for children, and then I realized that for once we're on our own. No child."

She glanced at the hordes of tourists spilling from the ferry and gave him a hesitant smile. "Not exactly on our own."

He was grateful for the crowds. Only the knowledge that he'd be arrested for indecency stopped him doing what he wanted to do. "So you left Lizzy with the twins. Good decision. Lisa is a responsible person, and the twins are sweet kids."

"They are." Her gaze slid to his. "I didn't think you liked kids, Ryan Cooper."

"I like them when they belong to someone else."

"I was talking to Lisa about the business." She was earnest and serious, but it made no difference because he already knew how much passion was simmering beneath that modest shirt. She dressed to hide her body, but curves like hers weren't easily disguised, and he'd already discovered what was underneath her clothes. He could still feel the dip of her small waist and the fullness of her breasts. He could taste the sweet flavor of her mouth as she'd opened to him, and he wanted to taste it again. He wanted to drag her into the nearest empty side street and indulge in the sort of sex she'd never be able to describe as "nice."

Realizing she was waiting for an answer, he cleared his throat. "That was kind of you."

"Not really." She looked uncertain. "It's probably driven by a selfish need to feel competent at something I'm doing. That certainly isn't child rearing. I need a crash course."

Her insecurity tugged at him. He remembered feeling the same way a million times.

"Anyone who feels competent at child rearing is deluding themselves. If it's going well, then you'd better realize it could change at any time. Just when you think you've got something nailed, they hit another phase, and suddenly you have no idea what you're doing."

"Was that how it was with Rachel?" Her earnest gaze made him slide deeper into the hole he'd dug for himself.

"Yeah. Losing my parents coincided with a difficult phase, so we never knew whether she was exhibiting grief or whether it was just normal behavior. We stumbled through it, making it up as we went along."

"I'm worried my lack of skills might be psychologically damaging."

He was pretty sure that being the child of Lana Fox would have done far more damage psychologically, but he kept that thought to himself. "I'm sure you're doing just fine."

"I ordered a ton of books, but so far I haven't had time to read them."

He could imagine her, focused on the internet, reading all the back cover copy in an attempt to decide which book would guarantee a safe future for Lizzy. "Parents never do. They're too busy being parents. And I'm not sure what books can teach you that your instincts can't."

"I'm not sure I have the right instincts." Her eyes were wide with uncertainty. "I know I don't have the right feelings for her, but I can protect her. That's my job. I'm trying to learn what she needs."

He wondered why she didn't recognize the feelings that were so obviously spilling over inside her. She had so much love to give it was like watching a balloon ready to burst.

Yet another reason to keep his distance.

"What she needs," he said slowly, "is to have some fun and lead a normal life with you in the background to guide her. Let her do the things other kids her age are doing."

A dimple appeared in the corner of her mouth. "You're saying that because you want to recruit people for your lobster bake."

He suddenly realized how much harder the evening would

be if she turned up to the lobster bake. "You're right. Forget it. I know a party on a beach would be your idea of a nightmare. You should stay away."

"WE ARE GOING to the lobster bake."

Skylar glanced up from the beads she was threading with Lizzy. "Are you serious?"

"Yes." Determined to do this before she could change her mind, Emily grabbed a large beach bag and started stuffing things inside. She had no idea what was needed for a trip to the beach, so she improvised, ignoring the part of her brain that told her she should be packing resuscitation equipment. "Get changed. Pack a sweater."

"We're going to the beach?" Lizzy erupted with excitement. "Can I take my bucket?"

Emily felt her stomach roll, but she reached for the bucket and stuffed it into the bag before she could think of all the reasons not to. "It's in. Anything else? Don't forget Andrew."

Skylar's eyebrows rose as Lizzy went running from the room. "Who is Andrew? Please, tell me he's some hot guy you have chained in your wardrobe for your nighttime pleasure."

"Andrew is the bear. He has to come everywhere." Some things she was learning.

"I don't know whether to be impressed or disappointed." Her friend sat back in the chair. "You are a different person."

"I learn from my mistakes. I only forget a bear once."

"I was talking about the beach."

"Oh."

"What changed your mind?"

"I realized that I have a responsibility to teach her to be safe around water, and avoiding it isn't going to achieve that." Emily added a pretty beach towel to the bag. "If I'm not careful, I'll make her scared and I don't want that."

"You're going to teach her to swim?"

"No. I can't swim myself." She thought about Ryan's offer

and dismissed it. There was no way she was putting as much as
a toe in the water, but she was prepared to go to a lobster bake
on the beach. That would be a start.

It had been Ryan's parting remark that had been responsible
for her change of heart.

A party on a beach would be your idea of a nightmare.

But not Lizzy's. And why should Lizzy be made to suffer because she was freaked out by water? The last thing she wanted
to do was pass her phobia on to the child.

Lizzy came back downstairs wearing pink sparkly flip-flops.
"Can we make a necklace to wear to the beach?"

"Great idea." Skylar pushed a box of beads toward her
and glanced at Emily. "We're fine here if you want to go and
change."

Leaving Lizzy to make jewelry with Skylar, Emily walk out
of the kitchen, but her friend's voice followed her up the stairs.

"Emily? Don't wear black."

CHAPTER ELEVEN

LOBSTER BAKES WERE a regular feature during the summer months. Anton, the chef from the Ocean Club, prepared the food the old-fashioned way, steamed in seaweed and cooked in wash kettles over open fires using water from the ocean. The event drew locals and tourists alike, all keen to savor the tradition and taste the very best seafood while enjoying an unparalleled view. Some did a little beachcombing, while others, the braver ones, chose to swim in the sea.

Overseeing it all, Ryan was in midconversation with Alec when he noticed Emily hovering at the edge of the beach. If it hadn't been for the fact that Lizzy and Skylar were by her side, he wasn't sure he would have recognized her. She'd swapped her usual discreet, dark colors for a dress that flowed around her curves in a swirl of purple and blue. The breeze breathed life into the fabric, playing with it so that it lifted and revealed a flash of toned leg.

Ryan lost the thread of the conversation. Hit by a punch of sexual awareness, his brain blanked.

Emily was holding Lizzy's hand firmly. That sight alone should have been enough to damp down the lust.

It didn't.

He wondered how long it had taken her to pluck up the courage to bring Lizzy to a party on a beach.

"Single mother," Alec reminded him, handing him another beer. "All your alarms should be going off right now."

"My alarm is malfunctioning."

"Then get it fixed. Last time my alarm system malfunctioned I found myself with an expensive divorce."

Ryan ignored him. "I need you to do me a favor."

"The answer is no."

"You don't know what I'm going to ask."

"Yes, I do." Alec drank. "You want me to babysit so that you can drag her back to your cave and get laid. We may have Wi-Fi and hot and cold running water, but that look on your face hasn't changed since the day man roamed the earth dressed in animal skins."

"I don't want you to babysit. I want you to be friendly to Skylar. And you can relax because I'm sure a woman as gorgeous and happy as she seems to be wouldn't need to ruin her day by getting involved with a moody bastard like you. If it helps, I think she's already in a relationship. Some guy running for senate."

"Makes sense. She seems the sort to be turned on by power."

Ryan didn't think Skylar seemed that sort at all, but he kept that thought to himself. "So, are you going to do it?"

"You do know you have a major problem, don't you?"

"You're talking about my choice of friends?"

"I'm talking about the fact that in order to get the girl, you're going to have to deal with the child." Alec lifted his beer to his lips. "For you, that's like walking through a ring of fire."

"All I had in mind was a drink and conversation. You've gone straight from a single look to divorce in sixty seconds."

"Every divorce begins with a single look. Never forget that."

"No chance while I'm hanging around with you. When is this cynicism going to die?"

"Never. It's keeping me safe."

"It's keeping you single."

"Same thing."

Ryan shook his head. "I thought you came here to heal."

"I came here to work."

But Ryan knew that wasn't the whole story. For plenty of people, Puffin Island was a sanctuary. It was the reason Lisa had chosen to uproot two small children in an attempt to build a new life. It was the reason Brittany had offered her cottage to Emily.

It was a place where wounds could heal, bathed by the beauty of nature.

Some wounds, he thought. *Not all.*

He saw Emily tighten her grip on Lizzy's hand and linger at the edge of the beach as if she were about to step into a pit of alligators. Her anxiety was almost painful to witness. He wanted to stride across the sand, fold her into his arms and stand between her and the sea. It was as if she were frozen.

Another panic attack?

Remembering how she'd been that day Lizzy had wandered onto the beach, Ryan cursed under his breath.

"Damsel in distress," Alec said flatly, "the most dangerous kind of all. They wait for you to show your soft side, and then they go in for the kill."

Ryan didn't think there was a single part of himself that could be classed as "soft" right at that moment. And he knew that nothing his friend had said applied to Emily. "That isn't what's happening here."

The water was her phobia.

The fact that she was here, facing up to the thing she feared most, simply increased his respect for her.

Shit.

"It's my job to greet guests, so I'm going over there—"

"Of course you are. Since that was always going to be the outcome, you should have done it five minutes ago."

Ryan ground his teeth. "Next time we're out in the boat, I hope the beam cracks your skull."

"I'm not the one who needs a smack round the head."

"You can stay here growling if you like, but I'm going to be sociable."

"You mean you're going to see if there's any chance comfort could lead to grateful sex."

Ryan gave a half smile. "Brittany asked me to look out for a friend in trouble. That's what I'm doing."

Part of him recognized that he might be the one in trouble, but he decided to ignore that along with the speculative look from Alec.

He strolled across the sand, checking everyone had what they needed and that there were no problems simmering. South Beach was one of the best beaches for swimming on the island, a curve of sand where the sea shelved gently and lacked the strong undertows characteristic of other parts of the island. One end of the beach was rocky, but those large gray slabs of granite provided a perfect platform for jumping into the water. Some of the braver individuals were swimming, their shrieks cutting through the air as they dipped into the cold waters of the Atlantic. Ryan might have joined them if it hadn't been for the woman hovering on the edge of the party. He'd put two of the guys who worked behind the bar on lifeguard duty. Kirsti was handing out drinks and welcoming people with her own individual brand of warmth that involved a significant amount of matchmaking.

As Ryan walked past her, she handed him a couple of extra beers from a bucket brimming with ice and winked.

He took the beers, ignored the wink and joined Skylar and Emily.

"This is a surprise." He handed over the beers and then dropped to his haunches to greet Lizzy, noticing the bows in her hair. "Pretty necklace."

Lizzy fingered it. "I made it with Skylar."

"Emily!" Lisa arrived with the twins, holding on to each hand. "Can Lizzy join us? We're hunting for shells on the far side of the beach with Rachel."

The request seemed to stir Emily from her trance. "Rachel?"

"My sister," Ryan murmured in response to her blank expression. "Even on her day off she doesn't miss the opportunity to grab a group of young children and stimulate their minds."

Emily held tight to Lizzy's hand. "That sounds like fun." The tone she used told a different story. "I'll come, too."

Ryan understood that for Emily, being here was an enormous step. It was too much to expect for her to leave the child in someone else's care. Blocking out Alec's comment that in order to get the girl he had to deal with the child, he swung a giggling Lizzy onto his shoulders.

"Now you have a seagull's view."

He ignored Kirsti's approving glance and strolled across the sand, wincing as Lizzy's small hands tugged at his hair.

"Hey, that's attached to me."

"I'm too high up. I don't want to fall." But she was giggling, and he saw Emily glance at the child and smile, too.

By the time he reached Rachel and the twins, his scalp was sore from being pulled, and he swung Lizzy down, forgetting to make allowances for his injury.

He said nothing, but something must have shown on his face because Emily reached out and touched his shoulder gently.

"You hurt yourself?"

"It's fine." He could feel the warmth of her hand through his shirt. He remembered those fingers sliding under his shirt and resting lightly on his back. Sliding over his jaw and into his hair. Locked with his as he'd lifted her arms above her head and plundered her mouth.

Her gaze lifted to his, and he knew she was remembering the same thing.

She withdrew her hand quickly.

"Ryan?" Rachel was glancing between them curiously, and

Ryan pulled himself together and introduced Emily and Lizzy. After that, all he had to do then was stand back and watch while his sister worked her magic. Even as a child, Rachel had wanted to be a teacher. He remembered her lining up all her toys and standing up to teach the "class."

The tide was far out, exposing granite boulders crowded with rockweed, barnacles, whelks and mussel shells. Within seconds Lizzy was holding Rachel's hand and searching nearby tide pools for sea creatures while Emily stood tense as a bow.

"I should go with them."

He wondered whether it was the sexual chemistry that was responsible for her tension or the proximity of the water.

"She'll be safe with my sister." He saw Rachel point out where Lizzy should step to be safe on the rocks. "Rachel is the best teacher Puffin Elementary has ever had. She adores the kids, and she knows exactly how to handle them. And she'll be working at Camp Puffin all summer. Relax."

"We're on a beach," she muttered. "I don't think relaxing is possible."

"Try." Against his better judgment, he put a comforting hand on her back. He felt her stiffen and then relax into the reassuring pressure and draw a deep, shuddering breath through her body.

"Pathetic."

"Who is pathetic?"

"I am." She kept her eyes fixed on Lizzy the whole time, every muscle in her body tense and ready to move in an instant.

"You're here. You're standing on a beach. That's not pathetic. It's brave."

"Brave would be getting in the water."

He glanced at her profile. "One step at a time."

"They're having fun." She watched a group of mothers play with their children in the shallows, an activity punctuated by much delighted squealing.

"You sound surprised."

"I guess for me beaches are more about fear than fun."

"I didn't expect you to be here."

"Would you rather I hadn't come?"

"No." He was beginning to wonder why he was fighting it. He glanced at her, wondering if she felt it, too, but she was staring at Lizzy, her green eyes focused on the child. Emily's hair was loose and softly curling, strands of blond and caramel floating around blush-tinted ivory skin that reminded him of the strawberries-and-cream flavor Lisa served in Summer Scoop.

If she were a dessert, he would have eaten her in two mouthfuls.

She stirred, her arm brushing against his. "I came because of you."

"Me?" For a moment he thought she was propositioning him, and then he realized their minds were working along different tracks, and she was still thinking about Lizzy.

"You told me she needed to have fun and lead a normal life. On Puffin Island a beach picnic is normal. I don't want her to be afraid of the water."

"Can she swim?"

"I have no idea." She turned slightly green. "You're worried she might fall in?"

"No, but swimming is an important life skill. It will give her confidence. In the summer, the pool at the Ocean Club is closed to the public in the mornings so that Rachel can give swimming lessons to the kids as part of Camp Puffin. I'm sure she'd take Lizzy."

Emily's expression showed an agony of indecision, and then she nodded. "Yes. It's a good idea." She said it as if it were the worst idea in the world.

"Every kid should be able to swim."

"Yes." She stared straight ahead, and he knew she was wondering whether she might have been able to prevent what had happened if she'd known how to swim.

"It wouldn't have made a difference." He spoke softly, so they couldn't be overheard. "You were too little. Most grown-ups don't know what to do when they're caught in a riptide. Even if you'd been able to swim, there is no way you would have been able to save her."

"I'll never know. You're right. I'll ask Rachel if she'll teach Lizzy." She watched as Lizzy scooped water from a tide pool into her bucket. When it was too dark to play any longer, they picked their way back across the rocks, juggling children, brimming buckets and sandy feet.

Anton and his team were layering potatoes, onions and garlic on top of the lobster in four large kettles over open fires. Then came corn and hot dogs and finally the whole meal was sealed to keep in the steam. Small tables were groaning under the weight of various appetizers, freshly baked bread and mixed salads. As well as hot dogs, the menu included hamburgers for the children, and the smell of cooking scented the air, mingling with the scent of the sea.

At the far edge of the beach, the forest crowded the edge of the water, and the setting sun sent a mosaic of warm light over the treetops and the sand.

Lizzy was clutching the bucket Ryan had given her, now filled with shells and other interesting objects she'd found in the pools.

As they sat down on blankets near the fire, Emily examined the contents of the bucket.

"That's pretty." Skylar leaned across and helped herself to a piece of turquoise sea glass, the ends of her hair sweeping the sand. "Polished up, that would be gorgeous."

"Ryan, look!" Lizzy crawled over to him and dropped a shell in his lap.

He picked it up and duly admired it. It was impossible not to respond to Lizzy's enthusiasm, and he caught his sister watching him curiously.

It was obvious from her expression she was wondering what he was doing.

He was wondering the same thing.

To give himself space from Lizzy's impromptu show-and-tell, he rose to his feet and excused himself on the pretext of checking in with Anton, but Rachel reached him before he made it halfway across the beach.

"What's going on, Ryan?"

"What do you mean?"

"Oh, please—" she anchored her dark hair with her hand "—you're carrying Lizzy on your shoulders and looking at shells. Who are you and what have you done with my brother?"

"You're not funny."

"No, what isn't funny is you using a child to get access to Emily's body!"

He ground his teeth. "Do you want to speak a little louder? I don't think they heard you in Boston."

"It's not fair, Ryan."

He swore under his breath and dragged his fingers through his hair. "That isn't what I'm doing."

"Then what are you doing?"

"Honestly? I don't know."

"But you like Emily."

Like? Such an insipid word didn't even begin to describe his complex feelings. "I sympathize with her situation."

"That wasn't sympathy I saw in your eyes when you looked at her."

"Back off."

"We both know you're not interested in taking on anyone's kids long-term, so just be careful, Ryan. I'm thinking of Lizzy. She's young. Kids get attached."

"Are you lecturing me?"

"Yeah, so now you know how it feels." She punched him lightly on the arm and walked back to the group at the far side of the beach, leaving him staring after her.

She was right, of course.

He wasn't interested in taking responsibility for a child.

He thought about Lizzy's hands locked in his hair and the delicious sound of her giggle as he'd bounced her across the sand.

What the hell was he doing?

He'd told Rachel to back off, but he was the one who needed to back off.

He talked to Anton for a few minutes, exchanged small talk with a few locals and then returned to where the others were sitting.

Instantly Lizzy slid across the blanket to show him another shell, but this time he encouraged her to show Skylar instead and sat detached while they continued to sift through their personal hoard of treasure.

When the food was ready, they used rocks to crack open the lobsters and ate until they were full.

Ryan watched Emily, wondering why he'd never before seen a beach picnic as a sensual activity. There was too much licking of lips and sucking of fingers for his own personal comfort.

The twins and Lizzy, tired from so much outdoor activity, fell asleep in a heap between Rachel and Lisa who were talking about plans for the summer. Skylar was still sorting through sea glass and shells, holding up each piece to the light of the fire to take a closer look.

Emily leaned forward, too, and the soft fabric at the neckline of her dress gaped slightly, giving him an uninterrupted view of smooth, full breasts.

Remembering exactly how they looked bare and aching for his touch, Ryan felt a raging hunger that had nothing to do with food.

Lust was hot, liquid and brutal. The final straw was when he saw a couple of the male swimming instructors from the Ocean Club pool almost fall on their faces as they tried to get a better look at Emily's luxuriant curves. Ryan gave them an icy glare that had them backing away, and then sprang to his feet.

"I need to talk to Anton again."

Emily glanced up at him in surprise. "You're leaving?" Her disappointment was so obvious he almost changed his mind.

And then he saw his sister's eyes narrow and knew he was in trouble.

"I'll be back." He stumbled and planted his foot on a shell, earning his sister's wrath.

"Ryan! Get your great big feet off the blanket. Ugh. You have no idea how many of my paintings he ruined when I was little."

He turned his back on seashells, children and Emily's curves and walked across the beach.

Alec was deep in conversation with a couple of marine biologists, and Kirsti was dancing with one of the instructors from the kayak school.

Across the sand he saw Jared end a conversation with a couple of lobstermen and glance toward Rachel.

Ryan ground his teeth and carried on walking.

His sister was right, her life was her business.

He had his own problems.

His problem caught up with him as he reached the edge of the beach.

"Ryan!" She sounded breathless, and he clenched his jaw and turned.

"What?"

"I thought you were going to talk to Anton?"

"He's busy." The truth was he'd forgotten about Anton; he'd been so intent on giving himself some space.

"Is everything all right? Lizzy was all over you. I hope she didn't make you feel uncomfortable. Or irritated."

Uncomfortable, he could have handled. Irritated, he could have handled. What he couldn't handle was the fact he'd found her adorable. "She was great. Every kid loves the beach." Too late, he remembered that she hated it. "Listen, Emily—"

"It's fine. You don't have to walk on eggshells—or maybe I should say seashells." A dimple appeared at the corner of her mouth. "Can I walk with you for a minute? I could use five minutes of adult time."

Unable to find a response that wouldn't seem rude, he nodded. "Are you cold? Do you need a wrap or something?"

"I'm fine."

It was a good job one of them was, he thought dourly, fixing his gaze on the rocks ahead. "When the tide is out you can walk right around to the next beach."

"It's pretty. I was thinking about what you said the other day," she said quickly, "about teaching me to swim. If you meant it, then I'd like to."

"You want to swim?"

She pulled a face. "No, but I think I should. It's important for Lizzy. I'm sending the message that water is scary and to be avoided, and that's not only unfair, it's dangerous. She needs to learn how to swim, and once she's learned, I need to be able to take her."

"What changed your mind?"

"Watching the kids in the water. They were having so much fun. And listening to Rachel and Lisa talking about all the summer activities they have planned at Camp Puffin. Beach camp, kayaking, sailing. I want her to be able to do those things one day. I thought maybe Agnes would be willing to watch Lizzy for an hour while you teach me. Would you do it?"

He wanted to refuse. "Are you sure you want to do this?"
Say no.

"I'm sure. What would I need to bring?"

His mouth was dry. "Just yourself and a bathing suit. But if you don't have a suit, then—"

"I have one."

He hoped to hell it hadn't been chosen by Skylar, or they would both be in serious trouble. He was tempted to suggest a wet suit but then decided that wasn't going to hide much, either. "Maybe you should wait a few weeks and—"

"I don't want to wait. Let's set a time. That way I can't change my mind."

He felt sweat bead on his forehead. "I need to look at my schedule."

"How about tomorrow? It's Sunday."

"Weekends are our busiest time at the Ocean Club. Lunches are always crazy, and we're fully booked for dinner."

"So how about five o'clock?"

They'd walked as far as the next beach where the rocks opened up into a cave. When the tide was in, it filled with water, but right now it was a moonlit, cavernous grotto.

It was a favorite tourist spot on the island.

It was also a favorite haunt for teenagers looking for somewhere to have sex.

"Ryan?"

"Yeah." His voice didn't sound like his own. He was wishing he'd walked in the opposite direction. "Five o'clock should work. But if you change your mind, just let me know."

"Don't let me change my mind, even if I go on my knees and beg you."

The thought of her on her knees almost made him stumble. "Emily—"

"Look!" She tugged her hand from his and walked toward the cave. "This place is amazing. Did you know it was here?" Her almost childlike wonder was in direct contrast to the dark, carnal thoughts that filled every inch of his brain.

"Yes." He was so aroused, it was difficult to walk. "Be careful. The sea gets trapped in a few places and the pools can be deep."

"How far back does it go?"

"When the tide is out, you can walk through to the next beach." Or you could stop halfway and—

"Lizzy would love it."

Even the mention of a child right now seemed inappropriate given that his thoughts were definitely adult only. "It's a dangerous place. It fills up when the tide comes in. The coast guard has rescued more people from here than any other part of Puffin Island. Promise me you won't come here without someone who knows the tides."

"I promise." Her voice was soft, and she slid her arm into his. "And thank you."

"For what?"

"For not making fun of the fact I'm scared of water. For caring enough to warn me. I appreciate it."

He had a feeling she wouldn't be thanking him if she could read his mind.

The sound of music wafted on the breeze, and he knew a few people would be dancing on the beach.

"We should go back."

"In a minute. Rachel is lovely. So warm and sweet-natured. Lizzy loved her instantly."

"Yes. Fortunately she's nothing like me."

"You're kind, too."

The breath hissed through his teeth. "I've already told you, I'm not kind."

"You've been very kind to me. You stayed with me when I had a panic attack. Most men would have run. You're patient with Lizzy, even though I know you've already done all the child rearing you intend to do. And now you've offered to teach me to swim."

He must have been out of his mind. "About that—"

"Thank you." She stood on tiptoe and put her arms around him. "I'm so sorry I yelled at you."

He caught her arms in his hands. "Emily, I lied to you. You were right to yell at me. And I'm not kind."

"I think you are. And you lied because you didn't want me to freak out. It was the right decision."

"Emily—"

"I know you didn't do it for me exactly, you did it for Brittany, but that makes you a loyal friend and I respect that."

His control snapped. "You want to know how kind I am? Right now I'm thinking of all the ways I could have sex with you in this cave without one of us injuring ourselves on the rocks."

She went still. "Here? Right now?" Her voice was breathy with shock. "Someone might come."

Yeah, you, he thought, but he managed to trap the words inside his brain for once instead of letting them escape from his mouth.

"I tell you I want to have sex with you in an infinite number of positions and that's what worries you?" He waited for her to pull away but she didn't.

Instead, she looked at his mouth. "Maybe if we did it quickly, we wouldn't be caught." Her voice was a whisper, and the gleam in her eyes made everything inside him tighten.

"I'm going to pretend you didn't just say that to me."

"Have you ever had sex in this cave?"

"I'm going to pretend you didn't say that, either."

Her eyes danced. "I'm pretty sure you're not a virgin, Ryan."

And he was pretty sure she was close to being one. He wondered how many lovers she'd had before Neil and decided he didn't want to know the answer.

She was certainly an outdoor-sex virgin, and he wasn't going to be the one to do something about that.

"We should go back."

"Not yet." She rested her hand on his chest, her features indistinct in the moonlit cave. "I've been thinking a lot about that kiss. I wondered if you'd thought about it, too."

He'd been trying not to. "We should definitely go back."

"There's something I want to do first." She stood on tiptoe again and brushed her mouth over his, and his grip on control unraveled like the chain of an anchor that had been tossed overboard. When her tongue licked into his mouth, he could no longer remember why he was fighting this.

Forgetting Rachel, Lizzy and all the obstacles he'd been trying to keep in the foreground of his brain, he buried his hands in her hair, angled his mouth over hers and kissed her back, opening her mouth with his, exploring those sweet depths with skilled, ruthless strokes of his tongue.

He tasted the delicious sweetness of her and buried his hands in that glorious hair. She smelled of summer blossoms and rose petals, everything about her silky smooth and feminine. She pressed her luscious curves against him, winding around him like a delicate plant growing up a rough rock face.

He felt her tug at his shirt and then slide her hands over his skin, and the feel of her brought him to his senses.

The cave magnified sound. Her gasps blended with soft echoes and the hollow drip of water sliding off rock. From beyond the cave came the faint rush of moonlit waves hitting the sand and the distant sound of laughter.

It was the laughter that penetrated his desire-clouded brain.

He eased his mouth from hers and heard her moan a protest.

"Ryan—" She breathed his name and opened her eyes reluctantly. "I want—"

"I know what you want." Despite the dim light, he could see the dark streaks of color on her cheeks.

"But you don't want the same thing. You're not interested."

He wondered how the hell she could think he wasn't interested, given that seconds ago she'd been welded against a part of him that should have told her exactly how he felt on that subject.

He thought about what Rachel had said. He thought about Lizzy. "We should get back. People will wonder where we are."

She registered the rejection. "You're right, we should get back." She stepped away unsteadily, like someone absorbing a punch. "It was unfair of me to ask you to teach me to swim when you're so busy. I'll book with one of the swimming instructors."

He thought about the two swimming instructors who worked at the Ocean Club, both of who had almost fallen on their faces trying to look down Emily's dress.

"I'll do it."

"That isn't necessary. I can—"

"I said, I'll do it."

"In that case, I'll see you at the pool tomorrow." The exchange was awkward and stilted.

"Sounds good."

It didn't sound good at all.

CHAPTER TWELVE

EMILY STOOD BY the entrance of the Ocean Club pool, shivering.

If someone had told her a month ago she'd be dancing at a beach barbecue and learning to swim, she would have called them deluded.

But here she was, with a bathing suit tight and uncomfortable under her clothes.

When she'd first noticed it in the bag of clothes Skylar had delivered, she'd ignored it, thinking she'd have no possible use for it. As a result, she hadn't taken a close look until five minutes before she was ready to leave the cottage.

She'd always assumed one piece bathing suits were less revealing than bikinis, but not this one. Or maybe it was just that her shape wasn't designed for it. And instead of sober black, the color that denoted seriousness in all things, it was red.

Red for danger, Emily thought, which pretty much described her situation right now. Not just because of the water, but because of the man. Still, Ryan had made it clear he didn't want to take their relationship further, so she didn't need to worry about how she looked in the damn swimsuit. She could focus on the water itself.

Fighting the urge to change her mind, she undressed in the

changing room, pushed her clothes into a locker and wrapped herself in a towel.

Ryan was alone in the pool, cutting through the water with powerful strokes that suggested an above-average athletic ability.

Remembering what he'd told her about his shoulder, she wondered if he'd used the pool as part of his recovery from his injuries.

When he reached the edge, he pulled himself out of the water in a lithe, fluid movement. His muscles bunched, and water streamed off those broad shoulders, droplets clinging to the dark hair that shadowed his chest. He was all sleek planes and streamlined power. Dazed by the vision of raw male strength, Emily blinked, reflecting on the unsettling discovery that apparently the mere sight of a man's half-naked body could turn a thinking woman stupid. Everything around them faded, and she could see nothing except the glitter of his eyes as he scanned her from head to foot.

Mouth dry, she tightened her grip on the towel.

Her physical awareness was so acute she wondered how on earth she was supposed to concentrate on swimming with him in the pool.

Even without her fear issues, she'd drown.

"Hi." He barely glanced at her before turning to pick up a towel from the bench near the water. In that moment she saw the vicious scars that curved over his shoulder and down his back. It looked as if he'd been mauled by a tiger.

Those scars told her everything he hadn't and filled in details he'd omitted in his sparse recounting of the incident that had killed his friend and left him severely injured.

She wanted to ask him about it, but he'd already made it clear the subject was off-limits, so she stayed silent while he wiped his face and looped the towel around his neck. Leaning forward, he picked up a long float shaped like a fat piece of spaghetti and bent it in half.

"We're going to put this around your middle until you're confident."

She was pretty sure that was going to be never, but she kept that thought to herself.

"All right."

He strolled across to her. "You're planning on swimming in a towel?"

If it had been an option, then she would have taken it. He might be unselfconscious about his body, but she wasn't. She wished now she'd just walked out of the changing room in the suit, instead of drawing attention to herself. Better still, she wished she'd picked out a suit herself. Surf and Swim in the harbor would probably have stocked at least ten swimsuits more suitable than this one. Something actually designed for swimming. This one looked as if she was trying to seduce him.

Knowing that the longer she left it, the worse it would be, she let the towel fall.

Face burning, she met his gaze. "You're thinking I should have worn a more serious swimsuit, but I don't really have the shape for any sort of suit, and Skylar bought me this one—" Her voice tailed off, and her cheeks grew redder by the second. "Do you want me in the water?" *Oh, God, why had she phrased it that way?* Now it sounded as if she were propositioning him.

"That would help." His voice was roughened and raw, and he flung the towel back on the bench and slid back into the water himself.

Dying of embarrassment, Emily sat on the side and dangled her legs in the water. Staring down into the blue depths, embarrassment gave way to another emotion. A hollow pit of fear sat where her stomach was supposed to be.

Through the spangled surface of the pool she could see the bottom, but sliding into water seemed like the most unnatural thing in the world.

She probably would have sat there forever had Ryan not moved in front of her.

"Are you sure you want to do this?"

No. "Yes."

"In that case, put your hands on my shoulders." His firm command cut through her building panic.

"You want me to slide in?"

"Yes. You're going to be fine."

"Lizzy had her first lesson with Rachel this morning. She can't stop talking about it."

"Emily." His voice softened a little. "Put your hands on my shoulders. I won't let you fall, and I won't let you go under the water."

Unable to postpone the moment any longer, she steeled herself and put her hands on his shoulders. Her palms made contact with hard, unyielding muscle.

"I don't want to hurt your shoulder."

"You're not hurting me."

"You're gritting your teeth."

"That's not—" He closed his eyes briefly and shook his head. "Never mind. Just do this. Every moment you hesitate makes this harder."

Taking a deep breath, she slid into the water. It was deliciously cool against her heated skin, and that might have been a relief if it hadn't been for the fact that the movement of sliding in brought her body in close contact with his.

Her thigh brushed against the hardness of his, and she heard him curse softly.

"Sorry—" Anxiety made her clumsy, and she gripped his shoulders with her hands, then realized she might be hurting him and forced herself to relax her grip.

"You're doing fine." He put the float around her, demonstrating how it would support her weight, showing her how to move her limbs.

"For now, get used to being in the water. You won't go under the surface because you have the float and you have me. We'll stay in the shallow end."

For a man whose defining characteristic was restless impatience, he was a remarkably patient teacher.

An hour later she swam the width of the pool with just the float, and he complimented her on her style.

Her confidence rose. "Can I try it without the float?"

"I think you've done enough for one day."

"I think it would help my confidence to try."

"It won't help your confidence if you go under and never want to get back in the water again."

"You could stay close by. Grab me if I look as if I'm going under."

If other people could swim without a float, then so could she.

Determined to do this, she put her float on the edge of the pool.

She pushed forward, and instantly her body felt heavy and strange. Without the float she no longer felt buoyant. Starting to sink, panic fluttered inside her, and then she felt his hand on her stomach, lifting her, giving her that extra support.

"You're doing fine." His voice was calm. "It feels different without the float, but the movements are the same. Keep kicking. Keep using your arms. You won't go under, I promise. I won't let you."

And suddenly instead of thinking about drowning, she was thinking about that hand on her stomach. About how it would feel if he moved it a little lower. It made her feel safe from drowning but unsafe in every other way.

She didn't dare look at him, so she focused on the side of the pool instead, kicked and used her arms, and suddenly she was swimming, really swimming, not elegantly but staying afloat without help. She kept kicking and moving her arms, spurred on by his encouragement, until finally she reached the side and grabbed it.

"Good job." Ryan was right next to her, and at last, now that the possibility of drowning seemed to have passed, she allowed herself to look at him.

His dark hair was slick, and droplets of water clung to the powerful muscles of his shoulders.

He was the sexiest man she'd laid eyes on.

And he wasn't interested in her.

She gave a bright smile. "Thank you. That was brilliant."

He didn't smile back. Instead, he eyed the changing room door, as if judging how fast he could get out of here. "You did well. Do you always work that hard at things?"

"If it's something important."

His gaze slid back to hers. "I think that's enough for one day. I need to get back to work."

"Of course. Thank you for taking the time to teach me. I can do it by myself from now on."

He frowned. "You can't do that."

"I'll stay in the shallow end, but I need to practice."

"Tell me when you're going to practice. I'll make sure I'm here."

"You're busy. You don't want to—"

"Damn it, Emily! The purpose of this exercise is to increase your confidence around water, and that's not going to happen if you're on your own, so just say yes."

"Yes. Tomorrow," she murmured. "Same time. But you don't seem very happy about it."

"I'm happy."

"Ryan, you're speaking through your teeth, and you can't wait to get out of this pool."

"Because you're standing next to me in a swimsuit that looks like something from a porn movie."

She stared at him, her heart pounding. "You said—I thought—"

"What did you think?"

"That you weren't interested. That this was all too complicated for you. That—" she hesitated "—that I'm not your type. I don't know enough about sex. I—I'm not exciting enough."

There was a long pause.

The only sound was the soft lap of water against the side of the pool and her own breathing.

"If you were any more exciting I'd need medical attention."

Her stomach dropped, but this time the feeling had nothing to do with fear.

The air was punctuated by a tension as unfamiliar and alien to her as the swimming.

"I thought— Then why—"

"Because you don't want what I'm offering."

"How can you possibly know what I want when you haven't asked me?"

His gaze held hers, and in that single moment the world consisted of the two of them and nothing else.

How could a single look be so arousing?

How could he do this to her?

"Emily—" He cradled the side of her face in his hand, stroking her cheek with his thumb as he looked down at her as if he was making a decision about something.

She was terrified he was going to change his mind. Walk away as he had the night before.

Instead, he lowered his head with a slow inevitability that made her wonder if anyone had ever died of anticipation.

His mouth brushed over hers with unhurried, skilled deliberation, the gentleness at odds with the leashed strength of his body. His eyes looked darker than usual, almost drowsy, clouded with emotions she found impossible to read.

And then the kiss altered. Instead of a lazy, exploratory brush of his mouth, it became hungry and urgent, and she felt the strength in his hands as he cupped her bottom and pulled her hard against him, the movement bold and blatantly sexual. She felt the hard, thick ridge of his erection through the thin fabric of her suit and the slick stroke of his tongue against hers as he slanted his mouth over hers and kissed her deeply.

Her hands gripped the brutal swell of his biceps and then slid upward over his wide shoulders and into the thickness of his hair.

He held her hard against him and kissed her with skill and purpose, the cool of the water contrasting with the heat of his mouth and the burning fire that blazed inside her. She was weightless in the water, slippery as a sea creature, and they kissed like demons, locked together and frantic.

He made a sound deep in his throat and then buried his mouth in her neck, and she tipped her head back, eyes closed, shaken and aroused as sensation ripped through her.

He backed her against the side of the pool and trapped her there. "I want you," he growled the words against her mouth. "Can you feel how much I want you?"

Yes, she could feel it. The hard, intimate pressure of his body against hers. The rough demands of his hands and mouth.

She drove her fingers into his hair, her mouth colliding with his in a kiss that stripped away reservations and inhibitions. "I want you, too." She felt his hand slide upward and cup the weight of her breast. Then his thumb made a slow slide over her nipple, teasing it into an aching peak until she squirmed against him, engulfed in exquisite sensation and delicious anticipation.

Her mind shut down. All of her senses were focused on him, on his hands, his mouth, on the dangerous heat that burned through her body.

She hadn't known it was possible to want someone this much.

They were doing everything except having sex, and just when she was hoping he'd cross that line sometime very soon, there was the sound of a door in the distance, and he released her.

"We've got company." His voice was husky and uneven, and he kept his hand on her waist until he was sure she was steady on her feet.

Emily looked at him dizzily, thinking that it was a good thing her feet could touch the floor of the pool; otherwise she definitely would have drowned.

Gradually it dawned on her that they were in a semi-public place.

One of them needed to say something, and she decided that since he'd taken the lead on everything else, she'd do that part.

"If I'd known swimming was this much fun, I would have done it years ago."

He made a sound that was half laugh, half groan and brought his mouth back to hers. "Leave Lizzy with Agnes tonight. We can watch the sunset from my bed."

She eased away, feeling the pull of regret. "I can't."

"Why not? She'd be safe."

Lizzy would be, but what about her? Up until the past few weeks, she'd never thought of herself as particularly sexual. What if they got as far as bed and she disappointed him? This was a small island. She could be committing herself to a summer of awkward encounters.

Her nerve fled. "I'll get changed and we'll forget it ever happened."

"Sure. That should work, as long as no one looks at the surveillance footage."

She glanced up and saw a camera focused on the pool. "There are cameras?"

"Yeah, we just starred in our own private movie."

Emily gave an embarrassed laugh. "Well, hopefully no one will ever have reason to examine the footage." She didn't trust her arms to be able to haul herself out of the pool the way he did, so to avoid a potentially ungainly accident, she chose to use the steps. She could feel him watching her every step of the way from the pool to the changing room.

"Emily—"

She turned her head. "Yes?"

"If you change your mind, you know where I live."

AFTER THAT SWIMMING LESSON, everything changed.

Or maybe the change had been happening gradually, and he hadn't noticed it.

Either way, Emily went from hiding away in Castaway Cottage to being a visible part of the Puffin Island community.

She and Lizzy visited Agnes every morning to walk Cocoa,

only now whenever Ryan called on his grandmother, he noticed small gifts on the kitchen table. Gifts that revealed exactly how Emily was spending her time with her niece. A bowl heaped with blueberries picked fresh from the bush. A plate of home-baked cookies and a picture of a boat bobbing on the waves painted by Lizzy.

"I think that girl is enjoying doing things she's never done before," was all that Agnes would say when he questioned her about the gifts that kept appearing.

"Lizzy?"

"I meant Emily, but that statement is probably true of both of them."

Judging from the interesting shape of the cookies, Emily was as experienced a cook as she was a swimmer, but he wasn't about to diminish her attempts to entertain the child and become part of the local island community at the same time.

A week after the first swimming lesson, he walked in to find Agnes wearing a necklace of glittery pink beads.

Recognizing Lizzy's signature color, Ryan refrained from reaching for his sunglasses. "Nice necklace."

"Lizzy made this with Emily. The child has an eye for anything that sparkles. I guess she inherited that from her mother."

"Does she talk about her mother?"

"A little, to Emily. They've made a scrapbook together, with pictures and news stories." His grandmother gave a faint smile. "Positive ones."

Aware of the rumors that had surrounded Lana Fox's colorful love life, Ryan wondered how long Emily had toiled to find material suitable for young eyes. He could imagine her, those green eyes serious as she'd searched for images to keep Lana's memory alive for her daughter.

"I came to see if any of your group need a ride to your book club meeting tonight, apart from Hilda."

"Emily is picking Hilda up. She offered to take me, too, but I didn't want to stop giving you a reason to call by."

"I don't need a reason to call by." Ryan frowned. "Emily is making the trip specially?"

"She's a kind girl. She and Lizzy have baked a blueberry pie for our meeting. But, no, she isn't making the trip just for that. Once she's dropped Hilda off, she's going around to Lisa's to talk business. She's put together a plan to save Summer Scoop." Agnes said it as if it were a sure thing, and Ryan felt a flicker of unease.

"She's not a magician."

"No, she's something better." Agnes glanced at him over the top of her glasses. "She's a management consultant. We've never had one of those on the island before."

Ryan refrained from pointing out there wasn't much of a demand for management consultants on Puffin Island.

Much as he admired Emily's generosity in offering to help, he was more circumspect about her chances of being able to do anything that would substantially boost the profits of a business that had been struggling from the outset.

"I hope she comes up with a plan."

"She will." His grandmother sounded sure. "Emily is a smart young woman, and she is determined to help make the business work. Lisa has a smile on her face for the first time in months. It broke my heart when I heard she'd bought the place, a widow with two young children. Summer Scoop has been struggling to survive since Doris Payne first opened it forty years ago. The whole community has been trying to find ways to help the girl, but there's only so much ice cream a person can consume without their arteries exploding. If Emily can find a way to sell more of it to the summer crowd, then we'll all be in her debt. How is the swimming going? That's assuming 'swimming' is all you're doing in that hour and a half you spend together every night." She picked up her purse and her keys and took his arm as they walked to the car.

Ryan kept his expression blank. "It's all we're doing."

"Shame." His grandmother gave him a look. "She's perfect for you."

"You've been talking to Kirsti."

"Rachel. And I have eyes. Don't make that mistake of thinking age means I don't see."

"You wear glasses."

"Which make my vision near perfect. That girl is longing for a family and a home."

"Maybe those glasses of yours need changing because she's been running from both those things most of her life."

"Sometimes you run from the things you want most, because those are the things that scare you." His grandmother looked at him pointedly, but Ryan chose not to engage in that particular conversation.

He wasn't scared. He just didn't want that.

After that first session in the pool, he'd made a point of not touching her, choosing instead to stay close enough to help if she found herself in trouble, but far enough away to ensure they focused on her swimming and not the sexual heat that underpinned every encounter.

Having made the decision to conquer her fear of water, she refused to let anything stand in her way. Not her own nerves or even an incident when she'd slid on the side of the pool and plunged into the deep end. She'd come up spluttering, wild-eyed, but had rejected his offer of assistance and instead choked and splashed her way to the side of the pool without help.

He suspected she'd lowered the water level by swallowing half of the pool, but he respected her determination to do it by herself.

He dropped his grandmother at her book group, but instead of driving back to the Ocean Club, he parked outside Summer Scoop.

The store was closed, and Lisa answered the door with a glass of wine in her hand. "Ryan!" She opened the door to let him in. "Emily is here. We're having a Save Summer Scoop meeting."

He looked at the wine. "That involves wine?"

"It definitely does. Emily brought it. It's delicious. Come and join us."

He followed Lisa into the small kitchen, noticing the toys piled hastily into a box in the corner. Emily had papers spread all over the kitchen table and her laptop open.

This was an Emily he hadn't seen before.

She was dressed in skinny jeans and a turquoise T-shirt that hugged her curves. Distracted by those curves, Ryan lost orientation and banged into the door frame. Pain exploded through his shoulder, and he decided life had been more comfortable when she'd worn black, voluminous tops.

He thought back to a disturbingly frank conversation they'd had the day before when she'd told him how hard it was to find clothes when you were big breasted. She'd explained that cute underwear was hopeless and that bras needed serious engineering to have any hope of offering support, and that when she exercised she had to wear two support bras. She'd explained that shirts that buttoned down the front were no good because they always gaped and that she couldn't wear long necklaces because they dangled off her breasts.

By the time she'd finished talking, he'd been relieved he wasn't a woman.

As he waited for the pain in his shoulder to die down, she lifted her head from the laptop and flashed him a smile.

"Hi, Ryan." She was keying numbers into a spreadsheet, her fingers swift. An untouched glass of wine sat by her elbow.

"So—" dragging his gaze from her hair, he eyed the papers spread across the table "—you're finding ways to attract tourists and put me out of business?"

"Competition is healthy, Ryan." Emily hit Save. "It will be good for you."

He was fairly sure that what would be good for him was a few hours with her naked in an oversize bed, but he kept that thought to himself. "I had no idea you had such a ruthless streak."

Lisa handed him a glass of wine. "She's amazing. We've been looking at ways to reduce costs. Emily thinks I should talk to Doug Mitchell about the rent on this place."

Ryan thought about Doug, who never gave anyone anything for free if he could charge for it. "Doug isn't known for his financial generosity or his gentle heart. Don't get your hopes up."

"He's a businessman." Emily printed out a document. "He's charging almost twice what he should, and if Summer Scoop closes, he won't be getting any rent at all."

"Unless he finds another dreamer like me." Lisa topped up her own wineglass.

"You're going to speak to him tomorrow." Emily rescued the pages from the printer, clipped them together and slipped them into a file. "Show him these numbers."

"Can I do it on the phone with a script?"

"It's harder to say no to someone face-to-face. We can rehearse it, if it would make you feel better."

Lisa looked gloomily at Ryan. "I had no idea she could be this scary."

He didn't answer. There was plenty about Emily he found scary, the biggest thing being just how much he wanted to drag her back to his place. "If it persuades Doug to reduce the rent, it will be worth it."

"If he does, then there might be some hope for me. Look at all these ideas." Perking up, Lisa picked up a sheaf of papers. "Scoop of the Day. Every day we pick a different flavor and promote it. Happy Hour—half price ice cream between 3:00 p.m. and 4:00 p.m. every day. Name an ice cream—every time you buy an ice cream, you enter into a competition to have an ice cream named after you."

Ryan wondered if anyone would buy an ice cream called "Hot and Desperate."

To distract himself, he glanced over Emily's shoulder at the spreadsheet, and immediately her scent wrapped itself around him. "How will discounting increase profits?"

"Because we're going to drive more traffic toward the store." Emily pushed a piece of paper toward him. "We're going to ask the town council for permission to put a sign up next to the place where the ferry docks. Also to put some pretty tables and chairs outside, so that people can sit for a while and watch the boats."

Ryan refrained from pointing out that they could sit and watch the boats from the deck of the Ocean Club. "And when the fog rolls in and folks are trapped indoors?"

"They can be trapped indoors here." Visibly excited, Lisa started sketching out ideas using the twins' art materials. "We're going to paint the place and put tables and chairs inside. We're going to have things for the kids to do, like coloring and jewelry making."

"Won't that have a significant cost implication?"

"It shouldn't." Emily made a note to herself. "Skylar knows plenty of suppliers."

"I thought her work was high end."

"It is now, but before she started designing jewelry for the rich and famous, she used to do the occasional children's party. She's very creative."

Lisa snapped the top off a blue pen. "And Emily's biggest idea? A stand on the waterfront just beyond the harbor and near the beach."

Emily pushed a sketch toward him. "If they won't come to the ice cream, then we'll take the ice cream to them. What do you think?"

It was so obvious Ryan wondered why no one had thought of it before. "You'll need a food truck license."

The anxiety was back on Lisa's face. "Will that be hard? Would they refuse me?"

"I don't see why, when everyone is so keen to see Summer Scoop work. And they gave a license to Chas when he wanted to serve gourmet burgers. Seems to me that gourmet ice cream right next door would make perfect sense. He might even be prepared to lease you the stand next to his. He owns both of them." Ryan caught Emily's eye. "Let me speak to a few people. Assuming there is no problem with the license and Chas is willing to help, who would run it? You don't have the budget to employ anyone, do you?"

Emily finished her wine. "Lisa could run it at lunchtimes and weekends when the island is at its busiest. I've been going through the numbers, and her quietest time here in the store is lunchtime—I guess because people are either already on the beach or they're in one of the restaurants or cafés. If we get the go-ahead with the license, we're going to try it for a month. See what happens."

"Leave it with me." Ryan put the papers back on the table, and Lisa passed the wine across to him.

"Drink. You've earned it. You're now officially part of the rescue team. I'm especially grateful since I know we're in competition."

"I can stand a little competition."

"In that case, next time you hold a lobster picnic on the beach, Lisa is going to provide the ice cream." Emily pushed the laptop toward him. "Take a look at these numbers, and tell me if you can see anything I've missed."

He couldn't see anything except those smoky green eyes and that soft mouth, but he forced himself to look at the screen. "Seems to me you've pretty much covered everything." Up until now he'd only ever seen her out of her depth, literally and figuratively. It was interesting seeing her comfortable and confident. "Where's Lizzy tonight?"

"Snuggled in the twins' bedroom." Lisa topped up all the glasses. "Hard to know which of them is more excited. Lizzy looks so much like them, they could be triplets."

"She's staying the night?"

"No, I'll scoop her up when we're ready to go home." Emily shut down the spreadsheet and closed the laptop. "Which I guess is now."

"You could leave her here and pick her up in the morning." Lisa said it casually, but Emily shook her head.

"We're taking this a step at a time."

"You mean you're taking it a step at a time."

She smiled. "You're right, that's what I mean. Letting Lizzy sleep over is a step I haven't reached yet."

"Think what you'd be able to do with a whole night off." Lisa grinned at her. "Adult company. Sleeping in."

"I have to go." Trying not to think of what he'd do with Emily if he had her in his bed for a night, Ryan stood up. "I need to work late to make sure you're not going to put me out of business."

Lisa laughed and walked him to the door.

"It's a crime that a man with a body like that should be allowed to wear clothes." Lisa sat back down at the table. "That's the worst thing about being a widow. No sex. Actually, it's not the worst thing. The worst thing are the rules you don't even know exist."

Emily slid her laptop back into her bag. Having Ryan there had seriously disturbed her concentration. "Rules?"

"I call them Rules for Widows. Society has unwritten rules about when it's decent to start seeing other men. The problem is that none of those rules take into account the quality of the relationship."

"You were unhappy?"

Lisa stood up and walked to the bottom of the stairs, checking there was no sound from the bedroom. Then she closed the kitchen door carefully so there was no chance they could be overheard. "Miserable. My husband had three affairs that I know about, one when I was pregnant with the twins. There were plenty of times when I could have killed the bastard myself, so it makes no sense that I got lumbered with all this guilt when he died. Why should I feel guilty? I want to smack it out of myself."

"Oh, Lisa—"

"Hey, life doesn't always send us what we want, as we both know."

A month ago Emily would have agreed wholeheartedly. Now she didn't even know what she wanted. The feeling of panic that had been her constant companion when she'd first arrived had receded to manageable levels. She and Lizzy had found an easy rhythm that was unexpected. But most unexpected of all was how much she enjoyed her swimming lessons with Ryan. Not just being with him, but the actual swimming. It gave her a feeling of strength to have overcome a fear that had been part of her life for so long.

"Why did you choose Puffin Island?"

"Because it had happy memories for me." A dreamy look crossed Lisa's face. "My parents brought me every summer. Dad was a marine biologist, and he worked at the university, so we used to come for the whole vacation. We hired a cottage near South Beach and did all the usual beach-based things. Poking around in tide pools, kayaking—I loved it. I spent a couple of summers at Camp Puffin, but the happiest one was when I turned seventeen."

"You met someone?"

"Took me five minutes to fall in love." She reached for her wine. "Do you remember that exciting feeling of discovering your own sexuality as a teenager?"

For Emily, it hadn't happened as a teenager, it had happened a few weeks before when she'd first met Ryan. And the discovery process was ongoing. She was beginning to think she didn't know herself at all. "What happened?"

"I met him a week before we were due to go back to Boston. Something clicked between us. I'd never met anyone I could talk to the way I could talk to him. We spent every moment together." Lisa gave a humorless laugh. "I often wonder if that's been the root of my problems. That one perfect week ruined me for anything afterward."

"You didn't stay in touch?"

"I tried. I sent him emails, but they bounced so I guess he gave me an email that didn't work." Lisa shrugged. "I thought about him all the time, but then I met Mike. I've often wondered if it was my fault he had all those affairs. Because I was too closed off. My heart hurt, and I didn't want it to hurt again. Does that make any sense?"

Emily thought about the way she'd protected herself after her sister had died. "Perfect sense."

"Maybe Mike knew there was a tiny part of me I kept from him."

"Or maybe that had nothing to do with it. Did you think about leaving him?"

"All the time, but I didn't want my babies to grow up without a father, and he was a good dad. If he'd been a terrible father I could have left for their sakes, but leaving for my own sake felt like the ultimate in selfishness."

"Is it selfish to want a good life for yourself?"

"He was with one of his lovers when he died." Lisa blurted the words out. "They had to cut both of them out of the car. I'm worried that one day the kids will look up the press coverage and find out the truth."

"Oh, Lisa—" Emily reached across and took her hand.

"I just want to protect my babies." Lisa's eyes filled, and she groped for a tissue. "I want to stop anything bad happening to them. Isn't that ridiculous?"

Emily's mouth was dry as sand. "Why is it ridiculous?"

"Because you can't control everything. It took me a long time to see that and realize there wasn't anything I could have done. I couldn't stop their father having an affair. I couldn't stop him dying with his latest girlfriend in the car. I couldn't stop the press finding out. All I could do was teach them to cope with whatever life threw at them. That's the best lesson of all, isn't it? I wanted to make sure they grew up strong and able to look after themselves. I didn't want to fill their heads with my baggage because, life being what it is, I knew they'd probably pick up plenty of their own."

"Don't talk to me about baggage." Emily sat back in her chair. "I suspect Lizzy and I could fill a cargo plane with no space left over."

"But you have skills. You're supporting yourself and Lizzy. I brought the twins here because I thought hard work and a dream would be enough. I wanted to get away from the sympathy and the pitying looks and live in a place where people didn't know my rat bastard cheating husband had died in a car with his skinny lover." She sniffed. "I wanted to show the twins I was strong, but all I've done is show them I have bad judgment. I've failed."

"What you've shown them is that you're not afraid to go after what you want. And if it doesn't work out, then you'll find a way to pick yourself up, and that's a good lesson for any child because life is about falling and then getting up again. But it's going to work out. You're not going to fall. Not this time."

"You don't know that."

"Yes, I do." Now that she knew the full story, she was even more determined to do what she could, even if she had to eat all the ice cream herself. "Providing Doug drops the rent and we can reduce some of your other costs, you'll make enough to keep going. But we're aiming for better than that. The boy you met that summer—you haven't seen him since you've been back on the island?"

Lisa shook her head. "No. And he isn't a boy now. Late twenties, I guess."

"What did he look like?"

"Tall and dark. A bit like Ryan. He likes you, by the way."

"Ryan?" Emily didn't think "like" described what was going on between them. "He was Brittany's best man. He's keeping an eye on me because she threatened to kill him if he doesn't."

Lisa laughed. "Somehow I don't think that's what's going on here. Are you interested?"

Emily thought about the slow kisses and the wild heat.

She was interested. And scared. The greater the emotion, the greater the capacity for hurt, and she knew this relationship could go nowhere.

"I have Lizzy. That's more than enough to adjust to for now. And children are the perfect contraception."

"True. On the other hand I might be able to help with that. Would you trust me with Lizzy?"

"I have trusted you with Lizzy. She's sleeping upstairs with your kids."

"I mean overnight. I swear if a photographer knocks on the door, I'll kill him with my bare hands. Even if I didn't already hate them after everything they printed about Mike's accident, I wouldn't let anything happen to Lizzy. I already love her."

"I trust you, Lisa. It isn't you, it's me. I have a problem with letting go." Over a glass of wine, she'd told Lisa the truth about Lizzy's identity, but she hadn't shared the story about Katy. "I want to be there the whole time to protect her."

"Are you really worried the photographers will come here?"

"Every day that passes makes it less likely. Ryan thinks the trail will have gone cold. That they've lost interest."

"So leave her with me," Lisa urged. "Go on a date. Have a night of wild sex. Believe me, if that is ever an option for me, I'll be dropping the twins with you!"

A wild night of sex.

Was she the only person in the world for whom sex had never been wild?

Feeling inadequate, Emily shook her head. "That isn't going to happen."

CHAPTER THIRTEEN

TWO DAYS LATER Ryan was on his way to deal with a problem at the marina when he saw Emily walking hand in hand with Lizzy toward the section of the harbor reserved for the boat tours. The child was talking nonstop, and Emily was listening attentively, occasionally nodding and interjecting.

He compared it to the first day when she'd sat in the Ocean Club staring at Lizzy as if she were a bomb that might detonate at any moment.

Instead of using the path down to the marina, Ryan diverted and joined them on the waterfront. "Taking a trip?"

"Yes." Lizzy was so excited she was almost dancing. "We're going on the boat. I swam on my own yesterday for the first time, and now Emily is taking me to see the puffins before they fly away for the winter."

It was impossible not to respond to that excitement. Also impossible not to wonder how much of a treat it would be for Emily.

"Sounds like fun." He cast a look at Emily and saw shades of pale under the bright smile. It was her skin color that made up his mind. "Why don't I take you myself?"

Emily shook her head. "That's not necessary. I know you're busy."

Ryan thought about the meeting he had scheduled with the multimillionaire yacht owner who wanted to negotiate the fee for using the Ocean Club facilities. He'd been looking forward to the cut and thrust of a negotiation that would end in him taking a generous chunk of the guy's money, but the anticipation was clouded by the thought of what might happen if Emily had a panic attack while Doug was in the middle of the bay. "Doug crams as many people on the boat as he can to make money. Sometimes the kids can't even see properly. You'd be more comfortable with me."

"There isn't—"

"I want to go with Ryan! Please?" Lizzy was visibly excited at the proposed change of plan, and Ryan drew Emily aside. He breathed in the scent of blossoms and lemons and wondered why he was doing this to himself.

"Are you sure this is a good idea?"

"A boat trip? Yes. I promised."

And she would never break a promise, he knew that.

"Then let me take you."

"No, but thank you for offering."

"Are you refusing because of what happened in the pool?"

Her gaze skidded to his and away again. "I'm refusing because this is a child-centered day, and you have better things to do with your time."

He certainly had other things to do with his time. Whether they were better or not, he wasn't sure. "I can manage one boat trip, Emily. I'll make sure you're both safe, and you can wear life jackets the whole time. You'll be happier, I promise." He saw her gaze flicker to the tourist boat where Doug was taking money from people as they boarded. The boat was filling up, and he knew that it was going to be at full capacity. "With me, if you discover you hate it, or if she hates it, we can turn around any time and come back to the harbor. You can't do that with Doug."

"I thought you sailed a flashy racing boat."

"I do, but I'll borrow Alec's sloop. It's a traditional wooden boat. You'll love it."

Her expression told him she didn't think there was anything to love about boats. "Lizzy isn't too young for that type of boat?"

"I took Rachel sailing for the first time when she was four. Spent a whole summer teaching her knots. Bowlines, hitches, figure of eights. By the time she was eight she was sailing a Sunfish by herself."

"I don't even know what that is."

"It's a dinghy. It has a habit of capsizing." Remembering made him smile and then he saw she'd turned green. "Alec's boat is stable."

"It doesn't need a crew to sail it?"

"I can sail it alone. And I'd be happy to take a couple of passengers." He saw her glance from Lizzy to the now heaving boat in the harbor.

"Well—if you're sure. Thank you."

Ryan glanced at his watch. "Can you give me an hour? I'll meet you at the marina." He figured that would give him time to part the multimillionaire from enough of his cash to ensure the Ocean Club had a good summer.

AN HOUR LATER Emily stood nervously at the marina, listening to the clink and creak of masts and the shriek of seagulls.

Was she crazy?

Learning to swim had given her a confidence boost, but not for a moment did she kid herself that swimming in a calm pool under Ryan's watchful gaze would be anything like swimming in the choppy waters of Penobscot Bay. If Lizzy fell overboard, she doubted her ability to save her.

The only thing stopping her from backing out was the knowledge that this was her problem, not Lizzy's.

Emily had spoken to the grief counselor regularly and been advised that outdoor activities were to be encouraged. Since Lizzy had started her swimming lessons with Rachel, there had been no more bad dreams, and she was sleeping in her own bed.

"There's Ryan! And he brought Cocoa." She sprinted toward him before Emily could stop her.

"Lizzy!" Her heart rate doubled, but she saw Ryan lengthen his stride and scoop the child into the safety of his arms.

"No running by the water. You might fall."

"Yes, Captain Ryan." Lizzy was grinning and wriggling like a fish in a net. As soon as Ryan put her down, Cocoa was in her arms.

Emily watched as dog and child greeted each other with mutual adoration. "The dog has her own life jacket?"

"Everyone does. Let's start with Lizzy." Once Lizzy was wearing a life jacket, he turned to Emily. "You're going to wear this the whole time, and if you don't feel safe or you want me to turn back, tell me." He secured the jacket with strong, sure hands, and she thought to herself that feeling safe had more to do with the way he made her feel than a flotation device.

"If Lizzy falls in—"

"She's not going to fall in." His hands were firm on her waist, his gaze holding hers. "Do you trust me?"

It was hard to focus on anything when he was standing this close to her. She dropped her gaze, but that move gave her an eyeful of his chest and biceps.

"Yes, but even you can't control the sea."

"But I can ensure Lizzy's safety." He tightened the life jacket "And yours."

"You have to sail the boat, and if she falls in—"

"No one is going to fall in. Unless you're planning on stripping down to that red swimsuit, in which case it will be a case of man overboard, and you'll be rescuing me." Beneath the mild humor, she heard male appreciation and felt her stomach drop.

He was the only man who had ever made her feel this way, and she had no idea how to handle her feelings.

He whistled to Cocoa who clearly recognized it as some sort of signal because she wagged her tail enthusiastically and sprang onto the boat.

Next he scooped up Lizzy and put her safely on the deck with instructions to sit down and not move until he told her what to do, and finally he held out his hand to Emily.

The rise and fall of the boat mirrored the feeling in her stomach. "I could have spent the afternoon painting or making jewelry."

"Which would have been a thousand times more boring than going to see seals and puffins." Letting go of her hand, Ryan picked up a short length of rope from a bag he'd put on the deck.

"We're going to see puffins!" Lizzy was finding it hard to keep her bottom on the seat.

"Yes, but first you're going to learn to tie a knot, because all good sailors learn knots." He squatted down in front of the child with the rope in his hands. "Watch closely. First you make a rabbit hole—" he formed a loop with the rope "—out comes the rabbit, around the tree, back down the hole." He showed her again and then handed the length of rope to Lizzy, who copied it perfectly.

"Like that?"

"Great job." He stood up. "Keep practicing."

He maneuvered the boat skillfully out of the marina, guided it through the markers and out into the bay. He stood easily on the deck, loose-limbed and relaxed as he absorbed the rise and fall of the boat. As they left the sheltered harbor of the island, Emily felt the wind pick up and gripped the seat, but there was something undeniably magical about being out on the water with the sunlight dancing over the surface of the sea.

She decided that if he was relaxed, then maybe she could be, too. She forced the tension from her muscles and took a few breaths.

Ryan pointed the boat into the wind, and it rocked gently while he hauled up the sails, first one, then another. Then he returned to the wheel, adjusted the angle and worked the lines until the wind filled the sails, and the boat seemed to come alive in the water. And then they were moving, skimming the surface of the water at a speed that took her breath away. It felt like flying, and Emily felt a sharp stab of anxiety. Then he turned his head and shot her a smile, and anxiety gave way to exhilaration. The wind whipped at her hair, and the spray of the sea showered her skin, and in that brief moment she understood why so many considered sailing to be the ultimate adventure. There was a rhythm to it that she hadn't expected, a beauty to the curve of the sails and the gleam of sunshine on the polished wooden deck.

Ryan stood at the wheel, legs apart and braced against the rise and fall of the boat as he judged tide and wind. He sailed along the rocky coast of Puffin Island, past the lighthouse that guarded the rocks by Shipwreck Cove, and across the inlet. They saw large houses tucked along the shoreline, children exploring the mysteries of the tide pools. From here she could see where the forest touched the sea and rocky outcrops that provided home to a variety of nesting seabirds.

It was a clear day, with not a hint of the fog that had a habit of shrouding the sea in the summer months.

As they sailed away from the island toward Puffin Rock he pointed out Castaway Cottage and Shell Bay.

He allowed Lizzy to steer the boat, an offer that resurrected Emily's anxiety until she saw him put the little girl between himself and the wheel and cover her hands with his.

They dropped anchor in a little cove, and Ryan pointed out a seal pup and its mother lying on a sunny ledge.

"Take a look at the puffins." He helped Lizzy adjust binoculars. "Puffins only come on land when they're breeding."

"They live on the sea?"

"Yes. They're skilled divers, and, here's the coolest thing of all—" he crouched down behind her, helping her focus in the right place "—when they're flying, they beat their wings up to four hundred times a minute and reach speeds of around fifty miles an hour."

"How do you know?"

"Because biologists study them." Ryan took the binoculars from her, and Lizzy peered over the side of the boat.

"My mom said I should be an actor or a ballerina, but I think I might want to be a biologist or the captain of a boat and do this every day. Can women be captains?"

"Women can be anything they want to be." Ryan handed the binoculars back to her, and Emily thought again that for a man who didn't want the responsibility of children, he was remarkably good with them.

Ryan opened the cooler, and they ate a picnic of delicious sandwiches he'd ordered from the kitchen of the Ocean Club, and then sailed the boat farther out into the bay before giving both of them a brief lesson on tacking.

It made her happy to see how much Lizzy was enjoying herself. She was swift and nimble in the boat and a fast learner.

Emily found it more exciting than she would ever have imagined. It was impossible to picture anything bad happening while Ryan was in charge, so she closed her eyes and enjoyed the feel of spray on her face, the warmth of the sun and the smell of the sea. By the time they arrived back at the marina, she'd decided that maybe, just maybe, she didn't want to move to Wyoming.

Ryan sprang off the boat, secured it and then reached for Lizzy. "How does pizza sound?"

"I'm going for a sleepover."

"It's the twins' birthday," Emily explained as he glanced at her in surprise, "and she really wanted to." And she was trying hard not to show how nervous she was about it. One of the hardest things about parenthood, she was discovering, was not transferring her own hang-ups to Lizzy.

"You're not meant to call them 'the twins.'" Lizzy grabbed Cocoa. "They're separate people."

"You're right. Thank you for reminding me. It's just that 'twins' is so much quicker to say than 'Summer and Harry.'"

"We're going to eat pizza, birthday cake and then watch a movie in our pajamas."

"Sounds like a perfect evening." Ryan strolled across to Emily and took her hand as she stepped off the boat. "So, you're on your own tonight." The way he said it made her heart beat faster.

"Yes."

"Have dinner with me." He spoke quietly, checking that Lizzy was still occupied with Cocoa. "I'll book a table at The Galleon. Fine dining. Candles. Lobster. Adult company."

The invitation took her breath away.

The three years she'd spent with Neil hadn't prepared her for the intensity of feelings, and she wasn't naive enough to think that an evening with Ryan would end with dinner.

"You wouldn't be able to get a table at this short notice in the summer."

"Are you looking for an excuse to say no?"

"No, but people book months in advance, the moment they know they're coming on holiday."

He simply smiled. "So, is that a yes?"

"I'm covered in sea spray and I'm a mess."

His gaze traveled slowly from her hair to her mouth. "Option one," he murmured, "is for you to shower at my place."

Her breath caught in her throat. "Ryan—"

"Option two is that you go back to the cottage and change."

"Or there's option three," she croaked, "which is that I stay home alone."

His eyes were hooded. "I didn't give you an option three."

They'd reached a crossroads. A point where a decision had to be made.

Feeling as if she were plunging into the deep end of the swimming pool, she took a deep breath. "I'll take option two."

As she dropped Lizzy off with Lisa and the twins, she felt like a teenager on her first date, and the nerves increased as she drove back to the cottage to shower and change. By the time she walked up the steps to Ryan's apartment, she felt slightly sick, and the feeling intensified as he opened the door.

This wasn't an afternoon with Lizzy as the focus. It wasn't a swimming lesson where the objective was improving her stroke and confidence in water. This was a date. Just the two of them. Man and woman.

Amusement flickered in his eyes. "Don't tell me—you've spent the last two hours thinking of all the reasons you shouldn't be doing this."

"Maybe it's a mistake."

"Maybe." He stood to one side to let her in. "But most mistakes don't smell the way you do, so I'm willing to take that chance. I have champagne in the fridge. Hopefully that will numb your panic."

Was it panic? She wasn't sure. It felt more like excitement with a heavy dose of nerves. It was the first time she'd been in his home, and it took her breath away. Acres of glass offered spectacular views over the bay, and the setting sun sent slivers of gold across the darkening ocean. The place was designed to make you feel as if you were part of the scenery, not just an observer. You could almost smell the sea and feel the wind in your hair. It should have unsettled her, but didn't. Maybe it was because she was slowly getting used to the sea, or maybe it was because from up here it felt as if they were suspended above it, safe from the dangerous lash of the waves.

As for the apartment, the decor was exactly as she would have predicted: sophisticated, minimalist and masculine, everything chosen for its clean lines and simplicity. The kitchen area was a gleaming run of polished steel, sleek and practical. The walls that weren't glass were lined with bookcases, and in one corner a spiral staircase wound its way up to a sleeping shelf.

"What's up there? Your bedroom?"

"No. An obscenely large TV and my state-of-the-art sound system."

She laughed. "It's amazing." It was also the least child-friendly apartment she'd ever seen. "It has the feel of a loft. This will probably surprise you, but I could sit and look at this view all day."

"Me, too. Sometimes I'm tempted to do just that. Then I remind myself that if I don't get off my butt and earn money, I won't be able to afford to look at the view." He stood next to her, his shoulder brushing against hers. "When I was in the hospital, I thought about this place all the time. Even as a kid I knew these buildings had potential. I used to lie there, planning what I'd do with it. It took my mind off the pain."

"You've built a successful business."

"Winters are still lean, but even they are picking up since we started to pull in the winter outdoor crowd. And a few artists have shown interest in renting these apartments for the winter months. North light. I'm lucky to be able to build a life here." He strolled across to the fridge, removed a bottle and scooped two slender stemmed glasses from one of the cabinets.

"What are we celebrating?"

"The fact that you've learned to swim? Your first boat trip? Your first night without a six-year-old sleeping in the room next door? Adult time? The list of possibilities is endless." Under his gentle persuasion the cork came free with a gentle pop, and he poured the champagne and handed her a glass. "Or maybe we should drink to courage."

"Courage?"

"Swimming, sailing and sleepover. Knowing how hard all of those things must have been for you, I think it's an appropriate toast."

Remembering the vicious scars on his shoulder she decided

he wasn't low on courage himself. "I loved the sailing. And you were so patient with Lizzy."

"She's a great kid. Gutsy, funny—she reminds me a little of Rachel at the same age. Were you scared to let her go tonight?"

"Yes. But she wanted to do it so badly, and I trust Lisa."

"Does she know the truth?"

"About Lizzy's identity, yes. She had a bad experience with journalists herself, so she was sympathetic." She wondered if she'd been tactless given his past profession, but he shook his head, reading her mind.

"I'm not about to defend the actions of the guy you told me about."

"It's been almost a month. Do you think they could still come?"

"It's less likely with every day that passes."

She stared down into her glass, watching the bubbles rise. "It's weird. This is the first time I've been on my own for a month, and instead of feeling free, I miss her."

"Kids have a habit of sneaking up on you. Before you know it, they've hooked you and you can't get free." He finished his champagne. "We should leave. They're holding our table."

The Galleon restaurant was situated a short walk from the harbor, with views over the ocean and the passing yachts. Despite the island location, or perhaps because of it, they'd managed to secure themselves a reputation as one of the top restaurants in Maine. They operated six months of the year, and during the winter months the owner and chef, Sallyanne Fisher, spent time traveling the world on the hunt for new recipes. As a result the menu was eclectic and interesting.

Sallyanne herself greeted Ryan with a kiss and showed them to a secluded table in the corner of the restaurant with a view over the water.

"Who did she have to disappoint to give you this table?" Emily slid into the chair with the view, noticing that they were partially hidden from their neighbors.

Ryan smiled. "I fixed her boat last summer. She's been grateful ever since. And on an island this small it's impossible not to know your neighbors and your competition."

"It doesn't bother you?"

"Why would it? The quality of the food here is attracting foodies from everywhere. It's good for all of us."

It certainly was good.

They ate sautéed jumbo shrimp with roasted garlic and baby spinach, followed by fresh Maine lobster washed down with a Californian white that was cool and so delicious, Emily drank more than she'd intended to.

They finished off by sharing a blueberry cheesecake. As she took the last mouthful, Emily moaned and closed her eyes. "This is so good. I'm going to tell Lisa to find a way to make this into an ice cream."

"It's generous of you to help her."

"I'm doing it for selfish reasons. After everything that has happened lately, I need to feel competent at something."

He picked up his glass. "You're competent at a lot of things."

"Not swimming or parenting."

"There's nothing wrong with your parenting skills. Just your confidence. But you're pushing yourself out of your comfort zone on a daily basis. And you're loving it."

She put down her glass. "How do you know that?"

"It shows on your face." He glanced at the dress. "It shows in everything."

"It isn't just about Lizzy. It's about me. I never did these things. I never sat on a beach and tried to eat ice cream before it melted over my fingers, I never pushed my fingers into a heap of flour and made my own pizza base, I never made necklaces out of flowers. Lisa showed me how to make the perfect pirate map. You soak paper in tea, dry it out and then burn the edges."

He smiled. "So ballerina is definitely off her list."

"Seems that way." She put her spoon down. "The thing about kids is that they make you pay attention to the small things.

Things that as an adult you rush past on your way to something else."

"That's exactly what drove me crazy as a teenager. I wanted to rush past it on my way to something else."

She nodded. "You were at an age when everything was changing radically. You were trying to work out who you were, and suddenly you were expected to be responsible for other people. That's scary, but also rewarding. Lizzy's reading is coming on so fast. Agnes has been reading to her, too. She gave us lots of Rachel's old books."

He sat back in his chair, studying her across the table. "Still worried you can't love her?"

"She's very easy to love."

"And that scares you."

"Yes, but lately I'm doing everything that scares me, so I guess this is just one more thing."

"You're an impressive person, Emily Donovan. You took on a child you'd never even met and agreed to live a life you didn't think you wanted. Most people in your position would have put her in foster care."

"I don't think so." She took a deep breath. "I think most people would have done what I did. Spending time with Lizzy makes me wish I'd tried harder to have a relationship with Lana. I blame myself for that."

"How was that your fault?"

"I keep wondering whether if the accident hadn't happened, or if I hadn't reacted so badly to it, maybe things would have been different. Maybe we would have been closer."

"Or maybe she was never going to be the sort of person who wanted that."

Emily thought about her half sister and the uncomfortable similarities to her mother. "She was so beautiful, and yet she seemed to need to have that confirmed all the time. Maybe that was my mother's fault because looks were the only thing she valued."

Maybe it was because he was such a good listener, but suddenly she was telling him everything, about how she'd been teased in school about her body, how she'd tried to disguise her shape, how she'd mistrusted relationships.

The conversation wasn't all one-sided. He talked a little about how he'd felt stifled by looking after his younger siblings and about how guilty he'd felt leaving his grandmother to cope when he'd taken up a place at college.

"She wanted that for you."

"Didn't stop me feeling guilty."

"But by then the children were older. And the fact that you wanted to leave doesn't change the fact that you loved them."

"Like the fact that wearing black doesn't disguise the fact you're the sexiest woman alive."

The shift in the atmosphere rocked her off balance, and she felt her pulse quicken. "How much of that wine have you drunk? Your brain is malfunctioning."

"My brain has been malfunctioning since you wore those pajamas."

She stared at him across the table. He was sensationally attractive, those eyes dark as flint in a face where every line and angle spoke of strength and masculinity. The air was alive with a tension she had only ever experienced around this man.

The sexual energy was palpable, and by the time they returned to his apartment, she was feeling light-headed from a heady mixture of wine and anticipation.

He found his keys, opened the door and flicked a switch that turned on a couple of lamps and sent a warm glow over the spacious room.

"It's late," she murmured. "I should probably go home." Because she was nervous, she walked to the window, and he threw his keys down on a small table near the door and followed her.

"Is that what you want?" He stood behind her, and his hands closed over her arms.

She closed her eyes. "It would be sensible."

"And do you always do what's sensible?"

"Always. I like order and predictability. I'm only interested in things I can control." She kept her eyes forward, staring into the darkness of the bay. Lights from boats sent a warm glow flickering across the water. "With you, I feel out of control. As if I've lost my balance."

"Good." He moved her hair aside gently, and she could feel the warmth of his breath on the back of her neck. "I'm pleased I unbalance you."

"I'm worried the reality will be a letdown."

"It won't be." He turned her to face him. His gaze was slumberous, and all she saw in his eyes was liquid desire that mirrored hers. "Are you nervous?"

"Yes. I don't feel any of the right things when I'm in bed with a man. It's as if something inside me isn't switched on."

His smile was slow and sure. "Maybe it's a question of knowing where to find the switch. Why don't you leave that part to me?"

"I think there might be something wrong with me."

"Honey, there's nothing wrong with you. I have surveillance footage that proves it."

She thought about that night in the pool and leaned her forehead against his chest. "I thought you said it would be wiped."

"After sixty days." His fingers gently massaged her hair. "So for the next few weeks I have visual evidence that you're not who you think you are. Or we could try a different way to prove the same thing."

Her heart was pounding so fast she felt sure he must be able to feel it. "Are you always so sure about everything?"

"Not everything." He lowered his head so that his mouth was a breath away from hers. "But this I'm sure about." His hand slid to the nape of her neck, and he held her head while he kissed her slowly, taking his time as he explored her mouth, her jaw, the hollow of her neck until the urgency inside her was a primal, desperate beat.

She wrapped her arms around him, felt him haul her close so that she was anchored against hardness and strength. And still he kissed her, his mouth exploring hers with leisurely skill until all she could hear was the soft thrumming of her own pulse in her ears and his murmured words of encouragement. If he hadn't been holding her, she would have sunk to the floor in a pool of molten desire. She was dizzy with it. Disoriented. All she knew was that of all the things that had happened over the past month, this felt the most right. Her hands were in his hair, her mouth responding to the erotic rhythm of his kiss.

She slid her hands down his back and tugged at his shirt.

She pressed against him, feeling the rigid thickness through the thin fabric of her dress.

"Steady." He whispered the words against her mouth. "We have all night."

She wanted to tell him that she wasn't going to last five minutes, let alone all night, but at that moment his hand slid from her hip to her rib cage, and she felt his fingers brush the underside of her breast. It was such a relief that she moaned, but then he drew his hand away and smoothed her back instead, leaving her body vibrating with frustration.

"Ryan—" She'd never felt this desperate for anything in her life before, but even her pleading didn't persuade him to alter his pace.

He continued to kiss her, long and deep, until she was trembling and shivering, until thick syrupy pleasure spread through her body. She was wondering what would happen when he finally touched her, when he slid the zipper on her dress and she felt his fingers slowly trace the length of her spine. His hands moved to her shoulders, and the dress slithered onto the wooden floor in a whisper of silk, leaving her standing in her underwear.

He eased her away from him, and the look he gave her from under those thick, dark lashes sent a lick of fire burning across her skin.

She trembled with arousal. "I wish—"

"You wish?" His voice was husky and deep, and she lifted her hands to the front of his shirt and started undoing the buttons. Because she was shaking, she fumbled, but he didn't help her, just stood and waited, holding himself still while she struggled to get him naked.

In the end she gave up and ripped at the last few, sending buttons bouncing across the floor.

She heard him laugh, and then he scooped her into his arms as if she weighed nothing and carried her across the room, through slivers of dark and moonlight, to his bedroom. She saw briefly that it had the same incredible view, the same canvas of sea and stars, and then he was lowering her onto the bed, the muscles of his shoulders bunched as he supported her weight.

Clumsy, she fumbled with his belt, but her fingers were useless, and instead she gave up, frustrated, and covered him with the flat of her hand. He made a sound somewhere between a groan and a laugh and finished what she'd started. She stroked her hands over his powerful shoulders, lingered on the rough texture of his scar and slid lower. She felt the roughness of his thigh brush against the softness of hers, and then he shifted, giving himself full access to her body.

She started to remove her underwear, but he stopped her, pressing her flat to the bed with a wicked smile.

"That's my job."

"But—"

"Be patient." He kissed her throat, and then his mouth moved lower to the full swell of her breasts, now pushing hard against the supportive fabric of her bra. His fingers brushed against the thrusting tip, and liquid heat pooled deep in her pelvis. For a moment she wondered whether his patience and control signified a lack of desire, but then she saw the dangerous glitter in his eyes and knew he was balanced on the edge, just as she was.

And then he was kissing her again, and she felt him remove her bra, leaving her breasts full and exposed.

"With a body like yours it's a sin to wear clothes— ever."

Her hips shifted against the softness of his sheets, her body arched, and still he explored, tasted, teased until she was sobbing his name, her fingers digging hard into the powerful muscles of his shoulders.

"Ryan—"

"Not yet." But his hand finally moved between her thighs, lingered there, stroked through the sheer fabric of her panties and then slid inside, parting delicate folds until she was gasping. When she didn't think she could stand it any longer, he stripped off the last of her underwear, and his fingers explored her with slow, skillful strokes and then slid deep, touching her in a way that was new to her until sensation built with suffocating intensity. She felt the first flutters of her body, but instead of finishing what he'd started, he moved down her body, kissing her stomach and lower until he was settled between her thighs.

Desperation gave way to acute shyness. This was something she'd never done with Neil, and she tried to wriggle away, but Ryan held her firmly, urging her to relax, to just breathe, to trust him, and then she felt the silky stroke of his tongue and the warmth of his breath against exposed, slippery flesh. He held her there, trapped and helpless, while he explored and exposed all of her body's secrets, until she could no longer keep still. Finally, when she was sobbing and desperate, she felt him pause and reach for something from the nightstand and then he shifted over her, hard and heavy.

"Look at me." His soft command penetrated her clouded brain, and she opened her eyes, met the burning intensity of his and then moaned as she felt him enter her with a series of slow, deliberate thrusts. She felt her body yield to the invasion of his, felt her muscles ripple against the swollen thickness and moaned his name.

"Am I hurting you?"

She was drowning in pleasure. "No! I just— I need—"

"I know what you need." His voice thickened, he lowered his mouth to hers and rocked into her, deeper, harder, until each stroke, each driving relentless thrust propelled her closer to ecstasy.

Inhibition fled. Her only fear was that he might stop, that he might once again delay the pleasure. But not this time. Instead, he shifted the angle so that the combination of masculine thrust and delicious friction finally opened the gate to that elusive peak.

Pleasure rushed at her like a wave, slamming into her, the intensity of her climax catching her by surprise. She heard him groan her name, and then he was kissing her, stealing every sob, every cry with his mouth as the ripples of her body tipped him into his own shuddering release.

Afterward she lay, eyes closed, shaken by the depth of her own feelings. He gathered her close, soothing her with gentle hands and soft words, and then she was dimly aware of him leaving the bed. In the distance she heard the sound of water coming from the bathroom, and then he returned to the bedroom, scooped her boneless, pliant body easily into his arms and carried her through to the steamy, scented heaven.

"I never take baths, just showers." She slid into the water with a groan. "I might drown. I need a life jacket."

"You're not going to drown."

She heard the smile in his voice and opened her eyes. Confronted by the hard planes of his body, her gaze lingered on the dip and swell of muscle, the strength of those shoulders, the board-flat abdomen and the hair-roughened length of his thighs.

Catching her looking at him, he raised one eyebrow questioningly, as unselfconscious as she was anxious and unsure.

"You cannot possibly be shy after what we just did." His voice was deep pitched, roughened by desire, and she discovered that far from being sated, it was as if her body had woken from a deep sleep.

"Maybe. You could turn the lights off if you like."

"Honey, your body is so perfect anything less than a spotlight is a waste." He slid into the water next to her, and she silenced the voice that questioned why he'd installed a tub big enough for two.

Her hair hung damp and curling in the steam, the ends heavy and wet as they clung to her neck. He pushed it aside and brought his mouth down on hers.

"You're beautiful."

She straddled him, her skin sliding against his, the warmth of the water mingling with the heat of his skin. She pressed her mouth to the rough texture of his jaw, felt the rhythm of his breathing change as her hands moved down his body.

By the time morning came they'd done everything except sleep.

They lay, wrapped up in each other, watching dawn break over an ocean as smooth and still as glass.

"I've never had a date like this one." Her voice broke the sleepy silence, and she felt him stir and tighten his grip.

"It's good to try new things." His voice was husky, and he shifted her under him and looked down at her through lowered lids. "Still think there's something wrong with you?"

"No." She slid her arms around his neck. "You obviously have special powers."

He lowered his mouth to hers, smiling against her lips. "Sweetheart, I haven't even started. Any time you want another display of my special powers, let me know."

She felt the weight of him on her, dominating and unbelievably arousing. "It's dawn. I'm picking up Lizzy in three hours, and the thing about having children is that there isn't a whole lot of opportunity for sleeping in the day."

"True. Sleepless nights suck. Unless the reason for it is sex." He rolled on to his back, but he kept hold of her, locking her body against his. "I want to know more about you. Tell me something. Anything. Did you like school?"

"Mostly, yes. I liked the learning and the routine. There was a consistency that wasn't ever present at home. Once I walked through those gates, I knew what was going to happen. The peo-

ple behaved in a predictable way. I was never going to walk in
and find them drunk or naked with a guy I'd never met before."

"I've heard a lot of reasons for enjoying school but never
that one."

"Was there a teacher that stood out for you? For me it was
Mrs. White. We used to wonder if she'd had her hair dyed to
match her name, but she was the best math teacher. I was good
at numbers. There was a beauty to it, a logic, that wasn't present
in anything else in my life. I had a gift, I think, and she saw it.
She took me under her wing. I don't know if she guessed what
was happening at home, or whether she was just one of those
people who are really good at bringing out the best in every
child. Either way, she helped me. I was always the last kid in
the building."

"You didn't want to go home."

"To begin with that was the reason, but after a few years it
was because I didn't want to leave. School was a place full of
possibilities. Mrs. White made me believe education was the
key to another world. I wanted that key so badly. For the first
time ever, the future looked exciting. I made it into college because of her. Every night when I left she gave me a new book
to read, and every morning I gave it back and exchanged it for
a different one."

"You read a book a night?"

"I read from the moment I arrived home until I fell asleep.
If the book was good, I didn't sleep much. Sometimes I'd talk
about the books with my stepfather, but mostly I just lived in
my own world, and he respected that."

"And your mom?"

"She didn't care what I was doing." She ran her hand over
his shoulder, feeling the uneven texture of his skin under her
fingers. "Does it hurt? And don't lie to me."

"It's worse when the weather is cold and occasionally when
I use it without thinking. But I don't mind." He hesitated. "At
the beginning when I was going through the endless surgery

and rehabilitation and taking the pain and frustration out on my family, I kept thinking of Finn. Every time I was tempted to feel sorry for myself, I thought about him. And the pain reminds me to live in the moment."

"I wish I was more like that. I spend half my life—no, more than half my life—" she corrected herself "—worrying about stuff that hasn't happened yet."

"You're not alone. Most of us go through life thinking about tomorrow, and we miss today. That was one of the things that made Finn such a great companion on our trips into dangerous territory. He noticed the small things that other people missed. It was also what made him a great photographer."

"You don't talk about him much. You don't talk about any of it much."

His fingers moved slowly up and down her arm. "The past is useful if it teaches you something about how you should be living in the present. Other than that, it's just the past."

Emily thought about her sister. "I think I've been living my whole life governed by the past. I didn't think about it and didn't talk about it, but it was there in everything I did. Skylar said that to me once and she was right. If it hadn't been for Lizzy, I probably would have stayed that way forever."

"And now?"

"Children have a way of making you live in the present. She doesn't see further than the next meal or the next activity." But she knew it wasn't just Lizzy who was responsible for the change in her. It was Ryan.

He turned his head to hers, the gleam in his eyes telling her he knew what she was thinking. "If you need a suggestion for what the next activity could be, just ask."

CHAPTER FOURTEEN

SHE LEFT BEFORE Ryan woke, tiptoeing out of his apartment as
sunlight shimmered through the wall of glass.

The trail of clothes strewn around the room told the story
of the night before, and she gathered them up, dressed swiftly
and quietly closed the door behind her.

As she walked down the steps that led from his apartment,
she wished she'd thought to bring something else to wear.

She was acutely conscious, not only of the dress that announced to the entire island where she'd spent the night, but of
the small things. The slight whisker burns on the sensitive skin
of her neck and the fact that her body ached in unusual places.
And then there were the other things. Emotions she didn't recognize. Feelings that were unfamiliar.

It was as if she'd gone to sleep as one person and woken as
another.

She arrived to pick up Lizzy and was grateful that Lisa said
nothing about the fact Emily was overdressed. Instead, she supplied a strong cup of coffee and proceeded to make small talk
about her plans for the makeover of Summer Scoop.

On the drive home Lizzy talked nonstop about her sleepover,
an evening apparently bursting with pizza and popcorn.

Emily parked outside the cottage and stared at Shell Bay.

Had Ryan woken up?

Maybe she should have left a note, but what would she have said?

Thanks for the best sex of my life.

"Can we dig in the sand?" Lizzy sounded hopeful, and Emily turned to look at her, wondering why everything felt different.

"Yes. Let's do it. Right now." Before this new version of herself vanished. Before she went back to being the person she'd been the day before.

They both changed into swimming things and pulled on shorts and T-shirts. Then Emily gathered up a blanket along with the bucket and spade and walked along the short sandy path that led directly to the beach.

Most of the tourists chose to stay on the beaches close to the harbor, and there was only one other family on Shell Bay.

Emily put the blanket down, and Lizzy stripped down to her swimsuit and started digging. "Can we build a boat?"

Emily would have preferred something a little less challenging for her first sand sculpture, but she gamely set her mind to scooping out the hull of a boat, using her hands to fashion seats and a prow while Lizzy filled and refilled the bucket.

They dug together for half an hour, and then Emily straightened and stripped off her shorts and tee. She dug her hand into her bag and surreptitiously checked her phone, but there were no messages.

Disappointment hovered like a cloud over her happiness.

Lizzy glanced up at her. "Skylar says red is your color."

"Does she? And what's your color? Pink?"

Lizzy shook her head and patted down the sand. "Turquoise. Like the sea."

Close by, the other family was playing a ball game, and when the ball came flying in their direction, Emily caught it and threw it back.

She hadn't intended to walk to the water's edge, but somehow that was where she ended up, and she stood with her toes curling into the damp sand, feeling the lick of the tide on her ankles. Ahead of her lay the vastness of the ocean, an infinity of blue merging with the summer sky on a horizon so straight it could have been drawn by a child with a ruler.

The expanse of water made her catch her breath, and she turned her head, needing to see land, and there right behind her was Castaway Cottage, looking over the beach like a benevolent friend. It was impossible to believe anything bad could happen within sight of the cottage and easy to see why Kathleen had bought it all those years ago. It was the perfect Maine beach house, a retreat that most people could only dream of owning.

Lizzy dropped the bucket and ran to her side. "Are you going in the sea?"

"Yes." Up until that point, she hadn't realized that had always been her intention. "I am."

"Can I come? I haven't swum in the sea yet, but Rachel said I was ready."

She wanted to refuse. She still wasn't sure she was ready to do it herself, let alone take someone else with her.

On the other hand, if this was a test, then she might as well make it the ultimate test.

"I want you to use your float."

Lizzy ran off and returned moments later carrying it.

Maybe she should have waited for Ryan. He would have come with her, she knew, but she also knew this was something she had to do by herself. It was her fear to conquer, and no one could do that for her. It felt as if she'd climbed almost to the top of Everest and was only a few steps from the summit. She didn't have to do this, but she knew she would never feel whole until she did.

She told herself that she knew this beach, that she'd watched the ebb and flow of the tide enough times to know how the beach shelved. Here, in the perfect curve of Shell Cove, there were no dangerous currents, no riptides. The safety of the swimming was one of the many reasons Brittany was constantly being bothered by people wanting to buy the land. There was surely no more perfect spot in the whole of Maine.

She took a single step forward, and Lizzy took her hand, dancing over the small waves without fear.

"It's freezing!" She squealed and laughed, while Emily watched, entertained and a little envious.

Had she ever been that carefree?

Had there ever been a time when she enjoyed the moment without worrying that something bad was about to happen? *Had she ever lived without protecting herself?*

"Aunt Emily—" Lizzy tugged her hand impatiently "—come on!"

And she realized that living in the moment was a choice, and she stepped forward and kept walking until the water was above her knees.

Another family joined them in the water, the children squealing as the father swung them high into the air.

Reassured by their presence, Emily scooped Lizzy into her arms and held her out of reach of the waves.

The water was midthigh, and she knew she didn't need to go any deeper. This was enough for now. The ocean stretched ahead of her, calm today, sleeping in the warm afternoon sunshine. The surface sparkled, inviting, and Emily knew that it had to be now. It was the perfect time.

"Are you ready?" Steeling herself, she lowered Lizzy to the water and watched her kick out, confident as she started to swim. "Swim parallel to the shore. Stay in line with the beach. That's it."

Without allowing herself to think too much, Emily slid forward into the water, gasping as the coldness closed over her shoulders. Immediately she had the urge to stand up, to feel the reassuring pressure of the sand beneath her feet, but she fought the panic and forced herself to breathe and move her arms and legs in the same rhythmic strokes she'd used in the pool. She felt the gentle lift and fall of the water as she swam, felt the sea lick at the edges of her hair and her face, playful, not threatening.

Panic was replaced by calm and then by pleasure and no small degree of pride. She was swimming, really swimming. She'd learned a new skill. The sea was in control, she knew that. But if she was careful, they could coexist.

Next to her Lizzy splashed and swam, chin raised like a dog out of the water, and Emily murmured words of encouragement, telling her to keep going, keep kicking, and she wasn't sure if she was saying the words to herself or the child.

They swam halfway along the cove before Lizzy declared that her arms were too tired, and Emily stood up, feeling the reassuring pressure of the sand beneath her feet. The water was still at midthigh but too deep for Lizzy, and she scooped her up and held her tightly, safely out of reach of the water.

"You swam so well."

She felt Lizzy's arms creep around her neck and the softness of her curls brush against her chin. She breathed in the smell of salt and sea and closed her eyes, rocked by the tight squeeze of those skinny arms and the priceless gift of trust. Something inside her that she'd thought had died sprang to life and bloomed. She wasn't sure how it happened or even why, but at some point holding turned to hugging. The deep chill that had become part of her slowly thawed as they stood, tangled together, intertwined and close.

"I like living here." Lizzy's voice was soft, and Emily felt her eyes sting.

"I like living here, too."

"Can we have a puppy?"

Eyes stinging, Emily started to laugh. "Let's take this a step at a time, shall we?"

"A puppy would be the best thing ever. I love Cocoa, but she's Agnes's best friend, so we can't have her."

"No, we can't." A puppy. Realizing she was actually considering it, Emily shook her head in disbelief. "Let's go indoors and wash off all this sand." Holding Lizzy on her hip, she waded back to shore. "Oh, wait, let's finish our sand yacht."

By the time they'd finished their impressive structure, the sun was dipping down below the horizon and clouds were gathering.

They ran indoors trailing sand and laughter into the house, showered, changed and then picked blueberries from the bushes in the garden and made a pie.

"Push your hands into the flour—" Emily stood Lizzy on a chair, and together they weighed and stirred and mixed while outside the sky darkened and thunder rumbled.

"Will we live here forever?" Lizzy had somehow managed to cover every available surface and herself with flour.

Emily poured the blueberries into the pie dish. "Castaway Cottage isn't ours. It belongs to Brittany, my friend."

"If she comes home, where will we live?"

Emily paused, understanding the child's need for security in a world that had crumbled around her. "We'd stay here until we found somewhere perfect for us." She sent mental thanks to her friend and the pact they'd made all those years before.

"Will we stay on Puffin Island?"

It was something she hadn't considered until the past few days. "That's something we'll have to talk about."

"I want to live here. I don't want to leave Cocoa. Or the puffins. I like swimming. Rachel says if I'm still here when school starts after the summer, she'd be my teacher."

Emily leaned across and wiped the flour from her mouth. "You'd have to call her Miss Cooper."

Lizzy grinned. "I'd be with Summer and Harry."

"That sounds like fun. Are you done making pastry? I'll finish off and then we can clean up and read a book while our pie is cooking."

She heard the front door open and then the sound of paws on the floor as Cocoa sprinted into the kitchen.

"Cocoa!" Abandoning her duties as pastry maker, Lizzy

jumped off the chair and hugged the dog, spreading flour and goodwill in equal measure.

Emily's heart lifted as Ryan walked into the room, wiping droplets of rain from his face. "She's learned *sit*, but *stay* is still giving us a problem."

His gaze connected with hers briefly, and the look he gave her sent heat rushing to her cheeks.

"Would you like to stay for dinner? It's Lizzy's favorite gourmet treat. Mac and cheese followed by blueberry pie."

"That sounds like the best invitation I've had in a long time." He hunkered down next to Lizzy. "I saw a boat on the beach. A boat that is even better than mine. No idea how something that spectacular could have just shown up on the sand like that. Any ideas?"

Lizzy was giggling, her hands full of Cocoa. "Emily and I made it. We copied yours."

"It's a better-looking boat than mine. Any time you want to build me a proper boat, go right ahead." He rose to his feet. "So, you played in the sand."

"And the sea. I swam."

His eyebrows rose. "With Rachel?"

"With Emily."

"Emily swam in the sea?" There was a strange note to his voice, and Emily slid the pie into the oven.

"I remembered everything you taught me."

"You should have told me you wanted to do that. I would have come with you."

"It wasn't something I planned. And I needed to do it by myself."

He nodded slowly. "And how did it feel?"

She thought about the sensation of the water on her limbs, the terror of feeling the waves tug at her and the satisfaction of having confronted something that frightened her so badly. "It felt good. I don't think I'll be swimming to the mainland anytime soon, but it was a start."

Lizzy scrambled to her feet. "Ryan, will you read a story?"

"Sure." He lifted her into his arms. "What's it to be? *Green Eggs and Ham*?"

Knowing how badly Lizzy needed to be wrapped in that security blanket right now, Emily sent him a grateful look. "I'll fetch the book."

"Not that one." Lizzy's arms were around his neck. "I want the one in your head. The one you told me that time Emily was sick, about Abbie, the lighthouse keeper's daughter who kept the lights burning when her father couldn't get back to the island."

Ryan sat down at the table with Lizzy on his lap and started telling the story while Emily made sauce for the mac and cheese. Thunder boomed outside the cottage, and Lizzy flinched against Ryan, who carried on telling the story in his calm, steady voice.

"It was one of the worse storms ever—"

"Worse than this one?"

"Much worse than this one…"

Lizzy kept interrupting, asking questions. Did Ryan think Abbie had been afraid? Why hadn't she used a boat to escape? Could the waves have covered the lighthouse?

He answered everything with the same quiet patience, returning each time to the story until another clap of thunder came from overhead. This one was so loud even Emily flinched, and Lizzy hid her face in Ryan's chest and clutched his shirt.

"I don't like storms."

"Plenty of people feel the same way." His hand smoothed her spine, gentle and reassuring. "Rachel was the same, but don't tell her I told you."

"But she's big and brave."

"Yeah, but she doesn't like storms. Everyone is afraid of something."

He'd used the same calm tone with her, Emily remembered. On the day of her meltdown, it had been his voice as much as his presence that had calmed her. When Ryan spoke, it was impossible to believe anything bad could happen, that the world could be anything other than a safe place.

Lizzy relaxed her hold on his shirt. "Are you afraid of storms?"

"Not storms, but there are plenty of other things that scare me."

"Like what?"

He hesitated. "I don't like hospitals. I don't like the way they smell or sound. I'll do just about anything to avoid going into one."

Lizzy pondered. "But what if the doctor said you had to go to the hospital?"

"Then I'd go." His hand stroked her hair. "Being afraid doesn't mean you don't do something, it just means it isn't easy and you have to try a little harder than other people."

"Aunt Emily?" Lizzy was looking at her. "What scares you?"

Loving and losing.

And she hadn't faced that fear. Instead, she'd done everything she possibly could to live her life in a way that meant she could avoid it.

Emily stirred the sauce in a mindless, rhythmic movement that required no attention.

The only sound in the kitchen was the faint simmer of liquid and the heavy patter of rain against the window.

"Aunt Emily?"

"The sea," she croaked. "Until today I was afraid of the sea. You have to let Ryan finish the story."

His eyes fixed on hers, he carried on with the story, his tone and the words he used making it all too easy to picture Abbie's struggle during that terrible storm.

As the rain sheeted down the windows, Emily found herself picturing the girl trying to keep the lamps burning in the lighthouse and take care of her three sisters and sick mother, while the sea boiled and lashed at her home.

Lizzy listened, absorbed. "What do you think Abbie was afraid of?"

"I don't know. Whatever it was, she didn't let it stop her keeping those lamps alight and protecting the shipping in that terrible storm."

"I want to hear the part where she rescues the hens—"

He'd already told that part of the story, but Ryan repeated it, and Emily sent him a grateful look. There was something intimate about sharing a thought that came with no words, and her chest warmed as she turned back to her sauce. She could feel his eyes on her, feel him watching every movement as she stirred the sauce until it was smooth and perfect.

"I love the sound of the rain on the roof," she said. "Close your eyes and listen."

Lizzy closed her eyes. "It sounds like an army with heavy boots."

Emily smiled. "It does." She looked at Ryan. His jaw was dark with stubble, his hair curling slightly from the rain. She wanted so badly to touch it, to slide her fingers into it and drag his mouth down to hers as she had the night before. The atmosphere was heavy, filled with unspoken need, the silence eloquent. His smile was intimate and deeply personal, and her response to that smile was so powerful it was hard to breathe through it.

She'd never realized that not touching could be so arousing.

He must have felt the same way because he shifted slightly in his seat.

Lizzy opened her eyes and tightened her grip like a monkey. "I don't want you to go."

"I'm not going anywhere." His voice was husky. "But I need to help Emily, so will you cuddle Cocoa? She hates storms, too."

Distracted by this new responsibility, Lizzy scrambled under the table with Cocoa.

Emily's heart rate quickened as Ryan stood next to her. He

covered her hand with his and stirred the sauce, his mouth close to her ear

"I'm hungry."

She didn't dare look at him. "The food won't be long."

"That isn't going to help me." His voice shimmered with wry humor.

The urge to kiss him was almost unbearable, and she wondered how she was going to make it through an evening without being allowed to touch him.

"Ryan?" Lizzy's voice came from under the table, making them both jump.

He kept his eyes on Emily's face. "Yeah?"

"You should hug Emily, too, in case she's scared."

"Oh!" Flustered, Emily almost dropped the spoon. "There isn't any need—"

"Great idea." Ryan removed the spoon from her hand, slid his arm around her and pulled her against him. "Are you scared, Emily?"

She placed her hand on his chest, intending to make a flippant remark and push him away, but she could feel the steady beat of his heart against her palm, and instead of pulling back she curved her hand up to his shoulder.

"I'm not afraid of storms," she said quietly.

"But you're afraid of other things." His voice was low, and she knew this conversation was no longer for Lizzy's benefit.

She was afraid. Not of the storm and not of him, but of her own feelings.

His cheek brushed against her hair, and she could feel the warmth of his hand low on her spine. She was pressed against thick, hard masculine pressure, and desire blurred her vision and her thoughts. It was obvious that his frustration matched hers. She wanted his mouth on hers so badly she almost dragged his head to hers right there and then.

The effort of holding back simply increased the erotic intensity of the moment.

Every sense was exaggerated. She could hear the relentless patter of rain on the roof and the soft bubbling of the sauce on the stove. She felt the warmth of his breath on her neck and the slow stroke of his fingers on her spine.

His hand cupped her cheek, and when she looked into his eyes she saw heat and raw desire.

She'd never wanted anything or anyone as badly as she wanted him.

Her stomach tightened.

His mouth was so close to hers he was almost touching her.

"Emily?" Lizzy's voice came from under the table where she was still playing with Cocoa. "I can smell burning."

The moment was broken.

They rescued the sauce, and later, much later, after a supper of mac and cheese followed by blueberry pie, Emily tucked Lizzy into bed.

The thunder had moved on, leaving only the rain, and Emily flicked on the tiny lamp by Lizzy's bed. "I'm going to leave the door open, so if you want me you just have to call out."

"Will you be downstairs?"

"The whole time. I'll be able to hear you."

"Will Ryan be there, too?"

"For a while, but then he'll be going home."

"I like it when he's here. I wish he could stay."

I wish he could stay, too.

"He has to go home." Emily tucked the patchwork quilt around the little girl and the bear. "And you need to go to sleep."

"Maybe he could do a sleepover one night, like I did with Summer and Harry."

Emily felt her tummy tighten. "We'll talk about that another time."

"Can Cocoa sleep on my bed tonight in case the storm comes back?"

"I'll ask Ryan."

"Can we swim in the sea again tomorrow?"

The questions were endless, a ruse to postpone the moment when Emily left the room.

"It depends on the weather." She sat on the edge of the bed and stroked Lizzy's hair. "Are you still scared? I could sit with you if you like."

"No." Lizzy's eyes were drifting shut. "I'm going to think about Abbie in the storm. She was brave."

"She was."

"Emily?"

She paused, waiting for another question. "Yes?"

"I love you."

Caught off guard, Emily felt her heart miss a beat and the breath jam in her throat.

It hadn't been a question, but still a declaration like that demanded a response and how was she going to respond?

Of all the things that scared her in life, this scared her the most.

More even than walking into the sea and swimming.

She thought of what Ryan had said about fear. She thought of Abbie keeping the lamps burning in the storm.

And then she closed her eyes and took the leap. "I love you, too."

"Is SHE ASLEEP?" Ryan offered her a beer, but Emily shook her head and walked to the window, her expression dazed. "What's wrong?"

"Everything." She wrapped her arms around herself, staring straight ahead. "I've lived my whole life trying to stop this happening."

Ryan put his hands on her shoulders and turned her to face him. "What?"

"She told me she loved me." Her voice shook slightly, and he saw emotion shimmer in those green eyes, along with something else.

"And that scared the hell out of you."

"Yes." She took a deep breath. "I can't do this, Ryan. I don't want this."

"You don't want her to love you? You're scared because she's putting all her trust in you, depending on you?"

There was a long silence, and then she lifted her face to his. "No, I'm scared because I love her back."

"Emily—"

"She's been with me for a matter of weeks, and I was so sure I had this under control."

"Feelings are the hardest thing in life to control."

She raked shaking fingers through her hair. "What am I going to do?"

"Same thing everyone else does. You're going to take life a day at a time, enjoy the good parts and deal with the bad."

"The bad broke me."

"You were a child and you were alone. You're not alone now." He pulled her against him and lowered his mouth to hers. "Tell me why you ran out on me this morning."

"I needed to pick up Lizzy."

"Next time, wake me." He kissed her and heard her moan softly. "How soon do you think Lizzy will want to go for another sleepover?"

"Not for a while."

"In that case I am going to be taking a lot of cold swims in the sea." He lifted his head and smoothed her hair back, searching her face. "Do you regret it?"

She shook her head. "Do you?"

It had been the best sex of his life. "No." He could feel her curves against him and had to use all his willpower not to strip her naked and press her back against the sofa. "But Kirsti saw you leaving, and I had to endure half an hour of questions, none of which I answered."

"Oops. Awkward."

"Not really. I'm immune to Kirsti. Let me know when you and Lizzy want to go out on the boat again."

"You'd take her again?"

"Of course. Why wouldn't I?"

She gave him a long look. "I guess I'm a little surprised. You make no secret of the fact your preference is for a child-free life."

"I'm suggesting a boat trip, not inviting her to move in. I like Lizzy. She's been through a trauma, and I know how that feels. And it's the only way I can spend time with you."

There was nothing more to it than that.

He had no idea why people insisted on making things more complicated than they were.

CHAPTER FIFTEEN

THE REGENERATION OF Summer Scoop took place the following weekend.

Lisa had bought the paint and supplies, and Ryan had managed to enlist an army of volunteers from the students who frequented the island over the summer months. They arrived in a minivan emblazoned with the logo of the Marine Center, ready to pitch in for the reward of free ice cream.

Skylar, who had flown in for the weekend, put herself in charge of the interior. She'd discarded the option of plain walls in favor of a mural. She and Lisa had pored over designs, before finally agreeing on an ocean theme.

"It needs puffins," Lizzy had announced firmly, and so puffins had been added to the design.

Skylar had given all three children paintbrushes and small pots of paint, and put them in charge of painting the sand under her strict supervision.

"She should be a teacher," Rachel murmured as she joined the group outside, painting the exterior. "I'm going to try and tempt her to do a few weeks at Camp Puffin next summer."

Years of weathering and chipped paint vanished under several coats of glossy blue that added cheer to the front of Summer Scoop.

Lisa had bought wrought-iron bistro tables and chairs from an online auction site and was busy cleaning them up. "I bought them from a lady in Bar Harbor who is moving to live with her daughter in Canada."

"They're fantastic." Emily watched with half an eye as Lizzy painstakingly added to the sand. "Did you talk to Doug about lowering the rent?"

"Yes. I said exactly what you said I should say and he agreed."

"I thought he might."

"I can't thank you enough." Lisa wiped her forehead on her forearm. "Finally, I feel as if there might be hope. Without you I think I would have given up."

"You wouldn't have."

"I certainly wouldn't have thought of all this. And I wouldn't have been able to persuade everyone to help."

"That was Ryan. He always says that islanders can be the most irritating people alive until you're in need, and then they're the best."

"He's right. And your friend Skylar is a talented artist."

Emily glanced across to Skylar who was painting a puffin on the rock. "Yes. Her career is taking off. She has an exhibition in London in December."

"Jewelry?"

"Among other things. She's produced some stunning glass sculptures inspired by photos a colleague of Brittany's sent her from Greece. Lily is an expert in Minoan ceramics, and Sky has been working with her. This new collection will be a modern take on ancient artifacts or something. The colors were inspired by Greek islands so lots of swirling blue and white. She's calling it *Ocean Blue*."

"Does she have a studio?"

"She rents space in another artist's studio. He's a glass artist."

Her friend had confided that Richard hadn't seemed pleased

either with the amount of time Skylar was spending in the studio, or her growing success.

Emily wished they'd had more time to talk about that, but in between entertaining Lizzy and giving Summer Scoop a face-lift, there hadn't been time to explore the personal.

They worked through the day, pausing just long enough to eat the pizzas Ryan ordered from the Ocean Club.

While Lisa supervised the children, Emily sat on one of the chairs next to Ryan.

"Why is it that whenever I see you there are a million people around?" He spoke in an undertone, and she glanced at the small crowd who were transforming Summer Scoop.

"They're working miracles."

"Leave Lizzy with Lisa, come back to my place and I'll work some miracles of my own."

She felt her cheeks warm. "I'm helping the community."

"I'm a member of the community, too." He pushed the pizza toward her. "And talking of that, an oceanfront cottage has come up at the Puffin Retirement Community."

She paused, a slice of pizza in her hand. "Are you thinking about Agnes?"

"I'm not thinking about it—she is. She's struggling to cope in Harbor House. The truth is the house is too big for her, and it's hard for her to see her friends. She's been thinking about next steps. She's asked me to take her to see it on Monday."

"Doesn't Hilda already live there?"

"Yes. That's part of the reason Gran wants to move. To be closer to her friends."

"And you don't want her to go? It upsets you that she is thinking of leaving the house. You feel you should be able to do something to keep her there."

"She's lived there most of her life."

"But people's lives change, their needs change. What was right for a person five years ago or even a year ago, might not be right now." She realized that she could have been talking about herself.

"She loves that house. Even on days when her arthritis is bad, she loves sitting and watching the boats and the people coming and going on the ferry. I'm worried she's thinking of leaving because she doesn't want to be a burden to me."

"Have you tried asking her what she really wants?"

"She wouldn't give me a straight answer."

"She might if you were honest with her. I think you should take her to see it. I think you should keep your mouth zipped, let her look around and do what she needs to do to make a decision. Then you should talk. This isn't about you, Ryan. It's not about what you're doing or not doing. It's about what she needs and wants."

They returned to the painting, and finally, as the sun was dipping down over the horizon, they finished. Lisa stood back and admired the freshly painted frontage with the new sign and the beautiful mural visible through the large window.

"I love it. I might cry."

"Don't cry," Ryan drawled. "I hate bawling women."

Emily noticed his eyes narrow slightly as Jared looped his arm around Rachel's shoulders and kissed her on the head. "She's an adult now," she said quietly, and he pulled a face.

"I know. I still want to kick his ass for kissing my sister."

"She looks happy."

"She's too trusting. And if he breaks her heart I *will* kick his ass." He frowned. "Oops. Lizzy is crying. Someone is tired. Do you want me to——?"

"No. I'll go to her." Concerned, Emily scooped up Lizzy and knew immediately something wasn't right. She put her hand on the child's forehead and frowned. "You're burning up. Are you not feeling well? Lisa, I'm sorry, I'm going to have to take her home."

"Of course. Thank you for everything. Do you have medicine? It's probably just a cold or something. Give me a call later and let me know how she is."

Ryan walked with Emily to the car. "I guess we'll have to postpone that romantic night."

"She was fine when she woke up, and she was painting happily all day. It's come on very suddenly." She pressed her hand to Lizzy's forehead again and felt a flash of unease. She was relieved Skylar was staying another night. It would be moral support.

"Give her lots of fluids." Ryan opened the car door for her. "Don't let her overheat, and if you're worried get in touch with the medical clinic. You have the number?"

"Stuck to the fridge."

"If you're worried, call me. I'd come back with you, but we have a wedding at the Ocean Club tomorrow and things are a little crazy."

"We're fine, Ryan." She strapped Lizzy into her seat. "I should go."

She closed the door, and Ryan put an arm on either side of her, caging her. "As soon as Lizzy is better, we need to arrange another sleepover."

For a moment she thought he was going to kiss her right there in public, but then he pulled away and she saw Skylar walking toward them, loaded down with art materials.

"Have I kept you waiting? I was taking photographs of the mural for my website. How's poor Lizzy?"

"Feverish." Emily knew she was going to be answering a hundred questions from her friend the moment they were on their own. "I'm going to get her home."

"Keep her cool," Ryan advised. "Don't let her overheat." He stood back so that Emily could slide into the driver's seat. "I'm sure she'll be better tomorrow."

TOMORROW CAME AND Lizzy was worse. She was restless and fractious all morning, and by the time Emily dropped Skylar at the airport at lunchtime her temperature was high.

Skylar stared up at the sky. "Storm blowing in. I wish I could stay, but I have a meeting with the gallery. They've sold some of my pieces and need more, and I really have to do some work on my collection for the exhibition in December."

"Of course you can't stay. We'll be fine. It's just a cold, I'm sure." She ignored the uneasy twinge in her stomach that told her it was something more.

She was a worrier, so she had to counteract that by forcing herself to be rational.

All the same she was up all night, checking Lizzy and keeping her cool. By morning, Lizzy was worse, not better. It was when Emily was changing her soaked T-shirt for the second time that she noticed the rash.

Icy calm, shaking, she bundled her into the car along with Andrew and drove her to the medical clinic, telling herself that it was probably just a virus, that kids got sick all the time and then got better again. Taking no chances, she called ahead to warn the clinic that she was coming.

She badly wanted to call Ryan, but she knew he'd spent his formative years dealing with this sort of thing and now avoided it. And anyway, today was the day he was taking Agnes to see the retirement home. He already had enough demands on his time.

The threatened storm had been building for days, and huge angry clouds hovered above them. Out in the bay the sea bounced and foamed with anger. By the time Emily reached the medical clinic, fat raindrops were pelting the car.

The nurse practitioner was busy, but one of the physicians who covered the clinic on a periodic basis was available.

Emily almost stumbled as she gave Lizzy's full name, reluctant to disclose her identity even to a medical professional bound to keep such details confidential.

If the doctor was surprised to find the daughter of Lana Fox on a remote island in Maine, she kept the thought to herself.

It took her less than five minutes to decide Lizzy should be transferred to the hospital on the mainland.

"My instinct is that it's just a virus. Her throat is clear, her ears look fine, and normally I'd suggest waiting a few hours. But we have bad weather coming in, and I don't want you trapped here with no access to a higher-level of medical care if she gets worse, especially as I can't find an obvious source for the infection."

Emily felt her stomach lurch. The fact that the doctor was sufficiently concerned to suggest a transfer to the mainland snapped the leash on her anxiety.

She wished she'd had the foresight to pack a bag.

And she wished yet again that Ryan were here.

While Lizzy lay, eyes closed, Emily pulled the doctor to one side. "I'm worried that it could be meningitis. Please, tell me I'm overreacting."

The doctor hesitated a few seconds longer than was reassuring. "That's just one of the options on the list. There are many others. I think it's unlikely, but she has a high temperature and a rash so I have to treat it as a possibility until we've ruled it out. I'm going to give her an injection. The hospital will be able to do more tests. Try not to worry."

Emily wondered why doctors said that when it was clearly asking the impossible. "What can I do?"

"Stay here while I call them. You'll be more comfortable here than in the waiting room, and you're my last patient."

As the door closed behind her, Emily was engulfed by silence.

Looking at Lizzy's listless form, anxiety overwhelmed her. Her heart, protected for so long, was exposed and vulnerable.

Desperate to hear Ryan's voice, she pulled her phone out of her bag and was dialing his number when the doctor walked back into the room.

The phone slipped back into her bag, forgotten.

"I've spoken to the pediatric department on the mainland, and, given the weather forecast and the lack of facilities here on the island, they want you to come in. They're expecting you."

Emily stood up, on legs that felt more like water than flesh and bone. "I'll take the ferry."

"The last ferry left early because of the storm. There won't be another crossing today."

"Can we fly out?"

"Island Air has grounded all flights." The doctor hesitated. "There is a private pilot willing to take you, but it's your decision."

In Emily's mind there was no decision to be made. "Where can I find him?"

"Up at the airfield, but you need to hurry. The winds are increasing. Is there anything you need before you go? Anyone you want to call to be with you?"

She thought about Ryan, taking Agnes to the home. She thought about Skylar, back in Manhattan and Brittany digging somewhere in Crete.

She was on her own with this.

Emily looked at the bear in Lizzy's arms. "We have the essential items."

The doctor handed Emily a letter. "Give this to the doctors. My number is on there, so they can call me. The pilot's name is Zachary Flynn."

Zach.

The man who had broken Brittany's heart.

The man whose photo had been stuck on Brittany's wall for those first few months of college, so that they could all draw on it.

A million objections crowded her brain, and in among them was the fact that Zach was a man not known for being reliable.

Why was he prepared to fly when no one else was?

The doctor was still talking. "I'll arrange for an ambulance to meet you when you land and transfer you to the hospital."

Despite her panic, Emily forced herself to drive carefully on the slick roads. The filthy weather had driven the tourists indoors, so she encountered very little traffic on her way to the airfield on the north of the island.

Glancing in her rearview mirror, she checked on Lizzy who was lying with her eyes closed, her face flushed with fever.

The wind buffeted her car, and rain almost obscured her view. What if even Zach decided it was too dangerous to fly? What if the weather transpired against them and trapped them here?

Creating disaster in her head, she parked, grabbed her bag and scooped Lizzy out of her seat, knowing that every second she waited increased the risk that Zach would decide he didn't need to risk his neck for a woman and a child that weren't his responsibility.

From what Brittany had told them, he wasn't big on responsibility or social conscience.

The plane sat on the runway, small and insignificant compared to the driving force of the weather.

Emily glanced at the wild, foaming fury of the sea, so different now from the still calm that had allowed her to swim with Lizzy only days before. Struggling to walk against the wind, she realized how tired she was. After two nights with virtually no sleep, her legs threatened to give way.

"I've got her." She heard a deep, male voice through the relentless howl of the wind and felt strong arms lift Lizzy from her.

Only when they were safely inside did she allow herself to look at the man she was entrusting with their lives, and decided that the photo Brittany had pinned to the wall all those years ago hadn't done him justice. Years had passed, of course, but muscles and maturity had only improved Zachary Flynn.

There was a daredevil gleam in his eyes that she would have expected to see in a man who had tempted her friend to throw away everything for love. There was also hardness, a toughness that suggested he knew more about life than most people ever would. Brittany had told them his childhood had been bad, but they'd all agreed that nothing excused the way he'd treated Brittany.

And now here was Emily, needing him, relying on him.

She felt like a traitor.

"Strap in," he ordered. "It's going to be rough up there."

Reciting apologies to Brittany in her head, she did as he ordered. "But visibility is good?"

"Yeah. That's because we have a hell of a crosswind. Wind gives great visibility."

Digesting the news that the visibility was bad news, not good, Emily sank back in her seat. "But you're confident? You think it's safe to fly?"

His gaze flickered to Lizzy. "I'll get you there safely, but you're going to be shaken up some."

She sensed from his low drawl that it was an understatement and took her eyes off Lizzy long enough to glare at him.

"I just hope you're a better pilot than you were a husband." The words left her mouth before she could debate the wisdom of antagonizing the man responsible for their lives.

He gave her a long, steady look and then turned back to the controls without comment.

Emily breathed deeply, hoping this wasn't going to turn out to be the worst decision of her life.

She heard him talking over the radio, but she had no anxiety to spare for the pilot or the fate of the plane. Everything was focused on Lizzy who lay with her eyes still closed.

She felt another lurch of fear.

Was it going to happen again?

Was she going to love, only to have the person she loved ripped away from her?

She barely noticed the plane lifting off, gave no thought to the yawning expanse of the bay or the hungry bite of the wind, both ready to consume a small plane in a moment if the pilot made any mistakes.

Zach made no mistakes.

The flight was bumpy, but Emily was too occupied with Lizzy to dwell on the possibility of plummeting into the ocean. If she hadn't been so worried, she would have thanked him for what she was sure was flawless and courageous flying. But there was no room for anything in her head but the panic.

They landed smoothly, and from there it was a short transfer by ambulance to the medical center where the pediatric team was waiting.

Lying in the room, surrounded by medical equipment, Lizzy opened her eyes. She looked ridiculously small and vulnerable. "Are you going to leave me here?"

"No." Emily was appalled she would even think it. "I'm not going anywhere."

"My mom always left if I was sick. She didn't want to catch anything. She said being ill made her ugly."

"I'm right here and I'm staying right here." Emily felt an ache in her chest, and she took the little girl's hand. "I won't leave you."

"Where's Ryan? I want Ryan."

The pitiful plea shot straight through Emily's heart, and her only thought was *me, too.*

"He can't be here, sweetie."

It shocked her just how badly she wanted him to be.

The doctor wrote something on a chart. "Is there someone you need us to call? If you give us this Ryan's number we can contact him."

"No. He's—" How to describe their relationship? "He's just a friend." A friend with other commitments. Other priorities. "There's no one."

The doctor accepted that and then sat down to take a medical history.

Emily realized how impossible this was. How had she ever thought Lizzy's past could be kept a secret? "I don't know much about her history," she admitted. Left with no choice, she briefly told the doctor all she knew.

"So you don't know the identity of Juliet's father?"

"No. And I know nothing about her health as a child, although the lawyers did give me details on her vaccinations."

"Do you have those?"

Emily pulled the papers out of her bag, telling herself that it was ridiculous to be concerned that they knew Lizzy's identity. The medical team had to know. And everything here was confidential, wasn't it?

"We need to take blood, Miss Donovan. If you'd rather wait outside—"

"I'm staying." She didn't even let him finish the suggestion. "You can work around me." She kept hold of Lizzy's hand, talking to her about the puffins, Ryan and the twins, anything to distract her while the medical team worked.

The next few hours were a blur of tests, bright lights and beeping machines. Of needles, sterility and stress.

Lizzy barely reacted, her eyes closed, the blotches on her skin vivid against the white background.

The walls were covered in a mural, a farm scene, and Emily stared blankly at brightly colored fields until the white dollops of paint started to look more like clouds with legs than sheep.

Her eyes were gritty and her head throbbed.

Staff came and went. Emily desperately wanted reassurance, but no one had answers for her questions.

At one point a nurse dimmed the lights, gave Emily a blanket and advised her to sleep, but she was too afraid to close her eyes, so she curled up in the chair, holding Lizzy's hand in hers.

Outside the wind howled and whipped the rain against the window, and she recited *Green Eggs and Ham* quietly, wondering how her life could have changed so much in less than a month.

She thought about the night she'd arrived, and how much she'd wanted to return to the safe, predictable life she'd carefully constructed for herself. She'd struggled against it, but gradually her new life had peeled away the layers of protection she'd worn for so long.

She'd believed that having Lizzy was the worst thing that could have happened to her, but it had turned out to be the best.

Despite her attempts to stay awake, she must have dozed for a little while, and when she opened her eyes Lizzy was looking at her.

"Why are you sleeping in a chair?"

"I didn't want to leave you." Groggy, Emily shook off the fog of sleep and felt Lizzy's chest. Her skin was cool to touch, and the rush of relief was so acute her eyes stung with tears. "How are you feeling?"

"I had a bad dream."

"Oh, baby—" Emily scooped her into her arms and held her. "You're safe. I'm here. I'll always be here."

"Why doesn't Ryan come? I love Ryan."

Emily held her tightly. Cold spread across her skin and penetrated her heart, and she realized with a rush of alarm that she'd made a mistake letting Ryan become so closely entangled in their lives. She'd only thought about herself, not Lizzy. Their relationship was fun, but she knew that for him it ended there. He didn't want the responsibility of anything more.

"I know you like Ryan a lot."

"I don't like him, I love him. And he loves me. He reads to me, and he takes me to see the puffins. He taught me knots. He's going to teach me to sail this summer. He promised."

Guilt sucked her down like water in a whirlpool. How did you explain to a child of six that a man had other things to do with his time?

She stroked the child's hair, trying to calm her. "There are lots of people on the island who can teach you to sail. Rachel, for instance."

"I want Ryan to do it. I love Ryan and so do you."

"That's not true." How could the words of a child cause this sudden feeling of panic? "I like Ryan a lot, but I don't love him."

"Yes, you do. He makes you smile. That day on the beach when you were sick, he took care of you. And he taught you to swim. You wanted him to do it and no one else."

"I—"

"Rachel says it's because you trust him. And that's why you wanted him to take us in his boat."

"Trust, yes. But not love." Emily's mouth was dry. She told herself children said things they didn't understand. "I don't love him."

"Why doesn't he come?"

"Because he doesn't know you're in the hospital."

"He'd want to know." She said it firmly, and Emily forced herself to breathe slowly.

"It's complicated, Lizzy. When you're older, I'll explain it to you."

"I already know why."

"You do?"

"Yes. It's because he's scared of hospitals. He said so."

"That isn't why. We're his friends, Lizzy, but we're not his family. He doesn't love us in that way."

"Skylar says friends can be better than family. She says you, she and Brittany are like sisters."

"That's true, we are, but—" How did you explain this to a child? "That isn't the way it is with Ryan. He has other people in his life to think about. He's taking his grandmother to look at somewhere new to live today. She'll be able to tell us all about it when we see her next."

"I already know. She wants a house that isn't so big." Lizzy's face crumpled. "I want Ryan. I want him to tell me the story about Abbie and the hens."

"As soon as we're back home, I'll ask him to come and tell you the story." She stroked Lizzy's hair and then looked up as a nurse came into the room. "She just woke up. She feels cooler."

The nurse checked the reading. "Her temperature is down. That's a good sign."

Emily was willing to grab any piece of good news. "What happens now?"

"We wait for these results, but she seems to have turned a corner."

Emily discovered she wasn't good at waiting.

While Lizzy slept and nurses walked in and out of the room checking her temperature and the rate of the IV, she sat there thinking about Ryan and everything Lizzy had said.

It was true that she'd asked him to teach her to swim and take them out on the boat, but that was because he understood her situation.

And the sex had been incredible, but it was still just sex, and she wasn't going to make the mistake of thinking it meant more than it did.

The door opened, and Emily glanced up, expecting it to be one of the doctors, but it was Ryan who stood in the doorway. His hair was sleek from the rain, his shirt clinging to his broad shoulders.

Seeing him there brought a rush of pure emotion. Elation. Relief. And something far deeper and infinitely more terrifying. She could hear Lizzy's words in her head.

You love him. You love Ryan.

Heart pounding, she managed to speak. "What are you doing here?"

He strode into the room scattering droplets of rain. "You're in the hospital. Where did you think I'd be? How sick is she?"

"Ryan!" Disturbed by the noise, Lizzy opened her eyes and her face brightened. "You came."

"I would have come sooner if I'd known." He walked straight to the bed, put down the large bag he was carrying and sat next to Lizzy. "Hi, tiger. What have you been doing to yourself?"

"I'm sick."

"I can see that." He picked up the bear. "And how is Andrew? Did he get sick on the flight over?"

Lizzy managed her first smile for days. "I held him all the way."

"You need to get well fast because the puffins miss you. And talking of puffins—" he reached into the bag and pulled out a stuffed puffin, complete with brightly colored felt beak "—I thought Andrew might like company." He snuggled it next to her as the door opened and a nurse walked in.

She frowned when she saw Ryan. "Relatives only."

"I'm a relative." Cool and self-assured, Ryan didn't budge, and the nurse looked at him curiously.

"Are you Ryan by any chance?" Her severe expression softened when he nodded. "She's been asking for you. Maybe now you're here you can persuade Emily to go and eat something. She hasn't left the room since she arrived."

"I didn't want to." Emily stayed firmly in the chair, trying to understand what was going on. He claimed not to want the attachment of a family, and yet he'd flown through filthy weather to get here.

She tried to work it out, but her brain wasn't functioning properly. She was so tired she wondered if she'd even have the ability to stand up when the moment came. Her short nap in the chair had made her feel worse, not better, as if the taste of sleep had reminded her brain what she'd been missing. Now that the danger had passed, the adrenaline that had kept her going vanished, taking energy with it.

"I wanted you to come," Lizzy said sleepily, "but Emily said you wouldn't because you don't love us the way we love you."

Oh, crap.

Meeting Ryan's questioning gaze, Emily felt herself turn scarlet. "The fever has made her very confused."

"I'm not confused," Lizzy murmured. "Do you love us, Ryan?"

Emily held her breath. How on earth was he going to deal with a question like that?

"Of course I love you." He didn't miss a beat. "You think I'd endure a ride in that bumpy plane if I didn't love you?"

"You see?" A satisfied smile curved at the corners of Lizzy's mouth. "I told you."

Emily felt a wash of cold spread over her skin. His answer was designed to soothe but he was making things worse, not better. He was using words like a comfort blanket, wrapping them around a sick child. What would happen when the blanket was ripped away and the child was left freezing and shivering? "Lizzy—"

"Are you scared?" Lizzy was still looking at Ryan.

"Scared?"

"You said you were scared of hospitals." Her eyes closed. "You can hold my hand. I'm not scared of hospitals, only storms. I'm glad you're here. I wanted you to tell me about Abbie and the hens." But she was already asleep, and Emily sat, thinking about the way she'd felt when Ryan had walked into the room.

It was as if the sun had come out in her life.

The nurse put her hand on her shoulder. "She's going to be fine. The doctor will be here in an hour to talk to you. Why don't you go and get a cup of coffee? I'll be right here, and if she wakes, I'll call you. There's no need to look so anxious."

Yes, there was, because Lizzy was right.

She was in love with Ryan.

CHAPTER SIXTEEN

IT WAS TRUE that he hated hospitals. He hated them so much he could hardly bring himself to walk into one. Something about the paint and the clinical smell took him right back to those months after his injury. As soon as he stepped through the door it came rushing back. The white light of the explosion, the pain and the sick empty feeling that came from knowing Finn wasn't in the hospital with him. Normally he blocked it out, but not today. Today the memories were playing like a movie in his head. The pitch-black of the helicopter, the rattle and sway, the bouncing beam of light from the headlamp of the flight medic. And the pain. Unimaginable pain.

Hoping they discharged Lizzy fast, he coaxed two cups of coffee from a temperamental machine and took them back to the waiting room.

Emily was standing in front of the window, staring into space.

Shock, he thought. Shock and exhaustion.

"Here—" He handed her the coffee. Remembering the last time she'd keeled over, he put his own down on the table. "Why the hell didn't you call me?"

She looked at him blankly, like someone emerging from a

long coma, seeing the world for the first time. "It wasn't your responsibility."

He remembered the sharp kick of fear he'd felt when he'd heard about their white-knuckle flight across the bay to the hospital, about the sleepless night he'd had waiting for the wind to die down sufficiently for him to make the crossing to the mainland. His mind had conjured a dozen nightmare scenarios, all of which involved Emily coping alone with a steadily deteriorating Lizzy. By the time he'd arrived at the hospital he'd almost caused casualties in his haste to reach her bedside.

Only when he'd seen Lizzy, awake and improving, did his own feelings about hospitals resurrect themselves.

He picked up his coffee, noticing with a twinge of wry humor that his hands were shaking.

Jesus, he couldn't even walk into a hospital without falling apart. He was meant to be supporting Emily, and he was in a worse state than she was.

What a hero.

Her silence was starting to disturb him. Retrieving his journalistic skills, he tried to think like her. Tried to get into her head. She'd be scared. Scared of losing another child. Of letting her down. "You're doing a brilliant job, Emily. You're taking good care of her."

Still there was no reaction, and he wondered if she'd even heard him.

"You're not going to lose her, Emily. She's going to be just fine. Kids get sick fast, and then they recover fast. The same thing happened when Rachel was young. You don't need to panic."

But she didn't seem to be panicking. She looked numb. Catatonic.

"It was Zach who called me." He ignored the fact that he seemed to be having a conversation with himself, and finally she stirred.

"Why would he call you?"

He couldn't believe she'd asked that question. "I guess he heard the rumor that you'd left my apartment wearing the same dress you'd worn to dinner and thought I might like to know." If she'd picked up on the dig that she should have been the one to call him, there were no visible signs of it.

"He was brave. Please, thank him from me."

"He's a gifted pilot."

She didn't argue. "Does Brittany know that he's back on the island yet?"

"I don't know. I still haven't told her. Who knows how long he'll stay, and she isn't here anyway, so why bring it up?" The last time he'd interfered with their relationship he'd made things worse. "Why the hell are we talking about Zach and Brittany? They're both old enough to sort out their own relationship. The fact that they don't is their business, not ours. Are you going to drink that coffee?"

She sipped mindlessly and pulled a face. "You put sugar in it?"

"You need the energy, and this stuff tastes disgusting with or without sugar. When did you last eat?"

"I'm not hungry."

He was willing to bet she hadn't slept, either. Looking at the dark shadows under her eyes, he decided she was too tired to be able to decide whether to move forward or backward.

She'd been going through torture, and she'd been going through it alone.

Anger and frustration simmered beneath his own layers of tension. "Hell, Emily, why didn't you call me? We're friends."

Her gaze flickered to his and away again. "We are friends. And as a friend, I respect your boundaries."

"Boundaries?" He lowered his voice. "You talk to me about boundaries after what we did in bed together the other night?"

"That's different. This was a problem, and it wasn't yours to deal with."

She was the one who was different, and he had no idea why.

Was it tiredness? The stress and anxiety of coping alone? Worry about Lizzy?

He decided the hospital was driving them both crazy, and the sooner he got them both home to Puffin Island, the better.

THEY KEPT LIZZY in the hospital for another twenty-four hours.

Despite Emily's protestations, Ryan insisted on returning the following morning to drive them back to the island.

She'd suffered another sleepless night, but this time her concerns were for herself as well as Lizzy. How had she managed to fall in love? She didn't understand how it had happened. All she knew was that she had to reverse the feeling fast. She had to fall out of love with him, and, more important, she had to help Lizzy fall out of love with him, too.

"So, the final verdict was a virus?" He slid behind the wheel. "*Virus* is a word doctors use when they don't have a clue what's going on."

Exhausted, Emily fought the urge to rest her throbbing head against those wide shoulders.

"They don't really know what it was, but it wasn't meningitis, and she's on the mend, so that's all that matters."

Now that the immediate panic about Lizzy had passed, she knew she had to think about the future. She'd woken up to the mistakes she'd made. Her mind was trying to make sense of it all, but the stress of the past few days caught up with her, and the smooth purr of the engine rocked her to sleep.

She woke as they drove off the ferry along with carloads of summer visitors.

John, the harbormaster, waved them over, and Ryan pulled up.

"She's doing fine, John."

"Good to know." Needing to check for himself, John stepped forward and looked at Lizzy. The smile spread along his weathered face. "We missed you, pumpkin. Ryan has been keeping us updated. Wait there. I have something for you." He vanished into his hut and emerged moments later holding a miniature version of the ferry, handmade and beautifully carved. "I've called her the *Captain Lizzy*. I made it in my workshop."

"For me?" Lizzy reached for it, enchanted. "It's like the *Captain Hook*. Does it float?"

"Should do. You'll have to take it down to the beach and test it. Let me know."

"Will you come?"

"To the beach?" John scratched his beard. "Maybe I will. Dora and I enjoy a walk on the sand. I appreciate the invitation."

"Look." Lizzy leaned forward to show Emily, and she examined the boat, marveling at the detail. There was a ramp that lifted and lowered and a little chain that fastened across the back.

"It's perfect. Thank you, John." She admired the craftsmanship, touched by the sentiment as much as the hours he'd obviously spent. She remembered how afraid of him she, Sky and Brittany had been.

As Ryan drove away, she mentioned it to him. "We used to be scared of him."

"Plenty of folk are. It's a trick he uses to stop people messing around near the ferry."

"I thought Lizzy had driven him crazy asking questions."

"John loves anyone who shows interest in the *Captain Hook*." He eased the car along the crowded roads. "And you're an honorary islander."

"Because I'm staying in Brittany's cottage?"

"Not just because of that. You've contributed to the community. Not only have you earned Hilda's approval, but Summer Scoop's business has doubled in the past few days. And all the islanders were worried about Lizzy. I couldn't walk down the street without being accosted for information, so in the end I had Kirsti put out a tweet on the Ocean Club Twitter account. Hope you don't mind." He slowed for a group of tourists who were loaded down with beach bags and coolers. "It's the silly season."

"This is why the business has doubled. It's the summer crowd."

"Not true. You had some great ideas."

"What's it like on the island in winter?"

"Quiet. I love it, although obviously the weather can be brutal. It can also be fun. I'll take you snowmobiling."

He was making the assumption she'd still be here in the winter.

Realizing they were leaving the harbor, Emily reached for her purse. "Could you take me via the airfield? I need to pick up my car."

"Jared drove it home for you yesterday."

"Jared?"

"The guy who is dating my sister. The guy I'm trying not to punch."

"But I've never even met him. Why would he help me? And where did he get the keys?"

Ryan glanced at her. "You left them in the car. I guess you had other things on your mind."

"I—" She'd left them in the car? "That doesn't explain why he'd help me, a stranger."

"Apart from the fact he can't keep his hands off my sister, he's a decent guy. And as I said, you're an honorary islander." Ryan took the coast road, and Emily looked out of the window at the islands dotted around the bay.

An honorary islander.

A month ago she hadn't been able to imagine living here. Now she couldn't imagine leaving.

When she'd arrived on that first night, she would have turned around and left again had there been some way of getting across the water; but at some point leaving had ceased to be a priority. The charm of the island had sneaked up on her, like the slow merging of the seasons.

The contrast to the night of the storm was incredible. The rain had stopped, the sky had cleared and visibility was perfect. It was as if it had never happened.

When they reached Castaway Cottage, she stepped out of the car and felt the breeze on her face. The scent of salt and sea expunged the last memories of clinical sterility. Shell Cove lay in front of her, a perfect crescent of golden tones, and she wondered why she'd wasted all those summers keeping her back to the water.

She realized she didn't feel trapped or scared, she felt free. For the first time in her life, she felt as if she'd come home.

Turning back to the car, she bumped into Ryan.

"Sorry—" He put his hands on her arms to steady her, and she stood for a few seconds, disoriented by his closeness and the terrifying depths of her feelings. Her eyes were level with the tanned skin at the base of his throat and the dark stubble that shaded his jaw.

Scooping up Lizzy, she carried her to the cottage and waited while Ryan unlocked the door.

"I should have asked you to stop at the harbor so we could pick some things up."

"You won't need anything." He walked through to the kitchen, and she saw the table was heaped high with bags and parcels.

"What's all this?"

"This," Ryan said dryly, "is all courtesy of your neighbors. Welcome to Puffin Island, where everyone knows what you like to eat for dinner. And if you're in trouble, they provide it." There was humor in his eyes as he pulled open the fridge and stepped to one side, so that she could see the contents.

Emily gaped and Lizzy wriggled out of her arms.

"There's so much food!"

"There is." Emily felt weak. "Was this you? Did you do this?"

"It was everyone. The town council sent out an email to everyone and coordinated people's contributions. They thought you wouldn't want to be thinking of food for a few days while you settle back in."

"The town council emailed?"

"That's nothing. If you stay here much longer you'll be expected to give them your phone number. Then you'll get a call or a text in an emergency."

Still looking at the food in disbelief, Emily shook her head. "What sort of emergency?"

"Well, let's see—" he leaned back against the counter "—there was the time two years ago when the Ratners' barn caught fire, and they needed as many people as possible to help. Then there was the time when the power went out last January, and they needed volunteers to check on the elderly and vulnerable. It's a good way of communicating to a wide number of people in the shortest space of time."

"I'm really touched." She opened one of the bags and pulled out a doll and a pile of books for Lizzy. "That's so thoughtful." Tears thickened her throat, and she realized with a flash of horror that she was going to cry.

Tired, she thought. She was just tired, that was all.

"I need to get Lizzy to bed." Forcing herself to keep moving, she carried Lizzy up to her bedroom and tucked her in.

"Will you open the window? I want to listen to the sea."

Emily opened the window, realizing that she no longer shrank from the sound. "Better?"

"Can Ryan read me a story?"

"I think you need to sleep."

"But could I have a story first?"

Ryan, Ryan, Ryan.

"It's my turn to read to you." She sat on the edge of the bed, picked a story and started to read. Lizzy was asleep by the end of the first page.

Emily stayed for a few minutes, staring down at tumbled blond hair and vulnerability.

She'd been almost the same age when she'd lost her sister.

She'd been alone with her feelings. There had been no one to comfort her. No one to protect her.

Reaching out, she stroked the curls away from Lizzy's face and bent to kiss her.

Lizzy wasn't alone, and she was going to do her best to protect her. A few weeks earlier the responsibility had almost sent her running. Not now. Now, the fierceness, the desire to protect came not from duty but from somewhere deep inside. A place she hadn't accessed for a long time. And finally she knew what she had to do.

Ryan was in the kitchen with his back to her, staring out of the window to the garden. He turned when he heard her walk in. "The storm flattened some of the plants."

"I'll deal with it tomorrow." She looked at those broad shoulders, at his handsome face, *at the man she loved.* "Thank you for what you did. Coming to see us. Bringing us home. All this—" She glanced at the surfaces, covered in gifts and donations of food. "I'm grateful."

"I didn't do it for your gratitude." His eyes darkened. "I missed you."

Her heart bumped against her chest. "Ryan—we can't do this—"

"I know that. You're exhausted."

"I don't mean now. I mean ever. Whatever there was between us, it has to stop."

There was a long, pulsing silence. "Because you don't want a relationship?"

It was a fair question. She hadn't thought anyone would break through the layers of protection she'd woven around herself, but Ryan Cooper had managed it.

"Because *you* don't. And it isn't fair to Lizzy."

Those dark brows met in a frown. "What's between us has nothing to do with Lizzy."

"How can it have nothing to do with Lizzy? She's part of

my life, Ryan. She was asking for you just now. She wanted you to read to her."

"You should have called me. I would have been happy to read to her."

"This time." Her mouth felt as if she'd swallowed sand. "She's growing too attached to you. She asks for you all the time. Every other word is *Ryan*. In the hospital she was crying for you—"

A muscle flickered in his cheek. "You should have called me—"

"Why? You don't want that level of attachment. She's starting to expect things, and you don't want anyone to expect things from you. You've told me that often enough.".

"So you're going to tell her I won't read her a story? Is that fair?"

The words goaded her temper. She thought back to the hospital, with Lizzy sick and missing him. "What's not fair is you telling her you love her. Behaving as if she's important in your life."

"She's a sweet kid, and—"

"Yes, she's a sweet kid, but we both know you're not interested in kids, Ryan, no matter how sweet they are. You've made that perfectly clear, and I respect that, but then you confuse everything by saying you love her!"

"You're overreacting. She was sick. She needed reassurance and I gave it. It's as simple as that."

"It's not simple. Thanks to you, it's complicated! And she didn't need lies! What happens when she's well, Ryan? Have you thought about that?"

"We'll handle that when she's well."

"*I'll* be the one who has to handle it. I'll be the one who will have to answer questions about where you are and why you don't want to spend time with her. I'll be the one who has to handle a child who feels miserable and let down, who has expectations that are never met." Her voice rose. "We both know this relationship of ours is just for fun, but that isn't how she sees it. What's going to happen when you've had enough of teaching her knots and taking her to see the puffins? She's a child. She doesn't understand the complexity of adult relationships. Children need consistency. They need to know where they stand. Love can't be given and then withdrawn. It doesn't come and go like the tide. I appreciate you bringing us home. It was kind of you, but now it's over."

But instead of walking away, Ryan strode across the room and took her face in his hands. "And what about us?" His eyes demanded all the answers she wasn't voicing. "You've talked a lot about Lizzy, but what about us?"

Dreams flitted into her head, and she pushed them brutally aside.

"There is no us." She fought the temptation to slide her arms around his neck and bring her mouth to his. "I love living here. I never thought I'd feel this way about living on a small island surrounded by water, but I do. I know we can't stay in this cottage forever, but whatever we do, I don't want to leave the island. I want us to stay. I want to build a life here. I don't want things to feel awkward between us." She stared up at him, rocked by the emotion in his eyes.

"So, you're ending this because of Lizzy. What about you?"

What about her? Despite having protected herself fiercely, she'd managed to fall in love twice. First with Lizzy and then with him.

Being with him had taught her she still had the ability to love deeply, but now she had to learn to switch it off again.

"I won't compromise Lizzy's happiness for sex. Even clothes-ripping, mind-blowing, wild animal sex."

"That's what it was to you?"

"Of course."

For a moment she thought he was going to say something else, but then he stepped back, his face expressionless.

"In that case there's nothing more to say. Call me if you need anything. Puffin Island is a small community. We look out for each other."

Because she didn't trust herself not to cave in and chase after him, she turned away, watching the last drips of sunlight bathe the garden, listening to his footsteps as he walked to the door.

As it closed behind him, she flinched. And remembered exactly why she'd spent all those years making sure she didn't love.

CHAPTER SEVENTEEN

"THERE'S NOT ENOUGH storage space." Ryan slammed one door shut and dragged open another. "Murph Compton should be shot. He expects everyone to live in a damn rabbit warren, so that he can live in a mansion."

"You're describing my future home," his grandmother said mildly, "and the storage space is perfect for my needs, providing you don't break the doors before I move in."

Ryan strode moodily across the small sunny kitchen and opened another door. *What the hell had Emily meant when she'd said he'd confused Lizzy?* "The contents of one of your kitchen cupboards would fill this whole place."

"I've been clearing out. It's called downsizing."

"There's no room for a toaster on that counter."

"I didn't realize you had such an emotional connection with my toaster, but if its welfare is that important to you, then, please, consider it a gift." Agnes sighed. "What's wrong, Ryan?"

"Nothing is wrong. I just can't understand why you want to live here, that's all." He strode back through to the airy living room and tried to forget about the confrontation with Emily. The whole "cottage" would have fit into half the downstairs space at Harbor House. "Where are you going to store everything?"

"I don't intend to store anything. I intend to declutter my life. Does the thought of that make you angry?"

He looked at her blankly. "What?"

"You're angry."

"No. Yes." He thumped his fist against the wall. "She's cut me out. She doesn't want to see me again."

Agnes eyed the wall and then her grandson. "I assume we're talking about Emily."

"She says it's confusing for Lizzy. That she's getting too attached."

"I see."

"Do you? Because I don't." It had been stewing inside him since the conversation a few days earlier. "Can you believe she didn't call me when she was in the hospital?"

"I expect she didn't want to bother you. You're a busy man. A busy, *single* man."

"You could have said that without the emphasis and the look."

"Everyone has the right to make their own choices in life. You've made yours. You need to allow Emily to make hers. She's a smart woman."

Smart and sexy. "Damn it, she was on her own there. It must have half killed her to have Lizzy in the hospital and she didn't call me."

"Perhaps she didn't feel that was the nature of your relationship."

He eyed his grandmother, wondering exactly how much she knew about their relationship. "Lizzy was asking for me."

"Was she?" His grandmother looked thoughtful. "That explains a great deal."

"Does it?"

"She's afraid the child will look forward to seeing you, and the next step on from that is *expecting* to see you, and you don't want that, do you? It's one thing to take a little girl on a boat trip when it fits into your day, but you don't want to feel pressure to do it. Same goes for swimming, sailing, walking Cocoa and all those other things." Agnes opened one of the windows to let air into the room. "Better not to do them at all. That way you can be sure of protecting your personal space and making sure you live life alone, the way you prefer it. No one is ever going to want anything, expect anything or demand anything of you. You're free to go wherever the wind blows you."

Ryan looked at his grandmother in exasperation. "You're a conniving, manipulative—"

"I'm describing your life, Ryan. That's all. The life you chose. The life you want. I don't see how that makes me conniving or manipulative."

"You're trying to make me question my choices."

"If it's the right choice, then no one can make you waver. Take me as an example—" she stood back and looked around her "—you can tell me I'm making the wrong decision as many times as you like, but I'm not going to doubt myself even for a second."

"Are we talking about my life or the house? Because if it's the house, my opinion is that it's a big step. You should take some time to think about it."

"When you reach my age, you don't waste precious time letting your brain talk you out of something your heart already knows is right."

Ryan stared at her. "She made it sound as if I didn't care. As if Lizzy doesn't matter to me."

"And does she?"

"Of course! I was as worried about Lizzy as she was. And I was worried about her." And the thought of her, anxious and alone in the hospital with no one to support her had driven him demented when he'd been trapped. "I thought I'd proved that by flying through a storm to get to the hospital—a place, I might add, that makes me want to swallow alcohol in large quantities." He paced to the other side of the room which, given the distance, didn't do anything to relieve his tension. "Can we talk about something else?"

"You can talk about anything you like. I believe you were expressing your opinion on my new home." The words were infused with patience and love, and Ryan felt a rush of guilt.

"I'm sorry." He pressed his fingers to the bridge of his nose and sent her an apologetic look. "It's been a stressful few days. First, Lizzy being sick—"

"Yes, that was a worrying time for the whole island. I know people were very relieved when Kirsti put that message up at the Ocean Club."

"She had people asking her every two minutes." His insides felt ripped and raw. He wondered if it was the hospital visit that had affected his mood so profoundly. "I guess I thought Emily and I were friends."

"I'm sure you are. But Emily has been thrown into the role of mother and she's trying to protect Lizzy."

He knew how important that was to her, but he hated to think she saw him as a threat to Lizzy's happiness. "I don't see why I'm such a threat. Emily is planning on staying on the island, and I'm not going anywhere."

"I think she's more concerned about your emotional presence than your geographical location." His grandmother removed her glasses and tucked them into her purse. "Whereas you seem very concerned about my geographical location. Does it bother you where I live?"

"I guess I find it hard to imagine you living anywhere but Harbor House. You've lived there since—" He broke off, and she nodded slowly.

"Since your parents died. I know how long I've lived there, Ryan. My brain is perfectly fine. It's my joints that aren't be-having themselves. I moved in to that big old house because I had my four wonderful grandchildren to care for. You'd lost your parents, and I didn't want you to lose your home, too. But things change. Needs change. This will be better for me. I can walk as far as Hilda's cottage, and I know most of the people living here. I won't have to rely on you and Rachel for lifts."

"We don't mind."

"I mind. I already made you take too much responsibility in your life. I see that now. I made mistakes."

"That's not true."

"It is true. You'd lost your parents. Your life changed overnight, and suddenly instead of riding your bike and your skateboard, you were reading bedtime stories and learning how to braid hair. And you did a fine job. It's because of you that Rachel has kept her sweet, generous nature. You gave her the security she'd lost. You were there when she needed you, but you were a child, too, and you shouldn't have had to take that on."

Thinking of Rachel raised his stress levels. "She's seeing Jared."

"I know."

"He's a decade older than her."

"I know that, too." His grandmother straightened, rubbing her hand over her back. "She's grown up, and you have to let her make her own decisions, even if some of those decisions aren't the ones you would have made. Do you think I wanted to see you fly off to dangerous places? No." It was the first time she'd ever voiced her feelings on the subject, and he realized how selfish he'd been back then, his one and only thought to get away and live his life.

"You never said anything."

"Because it wasn't about what I wanted, it was about what you wanted. And you wanted to see the world with nothing and no one holding you back. You had so much hunger inside you. There were so many things you wanted to do. When you left this island, there was a time when I wondered if we'd see you again. You were desperate for an adventure."

"That didn't end the way I thought it would." He thought about Finn, who right at the end had decided the next adventure in his life was going to be home and family.

"When I visited you in that hospital I wished you'd chosen a different path. I went back home at night and cried, but then

I pulled out every piece you ever wrote and reminded myself how important those stories were, and I realized that if people like you weren't telling them, the rest of us wouldn't know what was happening in the world. I'm proud of you. I probably don't say that enough. You made the decision that was right for you."

"Is this your way of telling me to butt out of your decision to sell the house?"

"Who said anything about selling the house?" Agnes walked to the window and stared over the sea. "Moving feels right. Selling doesn't, and I'm in the lucky position not to have to take that step. I'm not selling Harbor House, I'm giving it to you."

Ryan couldn't have been more surprised if she'd told him she was taking up Zumba. "Me?"

"It's a family house and I rattle around. And before you say anything, I've discussed it with the twins and Rachel. They all agree this should be yours. I've never been afraid of moving on, Ryan. You shouldn't be afraid, either."

"I'm not afraid."

"No? I shouldn't be interfering when I've just told you Rachel is a grown-up who can make her own decisions, but I'm going to anyway, because the truth is, I feel responsible."

"Responsible for what?"

"For the fact that you don't have a family."

Ryan straightened his shoulders. "How can you be responsible? That's my choice."

"Do you think I don't know why you've chosen to live your life free of commitment? Do you think I don't know how it was for you? You were helping me at an age when you shouldn't have had a care in the world."

"Teenagers always have cares."

"But they are different cares. What you want to do with your future, whether you'll ever date that cool brunette in your class, whether you'll be tall enough, smart enough—"

"In other words, selfish cares."

"Normal cares. Your cares were deeper and heavier and most

of the time didn't include you. You felt as if you had a leash tied to you, and it grew tighter every year. Because of that, you saw family as something that holds you back. You've been avoiding it ever since."

"I've been living my life."

His grandmother smiled. "Having a family doesn't stop you living your life, although I can see why you would think that way after what happened. I treated you like an adult, but you were still a child. You were still working out what sort of place the world was and how you fit into it."

"It probably did me good. I needed to think about someone other than myself." And he realized he needed to do that now. "If you love this place, then that's all I need to hear. Tell me how I can help."

"I have one remaining box of Rachel's old books and toys you can take over to Emily."

He knew he wouldn't be welcome. "Just leave a message on Emily's phone. She can pick them up when she's next in town."

"She may not be in town for a while. She'll want to keep Lizzy at home until she's back on her feet. I'd like you to take it over for me. I remember when Rachel was sick, she loved having something new to play with and read."

"I can't do that." He paced to the window, staring out over the ocean as he replayed the conversation. "She's shut me out. I was going to offer to take Lizzy on the boat again. She's showing all the signs of being a natural sailor. I enjoyed teaching her."

"Help out at Camp Puffin if you want to do those things with children."

"I don't." He wanted to do them with Lizzy. He remembered the look of concentration on her face when she'd mastered her first knot, the excited gasp the first time the wind had snapped the sails tight. Most of all, he remembered her look of happiness when he'd walked into the room at the hospital.

"I don't understand why this bothers you. You love your freedom, Ryan. I would have thought you'd be feeling relieved not to be towing a little girl out to see puffins and digging in the sand."

He realized that those moments had been the happiest he'd had in a long time. Those moments, and the ones he'd spent with Emily.

"Has it occurred to you that this isn't all about me? Emily is in this relationship, too. And it's a casual relationship. She doesn't want it to be more than that. She isn't interested."

His grandmother looked at him for a long moment. "You're many things, but I never thought you were a fool, Ryan. Can you lend me your phone? I want to call Murph and tell him I'll pick up the keys tomorrow."

"You can't pick up the keys until you own the place."

"I do own the place."

Ryan stared at her. "It only came on the market recently. You only just saw it."

"Murph called me the instant it happened, and he drove me over to take a look."

Ryan digested that. "And you didn't tell me?"

"You had a lot on your mind." She patted him on the arm. "Now, take me home and help me pack up some boxes."

IT WAS THEIR first trip to the harbor since they'd come back from the hospital, and they could barely take a step without being accosted by well-wishers.

Emily kept a close eye on Lizzy and tried not to fuss. "What would you most like to do?"

"Can we have waffles and chocolate milk?"

She'd been steeling herself for that inevitable request. Waffles and chocolate milk would mean visiting the Ocean Club and possibly bumping into Ryan. She'd discovered that asking him to keep his distance hadn't stopped her from thinking about him, nor had it stopped Lizzy talking about him. She'd reached the stage where she was ready to scream and cover her ears and had distracted herself by making endless collages with seashells found on the beach outside the door. But that pastime had only held Lizzy's attention for a short time. She'd discovered that a recovering Lizzy was harder to handle than a sick Lizzy. She wanted to be out on the water, swimming, seeing the puffins, anything other than staying trapped indoors.

Emily had suggested a trip to Summer Scoop, but it was clear that no activity was going to match the awesome experience of waffles and chocolate milk, so she surrendered to the inevitable. Why not? If they were staying on the island, then they were going to bump into Ryan sooner or later.

Lizzy insisted on taking both Andrew and her new puffin, and they were met by a smiling Kirsti, who showed them to their usual table.

Once again a large crowd of students had the table next to them, but this time Emily barely spared them a glance.

"One extra-chocolatey chocolate milk for an extra special guest." Kirsti placed the tall glass in front of Lizzy with a flourish and did the same with Emily's coffee. "Can I get you anything else?"

Lizzy looked around hopefully. "Is Ryan here?"

"No." Kirsti gave her a sympathetic look. "We haven't seen him this morning. He's dealing with some business down at the marina. Some guy whose ego is bigger than his yacht, and that's saying something." She walked off with a wink and a smile to serve another table of customers, and Lizzy's shoulders drooped.

She clutched the puffin in both hands, Andrew lying forgotten on one of the vacant chairs. "Why don't we see Ryan anymore?"

"He's busy, honey." It horrified her how badly she wanted to see him.

Was she really going to be able to live in such close proximity, or was she fooling herself?

Misery was a cold hard lump inside her. It was impossible not to second-guess herself. Maybe she should have let the relationship take its course. But how would that have worked?

Eventually he would have moved on, and that would have made the situation even more awkward.

The best option would have been not to fall in love with him in the first place, but it was too late for that.

Lizzy put the puffin down carefully and reached for her milk. "He said he loved us."

"He does love us in his own way, but he has a job to do and his own life."

And that life wasn't going to include them.

She couldn't wallow in self-pity; she had to move on. She had to keep Lizzy busy and introduce new people into her life.

Lizzy stared miserably across the restaurant, and then the chocolate milk slipped from her hands and spilled across the table, splattering Emily.

With lightning reflexes, she rescued puffin and Andrew, but before she could speak, Lizzy shrank down in her chair.

"He's here."

Emily was busy trying to stem the flood with a couple of napkins. "Ryan?"

"The man with the camera. The one who climbed into the house."

It took a few seconds for the words to sink in, and when they did, Emily dropped the napkins and slowly turned her head. The man was standing between her and the door, blocking the only exit. He scanned the restaurant as if searching for someone, and, after a few moments, he approached a couple at the table nearest to him and showed them a photograph. Heart thumping, Emily pushed both toys into Lizzy's hands. "Get under the table, sweetheart."

"But—"

"Get under the table, and whatever happens, don't move." She positioned herself with her back to the restaurant, hoping to block the man's view.

She was thinking hard about her options when she heard Ryan's deep voice behind her.

"We're busy today. I'm going to have to ask if you mind sharing your table."

Melting with relief, Emily turned her head to warn him, but he put his hand on her shoulder and gave it a firm squeeze.

"I've got this. Just crowd around and pull up a few extra chairs." He smiled at the students at the table next door, and they swiftly decamped to Emily's table, laughing, chatting and crowding around as he'd instructed. "Anna, give Emily your hat. She's in full sun there."

The girl next to her slid her hat from her head and passed it to Emily.

She glanced down and saw the words Marine Center embroidered on the front.

"Put it on," Ryan said softly. "Keep your back to the room and leave the rest to me."

"Here—" Anna pushed a copy of *Marine Biology* into her hand. "Get stuck into that. Don't look so panicked. Ryan has got this. We've all got this."

Two bulky guys with windswept hair sat either side of her, and one of them put his backpack carefully on the floor in front of Lizzy. With so many legs and backpacks, it would be next to impossible for anyone to see her.

Even so, Emily's heart was thudding as he approached the table.

"Hi." His smile was warm and friendly. "You guys live on the island?"

Anna smiled back. "During the summer. You?"

"Sadly, mine is a short visit. I wondered if you'd seen this little girl around." He handed a photo of Lizzy to Anna, who studied it carefully, shook her head and then passed it across the table to another girl.

Their eyes locked, their fingers brushed, and the photo fell into a sticky pool of chocolate milk.

Anna tutted. "Rita, you are so clumsy." She made a fuss of wiping it and tore the edge. "Oh, no! Now I'm the clumsy one."

The man gritted his teeth as he took it back. "I thought you might have seen her? She's traveling with her mother, a woman called Emily."

"Your wife and child?"

"My sister and her little girl. There are marital problems. I promised I'd help her."

"Your niece?" Anna took another look at the photo. "She doesn't look anything like you. But, no, I don't remember seeing her."

"The address is Castaway Cottage, but it's not listed anywhere, and no one I ask seems to know where it is."

"Castaway Cottage?" Anna looked vague. "Never heard of it, and this is my third summer on the island. You could try asking Pete—he drives the island cab."

"I did. He said there is no Castaway Cottage." The man looked frustrated. "But I know that's the address."

"Not on this island. Let me see that photo." Ryan took it from the man. "She looks like Summer. Her mother owns Summer Scoop just along Main Street. Or maybe not. It's not a great picture."

"If you wanted to rent somewhere out of the way on this island where no one would look for you, where would you stay?"

Ryan didn't hesitate. "White Pine House. But there's no way she'd stay there."

"Why?"

"Because getting there is a nightmare. It's in the middle of the island at the top of a trail that is impassable in bad weather. I wouldn't even try it if I were you."

"Can you give me directions?"

Ryan shrugged. "They're your tires. Do you have a map? I can show you." He was polite and friendly as he took the map of the island from the man's hand. "You want to take a right at the forest trail. It's a pretty rough road, but it's the only way up to Heron Pond. Be careful as you take Pond Bridge. There was some structural damage over the winter, and repairs haven't been finished yet. You might want to park and walk."

The guy stepped away with a nod of thanks.

"What a douche," Anna muttered as he walked away. "Please tell me he's going to blow out his tires on the way to the pond."

"He will." Ryan was calm. "And if by chance he makes it as far as the bridge, he'll probably take a swim."

"He's going to be calling for help," Anna said happily, and Ryan smiled back.

"He'll try. There is no cell phone coverage by the pond. He's going to have a long, tiring walk back down to the road."

Emily wasn't so easily reassured. "He knows about Castaway Cottage. He must have gotten the details from the hospital." She was sickened by it. "What if someone tells him where it is?"

"How can they, when none of us has ever heard of Castaway Cottage?" Ryan winked at her and then called Kirsti over. "Is it done?"

"It was done twenty seconds after you gave me the nod. Check your phone. And for those who don't text, we've been calling around leaving messages."

Ryan pulled his phone out of his pocket, smiled and handed it to Emily. There on the screen was a text warning the islanders about the journalist, complete with a photograph.

"How did you take that without him noticing?"

Kirsti smiled. "I'm sneaky."

Emily couldn't relax that easily. "What if he comes back?"

"I guarantee you by the time he leaves the island, he won't want to come back in a hurry." Ryan dropped to his haunches and grinned at Lizzy. "Hi there, tiger. Time to come out."

"Ryan!" Lizzy wriggled through legs and backpacks and launched herself into his arms. "It was him."

"I know, honey, but he'll be leaving again soon. In the meantime, how do you feel about spending the day at Harbor House with Agnes? She really needs your help with Cocoa while she packs boxes." He stroked her back gently, and Lizzy wrapped her arms and legs around him like a monkey.

"Will you be there, too?"

Across the top of Lizzy's head, Ryan's gaze met Emily's. She saw something flicker in the depths of his eyes, and then he set the child down, peeling her arms from around his neck.

"Later." His voice was husky. "First, I'm going to make sure Mr. Photographer never bothers you again." He turned to Emily. "Don't leave until I text you. John Harris is going to let me know as soon as he's safely on the ferry."

She nodded. Without his quick thinking, Lizzy's presence would have been exposed, and she wanted to express her gratitude. She wanted to pull back all the things she'd said, but then she saw Lizzy slide her arms around his legs and cling, and knew she had to stand firm.

"Thank you." She told herself it was the overwhelming gesture of warmth from the community that made her feel like sitting down and sobbing her heart out. For her whole life she'd felt like a small piece of a jigsaw puzzle that had been dropped on the floor and lost, fitting nowhere. Now she felt as if she'd found her place. A small piece, fitting perfectly into a bigger picture. For the first time in her life, she felt as if she belonged. There were people looking out for her.

The price she had to pay for that was not being with Ryan. She'd thought that was the simple option.

Now she was wondering if it might kill her.

EMILY SPENT THE rest of the day packing boxes with Agnes and picking up texts from various islanders determined to give her a nonstop commentary on what was happening. She was grateful for any activity that stopped her thinking about Ryan.

"The journalist got the car stuck on Pond Bridge and had to walk back down to the harbor." She gave Agnes an update. "He called a cab."

Agnes looked interested. "And how did that turn out for him?"

Emily scrolled through her texts. "Not well. Peter told him his cab had been booked all day by a family from Boston, so he tried Larry, but his cab was in the garage having the brakes fixed."

"It's a terrible thing that island transport is so bad."

"Before he left, he went into Summer Scoop and showed Lisa the photograph."

"Did she bury it deep in vanilla ice cream?"

"No, she said the little girl in the picture looked like Summer. Then she asked if she could keep the photograph because she objected to people taking pictures of her daughter without permission."

Agnes laughed as she wrapped up two candlesticks. "That was smart of her. And there is just enough of a resemblance between Summer and Lizzy that he might believe it."

"He asked the Realtor on Main Street if he'd ever heard of Castaway Cottage, and she suggested he try Bar Harbor."

"That will be Tilly Hobson. She believes houses choose people, not the other way around." Agnes sealed the box, and Emily scrambled to her feet.

"Don't lift that. I'll do it. I've met Tilly. I spoke to her a few days ago."

"You're looking for property?"

"Yes. It was kind of Brittany to let us use Castaway Cottage, but we can't stay there forever. We need somewhere of our own, but houses don't come up that often on Puffin Island." She lifted the box and stacked it with the others and then heard her phone beep. "That will be Ryan with another update."

But it turned out to be a text from Brittany, and when Emily read it she sat down on the chair with a thump.

Agnes paused with a stack of table mats in her hand. "Another update?"

"No. This time it's Brittany. She fell on the archaeological dig in Greece. She's broken her wrist." She pulled a face and sent a text back. "Poor Brit. You know how active she is—she'll go crazy with her right hand out of use."

"What's her plan?"

"To come home while she heals and then make some life decisions. Her postgraduate work at Oxford University has finished. This dig was something she was doing for fun while she decided what to do next." Emily absorbed the implications of that. "Looks like I might have need of Tilly's services sooner than expected."

"Brittany wouldn't want you to move out. I wouldn't rush into anything." Agnes looked vague. "Something might turn up."

Emily, who believed in structuring her life as much as she could, wasn't reassured. "I'm sure we can stay with Brittany for a while, but I feel, for Lizzy's sake, it's time we found somewhere that's ours. I want her to have security." She wanted Lizzy to have everything she'd never had herself. "I've enrolled her in school for September. She might even have Rachel as her teacher."

Agnes's face softened. "Lucky Lizzy. That girl has the sweetest nature. When Ryan was injured I couldn't drag Rachel from the hospital. Those two are very close. For weeks, she slept in the chair, and when he started the long rehabilitation process, she was the one bullying him into doing those exercises and pushing a little harder each day."

"He's very protective of her."

"Always has been. He took some serious teasing in school for looking out for his little sister. I remember one time the class had to take the thing they loved most into school for show-and-tell. It was meant to be a toy or a book. Rachel insisted on taking Ryan. They had to excuse him from math so he could sit on the mat with her. His friends gave him hell over that one, but he showed up, anyway." Agnes's eyes misted. "Oh, that little girl loved her big brother. He was a hero to her, and I've never seen anyone so patient as he was with his sister."

The lump in Emily's throat made it difficult to swallow. "He's been great with Lizzy. That day we went sailing, he was so patient with her." And she had to keep reminding herself that it had been a happy afternoon, that was all. Just because he was good with Lizzy, didn't mean he wanted to do it more often.

There was no room in life for dreaming.

She picked up a painting from the floor and paused, scanning the beautiful beach scene. "Is this one of Skylar's?"

"It's a watercolor she did when she was eighteen. She gave it to Kathleen as a thank-you for having her to stay. I admired it, and Kathleen left it to me. I love the colors. It's like bringing part of the beach indoors."

"Sky would be proud to know you love it enough to hang it on your wall." Emily wrapped it carefully. "I know it meant a lot that Kathleen believed in her. Whenever we stayed, she made sure Sky had a place to paint. Her own parents didn't do that for her. They thought her artistic talents detracted from what was important in life." She slid the painting carefully into the box. "She comes from a family of lawyers, and they wanted her to be a lawyer, too."

Agnes handed her a piece of tape. "The job of a parent is to nurture and guide, not kill dreams. What about you? What was your dream?"

"There wasn't any room in my life for dreams."

"And now?"

Something in the way Agnes was looking at her made her wonder if she'd guessed.

"I find it safer to focus on reality." Emily kept her eyes down, closed the box and secured it with tape. "I'm going to find a house that will be a good home for us. Then think about work. There's a property vacant on Harbor Road, not far from Summer Scoop. I'm thinking of maybe opening a boutique gift shop with a beach theme." The idea had come to her in the night, and she'd felt a rush of excitement and anticipation. Instead of helping with other people's businesses, why not start her own?

"I want to sell everything from jewelry to shells and maybe small pieces for the home. I have to run some numbers. Ask a few questions. Do you think it's a crazy idea?"

"I think it's a good idea." Agnes pushed another empty box toward her, and together they filled it while Emily waited for another text from Ryan telling them it was safe to go home. It never came. Instead, he came himself, taking the steps to Harbor House two at a time as the last ferry of the day sailed out into the bay on its journey across to the mainland.

Emily watched his approach from the large bay window and wondered if there was ever going to be a time when she could look at him and not want him.

Seeing him made her light-headed, as if she'd walked from darkness into the full glare of sunlight.

Fortunately she had herself under control by the time he walked into the room, and he answered her question before she asked it.

"He's headed home. He won't be bothering us again. Good thing he isn't a travel journalist, or Puffin Island would be in for some seriously negative publicity about the state of our roads and the clueless nature of its inhabitants. He was persistent, I'll give him that. He must have questioned every damn person on the island, even Hilda."

"Hilda?" Emily put down the painting she'd been wrapping. "What did poor Hilda say?"

"She pretended to be deaf. She made him shout so loudly he had an audience stretching from the harbor to Puffin Point."

Agnes laughed and walked to the door. "Talking of Lizzy, I'm going to see how she's getting on with that doll's house of Rachel's." She walked out of the room, leaving them alone, and Emily wondered how it was possible to feel self-conscious and awkward after everything they'd done together.

"I can't believe everyone did that for Lizzy."

"And you." His voice softened. "They did it for you, too. It can take a long time for mainlanders to be accepted here, but you've thrown yourself into island life and you've been officially adopted."

"Oh—" Her eyes filled, and she realized how ridiculous it was to feel like crying over something she should be celebrating.

And she knew her tears had nothing to do with her status as an islander, and everything to do with the way she felt about him.

In the past few weeks, she'd learned so many things and faced things she'd buried for most of her life. Now, instead of protecting herself from emotion, she was flooded by it.

She was starting to wonder if the dream of living here was really going to work.

Now she'd started feeling again, she didn't want to stop. And she wasn't sure she could hide it.

"Thank you. I don't even want to think about how that might have turned out if you hadn't done what you did. All of you. And please thank the group from the marine center." She scrambled to her feet. "Lizzy and I will come back tomorrow and help Agnes finish up."

"Why would you leave?"

"Because in a minute Lizzy will come downstairs and see you, and then she won't want to let you go." Avoiding his gaze, she stacked the last of the boxes by the door. "The ones with the black mark can be recycled. The red mark means they can go to the charity store. The green means Agnes is taking it when she moves."

There was a tense silence.

"What if I don't want to let her go? What if I don't want to let *you* go?"

"I'm taking the box by the door over to Lisa because there are some toys that Summer and Harry might—" She broke off and stared at him. "What did you just say?"

"What if I don't want to let you go?"

There was a clatter and thump from upstairs, but for once

Emily didn't rush to investigate. She trusted Agnes, and anyway, her feet were glued to the floor. "I don't know what you mean."

He closed the door, giving them privacy. "I want to talk about us."

Us.

Such a small, simple word to hold such deep significance. "There can't be an us, Ryan."

"There already is." He crossed the room to her and took her face in his hands. "There's been an 'us' from the first day you opened the door to me. There was an 'us' when you trusted me with your secret, when you asked me to teach you to swim, when you let me take you out in a boat and when you let me take you to bed. There was an 'us' when I came to the hospital, and when you told me you didn't want me in your life. If there hadn't been an 'us,' you wouldn't have felt the need to say that."

"I said it because Lizzy fell in love with you. I'm protecting her feelings."

"And what about you?" His voice was soft, his gaze holding hers. "What about your feelings?"

"How I feel doesn't matter. I can't let it matter. There's too much at stake." She felt as if she were teetering on the edge of a crumbling cliff with everything secure about to disintegrate beneath her feet.

"Do you know what I think, Emily Donovan?" His voice was husky and warm. "I think you're using Lizzy as an excuse. I think the reason you can't let it matter isn't because you're afraid for Lizzy, but because you're afraid for yourself. I think what's at stake isn't Lizzy's heart, but your own. You're scared. You've gone through life avoiding anything that threatens your emotions and that included picking men who wouldn't make you feel deeply."

She swallowed hard. "What does that say about me?"

"That you were scared. Love scares you, so you stayed in the shallow end of the relationship pool, picking guys who could never put your heart in danger. But I taught you to swim, Emily."

He ran his thumb gently over her cheek. "I taught you how to kick and stay afloat. I taught you what to do when a riptide grabs you. It's important to make good decisions, but you don't have to let fear hold you back, sweetheart."

The endearment ripped at her. "Are we talking about love or swimming?"

"Both. Loving Lizzy has been hard for you, and I think it's scary for you to admit you love me, too."

Her heart skipped a beat. The fact that he knew left her feeling raw and exposed, like a sea creature left stranded on the beach when the tide retreated. "Aren't you a little sure of yourself?"

His mouth tilted into a crooked smile. "Honey, I wasn't sure at all. I was upset that you'd pushed me away. I thought you weren't interested. It was Agnes who made me see the truth. You associate love with being hurt, and you're afraid I'll hurt you. You're protecting yourself."

Why would she deny the truth? If she was honest, maybe he'd respect her wishes and stay away, instead of making things harder. "Yes."

"You've lived your life doing that, caring for yourself, protecting yourself. You learned how to heal yourself, nurture yourself, and part of the way you did that was to cut out the things that threatened you. Children. Love."

"It worked better for me that way. But Lizzy is my family now. I had no choice about that, but now I wouldn't have it any other way. Skylar was right that sometimes the worst things can turn out to be the best. When the time is right, I'm going to formally adopt her."

"It never crossed my mind you'd do anything else. What would you say if I told you what I want is to spend the rest of my life trying to stop anything from hurting you and Lizzy? What would you say if I told you I want you both in my life?"

She took a few unsettled breaths, trying to listen to her head and not her heart. Trying to use reason and not emotion. "You value your independence. The ability to come and go as you please. You told me you didn't plan on giving that up anytime soon. This relationship can't be a revolving door, Ryan. You can't come and go as it suits you." Because she didn't trust emotion not to defeat reason, she pulled away from him and started to walk across the room, but he caught her arm and hauled her back to him.

"Damn it, Emily, I don't want a revolving door. I want to walk through it and stay. I want to lock it and throw away the key. I'm telling you I want to be with you. Both of you. I'm telling you I love you."

At first the words floated on the surface of her brain without penetrating. Then she assumed she'd misheard. "I— What?" She wondered if wishful thinking had conjured the words in her head. Had he really said that aloud?

"I love you."

"No, you don't. You love your freedom. You love being able to go with the wind and the tide."

"Yes. But there comes a time when what feels right is to drop anchor and stay a while in the same place. For me, that time is now."

She looked at him and saw her feelings mirrored in his eyes. "Ryan—"

"If this new, fledgling family of yours is looking for extra members, I thought I might apply. I can give you my résumé if you like, but you'll find I'm well qualified in certain aspects of child care including, but not limited to, rescuing soft toys from dangerous circumstances."

In all her life she'd never known a feeling like this one. She didn't know how to express everything in her head and her heart.

"I—Ryan—I don't know what to say."

"I want you to say yes to my question."

"Did you ask me a question?"

"Not yet, but I'm about to." He pulled his hand out of his pocket and handed her a box. "Will you marry me?"

Emotion swelled inside her, and her eyes filled. She opened the box and stared down at the sparkling diamond through eyes misted with tears.

"Ryan—"

"Will you trust me with Lizzy? Will you trust me with your heart? Can you do that?"

The cliff gave way beneath her feet, but instead of falling she was flying. "Yes." The word was almost inaudible, so she said it again. "Yes. Oh, yes."

And then he was kissing her, his mouth hard and demanding, his hands possessive and protective. Somewhere through the mists of passion, she heard the door opening, and she pulled away to see Lizzy peeping around the door with Agnes behind her.

"Can we come in, Ryan? Have you done it?"

Her hand still locked in the front of his shirt, Emily glanced up at him. "You told her to stay away?"

"I told her I had something important to ask you."

"He said it was private." Lizzy skipped across the room, and he scooped her up.

Watching the two of them together, Emily felt her heart flutter.

"Lizzy, we have something to tell you."

"I already know." She leaned her head against Ryan's shoulder, blond curls brushing against dark. "Ryan loves us. I told you that in the hospital, but you didn't believe me. Can we go and see the puffins again soon? Can we go sailing and eat waffles?"

"Yes." Emily's voice was muffled as Ryan pulled her close with his other arm. "Yes, we can do all those things."

Agnes walked into the room, a smile on her face. "Tilly is on the phone. You called her about a rental, but I told her it was a mistake."

Emily eased away from Ryan's grip, wondering how she was

supposed to focus on the practical when her head was spinning. "But Brittany is coming home, and I still need to find somewhere to live."

She saw Ryan exchange a look with Agnes and smile.

"You don't need to find somewhere to live." He lowered Lizzy to the window seat that overlooked the harbor. "I happen to know of a large family home with a sea view that's not even on the market yet. It will be perfect for us."

* * * * *

ACKNOWLEDGMENTS

Without my brilliant editor, Flo Nicoll, writing would be nowhere near as much fun or as productive. I'm grateful for her wise comments and the insight she offers on each book.

I'm thankful to my agent, Susan Ginsburg, and the team at Writers House who continue to be a wonderful source of support and encouragement in my career, and to the fantastic teams at Harlequin UK and HQN in the US who work so hard to put my books into the hands of readers.

Thanks to my husband for answering my questions on sailing, for not drowning me whenever he's taken me out on the water and for not rolling his eyes when I hung over the side moaning like a drama queen.

Developing a new series is always fun and exciting. I'm grateful to fellow author and friend Nicola Cornick for always being on the end of the phone when I hit a plot problem and to Andrew Cornick for generously allowing me to use his beautiful photographs of puffins on my website.

My two sons bought me a colony of soft toy puffins to act as inspiration on my desk, thus providing further proof of my family's support of my unusual profession.

My final thanks go to my readers, who cheer me daily with their kind emails, Tweets and Facebook comments. Thank you for buying my books. You're the best.

Sarah
xxx

Playing By The Rules

To the wonderful Joanne Grant,
for her enthusiasm and encouragement
and for always keeping the door open.

CHAPTER ONE

LILY PULLED HER hat down to shade her eyes from the burn of the hot Greek sun and took a large gulp from her water bottle. 'Never again.' She sat down on the parched, sunbaked earth and watched as her friend carefully brushed away dirt and soil from a small, carefully marked section of the trench. 'If I ever, *ever* mention the word "love" to you, I want you to bury me somewhere in this archaeological site and never dig me up again.'

'There is an underground burial chamber. I could dump you in there if you like.'

'Great idea. Stick a sign in the ground. *"Here lies Lily, who wasted years of her life studying the origin, evolution and behaviour of humans and still couldn't understand men".*' She gazed across the ruins of the ancient city of Aptera to the sea beyond. They were high on a plateau. Behind them, the jagged beauty of the White Mountains shimmered in the heat and in front lay the sparkling blue of the Sea of Crete. The beauty of it usually lifted her mood, but not today.

Brittany sat up and wiped her brow with her forearm. 'Stop beating yourself up. The guy is a lying, cheating rat bastard.' Reaching for her backpack, she glanced across the site to the group of men who were deep in conversation. 'Fortunately for all of us he's flying back to London tomorrow to his wife. And all I can say to that is, God help the woman.'

Lily covered her face with her hands. 'Don't say the word "wife". I am a terrible person.'

'Hey!' Brittany's voice was sharp. 'He told you he was single. He *lied*. The responsibility is all his. After tomorrow you won't have to see him again and I won't have to struggle not to kill him.'

'What if she finds out and ends their marriage?'

'Then she might have the chance of a decent life with someone who respects her. Forget him, Lily.'

How could she forget when she couldn't stop going over and over it in her head?

Had there been signs she'd missed?

Had she asked the wrong questions?

Was she so desperate to find someone special that she'd ignored obvious signs?

'I was planning our future. We were going to spend August touring the Greek Islands. That was before he pulled out a family photo from his wallet instead of his credit card. Three little kids wrapped around their dad like bindweed. He should have been taking them on holiday, not me! I can't bear it. How could I have made such an appalling error of judgement? That is a line I *never* cross. Family is sacrosanct to me. If you asked me to pick between family and money, I'd pick family every time.' It crossed her mind that right now she had neither. No money. No family. 'I don't know which is worse—the fact that he clearly didn't know me *at all*, or the fact that when I checked him against my list he was perfect.'

'You have a list?'

Lily felt herself grow pink. 'It's my attempt to be objective. I have a really strong desire for permanent roots. Family.' She thought about the emotional wasteland of her past and felt a sense of failure. Was the future going to look the same way? 'When you want something badly it can distort your decision-making process, so I've put in some layers of protection for myself. I know the basic qualities I need in a man to be happy. I never date anyone who doesn't score highly on my three points.'

Brittany looked intrigued. 'Big wallet, big shoulders and big—'

'No! And you are appalling.' Despite her misery, Lily laughed. 'First, he has to be affectionate. I'm not interested in a man who can't show his feelings. Second, he has to be honest, but short of getting him to take a lie detector test I don't know how to check that one. I thought Professor Ashurst was honest. I'm never calling him David again, by the way.' She allowed herself one glance at the visiting archaeologist who had dazzled her during their short, ill-fated relationship. 'You're right. He's a rat pig.'

'I didn't call him a rat pig. I called him a rat b—'

'I know what you called him. I never use that word.'

'You should. It's surprisingly therapeutic. But we shouldn't be wasting this much time talking about him. Professor Asshat is history, like this stuff we're digging up.'

'I can't believe you called him that.'

'You should be calling him far worse. What's the third thing on your list?'

'I want a man with strong family values. He has to want a family. But not several different families at the same time. Now I know why he gave off all those signals about being a family man. Because he already *was* a family man.' Lily descended into gloom. 'My checklist is seriously flawed.'

'Not necessarily. You need a more reliable test for honesty and you should maybe add "single" to your list, that's all. You need to chill. Stop looking for a relationship and have some fun. Keep it casual.'

'You're talking about sex? That doesn't work for me.' Lily took another sip of water. 'I have to be in love with a guy to sleep with him. The two are welded together for me. How about you?'

'No. Sex is sex. Love is love. One is fun and the other is to be avoided at all costs.'

'I don't think like that. There is something wrong with me.'

'There's nothing wrong with you. It's not a crime to want a relationship. It just means you get your heart broken more than the average person.' Brittany pushed her hat back from her face. 'I can't believe how hot it is. It's not even ten o'clock and already I'm boiling like a lobster.'

'And you know all about lobsters, coming from Maine. It's summer and this is Crete. What did you expect?'

'Right now I'd give anything for a few hours back home. I'm not used to summers that fry your skin from your body. I keep wanting to remove another layer of clothing.'

'You've spent summers at digs all over the Mediterranean.'

'And I moaned at each and every one.' Brittany stretched out her legs and Lily felt a flash of envy.

'You look like Lara Croft in those shorts. You have amazing legs.'

'Too much time hiking in inhospitable lands searching for ancient relics. I want your gorgeous blonde hair.' Brittany's hair, the colour of polished oak, was gathered up from her neck in a ponytail. Despite the hat, her neck was already showing signs of the sun. 'Listen, don't waste another thought or tear on that man. Come out with us tonight. We're going to the official opening of the new wing at the archaeological museum and afterwards we're going to try out that new bar on the waterfront. My spies tell me that Professor Asshat won't be there, so it's going to be a great evening.'

'I can't. The agency rang this morning and offered me an emergency cleaning job.'

'Lily, you have a masters in archaeology. You shouldn't be taking these random jobs.'

'My research grant doesn't pay off my college loans and I want to be debt free. And anyway, I love cleaning. It relaxes me.'

'You love cleaning? You're like a creature from another planet.'

'There's nothing more rewarding than turning someone's messy house into a shiny home, but I do wish the job wasn't tonight. The opening would have been fun. A great excuse to wash the mud off my knees and dress up, not to mention seeing all those artefacts in one place. Never mind. I'll focus on the money. They're paying me an emergency rate for tonight.'

'Cleaning is an emergency?'

Lily thought about the state of some of the houses she cleaned. 'Sometimes, but in this case it's more that the owner decided to arrive without notice. He spends most of his time in the US.' She dug in her bag for more sunscreen. 'Can you imagine being so rich you can't quite decide which of your many properties you are going to sleep in?'

'What's his name?'

'No idea. The company is very secretive. We have to arrive at a certain time and then his security team will let us in. Four hours later I add a gratifyingly large sum of money to my bank account and that's the end of it.'

'Four hours? It's going to take five of you four hours to clean one house?' Brittany paused with the water halfway to her mouth. 'What is this place? A Minoan palace?'

'A villa. It's big. She said I'd be given a floor plan when I arrive, which I have to return when I leave and I'm not allowed to make copies.'

'A *floor plan*?' Brittany choked on her water. 'Now I'm intrigued. Can I come with you?'

'Sure—' Lily threw her a look '—because scrubbing out someone's shower is so much more exciting than having cocktails on the terrace of the archaeological museum while the sun sets over the Aegean.'

'It's the Sea of Crete.'

'Technically it's still the Aegean, and either way I'm missing a great party to scrub a floor. I feel like Cinderella. So what about you? Are you going to meet someone tonight and do something about your dormant love life?'

'I don't have a love life, I have a sex life, which is not at all dormant fortunately.'

Lily felt a twinge of envy. 'Maybe you're right. I need to lighten up and use men for sex instead of treating every relationship as if it's going to end in confetti. You were an only child, weren't you? Did you ever wish you had brothers or sisters?'

'No, but I grew up on a small island. The whole place felt like a massive extended family. Everyone knew everything, from the age you first walked, to whether you had all A's on your report card.'

'Sounds blissful.' Lily heard the wistful note in her own voice. 'Because I was such a sickly kid and hard work to look after, no one took me for long. My eczema was terrible when I was little and I was always covered in creams and bandages and other yucky stuff. I wasn't exactly your poster baby. No one wanted a kid who got sick. I was about as welcome as a stray puppy with fleas.'

'Crap, Lily, you're making me tear up and I'm not even a sentimental person.'

'Forget it. Tell me about your family instead.' She loved hearing about other people's families, about the complications, the love, the experiences woven into a shared history. To her, family seemed like a multicoloured sweater, with all the different coloured strands of wool knitted into something whole and wonderful that gave warmth and protection from the cold winds of life.

She picked absently at a thread hanging from the hem of her shorts. It felt symbolic of her life. She was a single fibre, loose, bound to nothing.

Brittany took another mouthful of water and adjusted the angle of her hat. 'We're a normal American family, I guess. Whatever that is. My parents were divorced when I was ten. My mom hated living on an island. Eventually she remarried and moved to Florida. My dad was an engineer and he spent all his time working on oil rigs around the world. I lived with my grandmother on Puffin Island.'

'Even the name is adorable.' Lily tried to imagine growing up on a place called Puffin Island. 'Were you close to your grandmother?'

'Very. She died a few years ago, but she left me her cottage on the beach so I'd always have a home. I take several calls a week from people wanting to buy the place but I'm never going to sell.' Brittany poked her trowel into the ground. 'My grandmother called it Castaway Cottage. When I was little I asked her if a castaway ever lived there and she said it was for people lost in life, not at sea. She believed it had healing properties.'

Lily didn't laugh. 'I might need to spend a month there. I need to heal.'

'You'd be welcome. A friend of mine is staying at the moment. We use it as a refuge. It's the best place on earth and I always feel close to my grandmother when I'm there. You can use it any time, Lil.'

'Maybe I will. I still need to decide what I'm going to do in August.'

'You know what you need? Rebound sex. Sex for the fun of it, without all the emotional crap that goes with relationships.'

'I've never had rebound sex. I'd fall in love.'

'So pick someone you couldn't possibly fall in love with in a million years. Someone with exceptional bedroom skills, but nothing else to commend him. Then you can't possibly be at risk.' She broke off as Spyros, one of the Greek archaeologists from the local university, strolled across to them. 'Go away, Spy, this is girl talk.'

'Why do you think I'm joining you? It's got to be more interesting than the conversation I just left.' He handed Lily a can of chilled Diet Coke. 'He's a waste of space, *theé mou.*' His voice was gentle and she coloured, touched by his kindness.

'I know, I know.' She lifted the weight of her hair from her neck, wishing she'd worn it up. 'I'll get over it.'

Spy dropped to his haunches next to her. 'Want me to help you get over him? I heard something about rebound sex. I'm here for you.'

'No thanks. You're a terrible flirt. I don't trust you.'

'Hey, this is about sex. You don't need to trust me.' He winked at her. 'What you need is a real man. A Greek man who knows how to make you feel like a woman.'

'Yeah, yeah, I know the joke. You're going to hand me your laundry and tell me to wash it. This is why you're not going to be my rebound guy. I am not washing your socks.' But Lily was laughing as she snapped the top of the can. Maybe she didn't have a family, but she had good friends. 'You're forgetting that when I'm not cleaning the villas of the rich or hanging out here contributing nothing to my college fund, I work for the ultimate in Greek manhood.'

'Ah yes.' Spyros smiled. 'Nik Zervakis. Head of the mighty ZervaCo. Man of men. Every woman's fantasy.'

'Not mine. He doesn't tick a single box on my list.'

Spy raised his eyebrows and Brittany shook her head. 'You don't want to know. Go on, Lily, dish the dirt on Zervakis. I want to know everything from his bank balance to how he got that incredible six pack I saw in those sneaky photos of him taken in that actress's swimming pool.'

'I don't know much about him, except that he's super brilliant and expects everyone around him to be super brilliant, too, which makes him pretty intimidating. Fortunately he spends most of his time in San Francisco or New York so he isn't around much. I've been doing this internship for two months and in that time two personal assistants have left. It's a good job he has a big human resources department because I can tell you he gets through *a lot* of human resources in the average working week. And don't even start me on the girlfriends. I need a spreadsheet to keep it straight in my head.'

'What happened to the personal assistants?'

'Both of them resigned because of the pressure. The workload is inhuman and he isn't easy to work for. He has this way of looking at you that makes you wish you could teleport. But he *is* very attractive. He isn't my type so I didn't pay much attention, but the women talk about him all the time.'

'I still don't understand why you're working there.'

'I'm trying different things. My research grant ends this month and I don't know if I want to carry on doing this. I'm exploring other options. Museum work doesn't pay much and anyway, I don't want to live in a big city. I could never teach—' She shrugged, depressed by the options. 'I don't know what to do.'

'You're an expert in ceramics and you've made some beautiful pots.'

'That's a hobby.'

'You're creative and artistic. You should do something with that.'

'It isn't practical to think I can make a living that way and dreaming doesn't pay the bills.' She finished her drink. 'Sometimes I wish I'd read law, not archaeology, except that I don't think I'm cut out for office work. I'm not good with technology. I broke the photocopier last week and the coffee machine hates me, but apparently having ZervaCo on your résumé makes prospective employers sit up. It shows you have staying power. If you can work there and not be intimidated, you're obviously robust. And before you tell me that an educated woman shouldn't allow herself to be intimidated by a guy, try meeting him.'

Spyros rose to his feet. 'Plenty of people would be intimidated by Nik Zervakis. There are some who say his name along with the gods.'

Brittany pushed her water bottle back into her backpack. 'Those would be the people whose salary he pays, or the women he sleeps with.'

Lily took off her hat and fanned herself. 'His security team is briefed to keep them away from him. We are not allowed to put any calls through to him unless the name is on an approved list and that list changes pretty much every week. I have terrible trouble keeping up.'

'So his protection squad is there to protect him from women?' Brittany looked fascinated. 'Unreal.'

'I admire him. They say his emotions have never played a part in anything he does, business or pleasure. He is the opposite of everything I am. No one has ever dumped him or made him feel less of a person and he always knows what to say in any situation.' She glanced once across the heat-baked ruins of the archaeological site towards the man who had lied so glibly. Thinking of all the things she could have said and hadn't plunged her into another fit of gloom. 'I'm going to try and be more like Nik Zervakis.'

Brittany laughed. 'You're kidding, right?'

'No, I'm not kidding. He is like an ice machine. I want to be like that. How about you? Have either of you ever been in love?'

'No!' Spy looked alarmed, but Brittany didn't answer. Instead she stared sightlessly across the plateau to the ocean.

'Brittany?' Lily prompted her. 'Have you been in love?'

'Not sure.' Her friend's voice was husky. 'Maybe.'

'Wow. Ball-breaking Brittany, in love?' Spy raised his eyebrows. 'Did you literally fire an arrow through his heart?' He spread his hands as Lily glared at him. 'What? She's a Bronze Age weapons expert and a terrifyingly good archer. It's a logical suggestion.'

Lily ignored him. 'What makes you think you might have been in love? What were the clues?'

'I married him.'

Spyros doubled up with soundless laughter and Lily stared. 'You—? Okay. Well that's a fairly big clue right there.'

'It was a mistake.' Brittany tugged the trowel out of the ground. 'When I make mistakes I make sure they're *big*. I guess you could call it a whirlwind romance.'

'That sounds more like a hurricane than a whirlwind. How long did it last?'

Brittany stood up and brushed dust off her legs. 'Ten days. Spy, if you don't wipe that smile off your face I'm going to kick you into this trench and cover your corpse with a thick layer of dirt and shards of pottery.'

'You mean ten *years*,' Lily said and Brittany shook her head.

'No. I mean days. We made it through the honeymoon without killing each other.'

Lily felt her mouth drop open and closed it again quickly. 'What happened?'

'I let my emotions get in the way of making sane decisions.' Brittany gave a faint smile. 'I haven't fallen in love since.'

'Because you learned how not to do it. You didn't go and make the same mistake again and again. Give me some tips.'

'I can't. Avoiding emotional entanglement came naturally after I met Zach.'

'Sexy name.'

'Sexy guy.' She shaded her eyes from the sun. 'Sexy rat bastard guy.'

'Another one,' Lily said gloomily. 'But you were young and everyone is allowed to make mistakes when they're young. Not only do I not have that excuse, but I'm a habitual offender. I should be locked up until I'm safe to be rehabilitated. I need to be taken back to the store and reprogrammed.'

'You do not need to be reprogrammed.' Brittany stuffed her trowel into the front of her backpack. 'You're warm, friendly and lovable. That's what guys like about you.'

'That and the fact it takes one glance to know you'd look great naked,' Spy said affably.

Lily turned her back on him. 'Warm, friendly and lovable are great qualities for a puppy, but not so great for a woman. They say a person can change, don't they? Well, I'm going to change.' She scrambled to her feet. 'I am not falling in love again. I'm going to take your advice and have rebound sex.'

'Good plan.' Spy glanced at his watch. 'You get your clothes off, I'll get us a room.'

'Not funny.' Lily glared at him. 'I am going to pick someone I don't know, don't feel anything for and couldn't fall in love with in a million years.'

Brittany looked doubtful. 'Now I'm second-guessing myself. Coming from you it sounds like a recipe for disaster.'

'It's going to be perfect. All I have to do is find a man who doesn't tick a single box on my list and have sex with him. It can't possibly go wrong. I'm going to call it Operation Ice Maiden.'

NIK ZERVAKIS STOOD with his back to the office, staring at the glittering blue of the sea while his assistant updated him. 'Did he call?'

'Yes, exactly as you predicted. How do you always know these things? I would have lost my nerve days ago with those sums of money involved. You don't even break out in a sweat.'

Nik could have told him the deal wasn't about money, it was about power. 'Did you call the lawyers?'

'They're meeting with the team from Lexos first thing tomorrow. So it's done. Congratulations, boss. The US media have turned the phones red-hot asking for interviews.'

'It's not over until the deal is signed. When that happens I'll put out a statement, but no interviews.' Nik felt some of the tension leave his shoulders. 'Did you make a reservation at The Athena?'

'Yes, but you have the official opening of the new museum wing first.'

Nik swore softly and swung round. 'I'd forgotten. Do you have a briefing document on that?'

His PA paled. 'No, boss. All I know is that the wing has been specially designed to display Minoan antiquities in one place. You were invited to the final meeting of the project team but you were in San Francisco.'

'Am I supposed to give a speech?'

'They're hoping you will agree to say a few words.'

'I can manage a few words, but they'll be unrelated to Minoan antiquities.' Nik loosened his tie. 'Run me through the schedule.'

'Vassilis will have the car here at six-fifteen, which should allow you time to go back to the villa and change. You're picking up Christina on the way and your table is booked for nine p.m.'

'Why not pick her up after I've changed?'

'That would have taken time you don't have.'

Nik couldn't argue with that. The demands of his schedule had seen off three assistants in the last six months. 'There was something else?'

The man shifted uncomfortably. 'Your father called. Several times. He said you weren't picking up your phone and asked me to relay a message.'

Nik flicked open the button at the neck of his shirt. 'Which was?'

'He wants to remind you that his wedding is next weekend. He thinks you've forgotten.'

Nik stilled. *He hadn't forgotten.* 'Anything else?'

'He is looking forward to having you at the celebrations. He wanted me to remind you that of all the riches in this world, family is the most valuable.'

Nik, whose sentiments on that topic were a matter of public record, made no comment.

He wondered why anyone would see a fourth wedding as a cause for celebration. To him, it shrieked of someone who hadn't learned his lesson the first three times. 'I will call him from the car.'

'There was one more thing—' The man backed towards the door like someone who knew he was going to need to make a rapid exit. 'He said to make sure you knew that if you don't come, you'll break his heart.'

It was a statement typical of his father. Emotional. Un-guarded.

Reflecting that it was that very degree of sentimentality that had made his father the victim of three costly divorces, Niklaus strolled to his desk. 'Consider the message delivered.'

As the door closed he turned back to the window, staring over the midday sparkle of the sea.

Exasperation mingled with frustration and beneath that surface response lay darker, murkier emotions he had no wish to examine. He wasn't given to introspection and he believed that the past was only useful when it informed the future, so finding himself staring down into a swirling mass of long-ignored memories was an unwelcome experience.

Despite the air conditioning, sweat beaded on his forehead and he strode across his office and pulled a bottle of iced water from the fridge.

Why should it bother him that his father was marrying again?

He was no longer an idealistic nine-year-old, shattered by a mother's betrayal and driven by a deep longing for order and security.

He'd learned to make his own security. Emotionally he was an impenetrable fortress. He would never allow a relationship to explode the world from under his feet. He didn't believe in love and he saw marriage as expensive and pointless.

Unfortunately his father, an otherwise intelligent man, didn't share his views. He'd managed to build a successful business from nothing but the fruits of the land around him, but for some reason he had failed to apply that same intellect to his love life.

Nik reflected that if he approached business the way his father approached relationships, he would be broke.

As far as he could see his father performed no risk analysis, gave no consideration to the financial implications of each of his romantic whims and approached each relationship with the romantic optimism entirely inappropriate for a man on his fourth marriage.

Nik's attempts to encourage at least some degree of circum-spection had been dismissed as cynical.

To make the situation all the more galling, the last time they'd met for dinner his father had actually lectured him on his life-style as if Nik's lack of divorces suggested a deep character flaw.

Nik closed his eyes briefly and wondered how everything in his business life could run so smoothly while his family was as messy as a dropped pan of spaghetti. The truth was he'd rather endure the twelve labours of Hercules than attend another of his father's weddings.

This time he hadn't met his father's intended bride and he didn't want to. He failed to see what he would bring to the pro-ceedings other than grim disapproval and he didn't want to spoil the day.

Weddings depressed him. All the champagne bubbles in the world couldn't conceal the fact that two people were paying a fortune for the privilege of making a very public mistake.

LILY DUMPED HER BAG in the marble hallway and tried to stop her jaw from dropping.

Palatial didn't begin to describe it. Situated on the headland overlooking the sparkling blue of the sea, Villa Harmonia epit-omised calm, high-end luxury.

Wondering where the rest of the team were, she wandered out onto the terrace.

Tiny paths wound down through the tumbling gardens to a private cove with a jetty where a platform gave direct swim-ming access to the sea.

'I've died and gone to heaven.' Disturbed from her trance by the insistent buzz of her phone, she dug it out of her pocket. Her simple uniform was uncomfortably tight, courtesy of all the de-licious thyme honey and Greek yoghurt she'd consumed since arriving in Crete. Her phone call turned out to be the owner of the cleaning company, who told her that the rest of the team had been involved in an accident and wouldn't make it.

'Oh no, are they hurt?' On hearing that no one was in hospital but that the car was totalled, Lily realised she was going to be on her own with this job. 'So if it normally takes four of us four hours, how is one person going to manage?'

'Concentrate on the living areas and the master suite. Pay particular attention to the bathroom.'

Resigned to doing the best she could by herself, Lily set to work. Choosing Mozart from her soundtrack, she pushed in her earbuds and sang her way through *The Magic Flute* while she brushed and mopped the spacious living area.

Whoever lived here clearly didn't have children, she thought as she plumped cushions on deep white sofas and polished glass tables. Everything was sophisticated and understated.

Realising that dreaming would get her fired, Lily hummed her way up the curving staircase to the master bedroom and stopped dead.

The tiny, airless apartment she shared with Brittany had a single bed so narrow she'd twice fallen out of it in her sleep. *This* bed, by contrast, was large enough to sleep a family of six comfortably. It was positioned to take advantage of the incredible view across the bay and Lily stood, drooling with envy, imagining how it must feel to sleep in a bed this size. How many times could you roll over before finding yourself on the floor? If it were hers, she'd spread out like a starfish.

Glancing quickly over her shoulder to check there was no sign of the security team, she unclipped her phone from her pocket and took a photo of the bed and the view.

One day, she texted Brittany, I'm going to have sex in a bed like this.

Brittany texted back, I don't care about the bed, just give me the man who owns it.

With a last wistful look at the room, Lily tucked her phone carefully into her bag and strolled into the bathroom. A large tub was positioned next to a wall of glass, offering the owner an uninterrupted view of the ocean. The only way to clean something so large was to climb inside it, so she did that, extra careful not to slip.

When it was gleaming, she turned her attention to the large walk-in shower. There was a sophisticated control panel on the wall and she looked at it doubtfully. Remembering her disastrous experience with the photocopier and the coffee machine, she was reluctant to touch anything, but what choice was there?

Lifting her hand, she pressed a button cautiously and gasped as a powerful jet of freezing water hit her from the opposite wall.

Breathless, she slammed her hand on another button to try and stop the flow but that turned on a different jet and she was blasted with water until her hair and clothes were plastered to her body and she couldn't see. She thumped the wall blindly and was alternately scalded and frozen until finally she managed to turn off the jets. Panting, her hair and clothes plastered to her body, she sank to the floor while she tried to get her breath back, shivering and dripping like a puppy caught in the rain.

'I hate, hate, *hate* technology.' She pushed her hair back from her face, took it in her hands and twisted it into a rope, squeezing to remove as much of the water as she could. Then she stood up, but her uniform was dripping and stuck to her skin. If she walked back through the villa like this, she'd drip water everywhere and she didn't have time to clean the place again.

Peeling off her uniform, she was standing in her underwear wringing out the water when she heard a sound from the bedroom.

Assuming it must be one of the security team, she gave a whimper of horror. 'Hello? If there's anyone out there, don't come in for a moment because I'm just—' She stilled as a woman appeared in the doorway.

She was perfectly groomed, her slender body sheathed in a silk dress the colour of coral, her mouth a sheen of blended lipstick and lip-gloss.

Lily had never felt more outclassed in her life.

'Nik?' The woman spoke over her shoulder, her tone icy. 'Your sex drive is, of course, a thing of legend but for the record it's always a good idea to remove the last girlfriend before installing a new one.'

'What are you talking about?' The male voice came from the bedroom, deep, bored and instantly recognisable.

Still shivering from the impact of the cold water, Lily closed her eyes and wondered if any of the buttons on the control panel operated an ejector seat.

Now she knew who owned the villa.

Moments later he appeared in the doorway and Lily peered through soaked lashes and had her second ever look at Nik Zervakis. Confronted by more good looks and sex appeal than she'd ever seen concentrated in one man before, her tummy tumbled and she felt as if she were plunging downhill on a roller coaster.

He stood, legs braced apart, his handsome face blank of expression as if finding a semi-naked woman in his shower wasn't an event worthy of an emotional response. 'Well?'

That was all he was going to say?

Braced for an explosion of volcanic proportions, Lily gulped. 'I can explain—'

'I wish you would.' The woman's voice turned from ice to acid and her expensively shod foot tapped rhythmically on the floor. 'This should be worth hearing.'

'I'm the cleaner—'

'Of course you are. Because "cleaners" always end up naked in the client's shower.' Vibrating with anger, she turned the beam of her angry glare onto the man next to her. 'Nik?'

'Yes?'

Her mouth tightened into a thin, dangerous line. 'Who is she?'

'You heard her. She's the cleaner.'

'*Obviously* she's lying.' The woman bristled. 'No doubt she's been here all day, sleeping off the night before.'

His only response to that was a faint narrowing of those spectacular dark eyes.

Recalling someone warning her on her first day with his company that Nik Zervakis was at his most dangerous when he was quiet, Lily felt her anxiety levels rocket but apparently her concerns weren't shared by his date for the evening, who continued to berate him.

'Do you know the worst thing about this? Not that you have a wandering eye, but that your eye wanders to someone as fat as her.'

'*Excuse* me? I'm not fat.' Lily tried vainly to cover herself with the soaking uniform. 'I'll have you know that my BMI is within normal range.'

But the woman wasn't listening. 'Was she the reason you were late picking me up? I *warned* you, Nik, no games, and yet you do this to me. Well, you gambled and you lost because I don't do second chances, especially this early in a relationship and if you can't be bothered to give an explanation then I can't be bothered to ask for one.' Without giving him the chance to respond, his date stalked out of the room and Lily flinched in time with each furious tap of those skyscraper heels.

She stood in awkward silence, her feelings bruised and her spirits drenched in cold water and guilt. 'She's very upset.'

'Yes.'

'Er—is she coming back?'

'I sincerely hope not.'

Lily wanted to say that he was well rid of her, but decided that protecting her job was more important than honesty. 'I'm *really* sorry—'

'Don't be. It wasn't your fault.'

Knowing that wasn't quite true, she squirmed. 'If I hadn't had an accident, I would have had my clothes on when she walked into the room.'

'An accident? I've never considered my shower to be a place of danger but apparently I was wrong about that.' He eyed the volume of water on the floor and her drenched clothing. 'What happened?'

'Your shower is like the flight deck of a jumbo jet, that's what happened!' Freezing and soaked, Lily couldn't stop her teeth chattering. 'There are no instructions.'

'I don't need instructions.' His gaze slid over her with slow, disturbing thoroughness. 'I'm familiar with the workings of my own shower.'

'Well I'm not! I had no idea which buttons to press.'

'So you thought you'd press all of them? If you ever find yourself on the flight deck of a Boeing 747 I suggest you sit on your hands.'

'It's not f-f-funny. I'm soaking wet and I didn't know you were going to come home early.'

'I apologise.' Irony gleamed in those dark eyes. 'I'm not in the habit of notifying people of my movements in advance. Have you finished cleaning or do you want me to show you which buttons to press?'

Lily summoned as much dignity as she could in the circumstances. 'Your shower is clean. Extra clean, because I wiped myself around it personally.' Anxious to make her exit as fast as possible, she kept her eyes fixed on the door and away from that tall, powerful frame. 'Are you sure she isn't coming back?'

'No.'

Lily paused, torn between relief and guilt. 'I've ruined another relationship.'

'Another?' Dark eyebrows lifted. 'It's a common occurrence?'

'You have no idea. Look—if it would help I could call my employer and ask her to vouch for me.' Her voice tailed off as she realised that would mean confessing she'd been caught half naked in the shower.

He gave a faint smile. 'Unless you have a very liberal-minded employer, you might want to rethink that idea.'

'There must be some way I can fix this. I've ruined your date, although for the record I don't think she's a very kind person so she might not be good for you in the long term and with a body that bony she won't be very cuddly for your children.' She caught his eye. 'Are you laughing at me?'

'No, but the ability to cuddle children isn't high on my list of necessary female attributes.' He flung his jacket carelessly over the back of a sofa that was bigger than her bed at home.

She stared in fascination, wondering if he cared at all that his date had walked out. 'As a matter of interest, why didn't you defend yourself?'

'Why would I defend myself?'

'You could have explained yourself and then she would have forgiven you.'

'I never explain myself. And anyway—' he shrugged '—you had already given her an explanation.'

'I don't think she saw me as a credible witness. It might have sounded better coming from you.'

He stood, legs spread, his powerful shoulders blocking the doorway. 'I assume you told her the truth? You're the cleaner?'

'Of course I told her the truth.'

'Then there was nothing I could have added to your story.'

In his position she would have died of humiliation, but he seemed supremely indifferent to the fact he'd been publicly dumped. 'You don't seem upset.'

'Why would I be upset?'

'Because most people are upset when a relationship ends.'

He smiled. 'I'm not one of those.'

Lily felt a flash of envy. 'You're not even a teeny tiny bit sad?'

'I'm not familiar with that unit of measurement but no, I'm not even a "teeny tiny" bit sad. To be sad I'd have to care and I don't care.'

To be sad I'd have to care and I don't care.

Brilliant, Lily thought. *Why* couldn't she have said that to Professor Ashurst when he'd given her that fake sympathy about having hurt her? She needed to memorise it for next time. 'Excuse me a moment.' Leaving a dripping trail behind her, she shot past him, scrabbled in her bag and pulled out a notebook.

'What are you doing?'

'I'm writing down what you said. Whenever I'm dumped I never know the right thing to say, but next time it happens I'm going to say *exactly* those words in exactly that tone instead of producing enough tears to power a water feature at Versailles.' She scribbled, dripping water onto her notebook and smearing the ink.

'Being "dumped" is something that happens to you often?'

'Often enough. I fall in love, I get my heart broken, it's a cycle I'm working on breaking.' She wished she hadn't said anything. Although she was fairly open with people, she drew the line at making public announcements about not being easy to love.

That was her secret.

'How many times have you fallen in love?'

'So far?' She shook the pen with frustration as the ink stalled on the damp page, 'Three times.'

'*Cristo*, that's unbelievable.'

'Thanks for not making me feel better. I bet you've never been unlucky in love, have you?'

'I've never been in love at all.'

Lily digested that. 'You've never met the right person.'

'I don't believe in love.'

'You—' She rocked back on her heels, her attention caught. 'So what do you believe in?'

'Money, influence and power.' He shrugged. 'Tangible, measurable goals.'

'You can measure power and influence? Don't tell me—you stamp your foot and it registers on the Richter scale.'

He loosened his tie. 'You'd be surprised.'

'I'm already surprised. Gosh, you are *so* cool. You are my new role model.' Finally she managed to coax ink from the pen. 'It is never too late to change. From now on I'm all about tangible, measurable goals, too. As a matter of interest, what is your goal in relationships?'

'Orgasm.' He gave a slow smile and she felt herself turn scarlet.

'Right. Well, that serves me right for asking a stupid question. That's definitely a measurable goal. You're obviously able to be cold and ruthlessly detached when it comes to relationships. I'm aiming for that. I've dripped all over your floor. Be careful not to slip.'

He was leaning against the wall, watching her with amusement. 'This is what you look like when you're being cold and ruthlessly detached?'

'I haven't actually started yet, but the moment my radar warns me I might be in danger of falling for the wrong type, *bam*—' she punched the air with her fist '—I'm going to turn on my freezing side. From now on I have armour around my heart. Kevlar.' She gave him a friendly smile. 'You think I'm crazy, right? All this is natural to you. But it isn't to me. This is the first stage of my personality transplant. I'd love to do the whole thing under anaesthetic and wake up all new and perfect, but that isn't possible so I'm trying to embrace the process.'

A vibrating noise caught her attention and she glanced across the room towards his jacket. When he didn't move, she looked at him expectantly. 'That's your phone.'

He was still watching her, his gaze disturbingly intent. 'Yes.'

'You're not going to answer it?' She scrambled to her feet, still clutching the towel. 'It might be her, asking for your forgiveness.'

'I'm sure it is, which is why I don't intend to answer it.'

Lily absorbed that with admiration. 'This is a perfect example of why I need to be like you and not like me. If that had been my phone, I would have answered it and when whoever was on the end apologised for treating me badly, I would have told him it was fine. I would have forgiven them.'

'You're right,' he said. 'You do need help. What's your name?'

She shifted, her wet feet sticking to the floor. 'Lily. Like the flower.'

'You look familiar. Have we met before?'

Lily felt the colour pour into her cheeks. 'I've been working as an intern at your company two days a week for the past couple of months. I'm second assistant to your personal assistant.' *I'm the one who broke the photocopier and the coffee machine.*

Dark eyebrows rose. 'We've met?'

'No. I've only seen you once in person. I don't count the time I was hiding in the bathroom.'

'You hid in the bathroom?'

'You were on a firing spree. I didn't want to be noticed.'

'So you work for me two days a week, and on the other three days you're working as a cleaner?'

'No, I only do that job in the evenings. The other three days I'm doing fieldwork up at Aptera for the summer. But that's almost finished. I've reached a crossroads in my life and I've no idea which direction to take.'

'Fieldwork?' That sparked his interest. 'You're an archaeologist?'

'Yes, I'm part of a project funded by the university but that part doesn't pay off my massive college loans so I have other jobs.'

'How much do you know about Minoan antiquities?'

Lily blinked. 'Probably more than is healthy for a woman of twenty-four.'

'Good. Get back into the bathroom and dry yourself off while I find you a dress. Tonight I have to open the new wing of the museum. You're coming with me.'

'Me? Don't you have a date?'

'I had a date,' he said smoothly. 'As you're partially responsible for the fact she's no longer here, you're coming in her place.'

'But—' She licked her lips. 'I'm supposed to be cleaning your villa.'

His gaze slid from her face to the wash of water covering

the bathroom floor. 'I'd say you've done a pretty thorough job. By the time we get home, the flood will have spread down the stairs and across the living areas, so it will clean itself.'

Lily gave a gurgle of laughter. She wondered if any of his employees realised he had a sense of humour. 'You're not going to fire me?'

'You should have more confidence in yourself. If you have knowledge of Minoan artefacts then I still have a use for you and I never fire people who are useful.' He reached for the towel and tugged it off, leaving her clad only in her soaking wet underwear.

'What are you doing?' She gave a squeak of embarrassment and snatched at the towel but he held it out of reach.

'Stop wriggling. I can't be the first man to see you half naked.'

'Usually I'm in a relationship when a man sees me naked. And being stared at is very unnerving, especially when you've been called fat by someone who looks like a toast rack—' Lily broke off as he turned and strolled away from her. She didn't know whether to be relieved or affronted. 'If you want to know my size you could ask me!'

He reached for his phone and dialled. While he waited for the person on the other end to answer, he scanned her body and gave her a slow, knowing smile. 'I don't need to ask, *theé mou*,' he said softly. 'I already know your size.'

CHAPTER TWO

Nik lounged in his seat while the car negotiated heavy evening traffic. Beside him Lily was wriggling like a fish dropped onto the deck of a boat.

'Mr Zervakis? This dress is far more revealing than anything I would normally wear. And I've had a horrible thought.' Her voice was breathy and distracting and Nik turned his head to look at her, trying to remind himself that girls with sweet smiles who were self-confessed members of Loveaholics Anonymous were definitely off his list.

'Call me Nik.'

'I can't call you Nik. It would feel wrong while I'm working in your company. You pay my salary.'

'I pay you? I thought you said you were an intern.'

'I am. You pay your interns far more than most companies, but that's a different conversation. I'm still having that horrible thought by the way.'

Nik dragged his eyes from her mouth and tried to wipe his brain of X-rated thoughts. 'What horrible thought is that?'

'The one where your girlfriend finds out you took me as your date tonight.'

'She will find out.'

'And that doesn't bother you?'

'Why would it?'

'Isn't it obvious? Because she didn't believe I was the cleaner. She thought you and I—well...' she turned scarlet '...if she finds out we were together tonight then it will look as if she was right and we were lying, even though if people used their brains they could work out that if she's your type then I couldn't possibly be.'

Nik tried to decipher that tumbled speech. 'You're concerned she will think we're having sex? Why is that a horrible thought? You find me unattractive?'

'That's a ridiculous question.' Lily's eyes flew to his and then away again. 'Sorry, but that's like asking a woman if she likes chocolate.'

'There are women who don't like chocolate.'

'They're lying. They might not eat it, but that doesn't mean they don't like it.'

'So I'm chocolate?' Nik tried to remember the last time he'd been this entertained by anyone.

'If you're asking if I think you're very tempting and definitely bad for me, the answer is yes. But apart from the fact we're totally unsuited, I wouldn't be able to relax enough to have sex with you.'

Nik, who had never had trouble helping a woman relax, rose to the challenge. 'I'm happy to—'

'No.' She gave him a stern look. 'I know you're competitive, but forget it. I saw that photo of you in the swimming pool. No way could I ever be naked in front of a man with a body like yours. I'd have to suck everything in and make sure you only saw my good side. The stress would kill any passion.'

'I've already seen you in your underwear.'

'Don't remind me.'

Nik caught his driver's amused gaze in the mirror and gave him a steady stare. Vassilis had been with him for over a decade and had a tendency to voice his opinions on Nik's love life. It was obvious he thoroughly approved of Lily.

'It's true that if you turn up as my guest tonight there will be people who assume we are having sex.' Nik returned his attention to the conversation. 'I can't claim to be intimately acquainted with the guest list, but I'm assuming a few of the people there will be your colleagues. Does that bother you?'

'No. It will send a message that I'm not broken-hearted, which is good for my pride. In fact the timing is perfect. Just this morning I embarked on a new project. Operation Ice Maiden. You're probably wondering what that is.'

Nik opened his mouth to comment but she carried on without pausing.

'I am going to have sex with no emotion. That's right.' She nodded at him. 'You heard me correctly. Rebound sex. I am going to climb into bed with some guy and I'm not going to feel a thing.'

Hearing a sound from the front of the car, Nik pressed a button and closed the screen between him and Vassilis, giving them privacy.

'Do you have anyone in mind for—er—Operation Ice Maiden?'

'Not yet, but if they happen to think it's you that's fine. You'd look good on my romantic résumé.'

Nik leaned his head back against the seat and started to laugh. 'You, Lily, are priceless.'

'That doesn't sound like a compliment.' She adjusted the neckline of her dress and her breasts almost escaped in the process. 'You're basically saying I'm not worth anything.'

Dragging his gaze from her body, Nik decided this was the most entertaining evening he'd had in a long time.

'THERE ARE PHOTOGRAPHERS.' As they pulled up outside the museum Lily slunk lower in her seat and Nik closed his hand around her wrist and hauled her upright again.

'You look stunning. If you don't want them all surmising that we climbed out of bed to come here then you need to stop looking guilty.'

'I saw several TV cameras.'

'The opening of a new wing of the museum is news.'

'The neckline of this dress might also be news.' She tugged at it. 'My breasts are too big for this plunging style. Can I borrow your jacket?'

'Your breasts deserve a dress like that and no, you may not borrow my jacket.' His voice was a deep, masculine purr and she felt the sizzle of sexual attraction right through her body.

'Are you flirting with me?' He was completely different from the safe, friendly men who formed part of her social circle. There was a brutal strength to him, a confidence and assurance that suggested he'd never met a man he hadn't been able to beat in a fight, whether in the bar or the boardroom.

Her question appeared to amuse him. 'You're my date. Flirting is mandatory.'

'It unsettles me and I'm already unsettled at the thought of tonight.'

'Because you're with me?'

No way was she confessing how being with him really made her feel. 'No, because the opening of this new museum wing is a really momentous occasion.'

'You and I have a very different idea of what constitutes a momentous occasion, Lily.' There was laughter in his eyes. 'Never before has my ego been so effectively crushed.'

'Your ego is armour plated, like your feelings.'

'It's true that my feelings of self-worth are not dependent on the opinion of others.'

'Because you think you're right and everyone else is wrong. I wish I were more like you. What if the reporters ask who I am? What do I say? I'm a fake.'

'You're the archaeologist. I'm the fake. And you say whatever you want to say. Or say nothing. Your decision. You're the one in charge of your mouth.'

'You have no idea how much I wish that was true.'

'Tell me why you're excited about tonight.'

'You mean apart from the fact I get to dress up? The new wing houses the biggest collection of Minoan antiquities anywhere in Greece. It has a high percentage of provenanced material, which means archaeologists will be able to restudy material from old excavations. It's exciting. And I love the dress by the way, even though I'll never have any reason to wear it again.'

'Chipped pots excite you?'

She winced. 'Don't say that on camera. The collection will play an active role in research and in university teaching as well as offering a unique insight for the general public.'

As the car pulled up outside the museum one of Nik's security team opened the door and Lily emerged to what felt like a million camera flashes.

'Unreal,' she muttered. 'Now I know why celebrities wear sunglasses.'

'Mr Zervakis—' Photographers and reporters gathered as close as they could. 'Do you have a statement about the new wing?'

Nik paused and spoke directly to the camera, relaxed and at ease as he repeated Lily's words without a single error.

She stared at him. 'You must have an incredible short-term memory.'

A reporter stepped forward. 'Who's your guest tonight, Nik?'

Nik turned towards her and she realised he was leaving it up to her to decide whether to give them a name or not.

'I'm a friend,' she muttered and Nik smiled, took her hand and led her up the steps to the welcome committee at the top.

The first person she spotted was David Ashurst and she stopped in dismay. In answer to Nik's questioning look, she shook her head quickly, misery and panic creating a sick cocktail inside her. 'I'm fine. I saw someone I didn't expect to see, that's all. I didn't think he'd have the nerve to show up.'

'That's him?' His gaze travelled from her face to the man looking awkward at the top of the steps. 'He is the reason you're hoping for a personality transplant?'

'His name is Professor Ashurst. He has a *wife*,' she muttered in an undertone. 'Can you believe that? I actually cried over that loser. Do I have time to get my notebook out of my bag? I can't remember what I wrote down.'

'I'll tell you what to say.' He leaned closer and whispered something in her ear that made her gasp.

'I can't say that.'

'No? Then how's this for an alternative?' Sliding his arm round her waist, he pressed his hand to the base of her spine and flattened her against him. She looked up at him, hypnotised by those spectacular dark eyes and the raw sexuality in his gaze. Before she could ask what he was doing he lowered his head and kissed her.

Pleasure screamed through her, sensation scorching her skin and stoking a pool of heat low in her belly. She'd been kissed before, but never like this. Nik used his mouth with slow, sensual expertise and she felt a rush of exquisite excitement burn through her body. Her nerve endings tingled, her tummy flipped like a gymnast in a competition, and Lily was possessed by a deep, dark craving that was entirely new to her. Oblivious to their audience, she pushed against his hard, powerful frame and felt his arms tighten around her in a gesture that was unmistakably possessive. It was a taste rather than a feast, but it left her starving for more so that when he slowly lifted his head she swayed towards him dizzily, trying to balance herself.

'Wh-why did you do that?'

He dragged his thumb slowly across her lower lip and released her. 'Because you didn't know what to say and sometimes actions speak louder than words.'

'You're an amazing kisser.' Lily blinked as a flashbulb went off in her face. 'Now there's *no* chance your girlfriend will believe I'm the cleaner.'

'No chance.' His gaze lingered on her mouth. 'And she isn't my girlfriend.'

Her head spun and her legs felt shaky. She was aware of the women staring at her enviously and David gaping at her, shell-shocked.

As she floated up the last few steps to the top she smiled at him, feeling strong for the first time in days. 'Hi, Professor Ass—Ashurst.' She told herself it was the heat that was making her dizzy and disorientated, not the kiss. 'Have a safe flight home tomorrow. I'm sure your family has missed you.'

There was no opportunity for him to respond because the curator of the museum stepped forward to welcome them, shaking Nik's hand and virtually prostrating himself in gratitude.

'Mr Zervakis—your generosity—this wing is the most exciting moment of my career—' the normally articulate man was stammering. 'I know your schedule is demanding but we'd be honoured if you'd meet the team and then take a quick tour.'

Lily kept a discreet distance but Nik took her hand and clamped her next to his side, a gesture that earned her a quizzical look from Brittany, who was looking sleek and pretty in a short blue dress that showed off her long legs. She was standing next to Spy, whose eyes were glued to Lily's cleavage, confirming all her worst fears about the suitability of the dress.

The whole situation felt surreal.

One moment she'd been half naked and shivering on the bathroom floor, the next she'd been whisked into an elegant bedroom by a team of four people who had proceeded to style her hair, do her make-up and generally make her fit to be seen on the arm of Nik Zervakis.

Three dresses had magically appeared and Nik had strolled into the room in mid phone call, gestured to one of them and then left without even pausing in his conversation.

It had been on the tip of Lily's tongue to select a different dress on principle. Then she'd reasoned that not only had he provided the dress, thus allowing her to turn up at the museum opening in the first place, but that he'd picked the dress she would have chosen herself.

All the same, she felt self-conscious as her friends and colleagues working on the project at Aptera stood together while she was treated like a VIP.

As the curator led them towards the first display Lily forgot to be self-conscious and examined the pot.

'This is early Minoan.'

Nik stared at it with a neutral expression. 'You know that because it's more cracked than the others?'

'No. Because their ceramics were characterised by linear patterns. Look——' She took his arm and drew him closer to the glass. 'Spirals, crosses, triangles, curved lines——' She talked to him about each one and he listened carefully before strolling further along the glass display cabinet.

'This one has a bird.'

'Naturalistic designs were characteristic of the Middle Minoan period. The sequencing of ceramic styles has helped archaeologists define the three phases of Minoan culture.'

He stared down in her eyes. 'Fascinating.'

Her heart bumped hard against her chest and as the curator moved away to answer questions from the press she stepped closer to him. 'You're not really fascinated, are you?'

'I am.' His eyes dropped to her mouth with blatant interest. 'But I think it might be because you're the one saying it. I love the way you get excited about things that put other people to sleep, and your mouth looks cute when you say "Minoan". It makes you pout.'

She tried not to laugh. 'You're impossible. To you it's an old pot, but it can have tremendous significance. Ceramics help archaeologists establish settlement and trading patterns. We can reconstruct human activity based on the distribution of pottery. It gives us an idea of population size and social complexity. Why are you donating so much money to the museum if it isn't an interest of yours?'

'Because I'm interested in preserving Greek culture. I donate the money. It's up to them to decide how to use it. I don't micromanage and gifts don't come with strings.'

'Why didn't you insist that it was called "The Zervakis Wing" or something? Most benefactors want their name in the title.'

'It's about preserving history, not about advertising my name.' His eyes gleamed. 'And ZervaCo is a modern, forward-thinking company at the cutting edge of technology development. I don't want the name associated with a museum.'

'You're joking.'

'Yes, I'm joking.' His smile faded as Spy and Brittany joined them.

'They're good friends of mine,' Lily said quickly, 'so you can switch off the full-wattage intimidation.'

'If you're sure.' He introduced himself to both of them and chatted easily with Spy while Brittany pulled Lily to one side.

'I don't even know where to start with my questions.'

'Probably just as well because I wouldn't know where to start with my answers.'

'I'm guessing he's the owner of Villa You-Have-to-be-Kidding-Me.'

'He is.'

'I'm not going to ask,' Brittany muttered and then grinned. 'Oh hell, yes I am. I'm asking. What happened? He found you in the cellar fighting off the ugly sisters and decided to bring you to the ball?'

'Close. He found me on the floor of his bathroom where I'd been attacked and left for dead by his power shower. After I broke up his relationship, he needed a replacement and I was the only person around.'

Brittany started to laugh. 'You were left for dead by his power shower?'

'You said you wouldn't ask.'

'These things only ever happen to you, Lily.'

'I am aware of that. I am really not good with technology.'

'Maybe not, but you know how to pick your rebound guy. He is spectacular. And you look stunning.' Brittany's curious gaze slid over her from head to foot. 'It's a step up from dusty shorts and hiking boots.'

Lily frowned. 'He isn't my rebound guy.'

'Why not? He is smoking hot. And there's something about him.' Her friend narrowed her eyes as she scanned Nik's broad shoulders and powerful frame. 'A suggestion of the uncivilised under the civilised, if you know what I mean.' Brittany put her hand on her arm and her voice was suddenly serious. 'Be careful.'

'Why would I need to be careful? I'm never setting foot in his shower again, if that's what you mean.'

'It isn't what I mean. That man is not tame.'

'He's surprisingly amusing company.'

'That makes him even more dangerous. He's a tiger, not a pussycat and he hasn't taken his eyes off you for five seconds. I don't want to see you hurt again.'

'I have never been in less danger of being hurt. He isn't my type.'

Brittany looked at her. 'Nik Zervakis is the man equivalent of Blood Type O. He is everyone's type.'

'Not mine.'

'He kissed you,' Brittany said dryly, 'so I'm guessing he might have a different opinion on that.'

'He kissed me because I didn't know what to say to David. I was in an awkward position and he helped me out. He did that for me.'

'Lily, a guy like him does things for himself. Don't make a mistake about that. He does what he wants, with whoever he wants to do it, at a time that suits him.'

'I know. Don't worry about me.' Smiling at Brittany, she moved back to Nik. 'Looks like the party is breaking up. Thanks for a fun evening. I'll post you the dress back and any time you need your shower cleaned let me know. I owe you.'

He stared down at her for a long moment, ignoring everyone around them. 'Have dinner with me. I have a reservation at The Athena at nine.'

She'd heard of The Athena. Who hadn't? It was one of the most celebrated restaurants in the whole of Greece. Eating there was a once-in-a-lifetime experience for most people and a never-in-this-lifetime experience for her.

Those incredible dark eyes held hers and Brittany's voice flitted into her head.

He's a tiger, not a pussycat.

From the way he was looking at her mouth, she wondered if he intended her to be the guest or the meal.

'That's a joke, right?' She gave a half-smile and looked away briefly, awkward, out of her depth. When she looked back at him she was still the only one smiling.

'I never joke about food.'

Something curled low in her stomach. 'Nik...' she spoke softly '...this has been amazing. Really out of this world and something to tell my kids one day, but you're a gazillionaire and I'm a—a—'

'Sexy woman who looks great in that dress.'

There was something about him that made her feel as if she were floating two feet above the ground.

'I was going to say I'm a dusty archaeologist who can't even figure out how to use your power shower.'

'I'll teach you. Have dinner with me, Lily.' His soft command made her wonder if anyone had ever said no to him.

Thrown by the look in his eyes and the almost unbearable sexual tension, she was tempted. Then she remembered her rule about never dating anyone who didn't fit her basic criteria. 'I can't. But I'll never forget this evening. Thank you.' Because she was afraid she'd change her mind, she turned and walked quickly towards the exit.

What a crazy day it had been.

Part of her was longing to look back, to see if he was watching her.

Of course he wouldn't be watching her. Look at how quickly he'd replaced Christina. Within two minutes of her refusal, Nik Zervakis would be inviting someone else to dinner.

David stood in the doorway, blocking her exit. 'What are you doing with him?'

'None of your business.'

His jaw tightened. 'Did you kiss him to make me jealous or to help you get over me?'

'I kissed him because he's a hot guy, and I was over you the moment I found out you were married.' Realising it was true, Lily felt a rush of relief but that relief was tempered by the knowledge that her system for evaluating prospective life partners was seriously flawed.

'I know you love me.'

'You're wrong. And if you really knew me, you'd know I'm incapable of loving a man who is married to another woman.' Her voice and hands were shaking. 'You have a wife. A family.'

'I'll work something out.'

'Did you really just say that to me?' Lily stared at him, appalled. 'A family is *not* disposable. You don't come and go as it suits you, nor do you "work something out". You stick by them through thick and thin.' Disgusted and disillusioned, she tried to step past him but he caught her arm.

'You don't understand. Things are tough right now.'

'I don't care.' She dug her fingers into clammy palms. Knowing that her response was deeply personal, she looked away. 'A real man doesn't walk away when things get tough.'

'You're forgetting how good it was between us.'

'And you're forgetting the promises you made.' She dragged her arm out of his grip. 'Go back to your wife.'

He glanced over her shoulder towards Nik. 'I never thought you were the sort to be turned on by money, but obviously I was wrong. I hope you know what you're doing because all that man will ever give you is one night. A man like him is only interested in sex.'

'What did you say?' Lily stared at him and then turned her head to look at Nik. The sick feeling in her stomach eased and her spirits lifted. 'You're right. Thank you so much.'

'For making you realise he's wrong for you?'

'For making me realise he's perfect. Now stop looking down the front of my dress and go home to your wife and kids.' With that, she stalked past him and spotted the reporter who had asked her identity on the way in. 'Lily,' she said clearly. 'Lily Rose. That's my name. And yes, Rose is my second name.'

Then she turned and stalked back into the museum, straight up to Nik, who was deep in conversation with two important-looking men in suits.

All talk ceased as Lily walked up to him, her heels making the same rhythmic tapping sound that Christina's had earlier in the evening. She decided heels were her new favourite thing for illustrating mood. 'What time is that restaurant reservation?'

He didn't miss a beat. 'Nine o'clock.'

'Then we should leave, because we don't want to be late.' She stood on tiptoe and planted a kiss firmly on his mouth. 'And just so that you know, whatever you're planning on doing with the dress, I'm keeping the shoes.'

CHAPTER THREE

THE ATHENA WAS situated on the edge of town, on a hill overlooking Souda Bay with the White Mountains dominating the horizon behind them.

Still on a high after her confrontation with David, Lily sailed into the restaurant feeling like royalty. 'You have no idea how good it felt to tell David to go home to his wife. I felt like punching the air. You see what a few hours in your company has done for me? I'm already transformed. Your icy control and lack of emotional engagement is contagious.'

Nik guided her to his favourite table, tucked away behind a discreet screen of vines. 'You certainly showed the guy what he was missing.'

Lily frowned. 'I didn't want to show him what he was missing. I wanted him to learn a lesson and never lie or cheat again. I wanted him to think of his poor wife. Marriage should be for ever. No cheating. Mess around as much as you like before if that's what you want, but once you've made that commitment, that's it. Don't you agree?'

'Definitely. Which is why I've never made that commitment,' he said dryly. 'I'm still at the "messing around" stage and I expect to stay firmly trapped in that stage for the rest of my life.'

'You don't want a family? We're very different. It's brilliant.' She smiled at him and his eyes narrowed.

'Why is that brilliant?'

'Because you're completely and utterly wrong for me. We don't want the same things.'

'I'm relieved to hear it.' He leaned back in his chair. 'I hardly dare ask what you want.'

She hesitated. 'Someone like you will think I'm a ridiculous romantic.'

'Tell me.'

She dragged her gaze from his and looked over the tumbling bougainvillea to the sea beyond. *Was she a ridiculous romantic?*

Was she setting herself unachievable goals?

Seduced by the warmth of his gaze and the beauty of the spectacular sunset, she told the truth. 'I want the whole fairy tale.'

'Which fairy tale? The one where the stepmother poisons the apple or the one where the prince has to deal with a heroine with narcolepsy?'

She laughed. 'The happy-ending part. I want to fall in love, settle down and have lots of babies.' Enjoying herself, she looked him in the eye. 'Am I freaking you out yet?'

'That depends. Are you expecting to do any of that with me?'

'No! Of course not.'

'Then you're not freaking me out.'

'I start every relationship in the genuine belief it might go somewhere.'

'I presume you mean somewhere other than bed?'

'I do. I have never been interested in sex for the sake of sex.'

Nik looked amused. 'That's the only sort of sex I'm interested in.'

She sat back in her chair and looked at him. 'I've never had sex with a man I wasn't in love with. I fall in love, then I have sex. I think sex cements my emotional connection to someone.' She sneaked another look at him. 'You don't have that problem, do you?'

'I'm not looking for an emotional connection, if that's what you're asking.'

'I want to be more like you. I decided this morning I'm going to have cold, emotionless rebound sex. I'm switching everything off. It's going to be wham, bam, thank you, man.'

The corners of his mouth flickered. 'Do you have anyone in mind for this project?'

She sensed this wasn't the moment to confess he was right at the top of her list. 'I'm going to pick a guy I couldn't possibly fall in love with. Then I'll be safe. It will be like—' she struggled to find the right description '—emotional contraception. I'll be taking precautions. Wearing a giant condom over my feelings. Protecting myself. I bet you do that all the time.'

'If you're asking if I've ever pulled a giant condom over my feelings, the answer is no.'

'You're laughing at me, but if you'd been hurt as many times as I have you wouldn't be laughing. So if emotions don't play a part in your relationships, what exactly is sex to you?'

'Recreation.' He took a menu from the waiter and she felt a rush of mortification. As soon as he walked away, she gave a groan.

'How long had he been standing there?'

'Long enough to know you're planning on having cold, unemotional rebound sex and that you're thinking of wearing a giant condom over your feelings. I think that was the point he decided it was time to take our order.'

She covered her face with her hands. 'We need to leave. I'm sure the food here is delicious, but we need to eat somewhere different or I need to take my plate under the table.'

'You're doing it again. Letting emotions govern your actions.'

'But he *heard* me. Aren't you embarrassed?'

'Why would I be embarrassed?'

'Aren't you worried about what he might think of you?'

'Why would I care what he thinks? I don't know him. His role is to serve our food and make sure we enjoy ourselves sufficiently to want to come back. His opinion on anything else is irrelevant. Carry on with what you were saying. It was fascinating. Dining with you is like learning about an alien species. You were telling me you're going to pick a guy you can't fall in love with and use him for sex.'

'And you were telling me sex is recreation—like football?'

'No, because football is a group activity. I'm possessive, so for me it's strictly one on one.'

Her heart gave a little flip. 'That sounds like a type of commitment.'

'I'm one hundred per cent committed for the time a woman is in my bed. She is the sole focus of my attention.'

Her stomach uncurled with a slow, dangerous heat. 'But that might only be for a night?'

He simply smiled and she leaned back with a shocked laugh. 'You are so *bad*. And honest. I love that.'

'As long as you don't love *me*, we don't have a problem.'

'I could never love you. You are so wrong for me.'

'I think we should drink to that.' He raised a hand and moments later champagne appeared on the table.

'I can't believe you live like this. A driver, bottles of champagne—' She lifted the glass, watching the bubbles. 'Your villa is bigger than quite a few Greek islands and there is only one of you.'

'I like space and light and property is always a good investment.' He handed the menu back to the waiter. 'Is there any food you don't eat?'

'I eat everything.' She paused while he spoke to the waiter in Greek. 'Are you seriously ordering for me?'

'The menu is in Greek and you were talking about sex so I was aiming to keep the interaction as brief as possible in order to prevent you from feeling the need to dine under the table.'

'In that case I'll forgive you.' She waited until the waiter had walked away with their order. 'So if property is an investment that means you'd *sell* your home?'

'I have four homes.'

Her jaw dropped. 'Four? Why does one person need four homes? One for every season or something?'

'I have offices in New York, San Francisco and London and I don't like staying in hotels.'

'So you buy a house. That is the rich man's way of solving a problem. Which one do you think of as home?' Seeing the puzzled look on his face, she elaborated. 'Where do your family live? Do you have family? Are your parents alive?'

'They are.'

'Happily married?'

'Miserably divorced. In my father's case three times so far, but he's always in competition with himself so I'm expecting a fourth as soon as the wedding is out of the way.'

'And your mother?' She saw a faint shift in his expression.

'My mother is American. She lives in Boston with her third husband who is a divorce lawyer.'

'So do you think of yourself as Greek American or American Greek?'

He gave a careless lift of his broad shoulders. 'Whichever serves my purpose at the time.'

'Wow. So you have this big, crazy family.' Lily felt a flash of envy. 'That must be wonderful.'

'Why?'

'You don't think it's wonderful? I guess we never appreciate something when we have it.' She said it lightly but felt his dark gaze fix on her across the table.

'Are you going to cry?'

'No, of course not.'

'Good. Because tears are the one form of emotional expression I don't tolerate.'

She stole an olive from the bowl on the table. 'What if someone is upset?'

'Then they need to walk away from me until they've sorted themselves out, or be prepared for me to walk away. I never allow myself to be manipulated and ninety-nine per cent of tears are manipulation.'

'What about the one per cent which are an expression of genuine emotion?'

'I've never encountered that rare beast, so I'm willing to play the odds.'

'If that's your experience, you must have met some awful women in your time. I don't believe you'd be that unsympathetic.'

'Believe it.' He leaned back as the waiter delivered a selection of dishes. 'These are Cretan specialities. Try them.' He spooned beans in a rich tomato sauce onto her plate and added local goat's cheese.

She nibbled the beans and moaned with pleasure. 'These are delicious. I still can't believe you ordered for me. Do you want to feed me, too? Because I could lie back and let you drop grapes into my mouth if that would be fun. Or you could cover my naked body with whipped cream. Is that the sort of stuff you do in bed?'

There was a dangerous glitter in his eyes. 'You don't want to know the sort of "stuff" I do in bed, Lily. You're far too innocent.'

She remembered what Brittany had said about him not being tame. 'I'm not innocent. I have big eyes and that gives people a false impression of me.'

'You remind me of a kitten that's been abandoned by the side of the road.'

'You've got me totally wrong. I'd say I'm more of a panther.' She clawed the air and growled. 'A little bit predatory. A little bit dangerous.'

He gave her a long steady look and she blushed and lowered her hand.

'All right, maybe not a *panther* exactly but not a kitten either.'

She thought about what lay in her past. 'I'll have you know I'm pretty tough. Tell me more about your family. So you have a father and a few stepmothers. How about siblings?'

'I have one half-sister who is two.'

Lily softened. 'I love that age. They're so busy and into everything. Is she adorable?'

'I've no idea. I've never met her.'

'You've—' She stared at him, shocked. 'You mean it's been a while since you've seen her.'

'No. I mean I've never seen her.' He lifted his champagne. 'Her mother extracted all the money she could from my father and then left. She lives in Athens and visits when she wants something.'

'Oh, my God, that's *terrible*.' Lily's eyes filled. 'Your poor, poor father.'

He put his glass down slowly. 'Are you crying for my father?'

'No.' Her throat was thickened. 'Maybe. Yes, a little bit.'

'A man you've never met and know nothing about.'

'Maybe I'm the one per cent who cares.' She sniffed and he shook his head in exasperation.

'This is your tough, ruthless streak? How can you be sad for someone you don't know?'

'Because I sympathise with his situation. He doesn't see his little girl and that must be so hard. Family is the most important thing in the world and it is often the least appreciated thing.'

'If you let a single tear fall onto your cheek,' he said softly, 'I'm walking out of here.'

'I don't believe you. You wouldn't be that heartless. I think it's all a big act you put on to stop women slobbering all over you.'

'Do you want to test it?' His tone was cool. 'Because I suggest you wait until the end of the meal. The lamb *kleftiko* is the best anywhere in Greece and they make a house special with honey and pistachio nuts that you wouldn't want to miss.'

'But if you're the one walking out, then I can stay here and eat your portion.' She helped herself to another spoonful of food from the dish closest to her. 'I don't know why you're so freaked out by tears. It's not as if I was expecting you to hug me. I've taught myself to self-soothe.'

'Self-soothe?' Some of the tension left him. 'You hug yourself?'

'It's important to be independent.' She'd been self-sufficient from an early age, but the ability to do everything for herself hadn't removed the deep longing to share her life with someone. 'Why did your dad and his last wife divorce?'

'Because they married,' he said smoothly, 'and divorce is an inevitable consequence of marriage.'

She wondered why he had such a grim view of marriage. 'Not all marriages.'

'All but those infected with extreme inertia.'

'So you're saying that even people who stay married would divorce if they could be bothered to make the effort.'

'I think there are any number of reasons for a couple to stay together, but love isn't one of them. In my father's case, wife number three married him for his money and the novelty wore off.'

'Does "wife number three" have a name?'

'Callie.' His hard tone told her everything she needed to know about his relationship with his last stepmother.

'You don't like her?'

'Are you enjoying your meal?'

She blinked, thrown by the change of subject. 'It's delicious, but—'

'Good. If you're hoping to sample dessert, you need to talk about something other than my family.'

'You control everything, even the conversation.' She wondered why he didn't want to talk about his family. 'Is this where you bring all the women you date?'

'It depends on the woman.'

'How about that woman you were with earlier—Christina?

She definitely wouldn't have eaten any of this. She had carb-phobia written all over her.'

Those powerful shoulders relaxed slightly. 'She would have ordered green salad, grilled fish and eaten half of it.'

'So why didn't you order green salad and grilled fish for me?'

'Because you look like someone who enjoys food.'

Lily gave him a look. 'I'm starting to understand why women cry around you. You basically called me fat. For your information, most women would storm out if you said that to them.'

'So why didn't you storm out?'

'Because eating here is a once-in-a-lifetime experience and I don't want to miss it. And I don't think you meant it that way and I like to give people the benefit of the doubt. Tell me what happens next on a date. You bring a woman to a place like this and then you take her back to your villa for sex in that massive bed?'

'I never talk about my relationships.'

'You don't talk about your family and you don't talk about your relationships.' Lily helped herself to rich, plump slices of tomato salad. 'What do you want to talk about?'

'You. Tell me about your work.'

'I work in your company. You know more about what goes on than I do, but one thing I will say is that with all these technology skills at your disposal you need to invent an app that syncs all the details of the women who call you. You have a busy sex life and it's easy to get it mixed up, especially as they're all pretty much the same type.' She put her fork down. 'Is that the secret to staying emotionally detached? You date women who are clones, no individual characteristics to tell them apart.'

'I do not date clones, and I don't want to talk about my work, I want to talk about your work. Your archaeological work.' His eyes gleamed. 'And try to include the word "Minoan" at least eight times in each sentence.'

She ignored that. 'I'm a ceramics expert. I did a masters in archaeology and since then I've been working on an internationally funded project replicating Minoan cooking fabrics. Among other things we've been looking at the technological shift Minoan potters made when they replaced hand-building methods with the wheel. We can trace patterns of production, but also the context of ceramic consumption. The word *ceramic* comes from the Greek, *keramikos,* but you probably already know that.'

He reached for his wine glass. 'I can't believe you were cleaning my shower.'

'Cleaning your shower pays well and I have college debts.'

'If you didn't have college debts, what would you be doing?'

She hesitated, unwilling to share her dream with a stranger, especially one who couldn't possibly understand having to make choices driven by debt. 'I have no idea. I can't afford to think like that. I have to be practical.'

'Why Crete?'

'Crete had all the resources necessary to produce pottery. Clay, temper, water and fuel. Microscopic ceramic fabric analysis indicate those resources have been used for at least eight thousand years. The most practical way of understanding ancient technology is to replicate it and use it and that's what we've been doing.'

'So you've been trying to cook like a Minoan?'

'Yes. We're using tools and materials that would have been available during the Cretan Bronze Age.'

'That's what you're digging for?'

'Brittany and the team have different objectives, but while they're digging I'm able to access clay. I spend some of my time on site and some of my time at the museum with a small team, but that's all coming to an end now. Tell me what you do.'

'You work in my company. You should know what I do.'

'I don't know *specifically* what you do. I know you're a technology wizard. I guess that's why you have a shower that looks like something from NASA. I bet you're good with computers. Technology isn't really my thing, but you probably already know that.'

'If technology isn't your thing, why are you working in my company?'

'I'm not dealing with the technology side. I'm dealing with people. I did a short spell in Human Resources—you keep them busy by the way—and now I'm working with your personal assistants. I still haven't decided what I want to do with my life so I'm trying different things. It's only two days a week and I wanted to see how I enjoyed corporate life.'

'And how are you enjoying "corporate life"?'

'It's different.' She dodged the question and he gave her a long, speculative look.

'Tell me why you became involved with that guy who looked old enough to be your father.'

Her stomach lurched. *Because she was an idiot.* 'I never talk about my relationships.'

'On short acquaintance I'd say the problem is stopping you talking, not getting you talking. Tell me.' Something about that compelling dark gaze made it impossible not to confide.

'I think I was attracted to his status and gravitas. I was flattered when he paid me attention. A psychologist would probably say it has something to do with not having a father around when I was growing up. Anyway, he pursued me pretty heavily and it got serious fast. And then I found out he was married.' She lowered her voice and pulled a face. 'I hate myself for that, but most of all I hate him for lying to me.' Knowing his views on marriage, she wondered if he'd think she was ridiculously principled but his eyes were hard.

'You cried over this guy?'

'I think perhaps I was crying because history repeated itself. My relationships always follow the same pattern. I meet someone I'm attracted to, he's caring, attentive and a really good listener—I fall in love, have sex with him, start planning a future and then suddenly that's it. We break up.'

'And this experience hasn't put you off love?'

Perhaps it should have done.

No one had ever stayed in her life.

From an early age she'd wondered what it was about her that made it so easy for people to walk away.

The dishes were cleared away and a sticky, indulgent dessert placed in the centre of the table.

She tried to pull herself together. 'If you have one bad meal you don't stop eating, do you? And by the way this is the best meal I've ever had in my whole life.' She stuck her spoon in the pastry and honey oozed over the plate. She decided this was the perfect time to check a few facts before finally committing herself. 'Tell me what happens in your relationships. We'll talk hypothetically as you don't like revealing specifics. Let's say you meet a woman and you find her attractive. What happens next?'

'I take her on a date.'

'What sort of date?' Lily licked the spoon. 'Dinner? Theatre? Movie? Walk on the beach?'

'Any of those.'

'Let's say it's dinner. What would you talk about?'

'Anything.'

'Anything as long as it isn't to do with your family or relationships.'

He smiled. 'Exactly.'

'So you talk, you drink expensive wine, you admire the romantic view—then what? You take her home or you take her to bed?'

'Yes.' He paused as their waiter delivered a bottle of clear liquid and two glasses and Lily shook her head.

'Is that raki? Brittany loves it, but it gives me a headache.'

'We call it *tsikoudia*. It is a grape liqueur—an important part of Cretan hospitality.'

'I know. It's been around since Minoan times. Archaeologists have found the petrified remains of grapes and grape pips inside *pithoi*, the old clay storage jars, so it's assumed they knew plenty about distillation. Doesn't change the fact it gives me a headache.'

'Then you didn't drink it with enough water.' He handed her a small glass. 'The locals think it promotes a long and healthy life.'

Lily took a sip and felt her throat catch fire as she swallowed. 'So now finish telling me about your typical date. You don't fall in love, because you don't believe in love. So when you take a woman to bed, there are no feelings involved at all?'

'There are plenty of feelings involved.' The look he gave her made her heart pump faster.

'I mean emotions. You have emotionless sex. You don't say *I love you*. You don't feel anything here—' Lily put her hand on her heart. 'No feelings. So it's all about physical satisfaction. This is basically a naked workout, yes? It's like a bench press for two.'

'Sex may not be emotional, but it's intimate,' he said softly. 'It requires the ultimate degree of trust.'

'You can do that and still not be emotionally involved?'

'When I'm with a woman I care about her enjoyment, her pleasure, her happiness and her comfort. I don't love her.'

'You don't love women?'

'I do love women.' The corners of his mouth flickered. 'I just don't want to love one specific woman.'

Lily stared at him in fascination.

There was no way, *no way*, she would ever fall in love with a man like Nik. She didn't even need to check her list to know he didn't tick a single one of the boxes.

He was perfect.

'There's something I want to say to you and I hope you're not going to be shocked.' She put her glass down and took a deep breath. 'I want to have rebound sex. No emotions involved. Sex without falling in love. Not something I've ever done before, so this is all new to me.'

He watched her from under lowered lids, his expression

unreadable. There was a dangerous stillness about him. 'And you're telling me this because—?'

'Because you seem to be the expert.' Her heart started to pound. 'I want you to take me to bed.'

CHAPTER FOUR

NIK SCANNED HER in silence. The irony was that his original plan had been to do exactly that. Take her to bed. She was fun, sexy and original but the longer he spent in her company the more he realised how different her life goals were from his own. By her own admittance, Lily wasn't the sort to emotionally disengage in a relationship. In the interests of self-protection, logic took precedence over his libido.

'It's time I took you home.'

Far from squashing her, the news appeared to cheer her. 'That's what I was hoping you'd say. I promise you won't regret it. What I lack in experience I make up for in enthusiasm.'

She was as bright as she was pretty and he knew her 'misunderstanding' was deliberate.

'*Theé mou*, you should *not* be saying things like that to a man. It could be taken the wrong way.'

She sliced into a tomato. 'You're taking it the way I intended you to take it.'

Nik glanced at the bottle of champagne and tried to work out how much she'd had. 'I'm not taking you to my home, I'm taking you to *your* home.'

'You don't want to do that. My bed is smaller than a cat bas-

ket and you're big. I have a feeling we're going to get very hot
and sweaty, and I don't have air conditioning.'

Nik's libido was fighting against the restraining bonds of
logic. 'I will give you a lift home and then I'm leaving.'

'Leaving?' Disappointment mingled with uncertainty. 'You
don't find me attractive?'

'You're sexy as hell,' he drawled, 'but you're not my type.'

'That doesn't make any sense. You don't like sexy?'

'I like sexy. I don't like women who want to fall in love, settle down and have lots of babies.'

'I thought we'd already established I didn't want to do any
of that with you. You don't score a single point on my checklist, which is *exactly* why I want to do this. I know I'd be safe.
And so would you!'

He decided he didn't even want to know about her checklist.
'How much champagne have you had?'

'I'm not drunk, if that's what you're suggesting. Ask me anything. Make me walk in a straight line. I'll touch my nose with
my eyes closed, or I'll touch *your* nose with my eyes closed if
you prefer. Or other parts of you—' She gave a wicked grin
and leaned forward. 'One night. That's all it would be. You
will not regret it.'

Nik deployed the full force of his will power and kept his eyes
away from the softness of her breasts. 'You're right. I won't,
because it's not going to happen.'

'I do yoga. I'm very bendy.'

Nik gave a soft curse. 'Stop talking.'

'I can put my legs behind my head.'

'*Cristo*, you should *definitely* stop talking.' His libido was
urging logic to surrender.

'What's the problem? One night of fun. Tomorrow we both
go our own ways and if I see you in the office I'll pretend I
don't know you. Call your lawyer. I'll sign a contract promising not to fall in love with you. A pre-non-nuptial agreement.
All I want is for you to take me home, strip me naked, throw

me onto that enormous bed of yours and have sex with me in every conceivable position. After that I will walk out of your door and you'll never see me again. Deal?'

He tried to respond but it seemed her confusing mix of innocence and sexuality had short-circuited his brain. 'Lily—' he spoke through his teeth '—trust me, you do *not* want me to take you home, strip you naked and throw you onto my bed.'

'Why not? It's just sex.'

'You've spent several hours telling me you don't do "just sex".'

'But I'm going to this time. I want to be able to separate sex from love. The next time a man comes my way who might be the one, I won't let sex confuse things. I'll be like Kevlar. Nothing is getting through me. Nothing.'

'You are marshmallow, not Kevlar.'

'That was the old me. The new me is Kevlar. I don't understand why you won't do this, unless—' She studied him for a long moment and then leaned forward, a curious look in her eyes. 'Are you *scared*?'

'I'm sober,' he said softly, 'and when I play, I like it to be with an opponent who is similarly matched.'

'I'm tougher than I look.' A dimple appeared in the corner of her mouth. 'Drink another glass of champagne and then call Vassilis.'

'How do you know my driver's name?'

'I listen. And he has a kind face. There really is no need to be nervous. If rumour is correct, you're a cold, emotionless vacuum and that means you're in no danger from someone like little me.'

He had a feeling 'little me' was the most dangerous thing he'd encountered in a long while. 'If I'm a "cold, emotionless vacuum", why would you want to climb into my bed?'

'Because you are *insanely* sexy and all the things that make you so wrong for me would make you perfect for rebound sex.'

He looked into those blue eyes and tried to ignore the surge of sexual hunger that had gripped him from the moment he'd laid eyes on that pale silky hair tumbling damp round her gleaming wet body.

Never before had doing the right thing felt so wrong.

Nik cursed under his breath and rose to his feet. 'We're leaving.'

'Good decision.' She slid her hand into his, rose on tiptoe and whispered in his ear. 'I'll be gentle with you.'

With her wide smile and laughing eyes, it was like being on a date with a beam of sunshine. He felt heat spread through his body, his arousal so brutal he was tempted to haul her behind the nearest lockable door, rip off that dress and acquaint himself with every part of her luscious, naked body.

Vassilis was waiting outside with the car and Nik bundled her inside and sat as far from her as possible.

All his life, he'd avoided women like her. Women who believed in romance and 'the one'. For him, the myth of love had been smashed in childhood along with Santa and the Tooth Fairy. He had no use for it in his life.

'Where do you live?' He growled the words but she simply smiled.

'You don't need to know, because we're going back to your place. Your bed is almost big enough to be seen from outer space.'

Nik ran his hand over his jaw. 'Lily—'

Her phone signalled a text and she dug around in her bag. 'I need to answer this. It will be Brittany, checking I'm all right. She and Spy are probably worried because they saw me go off with you.'

'Maybe you should pay attention to your friends.'

'Hold that thought—'

Having rebound sex. She mouthed the words as she typed. Speak to you tomorrow.

Nik was tempted to seize the phone and text her friends to come and pick her up. 'Brittany was the girl in the blue dress?'

'She's the female version of you, but without the money. She doesn't engage emotionally. I found out today that she was married for ten days when she was eighteen. Can you believe that? Ten days. I don't know the details, but apparently it cured her of ever wanting a repeat performance.' She pressed send and slid the phone back into her bag. 'I grew up in foster homes so I don't have any family. I think that's probably why my friends are so important to me. I never really had a sense of belonging anywhere. That's a very lonely feeling as a child.'

He felt something stir inside him, as if she'd poked a stick into a muddy, stagnant pool that had lain dormant and undiscovered for decades. Deeply uncomfortable, he shifted in his seat. 'Why are you telling me this?'

'I thought as we're going to have sex, you might want to know something about me.'

'I don't.'

'That's not very polite.'

'I'm not striving for "polite". This is who I am. It's not too late for my driver to drop you home. Give him the address.'

She leaned forward and pressed the button so that the screen closed between him and the driver. 'Sorry, Vassilis, but I don't want to corrupt you.' She slid across the seat, closed her eyes and lifted her face to his. 'Kiss me. Whatever it is you do, do it now.'

Nik had always considered himself to be a disciplined man but he was rapidly rethinking that assessment. With her, there was no discipline. He looked down at those long, thick eyelashes and the pink curve of her mouth and tried to remember when he'd last been tempted to have sex in the back of his car.

'No.' He managed to inject the word with forceful conviction but instead of retreating, she advanced.

'In that case I'll kiss you. I don't mind taking the initiative.' Her slim fingers slid to the inside of his thigh. He was so aroused he couldn't even remember why he was fighting this, and instead of pushing her away he gripped her hand hard and turned his head towards her.

His gaze swept her flushed cheeks and the lush curve of her mouth. With a rough curse he lowered his head, driving her lips apart with his tongue and taking that mouth in a kiss that was as rough as it was sexually explicit. His intention was to scare her off, so there was no holding back, no diluting of his passion. He kissed her hard, expecting to feel her pull back but instead she pressed closer. She tasted of sugar and sweet temptation, her mouth soft and eager against his as she all but wriggled onto his lap.

The heavy weight of her breasts brushed against his arm and he gave a groan and slid his hand into her hair, anchoring her head for the hard demands of his kiss. She licked into his mouth, snuggling closer like a kitten, those full soft curves pressing against him. It was a kiss without boundaries, an explosion of raw desire that built until the rear of the car shimmered with stifling heat and sexual awareness.

He slid his hand under her dress, over the smooth skin of her thigh to the soft shadows between her legs. It was her thickened moan of pleasure that woke him up.

Cristo, they were in the car, in moving traffic.

Releasing her as if she were a hot coal, he pushed her away. 'I thought you were supposed to be smart.'

Her breathing was shallow and rapid. 'I'm very, very smart. And you're an amazing kisser. Are you as good at everything else?'

His pulse was throbbing and he was so painfully aroused he didn't dare move. 'If you really want to come home with me then you're not as smart as you look.'

'What makes you think that?'

'Because a woman like you should steer clear of men like me. I don't have a love life, I have a sex life. I'll use you. If you're in my bed it will be all about pleasure and nothing else. I don't care about your feelings. I'm not kind. I'm not gentle. I need you to know that.'

There was a long, loaded silence and then her gaze slid to

his mouth. 'Okay, I get it. No fluffy kittens in this relationship. Message received and understood. Can this car go any faster because I don't think I've ever been this turned on in my life before.'

She wasn't the only one. His self-control was stretched to breaking point. Why was he fighting it? She was an adult. She wasn't drunk and she knew what she was doing. Logic didn't just surrender to libido, it was obliterated. All the same, something made him open one more exit door. 'Be very sure, Lily.'

'I'm sure. I've never been so sure of anything in my life. Unless you want to be arrested for performing an indecent act in a public place you'd better tell Vassilis to break a few speed limits.'

LILY WALKED INTO the villa she'd cleaned earlier, feeling ridiculously nervous. In the romantic setting of the restaurant this had seemed like a good idea. Now she wasn't quite so sure. 'So why did you hire a contract cleaning company?'

'I didn't.' He threw his jacket over the back of a chair with careless disregard for its future appearance. 'I have staff who look after this place. Presumably they arranged it. I didn't give them much notice of my return. I don't care how they do their job as long as it gets done.'

She paced across the living room and stared across the flood-lit shimmer of the infinity pool. 'It's pretty at night.' It was romantic, but she knew this had nothing to do with romance. Her other relationships had been with men she knew and cared about. This scenario was new to her. 'Do you have something to drink?'

'You're thirsty?'

Nervous. 'A little.'

He gave her a long look, strolled out of the room and returned moments later carrying a glass of water.

'I want you sober,' he said softly. 'In fact I insist on it.'

Realising they were actually going to do this, she suddenly

found she was shaking so much the water sloshed out of the glass and onto the floor. 'Oops. I'm messing up the floor I cleaned earlier.'

He was standing close to her and her gaze drifted to the bronzed skin at the base of his throat and the blue-shadowed jaw. Everything about him was unapologetically masculine. He wasn't just dangerously attractive, he was lethal and suddenly she wondered what on earth she was doing. Maybe she should have taken up Spy's offer of rebound sex, except that Spy didn't induce one tenth of this crazy response in her. A thrilling sense of anticipation mingled with wicked excitement and she knew she'd regret it for ever if she walked away. She knew she took relationships too seriously. If she was going to try a different approach then there was surely no better man to do it with than Nik.

'Scared?' His voice was deep, dark velvet and she gave a smile.

'A little. But only because I don't normally do this and you're not my usual type. It's like passing your driving test and then getting behind the wheel of a Ferrari. I'm worried I'll crash you into a lamppost.' She put the glass down carefully on the glass table and ran her damp hands over her thighs. 'Okay, let's do this. Ignore the fact I'm shaking, go right ahead and do your bad, bad thing, whatever that is.'

He said nothing. Just looked at her, that dark gaze uncomfortably penetrating.

She waited, heart pounding, virtually squirming on the spot. 'I'm not good with delayed gratification. I'm more of an instant person. I like to—'

'Hush.' Finally he spoke and then he reached out and drew her against him, the look in his eyes driving words and thoughts from her head. She felt the warmth of his hand against the base of her spine, the slow, sensitive stroke of his fingers low on her back and then he lifted his hands and cupped her face, forcing her to look at him. 'Lily Rose—'

She swallowed. 'Nik—'

'Don't be nervous.' He murmured the words against her lips. 'There's no reason to be nervous.'

'I'm not nervous,' she lied. 'But I'm not really sure what happens next.'

'I'll decide what happens next.'

Her heart bumped uncomfortably against her ribs. 'So—what do you want me to do?'

His mouth hovered close to hers and his fingers grazed her jaw. 'I want you to stop talking.'

'I'm going to stop talking right now this second.' Her stomach felt as if a thousand butterflies were trying to escape. She hadn't expected him to be so gentle, but those exploring fingers were slow, almost languorous as they stroked her face and slid over her neck and into her hair.

She stood, disorientated by intoxicating pleasure as he trailed his mouth along her jaw, tormenting her with dark, dangerous kisses. Heat uncurled low in her pelvis and spread through her body, sapping the strength from her knees, and she slid her hands over those sleek, powerful shoulders, feeling the hard swell of muscle beneath her palms. His mouth moved lower and she tilted her head back as he kissed her neck and then the base of her throat. She felt the slow slide of his tongue against supersensitive skin, the warmth of his breath and then his hand slid back into her hair and he brought his mouth back to hers. He kissed her with an erotic expertise that made her head spin and her legs grow heavy. With each slow stroke of his tongue, he sent her senses spinning out of control. It was like being drugged. She tried to find her balance, her centre, but just when she felt close to grasping a few threads of control, he used his mouth to drive every coherent thought from her head. Shaky, she lifted her hand to his face, felt the roughness of his jaw against her palm and the lean, spare perfection of his bone structure.

She slid her fingers into his hair and felt his hand slide down her spine and draw her firmly against him.

She felt him, brutally hard through the silky fabric of her dress, and she gave a moan, low in her throat as he trapped her there with the strength of his arms, the power in those muscles reminding her that this wasn't a safe flirtation, or a game.

His kisses grew rougher, more intimate, more demanding and she tugged at his shirt, her fingers swift and sure on the buttons, her movements more frantic with each bit of male muscle she exposed.

His chest was powerful, his abs lean and hard and she felt a moment of breathless unease because she'd never had sex with a man built like him.

He was self-assured and experienced and as she pushed the shirt from his shoulders she tried to take a step backwards.

'I'd like to keep my clothes on, if that's all right with you.'

'It's not all right.' But there was a smile in his voice as he slid his hand from her hips to her waist, pulling her back against him. His fingers brushed against the underside of her breast and she moaned.

'You look as if you spend every spare second of your life working out.'

'I don't.'

'You get this way through lots of athletic sex?'

His mouth hovered close to hers. 'You promised to stop talking.'

'That was before I saw you half naked. I'm intimidated. That photo didn't lie. Now I know what you look like under your clothes I think I might be having body-image problems.'

He smiled, and she felt his hands at the back of her dress and the slow slither of silk as her dress slid to the floor.

Standing in front of him in nothing but her underwear and high heels, she felt ridiculously exposed. It didn't matter that he'd already seen her that way. This was different.

He eased back from her, his eyes slumberous and dangerously dark. 'Let's go upstairs.'

Her knees were shaking so much she wasn't sure she could walk but the next moment he scooped her into his arms and she gave a gasp of shock and dug her hands in his shoulder.

'Don't you dare drop me. I bruise easily.' She had a close-up view of his face and stared hungrily at the hard masculine lines, the blue-black shadow of his jaw and the slim, sensual line of his mouth. 'If I'd known you were planning on carrying me I would have said no to dessert.'

'Dessert was the best part.' They reached the top of the stairs and he carried her into his bedroom and lowered her to the floor next to the bed.

She didn't see him move, and yet a light came on next to the bed sending a soft beam over the silk covers. Glancing around her, Lily realised that if she lay on that bed her body would be illuminated by the wash of light.

'Can we switch the lights off?'

His eyes hooded, he lowered his hands to his belt. 'No.' As he removed the last of his clothes she let her eyes skid downwards and felt heat pour into her cheeks.

It was only a brief glance, but it was enough to imprint the image of his body in her brain.

'Do you model underwear in your spare time? Because seriously—' Her cheeks flooded with colour. 'Okay so I think this whole thing would be easier in the dark—then I won't be so intimidated by your supersonic abs.'

'Hush.' He smoothed her hair back from her face. 'Do you trust me?' His voice was rough and she felt a flutter of nerves low in her belly.

'I—yes. I think so. Why? Am I being stupid?'

'No. Close your eyes.'

She hesitated and then closed them. She heard the sound of a drawer opening and then felt something soft and silky being tied round her eyes.

'What are you doing?' She lifted her hand but he closed his fingers round her wrist and drew her hands back to her sides.

'Relax.' His voice was a soft purr. 'I'm taking away one of your senses. The one that's making you nervous. There's no need to panic. You still have four remaining. I want you to use those.'

'I can't see.'

'Exactly. You wanted to do this in the dark. Now you're in the dark.'

'I meant that you should put the lights out! It was so you couldn't see me, not so that I couldn't see you.'

'Shh.' His lips nibbled at hers, his tongue stroking over her mouth in a slow, sensual seduction.

She was quivering, her senses straining with delicious anticipation as she tried to work out where he was and where he'd touch her next.

She felt his lips on her shoulder and felt his fingers slide the thin straps of her bra over her arms. Wetness pooled between her thighs and she pressed them together, so aroused she could hardly breathe.

He took his time, explored her neck, her shoulder, the underside of her breast until she wasn't sure her legs would hold her and he must have known that because he tipped her back onto the bed, supporting her as she lost her balance.

She could see nothing through the silk mask but she felt the weight of him on top of her, the roughness of his thigh against hers and the slide of silk against her heated flesh as he stripped her naked.

She was quivering, her senses sharpened by her lack of vision. She felt the warmth of his mouth close over the tip of her breast, the skilled flick of his tongue sending arrows of pleasure shooting through her over-sensitised body.

She gave a moan and clutched at his shoulders. 'Do we need a safe word or something?' She felt him pause.

'Why would you need a safe word?'

'I thought—'

'I'm not going to do anything that makes you uncomfortable.'

'What do I say if I want you to stop?'

His mouth brushed lightly across her jaw. 'You say "stop".'

'That's it?'

'That's it.' There was a smile in his voice. 'If I do one single thing that makes you uncomfortable, tell me.'

'Is embarrassed the same as uncomfortable?'

He gave a soft laugh and she felt the stroke of his palm on her thigh and then he parted her legs and his mouth drifted from her belly to her inner thigh.

He paused, his breath warm against that secret place. 'Relax, *erota mou.*'

She lifted her hands to remove the blindfold but he caught her wrists in one hand and held them pinned, while he used the other to part her and expose her secrets.

Unbearably aroused, melting with a confusing mix of desire and mortification, she tried to close her legs but he licked at her intimately, opening her with his tongue, exploring her vulnerable flesh with erotic skill and purpose until all she wanted was for him to finish what he'd started.

'Nik—' She writhed, sobbed, struggled against him and he released her hands and anchored her hips, holding her trapped as he explored her with his tongue.

She'd forgotten all about removing the blindfold.

The only thing in her head was easing the maddening ache that was fast becoming unbearable.

She dug her fingers in the sheets, moaning as he slid his fingers deep inside her, manipulating her body and her senses until she tipped into excitement overload. She felt herself start to throb round those seeking fingers, but instead of giving her what she wanted he gently withdrew his hand and eased away from her.

'Please! Oh, please—' she sobbed in protest, wondering what he was doing.

Was he leaving her?

Was he stopping?

With a whimper of protest, she writhed and reached for him and then she heard a faint sound and understood the reason for the brief interlude.

Condom, she thought, and then the ability to think coherently vanished because he covered her with the hard heat of his body. She felt the blunt thrust of his erection at her moist entrance and tensed in anticipation, but instead of entering her he cupped her face in his hand and gently slid off the blindfold.

'Look at me.' His soft command penetrated her brain and she opened her eyes and stared at him dizzily just as he slid his hand under her bottom and entered her in a series of slow, deliciously skilful thrusts. He was incredibly gentle, taking his time, murmuring soft words in Greek and then English as he moved deep into the heart of her. Then he paused, kissed her mouth gently, holding her gaze with his.

'Are you all right? Do you want to use the safe word?' His voice was gently teasing but the glitter in his eyes and the tension in his jaw told her he was nowhere near as relaxed as he pretended to be.

In the grip of such intolerable excitement she was incapable of responding, Lily simply shook her head and then moaned as he withdrew slightly and surged into her again, every movement of his body escalating the wickedly agonising pleasure.

She slid her hands over the silken width of his shoulders, down his back, her fingers clamping over the thrusting power of his body as he rocked against her. His hand was splayed on her bottom, his gaze locked on hers as he drove into her with ruthlessly controlled strength and a raw, primitive rhythm. She wrapped her legs around him as he brought pleasure raining down on both of them. She cried out his name and he took her mouth, kissing her deeply, intimately, as the first ripple of orgasm took hold of her body. They didn't stop kissing, mouths locked, eyes locked as her body contracted around his and dragged him over the edge of control. She'd never experienced anything like it, the whole experience a shattering revelation about her capacity for sensuality.

It was several minutes before she was capable of speaking and longer than that before she could persuade her body to move.

As she tried to roll away from him, his arms locked around her. 'Where do you think you're going?'

'I'm sticking to the rules. I thought this was a one-night thing.'

'It is.' He hauled her back against him. 'And the night isn't over yet.'

CHAPTER FIVE

NIK SPENT TEN minutes under a cold shower, trying to wake
himself up after a night that had consisted of the worst sleep of
his life and the best sex. He couldn't remember the last time he
hadn't wanted to leave the bed in the morning.

A ton of work waited for him in the office, but for the first
time ever he was contemplating working from home so that he
could spend a few more hours with Lily. After her initial shyness she'd proved to be adventurous and insatiable, qualities
that had kept both of them awake until the rising sun had sent
the first flickers of light across the darkened bedroom.

Eventually she'd fallen into an exhausted sleep, her body tangled around his as dawn had bathed the bedroom in a golden
glow.

It had proved impossible to extract himself without waking
her so Nik, whose least favourite bedroom activity was hugging, had remained there, his senses bathed in the soft floral
scent of her skin and hair, trapped by those long limbs wrapped
trustingly around him.

And he had no one to blame but himself.

She'd offered to leave and he'd stopped her.

He frowned, surprised by his own actions. He had no need

for displays of affection or any of the other meaningless rituals that seemed to inhabit other people's relationships. To him, sex was a physical need, no different from hunger and thirst. Once satisfied he moved on. He had no desire for anything deeper. He didn't believe anything deeper existed.

When he was younger, women had tried to persuade him differently. There had been a substantial number who had believed they had what it took to penetrate whatever steely coating made his heart so inaccessible. When they'd had no more success than their predecessors they'd withdrawn, bruised and broken, but not before they'd delivered their own personal diagnosis on his sorry condition.

He'd heard it all. That he didn't have a heart, that he was selfish, single minded, driven, too focused on his work. He accepted those accusations without argument, but knew that none explained his perpetually single status. Quite simply, he didn't believe in love. He'd learned at an early age that love could be withdrawn as easily as it was given, that promises could be made and broken in the same breath, that a wedding ring was no more than a piece of jewellery, and wedding vows no more binding than one plant twisted loosely around another.

He had no need for the friendship and affection that punctuated other people's lives.

He'd taught himself to live without it, so to find himself wrapped in the tight embrace of a woman who smiled even when she was asleep was as alien to him as it was unsettling.

For a while, he'd slept, too, and then woken to find her locked against him. Telling himself that she was the one holding him and not the other way round, he'd managed to extract himself without waking her and escaped to the bathroom where he contemplated his options.

He needed to find a tactful way of ejecting her.

He showered, shaved and returned to the bedroom. Expecting to find her still asleep, he was thrown to find her dressed.

She'd stolen one of his white shirts and it fell to mid-thigh, the sleeves flapping over her small hands as she talked on the phone.

'Of course he'll be there.' Her voice was as soothing as warm honey. 'I'm sure it's a simple misunderstanding…well, no I agree with you, but he's very busy…'

She lay on her stomach on the bed, her hair hanging in a blonde curtain over one shoulder, the sheets tangled around her bare thighs.

Nik took one look at her and decided that there was no reason to rush her out of the villa.

They'd have breakfast on the terrace. Maybe enjoy a swim.

Then he'd find a position they hadn't yet tried before sending her home in his car.

Absorbed in her conversation, she hadn't noticed him and he strolled round in front of her and slowly released the towel from his waist.

He saw her eyes go wide. Then she gave him a smile that hovered somewhere between cheeky and innocent and he found himself resenting the person on the end of the phone who was taking up so much of her time.

He dressed, aware that she was watching him the whole time, her conversation reduced to soothing, sympathetic noises.

It was the sort of exchange he'd never had in his life. The sort that involved listening while someone poured out their woes. When Nik had a problem he solved it or accepted it and moved on. He'd never understood the female urge to dissect and confide.

'I know,' she murmured. 'There's nothing more upsetting than a rift in the family, but you need to talk. Clear the air. Be open about your feelings.'

She was so warm and sympathetic it was obvious to Nik that the conversation was going to be a long one. Someone had rung in the belief that talking to Lily would make them feel better and he couldn't see a way that this exchange would ever end as she poured a verbal Band-Aid over whatever wound she was being asked to heal. Who would want to hang up when they were getting the phone equivalent of a massive hug?

Outraged on her behalf, Nik sliced his finger across his throat to indicate that she should cut the connection.

When she didn't, he was contemplating snatching the phone and telling whoever it was to get a grip, sort out their own problems and stop encroaching on Lily's good nature when she gestured to the phone with her free hand.

'It's for you,' she mouthed. 'Your father.'

His *father*?

The person she'd been soothing and placating for the past twenty minutes was his *father*?

Nik froze. Only now did he notice that the phone in her hand was his. 'You answered my phone?'

'I wouldn't have done normally, but I saw it was your dad and I knew you'd want to talk to him. I didn't want you to miss his call because you were in the shower.' Clearly believing she'd done him an enormous favour, she wished his father a cheery, caring goodbye and held out the phone to him. The front of his shirt gapped, revealing those tempting dips and curves he'd explored in minute detail the night before. The scrape of his jaw had left faint red marks over her creamy skin and the fact that he instantly wanted to drop the phone in the nearest body of water and take her straight back to bed simply added to his irritation.

'That's my shirt.'

'You have so many, I didn't think you'd miss one.'

Reflecting on the fact she was as chirpy in the morning as she was the rest of the day, Nik dragged his gaze from her smiling mouth, took the phone from her and switched to Greek. 'You didn't need to call again. I got your last four messages.'

'Then why didn't you call me back?'

'I've been busy.'

'Too busy to talk to your own father? I have rung you every day this week, Niklaus. Every single day.'

Aware that Lily was listening Nik paced to the window,

turned his back on her and stared out over the sea. 'Is the wedding still on?'

'Of course it is on! Why wouldn't it be? I love Diandra and she loves me. You would love her, too, if you took the time to meet her and what better time than the day in which we exchange our vows?' There was a silence. 'Nik, come home. It has been too long.'

Nik knew exactly how long it had been to the day.

'I've been busy.'

'Too busy to visit your own family? This is the place of your birth and you never come home. You have a villa here that you converted and you don't even visit. I know you didn't like Callie and it's true that for a long time I was very angry with you for not making more of an effort when she showed you so much love, but that is behind us now.'

Reflecting on exactly what form that 'love' had taken, Nik tightened his hand on the phone and wondered if he'd been wrong not to tell his father the unpalatable truth about his third wife. He'd made the decision that since she'd ended the relationship anyway there was nothing to be gained from revealing the truth, but now he found himself in the rare position of questioning his own judgement.

'Will Callie be at the wedding?'

'No.' His father was quiet. 'I wanted her to bring little Chloe, but she hasn't responded to my calls. I don't mind admitting it's a very upsetting situation all round for everyone.'

Not everyone, Nik thought. He was sure Callie wasn't remotely upset. Why would she be? She'd extracted enough money from his father to ensure she could live comfortably without ever lifting a finger again. 'You would really want her at your wedding?'

'Callie, no. But Chloe? Yes, of course. If I had my way she would be living here with me. I still haven't given up hope that might happen one day. Chloe is my child, Nik. My daughter. I want her to grow up knowing her father. I don't want her think-ing I abandoned her or chose not to have her in my life.'

Nik kept his eyes forward and the past firmly suppressed. 'These things happen. They're part of life and relationships.'

His father sighed. 'I'm sorry you believe that. Family is the most important thing in the world. I want that for you.'

'I set my own life goals, and that isn't on the list,' Nik drawled softly. Contemplating the complexity of human relationships, he was doubly glad he'd successfully avoided them himself. Like every other area of his life, he had his feelings firmly under con-trol. 'Would Diandra really want Chloe to be living with you?'

'Of course! She'd be delighted. She wants it as much as I do. And she'd really like to meet you, too. She's keen for us to be a proper family.'

A proper family.

A long-buried memory emerged from deep inside his brain, squeezing itself through the many layers of self-protection he'd used to suppress it.

It had been so long the images were no longer clear, a fact for which he was grimly grateful. Even now, several decades later, he could still remember how it had felt to have those im-ages replaying in his head night after night.

A man, a woman and a young boy, living an idyllic exis-tence under blue skies and the dazzle of the sun. Growing up, he'd learned a thousand lessons about living. How to cook with leaves from the vine, how to distil the grape skins and seeds to form the potent *tsikoudia* they drank with friends. He'd lived his cocooned existence until one day his world had crumbled and he'd learned the most important lesson of all.

That a family was the least stable structure invented by man. It could be destroyed in a moment.

'Come home, Niklaus,' his father said quietly. 'It has been too long. I want us to put the past behind us. Callie is no lon-ger here.'

Nik didn't tell him that the reason he avoided the island had nothing to do with Callie.

Whenever he returned there it stirred up the same memory of his mother leaving in the middle of the night while he watched in confusion from the elegant curve of the stairs.

Where are you going, Mama? Are you taking us with you? Can we come, too?

'Niklaus?' His father was still talking. 'Will you come?'

Nik dragged his hand over the back of his neck. 'Yes, if that's what you want.'

'How can you doubt it?' There was joy in his father's voice. 'The wedding is Tuesday but many of our friends are arriving at the weekend so that we can celebrate in style. Come on Saturday then you can join in the pre-wedding celebrations.'

'Saturday?' His father expected him to stay for four days? 'I'll have to see if I can clear my diary.'

'Of course you can. What's the point of being in charge of the company if you can't decide your own schedule? Now tell me about Lily. I like her very much. How long have the two of you been together?'

Ten memorable hours. 'How do you know her name?'

'We've been talking, Niklaus! Which is more than you and I ever do. She sounds nice. Why don't you bring her to the wedding?'

'We don't have that sort of relationship.' He felt a flicker of irritation. Was that why she'd spent so much time on the phone talking to his father? Had she decided that sympathy might earn her an invite to the biggest wedding of the year in Greece?

Exchanging a final few words with his father, he hung up. 'Don't ever,' he said with silky emphasis as he turned to face her, 'answer my phone again.' But he was talking to an empty room because Lily was nowhere to be seen.

Taken aback, Nik glanced towards the bathroom and then noticed the note scrawled on a piece of paper by his pillow.

Thanks for the best rebound sex ever. Lily.

The best rebound sex?

She'd left?

Nik picked up the note and scrunched it in his palm. He'd been so absorbed in the conversation with his father he hadn't heard her leaving.

The dress from the night before lay neatly folded on the chair but there was no sign of the shoes or his shirt. He had no need to formulate a plan to eject her from his life because she'd removed herself.

She'd gone.

And she hadn't even bothered saying goodbye.

'NO NEED TO ASK if you had a good night, it's written all over your face.' Brittany slid her feet into her hiking boots and reached for her bag. 'Nice shirt. Is that silk?' She reached out and touched the fabric and gave a murmur of appreciation. 'The man has style, I'll give him that.'

'Thanks for your text. It was sweet of you to check on me. How was your evening?'

'Nowhere near as exciting as yours apparently. While you were playing Cinderella in the wolf's lair, I was cataloguing pottery shards and bone fragments. My life is so exciting I can hardly bear it.'

'You love it. And I think you're mixing your fairy tales.' Aware that her hair was a wild mass of curls after the relentless exploration of Nik's hands, Lily scooped it into a ponytail. She told herself that eventually she'd stop thinking about him. 'Did you find anything else after I left yesterday?'

'Fragments of plaster, conical cups—' Brittany frowned. 'We found a bronze leg that probably belongs to that figurine that was discovered last week. Are you listening to me?'

Lily was deep in an action replay of the moment Nik had

removed the mask from her eyes. 'That's exciting! I'm going to join you later.'

'We're removing part of the stone mound and exploring the North Eastern wall.' Brittany eyed her. 'You might want to re-think white silk. So am I going to hear the details?'

'About what?'

'Oh, please—'

'It was fun. All right, incredible.' Lily felt her cheeks burn and Brittany gave a faint smile.

'That good? Now I'm jealous. I haven't had incredible sex since—well, let's just say it's been a while. So are you seeing him again?'

'Of course not. The definition of rebound sex is that it's just one night. No commitment.' She parroted the rules and tried not to wish it could have lasted a little more than one night. The truth was even in that one night Nik had made her feel special. 'Do we have food in our fridge? I'm starving.'

'He helped you expend all those calories and then didn't feed you before you left? That's not very gentlemanly.'

'He didn't see me leave. He had to take a call.' And judging from the reluctance he'd shown when she'd handed him the phone, if it had been left to him he wouldn't have answered it.

Why not?

Why wouldn't a man want to talk to his father?

It had been immediately obvious that whatever issues Nik might have in expressing his emotions openly weren't shared by his father, who had been almost embarrassingly eager to share his pain.

She'd squirmed with discomfort as Kostas Zervakis had told her how long it was since his son had come home. Even on such a short acquaintance she knew that family was one of the subjects Nik didn't touch. She'd felt awkward listening, as if she were eavesdropping on a private conversation, but at the same time his father had seemed so upset she hadn't had the heart to cut him off.

The conversation had left her feeling ever so slightly sick, an emotion she knew was ridiculous given that she hadn't ever met Kostas and barely knew his son. Why should it bother her that there were clearly problems in their relationship?

Her natural instinct had been to intervene but she'd recognised instantly the danger in that. Nik wasn't a man who appreciated the interference of others in anything, least of all his personal life.

The black look he'd given her had been as much responsible for her rapid exit as her own lack of familiarity with the morning-after etiquette following rebound sex.

She'd taken advantage of his temporary absorption in the phone call to make a hasty escape, but not before she'd heard enough to make her wish for a happy ending. Whatever damage lay in their past, she wanted them to fix their problems.

She always wanted people to fix their problems.

Lily blinked rapidly, realising that Brittany was talking. 'Sorry?'

'So he doesn't know you left?'

'He knows by now.'

'He won't be pleased that you didn't say goodbye.'

'He'll be delighted. He doesn't want emotional engagement. No awkward conversations. He will be relieved to be spared a potentially awkward conversation. We move in different circles so I probably won't ever see him again.' And that shouldn't bother her, should it? Although a one-night stand was new to her, she was the expert at transitory relationships. Her entire life had been a series of transitory relationships. No one had ever stuck in her life. She felt like an abandoned railway station where trains passed through but never stopped.

Brittany glanced out of the window at the street below and raised her eyebrows. 'I think you're going to see him again a whole lot sooner than you think.'

'What makes you say that?'

'Because he's just pulled up outside our apartment.'

Lily's heart felt as if it were trying to escape from her chest. 'Are you sure?'

'Well there's a Ferrari parked outside that costs more than I'm going to earn in a lifetime, so, unless there is someone else living in this building that has attracted his attention, he clearly has things he wants to say to you.'

'Oh *no*.' Lily shrank against the door of the bedroom. 'Can you see his face? Does he look angry?'

'What reason would he have to be angry?' Brittany glanced out of the window again and then back at Lily. 'Is this about the shirt? He can afford to lose one shirt, surely?'

'I don't think he's here because of the shirt,' Lily said weakly. 'I think he's here because of something I did this morning. I'm going to hide on the balcony and you're going to tell him you haven't seen me.'

Brittany looked at her curiously. 'What did you do?'

Lily flinched as she heard a loud hammering on the door. 'Remember—you haven't seen me.' She fled into the bedroom they shared and closed the door.

What was he doing here?

She'd seen the flash of anger in his eyes when he'd realised it was *his* phone she'd answered, but surely he wouldn't care enough to follow her home?

She heard his voice in the doorway and heard Brittany say, 'Sure, come right on in, Nik—is it all right if I call you Nik?— she's in the bedroom, hiding.' The door opened a moment later and Brittany stood there, arms folded, her eyes alive with laughter.

Lily impaled her with a look of helpless fury. 'You're a traitor.'

'I'm a friend and I am doing you a favour,' Brittany murmured. 'The man is seriously *hot*.' Having delivered that assessment, she stepped to one side with a bright smile. 'Go ahead. The space is a little tight, but I guess you folks don't mind that.'

'No! Brittany, don't—er—hi...' Lily gave a weak smile as

Nik strolled into the room. His powerful frame virtually filled the cramped space and she wished she'd picked a different room as a refuge. Being in a bedroom reminded her too much of the night before. 'If you're mad about the shirt, then give me two minutes to change. I shouldn't have taken it, but I didn't want to do the walk of shame through the middle of Chania wearing an evening dress that doesn't belong to me.'

'I don't care about the shirt.' His hair was glossy dark, his eyes dark in a face so handsome it would have made a Greek god weep with envy. 'Do you seriously think I'm here because of the shirt?'

'No. I assume you're mad because I answered your phone, but I saw that it was your father and thought you wouldn't want to miss his call. If I had a dad I'd be ringing him every day.'

His face revealed not a flicker of emotion. 'We don't have that sort of relationship.'

'Well I know that *now,* but I didn't know when I answered the phone and once he started talking he was so upset I didn't want to hang up. He needed to talk to someone and I was in the right place at the right time.'

'You think so?' His voice was silky soft. 'Because I would have said you were in the wrong place at the wrong time.'

'Depends how you look at it. Did you manage to clear the air?' She risked a glance at the hard lines of his face and winced. 'I'm guessing the answer to that is no. If I made it worse by handing you the phone, I'm sorry.'

He raised an eyebrow. 'Are you?'

She opened her mouth and closed it again. 'No, not really. Family is the most important thing in the world. I don't understand how anyone could not want to try and heal a rift. But I could see you were very angry that I'd answered the call and of course your relationship with your father is none of my business.' But she wanted to make it her business so badly she virtually had to sit on her hands to stop herself from interfering.

'For someone who realises it's none of her business, you seem to be showing an extraordinary depth of interest.'

'I feel strongly about protecting the family unit. It's my hot button.'

His searing glance reminded her he was intimately familiar with all her hot buttons. 'Why did you walk out this morning?'

The blatant reminder of the night before brought the colour rushing to her cheeks.

'I thought the first rule of rebound sex was that you rebound right out of the door the next morning. I have no experience of morning-after conversation and frankly the thought of facing you over breakfast after all the things we did last night didn't totally thrill me. And can you honestly tell me you weren't standing in that shower working out how you were going to eject me?' The expression on his face told her she was right and she nodded. 'Exactly. I thought I'd spare us both a major awkward moment and leave. I grabbed a shirt and was halfway out of the door when your father rang.'

'It didn't occur to you to ignore the phone?'

'I thought it might be important. And it was! He was *so* upset. He told me he'd already left a ton of messages.' Concern overwhelmed her efforts not to become involved. 'Why haven't you been home for the past few years?'

'A night in my bed doesn't qualify you to ask those questions.' The look in his eyes made her confidence falter.

'I get the message. Nothing personal. Now back off. Last night you were charming and fun and flirty. This morning you're scary and intimidating.'

He inhaled deeply. 'I apologise,' he breathed. 'It was not my intention to come across as scary or intimidating, but you should *not* have answered the phone.'

'What's done is done. And I was glad to be a listening ear for someone in pain.'

'My father is not in pain.'

'Yes, he is. He misses you. This rift between you is causing him agony. He wants you to go to his wedding. It's breaking his heart that you won't go.'

'Lily—'

'You're going to tell me it's none of my business and you're right, it isn't, but I don't have a family at all. I don't even have the broken pieces of a family, and you have no idea how much I wish I did. So you'll have to forgive me if I have a tendency to try and glue back together everyone else's chipped fragments. It's the archaeologist in me.'

'Lily—'

'Just because you don't believe in love, doesn't mean you have to inflict that view on others and judge them for their decisions. Your father is happy and you're spoiling it. He loves you and he wants you there. Whatever you are feeling, you should bury it and go and celebrate. You should raise a glass and dance at his wedding. You should show him you love him no matter what, and if this marriage goes wrong then you'll be there to support him.' She stopped, breathless, and waited to be frozen by the icy wind of his disapproval but he surprised her yet again by nodding.

'I agree.'

'You do?'

'Yes. I've been trying to tell you that but you wouldn't stop talking.' He spoke through clenched teeth. 'I am convinced that I should go to the wedding, which is why I'm here.'

'What does the wedding have to do with me?'

'I want you to come with me.'

Lily gaped at him. 'Me? Why?'

He ran his hand over the back of his neck. 'I am willing to be present if that is truly what my father wants, but I don't have enough faith in my acting skills to believe I will be able to convince anyone that I'm pleased to be there. No matter how much he tells me Diandra is "the one", I cannot see how this match will have a happy ending. You, however, seem to see happy endings where none exist. I'm hoping that by taking you, people will be blinded in the dazzling beam of your sunny optimism and won't notice the dark thundercloud hovering close by threatening to rain on the proceedings.'

The analogy made her smile. 'You're the dark thundercloud in that scenario?'

His eyes gleamed. 'You need to ask?'

'You really believe this marriage is doomed? How can you say that when you haven't even met Diandra?'

'When it comes to women, my father has poor judgement. He follows his heart and his heart has no sense of direction. Frankly I can't believe he has chosen to get married again after three failed attempts. I think it's insane.'

'I think it's lovely.'

'Which is why you're coming as my guest.' He reached out and lifted a small blue plate from her shelf, tipping off the earrings that were stored there. 'This is stylish. Where did you buy it?'

'I didn't buy it, I made it. And I haven't agreed to come with you yet.'

'You *made* this?'

'It's a hobby of mine. There is a kiln at work and sometimes I use it. The father of one of the curators at the museum is a potter and he's helped me. It's interesting comparing old and new techniques.'

He turned it in his hands, examining it closely. 'You could sell this.'

'I don't want to sell it. I use it to store my earrings.'

'Have you ever considered having an exhibition?'

'Er—no.' She gave an astonished laugh. 'I've made about eight pieces I didn't throw away. They're all exhibited around the apartment. We use one as a soap dish.'

'You've never wanted to do this for a living?'

'What I want to do and what I can afford to do aren't the same thing. It isn't financially viable.' She didn't even allow her mind to go there. 'And where would our soap live? Let's talk about the wedding. A wedding is a big deal. It's intimate and special, an occasion to be shared with friends and loved ones. You don't even know me.' The moment the words left her mouth she realised how ridiculous that statement was given the night they'd spent. 'I mean obviously there are *some* things about me you know very well, but other things like my favourite flower and my favourite colour, you don't know.'

Still holding her plate, he studied her with an unsettling intensity. 'I know all I need to know, which is that you like weddings almost as much as I hate them. Did you study art?'

'Minoan art. This is a sideline. And if I go with you, people will speculate. How would you explain our relationship to your father? Would you want us to pretend to be in a relationship? Are we supposed to have known one another for ages or something?'

'No.' His frown suggested that option hadn't occurred to him. 'There is no need to tell anything other than the truth, which is that I'm inviting you to the wedding as a friend.'

'Friend with benefits?'

He put the plate back down on the shelf and replaced the earrings carefully. 'That part is strictly between us.'

'And if your father asks how we met?'

'Tell him the truth. He'd be amused, I assure you.'

'So you don't want to pretend we're madly in love or anything? I don't have to pose as your girlfriend?'

'No. You'd be going as yourself, Lily.' A muscle flickered in his lean jaw. 'God knows, the wedding will be stressful enough without us playing roles that feel unnatural.'

It was his obvious distaste for lies and games that made up her mind. After David, a man whose instinct was to tell the truth was appealing. 'When would we leave?'

'Next Saturday. The wedding is on Tuesday but there will be four days of celebrations.' It was obvious from his expression he'd rather be dragged naked through an active volcano than join in those celebrations and a horrible thought crept into her mind.

'You're not going because you're planning to break off the wedding, are you?'

'No.' His gaze didn't shift from hers. 'But I won't tell you it didn't cross my mind.'

'I'm glad you rose above your natural impulse to wreck someone else's happiness. And if you really think it would help to have me there, then I'll come, if only to make sure you don't have second thoughts and decide to sabotage your father's big day.' Lily sank down onto the edge of her bed, thinking. 'I'll need to ask for time off.'

'Is that a problem? I could make a few calls.'

'No way!' Imagining how the curator at the museum would respond to personal intervention from Nik Zervakis, Lily recoiled in alarm. 'I'm quite capable of handling it myself. I don't need to bring in the heavy artillery, I'll simply ask the question. I'm owed holiday and my post ends in a couple of weeks anyway. Where exactly are we going? Where is "home" for you?'

'My father owns an island off the north coast of Crete. You will like it. The western part of the island has Minoan remains and there is a Venetian castle on one of the hilltops. It is separated from Crete by a lagoon and the beaches are some of the best anywhere in Greece. When you're not reminding me to smile, I'm sure you'll enjoy exploring.'

'And he *owns* this island? So tourists can't visit.'

'That's right. It belongs to my family.'

Lily looked at him doubtfully. 'How many guests will there be?'

'Does it matter?'

'I wondered, that's all.' She wanted to ask where they'd be sleeping but decided that if his father could afford a private island then presumably there wasn't a shortage of beds. 'I need to go shopping.'

'Given that you are doing me a favour, I insist you allow me to take care of that side of things.'

'No. Apart from last night, which wasn't real, I buy my own clothes. But thanks.'

'Last night didn't feel real?' He gave her a long, penetrating look and she felt heat rush into her cheeks as she remembered all the very real things he'd done to her and she'd done to him.

'I mean it wasn't really my life. More like a dreamy moment you know is never going to happen again.' Realising it was long past time she kept her mouth shut, she gave a weak smile. 'I'll buy or borrow clothes, don't worry. I'm good at putting together a wardrobe. Colours are my thing. The secret is to accessorise. I won't embarrass you even if we're surrounded by people dressed head to toe in Prada.'

'That possibility didn't enter my head. My concern was purely about the pressure on your budget.'

'I'm creative. It's not a problem.' She remembered she was wearing his shirt. 'I'll return this, obviously.'

A smile flickered at the corners of his mouth. 'It looks better on you than it does on me. Keep it.'

His gaze collided with hers and suddenly it was hard to breathe. Sexual tension simmered in the air and she was acutely aware of the oppressive heat in the small room that had no air conditioning. Blistering, blinding awareness clouded her vision until the only thing in her world was him. She wanted so badly to touch him. She wanted to lean into that muscled power, rip off those clothes and beg him to do all the things he'd done to her the night before. Shaken, she assumed she was alone in feeling that way and then saw something flare in his eyes and knew she wasn't. He was sexually aroused and thinking all the things she was thinking.

'Nik—'

'Saturday.' His tone was thickened, his eyes a dark, dangerous black. 'I will pick you up at eight a.m.'

She watched him leave, wondering what the rules of engagement were when one night wasn't enough.

CHAPTER SIX

NIK PUT HIS foot down and pushed the Ferrari to its limits on the empty road that led to the north-western tip of Crete.

He spent the majority of his time at the ZervaCo offices in San Francisco. When he returned to Crete it was to his villa on the beach near Chania, not to the island that had been his home growing up.

For reasons he tried not to think about, he'd avoided the place for the past few years and the closer he got to their destination, the blacker his mood.

Lily, by contrast, was visibly excited. She'd been waiting on the street when he'd arrived, her bag by her feet and she'd proceeded to question him non-stop. 'So will this be like *My Big Fat Greek Wedding*? I loved that movie. Will there be dancing? Brittany and I have been learning the *kalamatianós* at the *taverna* near our apartment so I should be able to join in as long as no one minds losing their toes.' She hummed a Greek tune to herself and he sent her an exasperated look.

'Are you ever *not* cheerful?'

The humming stopped and she glanced at him. 'You want me to be miserable? Did I misunderstand the brief, because I thought I was supposed to be the sunshine to your thundercloud. I didn't realise I had to be a thundercloud, too.'

Despite his mood, he found himself smiling. 'Are you capable of being a thundercloud?'

'I'm human. I have my low moments, same as anyone.'

'Tell me your last low moment.'

'No, because then I might cry and you'd dump me by the side of the road and leave me to be pecked to death by buzzards.' She gave him a cheery smile. 'This is the point where you reassure me that you wouldn't leave me by the side of the road, and that there are no buzzards in Crete.'

'There are buzzards. Crete has a varied habitat. We have vultures, Golden Eagle, kestrel—' he slowed down as he approached a narrow section of the road '—but I have no intention of leaving you by the side of the road.'

'I'd like to think that decision is driven by your inherent good nature and kindness towards your fellow man, but I'm pretty sure it's because you don't want to have to go to this wedding alone.'

'You're right. My actions are almost always driven by self-interest.'

'I don't understand you at all. I love weddings.'

'Even when you don't know the people involved?'

'I support the principle. I think it's lovely that your father is getting married again.'

Nik struggled to subdue a rush of emotion. 'It is not lovely that he is getting married again. It's ill advised.'

'That's your opinion. But it isn't what *you* think that matters, is it? It's what *he* thinks.' She spoke with gentle emphasis. 'And he thinks it's a good idea. For the record, I think it says a lot about a person that he is prepared to get married again.'

'It does.' As they hit a straight section of road, he pushed the car to its limits and the engine gave a throaty roar. 'It says he's a man with an inability to learn from his mistakes.'

'I don't see it that way.' Her hair whipped around her face

and she anchored it with her hand and lifted her face to the sun.
'I think it shows optimism and I love that.'

Hearing the breathy, happy note in her voice he shook his
head. 'Lily, how have you survived in this world without being
eaten alive by unscrupulous people determined to take advantage of you?'

'I've been hurt on many occasions.'

'That doesn't surprise me.'

'It's part of life. I'm not going to let it shatter my belief in
human nature. I'm an optimist. And what would it mean to give
up? That would be like saying that love isn't out there, that it
doesn't exist, and how depressing would *that* be?'

Nik, who lived his life firmly of the conviction that love
didn't exist, didn't find it remotely depressing. To him, it was
simply fact. 'Clearly you are the perfect wedding guest. You
could set up a business, weddingguests.com. Optimists-R-us.
You could be the guaranteed smile at every wedding.'

'Your cynicism is deeply depressing.'

'Your optimism is deeply concerning.'

'I prefer to think of it as inspiring. I don't want to be one of
those people who think that a challenging past has to mean a
challenging future.'

'You had a challenging past?' He remembered that she'd
mentioned being brought up in foster care and hoped she wasn't
about to give him the whole story.

She didn't. Instead she shrugged and kept her eyes straight
ahead. 'It was a bit like a bad version of *Goldilocks and the
Three Bears*. I was never "just right" for anyone, but that was
my bad luck. I didn't meet the right family. Doesn't mean I don't
believe there are loads of great families out there.'

'Doesn't what happened to you cause you to question the va-
lidity of any of these emotions you feel? The fact that the last
guy lied to you *and* his wife doesn't put you off relationships?'

'It was one guy. I know enough about statistics to know you
can't draw a reliable conclusion from a sample of one.' She

frowned. 'If I'm honest, I'm working from a bigger sample than that because he's the third relationship I've had, but I still don't think you can make a judgement on the opposite sex based on the behaviour of a few.'

Nik, who had done exactly that, stayed silent and of course she noticed because she was nothing if not observant.

'Put it this way—if I'm bitten by a shark am I going to avoid swimming in the sea? I could, but then I'd be depriving myself of one of my favourite activities so instead I choose to carry on swimming and be a little more alert. Life isn't always about taking the safe option. Risk has to be balanced against the joy of living. I call it being receptive.'

'I call it being ridiculously naïve.'

She looked affronted. 'You're cross and irritable because you're not looking forward to this, but there is no reason to take it out on me. I'm here as a volunteer, remember?'

'You're right. I apologise.'

'Accepted. But for your father's sake you need to work on your body language. If you think you're a thundercloud you're deluding yourself because right now you're more of a tropical cyclone. You have to stop being judgemental and embrace what's happening.'

Nik took the sharp right-hand turn that led down to the beach and the private ferry. 'I am finding it hard to embrace something I know to be a mistake. It's like watching someone driving their car full speed towards a brick wall and not trying to do something to stop it.'

'You don't know it's a mistake,' she said calmly. 'And even if it is, he's an adult and should be allowed to make his own decisions. Now smile.'

He pulled in, killed the engine and turned to look at her.

Those unusual violet eyes reminded him of the spring flowers that grew high in the mountains. 'I will not be so hypocritical as to pretend I am pleased, but I promise not to spoil the moment.'

'If you don't smile then you *will* spoil the moment! Poor Diandra might take one look at your face and decide she doesn't want to marry into your family and then your father would be heartbroken. I can't believe I'm saying this, but be hypocritical if that's what it takes to make you smile.'

'Poor Diandra will not be poor for long so I think it unlikely she'll let anything stand in the way of her wedding, even my intimidating presence.'

Her eyes widened. 'Is that what this is about? You think she's after his money?'

'I have no idea but I'd be a fool not to consider it.' Nik saw no reason to be anything but honest. 'He is mega wealthy. She was his cook.'

'What does her occupation have to do with it? Love is about people, not professions. And I find it very offensive that you'd even think that. You can't judge a person based on their income. I know plenty of wealthy people who are slimeballs. In fact if we're going with stereotypes here, I'd say that generally speaking in order to amass great wealth you have to be prepared to be pretty ruthless. There are plenty of wealthy people who aren't that nice.'

Nik, who had never aspired to be 'nice', was careful not to let his expression change. 'Are you calling me a slimeball?'

'I'm simply pointing out that income isn't an indicator of a person's worth.'

'You mean because you don't know the level of expenditure?'

'No! Why is everything about money with you? I'm talking about *emotional* worth. Your father told me about Diandra. He was ill with flu last winter after Callie left. He was so ill at one point he couldn't drag himself from the bed. I sympathised because it happened to me once and I hope I never get flu again. Anyway, Diandra cared for him the whole time. She was the one who called the doctor. She made all his meals. That was kind, don't you think?'

'Or opportunistic.'

'If you carry on thinking like that you are going to die lonely.

He met her when she cooked him her special moussaka to try and tempt him to eat. I *love* that he doesn't care what she does.'

'He should care. She stands to gain an enormous amount financially from this wedding.'

'That's horrible.'

'It is truly horrible. Finally we find something we agree on.'

'I wasn't agreeing with you! It's your attitude that's horrible, not this wedding. You're not only a judgemental cynic, you're also a raging snob.'

Nik breathed deeply. 'I am not a raging snob, but I am realistic.'

'No, what you are is damaged. Not everything has a price, Nik, and there are things in life that are far more important than money. Your father is trying to make a family and I think that's admirable.' She fumbled with the seat belt. 'Get me out of this car before I'm contaminated by you. Your thundercloud is about to rain all over my sunny patch of life.'

Your father is trying to make a family.

Nik thought about everything that had gone before.

He'd buried the pain and hurt deep and it was something he had never talked about with anyone, especially not his father, who had his own pain to deal with. What would happen when this relationship collapsed?

'If my father entered relationships with some degree of caution and objective contemplation then I would be less concerned, but he makes the same mistake you make. He confuses physical intimacy with love.' He saw the colour streak across her cheeks.

'I'm not confused. Have I spun fairy tales about the night we spent together? Have I fallen in love with you? No. I know exactly what it was and what we did. You're in a little compartment in my brain labelled "Once in a Lifetime Experiences" along with skydiving and a helicopter flight over the New York skyline. It was amazing by the way.'

'The helicopter flight was amazing?'

'No, I haven't done that yet. I was talking about the night with you, although there were moments that felt as nerve-racking as skydiving.' Her mouth tilted into a self-conscious smile. 'Of course it's also a little embarrassing looking at you in daylight after all those things we did in the dark, but I'm trying not to think about it. Now stop being annoying. In fact, stop talking for a while. That way I'm less likely to kill you before we arrive.'

Nik refrained from pointing out she'd been the only one in the dark. He'd had perfect vision and he'd used it to his own shameless advantage. There wasn't a single corner of her body he hadn't explored and the memory of every delicious curve was welded in his brain.

He tried to work out what it was about her that was so appealing. Innocence wasn't a quality he generally admired in a person so he had to assume the power of the attraction stemmed from the sheer novelty of being with someone who had managed to retain such an untarnished view of the world.

'Are you embarrassed about the night we spent together?'

'I would be if I thought about it, so I'm not thinking about it. I'm living in the moment.' Having offered that simple solution to the problem, she reached into the back of the car for her hat. 'You could take the same approach to the wedding. You're not here to fix it or protect anyone. You're here as a guest and your only responsibility is to smile and look happy. Is this it? Are we here? Because I don't see an island. Maybe your father might have changed the venue when he saw the black cloud of your presence approaching over the horizon.'

Nik dragged his gaze from her mouth to the jetty. 'This is it. From here, we go by boat.'

LILY STOOD IN the prow of the boat feeling the cool brush of the wind on her face and tasting the salty air. The boat skimmed and bounced over the sparkling ocean towards the large island in the distance, sending a light spray over her face and tangling her hair.

Nik stood behind the wheel, legs braced, eyes hidden behind a pair of dark glasses. Despite the unsmiling set of his mouth, he looked more approachable and less the hard-headed businessman.

'This is so much fun. I think I might love it more than your Ferrari.'

He gave a smile that turned him from insanely good-looking to devastating, and she felt the intensity of the attraction like a physical punch.

It was true he didn't seem to display any of the family values that were so important to her, but that didn't do anything to diminish the sexual attraction.

As far as she could tell, he couldn't be more perfect for a short-term relationship.

For the whole trip in the car she'd been aware of him. As he'd shifted gear his hand had brushed against her bare thigh and she'd discovered that being with him was an exciting, exhilarating experience that was like nothing she'd experienced before.

There had been a brief moment when they'd pulled into the car park that she'd thought he might be about to kiss her. He'd looked at her mouth the way a panther looked at its prey before it devoured it, but just when she'd been about to close her eyes and take a fast ride to bliss, he'd sprung from the car, leaving her to wonder if she'd imagined it.

She'd followed him to the jetty, watching in fascination as the group of people gathered there sprang to attention. If she needed any more evidence of the power he wielded, she had only to observe the way people responded to him. He behaved with an authority that was instinctive, his air of command unmistakable even in this apparently casual setting.

It was a good job he didn't possess any of the qualities she was looking for, she thought, otherwise she'd be in trouble.

Her gaze lingered on his bronzed throat, visible at the open neck of his shirt. He handled the boat with the same confident assurance he displayed in everything and she was sure that no electrical device had ever dared to misbehave under his expert touch.

Trying not to think about just how expert his touch had been, she anchored her hair and shouted above the wind. 'The beaches are beautiful. People aren't allowed to bathe here?'

'You can bathe here. You're my guest.' As they approached the island, he slowed the speed of the boat and skilfully steered against the dock.

Two men instantly jumped forward to help and Nik sprang from the boat and held out his hand to her.

'I need to get my bag.'

'They will bring our luggage up to the villa later.'

'I have a gift for your father and it's only one bag,' she muttered. 'I can carry a single bag.'

'You bought a gift?'

'Of course. It's a wedding. I couldn't come without a small gift.' She stepped out of the bobbing boat and allowed herself to hold his hand for a few seconds longer than was necessary for balance. She felt warmth and strength flow through her fingers and had to battle the temptation to press herself against him. 'So how many bedrooms does your father have? Are you sure there is room for me to stay?'

The question seemed to amuse him. 'There will be room, *theé mou*, don't worry. As well as the main villa, there are several other properties scattered around the island. We will be staying in one of those.'

As they walked up a sandy path she breathed in the wonderful scents of sea juniper and wild thyme. 'One of the things I love most about Crete is the thyme honey. Brittany and I eat it for breakfast.'

'My father keeps bees so he will be very happy to hear you say that.'

The path forked at the top and he turned right and took the path that led down to another beach. There, nestling in the small horseshoe bay of golden sand with the water almost lapping at the whitewashed walls, was a beautiful contemporary villa.

Lily stopped. '*That's* your father's house?' The position was idyllic, the villa stunning, but it looked more like a honeymoon hideaway than somewhere to accommodate a large number of high-profile international guests.

'No. This is Camomile Villa. The main house is fifteen minutes' walk in the other direction, towards the small Venetian fort. I thought we'd unpack and breathe for an hour or so before we face the guests.'

Witnessing his tension, she felt a rush of compassion. 'Nik—' She put her hand on his cheek and turned his face to hers. 'This is a wedding, not the sacking of Troy. You do not need to find your strength or breathe. Your role is to smile and enjoy yourself.'

His gaze locked on hers and she wished she hadn't touched him. His blue-shadowed jaw was rough beneath her fingers and suddenly she was remembering that night in minute detail.

Seriously unsettled, she started to pull her hand away but he caught her wrist in his fingers and held it there.

'You are a very unusual woman.' His voice was husky and she gave a faint smile, ignoring the wild flutter of nerves low in her stomach.

'I am not even going to ask what you mean by that. I'm simply going to take it as a compliment.'

'Of course you are.' There was a strange gleam in his eyes. 'You see positive in everything, don't you?'

'Not always.' She could have told him that she saw very little positive in being alone in the world, having no family, but given his obvious state of tension she decided to keep that confidence to herself. 'So how do you know we're staying in Camomile Villa? Cute name, by the way. Maybe your father has given it to one of the other guests. Shouldn't you go and check?'

'Camomile belongs to me.'

Lily digested that. 'So actually you own five properties, not four.'

'I don't count this place.'

'Really? Because if I owned this I'd be spending every spare minute here.' She walked up the path, past silvery green olive trees, nets lying on the ground ready for harvesting later in the year. A small lizard lay basking in the hot sun and she smiled as it sensed company and darted for safety into the dry, dusty earth.

The path leading down to the villa cut through a garden of tumbling colour. Bougainvillaea in bright pinks and purples blended and merged against the dazzling white of the walls and the perfect blue of the sky.

Nik opened the door and Lily followed him inside.

White beamed ceilings and natural stone floors gave the interior a cool, uncluttered feel and the elegant white interior was lifted by splashes of Mediterranean blue.

'If you don't want this place, I might live here.' Lily looked at the shaded terrace with its beautiful infinity pool. 'Why does anyone need a pool when the sea is five steps from the front door?'

'Some people don't like swimming in the sea.'

'I'm not one of those people. I adore the sea. Nik, this place is—' she felt a lump in her throat '—it's really special.'

He opened the doors to the terrace and gave her a wary look. 'Are you going to cry?'

'It's perfect.' She blinked. 'And I'm fine. Happy. And excited. I love Crete, but I never get the chance to enjoy it like a tourist. I'm always working.' And never in her life had she experienced this level of luxury.

She and Brittany were always moaning about the mosquitoes and lack of air conditioning in their tiny apartment. At night they slept with the windows open to make the most of the breeze from the sea, but in the summer months it was almost unbearable indoors.

'You are the most unusual woman I've ever met. You enjoy small things.'

'This is not a small thing. And you're the unusual one.' She picked up her bag. 'You take this life for granted.'

'That is not true. I know how fortunate I am.'

'I don't think you do, but I'm going to be pointing it out to you every minute for the next few days so hopefully by the time we leave you will.' She glanced around her and then looked at him expectantly. 'My bedroom?'

For a wild, unnerving moment she hoped he was going to tell her there was just one bedroom, but he gestured to a door that led from the large spacious living area.

'The guest suite is through there. Make yourself comfortable.'

Guest suite.

So he didn't intend them to share a room. For Nik, it really had been one night.

Telling herself it was probably for the best, she followed his directions and walked through an open door into a bright, airy bedroom. The bed was draped in layers of cream and white, deep piles of cushions and pillows inviting the occupant to lounge and relax. The walls were hung with bold, contemporary art, slashes of deep blue on large canvases that added a stylish touch to the room. In one corner stood a tall, elegant vase in graduated blues, the colour shifting under the dazzling sunlight.

Lily recognised it instantly. 'That's one of Skylar's pots.'

He looked at her curiously. 'You know the artist?'

'Skylar Tempest. She and Brittany were roommates at college. They're best friends, as close as sisters. I would know her work anywhere. Her style, her use of colour and composition is unique, but I know that pot specifically because I talked to her about it. Brittany introduced us because Skylar wanted to talk to me about ceramics. She's incorporated a few Minoan designs into some of her work, modernised, of course.' She knelt down and slid her hand over the smooth surface of the glass. 'This is from her *Mediterranean Sky* collection. She had a small exhibition in New York, not only glass and pots but jewellery and a couple of paintings. She's insanely talented.'

'You were at that exhibition?'

'Sadly no. I don't move in those circles. Nor do I pretend to claim any credit for any of her incredible creations, but I did talk to her about shapes and style. Of course the Minoans used terracotta clay. It was Sky's idea to reproduce the shape in glass. Look at this—' She trailed her finger lightly over the surface. 'The Minoans usually decorated their pots with dark on light motifs, often of sea creatures, and she's taken her inspiration from that. It's genius. I can't believe you own it. Where did you find it?'

'I was at the exhibition.'

'In New York? How did you even know about her?'

'I saw her work in a small artisan jewellers in Greenwich Village and I bought one of her necklaces for—' He broke off and Lily looked at him expectantly.

'For? For one of your women? We're not in a relationship, Nik. You don't have to censor your conversation. And even if we were in a relationship you still wouldn't need to censor it.'

'In my experience, most women do not appreciate hearing about their predecessors.'

'Yes, well the more I hear about the women you've known in your life, the more I'm not surprised. Now tell me about how you discovered Skylar.'

'I asked to see more of her work and was told she was having an exhibition. I managed to get myself invited.'

Lily rocked back on her heels. 'She never mentioned that she met you.'

'We never met. I didn't introduce myself. I went on the first night and she was surrounded by well-wishers, so I simply bought a few pieces and left. That was two years ago.'

'So she doesn't know she sold pieces to Nik Zervakis?'

'A member of my team handled the actual transaction.'

Lily scrambled to her feet. 'Because you don't touch real

money? She would be so excited if she knew her work was here in your villa. Can I tell her?'

He looked amused. 'If you think it would interest her, then yes.'

'Interest her? Of course it would interest her.' Lily pulled her phone out of her bag and took a photo. 'I must admit that pot looks perfect there. It needs a large room with lots of light. Did you know she has another exhibition coming up?' She slipped her phone back into her bag. 'December in London. An upmarket gallery in Knightsbridge is showing her work. She's really excited. Her new collection is called *Ocean Blue*. It's still sea themed. Brittany showed me some photos.'

'Will you be going?'

'To an exhibition in Knightsbridge? Sure. I thought I'd fly in on my private jet, spend a night in the Royal Suite at The Savoy and then get my driver to take me to the exhibition.' She laughed and then saw something flicker in his eyes. 'Er—that's exactly what you're going to be doing, isn't it?'

'My plans aren't confirmed.'

'But you do have a private jet.'

'ZervaCo owns a Gulfstream and a couple of Lear jets.' He said it as if it was normal and she shook her head, trying not to be intimidated.

For her, wealth was people and family, not money, but still—

'Seriously, Nik. What am I doing here? To you a Gulfstream is a mode of transport, to me it's a warm Atlantic current. I used to own a rusty mountain bike until the wheel fell off. I'm the one who works in a dusty museum, digs in the dirt in the summer and cleans other people's houses to give myself enough money to live. And living doesn't include jetting across Europe to a friend's exhibition. I have no idea where I'll even be in December. I'm job hunting.'

'Wherever you are, I'll fly you there. And for your information, I wouldn't be staying in the Royal Suite.'

'Because you already own an apartment that most royals

would kill for.' His lack of response told her she was right and she rolled her eyes. 'Nik, we had an illuminating conversation earlier during which you confessed that you think your new stepmother is only interested in your father's money. Money is obviously a very big deal to you, so I'm hardly likely to take you up on your offer of a ride in your private jet, am I?'

'That is different. I'm grateful that you agreed to come here with me,' he said softly, 'and taking you to Skylar's exhibition would be my way of saying thank you.'

'I don't need a thank you. And to be honest I'm here because of the conversation I had with your father. My decision didn't have anything to do with you. We had one night, that's all. I mean, the sex was great, but I had no trouble walking out of your door that morning. There were no feelings involved.' She shook her head to add emphasis. 'Kevlar, that's me.'

He gave her a long, steady look. 'I have never met anyone who less resembles that substance.'

'Up until a week ago I would have agreed with you, but now I'm a changed person. Seriously, I'm enjoying being with you. You're smoking hot and surprisingly entertaining despite your warped view of relationships, but I am no more in love with you than I am with your supersonic shower. And you don't owe me anything for bringing me here—in fact I owe you.' She glanced across the room to the terrace outside. 'This is the nearest I've come to a vacation in a long time. It's not exactly a hardship being here. I am going to lie in the sun like that lizard out there.'

'You haven't met my family yet.' He paused, his gaze fixed on hers. 'Think about it. If you change your mind about coming to Skylar's London exhibition, let me know. The invitation stands. I won't withdraw it.'

It was a different world.

What would it be like, she wondered, not to have to think about your budget? Not to have to make choices between forfeiting one thing to buy another?

This close she could see the flecks of gold in those dark eyes, the blue-black shadow of his jaw and the almost unbelievably perfect lines of his bone structure. If a scale had been invented to measure sex appeal, she was pretty sure he would have shattered it. She couldn't look at his mouth without remembering all the ways he'd used it on her body and remembering made her want it again. She wanted to reach out and slide her fingers into that silky dark hair and press her mouth to his. And this time she wanted to do it without the blindfold.

Aware that her mind was straying into forbidden territory she took a step back, reminding herself that money came a poor second to family and this man seemed to be virtually estranged from his father.

'I won't change my mind.'

Dragging her gaze from his, she dropped her bag on the floor and unzipped it. 'I need to hang up my dresses or they'll be creased. I don't want to make a bad impression.'

'There are staff over in the main villa who will help you unpack. I can call them.'

'Are you kidding?' Amused by yet more evidence of the differences between their respective lifestyles, she pulled out her clothes. 'This will take me five minutes at most. And I'd be embarrassed to ask anyone else to hang up a tee shirt that cost the same amount as a cup of coffee. So what happens next?'

'We are joining my father and Diandra for lunch.'

'Sounds good to me.'

The expression on his face told her he didn't share her sentiments. 'I need to make some calls. Make yourself at home. The fridge is stocked, there are books in the living room. Feel free to use the pool. If there is anything you need, let me know. I'll be using the office on the other side of the living room.'

What else could she possibly need?

Lily glanced round the villa, which was by far the most luxurious and exclusive place she'd ever stayed.

She had a feeling the only thing she was going to need was a reality check.

HE HADN'T BEEN back here since that summer five years before. It had been an attempt to put the past behind him, but ironically it had succeeded only in making things worse.

The memory of his last visit sat in his head like a muddy stain.

Nik strolled out onto the terrace, hoping the view would relieve his tension, but being here took him right back to his childhood and that was a place he made a point of avoiding.

With a soft curse, he walked back into the room he'd had converted into an office and switched on his laptop.

For the next hour he took an endless stream of calls and then finally, when he couldn't postpone the moment any longer, he took a quick shower and changed for lunch.

Another day, another wedding.

Mouth grim, he pocketed his phone and strolled through the villa to find Lily.

She was sitting in the shade on the terrace, a glass of iced lemonade by her hand and a book in her lap, staring out across the bright turquoise blue of the bay.

She hadn't noticed him and he stood for a moment, watching her. The tension left him to be replaced by tension of a different source. That one night he'd spent with her hadn't been anywhere near long enough.

He wanted to rip off that pretty blue sundress and take her straight back to bed but he knew that, no matter what she said, she wasn't the sort of woman to be able to keep her emotions out of the bedroom so he gave her a cool smile as he strolled onto the terrace.

'Are you ready?'

'Yes.' She slid her feet into a pair of silver ballet flats and put her book on the table. 'Is there anything I should know? Who will be there?'

'My father and Diandra. They wanted this lunch to be family only.'

'In other words your father doesn't want your first meeting

for a long while to be in public.' She reached for her glass and finished her drink. 'Don't worry about me while we're here. I'm sure I can find a few friendly faces to talk to while you're mingling.'

He looked down at the curve of her cheeks and the dimple in the corner of her mouth and decided she was the one with the friendly face. If he had to pick a single word to describe her, it would be approachable. She was warm, friendly and he was sure there would be no shortage of guests eager to talk to her. The thought should have reduced his stress because it gave him one less responsibility, but it didn't.

Despite her claims to being made of Kevlar, he wasn't convinced she'd managed to manufacture even a thin layer of protection for herself.

He offered to drive her to avoid the heat but she chose to walk and on the way up to the main house she grilled him about his background. Did his father still work? What exactly was his business? Did he have any other family apart from Nik?

His suspicion that she was more comfortable with this gathering than him was confirmed as soon as he walked onto the terrace.

He saw the table by the pool laid for four and felt Lily sneak her hand into his.

'He wants you to get to know Diandra. He's trying to build bridges,' she said softly, her fingers squeezing his. 'Don't glare.'

Before he could respond, his father walked out onto the terrace.

'Niklaus—' His voice shook and Nik saw the shimmer of tears in his father's eyes.

Lily extracted her hand from his. 'Hug him.' She made it sound simple and Nik wondered whether bringing someone as idealistic as Lily to a reunion as complicated as this one had been entirely sensible, but she and his father obviously thought alike because he walked towards them, arms outstretched.

'It's been too long since you were home. Far too long, but

the past is behind us. All is forgiven. I have such news to tell you, Niklaus.'

Forgiven?

His feet nailed to the floor by the past and the weight of the secrets his father didn't know, Nik didn't move and then he felt Lily's small hand in his back pushing, harder this time, and he then stepped forward and was embraced by his father so tightly it knocked the air from his lungs.

He felt a heaviness in his chest that had nothing to do with the intensity of his father's grip. Emotions rushed towards him and he was beginning to wish he'd never agreed to this reunion when Lily stepped forward, breaking the tension of the moment with her warmest, brightest smile and an extended hand that gave his father no choice but to release Nik.

'I'm Lily Rose. We spoke on the phone. You have a very beautiful home, Mr Zervakis. It's kind of you to invite me to share your special day.' Blushing charmingly, she then attempted to speak a few words of Greek, a gesture that both distracted his father and guaranteed a lifetime of devotion.

Nik watched as his dazzled father melted like butter left in the hot sun.

He kissed her hand and switched to heavily accented English. 'You are welcome in my home, Lily. I'm so happy you are able to join us for what is turning out to be the most special week of my life. This is Diandra.'

For the first time Nik noticed the woman hovering in the background.

He'd assumed she was one of his father's staff, but now she stepped forward and quietly introduced herself.

Nik noticed that she didn't quite meet his eye, instead she focused all her attention on Lily as if she were the lifebelt floating on the surface of a deep pool of water.

Diandra clearly had sophisticated radar for detecting sympathy in people, Nik thought, wondering what 'news' his father had for them.

Experience led him to assume it was unlikely to be good.

'I've brought you a small gift. I made it myself.' Lily delved into her bag and handed over a prettily wrapped parcel.

It was a ceramic plate, similar to the one he'd admired in her apartment, decorated with the same pattern of swirling blues and greens.

Nik could see she had real talent and so, apparently, did his father.

'You made this? But this isn't your business?'

'No. I'm an archaeologist. But I did my dissertation on Minoan ceramics so it's an interest of mine.'

'You must tell me all about it. And all about yourself. Lily Rose is a beautiful name.' His father led her towards the table that had been laid next to the pool. Silver gleamed in the sunlight and bowls of olives gleamed glossy dark in beautiful blue bowls. Kostas put Lily's plate in the centre of the table. 'Your mother liked flowers?'

'I don't know. I didn't know my mother.' She shot Nik an apologetic look. 'That's too much information for a first meeting. Let's talk about something else.'

But Kostas Zervakis wasn't so easily deflected. 'You didn't know your mother? She passed away when you were young, *koukla mou*?'

Appalled by that demonstration of insensitivity, Nik shot him an exasperated look and was about to steer the conversation away from such a deeply personal topic when Lily answered.

'I don't know what happened to her. She left me in a basket in Kew Gardens in London when I was a few hours old.'

Whatever he'd expected to hear, it hadn't been that and Nik, who made a point of never asking about a woman's past, found himself wanting to know more. 'A basket?' Her eyes lifted to his and for a moment the presence of other people was forgotten.

'Yes. I was found by one of the staff and taken to hospital. They called me Lily Rose because I was found among the flowers. They never traced my mother. They assumed she was a teenager who panicked.' She spoke in a matter-of-fact tone but Nik knew she wasn't matter-of-fact about the way she felt.

This was why she had shown so much wistful interest in the detail of his family. At the time he hadn't been able to understand why it would make an interesting topic of conversation, but now he understood that, to her, it was not a frustration or a complication. It was an aspiration.

This was why she dreamed of happy endings, both for herself and other people.

He felt something stir inside him, an emotion that was entirely new to him.

He'd believed himself immune to even the most elaborately constructed sob story, but Lily's revelation had somehow managed to slide under those steely layers of protection he'd constructed for himself. For some reason, her simply stated story touched him deeply.

Unsettled, he dragged his eyes from her soft mouth and promised himself that no matter how much he wanted her, he wasn't going to touch her again. It wouldn't be fair, when their expectations of life were so different. He had no concerns about his own ability to keep a relationship superficial. He did, however, have deep concerns about her ability to do the same and he didn't want to hurt her.

His father, predictably, was visibly moved by the revelation about her childhood.

'No family?' His voice was roughened by emotion. 'So who raised you, *koukla mou*?'

'I was brought up in a series of foster homes.' She poked absently at her food. 'And now I think we should talk about something else because this is *definitely* too much detail for a first meeting, especially when we're here to celebrate a wedding.' Superficially she was as cheerful as ever but Nik knew she was upset.

He was about to make another attempt to change the topic when his father reached out and took Lily's hand.

'One day you will have a family of your own. A big family.'

Nik ground his teeth. 'I don't think Lily wants to talk about that right now.'

'I don't mind.' Lily sent him a quick smile and then turned back to his father. 'I hope so. I think family makes you feel anchored and I've never had that.'

'Anchors keep a boat secured in one place,' Nik said softly, 'which can be limiting.'

Her gaze met his and he knew she was deciding if his observation was random or a warning.

He wasn't sure himself. All he knew was that he didn't want her thinking this was anything other then temporary. He could see she'd had a tough life. He didn't want to be the one to shatter that optimism and remove the smile from her face.

His father gave a disapproving frown. 'Ignore him. When it comes to relationships my son behaves like a child in a sweetshop. He gorges his appetites without learning the benefits of selectivity. He enjoys success in everything he touches except, sadly, his private life.'

'I'm very selective.' Nik reached for his wine. 'And given that my private life is exactly the way I want it to be, I consider it an unqualified success.'

He banked down the frustration, wondering how his father, thrice divorced, could consider himself an example to follow.

His father looked at him steadily. 'All the money in the world will not bring a man the same feeling of contentment as a wife and children, don't you agree, Lily?'

'As someone with massive college loans, I wouldn't dismiss the importance of money,' Lily said honestly, 'but I agree that family is the most important thing.'

Feeling as if he'd woken up on the set of a Hollywood romcom in which he'd been cast in the role of 'bad guy', Nik refrained from asking his father which of his wives had ever given him anything other than stomach ulcers and astronomical bills.

Surely even he couldn't reframe his romantic past as anything other than a disaster.

'One day you will have a family, Lily.' Kostas Zervakis surveyed her with misty eyes and Nik observed this emotional interchange with something between disbelief and despair.

His father had known Lily for less than five minutes and already he was ready to leave her everything in his will. It was no wonder he'd made himself a target for every woman with a sob story.

Callie had spotted that vulnerability and dug her claws deep. No doubt Diandra was working on the same soft spot.

A dark, deeply buried memory stirred in the depths of his brain. His father, sitting alone in the bedroom among the wreckage of his wife's hasty packing, the image of wretched despair as she drove away without looking back.

Never, before or since, had Nik felt as powerless as he had that day. Even though he'd been a young child, he'd known he was witnessing pain beyond words.

The second time it had happened, he'd been a teenager and he remembered wondering why his father would have risked putting himself through such emotional agony a second time.

And then there had been Callie...

He'd known from the first moment that the relationship was doomed and had blamed himself later for not trying to save his father from that particular mistake.

And now here he was again, trapped in the unenviable position of having to make a choice between watching his father walk into another relationship disaster, or potentially damaging their relationship by trying to intervene.

Lily was right that his father was a grown man, able to make his own decisions. So why did he still have this urge to push his father out of the path of the oncoming train?

Emotions boiling inside him, he glanced across the table to his future stepmother, wondering if it was a coincidence that she'd picked the chair as far from his as possible.

She was either shy or she was harbouring a guilty conscience.

He'd promised he wouldn't interfere, but he was fast rethinking that decision.

He sat in silence, observing rather than participating, while staff discreetly served food and topped up glasses.

His father engaged Lily in conversation, encouraging her to talk about her life and her love of archaeology and Greece.

Forced to sit through a detailed chronology of Lily's life history, Nik learned that she'd had three boyfriends, worked numerous low-paid jobs to pay for college tuition, was allergic to cats, suffered from severe eczema as a child and had never lived in the same place for more than twelve months.

The more he discovered about her life, the more he realised how hard it had been. She'd made a joke about Cinderella, but Lily made Cinderella look like a slacker.

Learning far more than he'd ever wanted to know, he turned to his father. 'What is the "news" you have for me?'

'You will find out soon enough. First, I am enjoying having the company of my son. It's been too long. I have resorted to the Internet to find news of what is happening with you. You have been spending a great deal of time in San Francisco.'

Happy to talk about anything that shifted the focus from Lily, Nik relaxed slightly and talked broadly about some of the technology developments his company was spearheading and touched lightly on the deal he was about to close, but the diversion proved to be brief.

Kostas spooned olives onto Lily's plate. 'You must persuade Nik to take you to the far side of the island to see the Minoan remains. You will need to go early in the day, before it is too hot. At this time of year everything is very dry. If you love flowers, then you will love Crete in the spring. In April and May the island is covered in poppies, daisies, camomile, iris.' He beamed at her. 'You must come back here then and visit.'

'I'd like that.' Lily tucked into her food. 'These olives are delicious.'

'They come from our own olive groves and the lemonade in your fridge came from lemons grown on our own trees. Diandra made it. She is a genius in the kitchen. You wait until you taste her lamb.' Kostas leaned across and took Diandra's hand. 'I took one mouthful and fell in love.'

Losing his appetite, Nik gave her a direct look. 'Tell me about yourself, Diandra. Where were you brought up?' He caught Lily's urgent glance and ignored it, instead listening to Diandra's stammered response.

From that he learned that she was one of six children and had never been married.

'She never met the right person, and that is lucky for me,' his father said indulgently.

Nik opened his mouth to speak, but Lily got there first.

'You're so lucky having been born in Greece,' she said quickly. 'I've travelled extensively in the islands but living here must be wonderful. I've spent three summers on Crete and one on Corfu. Where else do you think I should visit?'

Giving her a grateful look, Diandra made several suggestions, but Nik refused to be deflected from his path.

'Who did you work for before my father?'

'Ignore him,' Lily said lightly. 'He makes every conversation feel like a job interview. The first time I met him I wanted to hand over my résumé. This lamb is *delicious* by the way. You're so clever. It's even better than the lamb Nik and I ate last week and that was a top restaurant.' She went on to describe what they'd eaten in minute detail and Diandra offered a few observations of her own about the best way to cook lamb.

Deprived of the opportunity to question his future stepmother further, Nik was wondering once again what 'news' his father was preparing to announce, when he heard the sound of a child crying inside the house.

Diandra shot to her feet and exchanged a brief look with his father before scurrying from the table.

Nik narrowed his eyes. 'Who,' he said slowly, 'is that?'

'That's the news I was telling you about.' His father turned his head and watched as Diandra returned to the table carrying a toddler whose tangled blonde curls and sleepy expression announced that she'd recently awoken from a nap. 'Callie has given me full custody of Chloe as a wedding present. Niklaus, meet your half-sister.'

CHAPTER SEVEN

LILY SAT ON the sunlounger in the shade, listening to the rhythmic splash from the infinity pool. Nik had been swimming for the past half an hour, with no break in the relentless laps back and forth across the pool.

Whatever had possessed her to agree to come for this wedding?

It had been like falling straight into the middle of a bad soap opera.

Diandra had been so intimidated by Nik she'd barely opened her mouth and he, it seemed, had taken that as a sign that she had nothing worth saying. Lunch had been a tense affair and the moment his father had produced his little half-sister Nik had gone from being coolly civil to remote and intimidating. Lily had worked so hard to compensate for his frozen silence she'd virtually performed cartwheels on the terrace.

And she couldn't comprehend his reaction.

He was too old to care about sharing the affections of his father, and too independently wealthy to care about the impact on his inheritance. The toddler was adorable, a cherub with golden curls and a ready smile, and his father and Diandra had been so obviously thrilled by the new addition to the family Lily couldn't understand the problem.

On the walk back from lunch she'd tentatively broached the subject but Nik had cut her off and made straight for his office where he'd proceeded to work without interruption.

Trying to cure her headache, Lily had drunk plenty of water and then read her book in the shade but she'd been unable to concentrate on the words.

She knew it was none of her business, but still she couldn't keep her mouth shut and when Nik finally vaulted from the pool in an athletic movement that displayed every muscle in his powerful frame, she slid off her sunlounger and blocked his path.

'You were horrible to Diandra at lunch and if you want to heal the rift with your father, that isn't the way. She is *not* a gold-digger.'

His face was an uncompromising mask. 'And you know this on less than a few minutes' acquaintance?'

'I'm a good judge of character.'

'This from a woman who didn't know a man was married?'

She felt herself flush. 'I was wrong about him, but I'm not wrong about Diandra, and you have to stop giving her the evil eye.'

Droplets of water clung to his bronzed shoulders. 'I was not giving her the evil eye.'

'Nik, you virtually grilled her at the table. I was waiting for you to throw her on the barbecue along with the lamb. You were terrifying.'

'*Theé mou,* that is *not* true. She behaved like a woman with a guilty conscience.'

'She behaved like a woman who was terrified of you! How can you be so *blind*?' And then she realised in a flash of comprehension that she was the one who was blind. He wasn't being small-minded, or prejudiced. That wasn't what was happening. She saw now that he was afraid for his father. His actions all stemmed from a desire to protect him. In his own way he was displaying the exact loyalty she valued so highly. Like a gazelle approaching a sleeping lion, she tiptoed carefully. 'I think your perspective may be a little skewed because of what happened with your father's other relationships. Do you want to talk about it?'

'Unlike you, I don't have the desire to verbalise every thought that enters my head.'

Lily stiffened. 'That was a little harsh given that I'm trying to help, but I'm going to forgive you because I can see you're very upset. And I think I know why.'

'Don't forgive me. If you're angry, say so.'

'You told me not to verbalise every thought that enters my head.'

Nik wiped his face with the towel and sent her a look that would have frozen molten lava. 'I don't need help.'

Lily tried a different approach. 'I can see that this situation has the potential for all sorts of complications, not least that Diandra has been given another woman's child to raise as her own just a few days before the wedding, but she seemed thrilled. Your father is clearly delighted. They're happy, Nik.'

'For how long?' His mouth tightened. 'How long until it all falls apart and his heart is broken again? What if this time he doesn't heal?' His words confirmed her suspicions and she felt a rush of compassion.

'This isn't about Diandra, it's about you. You love your father deeply and you're trying to protect him.' It was ironic, she thought, that Nik Zervakis, who was supposedly so cold and aloof, turned out to have stronger family values than David Ashurst, who on the surface had seemed like perfect partner material. It was something that her checklist would never have shown up. 'I love that you care so much about him, but has it occurred to you that you might be trying to save him from the best thing that has ever happened in his life?'

'Why will this time be different from the others?'

'Because he loves her and she loves him. Of course having

a toddler thrown into the mix will make for a challenging start to the relationship, but—' She frowned as she examined that fact in greater depth. 'Why did Callie choose to do this now? A child is a person, not a wedding present. You think she was hoping to derail your father's relationship with Diandra?'

'The thought had occurred to me but no, that isn't what she is trying to do.' He hesitated. 'Callie is marrying again and she doesn't want the child.'

He delivered that news in a flat monotone devoid of emotion, but this time Lily was too caught up in her own emotions to think about his.

Callie didn't want the child?

She felt as if she'd been punched in the gut. All the air had been sucked from her lungs and suddenly she couldn't breathe.

'Right.' Her voice was croaky. 'So she gives her up as if she's a dress that's gone out of fashion? I'm not surprised you didn't like her. She doesn't sound like a very likeable person.' Horrified by the intensity of her response and aware he was watching her closely, she moved past him. 'If you're sure you don't want to talk then I think I'm going to have a rest before dinner. The heat makes me sleepy.'

He frowned. 'Lily—'

'Dinner is at eight? I'll be ready by then.' She steered her shaky legs towards her bedroom and closed the door behind her.

What was the matter with her?

This wasn't her family.

It wasn't her life.

Why did she have to take everything so *personally*?

Why was she worrying about how little Chloe would feel when she was old enough to ask about her mother when it wasn't really any of her business? Why did she care about all the potential threats she could see to his family unit?

The door behind her opened and she stiffened but kept her back to him. 'I'm about to lie down.'

'I upset you,' he said quietly, 'and that was not my intention.

You were generous enough to come here with me, the least I can do is respond to your questions in a civil tone. I apologise.'

'I'm not upset because you didn't want to talk. I understand you don't find it helpful.'

'Then what's wrong?' When she didn't reply he cursed softly. 'Talk to me, Lily.'

'No. I'm having lots of feelings of my own and you hate talking about feelings. And no doubt you'll find some way to interpret what I'm feeling in a bad way, because that seems to be your special gift. You twist everything beautiful into something dark and ugly. You really should leave now. I need to self-soothe.'

She expected to hear the pounding of feet and the sound of a door closing behind him, but instead felt the warm strength of his hands curve over her shoulders.

'I do not twist things.'

'Yes, you do. But that's your problem. I can't deal with it right now.'

'I don't want you to self-soothe.' The words sounded as if they were dragged from him. 'I want you to tell me what's wrong. My father asked you a lot of personal questions over lunch.'

'I don't mind that.'

'Then what? Is this about Chloe?'

She took a juddering breath. 'It's a little upsetting when adults don't consider how a child might feel. It's lovely that she has a loving father, but one day that little girl is going to wonder why her mother gave her away. She's going to ask herself whether she cried too much or did something wrong. Not that I expect you to understand.'

There was a long pulsing silence and his grip on her arms tightened. 'I do understand.' His voice was low. 'I was nine when my mother left and I asked myself all those questions and more.'

She stood still, absorbing both the enormity and the implications of that revelation. 'I didn't know.'

'I don't talk about it.'

But he'd talked about it now, with her. Warmth spread through her. 'Did seeing Chloe stir it all up for you?'

'This whole place stirs it up,' he said wearily. 'Let's hope Chloe doesn't ask herself those same questions when she's older.'

'I was a baby and I still ask myself those questions.' And she had questions for him, so many questions, but she knew they wouldn't be welcome.

'I appreciate you listening to me, but I know you don't really want to talk about this so you should probably leave now.'

'Seeing as I am indirectly responsible for the fact you're upset by bringing you here in the first place, I have no intention of leaving.'

'You should.' Her voice was thickened. 'It's the situation, not you. You've never even met your half-sister so you can't be expected to love her and your father is obviously pleased, but a toddler is a lot of work and he's about to be married. What if he decides he doesn't want Chloe either?'

'He won't decide that.' His hands firm, he turned her to face him. 'He has wanted her from the first day, but Callie did everything she could to keep the child from him. I have no idea what my father will say when Chloe is old enough to ask, but he is a sensitive man—much more sensitive than I am as you have discovered—and he will say the right thing, I'm sure.' His hands stroked her bare arms and she gave a little shiver.

She could see the droplets of water clinging to dark hair that shadowed his bare chest.

Unable to help herself, she lifted her hand to his chest and then caught herself and pulled back.

'Sorry—' She took a step backwards but he muttered something under his breath in Greek and hauled her back against him. Her brain blurred as she was flattened against the heat and power of his body, his arm holding her trapped. He used his other hand to tilt her face to his and she drowned in the heated burn of his eyes in the few seconds before he bent his head and kissed her. And then there was nothing but the hunger of his mouth and the erotic slide of his tongue and it felt every bit as good as it had the first time. So good that she forgot everything except the pounding of her pulse and the desperate squirming heat low in her pelvis.

Pressed against his hard, powerful chest she forgot about feeling miserable and unsettled.

She forgot all the reasons this wasn't a good idea.

She forgot everything except the breathtaking excitement he generated with his mouth and hands. His kiss was unmistakably sexual, his tongue tangling with hers, his gaze locked on hers as he silently challenged her.

'Yes, yes.' With a soft murmur of acquiescence, she wrapped her arms round his neck, feeling the damp ends of his hair brush her wrists.

The droplets of water on his chest dampened her thin sundress until it felt as if there were nothing between them.

She felt him pull her hard against him, felt his hand slide down her back and cup her bottom so that she was pressed against the heavy thrust of his erection.

'I promised myself I wasn't going to do this but I want you.' He spoke in a thickened tone, and she gave a sob of relief.

'I want you, too. You have no idea how much. Right through lunch I wanted to rip your clothes off and remove that severe look from your face.'

He lifted his mouth from hers, his breathing uneven, the smouldering glitter of his eyes telling her everything she needed to know about his feelings. 'Do I look severe now?'

'No. You look incredible. This has been the longest week of my life.' She backed towards the bed, pulling him with her. If he changed his mind she was sure she'd explode. 'Don't have second thoughts. I know this is about sex and nothing else. I don't love you, but I'd love a repeat of all those things you did to me the other night.'

With sure hands, he dispensed with her sundress. 'All of them?'

'Yes.' She wanted him so badly it was almost indecent and when he lowered his head and trailed his mouth along her neck she almost sobbed aloud. 'Please. Right now. I want your whole repertoire. Don't hold anything back.'

'You're shy, it's still daylight,' he growled, 'and I don't have a blindfold.'

'I'm not shy. Shy has left the party. I don't care, I don't care.' Her hands moved over his chest and lower to his damp swimming shorts. She struggled to remove them over the thrusting force of his erection but finally her frantic fumbling proved successful and she covered him with the flat of her hand.

He groaned low in his throat and tipped her onto the bed, covering her body with his, telling her how much he wanted her, how hard she made him, until the excitement climbed to a point where she was a seething, writhing mass of desire. She tore at his shirt with desperate hands and he swore under his breath and wrenched it over his head, his fingers tangling with hers.

'Easy, slow down, there's no rush.'

'Yes, there is.' She rolled him onto his back and pressed her mouth to the hard planes of his chest and lower until she heard him groan. She tried to straddle him but he flipped her onto her back and caught her shifting hips in his hands, anchoring her there.

Despite the simmering tension, there was laughter in his eyes. 'It would be a criminal waste to rush this, *theé mou.*'

'No, it wouldn't.' She slid her hands over the silken muscles of his back. 'It might kill me if you don't.'

It was hard to know which of them was most aroused. She saw it in the glitter of his eyes and heard it in his uneven breathing. Felt it in the slight shake of his fingers as he unhooked her bra and peeled it away from her, releasing her breasts, taking his time. Everything he did was slow, unhurried, designed to torture her and she wondered how he could exercise so much control, such brutal discipline, because if it had been up to her the whole thing would have been over by now. He kept her still with his weight, with soft words, with skilled kisses and the sensual slide of his hand that dictated both position and pace.

She felt the cool air from the ceiling fan brush the heated surface of her skin and then moaned aloud as he drew her into the dark heat of his mouth. Sensation was sweet and wild and she arched into him, only to find herself anchored firmly by the rough strength of his thigh. He worked his way down her body with slow exploratory kisses and she shivered as she felt the brush of his lips and the flick of his tongue. Lower, more intimate, his mouth wandered to the shadows between her thighs and she felt the slippery heat of his tongue opening her, tasting her until she could feel the pleasure thundering down on her. She was feverish, desperate, everything in her body centred on this one moment.

'Nik—I need—'

'I know what you need.' A brief pause and then he eased over her and into her, each driving thrust taking him deeper until she didn't know where she ended and he began and then he paused, his hand in her hair and his mouth against hers, eyes half closed as he studied her face. She was dimly aware that he was saying something, soft intimate words that blurred in her head and melted over her skin. She felt the delicious weight of him, the masculine invasion, the solidity of muscle, the scrape of his jaw against hers as he kissed her, murmured her name and told her all the things he wanted to do to her. And she moaned because she wanted him to do them, right now. He was controlling her but she didn't care because he knew things about her she didn't know herself. How to touch her, where to touch her. All she wanted was more of this breath-stealing pleasure and then he started to move, slowly at first, and then building the rhythm with sure, skilled thrusts until she was aware of nothing but him, of hard muscle and slick skin, of the frenzy of sensation until it exploded and she clung to him, sobbing his name as her body tightened on his, her muscles rippling around the thrusting length of him drawing out his own response.

She heard him groan her name, felt him slide his hand into her hair and take her mouth again so that they kissed their way through the whole thing, sharing every throb, ripple and flutter in the most intimate way possible.

The force of it left her shaken and stunned and she lay, breathless, trying to bring herself slowly back to earth. And then he shifted his weight and gathered her close, murmuring something in Greek as he stroked her hair back from her face and kissed her mouth gently.

They lay for a moment and then he scooped her up and carried her into the shower where, under the soft patter of steamy water, he proceeded to expand her sexual education with infinite skill until her body no longer felt like her own and her legs felt like rubber.

'Nik?' She lay damp and sated on the tangled sheets, deliciously sleepy and barely able to keep her eyes open. 'Is that why you don't like coming back here? Because it reminds you of your childhood?'

He stared down at her with those fathomless black eyes, his expression inscrutable. 'Get some sleep.' His voice was even. 'I'll wake you in time to change for dinner.'

'Where are you going?'

'I have work to do.'

In other words she'd strayed into forbidden territory. Somewhere in the back of her mind there was another question she wanted to ask him, but her brain was already drifting into blissful unconsciousness and she slid into a luxurious sleep.

NIK RETURNED TO the terrace and made calls in the shade, one eye on the open doors of Lily's bedroom.

So much for his resolve not to touch her again.

And what had possessed him to tell her about his mother? It

was something he rarely thought about himself, let alone spoke of to other people.

It was being back here that had stirred up memories long buried.

He ignored the part of him that said it was the prospect of another wedding that stirred up the memories, not the place.

To distract himself he worked until the blaze of the sun dimmed and he heard movement from the bedroom.

He ended the call he'd made and a few minutes later she wandered onto the terrace, sleepy eyed and deliciously disorientated. 'Have you been out here the whole time?'

'Yes.'

'You're not tired?'

'No.'

'Because you're stressed out about your father.' She sat down next to him and poured herself a glass of water. 'For what it's worth, I like Diandra.'

He studied the soft curve of her mouth and the kindness in her eyes. 'Is there anyone you don't like?'

'Yes!' She sipped her water. 'I have a deep aversion to Professor Ashurst, and if we're drawing up a list then I should confess I didn't totally fall in love with your girlfriend from the other night, but that might be because she called me fat. And I definitely didn't like you a few hours ago, but you redeemed yourself in the bedroom so I'm willing to overlook the offensive things you said on the journey.' A dimple appeared in the corner of her mouth and Nik felt the instant, powerful response of his body and wondered how he was going to make it through an evening of small talk with people that didn't interest him.

She, on the other hand, interested him extremely.

'We should get ready for the party. The guests will be arriving soon and my father wants us up there early to greet them.'

'Us? You, surely, not me.'

'He wants you, too. He likes you very much.'

'I like him, too, but I don't think I should be greeting his guests. I'm not family. We're not even together.' Her gaze slid to his and away again and he knew she was thinking about what they'd shared earlier.

He was, too. In fact he'd thought of little else but sex with Lily since she'd drenched herself in his shower a week earlier.

Sex had always been important to him, but since meeting her it had become an obsession.

'It would mean a lot to him if you were there.'

'Well, if you're sure that's what he wants. This all feels a bit surreal.'

'Which part feels surreal?'

'All of it. The whole rich-lifestyle thing. Living with you could turn a girl's head. You can snap your fingers and have anything you want.'

Relieved by the lightening of the atmosphere, he smiled. 'I will snap my fingers for you any time you like. Tell me what you want.'

She smiled. 'You can get me anything?'

'Anything.'

'So if I had a craving for lobster mousse, you'd find me one?'

'I would.' He reached for his phone and she covered his hand with hers, laughing.

'I wasn't serious! I don't want lobster mousse.' Her fingers were light on his hand. There was nothing suggestive about her touch. Nothing that warranted his extreme physical reaction.

'Then what?' His voice was husky. 'If you don't want lobster mousse, what can I get you?'

Her eyes met his and colour streaked across her cheeks. 'Nothing. I have everything I need.' She removed her hand quickly and said something, but her words were drowned out by the clacking of a helicopter.

Nik rose reluctantly to his feet. 'We need to move. The guests are arriving.'

'By helicopter?' Her eyes were round, as if it was only now

dawning on her that this wasn't an ordinary wedding party. 'Is this party going to be glamorous?'

'Very. Lunch was an informal family affair, but tonight is for my father to show off his new wife.'

'How many guests?'

'A very select party. No more than two hundred, but they're arriving from all over Europe and the US.'

'Two *hundred*? That's a select party?' Her smile faltered. 'I'm a gatecrasher.'

'You are not a gatecrasher. You're my guest.'

She pushed her hair back from her face. 'I'm starting to panic that what I brought with me isn't dressy enough.'

'You look lovely in everything you wear, but I do have something if you'd like to take a look at it.'

'Something you bought for someone else?'

'No. For you.'

'I told you I didn't want anything.'

'I didn't listen.'

'So you bought me something anyway. In case I embarrassed you?'

'No. In case you had a panic that what you'd brought wasn't dressy enough.'

'I should probably be angry that you're calling me predictable, but as we don't have time to be angry I'm going to overlook it. Can I see?' She stood up at the same time he did and her body brushed against his.

'Lily…' He breathed her name, steadied her with his hands and she gave a low moan.

'No.' Her eyes were clouded. 'Seriously, Nik, if we do it again I'll fall asleep and never wake up. The Prince is supposed to wake Sleeping Beauty, not put her to sleep with endless sex.'

He lifted his hand to her flushed cheek and gently stroked her hair back from her face. It took all his will power not to power her back against the wall. 'We could skip the party. Better still, we could grab a couple of bottles of champagne and have our own party here by the pool.'

'No way! Not only would that upset your father and Diandra, but I wouldn't get to ogle all those famous people. Brittany will grill me later so I need to have details. Am I allowed to take photographs?'

'Of course.' With a huge effort of will he let his hand drop. 'You'd better try the dress.'

THE DRESS WAS EXQUISITE. A long sheath of shimmering turquoise silk with delicate beads hand-sewn around the neckline. It fitted her perfectly.

She picked up her phone, took a quick selfie and sent it to Brittany with a text saying Rebound sex is my new favourite thing.

People were wrong when they thought rebound sex didn't involve any emotion, she mused. Yes, the sex was spectacular, but even though she wasn't in love that didn't mean two people couldn't care about each other. She cared about making this wedding as easy as possible for Nik, and he'd cared enough not to leave her alone when she was upset.

Somewhere deep inside a small part of her wondered if perhaps that wasn't how she was supposed to be feeling, but she dismissed it, picked up her purse and walked through to the living room.

'I could be a little freaked out by how well you're able to guess my size.'

He turned, sleek and handsome in a dinner suit.

Despite the undisputable elegance and sophistication, formal dress did nothing to disguise the lethal power of the man beneath.

Testosterone in a tux, she thought as he reached into his pocket and handed her something.

'What's this?' She took the slim, elegant box and opened it cautiously. There, nestled in deep blue velvet, was a necklace of silver and sapphire she immediately recognised. 'It's one of Skylar's. I admired the picture.'

'And now you can admire the real thing. I thought it would look better on your neck than in a catalogue.' He took it from her and fastened it round her neck while she pressed her fingers to her throat self-consciously.

'When did you buy this?'

'I had it flown in after you admired her pot.'

'You had it *flown in*? From New York? There wasn't time.'

'This piece was in a gallery in London.'

'Unbelievable. So extravagant.'

'Then why are you smiling?'

'Because I like pretty things and Skylar makes the prettiest things.' Smiling, she pulled her phone out of her purse again. 'I need to capture the moment so when I'm sitting in my pyjamas in a cramped apartment in rainy London I can relive this moment. It's a loan, obviously, because I could never accept a gift this generous.' She took a couple of photos and then made him pose with her. 'I promise not to sell these to the newspapers. Can I send it to Sky? I can say *Look what I'm wearing*.'

A smile touched the corners of his mouth. 'It's your photo. You can do anything you like with it.'

'Skylar will be over the moon. I'm going to make sure everyone sees this necklace tonight. Now, tell me how you're feeling.' She'd asked herself over and over again if his earlier confession was something she should mention or not. But how could she ignore it when it was clearly the source of his stress?

His expression shifted from amused to guarded. 'How I'm feeling?'

'This is a party to celebrate your father's impending wedding, which you didn't want to attend. Is it hard to be here thinking about your mother and watching your father marry again? It must make marriage seem like a disposable object.'

'I appreciate your concern, but I'm fine.'

'Nik, I know you're not fine, but if you'd rather not talk about it—'

'I'd rather not talk about it.'

She kept her thoughts on that to herself. 'Then let's go.' She slipped her hand into his. 'I guess everyone will be trying to work out whether you're pleased or not, so for Diandra's sake make sure you smile.'

'Thank you for your counsel.'

'Ouch, that was quite a put-down. I presume that was your way of telling me to stop talking.'

'If I want to stop you talking, I have more effective methods than a verbal put-down.'

She caught his eye. 'If you feel like testing out one of those methods, go right ahead.'

'Don't tempt me.'

She was shocked by how badly she wanted to tempt him. She considered dragging him back inside, but a car was waiting outside the villa for them. 'I didn't realise there were cars on the island. How do they get across here?'

'There is a ferry, but my father usually takes a helicopter to the mainland if he is travelling.'

'We could have walked tonight.'

'There is no way you'd be able to walk that far in those shoes, let alone dance.'

'Who says I'll be dancing?'

His gaze slid to hers. 'I do.'

'You seem very sure of that.'

'I am, because you'll be dancing with me.'

She felt a shiver of excitement, excitement that grew as they drew up outside the imposing main entrance. The villa was situated on the far side of the island, out of sight of the mainland. 'This is a mansion, not a villa. Normal people don't live like this.'

'You think I'm not a normal person?'

'I *know* you're not.' She took his arm as they walked past

a large fountain to the floodlit entrance of the villa. 'Normal people don't own five homes and a private jet.'

'The jet is owned by the company.'

'And you own the company.' It was hard not to feel over-whelmed as she walked through the door into the palatial en-trance of his father's home. Towering ceilings gave a feeling of space and light and through open doors she caught a glimpse of rooms tastefully furnished with antiques and fine art. 'Tell me again what your father does?'

Nik smiled. 'He ran a very successful company, which he sold for a large sum of money.'

'But not to you.'

'Our interests are different.'

There was no opportunity for him to elaborate because Di-andra was hovering and Lily noticed the nervous look she gave Nik.

To break the ice, she enthused over the other woman's dress and hair and then asked after Chloe.

'She's sleeping. My niece is watching her while we greet ev-eryone, then I'm going to check on her. It's been a very unset-tling time.' Diandra kept her voice low. 'I wanted to postpone the wedding but Kostas won't hear of it.'

'You're right, I won't.' Kostas took Diandra's hand. 'Nothing is going to stop me marrying you. You worry too much. She will soon settle and in the meantime we have an army of staff to attend to her happiness.'

'She doesn't need an army,' Diandra murmured. 'She needs the security of a few people she knows and trusts.'

'We'll discuss this later.' Kostas drew her closer. 'Our guests are arriving. Lily, you look beautiful. You will stand with us and greet everyone.'

'Oh, but I—'

'I insist.'

Lily quickly discovered that Nik's father was as skilled at getting his own way as his son.

Unable to extract herself, she stood and greeted the guests, feeling as if she were on a movie set as a wave of shimmering, glittering guests flowed past her.

'This isn't my life,' she whispered to Nik but he simply smiled and exchanged a few words with each guest, somehow managing to make everyone feel as if they'd had his full attention.

She discovered that even among this group of influential people everyone wanted a piece of him, especially the women.

It gave her a brief but illuminating insight into his life and she saw how it must be for him, surrounded by people whose motives in wanting to know him were as mixed up and murky as the bottom of the ocean.

She was beginning to understand both his reserve and his cynicism.

The evening was like something out of a dream, except that none of her dreams had ever featured an evening as glittering and extravagant as this.

What would it be like, she wondered, if this really *were* her life?

She pushed that thought aside quickly, preferring not to linger in fantasyland. Wanting a family was one thing, this was something else altogether.

Candles flickered, silverware gleamed and the air was filled with the heady scent of expensive perfume and fresh flowers. The food, a celebration of all things Greek, was served on the terrace so that the guests could enjoy the magnificent sight of the sun setting over the Aegean.

By the time Nik finally swung her onto the dance floor Lily was dizzy with it.

'I talked to a few people while you were in conversation with those men in suits. I didn't mention the fact I'm a penniless archaeologist.'

'Are you enjoying yourself?'

'What do you think?'

'I think you look stunning in that dress.' He eased her closer. 'I also think you are better at mindless small talk than I am.'

'Are you calling me mindless?' She rested her hand lightly on his chest. 'Did you know that the very good-looking man over there with the lovely wife owns upmarket hotels all over the world? He's Sicilian.'

He glanced over her shoulder. 'Cristiano Ferrara? You think he's good-looking?'

'Yes. And his wife is beautiful. They seem like a happy family.'

He smiled. 'Her name is Laurel.'

'Do you know everyone? She was very down-to-earth. She admired my necklace and he pulled me to one side to ask me for the details. He's going to surprise her for her birthday.'

'If Skylar sells a piece of jewellery to a Ferrara I can assure you she's made. They move in the highest circles.'

'Laurel wants an invitation to her exhibition in London. I have plugged Skylar's jewellery to at least ten *very* wealthy people. I hope you're not angry.'

He curved her against him in a possessive gesture. 'You are welcome to be as shameless as you wish. In fact I'm willing to make a few specific suggestions about how you could direct that shameless behaviour.'

A few heads turned in their direction.

'Thank you for telling this room full of strangers that I'm a sex maniac. Are you sure you don't want to dance with someone else?'

His eyes were half shut, his gaze focused entirely on her. 'Why would I want to dance with anyone else?'

'Because there are a lot of women in this room and they're looking at you hopefully. Me, they look as if they'd like to kill. They're wondering why you're with me.'

'None of the men are wondering that,' he drawled. 'Trust me on that.'

'Can I tell you something?'

'That depends. Is it going to be a deeply emotional confession that is going to send me running from the room?'

'You can't run anywhere because your father is about to make a speech and—oh—' she frowned '—Diandra looks stressed.' Taking his hand, she tugged him across the crowded dance floor towards Diandra, who appeared to be arguing with Kostas.

'Wait five minutes,' Kostas urged in a low tone. 'You cannot abandon our guests.'

'But she needs me,' Diandra said firmly and Lily intervened. 'Is this about Chloe?'

'She's woken up. I can't bear to think of her upset with people she doesn't know. It's already hard enough on her to have been left here by her mother.'

'Nik and I will go to her,' Lily said immediately and saw Nik frown.

'I don't think—'

'We'll be fine. Make your speech and then come and find us.' Without letting go of Nik's hand, Lily made for the stairs. 'I assume you know where the nursery is or should we use GPS?'

'I really don't think—'

'Cut the excuses, Zervakis. Your little sister needs you.'

'She doesn't know me. I don't see how my sudden appearance in her life can do anything but make things a thousand times worse.'

'Children are sometimes reassured by a strong presence. But stop glaring.' She paused at the top of the stairs. 'Which way?'

He sighed and led the way up another flight of stairs to a suite of rooms and pushed open the door.

A young girl stood there jiggling a red-faced crying toddler. Relief spread across her features when she saw reinforcements.

'She's been like this for twenty minutes. I can't stop her crying.'

Nik took one look at the abject misery on his half-sister's face and took her from the girl, but, instead of her being comforted by the reassuring strength in those arms, Chloe's howls intensified.

Sending Lily a look that said 'I told you so', he immediately handed her over.

'Perhaps you can do a better job than I can.'

She was about to point out that he was a stranger and that Chloe's response was no reflection on him when the toddler flopped onto her shoulder, exhausted.

'You poor thing,' Lily soothed. 'Did you wake and not know where you were? Was it noisy downstairs?' She continued to talk, murmuring soothing nothings and stroking the child's back until the child's eyelids drifted closed. She felt blonde curls tickle her chin. 'There, that's better, you must be exhausted. Are you thirsty? Would you like a drink?' She glanced across the room and saw Nik watching her, his expression inscrutable. 'Say something.'

'What do you want me to say?'

'Something. Anything. You look as if someone has released a tiger from a cage and you're expected to bag it single-handed.'

There was a tension in his shoulders that hadn't been there a few moments earlier and suddenly she wondered if his response to the child was mixed up with his feelings for Callie.

It was obvious he'd disliked his father's third wife, but surely he wouldn't allow those feelings to extend to the child?

And then she realised he wasn't looking at Chloe, he was looking at her.

He lifted his hand and loosened his tie with a few flicks of those long, bronzed fingers. 'You love children.'

'Well I don't love *all* children, obviously, but at this age they're pretty easy to love.' She waited for him to walk across the room and take his sister from her, but he didn't move. Instead he leaned against the doorway, watching her, and then finally eased himself upright.

'You seem to have this under control.' His voice was level. 'I'll see you downstairs when you're ready.'

'No! Nik, wait—' She shifted Chloe onto her other hip and walked across to him, intending to hand over the wriggling toddler so that he could form a bond with her, but he took a step back, his face a frozen mask.

'I'll send Diandra up as soon as she's finished with the speeches.' With that he turned and strode out of the room leaving her holding the baby.

CHAPTER EIGHT

NIK MADE HIS way through the guests, out onto the terrace and down past the cascading water feature that ended in a beautiful pool. Children cried for a million reasons, he knew that, but that didn't stop him wondering if deep down Chloe knew her mother had abandoned her. The fact that he'd been unable to offer comfort had done nothing for his elevated stress levels, but the real source of his tension had been the look on Lily's face.

He could see now he'd made a huge mistake bringing her here. *Cristos*, who was he kidding? The mistake had been taking her back to his place from the restaurant that night, instead of dropping her safely at her apartment and telling her to lock the door behind her.

She was completely, totally wrong for him and he was completely, totally wrong for her.

Cursing under his breath, he yanked off his tie and ran his hand over his jaw.

'Nik?'

Her voice came from behind him and he turned to find her standing there, her sapphire eyes gleaming bright in the romantic light of the pool area. The turquoise dress hugged the lush lines of her body and her blonde hair, twisted into Grecian braids, glowed like a halo. The jewel he'd given her sat at the base of her throat and suddenly all he wanted to do was rip it off and replace it with his mouth. There wasn't a man in the room who hadn't taken a second glance at her and he was willing to bet she hadn't noticed. He'd always considered jealousy to be a pointless and ugly emotion but tonight he'd experienced it in spades. He should have given her a dress of shapeless black, although he had a feeling that would have made no difference to the way he felt. It was a shock to discover that will power alone wasn't enough to hold back the brutal arousal.

'I thought you were with Chloe. Is she asleep?'

'Diandra came to take over. And you shouldn't have walked away from her.' She was stiff. Furious, displaying none of the softness and gentleness he'd witnessed in the nursery.

The wind had picked up and he frowned as he saw her shiver and run her hands over her arms. 'Are you cold? Crete often experiences high winds.'

'I'm not cold. I'm being heated from the inside out because I'm boiling mad, Nik. I don't think it's exactly fair of you to take your feelings for her mother out on a child, that's all.'

Nik took a deep breath, wondering how honest to be. 'That is not what is happening here.'

'No? Well there has to be some reason why you looked at Chloe as if she was a dangerous animal.'

'This is not about Chloe.'

'What then?'

There was a long, throbbing pause. 'It's about you.'

'Me?' She stared at him blankly and he cursed under his breath.

'You are the sort of woman who cannot pass a baby without wanting to pick it up. You see sunshine in a thunderstorm, happy endings everywhere you look and you believe family is the answer to every problem in the world.'

She stared at him with a total lack of comprehension. 'I do like babies, that's true, and I don't see any reason to apologise for the fact I'd like a family one day. I don't see sunshine in every thunderstorm, but I do try and see the positive rather than the negative because that's how I prefer to live my life. I put up an umbrella instead of standing there and getting wet. Sometimes life can be crap, I know that but I've learned not to focus on the crap and I won't apologise for that. But I don't see what that has to do with the situation. None of that explains why you behaved the way you did in that room. You looked as if you'd been hit round the head with a plank of wood and then you walked out. And you say it was about me, but how can it possibly—?'

Her expression changed, the shards of anger in her eyes changing to wariness. 'Oh. I get it. You're worried that because I want a family one day, that because I like babies, it makes me a dangerous person to have sex with, is that right?' She spoke slowly, feeling it out, watching his face the whole time and she must have seen something there that confirmed her suspicions because she made a derisive sound and turned away.

'Lily—'

'No! Don't make excuses or find a tactful way to express how you feel. It's sprayed over you like graffiti.' She hitched up her dress and started to walk away from him and he gritted his teeth because he could see she was truly upset.

'Wait. You can't walk back in those shoes—'

'Of course I can. What do you think I usually do when I'm out? I'd never been in a limo in my life before I met you. I walk everywhere because it's cheaper.' She hurled the words over her shoulder and he strode after her, wondering how to intervene and prevent a broken ankle without stoking her wrath.

'We should talk about this—'

'There is nothing to talk about.' She didn't slacken her pace. 'I cuddled your baby sister and you're afraid that somehow changed our relationship. You're worried that this isn't about sex any more, and that I've suddenly fallen in love with you. Your arrogance is shocking.'

He kept pace with her, ready to catch her if she twisted her ankle in those shoes. 'It is not arrogance. But that incident upstairs reinforced how different we are.'

'Yes, we're different. That's why I picked you for my rebound guy. It's true I want children one day, but believe me you're the last man on earth I'd want to share that with. I don't want a guy who describes a crying child as an "incident".'

'That is not—*Cristos,* will you *stop* for a moment?' He caught her arm and she shrugged him off, turning to face him.

'Believe me, Nik, I have never been *less* likely to fall in love with you than I am right at this moment. A little girl was distressed and all you could think about was how to extract yourself from a relationship you're not even having! That doesn't make you a great catch in my eyes so you're perfectly safe. I understand now why you have emotionless relationships. You're brilliant at the mechanics of sex, but that's it. I'd get as much emotional comfort from a laptop. Seriously, you should stick to your technology, or your investments or whatever it is you do—' She tugged her arm from his grip and carried on walking down the path, her distress evident in each furious tap of her heels.

He stared after her, stunned into silence by her unexpected attack and shaken by his own feelings. In emotional terms, he kept women at a distance. He'd never aspired to a deeper attachment and when his relationships ended he invariably felt nothing. He had no interest in marriage and didn't care about long-term commitment.

But he really, really cared that Lily was upset.

The feeling was uncomfortable, like having a stone in his shoe.

He followed at a safe distance, relieved when she reached the terrace and ripped off her shoes. She dumped them unceremoniously on a sunlounger and carried on walking. The braids of her Grecian goddess hairstyle had been loosened by the wind, and her hair slithered in tumbled curls over her bare shoulders.

A man with a sense of self-preservation would have left her to cool down.

Nik carried on walking. He walked right into the bedroom, narrowly avoiding a black eye as she swung the door closed behind her.

He caught it on the flat of his hand, strode through and slammed it shut behind him.

She turned, her eyes a furious blaze of blue. 'Get out, Nik.'

He shrugged off his jacket and slung it over the nearest chair. 'No.'

'You should, because the way I feel right now I might punch you. No, wait a minute, I know exactly how to make you back out of that door.' She tilted her head and her mouth curved into a smile that didn't reach her eyes. 'You should leave, Nik, because I'm—oh, seconds away from falling in love with your irresistible self.' Her sarcasm made him smile and that smile was like throwing petrol on flame. 'Are you laughing at me?'

'No, I'm smiling because you're cute when you're angry.'

'I'm not cute. I'm fearsome and terrifying.'

What was fearsome and terrifying was how much he wanted her but he kept that thought to himself as he strolled towards her. 'Can we start this conversation again?'

'There is nothing more to say. Stop right there, Nik. Don't take another step.'

He kept walking. 'I should not have left you with Chloe. I behaved like an idiot, I admit it,' he breathed, 'but I'm not used to having a relationship with a woman like you.'

'And you're afraid I don't understand the rules? Trust me, I not only understand them but I applaud them. I wouldn't *want* to fall in love with someone like you. You make Neanderthal man look progressive and I've studied Neanderthal man. And stop looking at me like that because there is no way I can have sex with you when I'm this angry. It's not happening, Nik. Forget it.'

He stopped toe to toe with her, slid his hand into her hair and tilted her face to his. 'You've never had angry sex?'

'Of course not! Until you, I've only ever had "in love" sex. Angry sex sounds horrible. Sex should be loving and gentle. Who on earth would want to—?' Her words died as he silenced her with his mouth.

He cupped her face, feeling the softness of her skin beneath his fingers and the frantic beat of her pulse. He took her mouth with a hunger bordering on aggression and felt her melt against him. Her arms sneaked round his neck and he explored the sweet heat of her mouth, so aroused he was ready to rip off her dress and play out any one of the explicit scenarios running through his brain.

He had no idea what it was about her that attracted him so much, but right now he wouldn't have cared if she was holding an armful of babies and singing the wedding march, he still would have wanted to get her naked.

Without lifting his mouth from hers, he hauled her dress up to her waist and slid his fingers inside the lace of her panties. He heard her moan, felt her slippery hot and ready for him, and then her hands were on his zip, fumbling as she tried desperately to free him. As her cool fingers closed around him his mind blanked. He powered her back against the wall, slid his hands under her thighs and lifted her easily, wrapping her legs around his hips.

'Nik—' She sobbed his name against his mouth, dug her nails into his shoulders and he anchored her writhing hips with his hands and thrust deep. Gripped by tight, velvet softness, he felt his vision blur. Control was so far from his reach he abandoned hope of ever meeting up again and simply surrendered to the out-of-control desire that seemed to happen whenever he was near this woman.

He withdrew and thrust again, bringing thick waves of pleasure cascading down on both of them. From that moment on there was nothing but the wildness of it. He felt her nails digging into his shoulders and the frantic shifting of her hips. He tried to slow things down, to still those sensuous movements, but they were both out of control and he felt the first powerful ripples of her body clenching his shaft.

'*Cristo*—' He gave a deep, throaty groan and tried to hold back but there was no holding back and he surrendered to a raw explosive climax that wiped his mind of everything except this woman.

It was only when he lowered her unsteadily to the floor that he realised he was still dressed.

He couldn't remember when he'd last had sex fully clothed.

Usually he had more finesse, but finesse hadn't been invited to this party.

He felt her sway slightly and curved a protective arm around her, supporting her against him. His cheek was on her hair and he could feel the rise and fall of her chest as she struggled for air.

Finally she locked her hand in the front of his shirt and lifted her head. Her mouth was softly swollen and pink from his kisses, her eyes dazed. 'That was angry sex?'

Nik was too stunned to answer and she gave a faint smile and gingerly let go of the front of his shirt, as if testing her ability to stand unsupported.

'Angry sex is good. I don't feel angry any more. You've taught me a whole new way of solving a row.' She swayed like Bambi and he caught her before she could slide to the floor.

'*Theé mou*, you are *not* going to use sex to solve a row.' The thought of her doing with anyone else what she'd done with him sent his stress levels soaring.

'You did. It worked. I'm not saying I like you, but all my adrenaline was channelled in a different direction so I'm feeling a lot calmer. My karma is calmer.'

Nik was far from calm. 'Lily—'

'I know this whole thing is difficult for you,' she said, 'and you don't need to make the situation more difficult by worrying about me falling in love with you. That is never going to happen. And next time your little sister is upset, don't hand her to someone else. I know you don't like tears, but I think you could make an exception for a distressed two-year-old. Man up.'

Nik, who had never before in his life had his manhood questioned, struggled for a response. 'She needed comfort and I have zero experience with babies.' He spoke through his teeth. 'My approach to all problems is to delegate tasks to whichever person has the superior qualifications—in this instance it was you. She liked you. She was calmer with you. With me, she cried.'

She gave him a look that was blisteringly unsympathetic. 'Every expert started as a beginner. Get over yourself. Next time, pick her up and learn how to comfort her. Who knows, one day you might even be able to extend those skills to grown-ups. If you didn't find it so hard to communicate you might not have gone so long without seeing your father. He adores you, Nik, and he's so proud of you. I know you didn't like Callie, but couldn't you have swallowed your dislike of her for the occasional visit? Would that really have been so hard?'

Nik froze. 'You know nothing about the situation.' Unaccustomed to explaining his actions to anyone, he took a deep breath. 'I did *not* stay away from my father because of my feelings about Callie.'

'What then?'

He was silent for a long moment because it was a topic he had never discussed with anyone. 'I stayed away from him because of her feelings for me.'

'That's what I'm saying! Because the two of you didn't get along, he suffered.'

'Not because I didn't like her. Because she liked me—a little too much.' He spoke with raw emphasis and saw the moment her expression changed and understanding dawned. 'That's right. My stepmother took her desire to be "close" to me to disturbing extremes.'

Lily's expression moved through a spectrum encompassing confusion, disbelief and finally horror. 'Oh, *no*, your poor father—does he know?'

'I sincerely hope not. I stayed away to avoid there ever being any chance he would witness something that might cause him distress. Despite my personal views on Callie I did not wish to see his marriage ended and I certainly didn't want to be considered the cause of it, because that would have created a rift that never would have healed.'

'So you stayed away to prevent a rift between you, but it caused a rift anyway and he doesn't even know the reason. Do you think you should have told him?'

'I asked myself that question over and over again, but I decided not to.' He hesitated. 'She was unfaithful several times during their short marriage and my father knew. There was nothing to be gained by revealing the truth and I didn't want to add to my father's pain.'

'Of course you didn't.' Lily's eyes filled. 'And all this time I was thinking it was because of your stubborn pride, because you didn't like the woman and were determined to punish him. I was *so wrong*. I'm sorry. Please forgive me.'

More unsettled by the tears than he was by her anger, Nik backed away. 'Don't cry. And there is nothing to forgive you for.'

'I misjudged you. I leaped to conclusions and I try never to do that.'

'It doesn't matter.'

'It does to me. You said that she had affairs—' Her eyes widened. 'Do you think that Chloe might not be—?'

He tensed because it was a possibility that had crossed his mind. 'I don't know, but it makes no difference now. My father's lawyers are taking steps to make sure it's a legal adoption.'

'But if she isn't and your father ever finds out—'

'It would make no difference to the way he feels about Chloe. Despite everything, I actually do believe she is my father's child. For a start she has certain physical characteristics that are particular to my family, and then there is the fact that Callie did everything in her power to keep her from him.'

'You really think she used her child as currency?'

'Yes.' Nik didn't hesitate and he saw the distress in her eyes. 'I think I dislike her almost as much as you do.'

'I doubt that.'

'I'm starting to see why you were worried about your father marrying again. Is Callie the reason you don't believe love exists?'

'No.' His voice didn't sound like his own. 'I formed that conclusion long before Callie.'

He waited for her to question him further but instead she leaned forward and hugged him tightly.

Unaccustomed to any physical contact that wasn't sexual, he tensed. 'What's that for?'

'Because you were put in a hideous, *horrible* position with Callie and the only choice you had was to stay away from your father. I think you're a very honourable person.'

He breathed deeply. 'Lily—'

'And because you were let down by a woman at a very vulnerable age. But I know you don't want to talk about that so I won't mention it again. And now why don't we go to bed and have apology sex? That's one we haven't tried before, but I'm willing to give it my all.'

HOURS LATER THEY lay on top of the bed, wrapped around each other while the night breeze cooled their heated flesh.

Lily thought he was asleep, but then he stirred and tightened his grip.

'Thank you for helping with Chloe. You were very good with her.'

'One day I'd love to have children of my own, but it isn't something I usually admit to out loud. When people ask about your aspirations, they want to hear about your career. Wanting a family isn't a valid life choice. And I'm happy and interested in my job, but I don't want it to be all there is in my life.'

'Why did you choose archaeology?'

'I suppose I'm fascinated by the way people lived in the past.

It tells us a lot about where we come from. Maybe it's because I don't know where I come from that it always interested me.'

There was a long silence. 'You know nothing about your mother?'

'Very little. I like to think she loved me, but she wasn't able to care for me. We assume she was a teenager. What I always wonder is why no one helped her. She obviously didn't feel she could even tell anyone she was pregnant. I think about that more than anything and I feel horrible that there wasn't anyone special in her life she could trust. She must have been so lonely and frightened.'

'Have you tried to trace her?'

'The police tried to trace her at the time but they had no success. They thought she was probably from somewhere outside London.' It was something she hadn't discussed with anyone before and she wondered why she was doing so now, with him. Maybe because he, too, had been abandoned by his mother, even though the circumstances were different. Or maybe because his honesty made him surprisingly easy to talk to. He didn't sugarcoat his views on life, nor did he lie. After the brutal shock of discovering how wrong she'd been about David Ashurst, it was a relief to be with someone who was exactly who he seemed to be. And although she'd accused Nik of arrogance, part of her could understand how watching her with Chloe might have unsettled him. That moment had highlighted their basic differences and the truth was that his extreme reaction to her 'baby moment' had been driven more by his reluctance to mislead her, than arrogance.

It was obvious that his issues with love and marriage had been cemented early in life.

What psychological damage had his mother caused when she'd walked out leaving her young son watching from the hallway?

What message had that sent to him? That relationships didn't last? If a mother could leave her child, what did that say to a young boy about the enduring quality of love?

He'd been let down by the one person he should have been able to depend on, his childhood rocked by insecurity and lack of trust. Everything that had followed had cemented his belief that relationships were a transitory thing with no substance.

'We're not so different, you and I, Nik Zervakis.' She spoke softly. 'We're each a product of our pasts, except that it sent us in different directions. You ceased to believe true love existed, whereas I was determined to find it. It's why we're both bad at relationships.'

'I'm not bad at relationships.'

'You don't have relationships, Nik. You have sex.'

'Sex is a type of relationship.'

'Not really. It's superficial.'

'Why are we talking about me? Tell me why you think you're bad at relationships.'

'Because I care too much. I try too hard.'

'You want the fairy tale.'

'Not really. When you describe it that way it makes it sound silly and unachievable and I don't think what I want is unrealistic.'

'What do you want?'

There was a faint splash from beyond the open doors as a tiny bird skimmed across the pool.

'I want to be special to someone.' She spoke softly, saying the words aloud for the first time in her life. 'Not just special. I'm going to tell you something, and if you laugh you will be sorry—'

'I promise not to laugh.'

'I want to be someone's favourite person.'

There was a long silence and then his arms tightened. 'I'm sure you're special to a lot of people.'

'Not really.' She felt the hot sting of tears and was relieved it was dark. 'My life has been like a car park. People come and go. No one stays around for long. I have friends. Good friends, but it's not the same as being someone's favourite person. I want to be someone's dream come true. I want to be the person they call when they're happy or sad. The one they want to wake up next to and grow old with.' She wondered why she was telling him this, when his ambitions were diametrically opposed to hers. 'You think I'm crazy.'

'That isn't what I think.' His voice was husky and she turned her head to look at him but his features were indistinct in the darkness.

'Thank you for listening.' She felt sleep descend and suppressed a yawn. 'I know you don't think love exists, but I hope that one day you find a favourite person.'

'In bed, you are definitely my favourite person. Does that count?' He pulled the sheet up over her body, but didn't release her. 'Now get some sleep.'

THE NEXT COUPLE of days passed in a whirl of social events. Helicopters and boats came and went, although tucked away on the far side of the idyllic island Lily was barely aware of the existence of other people. For her, it was all about Nik.

There had been a subtle shift in their relationship, although she had a feeling that the shift was all on her side. Now, instead of believing him to be cold and aloof, she saw that he was guarded. Instead of controlling, she saw him as someone determined to be in charge of his own destiny.

In between socialising, she lounged by the pool and spent time on the small private beach next to Camomile Villa.

She loved swimming in the sea and more than once Nik had to extract her with minutes to spare before she was expected to accompany him to another lunch or dinner.

He was absent a lot of the time and she was aware that he'd been spending that time with his father and, judging from the more harmonious atmosphere, that time had been well spent.

After that first awkward lunch, he'd stopped firing questions at Diandra and if he wasn't completely warm in his interactions with her, he was at least civil.

To avoid the madness of the wedding preparations, Nik was determined to show Lily the island.

The day before the wedding he pulled her from bed just before sunrise.

'What time do you call this?' Sleepy and fuzzy-headed after a night that had consisted of more sex than sleep, she grumbled her way to the bathroom and whimpered a protest when he thrust her under cold water. 'You're a sadist.'

'You are going to thank me. Wear sturdy shoes.'

'The Prince never said that to Cinderella and I am never going to thank you for anything.' But she dragged on her shorts and a pair of running shoes, smothering a yawn as she followed him out of the villa. She stopped when she saw the vintage Vespa by the gates. 'I hate to be the one to tell you this but something weird happened to your limo overnight.'

'When I was a teenager this was my favourite way of getting round the island.' He swung his leg over the bike with fluid predatory grace and she laughed.

'You are too tall for this thing.' But her heart gave a little bump as she slid behind him and wrapped her arms round hard male muscle. 'Shouldn't I have a helmet or a seat belt or something?'

'Hold onto me.'

They wound their way along dusty roads, past rocky coves and beautiful beaches and up to the crumbling ruins of the Venetian fort where they abandoned the scooter and walked the rest of the way. He took her hand and they scrambled to the top as dawn was breaking.

The view was breathtaking, and she sat next to him, her thigh brushing his as they watched the sun slowly wake and stretch out fingers of dazzling light across the surface of the sea.

'I could live here,' she said simply. 'There's something about the light, the warmth, the people—London seems so grey in comparison. I can't believe you grew up here. You're so lucky. Not that you know that of course—you take it all for granted.'

'Not all.'

He'd brought a flask of strong Greek coffee and some of the sweet pastries she adored and she nibbled the corner and licked her fingers.

'I don't believe you made those.'

'Diandra made both the coffee and the pastries.'

'Diandra.' She grinned and nudged him with her shoulder. 'Confess. You're starting to like her.'

'She is an excellent cook.'

'And a good person. You're starting to like her.'

'I admit that what I took for a guilty conscience appears to be shyness.'

You like her.

His eyes gleamed. 'Maybe. A little.'

'There, you said it and it didn't kill you. I'll make a romantic of you yet.' She finished the pastry, contemplated another and decided she wouldn't get into the dress she'd brought to wear at the wedding. 'That was the perfect start to the day.'

'Worth waking up for?' His voice was husky and she turned her head, met his sleepy, sexy gaze and felt her tummy tumble.

'Yes. Of course, it would be easier to wake up if you'd let me sleep at night.'

He lowered his forehead to hers. 'Do you want to sleep, *erota mou*?' He curved his hand behind her head and kissed her with lingering purpose. 'I could take you back to bed right now if that is what you want.'

Her heart was pounding. She had to keep telling herself that this was about sex and nothing else. 'What's the alternative?'

'There are Minoan remains west of here if you want to extend the trip.'

'There are Minoan remains all over Crete,' she said weakly, telling herself that she could spend the rest of her life digging around in Minoan remains, but after this trip was over she'd never again get the chance to spend time with Nik Zervakis. 'Bed sounds good to me.'

CHAPTER NINE

THE CREAM OF Europe's great and good turned up to witness the wedding of Kostas Zervakis and Diandra.

'It's busier than Paris in fashion week,' Lily observed as they gathered for the actual wedding.

Nik was looking supremely handsome in a dark suit and whatever reservations he had about witnessing yet another marriage of his parent he managed to hide behind layers of sophisticated charm.

'You're doing well,' Lily murmured, reaching down to rescue the small posy of flowers that Chloe had managed to drop twice already. 'I'm proud of you. No frowning. All you have to do is keep it up for another few hours and you're done.'

He curved his arm round her waist. 'What's my reward for not frowning?'

'Angry sex.'

There was laughter in his eyes. 'Angry sex?'

'Yes. I like that sort. It's good to see you out of control.'

'I'm never out of control.'

'You were totally out of control, Mr Zervakis, and you hate that.' She hooked her finger into the front of his shirt and saw his eyes darken. 'You are used to being in control of everything. The people around you, your work environment, your emotions—angry sex is the only time I've ever seen you lose it. It felt good knowing I was the one responsible for breaking down that iron self-control of yours. Now, stop talking and focus. This is Diandra's moment.'

The wedding went perfectly, Chloe managed to hold onto the posy and after witnessing the ceremony Lily was left in no doubt that the love between Kostas and Diandra was genuine.

'She's his favourite person,' she whispered in a choked voice and Nik turned to her, wry humour in his eyes.

'Of course she is. She cooks for him, takes care of his child and generally makes his life run smoothly.'

'That isn't what makes this special. He could pay someone to do that.'

'He *is* paying her.'

'Don't start.' She refused to let him spoil the moment. 'Have you seen the way he looks at her? He doesn't see anyone else, Nik. The rest of us could all disappear.'

'That's the best idea I've heard in a long time. Let's do it.'

'No. I don't go to many weddings and this one is perfect.' Teasing him, she leaned closer. 'One day that is going to be you.'

He gave her a warning look. 'Lily—'

'I know, I know.' She shrugged. 'It's a wedding. Everyone dreams at weddings. Today, I want everyone to be happy.'

'Good. Let's sneak away and make each other happy.' His eyes dropped to her mouth. 'Wait here. There's one thing I have to do before we leave.' Leaving Lily standing in the shade, he walked across to his new stepmother and took her hands in his.

Lily watched, a lump in her throat, as he drew her to one side. She couldn't hear what was said but she saw Diandra visibly relax as they talked and laughed together. And then they were joined by Kostas, who evidently didn't want to be parted from his new bride.

The whole event left Lily with a warm feeling and a genuine belief that this family really might live happily. Oh, there would be challenges of course, but a strong family weathered those together and she was sure that, no matter what had gone before, Kostas and Diandra were a strong family.

Just one dark cloud hovered on the horizon, shadowing her happiness. Now that the wedding was over, they'd both be returning to the reality of their lives.

And Nik Zervakis had no place in the reality of her life.

Still, they had one more night and she wasn't going to spoil today by worrying about tomorrow. She was lost in a private and very erotic fantasy about what the night might bring when Kostas drew her to one side.

'I have an enormous favour to ask of you.'

'Of course.' Her mind elsewhere, Lily wondered if it was time to be a bit more bold and inventive in the bedroom. Nik brought a seemingly never-ending source of energy, creativity and sexual expertise to every encounter and she wondered if it was time she took the initiative. Planning ways to give him a night he'd never forget, she remembered Kostas was talking and forced herself to concentrate.

'Would you take Chloe for us tonight? I am thrilled she is with us, but I want this one night with Diandra. Chloe likes you. You have a way with children.'

Lily's plans for an erotic night that Nik would remember for ever evaporated.

How could she refuse when her relationship with Nik was a transitory thing and this one was for ever?

'Of course.' She hid her disappointment beneath a smile, and decided that the news that they were sharing Camomile Villa with a toddler was probably best broken when it was too late for Nik to do anything about it, so instead of enlisting his help to transport Chloe's gear across to the villa, she did it herself, sending a message via Diandra to tell him she was tired and to meet her back there when he was ready.

She'd settled a sleepy Chloe into her bed at the villa when she heard his footsteps on the terrace.

'You should have waited for me.' Nik stopped in the door-way as she put her finger to her lips.

'Shh—she's sleeping.'

'*Who* is sleeping?'

'Chloe.' She pointed to where Chloe lay, splayed like a star-fish in the middle of the bed. 'It's their wedding night, Nik. They don't want to have to think about getting up to a toddler. And in case you're thinking you don't want to get up to a tod-dler either, you don't have to. I'll do it.'

He removed his tie and disposed of his jacket. 'She is going to sleep in the bed?'

'Yes. I thought we could babysit her together.' She eyed him, unsure how he'd react. 'I know this is going to ruin our last night. Are you angry?'

'No.' He undid the buttons on his shirt and sighed. 'It was the right thing to do. I should have thought of it.'

'She might keep us awake all night.'

His eyes gleamed with faint mockery. 'We've had plenty of practice.' He looked at the child on the bed. 'Tell me what you want me to do. This should be my responsibility, not yours. And I want to do the right thing. It's important to me that she feels secure and loved.'

Her insides melted. 'You don't have to "do" anything. And if you'd rather go to bed, that's fine.'

'I have a better idea. We have a drink on the terrace. Open the doors. That way we'll hear her if she wakes up and she won't be able to escape without us seeing.'

'She's a child, not a wild animal.' But his determination to give his half-sister the security she deserved touched her, and Lily stood on tiptoe and kissed him on the cheek. 'And a drink is a good idea. I didn't drink anything at the wedding because I was so nervous that something might go wrong.'

'I know the feeling.' He slid his hand behind her head and tilted her face to his. 'Thank you for coming with me. I have no doubt at all that the wedding was a happier experience for everyone involved because you were there.' His gaze dropped to her mouth and lingered there and her heart started to pound.

All day, she'd been aware of him. Of the leashed power concealed beneath the perfect cut of his suit, of the raw sexuality framed by spectacular good looks.

A cry from the bedroom shattered the moment and she eased away regretfully. 'Could you pick her up while I fetch her a drink? Diandra says she usually has a drink of warm milk before she goes to sleep and I'm sure today was unsettling for her.'

'It was unsettling for all of us,' he drawled and she smiled.

'Do you want warm milk, too? Because I could fix that.'

'I was thinking more of chilled champagne.' He glanced towards the bedroom and gave a resigned sigh. 'I will go to her, but don't blame me when I make it a thousand times worse.'

Perhaps because he was so blisteringly self-assured in every other aspect of his life, she found his lack of confidence strangely endearing. 'You won't make it worse.'

She walked quickly through to the kitchen and warmed milk, tension spreading across her shoulders as she heard Chloe's cries. Knowing that all that howling would simply ensure that Nik didn't offer to help a second time, she moved as quickly as she could. As she left the kitchen, the cries ceased and she paused in the doorway of the bedroom, transfixed by the sight of Nik holding his little sister against his shoulder, one strong, bronzed hand against her back as he supported her on his arm. As she watched, she saw the little girl lift her hand and rub the roughness of his jaw.

He caught that hand in his fingers, speaking to her in Greek, his voice deep and soothing.

Lily had no idea what he was saying, but whatever it was seemed to be working because Chloe's eyes drifted shut and her head thudded onto his broad shoulder as she fell asleep, her blonde curls a vivid contrast to the dark shadow of his strong jaw.

Nik stood still, as if he wasn't sure what to do now, and then caught sight of Lily in the doorway. He gave her a rueful smile at his own expense and she smiled.

'Try putting her back down on the bed.'

As careful as if he'd been handling delicate Venetian glass, Nik lowered the child to the bed but instantly she whimpered and tightened her grip around his neck like a barnacle refusing to be chipped away from a rock.

He kept his hand securely on her back and cast Lily a questioning look. 'Now what?'

'Er—sit down in the chair with her in your lap and give her some milk,' Lily suggested, and he strolled onto the terrace, sat on one of the comfortable sunloungers and let the toddler snuggle against him.

'When I said I wanted to spend the evening on the terrace with a woman this wasn't exactly what I had in mind.'

'Two women.' Laughing, she sat down next to him and offered Chloe the milk. 'Here you go, sweetheart. Cow juice.'

Nik raised his eyebrows. 'Cow juice?'

'One of my friends used to call it that because whenever she said "milk" her child used to go demented.' Seeing that the child was sleepy, Lily tried to keep her hold on the cup but small fingers grabbed it, sloshing a fair proportion of the contents over Nik's trousers.

To give him his due, he didn't shift. Simply looked at her with an expression that told her she was going to pay later.

'Thanks to you I now have "cow juice" on my suit.'

'Sorry.' She was trying not to laugh because she didn't want to rouse the sleepy, milk-guzzling toddler. 'I'll have it cleaned.'

'Let me.' He covered Chloe's small fingers with his large hand, holding the cup while she drank.

Lily swallowed. 'You see? You have a natural talent.'

His gaze flickered to hers. 'Take that look off your face. This is a one-time crisis-management situation, never to be repeated.'

'Right. Because she isn't the most adorable thing you've ever seen.'

Nik glanced down at the blonde curls rioting against the crisp white of his shirt. 'I have a fair amount of experience with women and I can tell you that this one is going to be high maintenance.'

'What gave you that idea? The fact that she wouldn't stay in her bed or the fact that she spilled her drink over you?'

'For my father's sake I hope that isn't a foreshadowing of her teenage years.' Gently, he removed the empty cup from Chloe's limp fingers and handed it back to Lily. 'She's fast asleep. Now it's my turn. Champagne. Ice. You.' His gaze met hers and she saw humour and promise under layers of potent sex appeal.

Her stomach dropped and she reached and took Chloe from him. 'I'll tuck her in.'

He rose to his feet, dwarfing her. 'I'll get the champagne.'

Wondering if the intense sexual charge ever diminished when you were with a man like him, Lily tiptoed through to the bedroom and tucked Chloe carefully into the middle of the enormous bed.

This time the child didn't stir.

Lily brushed her hand lightly over those blonde curls and stared down at her for a long moment, a lump in her throat. When she grew up was she going to wonder about her mother? Did Callie intend to be in her life or had she moved on to the next thing?

Closing the doors of the bedroom, Lily took the cup back to the kitchen. By the time she returned Nik was standing on the terrace wearing casual trousers and a shirt.

'You changed.'

'It didn't feel right to be drinking champagne in wet trousers.' He handed her a glass. 'She's asleep?'

'For now. I don't think she'll wake up. She's exhausted.' She sipped the champagne. 'It was a lovely wedding. For what it's worth, I like Diandra a lot.'

'So do I.'

She lowered the glass. 'Do you believe she loves him?'

'I'm not qualified to judge emotions, but they seem happy together. And I'm impressed by how willingly she has welcomed Chloe.'

She slipped off her shoes and sat on the sunlounger. 'I think Chloe will have a loving and stable home.'

He sat down next to her, his thigh brushing against hers. 'You didn't have that.'

She stared at the floodlit pool. 'No. I was a really sickly child. Trust me, you don't want the details, but as a result of that I moved from foster home to foster home because I was a lot of trouble to take care of. When you face the possibility of having to spend half the night in a hospital with a sick kid when you already have others at home, you take the easier option. I was never the easy option.'

He covered her hand with his. 'Was adoption never considered?'

'Older children aren't easy to place. Especially not sickly older children. Every time I arrived somewhere new I used to hope this might be permanent, but it never was. Anyway, enough of that. I've already told you far more than you ever wanted to know about me. You hate talking about family and personal things.'

'With you I do things I don't do with other people. Like attend weddings.' He turned her face to his and kissed her. 'You had a very unstable, unpredictable childhood and yet still you believe that something else is possible.'

'Because you haven't experienced something personally, doesn't mean it doesn't exist. I've never been to the moon but I know it's there.'

'So despite your disastrous relationships you still believe there is an elusive happy ending waiting for you somewhere.'

'Being happy doesn't have to be about relationships. I'm happy now. I've had a great time.' She gave a faint smile. 'Have I scared you?'

He didn't answer. Instead he lowered his head to hers again

and she melted under the heat of his kiss, wishing she could freeze time and make this moment last for ever.

When she finally pulled away, she felt shaky. 'I've never met anyone like you before.'

'Cold and ruthlessly detached? Wasn't that what you said to me on that first night?'

'I was wrong.'

'You weren't wrong.'

'You reserve that side of you for the people you don't know very well and people who are trying to take advantage. I wish I were more like you. You're very analytical. There's another side of you that you don't often show to the world, but don't worry—it's our secret.'

His expression shifted from amused to guarded. 'Lily—'

'Don't panic. I still don't love you or anything. But I don't think you're quite the cold-hearted machine I did a week ago.'

I still don't love you.

She'd said the words so many times during their short relationship and they'd always been a joke. It was a code that acted as a reminder that this relationship was all about fun and sex and nothing deeper. Until now. She realised with a lurch of horror that it was no longer true.

She wasn't sure at what point her feelings had changed, but she knew they had and the irony of it was painful.

She'd conducted all her relationships with the same careful, studied approach to compatibility. David Ashurst had seemed perfect on the surface but had proved to be disturbingly imperfect on closer inspection whereas Nik, who had failed to score a single point on her checklist at first glance, had turned out to be perfect in every way when she'd got to know him better.

He'd proved himself to be both honest and unwaveringly loyal to his family.

It was that honesty that had made him hesitate before finally agreeing to take her home that night and that honesty was part of the reason she loved him.

She wanted to stay here with him for ever, breathing in the sea breeze and the scent of wild thyme, living this life of barefoot bliss.

But he didn't want that and he never would.

THE FOLLOWING MORNING, Nik left Lily to pack while he returned Chloe to his father and Diandra, who were enjoying breakfast on the sunny terrace overlooking the sea.

Diandra took Chloe indoors for a change of clothes and Nik joined his father.

'I was wrong,' he said softly. 'I like Diandra. I like her a great deal.'

'And she likes you. I'm glad you came to the wedding. It's been wonderful having you here. I hope you visit again soon.' His father paused. 'We both love Lily. She's a ray of sunshine.'

Nik usually had no interest in the long-term aspirations of the women he dated, but in this case he couldn't stop thinking about what she'd told him.

I want to be someone's favourite person.

She said she didn't want a fairy tale, but in his opinion expecting a relationship to last for a lifetime was the biggest fairy tale of all. His mouth tightened as he contemplated the brutal wake-up call that awaited her. He doubted there was a man out there who was capable of fulfilling Lily's shiny dream and the thought of the severe bruising that awaited her made him want to string safety nets between the trees to cushion her fall.

'She is ridiculously idealistic.'

'You think so?' His father poured honey onto a bowl of fresh yoghurt. 'I disagree. I think she is remarkably clear-sighted about many things. She's a smart young woman.'

Nik frowned. 'She is smart, but when it comes to relationships she has poor judgement just like—' He broke off and his father glanced at him with a smile.

'Just like me. Wasn't that what you were going to say?' He poured Nik a cup of coffee and pushed it towards him. 'You think I haven't learned my lesson, but every relationship I've had has taught me something. The one thing it hasn't taught me is to give up on love. Which is good, because this twisty, turning, sometimes stony path led me to Diandra. Without those other relationships, I wouldn't be here now.' He sat back, relaxed and visibly happy while Nik stared at him.

'You're seriously trying to convince me that if you could put the clock back, you wouldn't change things? Try and undo the mistakes?'

'I wouldn't change anything. And I don't see them as mistakes. Life is full of ups and downs. All the decisions I made were right at the time and each one of them led to other things, some good, some bad.'

Nik looked at him in disbelief. 'When my mother left you were a broken man. I was scared you wouldn't recover. How can you say you don't regret it?'

'Because for a while we were happy, and even when it fell apart I had you.' His father sipped his coffee. 'I wish I'd understood at the time how badly you were scarred by it all and I certainly wish I could undo some of the damage it did to you.'

'So if you had your time again, you'd still marry her?'

'Without hesitation.'

'And Maria and Callie?'

'The same. There are no guarantees with love, that's true, but it's the one thing in life worth striving to find.'

'I don't see it that way.'

His father gave him a long look. 'When you were building your business from the ground and you hit a stumbling block, did you give up?'

'No, but—'

'When you lost a deal, did you think to yourself that there was no point in going after the next one?'

Nik sighed. 'It is *not* the same. In my business I never make decisions based on emotions.'

'And that,' his father said softly, 'is your problem, Niklaus.'

CHAPTER TEN

THE JOURNEY BACK to Crete was torture. As the boat sped across the waves, Lily looked over her shoulder at Camomile Villa, knowing she'd never see it again.

Nik was unusually quiet.

She wondered if he'd had enough of being with her.

No doubt he was ready to move on to someone else. Another woman with whom he could share a satisfying physical relationship, never dipping deeper. The thought of him with another woman made her feel ill and Lily gripped the side of the boat, a gesture that earned her a concerned frown.

'Are you sea sick?'

She was about to deny that, but realised to do so would mean providing an alternative explanation for her inertia so she gave a little nod and instantly he slowed the boat.

That demonstration of thoughtfulness simply made everything worse.

It had been so much easier to stay detached when she'd thought he was the selfish, ruthless money-making machine everyone else believed him to be.

Now she knew differently.

The drive between the little jetty and his villa should have been blissful. The sun beamed down on them and the scent of lavender and thyme filled the air, but as they grew closer to their destination she grew more and more miserable.

She was lost in her own deep pit of gloom, and it was only when he stopped at the large iron gates that sealed his villa off from the rest of the world that she realised his mistake.

She stirred. 'You forgot to drop me home.'

'I didn't forget.' He turned to look at her. 'I'll take you home if that's what you want, or you can spend the night here with me.'

Her heart started to pound. 'I thought—' She'd assumed he'd drop her home and that would be the end of it. 'I'd like to stay.'

The look in his eyes made everything inside her tighten in delicious anticipation.

He muttered something under his breath in Greek and then turned his head and focused on the driving, a task that seemed to cost him in terms of effort.

She knew he was aroused and her mood lifted and flew. He might not love her, but he wanted her. That was enough for now.

It wasn't one night.

They'd already had so much more than that.

He shifted gears and then reached across and took her hand and she looked down, at those long, strong fingers holding tightly to hers.

Her body felt hot and heavy and she stole a glance at his taut profile and knew he was as aroused as she was. In the short time they'd been together she'd learned to recognise the signs. The darkening of his eyes, the tightening of his mouth and the brief sideways glance loaded with sexual promise.

He wore a casual shirt that exposed the bronzed skin at the base of his throat and she had an almost overwhelming temptation to lean across and trace that part of him with her tongue. To tease when he wasn't in a position to retaliate.

'Don't you dare.' He spoke through his teeth. 'I'll crash the car.'

'How did you know what I was thinking?'

'Because I was thinking the same thing.'

It amazed her that they could be so in tune with each other, when they were so fundamentally different in every way.

'You need a villa with a shorter drive.'

He gave a laugh that was entirely at his own expense, and then cursed as his phone rang as he pulled up in front of the villa.

'Answer it.' She said it lightly, somehow managing to keep the swell of disappointment hidden inside.

'I'll get rid of them.' He spoke with his usual arrogant assurance before hitting a button on his phone and taking the call.

He switched between Greek and English and Lily was lost in a dream world, imagining the night that lay ahead, when she heard him talking about taking the private jet to New York.

He was flying to New York?

The phone call woke her up from her dream.

What was she doing?

Why was she hanging around like stale fish when this relationship was only ever going to be something transitory?

Was part of her really hoping that she might be the one that changed his mind?

The happiness drained out of her like air from an inflatable mattress.

She never should have come back here. She should have asked him to drop her at her flat and made her exit with dignity.

Taking advantage of the fact he was still on the phone, she grabbed her small bag and slid out of the car.

'Thanks for the lift, Nik,' she whispered. 'See you soon.'

Except she knew she wouldn't.

She wouldn't see him ever again.

He turned his head and frowned. 'Wait—'

'Carry on with your call—I'll grab a cab,' she said hastily, and then proceeded to walk as fast as she could back up his drive in the baking heat.

Why did his drive have to be so *long*?

She told herself it was for the best. It wasn't his fault that her feelings had changed, and his hadn't. Their deal had been rebound sex without emotion. She was the one who'd brought emotion into it. And she'd take those emotions home with her, as she always did, and heal them herself.

Her eyes stung. She told herself it was because the sun was bright and scrabbled in her bag for sunglasses as a car came towards her down the drive. She recognised the sleek lines of the car that had driven her and Nik to the museum opening that night. It slowed down and Vassilis rolled down the window.

He took one look at her face and the suitcase and his mouth tightened. 'It's too hot to walk in this heat, *kyria*. Get in the car. I'll take you home.'

Too choked to argue, Lily slid into the back of the car. The air conditioning cooled her heated skin and she tried not to think about the last time she'd been in this car.

She was about to give Vassilis the address of her apartment, when her phone beeped.

It was a text from Brittany.

Fell on site, broke my stupid wrist and knocked myself out. In hospital. Can you bring clothes?

Horrified, Lily leaned forward. 'Vassilis, could you take me straight to the hospital please? It's urgent.'

Without asking questions, he turned the car and drove fast in the direction of the hospital, glancing at her in his mirror.

'Can I do anything?'

She gave him a watery smile and shook her head. At least worrying about Brittany gave her something else to think about. 'You're already doing it, thank you.'

'Where do you want me to drop you?'

'Emergency Department.'

'Does the boss know you're here?'

'No. And he doesn't need to.' She was glad she'd kept the

sunglasses on. 'It was a bit of fun, Vassilis, that's all.' Impulsively she leaned forward and kissed him on the cheek. 'Thank you for the lift. You're a sweetheart.'

Scarlet, he handed her a card. 'My number. Call me when you're ready for a lift home.'

Lily located Brittany in a ward attached to the emergency department. She was sitting, pale and disconsolate, in a room where she was the only occupant. Her face was bruised and her wrist was in plaster and she had a smear of mud on her cheek.

Putting aside her own misery, Lily gave a murmur of sympathy. 'Can I hug you?'

'No, because I'm dangerous. I'm in a filthy mood. It's my right hand, Lil! The hand I dig with, type with, write with, feed myself with, punch with— Ugh. I'm so *mad* with myself. And I'm mad with Spy.'

'Why? What did he do?'

'He made me laugh! I was laughing so hard I wasn't looking where I was putting my feet. I tripped and fell down the damn hole, put my hand out to save myself and smashed my head on a pot we'd dug up earlier. It would be funny if it wasn't so tragic.'

'Why isn't Spy here with you?'

'He was. I sent him away.' Brittany slumped. 'I'm not good company and I couldn't exactly send him to pack my underwear.'

'What's going to happen? Are they keeping you in?'

'Yes, because I banged my head and they're worried my brain might be damaged.' Brittany looked so frustrated Lily almost felt like smiling.

'Your brain seems fine to me, but I'm glad they're treating you with care.'

'I want to go home!'

'To our cramped, airless apartment? Brittany, it will be horribly uncomfortable.'

'I don't mean home to the apartment. I mean home to Puffin Island. There is no point in being here now I can't dig. If

I've got to sit and brood somewhere, I'd rather do it at Castaway Cottage.'

'I thought you said a friend was using the cottage.'

'Emily is there, but there's room for two. In fact it will be three, because—' She broke off and shook her head dismissively, as if realising she'd said something she shouldn't. 'Long story. My friends and I lurch from one crisis to another and it looks as if it's my turn. Can you do me a favour, Lil?'

'Anything.'

'Can you book me a flight to Boston? I'll sort out the transfer from there, but if you could get me back home, that would be great. The doctor said I can fly tomorrow if I feel well enough. My credit card is back in the apartment.' She lay back and closed her eyes, her cheeks pale against the polished oak of her hair.

'Have they given you something for the pain?'

'Yes, but it didn't do much. I don't suppose you have a bottle of tequila on your person? That would do it. Crap, I am so selfish—I haven't even asked about you.' She opened her eyes. 'You look terrible. What happened? How was the wedding?'

'It was great.' She made a huge effort to be cheerful. 'I had a wonderful time.'

Brittany's eyes narrowed. 'How wonderful?'

'Blissful. Mind-blowing.' She told herself that all the damage was internal. No one was going to guess that she was stumbling round with a haemorrhaging wound inside her.

'I want details. Lots of them.' Brittany's eyes widened as she saw the necklace at Lily's throat. 'Wow. That's—'

'It's one of Skylar's, from her *Mediterranean Sky* collection.'

'I know. I'm drooling with envy. He *bought* you that?'

'Yes.' She touched her fingers to the smooth stone, knowing she'd always remember the night he'd given it to her. 'He had one of her pots in his villa—do you remember the large blue one? She called it *Modern Minoan* I think. I recognised it and when he found out I knew Skylar, he thought I might like this.'

'So just like that he bought it for you? How the other half lives. That necklace you're wearing cost—'

'Don't tell me,' Lily said quickly, 'or I'll feel I have to give it back.' She'd intended to, but it was all she had to remind her of her time with him.

'Don't you dare give it back. You're supporting Sky. Her business is really taking off. It's thrilling for her. In my opinion she needs to ditch the guy she's dating because he can't handle her success, but apart from that she has a glittering future. That is one serious gift you're wearing, Lily. So when are you seeing him again?'

'I'm not. This was rebound sex, remember?' She said it in a light-hearted tone but Brittany's smile turned to a scowl.

'He hurt you, didn't he? I'm going to kill him. Right after I put a deep gouge in his Ferrari, I'm going to dig out his damn heart.'

Lily gave up the exhausting pretence that everything was fine. 'It's my fault. Everything I did was my choice. It's not his fault I fell in love. I still don't understand how it happened because he is *so* wrong for me.' She sank onto the edge of the bed. 'I thought he didn't fit any of the criteria on my list, and then after a while I realised he did. That's the worst thing about it. I've realised there are no rules I can follow.'

'You're in love with him? Lily—' Brittany groaned '—a man like that doesn't *do* love.'

'Actually you're wrong. He loves his father deeply. He doesn't show it in a touchy-feely way, but the bond between them is very strong. It's romantic love he doesn't believe in. He doesn't trust the emotion.' And she understood why. He'd been deeply hurt and that hurt had bedded itself deep inside him and influenced the way he lived his life. His security had been wrenched away from him at an age when it should have been the one thing he could depend on, so he'd chosen a different sort of security—one he could control. He'd made sure he could never be hurt again.

She ached for him.

And she ached for herself.

Brittany took her hand. 'Forget him. He's a rat bastard.'

'No.' Lily sprang to his defence. 'He isn't. He's honest about what he wants. He would never mislead someone the way David did.'

'Not good enough. He should have seen what sort of person you were on that very first night and driven you home.'

'He did see, and he tried to.' Lily swallowed painfully. 'He spelled out exactly what he was offering but I didn't listen. I made my choice.'

'Do you regret it, Lil?'

'No! It was the most perfect time of my life. I can't stop wishing the ending was different, but—' She took a deep breath and pressed her hand to her heart. 'I'm going to stop doing that fairy-tale thing and be a bit more realistic about life. I'm going to "wise up" as you'd say, and try and be a bit more like Nik. Protect myself, as he does. That way when someone like David comes into my life, I'll be less likely to make a mistake.'

'What about your checklist?'

'I'm throwing it out. In the end it didn't prove very reliable.' And deep down she knew there was no chance of her making a mistake again. No chance of her falling in love again.

'Does he know how you feel?'

'I hope not. That would be truly embarrassing. Now let's forget that. You're the important one.' Summoning the last threads of her will power, Lily stood up and picked up her bag. 'I'm going to go back to our apartment, pack you a case of clothes and book you on the first flight out of here.'

'Come with me. You'd love Puffin Island. Sea, sand and sailing. It's a gorgeous place. There's nothing keeping you here, Lily. Your project is finished and you can't spend August travelling Greece on your own.'

Right now she couldn't imagine travelling anywhere.

She wanted to lie down in a dark room until she stopped hurting.

Brittany reached out and took her hand. 'Castaway Cottage is the most special place on earth. We may not have Greek weather, but right now living here is like being in a range cooker so you might be grateful for that. When I'm home, I sleep with the windows open and I can hear the birds and the crash of the sea. I wake up and look out of the window and the sea is smooth and flat as a mirror. You have to come. My grandmother thought the cottage had healing properties, remember? And it looks as if you need to heal.'

Was healing possible? 'Thanks. I'll think about it.' She gave her friend a gentle hug. 'Don't laugh at any jokes while I'm gone.'

She took a cab home and tried not to think about Nik.

Sweltering in their tiny, airless bedroom, she hunted for a top or a dress that could easily be pulled over a plaster cast.

It was ridiculous to feel this low. Right from the start, there had only been one ending.

She'd be fine as long as she kept busy.

But would he?

The next woman he dated wouldn't know about his past, because he didn't share it.

They wouldn't understand him.

They wouldn't be able to find a way through the steely layers of protection he put between himself and the world and they'd retreat, leaving him alone.

And he didn't deserve to be alone.

He deserved to be loved.

Through the window of her apartment she could see couples walking hand in hand along the street on their way to the nearest beach. Families with small children, the nice gay couple who owned Brittany's favourite bar. Everyone was in pairs. It was like living in Noah's ark, she thought gloomily, two by two.

She resisted the urge to lie down on the narrow bed and sob

until her head ached. Brittany needed her. She didn't have time for self-indulgent misery, especially when this whole thing was her own fault.

She found a shirt that buttoned down the front and was folding it carefully when she heard a commotion in the street outside.

Lily felt a flicker of panic. The cab couldn't be here already, surely?

She was about to lean out of the window and ask him to wait when someone pounded on the door.

'Lily?' Nik's voice thundered through the woodwork. 'Open the door.'

The ground shifted beneath her feet and for a moment she thought there had been a minor earthquake. Then she realised it was her knees that were trembling, not the floor.

What was he doing here?

Dragging herself to the door, she opened it cautiously. 'Stop banging. These apartments aren't very well built. A cupboard fell off the wall last week.' She took in his rumpled appearance and the tension in his handsome face and felt a stab of concern. 'Is something the matter? You look terrible. Was your phone call bad news?'

'Are you ill?' He spoke in a roughened tone and she looked at him in astonishment.

'What makes you think I'm ill?'

'Vassilis told me he took you to the emergency department. You *were* very pale on the boat. You should have told me you were feeling so unwell.'

He thought she'd gone to the hospital for herself? 'Brittany is the one in hospital. She had a fall. I'm on my way there now with some stuff. I really need to finish packing. The cab will be here soon.' Knowing she couldn't keep this up for much longer, she turned away but he caught her arm in a tight grip.

'Why did you walk away from me? I thought we agreed you were going to stay another night.'

'I didn't walk. I bounded. That's what happens after rebound sex. You bound.' She kept it light and heard him curse softly under his breath.

'You didn't need to leave.'

'Yes, I did.' Aware that her neighbours were probably enjoying the show, she reached past him and closed the door. 'I shouldn't have agreed to stay in the first place. I wasn't playing by the rules. And as it happened Brittany needed me, so your phone call was perfect timing.'

'It was terrible timing.'

Discovering that being in the same room as him was even harder than not being in the same room as him, Lily walked back to the bedroom and finished packing. 'So you're flying back to New York? That sounds exciting.'

'Business demands I fly back to the US, but I have things to settle here first.'

She wondered if she was one of the things he had to settle.

He was trying to find a tactful way of reminding her their relationship hadn't been serious.

The ache inside grew worse. She tried to think of something to say that would make it easy for him. 'I have to get to the hospital. Brittany fell on site and fractured her wrist. She's waiting for me to bring her clothes and things and then I have to arrange a flight for her back to Maine because she can't stay here. She has invited me to spend August with her. I'm going to say yes.'

'Is that what you want?'

Of course it wasn't what she wanted. 'It will be fantastic.' Her control was close to snapping. 'Did you want something, Nik? Because I have to ring a cab, take some clothes to Brittany at the hospital and then battle with the stupid Wi-Fi to book a ticket and it's a nightmare. I did some research before the Internet crashed and at best it's a nineteen-hour journey with two changes. She's going to have to fly to Athens, then to Munich where she can get a direct flight to Boston. I still have to research how she gets from Boston to Puffin Island, but I can guarantee that by the time she arrives home she'll be half dead. I'm going to fly with her because she can't do it on her own, but I hadn't exactly budgeted for a ticket to the US so I'm having to do a bit of financial juggling.'

'What if I want to change the rules?'

'Sorry?'

'You said you weren't playing by the rules.' His gaze was steady on her face. 'What if I want to change the rules?'

'The way I feel right now, I'd have to say no.'

'How do you feel?'

She was absolutely sure that was one question he didn't want answered. 'My cab is going to be here in a minute and I have to book flights—'

'I'll give you a lift to the hospital and arrange for her to use the Gulfstream. We can fly direct to Boston and she can lie down all the way if she wants to,' he said. 'And I know a commercial pilot who flies between the islands, so that problem is also solved. Now tell me how you feel.'

'Wait a minute.' Lily looked at him, dazed. 'You're offering to transport Brittany home on a private jet? You can't do that. When I told you I was going to have to do some financial juggling I wasn't fishing for a donation.'

'I know. It sounds as if Brittany's in trouble and I'm always happy to help a friend in trouble.'

It confirmed everything she already knew about him but instead of cheering her up, it made her feel worse. 'But she's my friend, not yours.'

He drew in a breath. 'I'm hoping your friends will soon be my friends. And on that topic, *please* can we focus on us for a moment?'

Her heart gave an uneven bump and she looked at him warily. 'Us?'

'If you won't talk about your feelings then I'll talk about mine. Before we left the island this morning, I had a long conversation with my father.'

Lily softened. 'I'm pleased.'

'I'd always believed his three marriages were mistakes, some-thing he regretted, and it wasn't until today that I realised he regretted nothing. Far from seeing them as mistakes, he sees them as a normal part of life, which delivers a mix of good and bad to everyone. Yes, there was pain and hurt, but he never once faltered in his belief that love existed. I confess that came as a surprise to me. I'd assumed if he could have put the clock back and done things differently, he would have done.'

Lily gave a murmur of sympathy. 'Perhaps it was worse for you being on the outside. You only had half the story.'

'When my mother left I saw what it did to him, how vulner-able he was, and it terrified me.' His honesty touched her but she resisted the temptation to fling her arms round him and hug him until he begged for mercy.

'You don't have to tell me this. I know you hate talking about it.'

'I want to. It's important that you understand.'

'I do understand. Your mother walked away from you. That was the one relationship you should have been able to depend on. It's not surprising you didn't believe in love. Why would you? You had no evidence that it existed.'

'Neither did you,' he breathed, 'and yet you never ceased to believe in it.'

She gave a half-smile. 'Maybe I'm stupid.'

'No. You are the brightest, funniest, sexiest woman I've met in my whole life and there is no way, *no way*,' he said in a raw tone, 'I am letting you walk out of my life.'

'Nik—'

'You asked me why I was here. I'm here because I want to renegotiate the terms of our relationship.'

She almost smiled at that. Only Nik could make it sound like a business deal. 'Is this because you know I have feelings for you and you feel sorry for me? Because, honestly, I'm going to be fine. I'll get over you, Nik. At some point I'll get out there again.' She hoped she sounded more convincing than she felt.

'I don't want you to get over me. And I don't want to think of you "out there", a pushover for anyone who decides to take advantage of you.'

'I can take care of myself. I've learned a lot from you. I'm Kevlar.'

'You are marshmallow-coated sunshine,' he drawled, 'and you need someone with a less shiny view on life to watch out for you. I don't want this to be a rebound relationship, Lily. I want more.'

Suddenly she found it difficult to breathe. 'What exactly are we talking about here? How much more?'

'All of it.' He stroked her hair back from her face with gentle hands. 'You've made me believe in something I never thought existed.'

'Fairy tales?'

'Love,' he said softly. 'You've made me believe in love.'

'Nik—'

'I love you.' He paused and drew breath. 'And unless my reading of this situation is completely wrong, I believe you love me back. Which is probably more than I deserve, but I'm self-ish enough not to care about that. When it comes to you, I'll take whatever I can get.'

'Oh.' She felt a constriction in her chest. Her eyes filled and she covered her mouth with her hand. 'I'm going to cry, and you hate that. I'm really sorry. You'd better run.'

'I hate it when you cry, that's true. I don't ever want to see you cry. But I'm not running. Why would I run when the one thing in life that is special to me is right here?'

A lump wedged itself in her throat. She was so afraid of mis-interpreting what he said, she was afraid to speak. 'You love me. So y-you're saying you'd like to see me again? Date?'

'No, that's not what I'm saying.' Usually so articulate, this time he stumbled over the words. 'I'm saying that you're my favourite person, Lily. And I apologise for proposing to you in a cramped airless room with no air conditioning but, as you know, I'm very goal orientated and as my goal is to persuade you to marry me then the first step is to ask you.' He reached into his pocket and pulled out a box. 'Skylar doesn't make engagement rings but I hope you'll like this.'

'You want to marry me?' Feeling as if she were running to catch up, she stared at the box. 'I'm your favourite person?'

'Yes. And when you find your favourite person it's important to hold onto them and not let them go.'

'You love me? You're sure?' She blinked as he opened the box and removed a diamond ring. 'Nik, that's *huge*.'

'I thought it would slow you down and make it harder for you to escape from me.' He slid it onto her finger and she stared at it, dazzled as the diamond caught the sun's rays.

'I'm starting to believe in fairy tales after all. I love you, too.' It was her turn to stumble. 'I knew I was in love with you, but I wasn't going to tell you. It didn't seem fair on you. You were clear about the rules right from the beginning and I broke them. That was my fault.'

With a groan, he pulled her against him. 'I knew how you felt. I was going to force you to talk to me, but then I had to take that phone call and you vanished.'

'I didn't want to make it awkward for you by hanging around,' she muttered and he said something in Greek and eased her away from him.

'What about you?' His expression was serious. 'This isn't a first for you. You've fallen in love before.'

'That's the weird thing—' she lifted her hand to take another look at her ring, just to make sure she hadn't imagined it '—I thought I had, but then I spent time with you and told you all those things and I realised that with you it was different. I think I was in love with the idea of love. I thought I knew exactly what qualities I wanted in a person. But you can't use a checklist to fall in love. With you, I wasn't trying and it happened anyway. I need to change. I need to find a new way to protect myself.'

'I don't want you to change. I want you to stay exactly the way you are. And I can be that layer of protection that you don't seem to be able to cultivate for yourself.'

'You're volunteering to be my armour?'

'If that means spending the rest of my life plastered against you that sounds good to me.' His mouth was on hers, his hands in her hair and it occurred to her that this level of happiness was something she'd dreamed about.

'I was going to spend August on Puffin Island with Brittany.'

'Spend it with me. I have to go to New York next week, but we can fly Brittany to Maine first. I have friends in Bar Harbor. That's close to Puffin Island. While I'm at my meeting in New York you could visit Skylar. Then we can fly to San Francisco and take some time to plan our life together. I can't promise you a fairy tale, but I can promise the best version of reality I can give you.'

'You want me to go with you to San Francisco? What job would I do there?'

'Well, they have museums, but I was thinking about that.' He brushed away salty tears from her cheeks. 'How would you feel about spending more time on your ceramics?'

'I can't afford it.'

'You can now, because what's mine is yours.'

'I couldn't do that. I don't ever want our relationship to be about money.' She flushed awkwardly. 'It's important I keep custody of my rusty bike so I'm going to need you to sign one of those pre-nuptial agreement things so I'm protected in case you try and snatch everything I own.'

He was smiling. 'Pre-nuptial agreements are for people whose relationships aren't going to last and ours will last, *theé mou*.' Those words and the sincerity in his voice finally convinced her that he meant it, but even that wasn't enough to convince her this was really happening.

'But seriously, what do I bring to this relationship?'

'You bring optimism and a sunny outlook on life that no amount of money can buy. You're an inspiration, Lily. You're willing to trust, despite having been hurt. You have never known a stable family, and yet that hasn't stopped you believing that such a thing is possible for you. You live the life you believe in and I want to live that life with you.'

'So I bring a smile and you bring a private jet? I'm not sure that's an equitable deal. Not that I know much about deals. That's your area of expertise.'

'It is, and I can tell you I'm definitely the winner in this particular deal.' He kissed her again. 'The money is going to mean I can spoil you, and I intend to do that so you'd better get used to it. I thought being an artist would fit nicely round having babies. We'll split our time between the US and Greece. Several times a year we'll come back here and stay in Camomile Villa so we can see Diandra and Chloe and you can have your fill of Minoan remains.'

'Wait. You're moving too quickly for me. You have to understand I'm still getting used to the idea that I've gone from owning a bicycle, to having part ownership of a private jet.'

'And five homes.'

'I have real-estate whiplash. But at least I know how to clean them!' But it was something else he'd said that had really caught her attention. 'A moment ago—did you mention babies?'

'Have I misunderstood what you want? Am I sounding too traditional? Right now my Greek DNA is winning out,' he groaned, 'but what I'm trying to say is you can do anything you like. Make any choices you like, as long as I'm one of them.'

'You'd want babies?' She flung her arms round him. 'You haven't misunderstood. Having babies is my dream.'

His mouth was on hers. 'How do you feel about starting right away? I used to consider myself progressive, but all I can think about is how cute you're going to look when you're pregnant so I have a feeling I may have regressed to Neanderthal man. Does that bother you?'

'I've already told you I studied *homo neanderthalensis*,' Lily said happily. 'I'm an expert.'

'You have no idea how relieved I am to hear that.' Ignoring the heat, the size of the room and the width of the bed, he pulled her into his arms and Lily discovered it was possible to kiss and cry at the same time.

'We've had fun sex, athletic sex and angry sex—what sort of sex is this? Baby sex?'

'Love sex,' he said against her mouth. 'This is love sex. And it's going to be better than anything that's gone before.'

* * * * *

Keep reading for an excerpt of
Cowboy's Redemption
by B.J. Daniels.
Find it in the
Heroes Blockbuster 2024 anthology,
out now!

CHAPTER ONE

RUNNING BLINDLY THROUGH the darkness, Lola didn't see the tree limb until it struck her in the face. It clawed at her cheek, digging into a spot under her right eye as she flung it away with her arm. She had to stifle the cry of pain that rose in her throat for fear she would be heard. As she ran, she felt warm blood run down to the corner of her lips. The taste of it mingled with the salt of her tears, but she didn't slow, couldn't. She could hear them behind her.

She pushed harder, knowing that, being men, they had the advantage, especially the way she was dressed. Her long skirt caught on something. She heard the fabric rend, not for the first time. She felt as if it was her heart being ripped out with it.

Her only choice was to escape. But at what price? She'd been forced to leave behind the one person who mattered most. Her thundering heart ached at the thought, but she knew that this was the only way. If she could get help...

"She's over here!" came a cry from behind her. "This way!"

She wiped away the warm blood as she crashed through the brush and trees. Her legs ached and she didn't know how much longer she could keep going. Fatigue was draining her. If they caught her this time...

She tripped on a tree root, stumbled and almost plunged

headlong down the mountainside. Her shoulder slammed into a tree trunk. She veered off it like a pinball, but she kept pushing herself forward because the alternative was worse than death.

They were closer now. She could feel one of them breathing down her neck. She didn't dare look back. To look back would be to admit defeat. If she could just reach the road before they caught up to her...

Suddenly the trees opened up. She burst out of the darkness of the pines onto the blacktop of a narrow two-lane highway. The glare of headlights blinded her an instant before the shriek of rubber on the dark pavement filled the night air.

CHAPTER TWO

MAJOR COLT MCCLOUD felt the big bird shake as he brought the helicopter low over the bleak landscape. He was back in Afghanistan behind the controls of a UH-60 Black Hawk. The throb of the rotating blades was drowned out by the sound of mortar fire. It grew louder and louder, taking on a consistent pounding that warned him something was very wrong.

He dragged himself awake, but the dream followed him. Blinking in the darkness, he didn't know where he was for a moment. Everything looked alien and surreal. As the dream began to fade, he recognized his bedroom at the ranch.

He'd left behind the sound of the chopper and the mortar fire, but the pounding had intensified. With a start, he realized what he was hearing.

Someone was at the door.

He glanced at the clock on his bedside table. It was after three in the morning. Throwing his legs over the side of the bed, he grabbed his jeans, pulling them on as he fought to put the dream behind him and hurry to the door.

A half dozen possibilities flashed in his mind as he moved quickly through the house. It still felt strange to be back here after years of traveling the world as an Army helicopter pilot. After his fiancée dumped him, he'd planned to make a career out of the military, but then his father had died, leaving him a working ranch that either had to be run or sold.

He'd taken a hundred-and-twenty-day leave in between assignments so he could come home to take care of the ranch. His father had been the one who'd loved ranching, not Colt. That's why there was a for-sale sign out on the road into the ranch.

Colt reached the front door and, frowning at the incessant knocking at this hour of the morning, threw it open.

He blinked at the disheveled woman standing there before she turned to motion to the driver of the car idling nearby. The engine roared and a car full of what appeared to be partying teenagers took off in a cloud of dust.

Colt flipped on the porch light as the woman turned back to him and he got his first good look at her and her scratched, blood-streaked face. For a moment he didn't recognize her, and then it all came back in a rush. Standing there was a woman he'd never thought he'd see again.

"Lola?" He couldn't even be sure that was her real name. But somehow it fit her, so maybe at least that part of her story had been true. "What happened to you?"

"I had nowhere else to go." Her words came out in a rush. "I was so worried that you wouldn't be here." She burst into tears and slumped as if physically exhausted.

He caught her, swung her up into his arms and carried her into the house, kicking the door closed behind him. His mind raced as he tried to imagine what could have happened to bring her to his door in Gilt Edge, Montana, in the middle of the night and in this condition.

"Sit here," he said as he carried her in and set her down in a kitchen chair before going for the first-aid kit. When he returned, he was momentarily taken aback by the memory of this woman the first time he'd met her. She wasn't beautiful in the classic sense. But she was striking, from her wide violet eyes fringed with pale lashes to the silk of her long blond hair. She had looked like an angel, especially in the long white dress she'd been wearing that night.

That was over a year ago and he hadn't seen her since. Nor had he expected to since they'd met initially several hundred miles from the ranch. But whatever had struck him about her hadn't faded. There was something flawless about her—even as scraped up and bruised as she was. It made him furious at whoever was responsible for this.

"Can you tell me what happened?" he asked as he began to clean the cuts.

"I... I..." Her throat seemed to close on a sob.

"It's okay, don't try to talk." He felt her trembling and could see that she was fighting tears. "This cut under your eye is deep."

She said nothing, looking as if it was all she could do to keep her eyes open. He took in her torn and filthy dress. It was long, like the white one he'd first seen her in, but faded. It reminded him of something his grandmother might have worn to do housework in. She was also thinner than he remembered.

As he gently cleaned her wounds, he could see dark circles under her eyes, and her long braided hair was in disarray with bits of twigs and leaves stuck in it.

The night he'd met her, her plaited hair had been pinned up at the nape of her neck—until he'd released it, the blond silk dropping to the center of her back.

He finished his doctoring, put away the first-aid kit, and wondered how far she'd come to find him and what she had been through to get here. When he returned to the kitchen, he found her standing at the back window, staring out. As she turned, he saw the fear in her eyes—and the exhaustion.

Colt desperately wanted to know what had happened to her and how she'd ended up on his doorstep. He hadn't even thought that she'd known his name. "Have you had anything to eat?"

"Not in the past forty-eight hours or so," she said, squinting at the clock on the wall as if not sure what day it was. "And not all that much before that."

He'd been meaning to get into Gilt Edge and buy some groceries. "Sit and I'll see what I can scare up," he said as he opened the refrigerator. Seeing only one egg left, he said, "How do you feel about pancakes? I have chokecherry syrup."

She nodded and attempted a smile. She looked skittish as a newborn calf. Worse, he sensed that she was having second thoughts about coming here.

She licked her cracked lips. "I have to tell you. I have to explain—"

"It's okay. You're safe here." But safe from what, he wondered? "There's no hurry. Let's get you taken care of first." He'd feed her and get her settled down.

He motioned her into a chair at the kitchen table. He could tell that she must hurt all over by the way she moved. As much as he wanted to know what had happened, he thought she needed food more than anything else at this moment.

"While I make the pancakes, would you like a hot shower? The guest room is down the hall to the left. I can find you some clothes. They'll be too large for you, but maybe they will be more comfortable."

Tears welled in her eyes. He saw her swallow before she nodded. As she started to get to her feet, he noticed her grimace in pain.

"Wait."

She froze.

"I don't know how to say this delicately, but if someone assaulted you—"

"I wasn't raped."

He nodded, hoping that was true, because a shower would destroy important evidence. "Okay, so the injuries were..."

"From running for my life." With that she limped out of the kitchen.

He had the pancake batter made and the griddle heating when

he heard the shower come on. He stopped to listen to the running water, remembering this woman in a hotel shower with him months ago.

That night he'd bumped into her coming out of the hotel bar. He'd seen that she was upset. She'd told him that she needed his help, that there was someone after her. She'd given him the impression she was running from an old boyfriend. He'd been happy to help. Now he wondered if that was still the case. She said she was running for her life—just as she had the first time they'd met.

But that had been in Billings. This was Gilt Edge, Montana, hundreds of miles away. Didn't seem likely she would still be running from the same boyfriend. But whoever was chasing her, she'd come to him for help.

He couldn't turn her away any more than he'd been able to in that hotel hallway in Billings last year.

Lola pulled out her braid, discarding the debris stuck in it, then climbed into the steaming shower. She stood under the hot spray, leaned against the smooth, cool tile wall of the shower and closed her eyes. She felt weak from hunger, lack of sleep and constant fear. She couldn't remember the last time she'd slept through the night.

Exhaustion pulled at her. It took all of her energy to wash herself. Her body felt alien to her, her skin chafed from the rough fabric of the long dresses she'd been wearing for months. Stumbling from the shower, she wrapped her hair in one of the guest towels. It felt good to free her hair from the braid that had been wound at the nape of her neck.

As she pulled down another clean towel from the bathroom rack, she put it to her face and sniffed its freshness. Tears burned her eyes. It had been so long since she'd had even the smallest creature comforts like good soap, shampoo and clean towels that smelled like this, let alone unlimited hot water.

When she opened the bathroom door, she saw that Colt had

left her a sweatshirt and sweatpants on the guest-room bed. She dried and tugged them on, pulling the drawstring tight around her waist. He was right, the clothes were too big, but they felt heavenly.

She took the towels back to the bathroom to hang them and considered her dirty clothing on the floor. The hem of the worn ankle-length coarse cotton dress was torn and filthy with dirt and grime. The long sleeves were just as bad except they were soiled with her blood. The black utilitarian shoes were scuffed, the heels worn unevenly since she'd inherited them well used.

She wadded up the dress and shoved it into the bathroom wastebasket before putting the shoes on top of it, all the time feeling as if she was committing a sin. Then again, she'd already done that, hadn't she.

Downstairs, she stepped into the kitchen to see Colt slip three more pancakes onto the stack he already had on the plate.

He turned as if sensing her in the doorway and she was reminded of the first time she'd seen him. All she'd noticed that night was his Army uniform—before he'd turned and she'd seen his face.

That he was handsome hadn't even registered. What she'd seen was a kind face. She'd been desperate and Colt McCloud had suddenly appeared as if it had been meant to be. Just as he'd been here tonight, she thought.

"Last time I saw you, you were on leave and talking about staying in the military," she said as he pulled out a kitchen chair for her and she sat down. "I was afraid that you had and that—" her voice broke as she met his gaze "—you wouldn't be here."

"I'm on leave now. My father died."

"I'm sorry."

He set down the plate of pancakes. "Dig in."

Always the gentleman, she thought as he joined her at the table. "I made a bunch. There's fresh sweet butter. If you don't like chokecherry syrup—"

"I love it." She slid several of the lightly browned cakes

onto her plate. The aroma that rose from them made her stomach growl loudly. She slathered them with butter and covered them with syrup. The first bite was so delicious that she actually moaned, making him smile.

"I was going to ask how they are," he said with a laugh, "but I guess I don't have to."

She devoured the pancakes before helping herself to more. They ate in a companionable silence that didn't surprise her any more than Colt making her pancakes in the middle of the night or opening his door to her, no questions asked. It was as if it was something he did all the time. Maybe it was, she thought, remembering the first night they'd met.

He hadn't hesitated when she'd told him she needed his help. She'd looked into his blue eyes and known she could trust him. He'd been so sweet and caring that she'd almost told him the truth. But she'd stopped herself. Because she didn't think he would believe her? Or because she didn't want to involve him? Or because, at that point, she thought she could still handle things on her own?

Unfortunately, she no longer had the option of keeping the truth from him.

"I'm sure you have a lot of questions," she said, after swallowing her last bite of pancake and wiping her mouth with her napkin. The food had helped, but her body ached all over and fatigue had weakened her. "You had to be surprised to see me again, especially with me showing up at your door in the middle of the night looking like I do."

"I didn't even know you knew my last name."

"After that night in Billings… Before I left your hotel room, while you were still sleeping, I looked in your wallet."

"You planned to take my money?" He'd had over four hundred dollars in there. He'd been headed home to his fiancée, he'd told her. But the fiancée, who was supposed to pick him up at the airport, had called instead with crushing news. Not only was she not picking him up, she was in love with one of his best friends, someone he'd known since grade school.

He'd been thinking he just might rent a car and drive home to confront the two of them, he'd told Lola later. But, ultimately, he'd booked a flight for the next morning to where he was stationed and, with time to kill, had taken a taxi to a hotel, paid for a room and headed for the hotel bar. Two drinks later, he'd run into Lola as he'd headed from the bar to the men's room. Lola had saved him from getting stinking drunk that night. Also from driving to Gilt Edge to confront his ex-fiancée and his ex-friend.

"I hate to admit that I thought about taking your money," she said. "I could have used it."

"You should have taken it then."

She smiled at him and shook her head. "You were so kind to me, so tender..." Her cheeks heated as she held his gaze and remembered being naked in his arms. "I'm sure I gave you the wrong impression of me that night. It wasn't like me to...with a complete stranger." She bit her lower lip and felt tears well in her eyes again.

"There is nothing wrong with the impression you left with me. As a matter of fact, I've thought of you often." He smiled. It was a great smile. "Every time I heard one of those songs that we'd danced to in my hotel room that night—" his gaze warmed to a Caribbean blue "—I thought of you."

She looked away to swallow the lump that had formed in her throat before she could speak again. "It wasn't an old boyfriend I was running from that night. I let you believe that because I doubted you'd have believed the truth. I did need your help, though, because right before I collided with you in that hallway, I'd seen one of them in the hotel. I knew it was just a matter of time before they found me and took me back."

"Took you back?"

"I wasn't a fugitive from the law or some mental institution," she said quickly. "It's worse than that."

He narrowed his gaze with concern. "What could be worse than that?"

"The Society of Lasting Serenity."

BRAND NEW RELEASE

Don't miss the next instalment of the Powder River series by bestselling author B.J. Daniels! For lovers of sexy Western heroes, small-town settings and suspense with your romance.

RIVER JUSTICE
—R—
A POWDER RIVER NOVEL

PERFECT FOR FANS OF YELLOWSTONE!

Previous titles in the Powder River series

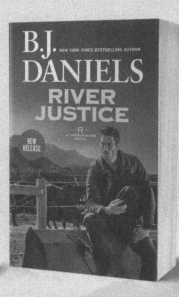

September 2023   January 2024   In-store and online August 2024